WHEN DEATH WON'T DO

A NOVEL

WILLIAM ARSENIS

For Jan

First published in the US and the UK in 2011 as TRUST MATTERS by Stingheart Press,
Chandler, AZ, 85226

ISBN: 0989623203
ISBN 13: 9780989623209
Library of Congress Control Number: 2013944450
Stingheart Press, Chandler AZ

STINGHEARTPRESS

PROLOGUE

He had never heard a sound like this before. Not surprising, considering the boy was only seven and most adults live a lifetime without hearing a shot fired indoors.

Damon van Luden found himself propped up against the headboard, only his feet still warm under the covers.

Then he realized his baby brother was crying.

Kory cried like that at night, even though he was almost two. When he was tiny, he yelled for food and for a change of diapers. Their mother said he sometimes has bad dreams.

Not completely awake, despite his brother's cries, Damon stared at the void, watching the gray shadows loiter in the darkness to form a nighttime rendition of his bedroom. The cherrywood armoire stood out first, looking as it always did at night: forming a dragon's head. A fiendish creature, without discernable beginning or end, like a mess of ink on blotting paper.

Damon tucked in his feet and in a sudden motion, hoping to catch the dragon off guard, he sprinted across the length of his bouncy bed and took a calculated leap into the dark. He missed the length of Persian carpet by a foot, making for the door with his arm ramrod-straight and his index finger forming the tip of a human lance. He hit the light switch on the first try, spinning around to see if the dragon was chasing after him. Annihilated by the now brightened room, only its unmoving cherrywood skeleton remained.

Satisfied the monster was vanquished, Damon cracked his bedroom door just enough to peep into the hallway, where he could see as far as Kory's room. Damon wedged his whole head through, but all he could make out was the wooden railing; the spiraling staircase beyond was lost in the darkness. Holding down a lungful of cool air, he ventured from the sanctuary of his room.

He stood in a hallway with no visible end, bare feet on a hardwood floor. From there, his brother's cries were louder.

They didn't call them crybabies for nothing.

The crying persisted. Damon waited for it to stop, but it wouldn't. He closed his eyes as tightly as he could, willing his brother to be quiet. It failed despite his efforts. The screaming turned into a coughing fit.

Damon opened his eyes, but the world still refused to make sense. *Mommy never lets Kory cry this long.*

As if in agreement, Kory recovered from his brief choking session and the yelling resumed.

Damon took a few timid steps, dragging his arm against the cold wall until he came to Kory's door. It was shut. Four doors down the corridor, a hint of light spilled through, just enough to guide Damon to his parents' room.

He froze at the sound of crying. There was no doubt in his mind: this time it wasn't Kory.

It was his mother.

PART I

DEFYING DAMON

December 4, 1953

This was madness.

A madness Kory van Luden was about to repeat for the third time.

He looked up and down the corridor again before he finally turned the doorknob and slipped into his big brother's room.

The windows were closed, like before, but Damon's room still felt as cold as a Soviet missile silo.

Such perfect order. Kory wondered how long it would take to mess it all up.

He could ruffle up the drum-tight bedcovers and use a pillow for a weapon to hurl at Damon's desk.

There wouldn't be much of a point doing that, of course. The only things on it were a black leather pad, an inkwell, a blotter, and a golden Waterman sheathed in a mahogany crystal clock-and-globe stand. No loose papers, no open notebooks, and no unfinished homework. Maybe if he were to swing the pillow hard enough, the crystal and the inkwell would shatter, and sharp little pieces of glass and splatters of ink would fly everywhere.

Kory shivered in his jacket.

Better still would be to find something like a diary in the desk drawer. There wouldn't be enough time to read it, but he could just open it and leave it on the desk so that Damon would think that the whole world was snickering at his stupid secrets.

Kory would never do any of those things. He didn't have a death wish.

What he was really about to do was just as bold, but there was a big difference: smashing up the room was a reckless fantasy, and this adventure was nothing of the kind. Most important, Kory had gotten away with it twice before, and he would get away with it this time.

But this was the last time.

He swore it was.

Absolutely the very, very last time.

Kory took off his shoes. They were clean—he'd checked twice—but his socks were even cleaner. He could have gone around the Persian rug, but then he would've had to lean over to get to the armoire. If he were to lose his balance, he could fall. Such a thing could generate enough noise to be heard on the floor below. He'd almost made that mistake the first time he'd tried this.

Kory found what he was looking for on the top shelf, in the exact same place it had been the week before and the week before that. Dollie never left the estate except to visit the vet. Her leash lay neatly coiled with the metal latch to the right. Kory made a mental picture of the shelf, just as he had the other two times. When this was over, he'd have to return every item exactly as it was.

He stuffed the leash into his coat, peeked out the bedroom door to make sure none of the servants were tending to the third floor, and closed the door behind him without making the slightest noise—one of the many things he'd learned from his brother over the years.

He walked quietly down the steps, though he wasn't worried about anybody seeing him at this point. The leash was hidden in the inside pocket of his coat. As far as anybody was concerned, he was just stepping outside to play with Dollie. No harm there.

Besides, at the moment, the only people who might see him were the butler, the servants, and the groundskeepers.

Damon was "training" with that weirdo neighbor. What he was training for, Kory did not know, and he did not care.

He didn't have to worry about his mother, either. As far as Martha knew, Kory was in his room doing homework and studying his chess books.

Also, Friday was the day she saw that lawyer guy. Every Friday at four. Kory wasn't sure what they talked about exactly, but it had something to do with money. Of course, Damon probably knew all about it. Martha told Damon everything.

It was cold outside, but they hadn't had the first snow of the year yet. Dollie was crazy about snow. She loved to leap around, diving in and out of the white powder like a dolphin at sea.

Kory spotted her, curled up by a tree.

He squatted down. Dollie tilted her head as if to say "Is that really you, Kory?" and galloped over to him, her tail wagging in floppy arcs.

Dollie had been a gift from their aunt Mary, from California.

Though Aunt Mary never said, "This puppy is for Damon, and Damon only," that's exactly what Kory's brother believed. Damon was the oldest, and he immediately took responsibility for feeding and training the dog. Nobody ever asked Kory if he wanted to care for Dollie. Kory didn't even have a say in naming her.

In the first six months, Damon had trained her to obey him without any voice commands. If there was something Damon did well, it was teaching obedience. Dollie obeyed all the signals she was taught instantly. Kory only knew a handful:

Assuming the crouching position meant *come.*

An open palm meant *stop and stay where you are.*

An index finger pointing up meant *sit,* a downward wave *lie down.*

Of course, Dollie never barked. Damon would have given her away in a heartbeat if she had. Maybe, in the very beginning, when she was just a small puppy, she'd let out an excited *woof.* Maybe. If so, Kory hadn't been around to hear it.

Kory sometimes wondered if, at first, Damon had hit Dollie the way Damon hit him. Probably not.

Dollie was the smartest dog around. She learned new tricks quickly and without a fuss. Rebellion wasn't in her heart. She would never have given Damon a reason to hit her.

And Damon always needed a reason.

Kory rolled on the ground as she licked his face. If Damon had been there to see, he'd give Kory a good beating for teaching the dog bad habits. After coming over, the dog was supposed to automatically sit and await her master's next command. Only after remaining in the sit position for a while should she be rewarded.

Kory threw a stick as hard as he could, just as he'd done before. Instead of simply waiting for Dollie to retrieve it, he ran after the prize as well, as if he stood a chance of getting there before his four-legged friend. This, too, would have made Damon's blood boil—he always said that a master should never be running after his dog.

Kory repeated this racing event until he'd traversed the long mile to the main gate. If any of the groundskeepers were watching, they'd think Kory was just playing a new kind of fetch. Going this far from the mansion on foot was unusual, but as long as Kory remained on estate grounds, it wasn't expressly forbidden.

Of course, Damon could go anywhere he pleased, anytime he pleased. Damon was fourteen and got to waltz around free as a birdie while Kory, who was nine—ten in just a month and twenty-one days—needed permission from his brother to do almost anything, except for studying his father's chess books and going to school. Of course, Damon always said these were Martha's rules and they were for Kory's own good.

Kory knew better.

He leaned against the stone pillar and looked around. The front of the estate was clear for as far as he could see. He put the leash on Dollie and pushed open the wrought-iron gate. This was the third time he had opened it himself, but he was still surprised at how heavy it felt.

The normal way to Rhodes Park would be to take a left along the road outside the gate and then walk down Henson Street. But there were estates along that road, and closer to the park there were properties small enough for people to spot him from their living rooms. Would somebody actually call his mother and tell her what he was up to? Probably not, but you never could be sure with some people. On his first venture outside the grounds, he'd chosen a path that led straight across the road and down a thicket of trees. That plan seemed as good this time as it did on the last two outings.

Dollie loved the new scents of the forest and the park beyond. For some reason, even though Schoongelegen had more land than any other estate in Rhodes—who knows, maybe even in all of New York State—she found it boring, and never ran or played unless someone else was there to play with her.

It was four twenty. Soon, he would be on the rock, his favorite spot to watch the setting sun.

Kory had been able to sense the time since he was a little boy. He probably kept better track of time than that golden watch Martha had given to Damon two years ago on his birthday.

After slaloming downhill between tall pine trees, Kory and Dollie reached an even steeper section, which marked the point where the thicket came to an end at Route One. On the other side of the two-way road was the green manicured expanse of Rhodes Park. Kory wrapped the leash tightly around his wrist.

Now, he knew full well Damon had crossed Route One here, though Martha had warned them about the dangers of that road. You could slice off a full ten minutes going to town that way, so why wouldn't Damon choose the quickest path? Especially since Damon could do pretty much anything he wanted knowing his mother would look the other way.

Martha had told Kory several horror stories about Route One. The cleaned-up versions, of course.

Twelve years earlier, during the war, two cars had met in a head-on collision. It was daylight, but good visibility wasn't enough to prevent disaster. The crash had happened on the curve just a few yards from where Kory and Dollie were standing. Route One had a lot of nasty turns as it snaked through Rhodes, but this one was the worst of them all. The driver who caused the accident was speeding and ended up skidding onto the opposite lane. Both cars went up in flames; three people died instantly. A fourth ended up in the hospital with third-degree burns.

There was also the story of Freddie Stone. Kory didn't know if it was basically true, only kind of true, or just plain old make-believe. Either way, Martha wasn't the one who told Kory about it. She probably thought it was too gruesome for his "young, sensitive ears."

She might have told Damon; Kory did not know. They spoke about a lot of things. They spoke alone, in the conference room; or else very softly, so only they could hear.

The story, as the kids in school loved to tell it, was about a guy named Fred, who, in the winter of 1951, had crossed Route One half a mile down the road to the east, at the worst possible time.

Fred slipped on a patch of ice. The driver of the semi saw him sit up, casual as can be, obviously still dazed from the fall. Had the fall knocked him out, he'd have still been alive—the semi would have driven right over him. Instead, he remained seated, screaming at the truck as if that would somehow help. And so, as the rhyme went, *"Dead Fred lost his head."* They found it, one eye open looking at the sky, on the grassy mound that formed the edge of Rhodes Park.

A sharp turn warning sign was posted at the junction of Route One and Henson, but that didn't help much.

Kory stood on the steep slope. In front of him, Route One curved like a twisted horseshoe. A wall of tall trees on his side of the road made it even harder for him to see. A Silver Cadillac whizzed by, its tires straining to grip the asphalt, followed closely by a light-blue Dodge. Just when he thought there was a break in the traffic, a cement truck roared by as the driver downshifted to make the turn.

Kory instinctively yanked on the leash. He waited there for two full minutes until he found an opening. He sprinted across, with Dollie pulling like a sleigh dog.

He was on the park green. Safe. Dollie knew where to go. He followed her to the rock. It looked like an unfinished sculpture of the Leaning Tower of Pisa. It stood almost five feet high, but was sufficiently inclined for Dollie to ascend. Its top was flat and smooth and there was room for both of them.

Kory lay on his back. It felt like he was on some giant molar tooth. Dollie stretched out next to him. She rested her head tenderly on his chest, as though she could read his mind and his wish instantly became her wish too.

He held her in a tight embrace as he watched the sun sink below the treetops.

They wouldn't be doing this ever again. He shouldn't have tried this even once, never mind three times. If he kept doing it, he'd surely be caught. Caught leaving the estate without permission *and* taking Damon's dog.

There was no telling what his brother would do to him if he found out.

He scratched Dollie's ears, and she rewarded him with a smile. They say dogs can't smile, but Dollie was more human than some people Kory knew.

The pink horizon was becoming a winter crimson.

Four forty-five . . . Oh God!

No, it was okay.

He could hear the blood pounding in his ears.

Damon had left for the Johnsons' at three forty-five and he'd be finished with whatever the hell it was they did there by six. So he'd be back by six fifteen at the latest, washed up and ready for supper at six thirty sharp. Martha was always done with her meeting by six, usually in time to welcome Damon when he got back home. For some reason this particular meeting was supposed to be extra-important, so six would be the earliest she'd be done. If Kory were home by five forty-five, he'd be plenty safe.

It was a quarter to five, so he had an hour before he had to be home. The walk uphill had taken him fifteen minutes last time, and eighteen the time before, so Kory decided to play it super-safe and give himself a full half hour. That left another half hour on the rock with Dollie. Thirty minutes, not a second more. He had to keep good track of the time, all the time.

This wasn't English class, where getting caught not paying attention to the lesson meant Mrs. Rakkowski would chew him out in front of everyone for daydreaming. The boys would shoot spitballs at him, and the girls would laugh, but that had never stopped him from playing chess in his mind.

This, however, was way different. One mess-up here meant he could end up having to deal with Damon. And Damon never chewed him out. Punishment was never that simple and pain-less. There was never any talk. No sound. A swift punch to the gut, and any chance that Kory might make a noise was gone.

The last time he was on the rock with Dollie, ten full min-utes had slipped by before Kory caught himself so deep in the middle of a game he'd lost all track of time. Ten minutes. If that had happened at the very end of his time allowance, and if Damon had for one reason or another come home earlier . . . Kory didn't want to even think about it.

Right then, he wanted to savor his last outing with Dollie.

Four fifty.

Kory wouldn't push it this time. He'd make it back without getting caught. He had to. He'd make it back and not a soul would ever find out. Only he would ever know.

And the next time Damon was dishing out a punishment, Kory would fight the pain by thinking about the times he took Dollie to the park.

The only hard part would be trying not to smile.

Ken Johnson watched as Damon ran the third lap around the periphery of the grounds. He had trained many young men in his day—although none quite as young as Damon—and this kid was by far one of the most promising he'd seen in his career as a staff sergeant with the Marines.

He'd first met the boy at a get-to-know-the-neighbors din-ner his wife had arranged five years earlier. Ken had learned that Damon's father had been a war hero. A Medal of Honor winner, no less.

The man was the first ever landlord in Rhodes history to volunteer for battle when the rest of the rich snobs stayed in their mansions, complaining because their servants had been drafted and nobody was left to wipe their blue-blood asses. Nicholas had come back a war hero, but a bullet fired on the beach of Normandy had nicked his spine and paralyzed his legs, leaving him with an agonizing pain that didn't let up until the day he died.

Nicholas van Luden had always believed his eldest son, Damon, would leave his mark on this world. Sergeant Johnson had decided right then and there he'd help the boy make his father's conviction a reality.

Martha van Luden seized the forty-page document from the older of the two attorneys seated across the mahogany conference table. "I've wasted almost four months listening to your advice. If everything is in order, then why the same questions?"

Bradley Chambers pointed a cautioning index finger at his younger colleague. "I'm sorry; if I have been somewhat persistent on this matter it is only because—"

"You're concerned for my well-being and that of my children," Martha said. "So you've said, but my late husband placed a great deal of faith in you, now all I ask is that you have the same faith in him and that you respect his dying wish."

Nicholas had passed away seven years earlier, yet she still missed him as much as she did then. He'd often spoken of creating a trust that would both ensure the continuation of the van Luden line, and safeguard a family estate that had taken many generations to become what it was. Only a week before his death, consumed in a pain even morphine could not appease, he'd asked her to carry forth his vision to protect the future of the van Luden name. Now, years later, Martha was going to fulfill her promise.

The young attorney, who must have been twenty-two but looked no more than eighteen, spoke before Mr. Chambers could stop him. "The marriage clause lends itself to problems, Mrs. van Luden."

She gave him a cold smile. "I was told you were here as a witness only." Addressing her attorney once more: "You assured me there were no more loopholes."

Bradley Chambers shifted in his seat. "That is correct; there are none. What I believe Mr. Halloway was trying to say is that this kind of stipulation is not common practice because it could, under highly extenuating circumstances, lead to . . . unpleasantness between the affected parties."

Martha glared at Mr. Halloway, wondering how this wet-behind-the-ears Harvard Law graduate had managed to get her family attorney to take him under his wing. "Bradley and I have already discussed this. He knows how distressing I find the suggestion that my boys might one day fall into the sordid class of those who would quibble over a will."

The young attorney turned crimson. "Forgive me, Mrs. van Luden, but this is no ordinary—"

"No, Mr. Halloway, I don't believe I shall be forgiving you; I've had quite enough of your insolence." She turned to her family attorney. "Either we proceed now or I'm afraid I will have to ask you and your ill-mannered colleague to leave."

Bradley Chambers handed her his pen and pointed: "Initial here. . . ."

Damon had just finished his three-mile run, coming to a stop two feet from Ken Johnson, where he dropped down to the ground to complete the routine.

For Damon, this was more an exercise in balance than physical strength.

Three.

Four.

He had to lower and raise his stiffened body over one hand, which punched into the earth with the knuckles of the index and middle fingers (to harden the "striking zone," as Sergeant Johnson had once explained); his other hand was locked behind his back.

Five.

Six.

Reaching fifty, Damon switched arms and continued the push-ups.

His T-shirt felt cold, heavy, and clammy. The salty sting of perspiration burned into his eyes. His count came out in puffs of steam. Damon loved the cold, especially during workouts.

Twenty-four.

Twenty-five.

Twenty-six.

"Slowly," ordered Sergeant Johnson. "You don't get a workout rushing."

Tweeenty-niiine.

"Is the arm burning, son?"

"Yes—"

Thiiirty . . .

"—sir!"

Thiiirty-one . . .

"You know what muscles are made of, son?"

Forty-two.

"Yes . . . sir . . . fiber . . . sir."

Sergeant Johnson shook his head as if Damon could see him. "Sweat. Good, old-fashioned sweat."

Damon finished the fiftieth push-up with his left hand and rolled over onto his back, crossed his hands over his chest mummy-style, bent his knees, and started on the sit-ups.

"Straighten that back. Come up slowly. Keep that back straight. *Slower.*"

"Yes, sir!"

Damon knew the routine well and didn't need to be told what to do next. After three sets of fifty sit-ups, it was time to work on hand-to-hand combat; and after that there would be more running, followed by more hand-to-hand. Sergeant Johnson had warned him that big men normally don't have the endurance it takes to be a Marine. He was going to push until Damon dropped and then some.

"On your feet," Sergeant Johnson ordered.

Damon used the momentum of his last sit-up to fling himself to his feet.

"We've covered basics in hand-to-hand, and we've worked on weapons, but we need to hone your skills against a blade.

No matter how good you are, if the guy with a knife is worth two flies on a pile of shit, you're in trouble. *Never* underestimate your opponent. When you fight him, imagine he's a *Marine*."

Without warning, Sergeant Johnson's hand shot down toward his right boot and in one motion he lunged forward, striking Damon on the chin with the palm of his left hand. Damon regained his balance in time to pivot away from the nine-inch rubber knife Sergeant Johnson had hidden in his boot. Damon was too late—the palm strike was used to give Sergeant Johnson the range he needed for a forward roll. With one foot he hooked under Damon's ankle and with the other he forced down hard just below the kneecap. Damon went down and Sergeant Johnson was over him, his knife pressing with dangerous force against Damon's throat.

"You're dead," Sergeant Johnson said with disgust.

Damon blinked, trying to keep the sweat from his eyes.

"What's wrong, son?" Sergeant Johnson asked, sheathing his knife. He was no longer angry; he was concerned. Damon could do better in his sleep.

They both got back on their feet.

Damon offered no response, peering vacantly at the setting sun instead.

Sergeant Johnson looked his student over. "We've been doing this for over a year now and that was one of the lousiest demonstrations of self-defense I've ever seen. I can tell when you're not with me, son. What is it? A girl problem?"

"No, sir!" Damon answered, hurt by the implication.

"Nothing wrong with girls, son."

"It's Kory," Damon said, lowering his voice.

"Kory? Your little brother?" He'd almost forgotten Damon had a brother.

Damon nodded.

"What's the problem? Is he sick?"

"No, sir." Damon paused for a moment. "I'm worried he's going to upset Mother again."

Sergeant Johnson's mouth became a straight line. "What's he been up to?"

"She doesn't want him taking the dog off the grounds. He knows that. He knows it full well. Kory could get himself into all kinds of trouble with a dog Dollie's size, and Mother worries." Damon took a deep breath, "The fact is, he's been disobeying her for some time now."

Sergeant Johnson waited.

"I'd just gotten back from my jog and my dog runs up to me like she always does when I get back from school. Jim—he's one of the groundskeepers—he says something like 'cute dog.' I ask him if he'd seen Kory because—"

Sergeant Johnson crossed his arms.

"—he was misbehaving and I wanted to keep an eye out. So Jim says, 'The dog is here, so Kory is probably in the main house.' So I say, 'What does Dollie have to do with anything?' He says Kory's probably in the house, since he's not *out* with the dog. *Out* as in *off the property*. He tells me he saw Kory waltzing out the gate with Dollie on the leash. He says—"

"And your kid brother knew he wasn't supposed to take the dog out?"

"Oh, he knows all right. It doesn't take much to upset Mother, and the doctor said—"

"What did you do about it?"

"I was about to track him down and set things right, then and there, but I didn't."

The sergeant squinted.

"Remember what happened with Hagginbrogh?" Damon asked.

"The snot-nosed punk you set straight?"

"Yeah, him. The principal said he had to make an example of me. Didn't matter that Hagginbrogh started it, or that he was a senior, or he was the school bully and everybody hated him. The principal saw me punching Hagginbrogh, so it all became my fault. I told the principal—I said I'd take any punishment, so long as he didn't tell Mother. I tried explaining about her weak heart, but he didn't care. The bastard called her anyway." Damon clenched his teeth. "She never said a thing to me, but I could tell it really got to her."

Sergeant Johnson flipped the rubber knife in his hand.

"Mother was home that day I found out about Kory taking my dog," Damon said. "If I had done something then, she would have heard because he purposely yells when I try to give him a hiding. No way could I risk upsetting her a second time."

The sergeant nodded but said nothing.

"I was going to ask your permission to leave early today . . . to check up on him. I think I know where he might have taken her—he likes hanging around in the park. Mother has a meeting now, and I was thinking, if I could find him, I could talk some sense into him before he gets back home."

Sergeant Johnson jabbed the knife back in his boot. "You do that, son." He nodded slowly. "Permission granted. Make sure you put an end to this, you hear? You're the man of the house—sounds like it's time to hand out some discipline."

"Yes, sir!" Damon said.

He knew Sergeant Johnson would understand.

Kory lay on the rock. He reached Move 17 in Game Three of the 1858, Paris, Anderssen-Morphy match. Like all the games he'd read about, he knew this one by heart.

As he pressed against her, he could feel Dollie's heat through his coat. Seated, she was like a lion. Majestic, with her chest sticking out and with all that puffy golden fur. Lying down, as she was doing at the moment, she was like a puppy again. She had the cutest way of tucking her head. And she had these long eyelashes. Her eyes were half closed, and she looked like she was sleeping, but she was just resting. Dollie was guarding him, he could tell. She was listening to everything, smelling everything.

How she loved to be rubbed behind her ears. Give her a massage there, and if she could purr, she would. She always gave him a big smile, but never did anything to distract him from his thoughts. There, on that rock with Dollie, playing chess in his mind, he didn't feel the cold. It was as though he had no body. Everything, even the hard, frigid surface of the rock, was as soft and dreamy as Dollie's silky-smooth fur.

He could see the text as clearly as if the book were in his hands. Page 223: "Apprehensive of the advance of Morphy's pawn on

King's Bishop Three, Anderssen plays Pawn to King's Knight Five. Morphy continues his onslaught with . . ." Kory quickly played out the next two moves in his mind so he could get to his favorite part, Move 20. "With the capture of the king's pawn, the rook sacrifice makes Anderssen's position hopeless and the great master resigns to the world champ—"

Dollie's head popped up. She cocked it the way she did when she saw someone she recognized. Before his eyes had a chance to focus, Dollie was on her feet.

It was then that he saw Damon. He was standing there, across the street, fused to the side of a tree, clearly visible in the twilight.

Damon crouched down.

In that instant, Dollie leaped off the rock. The leash, still wrapped around Kory's wrist, pulled him off the edge and slipped off midair as he fell.

Kory regained consciousness to the shrieking cry of tires burning on asphalt. He lifted his head, and at first thought the brown pickup was stopping for a Ford Thunderbird coming from the other direction.

There was a loud thump, like a punching bag striking the ground after a ten-story fall. Dollie was airborne. For a second, seeing a flying dog was almost funny. But the reality of what had happened hit him as if he'd been struck himself—the screeching sound he had heard was the convertible trying to stop for *Dollie.*

Kory felt a sickening weight in his stomach as the last few seconds started to make horrible sense.

By crouching down, Damon had intentionally commanded Dollie into the path of a speeding car.

For a moment, Kory's legs would not move—it was as if they belonged to someone else. Slowly they started working again and suddenly he was running as hard as he could, as though somehow he could still do something. Dollie lay on her back in the middle of the street, her four legs pawing frantically at the cold night air.

Dollie was moving.

She was just hurt, not dead, just hurt. Kory ran faster, almost tripping.

Before he reached her, she finished her strange dance and turned on her side, motionless, except for the steady rise and fall of her chest. She was breathing.

He would get the guy in the pickup to take her to a vet. There was still time.

There had to be.

Then he saw the blood. His chest tightened and his breathing came out in spasms. He was crying into his glasses.

A middle-aged man with salt-and-pepper hair and a Yankees cap got out of the pickup to calm down the two teenagers who were in the Thunderbird. The girl in the front seat was talking to herself in a continuous incoherent stream of words.

Her boyfriend stammered from the car. "I didn't see the dog—it came out of nowhere."

"Calm down, it wasn't your fault," the pickup driver said, but the teenager wouldn't listen.

He turned to his date as if she were a juror. "Really. I didn't see it. Shit, Linda, don't give me that look."

The dog was still breathing, her eyes open but dilated. Kory watched as two wobbling puddles of tears in the valleys of his lenses blurred what already seemed unreal. He was stroking Dollie's thick, smooth mane. Her pink tongue hung out lamely, resting in a swelling pool of blood. The breathing shallowed until there was no longer any movement for Kory to feel. He rested his hand firmly against her chest.

"I didn't see it coming. I didn't bust any speed limits—I swear. I really didn't. Is the dog going to be all right?"

Linda looked at her boyfriend, bit her lip, and shook her head.

Taking that as a definitive answer, the Thunderbird driver said, "Aw, kid, listen. Aw shit. I . . . I'm sorry, I didn't mean to—"

The man with the Yankees cap approached. "You need to take your dog to a vet. You have a vet, son?"

"Shhhh," Kory said.

Everyone fell into silence.

Kory felt her heartbeats fade, then slow. He pressed his ear to Dollie's chest.

There was a gentle *thump-thump* . . . *thump-thump* . . . and then there was nothing.

THE CONFERENCE ROOM

February 3, 1957
Three Years and Two Months Later

Kory was not permitted in the conference room. This was one rule he didn't mind. The only time he was allowed to be there was for family meetings. Thankfully, family meetings were extremely rare.

Damon eyed him from across the mahogany table, his mother seated at his side.

Martha's eyes were cast in Damon's direction, but Damon wasn't speaking. He was going to let Kory smolder in silence.

No one spoke of it, but it was no mystery to Kory why Damon held family meetings in this room.

It was a reminder.

As if Kory could ever forget. Lord knows he'd tried. But the images of that horrific day four Decembers ago had a will of their own. They came and went in his mind like rain showers in the tropics. They interrupted him when he was at peace, playing chess, when he thought it was safe.

But there more than ever, in that room, the memories replayed themselves as though it had all happened yesterday.

Martha had been sitting at the table, right where she was now, with that attorney of hers and some other fellow, a guy Kory had never seen before. Damon had made it into the room first. Not knocking, the huge door hanging ajar; Kory right behind him.

The vet, the sheriff, and the mess of people involved could do nothing to undo what had happened on that day.

Dollie was dead, and only a time machine would bring her back.

All that remained was for the culprit to be punished.

It all happened there, in that conference room. A place where liars became the unquestioned prophets of truth, and the real victims were decried as perpetrators.

Damon had spoken first. Kory would like to have fooled himself into believing that if he'd had the first word, events might have come to a different conclusion. That Martha, the lawyer, and that other guy, would all have believed Kory. Or at least listened to what he had to say.

But even that was wishful thinking.

Damon always had a way about him that commanded attention and respect. Even from adults.

If Kory had been the first to speak, and had used soft, tempered words instead of screaming as he had on that day, it would not have made a difference. Not in the least.

Even if Damon hadn't disappeared from the scene of his own crime. Even if the sheriff had caught and detained him. Even if Kory had made it to the conference room alone, with all the time he could've possibly wanted to explain how and why his psychopathic brother had killed Dollie in a sick act of revenge.

Even then, hours later, Damon would have somehow explained his way out of all culpability.

Lying and deceit came easily to Damon.

Kory had long since given up rethinking that day; sampling different words, different actions, playing them out like a sequence of moves on a chessboard. The best thing he could do was to try to block the memory.

But there, in the conference room, Kory stood no chance of saving himself from reliving that evening as it happened, in inexorable detail, from beginning to end.

What had really happened there on that day had taken place in a matter of seconds, yet the memory stretched on.

Kory took my dog and crossed Route One and now Dollie is dead.

That's all Damon had said. Those thirteen words.

Back when Kory was still in the business of analyzing that evening, he used to imagine what would have happened had he given his mother a chance to react to Damon's words. After the initial shock had subsided, Martha might have had the time to pose a question. A question would have invited a response. In this particular fantasy, Kory was always calm. He would admit to taking the dog without permission. He would admit to crossing Route One. And up to that point, everything worked as it should in the normal world. But when he tried explaining what Damon had done, somehow, Damon would take over control of Kory's fantasy. In some versions, after explaining that he was nowhere near the scene of the crime, Damon would bare his teeth in the world's largest grin, dissolving the daydream in two perfect rows of white.

The outcomes of these scenarios were somehow even worse than what had really happened, because they proved over and over again that no matter what Kory said, Damon would always come out being the hero.

Of course, that evening, Kory had not paused for the shock of Damon's words to settle, and neither had he waited for an invitation to defend himself.

Instead, he had started yelling; shouting words, at the top of his lungs, which in any other place or time would surely have vindicated him.

In that conference room, however, the reality of what had happened that day had fallen on deaf ears.

Nobody was even looking at Kory as he yelled the true account of what his brother had done.

It had taken him a moment to realize why.

His mother had collapsed.

She'd only fainted for a second, and the attorney had caught her before she'd had a chance to fall all the way to the ground, but suddenly the reality of Dollie's murder meant nothing to anyone except Kory.

The only thing they took with them that day was that by screaming, Kory van Luden had given his mother what Dr. Kleinkopf had said might have been anything from a fainting spell to a mild heart attack.

Naturally, despite the good doctor's reverence for scientific objectivity, everyone had concluded it was the latter.

Damon suddenly broke the silence, as though he'd been waiting all this time for the movie playing in his brother's head to come to a conclusion. "As you know, I'll be leaving for West Point in five months."

Kory did not need reminding—eighteen weeks and two days and then no more Damon. One hundred and twenty-eight days to freedom. It was what had been keeping Kory going all this time. His only hope.

Then without Damon saying another word, Kory understood.

Somehow, some way, Damon was going to rip away this last hope.

Kory was certain of this—family meetings always meant bad news. *Always.*

"There's a school in New Hampshire, the Livingsford School for Boys. It's one of the best in the nation—"

Kory had that sickening feeling in his gut.

"—it's a boarding school—"

Of course. There it was.

Kory looked at his mother in disbelief and managed to say "Boarding school?" before his throat shut down completely.

"Give your brother a chance to explain, Kory."

Kory had no choice. No further words would make it out of his mouth.

Damon had obviously planned this very well. He had memorized a brochure full of reasons why it would behoove Kory to attend Livingsford.

As if Damon cared about Kory's education or whether Kory would be going to "one of the most prestigious educational institutions in America."

Much of the reasoning was directed at Martha, as though she and Damon hadn't already discussed this and she hadn't already given her consent.

He wondered why Damon bothered with the whole charade.

"Naturally, Kory will be subjected to a stronger regimen of discipline than he's used to here in Rhodes, and at first, he might feel reluctant or even scared. But after a month or so at

Livingsford, he'll be more at home there than he is here. And the friends he'll make will be the friends he always wished he had."

Kory felt the sudden onset of nausea.

Martha smiled. "That sounds wonderful, dear."

It wasn't clear whom she was talking to. It didn't matter. She was completely under Damon's spell.

"Kory will graduate a highly skilled and cultivated young man with an academic edge over the rest, putting him on the short list for any college of his choosing. Whatever he ends up doing, whatever career he might wish to pursue, the values he will learn at Livingsford will remain with him for the rest of his life."

Martha turned to Kory. She was obviously expecting him to say something, but Kory still couldn't speak.

Damon continued his monologue, singing praises for the school, when suddenly Kory found his voice. "Why?"

Damon squinted, as if Kory had just asked the world's dumbest question.

"If you had been listening, you wouldn't be asking why."

"What I mean is, why *now?*"

Damon nodded. "Okay, that's a fair question." He regarded his mother, giving her an affectionate, yet concerned look. "As you know, Mother is not as well as we all would want. She needs her rest." Damon directed his cold gray eyes at Kory. "She's in no condition to care for an unruly teenager. A boy who resists becoming a man. A boy who has not yet matured to the point where he cares about the welfare and well-being of people other than himself. A maturity I guarantee he will acquire under the auspices of the Livingsford School for Boys."

"There's no way I'm going to boarding school, I won't—"

"There are two options, Kory. One, a solution that works for everyone: you go to boarding school, I go to the Academy, and Mother has the best nursing care money can buy. And two, we all stay here in Rhodes."

Damon waited, expecting Kory to speak.

But he didn't. Kory wasn't sure what Damon was up to, but he did know this was a trap. That knowledge wouldn't save

Kory, but by keeping silent, he hoped to deprive Damon of some satisfaction.

"Of course, if Kory stays, I'd have to stay as well. I'd be forced to attend a nearby college." Damon took in a long, deep breath, as if he were reconciling himself with the idea. "As a result I'd have to forfeit my once-in-a-lifetime opportunity to attend West Point."

Martha went pale. "You *can't* do that, I won't have it."

This was no act. Martha was as shocked as Kory was. Damon had obviously convinced his mother about the boarding school without pulling out his trump card and playing the martyr.

The nausea came back. This time, Kory had to physically resist the urge to throw up.

"Mother, the unfortunate reality is that you are not well enough to care for a child on your own."

"I'm not a child," Kory said. "I'm thirteen."

Damon returned a sad smile. "Unfortunately, being thirteen does not make you responsible. Regardless of any well-meaning intentions you might be feeling at this moment, I think history has demonstrated that instead of helping her, you'd be a burden."

Kory could see it in his brother's eyes: Damon was daring him to say something. *Anything.*

If Kory were to so much as open his mouth, Damon would bring up what happened on that fateful day. All he'd have to do was mention Dollie's name, and no argument against this preposterous boarding school scheme, no matter how eloquently disposed, no matter how logical, would work in Kory's favor.

Kory started breathing as though he'd just run a quarter-mile sprint. If he wasn't careful, he'd cry. And this was no time to be seen crying.

None of this would have happened had his father been alive. Kory was certain of this, though he did not remember Nicholas. Damon and Martha rarely mentioned him. Kory had seen a few pictures, but that was all.

With all those books in his library, Kory's father must have been brilliant at chess. Whenever Kory thought of Nicholas, he imagined a man who had an objective, calculating mind. A mind that would easily discern the logic behind Kory's arguments and the insanity of Damon's self-serving schemes.

His father had been a great soldier, that much they *had* told him. If anybody was strong enough to stop Damon, it had to have been his father. Kory replayed the fantasy he'd imagined so many times before: Damon, just about to strike him; his father sliding in out of nowhere, grabbing Damon's fist in mid-air, crushing it until Damon fell to his knees, begging his father to stop. Damon's begging never helped, and in some versions Damon would even break down in tears. But Nicholas doesn't let go, not until Damon finally admits to murdering Dollie and promises to leave Kory alone, now and forever after.

"What will it be?" Damon said. "Do you want to stay here in Rhodes or are you going to do what's right for everyone and go to boarding school?"

The room was still. Martha was looking at Kory with nervous, hopeful eyes.

Damon remained as eternally patient and unaffected as the painting of J. S. Bach on the wall behind him.

Kory met his brother's stare but he did not speak.

Nothing could be worse than spending another five years with Damon. *Nothing*. Not even boarding school.

Damon smiled, as though he had just read his brother's mind. "I'll take that as a yes to Livingsford."

THE DUKES OF DEATH

Friday, March 8, 1957

Damon got his books from his locker and made it outside in time to see the rush of students pouring out of the main door. Finally he spotted her, carrying her schoolbooks, her head appearing and disappearing in the crowd. She turned right, breaking away from the stream of kids, heading home on foot as she always did. Damon often wondered why her parents never dispatched anyone to come pick her up after school.

When she headed for Sherman Street, he followed her, maintaining a calculated distance. Across the street, four seniors wearing Dukes of Death leather jackets caught sight of her and jogged in her direction. Damon knew them all. Every one of them was a complete pussy with the exception of their leader, Vinnie Marcello, who'd actually been in a real gang back when he was living in Brooklyn. That was before Vinnie's dad had married an old widow with enough money to buy her way into the new section of Rhodes.

They were within ten feet of her now, but Damon was behind them, closing the gap quickly.

"Hey, sexy. Want some of this?" Vinnie made a rubbing motion.

Dorothy gave him an icy stare and told him to dance on a freeway. She was new to the area—she'd come in January for the second half of the school year—and this was her first encounter with the Dukes of Death.

"C'mon, baby, I'll make you feel gooood. Why deny before you try?" He grabbed her by the arm and spun her around.

Damon frowned, shaking his head. That idiot could have really hurt her.

She looked at Vinnie, her eyes dancing in the no-man's-land between panic and defiance. Then her gaze fell upon Damon.

Damon had seen her before, but this was the first time she'd looked right at him. Dorothy had large emerald-green eyes, a slightly curved classic nose, and golden blond hair grown halfway down to her hips. She dressed like a woman: white gloves, matching purse, classy skirt. She was taller and had bigger tits than most girls in her grade, but Dorothy was still too young. . . at least for now. She had a long way to go before making the jump from girlishly cute to womanly beautiful. More like grape juice than wine.

Dorothy made an attempt to kick Vinnie in the shin, but he pivoted out of the way easily, throwing her off balance. He yanked her toward him and began lapping his tongue inches from her face in an obscene offering.

Not one given to attacking from behind, Damon warned, "Hey, *asshole*."

Vinnie turned, his face twisted in surprise and annoyance.

The trick, Damon knew, was always to take out the leader— take him out fast and hard.

Without a word, Vinnie reached for his back pocket, producing a switchblade with the speed of a veteran street fighter, but he didn't have time to press the button. Damon jabbed him hard in the solar plexus. Vinnie's eyes bulged from the shock.

The gang leader wasn't used to being on the receiving end of pain, and he certainly wasn't expecting it this time. A snap-kick directed at the groin and the gang leader doubled over. Grabbing him by the scruff of the neck, Damon threw Vinnie, headfirst, at one of the other leather-bound gang members who was advancing with a full swing punch. The other two seemed ready to charge, but they hesitated. Damon went for the guy closest to him, taking him out with a palm strike to the side of the neck. As the kid fell to the ground, Damon lunged for the last one standing, but he'd already started running.

"Friends of yours?" Dorothy asked, her efforts to sound lighthearted betrayed by the tremor in her voice.

Taking her by the hand, Damon said, "Come on, I'm walking you home."

Thanks to Vinnie and the Dukes of Death, Damon would have a great story to one day tell his grandchildren. A story about how he met his bride-to-be.

MARTHA

Friday, May 17, 1957

Three months earlier, Damon had forced Kory to take the Livingsford admissions test, warning Kory that if he tried to weasel out by doing poorly, he would be sent to a military school for delinquents.

Taking the exam had been a step in the wrong direction, no question, but at least it didn't involve an actual commitment.

Monday. Now, that was another story. Monday could end up being just another day or it could be the beginning of the end. It was hard to see how anything Kory could do or say would stop the inevitable after that.

Which meant that the coming weekend was Kory's last chance to avoid boarding school. Okay, perhaps it really wasn't his very *last* chance, but it certainly felt that way because come Monday, if Kory didn't do some major convincing before then, Martha would be advising the Registrar's Office that her youngest son would not be attending Rhodes High in the fall.

Martha probably could call his school and say she'd had a change of heart. It was conceivable, but not likely. Practically speaking, it would be much harder to convince her to let him stay at home once she'd already begun the process of sending him away.

On Thursday, after school, Kory had managed to catch his mother alone, and was making good headway with his reasoning, when the butler interrupted them to ask Martha if the doctor had prescribed another change of diet. By the time she'd finished discussing the evening menu, Kory had only five minutes before Damon was expected to return from his training. Not willing to take the risk of having his brother walk in on their conversation, instead of trying to rekindle her interest in his cause, Kory had used his precious remaining time to get Martha to promise him an audience once more. In private— just the two of them with no interruptions.

That time had come.

Kory hesitated at the mezzanine where the two symmetrical stairways connecting the top five floors merged into one, descending from there to the foyer. If he were to lean forward, lose his balance, and fall over the mahogany railing, he would probably break his neck on the marble below. Suddenly, inhaling required thought, and he longed for water.

Forcing a deep breath he started slowly down the double-wide stairway.

His father would have known exactly what to do and what to say. Kory was certain. He imagined his father taking him by the hand as they walked up to Martha. Just having his father there, by his side, would have been enough to convince Martha to let Kory stay where he belonged—at home.

Kory put his attention on the red-and-black swirl pattern of the stairway carpeting. There was no point in taking sanctuary in yet another daydream. His father was not going to come back from the dead to save the day. He was gone. Forever. Kory was alone in this cause, and he alone would have to convince his mother to listen to reason, though to this day, the only person she had ever really listened to was Damon.

They hadn't arranged for a meeting place or time. Kory's mother had simply told him that she would be willing to talk with him again, while Damon was training. Kory decided to try the east wing. These days, she was either in her room, resting, or in the library.

She had contracted rheumatic fever as a child, which had eventually developed into rheumatic heart disease. Not long after Nicholas died, her condition had gotten worse. That was when Doctor Kleinkopf had told Damon his mother needed peace and quiet. At the time, Kory was just two, and though

Damon was only five years his senior, he'd already started administering his spirited, if unsophisticated beatings, punishing Kory every time, in Damon's estimation, his younger brother had done something to disturb the prescribed peace and quiet.

The louder Kory had cried, the harder Damon had slapped him. By the time Kory was seven and his older brother was twelve, the beatings had developed into an art form. If Kory made any noise, *any* noise whatsoever, Damon would take him aside, to one of the twenty-four empty rooms, and punch him full-force in the stomach. A technique Damon no doubt picked up from that lunatic Marine he'd started visiting around then. A punch like that created no visible marks. It left Kory gasping for air while Damon completed the remainder of the punishment, placing every blow with calculated precision.

The assaults continued until Damon had knocked the rebellion out of him. Killing Dollie had been Damon's final blow.

Since then, Damon hadn't been able to find an excuse for a beating no matter how hard he'd tried. Kory's room had been spotless and hadn't failed any of Damon's inspections in years. And Kory never made a sound, not so much as a squeak of his shoes on the floor. He always came straight home after school, went to his room, and did his homework. That was all he did, with the noted exception of studying his father's chess books, and because it had been Damon's idea in the first place, that activity had not once been deemed a transgression. For the past three years, five months, and thirteen days, Kory had kept out of trouble—and pretty much out of sight—day-in, day-out.

So what was Damon afraid was going to happen? He'd leave for the Academy, Kory would be alone with his mother, and then what? All of a sudden Kory would become a rebel, wear leather, and start playing the drums? Damon was no fool. He knew full well Kory wouldn't pose that kind of problem. Maybe Damon just couldn't stand the idea that Kory would have his mother all to himself, unchecked, unpoliced. God forbid Martha would take notice and remember that she has another son besides Damon.

No. That didn't make sense either. Damon couldn't be worried about that. Even given five years alone with her, nothing Kory could say or do would ever get his mother to think of him the way she thought of Damon. Everything Damon did was important and that would never change.

In the beginning of the year, all Martha would talk about was how Damon was going to West Point. Now the latest topic was that blonde, Dorothy. Kory was sick of hearing about the beautiful young girl with lovely green eyes and flowing golden hair. Even listening to stories about West Point was preferable. Kory wondered about that girl. Couldn't she see what kind of a screwed-up person Damon was? Martha didn't want to see, but that made sense, she was his mother. What was Dorothy's excuse?

The library was empty and smelled of old leather. A brochure rested neatly in the middle of Martha's rocking chair—the only sign of recent human presence. Even at this distance, the bold letters were easy to read:

UNITED STATES MILITARY ACADEMY

DUTY * HONOR * COUNTRY

WEST POINT ADMISSIONS

The setting sun shot a fuzzy bar through the window, filtered through the cream curtains, making a line diagonally across the brochure, it bent down over the contours of the chair stretching out across the room.

Kory walked down the long hallway, passing a portrait of his father's great-great-grandfather, Jan van Luden.

There was no point checking the ballroom, and Kory didn't want to go anywhere near the conference room.

His chest tightened as he remembered his brother's words. *I'll take that as a yes.*

Damon had not sealed Kory's fate. Not yet. This was *not* an exercise in futility. There was some hope. She'd listened to him yesterday . . . she'd really listened.

And Martha wasn't that unreasonable, at least when Damon wasn't there to mess with her mind.

This time he'd get her to agree to let him stay. He'd simply tell her he wanted to remain at home, with her. He'd promise to behave and never be a burden.

And yes, if he had to, he'd even apologize for yelling that one time, four years ago. He'd promise to never upset her again. When had he ever broken his word?

She was his mother.

Didn't she want him at her side?

What could she say to that?

Kory made his way across the foyer once more, passing the butler's pantry.

The morning-room windows were all shut, the curtains drawn, the shutters secured. He inspected the shadowy shapes, recognized each, and decided his mother wasn't there, either. Silly of him. What would she be doing in an unlit room?

She had to be in the house. He'd checked earlier: her Cadillac was still in the motor park. She hadn't left Schoongelegen in more than ten days.

Remembering his thirst he went to the kitchen for a glass of milk, and there he found his mother.

She lay on the white marble floor, one hand on her breast and the other raised high above her head. A strand of dribble hung out of the corner of her open mouth, refusing the call of gravity.

He stumbled backward a step, and regained his balance against the doorframe. Something inside the depths of his gut heaved, but he choked it down and managed not to vomit.

He worked his mouth, but no sound came out. Soon the convulsions from his stomach subsided into quick spasmodic breaths.

Time to split.

He'd just wasted thirteen precious seconds thinking about it. He could have done a lot of running in thirteen seconds.

With both hands on the knob, Kory pulled the kitchen door; it crashed shut with a hollow sound like an explosion from a crypt.

Kory scrambled for the front door, sensing another presence, but not soon enough. For a crazy moment, he imagined his mother lying there, clawing at him for help.

Instead it was Damon.

Damon was halfway up the stairs leading to the mansion's main entrance when he heard the sound of a slamming door. It was

Friday. Mother had her appointments with Mr. Chambers on Fridays, but rarely did their meetings last this long. The attorney wasn't supposed to be there now, but even if he were, it was highly unlikely for him to have caused the noise. Though the lawyer wasn't always as quiet as Damon would have liked, Mr. Chambers had never made anything close to this kind of ruckus.

Damon went to the front door. It burst open, at first, seemingly on its own.

Then he saw his little brother, staring right at him; Kory's eyes magnified by thick lenses.

Something was very wrong, he could read it in his brother's face: Kory looked slightly green, like he did before he had one of those fainting spells. Martha had thought that Kory might have inherited her weak heart. Typical of her to worry like that.

Kory seemed ready to run, but instead he stared. What was he afraid of? The slammed door? That had to be it. *Kory* had slammed the door.

Shit. This was exactly what Damon had hoped to prevent by leaving his training early. It had to be about that meeting Kory was going to have with Martha. The meeting Kory thought Damon knew nothing about. Kory must have realized there was no changing his mother's mind, and lost his cool.

Kory had slammed the door *on purpose*.

But there was something about the way Kory was looking at him. A madness in his eyes, a hysteria Damon had never seen before.

This wasn't just about boarding school or a door slamming, this had to be something even worse. Damon felt his temples pulse.

Under normal circumstances, Kory would have detected Damon's approach, even coming from the outside, with ample time to plot an alternative course, but nothing inside his brain seemed to function anymore.

It was as if his nightmares had prophesied this very day. In his dreams, Damon always wore his black overcoat. No matter how fast Kory ran, Damon emerged from a tree just in front of him, springing out from a squatting position, the stance he'd used to lure Dollie to her death. Damon would come for him, patiently, smiling at his brother's helplessness.

There was no way of telling how long he stood there frozen, as if his brother's cool gray eyes had the power of a Gorgon and had turned him to stone.

The instinct to survive emerged from the very core of his being, breaking the spell that bound him where he stood, and Kory ran past his brother, down the flight of marble stairs to the gravel path below. It felt like the best his muscles could do was a lazy Sunday jog, as though he were running in the quicksand of his dreams.

Approaching the gate, Kory skidded. He bent his knees and balanced himself with two outstretched arms. After two yards of gravel surfing, he managed to get his feet going again. Why run? If Damon wanted to catch him, he would. Kory had no delusions about that.

Damon would catch him even if Kory could swim across the Atlantic Ocean. Kory kept running, despite the certain outcome.

He struggled with the wrought-iron gate while eyeing the gatehouse. The groundskeepers usually sat there when they were done with the landscaping, but not this late in the day. It was usually empty at this hour. Kory heaved. The gate creaked but barely moved. He'd forgotten to pull up the latch bolt.

Kory ran across the street, not bothering to shut the gate behind him. A few moments later, he was dodging pines in the thicket.

He had been running through the very same trees four years earlier. Only then, Dollie had been with him, running ahead, the leash never slacking.

He tripped over a thick root and fell squarely on his face. His glasses were bent at the rim, but neither lens had broken. The metallic scent of blood filled his sinuses as a thin stream leaked out of his nostril to his lips. He got to his feet again, wiped off the blood from his nose, and brushed away the soil and dead leaves from his knees. Clamping his hand to his side, he tried to ignore the splitting pain and trotted on.

They were just the two of them now, and his brother had turned eighteen, one week to the day. Ergo, Damon would be his guardian. It made sense. It made sense like death made sense.

Alone in that house with Damon for the five years of school Kory had left. *Five years.* Kory doubted he would survive a week.

With his mother alive, there were limits; now Damon could do as he pleased, and for the first time he wouldn't care how loudly Kory screamed.

The incline grew steeper, and not wanting to risk another fall, Kory slowed to a fast walk.

It occurred to him that he had no plan. He didn't have much money in his pockets, either. Barely enough for a one-way ticket. And to where? Without a change of clothing and money for a hotel, he'd have trouble making it through the night.

The only safe haven for him was the Sheriff's Office. Damon wouldn't dare hurt him there. Kory needed to keep away from his brother just long enough for Damon to leave for the Academy. Though West Point wasn't that far away, Damon wouldn't have many opportunities to make his way to Rhodes. Kory remembered him mentioning something to Martha about not getting much time off, especially during his first year; and that certainly made sense, military academies being what they were. All that talk about going to a nearby college and living at home had to have been a bluff—Damon valued his military future above all else.

But Kory still had to make it across Rhodes Park and all the way to the new section of town. There were no guarantees he'd get that far. Even though he was running for his life, there was no telling; not when it came to outrunning Damon.

When he arrived at the edge, he ran across Route One without pausing.

A horn blared behind him.

For a second, Kory was horizontal, cradled in thin air.

He was unconscious the instant his head hit the road.

Damon watched as Kory burst into a sudden run, taking the steps two at a time.

The massive oak door hung open. "Mother?"

Damon realized he was shouting, and for some reason that didn't matter now. He darted through the foyer in the main wing. Nothing.

In the library, he saw the pamphlet on the rocking chair. It was closed. On the front cover was a picture of the Washington Monument at West Point. The general was seated on his stone horse, his arm held out to the right. Damon ran to the west wing. The doors were closed. Nobody in the halls.

The morning room was also empty.

He opened the door to the kitchen and for a second he was unable to process what he was seeing. It was the longest second of his life.

Kory had done it again. Only this time it was worse.

She was hurt.

Really hurt.

She wasn't even moving.

Damon fell to his knees and grabbed her arm. Frantically he searched for a pulse between her tendons.

He ran to the phone, called the operator, demanding to be connected to the police.

Answer . . . answer . . . *Goddammit,* answer.

"Sheriff's Office, who's calling?"

"I need an ambulance for my mother. She's had a heart attack."

"Okay, stay calm now."

"I am calm," Damon said. "I need an ambulance here on the double. Schoongelegen."

"Where?"

"*Schoongelegen.* The van Luden Estate."

"Oh, Schoongelegen. Okay, sir, I need you to remain—"

Damon had already dropped the receiver and was on his way back to the kitchen.

He squeezed his mother's throat with the tips of his fingers. Her flesh felt like cool plastic. He gripped harder, fixing his fingers around her jugular and then released. She didn't seem to be breathing, but there was no way to be certain.

Damon looked for a pulse, forgetting he already had. Somehow, he couldn't remember where to find it. He fumbled for her arm, searching for something there that would remind him. Seeing her wrist, he had a vague idea what needed to be done. He had learned this somewhere . . . someone had told him something about using his fingers like chopsticks.

He felt a tingling sensation. Was that coming from her? He didn't know. In a slow stutter, the kitchen started to sink, tilt, and whiten. Everything softened as the world came out of focus.

"An ambulance will be here very soon Mother, don't worry," Damon said in the oddly bright kitchen.

I'm not worried. I know you'll take care of me.

Damon smiled at her. "You mustn't talk, you'll tire yourself. Remember what the doctor said."

Oh, honey, but I must, and you have to listen carefully . . . I will not be here to guide you forever.

Damon nodded.

Listen. That Dorothy Saunders, she might be just a girl now, but she will grow into a fine young lady. She's meant for you. She needs some growing-up time, that's all.

Perfect matches are blessings that you cannot let slip by. I know; your father and I had that very same magic spark.

In a few years, she'll be of age. Marry her. Make me some beautiful grandchildren. Continue the van Luden line. Make me grandchildren; strong, healthy, and handsome like you.

Make me proud, my little soldier, make me proud.

Damon took his mother in his arms, locking her in a bear hug. Something inside his mother made a popping sound, but he didn't notice, he was weeping in convulsions now.

When the medics arrived, they tried to take Martha away. He explained to them about her heart condition, but they weren't listening. They were pounding on her chest and sticking her with needles.

Two more men came over. Not much older than Damon. They tried putting her on a stretcher. She needed to go to the hospital. Damon understood that, but he wasn't going to leave her alone. He had to be there, by her side, for when she recovered.

He kept a tight grip on to her hand as they carried the stretcher to the ambulance. Now she had a mask on her face, but that was okay, she still talked to Damon.

He could hear every word, gentle whispers in his head.

"Can you hear me?"

The sound was distant and nearby at the same time.

Kory's head was throbbing. He was lying down.

He tried having a look, but his eyelids did not respond.

"Son, can you hear me?"

His eyes finally came open. The room was painfully bright and completely out of focus. Where were his glasses?

"What happened?" Kory's voice was frail; his tongue thick and tasting of cotton. He tried the same question again with more force, but still couldn't get beyond a whisper.

"You've had an accident. You're lucky to be alive. The driver who hit you brought you here. He said you just shot across the road without looking. If he didn't get on the brakes when he did . . ."

"Where am I?"

"You're in the St. Francis Hospital," the man said. "I'm Sheriff Thompson."

Kory struggled for a memory and recalled running through trees to Route One. And then there was only the dark weight of missing time, with no way of telling how many minutes or hours had been stolen from his life.

He realized he was wearing a gown and nothing else under the covers. He imagined a nurse undressing him. Taking her time, while he lay on this bed, completely exposed.

Then he remembered what had made him run in the first place. He almost managed to sit up, but the movement made him immediately dizzy, and his head fell back on the pillow. The throbbing pressure took a long while to subside.

"Son, you need to stay put. Doctor's orders."

"My . . . my . . . mother . . ." Kory said.

The sheriff stepped closer; his fuzzy outline was becoming clearer now. He was at least six-four and overweight, but it was hard to tell how much of the man was muscle and how much was fat. He had viciously pocked skin that contrasted sharply with his kind brown eyes. The sheriff sighed. "The doctor says you need to get your rest. I had to promise I wouldn't keep you long."

Kory found his voice. "My mother was in the kitchen. On the floor."

The sheriff walked over to the bed, dragging a chair with him. He cleared his throat.

"She's dead, isn't she?" Kory's voice was still a whisper.

The answer came after a long silence. "I'm afraid so, son."

To Kory's surprise, he found himself bursting into tears. The agony in his head flared with every convulsion, but Kory couldn't stop crying. He grabbed his head as if trying to hold his skull together. The pain left little room for anything else, and Kory could barely feel the sheriff squeezing his shoulder.

Martha was dead. The convulsions gave way to shaking. He'd known she was dead from the very moment he'd seen her lying in the kitchen. Hope had found a hiding place somewhere within him, only showing itself the moment it was shattered.

I'm afraid so.

Gone. Forever.

The tears burned in his eyes. "Please . . . please . . . don't make me go back there. I . . . I couldn't bear it."

The sheriff gave Kory another squeeze. "It'll be all right. You'll be staying with the Johnsons. You know them, right?"

"Yes," Kory said, his voice steady with relief. *Anyone but Damon.*

"You will stay there until other arrangements are made."

"What other arrangements?"

"You have an aunt in California. Mrs. Johnson told me she would call her, to tell her . . . about your situation."

"You mean that I'm an orphan now."

The sheriff met Kory's gaze. "I mean that you'll be needing someone to take care of you. But first, we've got to get you well again. Okay, little buddy?"

Kory nodded.

"The doctor said you don't have any broken bones but he'll still need to keep you in the hospital for observation."

"How long?"

"Oh, a day or so, depending on how you're feeling. You've had a concussion, so he'll want to keep an eye on you for a while."

Kory made an effort to sit up.

The sheriff smiled. "Can you handle one more visitor?" Before Kory could respond, Sheriff Thompson added, "Your brother's outside waiting to see you."

BURIED

Sunday, May 19, 1957

"Oh, do stop. Haven't we finished with this?" Jane said, centering her husband's tie.

"No, in fact we haven't."

Ken sifted through his jackets to find the one matching his pants. He located it, on the far end, annoyed that Jane hadn't had the damned suit hanging out in the first place. "You never told me why you're so interested in this kid all of a sudden."

"Martha was a dear friend of mine."

"Your *only* friend in these parts," Ken corrected.

"Why, that's not true. There's Carolyn, there's Josephine, and—"

"I said in *these* parts. All your other friends are in New Rhodes."

He'd hit a nerve there, but what had to be said, had to be said. New Rhodes was for what Jane called the *nouveau riche*. For some reason, people like Jane considered that a bad thing, a low-class thing. Ken had been born to this earth with no class and no money. His parents, her parents—pretty much everyone—had said their marriage wouldn't work. Her mother had called it an "unabashedly adolescent maneuver." The rich didn't say anything directly, but Ken knew what they thought of him: he didn't have a fancy diploma, he didn't come with a pedigree (something like Kenneth S. Johnson III), and he certainly didn't have much in the way of money.

Shit, his entire family put together couldn't pay for a month's upkeep of the Rhodes mansion, not if they had a life-time to come up with the cash. And this was the third estate his in-laws had given their daughter.

What none of them had realized was that Ken was a Marine, and failure wasn't part of his vocabulary. He'd proven them all wrong. This year he and Jane would celebrate their twentieth wedding anniversary. Yes sir.

So he had let her put him through endless lunches and din-ners until they had pretty much met everyone in the Rhodes *Who's Who.* Except the van Ludens. Jane learned from her new neighbors that the van Luden family came to New York among the very first settlers, arriving before the *Mayflower,* some time in the mid-1600s. They didn't come more blue-blooded than that, Jane had said. Ken had wanted to point out that these people came from Holland; back then they were probably just a bunch of profit-hungry fur traders. You'd have to go back six generations to find a van Luden who put in an honest day's work. How did that make them better than anyone else? Ken hadn't said any of these things. If Jane needed to socialize with her kind, if that made her happy, he wouldn't stand in her way. He put up with her shit, and God knew she put up with his.

None of the van Ludens had come over to introduce them-selves or extend an invitation to dinner, or even just tea, and Jane had taken it personally. The neighbors had warned her that Mrs. van Luden no longer entertained and didn't accept invitations, either, but Jane just couldn't swallow the fact that she was being excluded. Ken could have said, "Welcome to the club," but he had held his tongue then, too.

Eventually, she'd broken down and called. Martha van Luden had accepted her dinner invitation. Jane had consid-ered this a great honor. Ken Johnson didn't give a rat's ass.

The growing bond between the two women had mystified Ken. He never understood what Jane could like in a cold blue-blooded bitch like Martha, but his wife came from a completely different world and he'd learned long ago not to mess with Jane's social life.

She took a seat at her vanity table. "What is your point?" Jane had her black dress on and had been at the hairdresser's earlier that morning; now all that was required was a modest application of makeup, the hat, and the veil.

"Do I really have to spell it out?"

Jane cocked her head. "Of all people, I wouldn't have expected *you* to object to my consorting with the occasional acquaintance of lesser heritage."

"Jane, honey, when you start with the fancy-dancy words, I know you're full of crap. This isn't about your friends in New Rhodes, and you know it."

"And *you* know I don't like that language."

"That's what you get for marrying a Marine."

He searched for a hint of a smile, but she wasn't in the mood to let this go.

Ken pressed. "If the kid wasn't worth four hundred million, you're telling me you'd still be interested?"

"Kenneth Johnson, *really*." She slapped the lipstick barrel into its gold mirror case. "How could you say such a thing? That's reprehensible, even for you."

"Maybe, but it's true."

"It is nothing of the kind."

"Then why do you keep moaning and groaning about money?"

Jane's parents had recently suffered what she referred to as "a series of unfortunate setbacks," and so her annual allowance had been reduced. By how much, he didn't know, and he didn't care.

"You needn't concern yourself with our finances, we have accountants for that. And I told you this was just temporary; my father has to reallocate significant portions of his stock. Have you even noticed the difference? Do you want for anything?"

"Don't turn this around. You know I don't give a damn about money."

"Kenneth."

"But *you* do."

"Even if that were true, which it isn't, I've already told you about the boys' trust fund. It's not something any outsider could simply lay claim to. It's complicated, my dear. You would hardly understand."

"Are you calling me stupid again?"

"Don't be silly. Martha said it was the most complex trust her attorney had ever drafted. She didn't go into specific details, but I do know the trust will pass on to the first to marry and then to his first male offspring."

"Yes, yes," Ken said, waving at her with annoyance. "You've told me. And believe it or not, even I can understand that."

"I know that, dear, but you must take in to account that there are many conditions and stipulations about which neither of us is aware. I can assure you that someone like Martha van Luden wouldn't leave her fortune to a poorly drafted trust." Jane did not take her eyes off her reflection in the mirror. "I happen to know that even as legal guardians, we'd have no claim to her estate."

"Maybe not directly."

"What you insinuate is no less than abhorrent. Kory is just thirteen, for heaven's sake. The dear child just lost his mother. Are you saying I'm so heartless as to take advantage of this child for petty financial gain?"

Ken was quiet for a while as he studied the image of his wife in the mirror. "See, now I really don't understand this: we're going to a funeral and you'll be wearing a veil—so what's the deal with all the makeup? I don't like makeup, and I've told you that, so why the hell do you wear it?"

"Now who's changing the topic?" Jane did not speak for a while, but she seemed deep in concentration. When at last she spoke, her voice had acquired a serrated edge. "Martha was a dear friend of mine and now she's passed away. Do you expect me to simply turn away from her two children? Would you like me to leave them on the sidewalk? Or would you rather we gave them to that incompetent trollop just because she's their aunt?"

"First of all," Ken replied, raising his voice above hers, "we're not talking about two kids here, Damon's an adult now. He can stay with us until the beginning of summer, but then he's got to report to West Point for Beastie Week. So we're just talking about Kory. Now he's thirteen, and that means it'll be five years before he leaves for college. Have you really thought about what it's going to be like dealing with that undisciplined kid for all that time? Besides, we have no legal claim on him.

You said that according to the will, we become the guardians only if there is no available and willing relative."

Jane coughed a laugh. "And who is available and willing? Martha's sister? She is the only living relative, and she couldn't hold on to a marriage, never mind a child. Besides, even if it were true that Kory has some problems, then we owe it to Martha to help him."

Ken paused for a moment. "If you insist on giving the kid a try, I won't stand in your way. But I happen to know the kid is trouble, and I'm telling you right now, there'll be discipline in this house. I won't put up with any of his snot-nosed crap. I don't care what he's worth. Damon had his hands full trying to discipline the kid. I'm telling you right now, if Kory turns out to be a spoiled brat, he's out. Am I clear?"

"You're creating problems where there are none," she said, trying on the hat. "Let's get guardianship first, and I promise you, there'll be no trouble from Kory."

The humidity in New York was insufferable, and her dress clung to her in wet patches. Funny how she'd forgotten what it was like. The sidewalks were swarming with people. The place was nuts. Mary felt like a lost sheep in the middle of a wildebeest stampede. The weather was always like this in the city, but it certainly hadn't been this congested when she was a child.

Mrs. Johnson had been the first to tell her. Mary had been shocked to hear of her sister's death, and receiving the bad news through a long-distance phone call from a complete stranger only made it worse. Fifteen minutes later, the phone had rung a second time. Brad Chambers had called, sounding lawyerly despite his clumsy attempts at compassion.

After he'd offered his condolences, for the second time that day, Mary had nothing intelligent to say. Brad, however, hadn't seemed the least bit at a loss for words. He'd just told her Martha was dead, and only seconds later he was all business. He wanted to settle the matter of custody for Kory. Damon had just turned eighteen, and didn't need caring for in the eyes of the law.

Damon was going to West Point, so effectively she was the only family Kory had. Brad had said that if she didn't want custody, he could arrange for the Johnsons to care for Kory.

Without pausing for air, Brad had paraphrased from clauses in Martha's will and had made several references to the trust fund. Mary hadn't been listening, although she did remember him saying something about going over this in greater detail at a later, more appropriate, time. How very thoughtful, Brad.

After those calls, she'd helped herself to a few extra drinks that evening. Not just out of sorrow for her sister's death—it was what Mrs. Johnson had said that had really bugged her. And *how* she'd said it. Mary was no fool; she got the hidden message. That Johnson woman knew, somehow, that Mary wouldn't want the responsibility of a teenage boy.

Naturally, how could a licentious divorcee like Mary bring up a child? God only knew what Martha must have told her.

How sweet and understanding Mrs. Johnson had sounded. What nerve of the woman to call her and talk to her as if they'd been lifelong friends.

Mrs. Johnson had told her the news of her sister's death using tactful, calculated words.

Of all the things she could have said, "Really?" had rolled out of Mary's mouth like a soft belch.

She should have said nothing—it would have been so much better that way. . . .

Or she could have hung up, or cried, or something like that; anything was preferable to what she'd said.

Why not just say, "So what?" or "Good for her," or just let out a long, hearty laugh?

Mary had made a complete mess of her life. They knew it in California, and they knew it back home. She couldn't even get pregnant. And it was her fault—that much was a medical certainty. Her first husband never forgave her for it, while her second had claimed not to care, perhaps because he'd found entertainment elsewhere.

She had suspected him for months before gathering the courage to hire a professional. The detective had produced a taped phone conversation, a manila envelope with twenty-four color photographs, and an outrageous bill. That had ended marriage number two.

Now Mary was alone, despite the ugly rumors to the contrary.

At the end of the block, a man in a white apron was selling soft drinks behind a hot-dog stand, where bottles of coke and root beer nested in a bucket of melting ice.

Her thirst was suffocating, but Mary didn't want to be seen sucking soda from a straw; there were some things she couldn't shake from her upbringing, although God knows she'd tried.

The price they were asking for that dress was outrageous; she should have bought it back in San Francisco. At least there she knew where to shop.

The saleslady at Best & Co. believed a funeral was an appropriate place for Mary to make a fashion statement, suggesting a black rayon crepe dress with a tambourine screening that fell in fancy fluid ribbons to the skirt hem, and a large orbital hat to house the veil. Saks Fifth Avenue had offered more of the same.

All Mary needed was a simple black dress, to be worn just this once. She didn't want to fuss over it; she didn't even want to think about it. So she had put an end to the problem and bought the damned thing at Saks without further ado.

Mary looked around for a place with air-conditioning, somewhere comfortable to sit, and where they served drinks in a glass. A red neon sign proclaiming STEAK, BBQ AND GRILL caught her attention.

As she nursed a Coca-Cola by the corner window, she thought again of Kory and Damon, her sister's two children, now totally alone in the world. And what a cruel world it was—a world where everyone is out for themselves. Out to get you. To take *advantage* of you.

Those two boys would be inheriting a fortune, and could easily fall prey to the many vultures out there. She didn't know Martha's neighbors, but she certainly didn't like the sound of that Mrs. Johnson. Mrs. Johnson's words hadn't set off warning bells at the time, but now Mary felt differently. Mrs. Johnson wasn't just some brainless gossip, and to think of her as such would be to underestimate the threat. She was one of the vultures.

Mrs. Johnson had been precise, placing each word with care: "I know what a shock this all must be to you, and I am sorry to have to be the bearer of such sad news, but I am afraid that there is another pressing issue, and that is your sister's children. As you well know, you are the only family they have left. Fortunately Martha did not presume to burden you with their care. She left you with a choice: Should you be unable or unwilling to care for them for any reason—and after the shock you have just been through that would be perfectly under-standable—she has named us as alternative guardians. There is plenty of time to decide, Mrs. Thorn. You needn't worry yourself with this. I only mention it because I didn't want you to think that you have to be bothered with such concerns at a time like this. The two children are in our care now."

Should you be unable or unwilling . . . hadn't Brad Chambers used those exact words just minutes after Mary had finished that phone conversation with Mrs. Johnson?

"I see," Mary had said. Not really seeing anything at all. "How are they taking it?"

"The youngest had an initial shock and ran off. There was a very minor accident . . . he was hit by a passing car."

"Heavens, is Kory okay?"

"Oh, yes. He's fit as a fiddle. The driver managed to slow down and Kory just ended up bumping his head."

"And Damon?"

"He's still quite upset . . . understandable, poor dear . . . and there was a bit of an incident . . . well, no point of going into that; they are both fine now."

"What incident?" Mary had asked, just as Mrs. Johnson must have hoped she would.

"Well, you see, Damon was quite shaken by the whole thing. He wouldn't leave her side and . . . well . . . there was a minor scuffle with one of the paramedics who tried to revive your sister."

"A scuffle?" Mary had inquired, not knowing then how mas-terfully Mrs. Johnson had manipulated her. Oh, but she could see it clearly now.

"Yes, I'm afraid so. Damon started shouting, insisting that his mother could be revived. The medic was patient and understanding, but this only frustrated the poor boy more and, well, as he tried getting to his mother he inadvertently gave the medic a rather strong push. You know how boys are; they don't know their own strength, especially Damon. Fortunately nobody was hurt. We apologized on Damon's behalf and there is no issue of a lawsuit."

"But is Damon okay now?"

There was a pause on the line. "Yes, you must understand, Mrs. Thorn, they've been through a terrible shock and will both need time to heal. But please don't worry, they are staying with us. We've always wanted children of our own and we're delighted to have them. You mustn't worry, both of them will be just fine."

In return for what, Mary thought now, a piece of the fortune? Or was Mary supposed to be stupid enough to believe that all this love, care, and protection was coming out of the goodness of their hearts?

And the way that woman so cleverly mentioned the episode with Damon. All designed to put Mary off any idea she might have had of taking Kory under her wing.

How stupid Mary had been. How petty and selfish. Those psychiatrists she'd wasted so much good money on all put indirect blame on something: her mother, her father, this or that complex, syndromes and neuroses with fancy Greek names.

What poppycock.

Mary glanced at the Saturday *New York Times,* which lay folded on the passenger seat of her rental car. The headlines read: BENNY HOOPER RESCUED. She had read the article while having breakfast at the hotel. Two hundred men worked to get a seven-year-old out of a well. He'd been trapped in there for twenty-four hours. The first thing the poor boy had asked for was his mommy.

Strange how this headline appeared to her now, at this very moment in her life. It was as if God were trying to tell her something.

The area was becoming very familiar, and soon she entered the outskirts of Rhodes.

Mary wondered how people like the Johnsons could live in such beauty and have such cold hearts. She drove through downtown Rhodes, past the fancy boutiques that had never been there when she was a child, past the old redbrick library. She turned right, on Franklin Street, and soon the shops gave way to trees, and at the other end of town she could see Rhodes High. Old architecture blended with new, and although she recognized the Main Hall, the other buildings had changed completely. After the football field, the last of the Rhodes High campus rolled by and now there was only country.

Mary parked the rental behind a long train of limousines, and she sat there staring out the window. People were walking, in slow procession, toward the rectangular gash in the lawn.

The last funeral she'd attended here, her sister had buried her soul along with her husband.

Now, Mary thought sadly, we bury her body.

Finally she pushed open the door, letting in a warm, rich smell of country air. It was an inappropriately beautiful day for the occasion, Mary thought, realizing her sister was probably thinking the same thing as she looked down on her own funeral.

Mourners, some she recognized, most she did not, had already taken their assigned places among four rows of chairs. The front row, normally sectioned off for relatives, was occupied by only three people: A woman in a wide black hat who had to be Mrs. Johnson, a man with a crew cut and black silk suit, and a tall boy whose head was wrapped with a wide bandage. Mary's eyes narrowed.

Kory just ended up bumping his head. . . .

That was no mere *bump.* How much of the rest of Mrs. Johnson's story had been twisted truth designed to leave Mary thinking everything was under control?

She regarded her nephew. The years had stretched Kory, head and body, into an awkward adolescence. She had expected to see him crying; instead he wore quite a different expression, no less intense but much harder to interpret. His brother wasn't seated, and neither could she spot him in the crowd. Where was Damon?

Mary walked over to the front row and the Johnsons stood. Kory followed their example. After the formal introductions, Mrs. Johnson said, "I'm so sorry, this is such a tragedy."

"Ma'am," Mr. Johnson said, "my condolences."

She nodded and turned to Kory.

"Kory? Honey?" She kissed him on the cheek, her temple brushing across the coarse cloth strapped around his head. He peered at her through thick lenses, his eyes so huge, irises cyan-gray just like his father's. There was a hint of a smile and then it was gone. She tried to understand what was wrong. The boy did not appear to be sad, he seemed frightened—terribly so. Suddenly, her heart sank. She felt such pity for her nephew. What had she been thinking? Of course he was frightened. He was *alone*, an orphan.

She couldn't leave them to strangers; she didn't care what the hell anybody might think.

Mary was not paying attention to the minister's eulogy. She was crying, the only one there in tears. Her sister was dead, but now Mary had an opportunity to have some semblance of her own family.

She took her nephew's hand in hers and squeezed. His arm was limp, his eyes looking nervously left and right.

The coffin was lowered slowly into the pit, and Martha disappeared into the face of the earth.

The minister grabbed a fistful of soil and let it slip between his fingers. "Dust unto dust, ashes unto ashes . . ."

Mary was still gripping Kory's hand as people stood and began to leave. She felt Kory tug in the opposite direction and realized Mrs. Johnson had Kory by the other hand.

Neither woman relinquished her grip.

"If you don't mind, Mrs. Johnson, I was thinking I'd take him in my car."

"Oh . . . all right . . . no problem . . . but please do call me Jane."

"Thank you, *Jane*. Feel free to call me Mary."

"Mary it is. We can dispense with silly formalities—after all your sister has said about you, I feel I have known you a long time. You are welcome to come to our place; I simply assumed that after the long drive from New York City, you'd want to rest at your hotel."

"That's very considerate of you, but I've already checked out."

"Oh? Leaving us so soon?"

"No, actually I'm not leaving, I'm staying."

"Oh, that's good. Because we haven't had time to chat, and there is so much to talk about . . . . So, how long will you be here with us, before you return to San Francisco?"

"I'm not going back to San Francisco. My responsibilities are here, with my nephews."

"Miss Thorn," Jane said, "forgive me, but a child is an enormous responsibility, and one mustn't make such decisions on the spur of the moment. You haven't seen either of them in years. I didn't want to tell you this over the phone," she lowered her voice as if Kory wouldn't hear even though he was standing between them, "but Damon really isn't taking this very well. He's insisted upon staying alone in Schoongelegen, with only the servants for company, and he refuses to talk to us or even his little brother. We were hoping he'd show up today, but as you can see . . ." Jane motioned with an open palm. "And there's young Kory—he's been awfully quiet."

Kory made eye contact with his aunt. Mary rubbed his hand with her thumb.

Jane was no longer whispering. "At the moment you must be emotionally distraught, and that is quite understandable, but you have had no experience bringing up children, and these two, although they *are* lovely boys, have been under tremendous strain—they are both quite affected by the loss of their mother. Come to our place and we can have a nice talk. Once you see what a wonderful home we have here in Rhodes, I'm sure you'll agree it's in the children's best interest to stay with us."

"Rest assured, *Jane*, the only thing on my mind is what's best for them. I don't know what my sister has told you about me, and I really don't care.

"It may have been years since I've seen the boys, but I've known them since they were born, and frankly I would have been surprised to hear that they'd taken lightly to the sight of their mother lying dead in the kitchen.

"The way I see it, I am at least as qualified to bring up children as you are, since neither of us have had any.

"I'm going to follow you to your house now, so Kory can gather his things."

"Miss Thorn, please—"

"Look, I'm sure you have a wonderful home, but if you want children, then go spawn your own."

John Saunders settled his newspaper on the coffee table, perched his pipe in a wooden ashtray Dorothy had made for him in art class, and let out a groan as he pushed himself out of his beloved easy chair, wondering who could be at the door. Just an hour ago, he'd bought two boxes of Girl Scout cookies.

At his doorstep stood a younger, stronger, blue-eyed version of Clark Gable, minus the mustache. It was the van Luden boy, Damon. John had only seen him once before, when Damon had taken his daughter on what she had insisted *wasn't* a date. Which of course meant it was. The whole thing had caught John off guard. The suddenness and utter formality of it all. Damon van Luden appearing in a suit just to take Dorothy for lunch in a diner? John knew Joey's Diner had to have been his daughter's idea, but still . . . a suit? And his mother calling beforehand, making it all so official. Martha van Luden, didn't she just . . . wasn't today her—

"Mr. Saunders?" Damon said, taking off his hat. "Forgive me for calling unannounced."

"Of course, of course, no problem."

The young man was dressed in black. Funereal black.

John tried to conceal his uneasiness. "Is Dorothy expecting you?"

"No. But it is imperative I speak to her."

Imperative. John did not like the sound of that, but there was a genuine quality of urgency in the young man's tone. Seeing him for the second time, the effect was no less surprising: he looked older than his age, like a man in his twenties, not a kid who'd just turned eighteen. Which made his interest in Dorothy even harder to swallow. She was just a little girl. Damon was older, much older, and physically overbearing. John wondered if this was going to set a precedent for boyfriends to come.

"Come in, and please, do sit down," John said, pulling up a chair for himself and pointing at the couch for Damon. The wooden chair was much easier to get out of, and John hoped, somehow, by sitting on it, the conversation would be similarly affected.

"I heard about your mother . . . what happened. I'm really sorry. I'm relatively new here . . . I only had that one conversation with her on the phone, but I had the impression she cared for you very much." John looked for reassurance, but his guest wasn't offering. "The funeral was today, wasn't it?"

John took the silence to mean yes. He should have known better than to ask; after all, the young man was obviously dressed for the occasion.

"Yes, well, like I was saying, I didn't know your mother very well, and . . . and funerals are for friends and family . . . but I *am* very sorry for your loss." Annoyed that the words refused to fall into place, John tried a more direct approach and the result sounded worse. "Now, what can I do for you?"

Damon waited for a few seconds, took another deep breath, and said, "I've come to say good-bye."

"You're leaving Rhodes?" John asked, raising his eyebrows.

"Yes, for now."

John shifted, and his chair—a relic from childhood he couldn't bring himself to part with—responded with a jarring groan against the wooden floor.

"I'll be heading for the city in a few hours," Damon said.

"You're going to Manhattan?"

"Until I start classes at the Academy, yes."

"Oh, that's right, Dorothy mentioned something about that. West Point, is it?"

Damon nodded. "I start on the second of July." He produced a calling card. "I'll be staying in our New York town house. I've written the telephone number on the back."

John took the card, regarded it politely, and put it next to the ashtray.

"I have to take care of certain matters regarding my mother," Damon explained.

John nodded. "Yes, of course. If you need anything—anything at all—you know where to reach me."

"Thank you, that is much appreciated, sir."

The funeral must have just ended, John decided. Damon must have come straight here, without changing attire. He appeared unsettlingly calm for an eighteen-year-old who'd just lost his mother, but John had read somewhere—it was either Dr. Spock or Anna Freud—of the effects shock can have on people, and how deceptive a composed appearance can be.

"I would have liked to have visited earlier, but my mother was not well, and I was needed at home."

"I understand," John said, making the chair squeak a second time.

"At least you had the chance to speak to her, even if it was just over the phone," Damon said.

John stopped himself, mid-frown. The young man was obviously upset, probably confused, not knowing where to turn for support.

"It pains me to have to leave Rhodes, but I cannot stay here any longer. I couldn't leave without saying good-bye."

"Why, thank you," John said, forming a clumsy smile.

"It is a pity that Mrs. Saunders isn't here; I would have liked to have paid my respects to her as well."

"Well . . . uh . . . yes, but she's . . . she's gone, I'm afraid," John said, halfway out of his seat. "Can I get you something to drink, Damon? Orange juice, Coca-Cola?"

"I'm sorry to hear that," Damon said.

John hovered over his childhood chair, and then realizing he wasn't going to be allowed the excuse to get a breather in the kitchen, he sat down, releasing his weight delicately.

"I understand what a tragedy the loss must have been for you," Damon said.

"Well . . . we were actually divorced at the time," John said, but it did not seem Damon had heard him.

"My mother said she met Father by the grace of God. It took them just two weeks to realize they were meant for each other. They seized the moment, and lived what little time they had together to the fullest."

John eyed his pipe as if it could help him figure out what to say. "Are you sure you don't want something to drink? It's actually quite warm out there, and you must be smoldering in that suit."

"I'm fine, thank you," Damon said.

John disagreed, but said nothing.

"I know Dorothy and I have only been on one date; I wish things had been different, but Mother's heart condition was getting worse, and I spent every moment of my free time with her until the very end."

"That must have been very hard for you."

"Your daughter is special. She's like no girl I've ever met. You know what I mean, you're her father."

John cracked an uneasy smile. "She's quite a handful, I'll grant you that."

"What I'm trying to say is that you never know when you'll lose a loved one. It could be your father, your mother, a friend, or the love of your life—"

"Well, I suppose that's true, but you're a young man with a long life full of prospects ahead of you. You should be thinking more of what you have than of what you might lose."

Damon nodded. "Yes, I didn't mean to sound ungrateful. Believe me, I know and value what I have."

Mr. Saunders fidgeted with his finger, and Damon wondered if he realized his daughter had been listening to most of the conversation.

Damon had seen Dorothy's head disappear at the top of the stairs. It had been a blur really, and he wasn't even quite inside the house yet when he'd noticed, but Damon wasn't one to miss something like that. How could her father not expect her to be curious about who was at the door? Hadn't Mr. Saunders heard Dorothy creeping down the steps? He seemed like a kindhearted man, just as Martha had said he was, but he certainly didn't keep much of an eye out for his only child.

"I'd like to see Dorothy one more time before I leave."

Clearly relieved at the excuse to get out of his seat, Mr. Saunders shouted, "Honey! There's someone here to see you."

Forgetting to pretend to open and close her bedroom door, and appearing a bit too soon, Dorothy made herself visible at the top of the stairs.

She was wearing a white dress with pink lace. Damon felt a vacuum from the depths of his stomach. Leaving her here was going to be difficult, especially knowing many would chase after her in his absence.

As she entered the living room, Mr. Saunders said, "I have to go to the supermarket, hon, can I get you anything?"

"No, thanks," Dorothy said.

Mr. Saunders extended his hand. "Damon, I wish you the best with your studies at the Academy, and do write us when you get the chance."

"I'll do that," Damon said, giving a tight handshake. Sergeant Johnson had taught him how to read a man from the way he grabs your hand. Mr. Saunders's grip was feeble and clammy.

"So, how have you been?" Damon asked, when he heard his father-in-law-to-be close the front door.

"Fine . . . and you?" Dorothy said, bowing her head.

"Sit down," Damon ordered gently.

He took a seat next to her, so close their legs were touching. "Dorothy, I'm afraid I have some bad news. I'm leaving . . . earlier than planned. Unfortunately—"

"Before you go on, I have a confession to make." She looked up at him. "I heard everything you said to my dad."

"Really?" Damon said, pleased by the admission.

"I think what you said was very sweet. And I've got another confession to make . . . I misjudged you—I didn't know you had such a sensitive side."

Damon smiled, putting something into her palm. "I want you to have this."

"Oh my." Dorothy covered her mouth as she looked at the golden watch. "I couldn't."

"Please," he said, closing her fingers over the watch, "my mother gave me one just like it. See? It's a Patek Philippe. These are very rare watches, handmade in Geneva. Not many people in the world own a watch like this." He pulled back his cuff to demonstrate and then he unpeeled her fingers and turned her wristwatch upside down to reveal the inscription on the back.

The rose gold was dazzling, and she had to angle the ladies' watch to read through the glare.

Forever Yours

"This is too much, really," Dorothy said softly.

"It belongs to you," Damon said.

Dorothy looked at the face of the watch as if it would tell her what to say next.

"I see you already have a watch, and if you don't like it—"

"Oh, no, it isn't that, it's just— "

"You can have it for special occasions," Damon said. "Keep it. Please. As something to remember me by."

"I don't know what to say." Her head popped down again and her cheeks were turning pink.

Damon lifted her chin.

"Do you understand how I feel about you?" Damon asked in a fragile whisper.

Dorothy frowned, and for a second became a younger version of her father. "I guess."

"I realize you're very young still—"

"I'm *fourteen*," Dorothy said, straightening as if in demonstration.

"Yes," Damon said, knowing she wouldn't even be fourteen until October. "You're young in years, is what I meant to say, and I know because you are mature, you can appreciate the significance of this gift, and why I want so much for you to keep it."

Dorothy nodded.

He raised her hand to his lips and kissed it softly. Then, giving her hand a gentle squeeze, he said, "I must go now, but I promise you I'll be back."

"When?" Dorothy asked as he picked up his hat and started for the door.

"As soon as they let me. I won't get time off during Plebe year, but after that, I'll come and visit you as often as I can."

Dorothy nodded. "You'll write, won't you?"

Damon smiled and kissed her cheek. "Every chance they give me."

Kory's hand was slippery under Mary's tight grip. The sun cut right into his eyes, and the band over his head felt heavy with sweat.

He'd half expected Damon to have come into the hospital room brandishing a butcher's knife and a brotherly smile. But Damon had come bearing neither knife nor smile. He'd pulled up a chair and had sat very close to the bed.

"I'm going to say this once. And don't make me repeat myself. Understood?"

Kory winced after producing a nod.

"I'm leaving town. I'll be staying at Father's place. The Johnsons have my number if you need to reach me. Aunt Mary is flying over from California. I don't know whom you'll be living with, the Johnsons or Aunt Mary. As far as I'm concerned, it's the same deal: I hear one peep about your behavior and I'm going to rain hell on you. Am I clear?"

Kory said yes, but it was barely audible. "Am I still going to that school?"

"That's for your guardian to decide, but whether you stay here or go to Livingsford, don't for one moment think I won't be checking up on you. I'll know exactly how you are doing both at school and at home . . . if you're at home."

"I have no doubt you will."

"Don't be a smartass. You're not a kid anymore. If you stay, you're going to be the one in charge of Schoongelegen. Not officially, of course, but you get my point."

Kory forced another head-throbbing nod.

"You don't see it. I know you don't, but let me tell you what you're facing: there are two paths ahead; one is the easy downhill path to Losersville; the other is a tough road full of obstacles made only for real men. Which road are you going to take, Kory?"

The road that takes me farthest from you. For a terrifying second, Kory was afraid the words might have actually escaped in a soft breath, but if they had, Damon seemed not to hear.

"I'm not going to be able to visit in the beginning, but I'll be coming over every chance I get after Plebe year. I need to keep an eye out for my kid brother."

"You needn't bother yourself on my account." This time, Kory did hear himself speak the words.

"It's not all about you. When are you going to grow up and understand that? It's about Mother. It's about Father. It's about *family.*"

That triggered the memory of a screeching sound followed by a loud thud. Something inside Kory snapped, cracking a temporary hole in the ball of fear that had been plugging his throat. "Family, as in *me, myself, and I.*"

Damon located a pressure point and squeezed.

"Aaaah!" Kory shrieked, as the white pain exploded through his arm.

"Like I said, it's about family."

As the people stood and headed for the reception, it occurred to Kory that his brother wasn't about to finish this suddenly, in some violent, bloody outburst. No, sir. Damon van Luden would torture him for many years to come. His plan was probably to keep Kory in fear. Make sure he always looked over his shoulder, always wondered when his time was about to come. Not showing up at the funeral was just the beginning.

It was a message; it had to be.

PART II

THE PARTY

September 1957

Private Eye Ioannis Stavridis was not pleased with the job he'd been tasked with for the past four months. It had all started at that meeting in the Wall Street main office.

The timing had been distasteful to say the very least: the van Luden fellow had just buried his mother only two days earlier and already he was in the office, discussing matters of business. Such a thing would not have happened in Greece.

Stavridis was also displeased that he was now stuck with two bosses. He was assured that nothing had essentially changed, that in reality he still answered to only one man, and that this was but a temporary arrangement. There wasn't a thing Stavridis could have said to change his employer's mind anyway.

So just days after Mrs. van Luden's death, under instructions from his boss—his *real* boss—he had to explain to her son what he'd been doing for her and ask him if he was interested in continuing the services or if he just wanted to settle accounts and be finished with the matter.

Mr. van Luden seemed completely unaffected by the news that his own mother had hired a detective to investigate his girlfriend.

He had wanted to know what information his mother had requested, and that was all. If this was what she'd wanted, it was what he wanted, and he had concluded stating that Mr. Stavridis was to remain under his employ until otherwise notified.

Twenty-three years here, and Stavridis still didn't understand these rich Americans.

According to Nancy, Todd's parents had a Fischer stereophonic system that produced a sound you could feel as well as hear. Dorothy had met Nancy at school, and after Damon had taken Dorothy on that first date, she'd confided in Nancy, sparing no detail, and asked that she tell no one. She might as well have placed a full-page ad in the *New York Times*.

Dorothy's classmates had suddenly started acting as though they were her lifelong friends.

While this had been an almost expected betrayal of confidence, it had still raised doubts in Dorothy's mind about her new best friend. Not that Nancy was a *real* best friend anyway. Dorothy had only moved to Rhodes at the beginning of the year, and so there hadn't been much time, and Nancy had seemed pretty nice. Her real one-and-only best friend was Patty Normandy. But she was in Boston, and that might as well have been Timbuktu. Dorothy missed the pajama parties and having someone with whom to share forbidden thoughts. Now they were no better than pen pals.

Dorothy couldn't talk with Nancy the way she used to with Patty, but she had to have a best friend, everyone else did. Dorothy had hoped her new friend would treasure the secret about Damon. Boy, had she been wrong.

"What?" Dorothy yelled over the music.

"You make *Rachelle* look like a square, and she brought a six-pack!"

Dorothy was the only one to have brought hard liquor to the party. It had been all she could find, except for the wine in the cellar and the Champagne in the refrigerator. The Champagne was out, for obvious reasons, and the wine meant a lot to her dad. If she'd taken even a single bottle, he'd have known it was missing. The liquor cabinet was always full, and had been her best option.

Dad worked out of the house much of the time, and clients would often ask for a drink or two while reviewing their—folders? Folios? *Portfolios.* That was what he called them. Dorothy wasn't sure what a portfolio was, but it had to do with money, that much she did know. Dad's job involved bookkeeping, accounting, and consulting. She wasn't about to call him an accountant so, when asked, she'd say he was a consultant. That sounded more sophisticated, and most of the time people didn't press for details.

Dorothy figured her dad wouldn't keep tabs on how many bottles he had and how much he had served to his clients. She only planned on doing this once, so what were the odds he would notice?

She had taken three bottles from the back of the cabinet, paying attention only to their shape and the color of the liquid inside them. The clear stuff she'd left behind, not wanting to go through all the risk just to show up with fancy bottled water.

She'd obviously done well, because Todd's eyes had widened when she'd handed him the bottles.

Dorothy didn't want to be square, and she certainly didn't want anyone finding out she was just thirteen. It was two weeks into the fall semester, and in nineteen days, Dorothy wouldn't have to worry anymore; she could say she was fourteen and it would be true. Besides, at least she knew she looked a lot older. Damon had said so, and he had been a senior. Now he was at West Point. Dorothy would have thought he'd have served as her carte blanche to any party. After all, she was Damon's girl, so if she was old enough and cool enough for him, that distinction should apply universally. Well, it didn't.

"Todd *is* really cute," Nancy said.

Dorothy wasn't biting. "He's cute, but he's no Damon."

Nancy nodded.

Two juniors, Alex and Cindy, were French-kissing in the corner. Jerry, a senior, had Jill—a sophomore or a junior, but certainly not a senior—by the hand, and as he passed by his friends, he gave them a wink and walked her upstairs. What a jerk.

Todd's parents were gone for the weekend, and had been dumb enough to trust him to take care of his brother. Poor little boy was probably crying his eyes out. If he was, nobody could hear him because Todd was playing "Jailhouse Rock" from his new album. Todd had planned this party for some time, and asked his friends to invite cool kids. That meant only guys who could bring the good stuff.

Nancy had gotten wind of this and cornered Dorothy as she was taking her math book out of her locker between classes. She'd said this was an unparalleled party opportunity; all Dorothy would have to do was bring something over and she'd be in. Dorothy had asked what Nancy was going to bring. Nancy had tried slipping out of that one, but Dorothy hadn't let her. Nancy had to confess that her father was a total square and didn't allow alcohol in the house.

Things were working out well. Dorothy was at a party full of seniors, and she and Nancy were the only kids under sixteen there. Nobody propositioned Dorothy. Not even for a dance. They were avoiding her because she was Damon's girl. That suited her fine; she certainly didn't want to have one of those guys sticking his tongue down her throat. That was just gross.

Dorothy looked down at the amber liquid in her glass. Todd had served her the drink first, which made sense since she'd brought the drink to the party in the first place. It made her warm, sleepy, and giddy. Dorothy could tell she was getting drunk. Still, she couldn't exactly refuse the second offer—if she did, they'd figure out this was her first time drinking.

Nancy leaned over, her face flushed. "I think Todd likes you. He's looking at you right now."

"How many times do I have to tell you? I'm not interested," Dorothy said, but she wasn't angry. Nancy was just being Nancy.

"All I know is that Todd is here and Damon is not," Nancy said. "You have an opportunity, why not take it?"

"I'm not that kind of girl," Dorothy said, but it sounded a bit like a question.

"Sure you're not."

"Why don't you ask him to dance, since *you're* so interested?"

"He's not really my type."

This surprised Dorothy. "Really, who is your type?"

"A guy with experience."

"And Todd's not experienced?"

Nancy shook her head. "Nope."

Dorothy frowned.

"You can just tell he's never done it before," Nancy said.

Dorothy laughed. "How can you tell *that?*"

"A girl can tell."

"Oh, really? So what am I, a doorpost?"

Nancy shrugged. "You're too young to understand."

"Too young? We're almost the same age. You just turned fourteen in April," Dorothy said, wishing she'd kept her mouth shut.

"Well, at least I'm not thirteen like other people I won't mention."

"You'd *better* not, so help me, Nancy."

Nancy smiled, leaning back into the sofa.

The couples in the living room had thinned out, leaving for the backyard and spots behind bushes. All rooms upstairs were already taken. It was getting chilly with the beginning of fall, but Dorothy guessed the juniors and seniors who had to go outside didn't have to worry much about keeping warm.

Todd lived on Pine Street, where the houses were close enough for music to disturb the neighbors. His parents had plenty of money, and anywhere else, this area would probably have been considered the rich neighborhood. In Rhodes, Pine Street was like the ghetto.

Red light chased by white brightened the front windows. The police had arrived.

There was knocking at the door. Neither Dorothy nor Nancy moved. Nobody else seemed to hear.

The knocking became more persistent, and after a pause, the door opened.

It was Sheriff Thompson.

A few heads turned and then everyone froze. There was an ear-piercing scrape as someone plucked the needle from the LP. People stopped making out.

"Is Mr. or Mrs. Endwise here?" Sheriff Thompson asked. He didn't wait long for a reply. "Todd Endwise?"

Nobody offered to point him out. Nobody had to; the sheriff was looking right at him. Todd tried diverting his eyes.

"Come over here, young man," Sheriff Thompson said.

Todd made his way through the living room to the front door, stumbling twice. "What?"

"You've been disturbing the peace here is what. Your neighbors are complaining, and I can see why. I can almost hear that trash you're playing from the station!" Sheriff Thompson looked around.

Dorothy followed his gaze. There was junk everywhere—potato-chip bags, empty bottles. Then he looked in her direction.

"I'd better not find out that those two girls"—the sheriff pointed at Dorothy and Nancy—"have been drinking."

Todd shrugged. "They brought it."

"Idiot," Nancy said.

Todd frowned. "I don't see the problem."

"You don't see the problem? Loud music and alcohol, and whatever else is going on in here is the problem, young man."

Todd gave a puzzled look.

"Do your parents know what you're doing here?"

Todd shifted uneasily, his gaze falling to the ground. "Uh, sorta."

"Sort of?" the sheriff said. "So if I were to call them at their hotel—and yes, Mrs. Crabtree told me where they're staying—if I were to call them, they'd be fine with all this?"

Todd suddenly went pale. "Oh, you don't need to do that. Please, Sheriff, my parents will kill me. Look . . . we were just having a little party and listening to some music. I'm sorry it was loud and I'm sorry we disturbed Mrs. Crabtree. We won't play it loud anymore. We won't play it at all—"

"I'm calling your parents, Todd. I don't have a choice. You've made a mess of the house, and you've been serving drinks to kids."

"But she brought it—" Todd said, cutting himself off.

"Is this true, young lady?"

Dorothy looked at the sheriff but did not offer a reply.

"It *is* true," Todd said.

"I'm not asking you," Sheriff Thompson snapped. "You're in deep enough as it is, young man."

Todd recoiled and hit his back on the open front door.

"Well? Is it true? Did you bring the drinks?" Sheriff Thompson said, his voice gentle now.

Dorothy shook her head. "Not *all* of them, just some."

Todd jumped at the opportunity. "All we had here was beer, that's all anybody brought. She came with the liquor. I didn't know anything about that. Honest."

The sheriff looked at Dorothy for confirmation.

Dorothy had sampled a full glass of her father's liquor, but that didn't prevent her from seeing what was happening. This could be a disaster or a unique opportunity to turn things in her favor. In trying to save himself, Todd had committed social suicide.

Dorothy smiled defiantly. "Everything Todd said is true."

Sheriff Thompson's brow turned into a stack of trenches.

"He didn't know I was bringing liquor, and I was the only one who did. Everyone else just brought beer."

Even Sheriff Thompson had nothing to say to this. Dorothy let the silence sit for a moment and then she said, "I was the only one who could."

The sheriff raised his voice and said, "Okay, folks, listen up. The party is over. I want everyone to go home. Right now." He motioned at Dorothy and Nancy. "You two girls are coming with me." Directing his gaze at Todd: "Anyone else in your party their age?"

Todd shook his head energetically. "No, no. I had no idea they were fourteen."

"I don't recall mentioning their age." The sheriff pointed a finger at the back of the house. "You tell the rest of your friends the party is over, you hear?"

Todd nodded reluctantly and headed to the backyard to start spreading the bad news.

"A regular Einstein," Sheriff Thompson mumbled to himself.

Nancy lived closer to Todd than Dorothy did, so Nancy was the first to be dropped off. Dorothy watched from the police car. She couldn't hear what was being said, but she could tell from the father's body language that Nancy would end up being grounded for life. Probably worse. The sheriff tipped his hat and walked back to the car.

Dorothy stood there outside her home, with the sheriff, waiting for her father to answer the door. It was her turn now, but it wouldn't be a repeat of what had just happened in Nancy's house. No way would her father react like that.

John Saunders stared at the sheriff and then at Dorothy. He looked very worried. "Is everything okay, Sheriff?"

Sheriff Thompson cleared his throat. "Were you aware that your daughter was at a party?"

John regarded his daughter, trying to read her face for clues. "Yes, she told me that she was going to a party."

Sheriff Thompson gave him a look of disapproval.

"At her friend Nancy's house," John added.

The sheriff shook his head. "No, sir. She was at the Endwises'. Their seventeen-year-old boy decided he was going to have himself a big party while his parents were gone. Loud music, alcohol, and sex."

The color drained from John's face. "Dorothy? Is this true?"

"No. I would never do *that* with a boy."

Sheriff Thompson nodded. "I didn't see her involved that way, sir, but you never know what can happen when you mix seventeen-year-olds in a party with pretty girls."

"Dorothy? Honey? You went to a party with seventeen-year-olds?"

"Yes, but I didn't do what he said."

"Maybe not, young lady, but you said you brought liquor to the party." Sheriff Thompson glanced at John. "And I'm sure your father can see, as I do, that you've been drinking."

Dorothy didn't know how to answer that.

John leaned toward his daughter and sniffed. His eyes widened. "Dorothy? Are you drunk?"

"She couldn't walk a straight line if her life depended on it," Sheriff Thompson said.

Dorothy could see that there was no way out of this. "Sorry, Dad."

"You're *sorry?*" He checked himself, shook his head, and looked at the sheriff. "My daughter and I obviously need to have a talk. I can assure you this won't happen again."

Sheriff Thompson nodded. That's exactly what he'd wanted to hear. "Okay, I'll be going then." The sheriff walked to the police car, stopped, and turned. "You might want to be more careful about the company you keep in the future, young lady."

"I thought you would be home with your family for Thanksgiving."

"Did they figure out who you are?"

"No. I'm not an amateur, Mr. van Luden. I was doing this before you were born."

"Look, there's a line of people waiting for the phone, I can't talk forever. Get to the point."

"There was a party. Some older students got together . . . they made a lot of noise, and they drank."

"Yes?"

"Your Dorothy was there. All of Rhodes is saying that she brought the alcohol."

"Dorothy? Are you sure?"

"Yes, but—"

"When did you say this was?"

"Wait," Stavridis said. Damon could hear the receiver landing on a hard surface as Stavridis rummaged through papers. "This was Saturday, September 14."

"You're telling me that Dorothy was at a party drinking with seniors?"

"I'm afraid so, Mr. van Luden. The sheriff had to take her back home in the police car." Stavridis listened to static over the line for a while.

"I need to think about this. I'll call you back."

Fifteen minutes later, Stavridis's phone rang.

"Stavridis?"

"Yes?"

"I need you to do something for me."

CHARLIE PATTERSON

1960
Three Years Later

"Honey, would you turn that thing down, I can't hear myself think!"

Dorothy gave her father a quick glance and turned back to their new twenty-four-inch Emerson.

"How do you think it makes me feel to have a daughter whose favorite star is a dog?" John Saunders said.

This time, Dorothy didn't move at all.

"Pumpkin, please, you'll go deaf with that on so loud."

"Hello, Mr. S. Hiya, Dorothy," Charlie said, peering into the living room. "I knocked but nobody answered, and then I heard the barking and figured Dorothy must be home watching *Lassie*."

John waved Charlie in, resigning hope for a quiet Sunday. "Just happened to be in the neighborhood again?"

"I just happen to live just two blocks away."

"Thanks for reminding us." John sat deeper in his seat. "Go ahead, Charlie, make yourself at home. You always do." The pipe went out again, and he gave it a few frustrated taps on the ashtray.

"I see that you are both very busy here."

John pried into his pipe. Dorothy didn't take her eyes off the television.

Lassie barked.

"*Ahem.* I've got something important you need to hear," Charlie said not nearly loud enough. He tried a second time, raising his voice.

John took a few deep puffs and his pipe started working again.

Charlie made a jumping-jack motion with his arms. "Hello? Come on, you absolutely have to listen to this!"

"Really now?" John replied. "Dorothy, maybe you ought to turn that down a bit. Let's hear what's so important."

Charlie knelt down in front of Dorothy. "Do you mind if I— " He gestured at the television.

"*Shhh,*" Dorothy said without looking away from the show.

"Come on, Dorothy, I've got breaking news here and you'd rather watch *Lassie*?"

Dorothy shifted forward, giving Charlie a push to the side. "You're not invisible, you know."

"Yeah, well I was beginning to wonder," Charlie replied. "Here I am, the perfect guy for you, and it's like you hardly notice me."

"Give it a rest. She's got too much of her father's common sense to pay attention to you, Charlie. And besides, I don't think Damon would approve."

"Damon?" Charlie used his hand as a visor, scanning the room. "Where?"

"He's at the Academy," Dorothy said, "as if you didn't know."

"Well, in that case, Damon *who*?" Charlie saw her smile. "Ooh, *that* Damon?" He punched his palm. "I could take him."

Dorothy laughed. "Where exactly would you take him, Charlie?"

"Far from you, that's for sure. We don't have to worry about Damon for a while 'cause spring break isn't until April and he's already used up one of his two weekends for this semester."

"You're well informed," Dorothy said.

"Hey," Charlie said, "a guy has to keep tabs on the competition."

John laughed. "What competition?"

"Good point, Dad."

Was that Dorothy rooting for Damon? John had to admit he had no idea what feelings his daughter currently had for that man. No question about Damon's infatuation for *her*, though. He'd sent Dorothy a letter every week, like clockwork.

These were modern times, and John Saunders prided himself on being a progressive thinker, although he had to admit at first he'd been concerned. And it wasn't the age difference—it boiled down to the fact that his Dorothy was a minor, whereas Damon was an adult and at a point in his life where there could be nothing innocent about his advances.

His first instinct had been to put an end to it, before Damon had a chance to hurt her, but during that first year, Damon hadn't once paid Dorothy a visit. John had wrongly assumed their association would quickly fizzle out, as had Dorothy's friendship with the girl from Boston.

The information came his way by virtue of John's Greek associate, who worked closely with the van Luden family and was surprisingly informed about each of them, especially Damon.

It turned out Damon wanted to come, but the Academy only allowed its first-year students to see two football games and that was the extent of it. Last year had been different, however. Damon had tried visiting during Christmas, but John had already made plans to take his daughter skiing in Vermont. The following year, Damon had managed two dates with Dorothy during spring break.

This year, oddly enough, Dorothy had stopped mentioning Damon's name. When John had asked her whether she would be seeing Damon this spring, she'd brushed off the question, as if she'd just been reminded of some unpleasantness. It was either that, or things were getting serious and she wanted her father out of the loop.

Just as she had pushed him away each and every time he confronted her about the missing alcohol and the drugs. The problem had reached the point where he'd felt it necessary to tell Dr. Rosenthal in person. That had been a very uncomfortable experience, speaking to her psychologist behind her back.

John told Dr. Rosenthal about the empty bottles under her bed, and the small bags of hashish he'd found in her desk. Dorothy claimed she didn't even know what hashish looked like and tried to convince him it had to be some of his tobacco.

John had quickly realized that pushing her wasn't helping. It was better to let Dr. Rosenthal handle it.

The psychologist had been quite concerned, stating that the deep depression and death angst caused by her mother's suicide may have developed into a chronic neurotic condition, a common symptom of denial. The alcohol and drugs served as self-medication, although peer pressure may have played some role.

Dr. Rosenthal said Dorothy subconsciously believed her father to be solely responsible for the divorce and that this schism in her parents' relationship had brought about the sorrow that led to her mother's death. Her confused feelings toward her father were compelling her to test him to see if he trusted her unconditionally, in which case she'd feel it was safe to reciprocate. This explained her rebellious actions and her denial.

Additionally, drugs served as a means to push the real world away—a way to disconnect herself without actually committing the act of suicide. Dorothy had tried taking her life once, shortly after her mother's death, but Dr. Rosenthal had assured John it had been more a device for attention than a genuine suicide attempt.

"Business before pleasure, my dear." Charlie stood up and rested his hand on Dorothy's shoulder. "I'll tell you some other time, perhaps." He patted her twice and then strolled over to her father's chair, sliding onto one of the thick arm supports. "I'm here on important business."

"What was that, Charlie?" John said.

"I was saying I'm here on important business."

"Hey, get off!" John nudged him with his elbow and Charlie slipped off the smooth leather. "I'll have you know I only put up with you because your father is a close friend and a good client of mine," John said with half a smile.

"Like I was saying, Mr. S, this is a business call. Oh, and speaking of my dad? He told me to tell you that you're on for tennis at nine." Charlie let this settle in. "But why bother? You know you'll lose."

John frowned. "So this is the *important* business, Charlie? You disturb the tranquility of my home to confirm a tennis match with your father?"

Lassie let out a sharp bark.

"Some tranquil home." Charlie went over to Dorothy, patted her on the head, and turned down the volume.

"Hey!" Dorothy said.

"Thank you, Charlie," John said with a smile. "That was the smartest thing I've seen you do."

Charlie settled himself down on the sofa. "Actually there *is* something more."

"I'm all ears."

"Tennis just isn't your game, Mr. S. You should play what you're good at." Charlie grinned, revealing two rows of bright whites. "Chess."

John cocked his head back. "I wasn't aware Andy played chess."

"He doesn't, but *you* do." Charlie looked at Dorothy, hoping she was listening, but she'd crept even closer to the television set.

John returned a tired smile. "You want me to play chess with you again, Charlie? You should have just asked; you know I don't turn down an offer to play chess—even with you."

"I couldn't beat you at chess any more than my father could—"

The credits were showing. Dorothy turned off the television, suddenly interested in the conversation.

Charlie leaned forward in the sofa. "But I know somebody who can."

"Really?" John said, leaning back into his chair. "Here? In Rhodes?"

"Yep. Right here in Rhodes."

"Okay, you've got my attention now. Who is it?"

Charlie leaned back and folded his arms across his chest.

"Come on, Geronimo," John said. "Let's hear it!"

"Kory."

"I haven't heard the name."

"Kory is Damon's brother," Dorothy said. "He's this skinny guy in Charlie's math class."

"That's the one," Charlie affirmed.

"A kid?" John said. "You want me to play chess with a kid?"

"He's no *kid*, he's my age," Dorothy said.

"Yes, darling, of course." John eyed his pipe for a moment and then gave Charlie a frown. "For a moment there, I thought you were serious. I should have known better."

"I *am* serious."

"Charlie, I play chess with you so that you can learn to use that thing upstairs referred to as a brain. But I'm not about to start giving lessons to every teenager in Rhodes."

"Mr. S," Charlie said, his eyes lighting up, "if anyone is going to be taught a lesson, it'll be you."

John laughed, but it sounded like a cough. "A lesson from a *boy*—" Dorothy gave him a stare. "Sorry: a teenager?"

"My chess might be almost as bad as your tennis, but I know enough to tell that Kory could beat the pants off anybody in this town. He plays games with himself in class."

"Playing chess in the middle of a lesson is hardly commendable, Charlie," John said, shaking his head.

"Yeah, well, Kory plays *without* a chess board."

"I'm impressed. Now please, Charlie, it is getting late and it is time we had dinner."

"Just tell me when he can come over, and I'll be gone."

"Thanks but no thanks. Believe it or not, I have more important things to do than entertain your friends."

"I'll tell you what. You play chess with him and if you're not convinced it was worth your time, I promise never to come over and bug you, or your lovely daughter, again." He nodded, coaxing for John to do the same. "How does that sound?"

"Like blackmail."

"I'll take that as a yes." Charlie bounced off the sofa, and blew a kiss in Dorothy's direction. "Don't worry, my dear, I'll be back. Kory won't let us down."

"All right then, how about *Gigi*," Mary asked.

"Gigi?"

"Yes," Mary said eagerly, "it's a musical picture. I saw it in the papers and it happens to be showing today."

"You took me to the movies last week. You've already gone through enough trouble. I'm quite all right here."

"No," Mary said loudly, startling them both. "That's just the point. You're not all right here. Everyone is out living life and having fun while you spend all your free time at home. You're only sixteen once."

"One is always a certain age only once."

She passed him another plate. He seemed no stranger to chores, yet he had grown up with servants all his life.

Van Luden Enterprises had come to the decision that the servants were no longer required and had them all dismissed with the exception of the groundskeepers. Mary certainly didn't need the trust to pay their salaries, but she really didn't mind cleaning and cooking, and it was fun playing the role of an average housewife. Kory seemed to have a natural affinity for orderliness.

This she had noticed from day one. His room was sterile. She supposed that there were many parents who would love to have a child like Kory. Good grades, no troubles. And polite; *too* polite.

If she'd only had the chance to bring him up from early childhood. She dismissed the thought.

Kory was waiting for another plate. She handed him one and said, "What do you say? We'll have fun."

"Thank you, but . . ."

"We had fun last time, didn't we?" Mary said quickly to keep Kory from coming up with another excuse. "Bicycle riding in Central Park, that seafood restaurant where you gobbled up an entire lobster on your own."

"Yes, that was very nice."

"And then we saw *Vertigo*, and I know you liked that."

Kory nodded. "I did, thank you."

Mary frowned.

Kory remembered Mary didn't like it when he said "thank you" too much. "I did like the movie," he said, "but I really don't want to suffer through a musical. Hitchcock is one thing, *Gigi* sounds like punishment."

Mary laughed. "Well, at least you have a sense of humor today. What if we just skip the picture and go for a nice walk in the park instead?"

"I'd rather stay here."

"And play chess," she finished for him.

Kory said nothing.

When Kory wiped off the last plate, Mary motioned to the white kitchen table. "Sit down."

Kory obeyed.

"I've been here with you, in this house, for almost three years now," Mary said.

"Two years, eight months, and sixteen days."

"That kind of accuracy is not very flattering."

"Sorry."

"You have everything going for you: you're young, good-looking, intelligent. Kory, do you know how many girls would be after you if you'd just put on a few more pounds and dress like a kid your age instead of a caretaker? Why are you shutting yourself off from the world?"

Kory sighed. They'd had this conversation before. "My world is chess."

"Oh, come on, that's just a game. You can't hide behind wooden chess pieces your whole life. I realize that things haven't been easy for you, but that's in the past now. It's time you look ahead."

"To you, chess is just a game, but—"

The bell rang with a loud *bing-bong*. Before Mary could make it to the front door, it rang three more times.

As she held the door open, Charlie passed under her arm, saying, "Good morning, Mrs. Thorn."

"Good morning, Charlie," she said, pleased to see him. She realized she probably wasn't going to make any headway with her nephew anyway.

He bumped into Kory, nudging him playfully in the ribs, and made for the refrigerator. Sticking his head inside, Charlie said, "What, no beer?"

"You won't find any alcohol in this household," Mary said as she came into the kitchen.

"What a shame," Charlie said from behind the refrigerator door. "Do you have any goldfish?"

"Goldfish?"

"Yeah, you know, the orange shiny things with fins on their rear ends?"

Mary laughed. "What in the world would you do with goldfish?"

"Practice. They say you have to swallow live goldfish to get into a good fraternity at Cornell. Isn't that so, Kory?"

"I wouldn't know. Why don't you try our reflection pond? You may not find any goldfish, but I'll bet you'll find a few frogs. If you can swallow some of those, you could pick and choose your fraternity."

"Gross. I'm not swallowing a Frenchman. I figured you'd know about the goldfish-swallowing thing, since you're an Ivy League shoo-in. You can't tell me you haven't looked into it."

"I can, and I haven't. Fraternities do not interest me, Charlie."

Mary ruffled Charlie's bright-orange hair. "Charlie, you're sixteen, I don't think that you have to worry about goldfish-swallowing for at least another two years."

"It never hurts to practice." Turning to Kory: "Speaking of practicing, Kory, have you been playing with yourself lately?"

"*Charlie*, really," Mary scolded, but she couldn't hold down a smile.

"*Chess*. I meant playing chess, of course."

"Of course," Mary said.

"No, really, Mrs. Thorn. Don't you know he can play games without a chessboard? He's a regular gold mine. You could make a million bucks!" He paused, making a mental correction, and turned around in a slow circle, surveying the west wing of the mansion. "*Another* million bucks."

Kory rolled his eyes. "A brilliant idea, Charlie. Perhaps you should consider a business major when you finally make it to Cornell—once you've perfected the art of goldfish-swallowing that is."

"Is it true, Kory?" Mary asked.

Kory regarded the marble floor. "Is what true?"

"Can you play chess without a chessboard?"

"Gee, thanks, Charlie. Next time I want the world to know something, I won't look for an advertising agency, I'll go straight to you."

Charlie smiled. "Come on, Kory. It's a sin to waste talent like yours, not to mention the potential money you could make."

"Please, enough! You come here—uninvited, as usual—demanding beer and goldfish. Next you'll want to turn me into a freak show for the Rhodes High summer party."

"How did you know?"

"I didn't until just now." Kory tried to make his voice sound harsh, but it refused to come out that way. Charlie always seemed to put him in the position of having to fake anger. "Forget it."

"I already have."

"Good. Then, if you don't mind, Aunt Mary and I were off to the movies."

"Oh, really?" Mary said. "That's news to me. Come on, Kory, don't be such a lousy host. That's no way to treat a friend. Why don't you two go out to the movies, or to Joey's Diner?"

"He's not my friend," Kory said, but it was a lie and all three of them knew it.

"I'm serious, Kory. I couldn't care less about the Rhodes summer party . . . Okay, I admit, it might have been in the back of my mind at some point, but I've got a *much* better idea."

"Spare me."

"No, listen, this is great—"

Kory raised an open palm, traffic cop–fashion. "I've had enough, I'm going to my room." Kory waved good-bye, slipped out through the kitchen door, and ran upstairs.

Mary looked at Charlie, and they both knew what the other was thinking. Charlie smiled, acknowledging their silent understanding, and chased after his friend.

Kory tried to close his bedroom door, but Charlie blocked it with his foot.

"Ow!"

"Leave me in peace."

Charlie slipped in. "It's not going to happen. Hey, ease off on the door or you're going to leave me in *pieces.*"

Kory wondered how Charlie always seemed to manage that foot-in-the-door maneuver. "Why are you so persistent?"

"You've got something, Kory, don't you see it?"

"I see you, in my house, and in my room. Now, if you don't mind, I want to be left alone."

"Watch what you wish for. One day we'll all be alone, and for a long, long time."

Kory folded his arms, tapping his foot.

"Do it. Show me one more time."

Kory didn't move.

Charlie jumped over Kory's bed and grabbed at the chessboard on the shelf. "One quick game. That's all I ask."

"And then you'll leave me alone?"

"I promise."

Kory thought about this for a moment, as if to prove he had a choice.

"Okay, fine, if that is what it takes." Kory sat back against the bed rest and closed his eyes.

"No peeking now," Charlie said.

"This is ridiculous."

"Pawn to King Four."

"Pawn to King Four," Kory answered in a new voice.

"Jesus, no matter how many times you do it, I still can't believe it," Charlie said, twenty-five moves later. He had lost his queen, and Kory had kept his eyes closed throughout the game.

"Kory?"

"What now?"

"You can open your eyes. I've got this thing about playing without a queen."

"Next time, it might help if you thought before you made a move."

"What's the point? I could think my brains into mush and you'd still wipe me off the board."

Charlie put the chess pieces back in their box. The white pieces on one side of the divider, the black pieces on the other. Kory watched, silently appreciative of the gesture.

"Kory?"

"Now what?"

"Would you please stop saying 'now what'?"

"Fine, I'll stop saying 'now what?' and now would you please kindly remove yourself from my house?"

"Yeah, I'll go, but you're coming with me."

"You're dreaming."

"Kory, I want you to play another game."

"*One* game. We said one game and you'd go. You had your game, and yet for a reason which completely eludes me, you're still here."

"With Mr. Saunders."

"Who?" Kory said.

"He's got an expert rating, and he competes at the Manhattan Chess Club."

Kory said nothing.

"Well?"

"I've never—" Kory stopped himself before saying anything more. He had told Charlie about the chess matches he played with himself, and now he was beginning to regret it. Charlie had been on his tail for the past six months, not just asking for friendship, but demanding it. This behavior would not have been surprising for an unpopular kid, yet everyone liked Charlie, so why did he relentlessly seek Kory's friendship?

"You never what?"

"I've never played chess before," Kory said, surprised to hear himself utter the words.

Charlie frowned, shaking his head. "What do you call what we just did?"

"That doesn't count," Kory said in a sigh, wondering why he was talking so much. "It's true, I really haven't."

Charlie detected the honesty in his friend's voice. "I don't get it."

"No, Charlie," Kory said, "you don't. I've played chess against myself and I've played a few of these silly circus games with you. What I mean is that I've never played chess against anyone other than you or myself. I've never played a *real* game."

"Gee, folks, I'm not certain, but I think I've just been insulted."

"Blindfold chess doesn't mean much. Even *you* could make rudimentary moves without a chessboard if you worked on it."

"Okay, maybe I could—after a zillion years of practice. But you completely destroy me, game after game, and I'm not *that* bad. Sorry, but no amount of practice could get me to play that well without a chessboard to look at."

"You think so?" Kory asked.

"Think so? I *know* so. You're like the superman of chess." Charlie stepped back and carved a square frame into the air with his index fingers. "I can see you on television. The kid genius from Rhodes, New York. We'll be famous. Well, you'll be famous, I'll be rich."

He hated calling from home. The whole thing was unpleasant enough without having to bring it into his very own household. That's why it paid so well, Stavridis reminded himself.

Christina was gone, shopping, but he still felt more comfortable using the bedroom phone.

The wiretaps had started two and a half years ago pursuant to Mr. van Luden's request for heightened surveillance on his girlfriend. In order to do all that was required, including monitoring the line every morning to midnight, a team of men had to be hired. The American had approved that as well.

To make the tap, Stavridis needed to gain access to Mr. Saunders's house. Initial surveillance had started with Martha van Luden. Since her death, the van Luden trust fund had been footing the bill, and had agreed to do so because this had been her request in the first place.

With prior consent from Van Luden Enterprises, in order to facilitate access to the Saunderses' home, Stavridis had offered John Saunders a job as a financial adviser and bookkeeper for the van Luden trust. Mr. Saunders had been told he could work out of his home, with Stavridis acting as the "company liaison." In this manner, Stavridis had given himself a unique opportunity to learn as much as possible directly from Dorothy Saunders's father.

Stavridis made a good show of listening to Mr. Saunders talk about the company finances. Of course, Van Luden Enterprises was not about to let this man have access to any of its real financial information—the books had been manufactured to make Mr. Saunders believe he was doing something for the money the company was paying him.

Stavridis could drink any man under the table, so loosening Mr. Saunders up with booze had been child's play. The first step was always to gain trust. To that end, Stavridis had fed Mr. Saunders the story of his life. The career part—the part about him being a businessman—was complete fiction; only the story about his family was true. Stavridis told him about his daughter. How he'd wanted a son, but had ended up with a girl. How he'd tried again, but his wife had been unable to conceive a second time. Stavridis mentioned all the problems his daughter went through as a teen. It wasn't long before Mr. Saunders had started talking about Dorothy.

In a few months, Stavridis had heard everything. About the bottles of empty gin under her bed. The hashish he found in her room while she was at school. Soon Mr. Saunders was even confiding in him about what the psychologist had said. Now that Stavridis had heard about the suicide attempt from Mr. Saunders's very lips, his hands were untied and he could mention it to Damon, should the need arise—it never hurt having an ace up one's sleeve.

"Anything I should be worried about?"

"The drugs, the alcohol . . . the company is not happy about this. Now everybody knows about Dorothy, so I had to tell the company, otherwise they would question my loyalty."

"We've been over this."

"I know, Mr. van Luden, but I have to say, I don't understand what you are doing. You put me in hard position."

"Hey, I'm paying you and the company is paying you, how tough can that be?"

"It is hard because with this drug things, the company does not want you involved with her. Are you purposely trying to make my boss unhappy?"

"I'll deal with the company; you do as I tell you. Now, what about Nancy?"

Stavridis sighed. "Nothing new. She pushes for trouble, understand? But so far Dorothy keeps away from the boys."

"How is Mr. Saunders?"

"I see him once a month. As always. I'm company liaison. After me, he talk to your aunt about the trust. It is simple arrangement. Under different situations, Mr. Saunders and me could have been friends. You should know, he is good man. He worries about his daughter."

"He should."

"And the company worries too."

"Let's not get into that again. You just—"

"Yes, yes, do my job. I know. Good-bye, Mr. van Luden."

Mr. Saunders's moves up to this point had been conservative, main-line Queen's Indian Defense.

Kory was going numb where the rim of the chair was cutting into him. He had to do something or both legs would soon fall asleep.

Mr. Saunders's next move was something Kory had never seen before. For the first time he was completely baffled. He studied the board for ten minutes and came up with nothing. Tactically, Mr. Saunders's move offered no immediate threats. It made no sense from a positional point of view either.

Kory's game was under siege, and he was powerless to prevent the onslaught. For years, chess had carried him to a safe haven, a world of clarity, purity, and simplicity he had found nowhere else. He had read all sixteen books, and he knew each one by heart, memorizing 327 championship games. Each move in those games had made perfect, beautiful sense. Yet now his mind was blank.

This had been a mistake. Kory shouldn't have come. He'd been wary of the idea from the moment Charlie had mentioned it, but the need to play with somebody—anybody—who was an expert at the game had gotten the better of him. Now Kory was going to suffer humiliation for giving in to Charlie's pressure.

He stared at the board and this time focused harder. He should have known this would happen. This was a real game, with a real opponent. Kory pushed his mind to its limits, probing ten moves ahead, but still came up with nothing.

Charlie sighed loudly, and Kory turned an angry face toward him. Reluctantly, Charlie sat back on the sofa, his arms akimbo.

Kory lost himself in the game once again. He was used to interruptions. It happened all the time when he played chess with himself in class. He still couldn't make any sense of Mr. Saunders's move. There wasn't even a hint of something. It was as if he'd gone mentally blind. He was suddenly feeling queasy, and for a while he wondered if he'd end up emptying his lunch on Mr. Saunders's cherrywood chessboard.

Charlie shifted on the sofa. Kory tried to concentrate on his move.

John Saunders picked up his new pipe, emptied the used ash with a loud *tap-tap* against the ashtray, and began the ritual of filling it and lighting it. Soon the room was rich with the sweet scent of pipe tobacco.

Kory looked at the grandfather clock. He'd spent fifteen minutes on his move so far. Yet, still, he needed more time.

John picked up a folded copy of the *New York Times* and cracked it open to a full spread.

There was nothing Kory could do but play a developing move. He was beginning to accept the fact that he wouldn't be able to see through his opponent's strategy no matter how much time he had.

The bishop felt very heavy in his fingers. "I moved."

"Excuse me?"

"Bishop to King Three."

John tipped the newspaper and peeped over it at the board. After a few seconds, he said, "Move my knight to King Five."

Kory obeyed. This move was even more baffling than the previous one. Kory had spent fifteen minutes analyzing all the best responses, yet this one had eluded him. He closed his eyes. His hands were cold and clammy.

Charlie leaned over, and seeing Kory sitting there with his eyes closed he shook his head. "I'm going to see what Dorothy's up to."

Kory did not reply. Dorothy. *Damon's* Dorothy. He'd never actually seen her before and he'd hoped today it would stay that way.

"This game is taking ages," Charlie said.

"Now, now, let the boy think," John said from behind his newspaper and a veil of blue smoke.

"Fine, just tell me if anything happens."

Kory had a move in mind. Another developing move, but he didn't want to make it until he figured out what Black was up to. His opponent's plan would eventually become obvious, but Kory was afraid it would be too late then.

He ran through as many variations as he could, but he was unable to spot the threat. Finally, Kory moved.

John heard the chair creak and the hollow sound of a piece being moved. The newspaper crumpled enough for John to see, and without hesitation he advanced his queen to the center ranks.

It came to Kory immediately, yet he refused to accept what his mind was telling him. The urge to move was almost irresistible, but Kory forced himself to analyze what he was certain was correct.

Sounds of laughter came from upstairs, and then Kory could make out two people coming down the stairs.

"How's the big game, Dad?" a young female voice shouted.

John turned in his easy chair and the newspaper crackled with surprising volume. Kory tried to focus on the game; he tried blocking out the sounds, but as Dorothy came into his periphery of vision, curiosity got the better of him, and with a will of their own, his eyes locked on to her.

The first thing that hit him was how short she was. She was purportedly mature for her age, at least according to Martha, and Kory had somehow translated this into an image of her being tall . . . at least tall enough to stand at Damon's side. She did have blond hair, but Kory would hardly call it golden. And green eyes, yes, but *emerald?* She was wearing a pink dotted dress more suited to a fifth-grader than a junior in high school.

"It's going fine, just fine, sugarplum," John said. Then, addressing Charlie: "Your friend plays well. He seems to know his openings, but don't forget I've been playing chess since long before he was born."

Charlie sat back on the sofa; Dorothy sat by the television facing the two chess players.

Kory moved, taking the King's rook pawn.

"What are you doing?" Charlie said, exasperated.

John frowned and shook his head slowly. "There's nothing behind that piece, son. I'll just capture it with my king. Would you like to take it back?"

"No, sir. The game is over."

"Well don't give up that easi—"

Kory shook his head "The game is over, sir. For *you.*"

Charlie bounced out of the couch. "Ha! I knew you wouldn't let me down, Kory. I *knew* it!"

John smiled sympathetically, and took Kory's bishop with his king. "As you wish."

Without hesitation Kory retreated his knight, attacking John's queen and exposing a check with his remaining bishop.

"*Roi, reine,*" Kory announced.

Now Charlie was standing over the board.

"What was that, son?"

"Check, and queen en prise," Kory said.

"Where?"

Kory pointed at the doomed pieces. John looked puzzled, and folding his newspaper he sank into deep thought for five minutes. His hand paused over his king before he grabbed it, moving it to safety.

"Mate in four," Kory said, placing his rook in the third rank.

Dorothy got up and slowly walked over to where Charlie was standing. Kory kept his eyes focused on the board, not even allowing himself another glance at the paradox that was Damon's taste in the opposite sex.

John Saunders bunched his eyebrows. How was the rook supposed to be a threat? His king wasn't in check, and Kory was a piece down. He struggled with a few ideas and decided to mount a counterattack. He moved his knight, threatening Kory's exposed rook.

Charlie looked at Kory for reassurance.

"Now it's mate in two," Kory said, sliding his queen to the king's corner of the board.

John grabbed the knight, but at that point all that was available to him was a delaying move. Charlie couldn't see any of it.

"Checkmate," Kory said, not feeling any rush at all. It wasn't supposed to be this way; he was visibly disappointed.

John stared at the board incredulously for a long time and finally he said, "You expect me to believe that you've never played this game before?"

"I've read a lot of books, Mr. Saunders."

"You can't learn to play chess like that from a *book*." John dropped his pipe in the ashtray. He softened his tone. "A rematch?" Without awaiting a reply he said, "This time I've got white."

Dorothy walked around the easy chair, hugging her father from behind. "Let me get this straight, Dad. You *lost?*"

"You bet he did," Charlie exclaimed, "and now that means I get to come over whenever I want. At last, Juliet, nothing will come between us!"

John didn't answer; he was resetting the board in a rush.

"Except two hundred pounds of Romeo," Kory said.

"That's it, Kory," Charlie said, "kill the moment."

Kory rolled his eyes.

"Dad? You lost to someone my age? A *kid?*"

"All right, honey, that's enough, you don't have to rub it in."

Dorothy went into the kitchen and came back with a wicker chair. She placed it next to her father and sat down.

"Hey, what about me? Don't I get a chair?" Charlie asked.

"Sit on it, Charlie!" Dorothy said.

"Dorothy!" John protested through a smile.

Charlie stood over Kory, his hand on his shoulder. "Don't pay any attention to them, Kory, you just do your thing."

The newspaper and the pipe lay to the side, abandoned. John tried the Ruy Lopez opening, hoping the memorized moves would carry him to a strong middle game. To his disappointment, Kory knew the opening well. Obviously, the boy really had read his share of chess books. John was beginning to think that the Lopez was not a prudent choice. But what was?

If he'd tried something unorthodox, he could have set himself up for a series of tactical disasters.

"Dad, you're not going to lose this one too, are you?" Dorothy said, prodding him on the back of his head.

"No, honey, now just let me think here."

Dorothy noticed an irritability in her father's voice she didn't often hear—at least, not directed at *her*. For the first time that afternoon, she took a good look at the strange boy on the other side of the chessboard. None of the conversation was affecting him. He was transfixed on the game, his baby face with those cute thick glasses looked suddenly grown-up.

And he was behaving as if she weren't even there. Baby-faced or not baby-faced, that was a first for any guy.

She saw him move. It looked like an attack on the queen's side of the board, but she wasn't sure.

"Atta boy, Kory!" Charlie shouted, though he had no clue what his friend was planning.

John leaned on the edge of his easy chair, his head only twelve inches from the chessboard. He knew his king was under siege now, and he was not going to let His Majesty down a second time.

Kory gave himself a five count, just to be certain, and moved. He had complete control of the game, and there were many ways to end it. All he had to do was pick and choose. It had never occurred to him that he'd been playing with a medi-ocre chess player. How could he have known? For years, he had only read about the *best* games ever played. Mr. Saunders had presented no challenges—positional, tactical, or strategic.

Kory had been looking for threats where there'd been none. He couldn't blame himself; Charlie had made Mr. Saunders sound like a chess master.

John had managed to defend his king from impending doom, but at the expense of a rook, a knight, and two pawns. He stared at the chessboard, shaking his head sadly. "Enough punishment for me, I resign."

"Yabba-dabba-doo!" Charlie exclaimed. "You did it, Kory—you beat the best in Rhodes."

John was about to say something in his defense but decided against it. Instead, he looked for consolation in the direction of his abandoned pipe. "Son, would you mind if I had a word with your father?"

Kory looked away and said in a small voice, "You can't."

"Excuse me?"

"He's dead."

"Oh." Then after some thought, "Well I'd like to speak to your mother, then."

"She's dead too."

Dorothy interjected, "Dad, I *told* you. Remember?" She lowered her voice, as if this would prevent Charlie and Kory from hearing what they both already knew. "He's *Damon's* brother."

John remembered it now. He hadn't paid attention or made the connection because, at the time, he wasn't in the least interested in playing chess with a boy.

He started filling his pipe. "I'm sorry, son, you really don't look anything like him." He regretted that, too. It wasn't meant to come out that way, although his observation couldn't have been truer. The young man was nothing like his older brother. He wasn't at all hard on the eyes, but Kory was too thin, and his facial features were still somewhat juvenile.

Dorothy squeezed her father's shoulders. She felt a pang of sympathy for Kory. A guy without a mother . . . or a father.

"That's okay, sir," Kory answered in a small voice.

"So who's taking care of you?"

"My aunt Mary."

"Would you mind if I had a word with her?"

"No, why?"

"I was thinking you might like to come with me to the Manhattan Chess Club. I'll be going down to New York on Tuesday. You could meet me there in the afternoon, when I've finished with business."

Charlie smiled. "Great idea, Mr. S. Can I come too?"

"Kory is the only one I'm taking to the club."

"Oh, I get it, you wanted me to stay here and take care of Dorothy, right?" Charlie said, offering his best smile.

"In your dreams." Dorothy laughed.

John smiled at his daughter and turned to the first person in Rhodes to defeat him in chess. "Kory? What do you say?"

"I don't know. I'd have to ask my aunt." Kory stood, offering his hand. "Thank you. I've always wanted to play with someone."

Someone. Two games with a kid and now John's expert rating felt both meaningless and commonplace. "Well, you're always welcome to come and play with me. It seems I've finally met my match." John got up and shook Kory's hand. He escorted him to the door and, opening it, said, "You really should come with me. You have talent. Think about it and let me know."

Charlie rushed over to the door before John could close it. "Kory! Hold on, wait for me! You're not getting off the hook that easy!"

Kory was already walking down the driveway. Charlie turned around, trying to get a few words in through the closing door. "I'm so sorry I have to leave you all alone, Dorothy, but duty calls. No manager worth his money would let an opportunity like Kory walk away." John shut the door. "I'll miss you too!" Charlie shouted, and then he ran after Kory.

When Charlie caught up with him, Kory said, "Why do you do that?"

"Why do I do what?" Charlie asked.

"Why do you make a joke of everything?"

"What do you mean?"

"You like Dorothy, don't you?"

"You bet."

"Then why joke around with her?"

"I like her, but I don't have a death wish, you know. Besides, you got something against a sense of humor?"

"If you don't have a death wish, and you're after Damon's girl, then you really don't know my brother at all."

"Hey, I know all I need to know."

Kory shook his head and snorted. "Ignorance is bliss."

"I like her, I joke around . . . It's who I am, okay? Who died and made you the expert on broads? A monk knows more than you do!"

"I'll have you know the Ruy Lopez was invented by a monk."

"The what?"

"The opening Mr. Saunders used. I thought you knew how to play chess."

"Hey, not everyone is a genius."

"I don't mean to put down Mr. Saunders's game, but it is certainly not what you made it out to be. Defeating him hardly elevates me to the ranks of genius, Charlie."

"I dunno, but I still don't see what this Roy Whateverhisnameis has to do with broads."

"*Ruy Lopez*," Kory said. "He was a monk, and he has absolutely nothing to do with *broads*."

"My point exactly."

Kory took two handfuls of his hair and pretended to pull hard. They'd reached Orange Street, and it was completely dark now.

Kory said, "This is it."

Before turning off on Orange Street, Charlie stopped, tilting his head toward the heavens. "*Wait*. I hear a voice."

Kory strained to listen—it was the first time anyone had ever heard a sound before he did.

"What was that?" Charlie asked the sky. "Oh, yeah, okay, I'll tell him."

Kory frowned.

"I heard a voice. From the holy saint of managers."

Kory rolled his eyes.

"Mock me if you will, but the Voice is rarely wrong."

"Uh-huh."

"Don't you want to hear what it said?"

"The suspense is killing me."

"The Voice commanded me to tell you that the Manhattan Chess Club is an opportunity not to be missed."

"How convenient, having a voice like that." Kory walked off in his own direction. "Bye, Charlie."

Charlie ran in front of him, blocking his path. "I know you want to play chess, so why fight it?"

"Charlie, I don't understand you. Why do you bug me so much? Why don't you just leave me alone? I'll lead my life, and you can lead yours, wherever that's going."

"I told you, Kory. I'm your manager," Charlie said, the hurt in his voice sounding genuine.

They stood there for a moment, then Kory sighed and said, "I didn't mean that."

"Yes, you did."

"No, I didn't. Feel free to bug me all you want."

"Really?"

"Yeah, really. What are friends for, right?"

"Right," Charlie said, recovering a smile. He thought of something and chuckled.

"What?" Kory asked.

"I've never heard you use the F word before."

"F word?"

"'Friends.'"

THE MATCH

1960

"Can I help you?" the man behind the desk said, seeing the tall lady come through the door followed by two teenagers. "Uh, if you're looking for your hotel room, you've got the wrong floor. This is—"

"The Manhattan Chess Club, Suite 1403, at the Woodrow. We can read signs, thank you."

"Sam? One member, three guests," John Saunders said, waving as he shut the door behind him.

"Oh. Mr. Saunders. I didn't see you there. You brought your family today?"

John took out his wallet. "She's my daughter and this is—"

"That'll be two dollars per guest. Tell your kids to keep it down and no talking to the players during a game."

"I know the rules, Sam," John said, producing a twenty.

"Don't you have anything smaller?" Sam grabbed the bill with disgust.

John looked at Mrs. Thorn apologetically.

"This is hardly a place for youngsters," Sam mumbled as he searched the drawers for change.

John was already regretting bringing Dorothy and Mary Thorn along.

Concerned that Kory's aunt might have reservations about allowing him to go to the chess club, John had been very convincing on the phone. As a result, she'd been so enthusiastic about the whole thing, she'd basically invited herself over.

That had taken John by surprise. He'd hung up wondering why she'd found it necessary to tag along; after all, Kory was Dorothy's age, and John was a parent. Didn't Mrs. Thorn trust him to take a teenager to New York and back?

He'd wanted to take Kory to the club and show off his find alone without Mrs. Thorn or anybody else. Still, he was relieved she'd said yes, and made the mistake of sharing the good news with Dorothy.

He'd been trying to get his daughter interested in chess for years, but she kept putting off his offer until he finally gave up on the idea of teaching her. It never occurred to him she'd want to come along. In a hurried attempt to dissuade her, he'd said that it would be something only a chess player would appreciate. If he'd just kept his mouth shut, Dorothy might never have shown interest. She took it as an implication that women weren't smart enough, that *she* wasn't smart enough, or worse, old enough, to enjoy the trip. The only way to get out of that mess had been to concede.

The ride down to the city had been better than he'd expected. Mary Thorn, as it turned out, was quite easy on the eyes, an interesting person, and an entertaining conversationalist.

John walked Dorothy and Kory into the club; Mary remained behind.

There were two long rows of tables, each with a chessboard set up for a game. All seats were empty, except for the one in the far corner occupied by a man with red suspenders, whose flesh seemed to overflow around his chair. He had no opponent, and the chess pieces had been pushed aside, some of them toppled over.

John Saunders walked over to him, his daughter by his side, Kory in tow.

John directed his attention to the huge man who hadn't taken his eyes off the board, even though there wasn't a single chess piece on it.

"Good afternoon, sir, I was wondering if you would be interested in playing a game with this young man over here." John groped behind him, caught one of Kory's long thin arms, and tugged him forward.

"What's the matter, boy? You got a mouth, use it." The words came in a rich, phlegmy garble.

Kory froze. The fat man was staring right at him with eyes so dark each appeared to have no iris. Thick lips glistened under an eggplant nose, pushing out from pale, bloated flesh.

"Look, I'm waiting to play a match and my opponent is late," the man said. "So do you want to play chess, or are you going to stand there like a moron?"

Kory took a seat.

The fat man pushed the pieces toward Kory. "Good, now set up the board."

Mary walked up to John and whispered like a conspirator, "A match, already?"

"Yes," he answered, cupping his hand over his mouth, "but we'd better keep the chatter down; this fellow is rather eccentric."

Mary nodded. "I'll pass it on to Dorothy."

"Where is she? I—"

A meaty fist came crashing down on the table, and several pieces went airborne. "*Hurry!*" It sounded like something deep within the recesses of the man's stomach was fighting to get out.

Kory hurried, half expecting his opponent to vomit all over the table. Instead, the fat man took the chess clock and gave the two dials behind it a vigorous twist. "Five-minute blitz."

Mr. Saunders leaned forward. "He doesn't know—I don't think he's ever used a clock."

"Who's playing here?" the fat man barked. "You or the kid?"

"My name is Kory," he said, extending his arm.

"Get your hand out of my face! I don't care what the hell they call you! Are we going to play chess or play house?"

"Chess, sir," Kory replied in a tiny voice.

"Don't give me that *sir* crap; you won't win any brownie points with that kind of shit."

John looked around for his daughter. This wasn't turning out as he'd hoped. The chess club was empty, with the exception of Sam and the fatso with the foul mouth, and Kory probably wouldn't get two moves in before John would have to put an end to the game. There was only so much he could tolerate in the presence of ladies.

John bent down and whispered in Kory's ear: "Make your move, then press the button on your clock; doing that will set off his. If you take a piece, make sure you put it on the table *before* you press your clock."

"No talking!" the fat man yelled.

John retreated.

Mary whispered, "What a vulgar man."

"I heard that," the fat man said with no trace of anger in his voice.

The game started with Kory playing white. He moved slowly, regarded the clock with distrust, and pressed his button. The fat man reacted instantly, slamming down his piece so hard, the whole board shook, but amazingly none of the pieces fell.

Kory played the King's Gambit, and on the twelfth move he sacrificed his bishop for a king's pawn.

The fat man stared at the board, looked up at Kory, and laughed. Kory imagined the man exploding. The laugh became a coughing fit and something yellow shot out of his mouth. It landed on the corner of the table. The fat man pulled out his pocket handkerchief, wiping off the phlegm as a matter of course. "You play like a barbarian. No—a frightened savage. That is why you like to make sacrifices. Am I right?"

Kory gave him a blank stare.

"Of course I'm right," the fat man said, resetting the chessboard.

"What are you doing?" Kory said.

"Your game was boring me! You cannot expect to win a sacrifice against Bandini!"

"I don't understand," Kory said.

"And I don't care." He looked in Sam's direction and saw no activity there. "My partner isn't here yet." He grabbed for the clock. "We'll try a ten-minute game."

John tried to remember the name. *Bandini.* It did sound vaguely familiar.

The opening went quickly, Bandini impaling the pieces into the board, Kory moving inaudibly. In the middle game, Kory saw his chance to mount an attack.

"More stupidities! You think you can win with this?" Bandini barked, causing a tide of stomach to roll over the tabletop. He smashed his knight into the seventh rank.

Kory went pale. The man was obviously planning a counterattack of lethal proportions. The knight sat there like an octopus, its crooked tentacles threatening havoc in Kory's sensitive ranks. The knight was going to end the game—Kory couldn't see how, but he could feel it. There were too many tactical possibilities to explore.

After reviewing several of the more obvious aggressive variations, Kory forced himself to limit his focus to defensive lines. If he were to delay any longer, he would eventually lose on time. Continuing with the attack was out of the question, but now even finding a defense seemed impossible. He needed more time. Kory played the safest move he could think of and Bandini reacted immediately with a smirk followed by a crash of wood on wood as he smashed his rook through an opening. They played for a few more minutes and Kory saw a variation that he normally would have ignored.

This was not Kory's style, but the sequence couldn't fail. "Check."

Bandini removed his king from harm's way.

"Check," Kory said, bringing in his bishop.

Disgusted, Bandini moved his king back.

"Check," Kory said, using the rook again.

Bandini gave Kory a hateful glare.

"Draw by repetition," Kory announced.

"You know nothing about chess," Bandini said, pounding both fists on the table.

This time the pieces did go flying.

Dorothy, who had joined her father and Mary long enough to see the ending said, "He does too!"

"What is this?" Bandini said, addressing everyone. "Chess is no game for women. This is a *man's* club." He looked at Kory: "Do you always bring along a cheerleader when you play?"

"Now, see here," John cut in. "I won't have you talking about my daughter like that."

Without bothering to turn his head toward John, Bandini said, "Show her the Empire State Building, take her to a ballet, just don't bring her here. Chess is ugly. If you don't like it, leave."

John said, "We drove all the way from Rhodes to show—"

Bandini put up a fat, fleshy hand and said to Kory, "It takes a lot more than just brains to play chess. You need character. I played you right out of a crushing attack."

Mary looked like she was about to say something, but John could see she held back the urge. John liked a woman with spunk, and a woman with enough finesse to know when to leave the talking to a man even more.

"What do you mean?" Kory said to Bandini.

John decided to follow Mary's example and remain quiet. It was probably best to let the boy stand up for himself.

"I'm talking about psychological chess," Bandini said, as if there'd been no interruption. "The average master would have resigned; he'd have seen how hopeless his position was and quickly handed you the game. You had a winning attack, but that alone isn't good enough. You can hold a gun to the enemy's temple and still end up dead. You've got to have guts to pull the trigger. I could see from the beginning: it's in your eyes. Fear. You reek of it. You're no man, you're a sniveling child.

"My knight was innocuous," he continued. "There was no real tactical potential there. I made you *believe* there was. I sniffed out a coward and you proved me right by going for a draw." Bandini smiled, his lips gleamed. "My opponents take one look at me and they've already lost. You handed me a draw when you could have had an easy win. What use is a brilliant game when you throw it all away and hand me a gift of half a point?

"You have to think of the entire match, not just about the individual game. I gave you the first game, just to get a feel for your style. See the difference? Why did you let me stop the first game? I'll tell you: because you didn't have the *nerve*. You needed your little cheerleading party to stand up for you. I learned about you from that first game, and yet you learned nothing about me. By the second game I knew your style, your weaknesses, and your spineless character.

"People like you are only good for correspondence chess—they spend their time analyzing games instead of playing them. You have to see the big picture. Winning the tournament, that's what it's all about. Chess is life and death."

"And what would you know about either?" It was a new voice, and all heads turned.

The newcomer was taller than Mary by at least an inch. He had a pleasant pink face with patches of irritated skin where the razor had cut too close. Gray-white hair put him closer to sixty than fifty. He wore a charcoal, pinstriped suit accented with a scarlet bow tie. Mary decided he must have been a handsome specimen in his day.

Bandini hacked a comet of phlegm into his handkerchief. "Goddammit, George, can't you ever come on time?"

George pointed at the clock on the wall. "I'm not late, it's precisely five."

Bandini shook his head. "This used to be a serious club, now all the good players are gone." He pointed a finger at George and addressed Kory. "Did you know they have a special name for his gutless style? They call it *Jewish* chess. Makes me want to puke."

John turned to the newcomer and offered his hand. "Mr. Schelowitz, John Saunders. I've heard you come from time to time, but I've not had the pleasure of meeting you."

"The pleasure is mine."

Kory stared, openmouthed. *International Grandmaster Schelowitz.* He was the world-renowned master of defense. Kory had studied every one of his great games. Although defensive chess had never been his preference, Kory had great respect for the man known as "The Wall."

Kory stood up, offering his seat to the grandmaster. He imagined Paul Morphy might have looked something like him. "Sir, I am honored to make your acquaintance."

Grandmaster Schelowitz started collecting the pieces off the floor, and Kory immediately got down on his knees to help. Bandini watched the two of them, amused.

Scraping for a pawn, Schelowitz said, "What did the old bulldog do? Pound his fists? Swear? Try to intimidate you into losing?"

Kory looked up at Schelowitz, speechless.

Schelowitz smiled. "Now that he's had his rabies shot, I can honestly say his bark is worse than his bite."

Kory heard Dorothy laugh. Did she really have to be here? Though she'd been laughing in his defense, it felt to Kory as though she were laughing *at* him. As though she carried Damon's voice all the way from West Point to Manhattan.

"You see what I'm talking about?" Bandini said to nobody in particular. "They've turned this chess club into a daycare center."

Schelowitz smiled. "Let's see if we can impale that impenetrable ego of his."

Bandini set the clock for five minutes.

Mary watched carefully, John Saunders and his daughter beside her. Mary had played a few games of chess as a child, but that had been the extent of it. She noticed a change in Kory. There was something different about him—an intensity she'd never seen before. No doubt this was the talent Mr. Saunders had been telling her about. She had been grateful for that phone call, for many reasons.

The game started off in a storm of crashing wood. There was nothing gutless in Schelowitz's manner. Bandini crashed the pieces down and Schelowitz pounded even louder.

Two minutes into the game, an image flashed in Kory's mind and his mouth worked before he could stop it: "Mate in five."

Schelowitz put his hand over the clock pressing both buttons with his long fingers, stopping the timer. "This one doesn't count."

No one said a thing while both Bandini and Schelowitz studied the board. Two minutes later, Schelowitz turned to the boy. "You saw this in the middle of a blitz?"

"I'm so sorry, sir. I don't know what came over me. I didn't mean to interrupt the game."

"And why not, young man?" Schelowitz said. "You spotted a solution to a position worthy of a puzzle book, smack in the middle of a blitz. I had him and I completely missed the opportunity."

"Yeah, well let him solve chess problems and leave the real chess to men," Bandini said.

"That wasn't real enough for you? Did you know Kory can play blindfold chess? I'll bet *you* can't!" Dorothy said.

Kory winced.

"'Blindfold chess'? Does this look like a circus to you?"

"You're avoiding her question." Mary stepped in. "Kory can play without a chessboard, can *you?*"

"A pointless and outdated exercise. Any master should be able to play blindfold chess; only the likes of Morphy and some of his antiquated colleagues were petty enough to flaunt their talents so shamelessly."

Kory turned crimson. "Don't talk about Paul Morphy like that."

"What's the big deal about Morphy? That was *old* chess. Nobody plays like that anymore," Bandini said, thrown off guard by the boy's tone.

"He was one of the greatest chess players ever. If he had access to the theory we have today—were he alive today—he would still be world champion."

"Relax, the man is dead," Bandini said, "and so, my boy is his game, and blindfold chess, for that matter."

"Pawn to King Four," Kory said.

"What?"

Kory sat down. "Pawn to King Four. Your move."

"I'm not interested. There are chessboards here, as you can see. I will not be part of a circus act."

"Fine, but blindfold chess is no circus act, nor was Paul Morphy. He was immortalized not only for his unfathomable genius but also for his generosity, his conduct, his demeanor. He was your antithesis. He was a *gentleman*."

Bandini coughed, said nothing.

"Touché," Schelowitz said. To Kory: "Bandini is like a diamond in a dung heap. One can learn a lot from him, believe it or not."

"I don't give lessons," Bandini spat.

"Do you, Mr. Schelowitz?" Mary asked.

"I suppose that would depend on the student." Schelowitz regarded Kory for a moment, as if he were determining whether the boy were just such a student. "Pawn to King Five."

Kory smiled, fully exorcised of his demonic rage. "Knight to Queen's Bishop Three."

Kory and Schelowitz chanted through the opening and in less than thirty seconds. This was blindfold chess with no time limit. Kory was completely within his element. Both of them had their eyes open, neither of them looking at anything in particular.

Bandini shook his head in disgust, but it was obvious that he was following the game just as closely as everyone else.

There was some commotion in the background. More members had arrived, and someone had set up a board on the other side of the room, frantically playing out the moves as they were being said. Mr. Saunders took his daughter and Mary across the room and they joined the tight circle around the chessboard. The group was whispering loudly. Someone said, "Write the moves down, Jim. Write them down or we'll mess up the postmortem."

A few members migrated toward Schelowitz and Kory, some pretending that they could follow the game without a chessboard, and others advanced enough to really do so.

"What's going on, Dad?" Dorothy asked, bewildered.

"Shh, honey, I'm trying to listen to what these guys are saying, I'll tell you in a second." Then he turned to Mary. "Just give me a moment here and I'll fill you both in."

A young man, with a collar several sizes too large, said, "The kid is crazy to attack, he's got to play positional. Attacking the likes of Schelowitz—might as well try piercing a tank with a spoon!"

"Good one, Frank," Sam said, abandoning his post at the reception desk. "So what would you do, play positional chess and just wait until Schelowitz finds a hole? I say, if you're going to lose, you might as well lose putting up a fight."

From the other side of the room Kory said, "Pawn to Bishop Five."

The circle around the board went quiet for almost a minute and then the whispers started again.

"The kid's violent," a bearded man said, centering a few pieces on the board.

"Playing positional chess would be playing Schelowitz's game," Sam said. "The kid's going to bite the dust, but he won't go down without drawing blood first."

John spoke up. "I agree, it doesn't make sense for him to play Schelowitz's game."

"Who says he's going to lose?" Dorothy said.

The bearded man answered, "I do. You just don't beat a grandmaster."

"I'm sure *you* don't," Dorothy said. "But you're not Kory."

Schelowitz said, "King to Rook One."

Mouths around the table dropped open almost in unison.

"What's happening, Dad?" Dorothy said.

"I don't know. Guys, what *is* going on?"

"Schelowitz is not taking the sacrifice!"

"And that means?" It was the bearded man.

"I guess it means that there's something to this kid after all," Sam said.

Mary said, "And you're the one who was lecturing me about kids not belonging in chess clubs."

"Nobody told me the kid was a prodigy," Sam said.

"Play it out. Play it out," Mr. Saunders said.

Frank said, "Play out the sacrifice?"

"Good idea," the bearded man said as he captured the bishop. The crowd stared at the board.

"What now? Rook takes pawn, check?"

"So?"

"I don't get it," Mr. Saunders said.

"What's happening, Dad?"

"We're trying to see what would happen if Schelowitz had accepted Kory's sacrifice. If you'd let me teach you chess, you'd be able to follow."

From across the room they heard Kory say, "Draw."

The circle split into a curve facing Schelowitz.

The grandmaster smiled. "No draw. Bandini may be a bit crass, but in his own misanthropic way, he was trying to help you. Can you see the point he was making?"

Kory cocked his head, holding his breath. The chess club had suddenly gone quiet, reminding Kory of his home in a time before Mary arrived. Everyone anticipated an explanation but Grandmaster Schelowitz offered none.

"Finish him off," Bandini spat.

Kory looked at Schelowitz and the grandmaster nodded his encouragement.

"Queen to Bishop Five," Kory said.

The circle re-formed and the bearded man shouted, "Set this board back to the position. Put that bishop back where it was!"

Sam replaced the bishop, and moved Kory's queen to the fifth rank. The circle examined the board. John turned to explain the position to his daughter, but she was already half-way across the room. For years he couldn't get her to play a single game. The transformation was remarkable. Bringing the ladies along hadn't been such a bad idea after all.

Dorothy walked up to Kory, whispering in his ear, "You can do it. You can beat him." His first impulse was to punish her with a hostile look for the interruption, but her Charlie-esque persistence was enough to make him hesitate, and for a fleeting moment he was not irritated by her presence. But in a flash Kory was back to the game, and everyone around him, Dorothy included, vanished from his world.

Bandini watched closely but remained silent.

The next sequence of moves left the circle speechless. Nobody had time to think of an intelligent comment.

Schelowitz said, "Queen to Queen Seven" and before the circle could play out the move, Kory replied, "Rook to Rook Six." The two fired moves at each other, already knowing what the other would say before he said it. This sequence lasted for five moves. Only Bandini knew what was happening. A smile was growing rapidly on his pasty face.

Schelowitz stretched out his hand, and with the word "Congratulations," he offered his resignation.

Bandini laughed, and spittle shot out of his mouth in wide blasts.

Schelowitz stepped back to avoid the spray and, turning to Kory, he said, "It is possible to play a ruthless game and still be a gentleman. Morphy did, and I assure you, given your winning position, he would have never offered a draw."

"There's an insult for you—getting a lesson in aggression from the king of cowardice himself," Bandini said.

Mary gave Bandini a disgusted look and said to Schelowitz, "Are you saying my nephew is gifted?"

"Without question," Schelowitz said, "but he needs guidance if he's going to be successful in tournaments."

Mary said, "Could you give him that guidance, Mr. Schelowitz?"

"Well . . . I don't give lessons, I never have," Schelowitz said, noticing Kory's head drop. "Madam, I've seen many a prodigy come and go. If I make an exception for this one, it would be because he's got the heart of a true gentleman, and not by virtue of his talent alone."

John walked up to Mary. "I come down once a week; I could bring him over."

"I go to the city frequently as well," Mary said, brightening. "If you can't make a lesson, I could take him."

"Or we can all go," Dorothy said, "just like we did today."

John put his arm around his daughter. "I never thought you'd take an interest in chess."

"I never thought *I* would either," Mary said, "until today."

THE FINAL DATE

1961
One Year Later

In his pent-up rage, Kory considered messing up his bed, or throwing a shirt on the floor, but the door opened, and it was too late for any of that.

For three years now, Damon had been coming to visit, tormenting him at `every opportunity.

That was for pleasure.

He didn't even have to do anything—his presence was torture enough. Damon pretended not to know the effect he had on his brother. He was like arsenic, sipped slowly, morning, noon, and evening.

But it wasn't all for amusement: there was a business part to Damon's visits as well, and that was to make sure the people who counted knew he was still in charge. Everyone reported to him. From Mary to the principal all the way down to the butler.

Well, this time Kory'd had enough.

What he was going to do about it, he didn't know. All he could feel was anger, the fantasies of beating his older brother to a pulp kept filling his mind, and instead of fighting them, now he was feeding them. Feeding them to feed his anger. The anger crowded away all rational thought.

Because nobody in his rational mind could stand up to Damon.

The door opened in one motion; there was no time to see the knob turning. Although Damon always had an affinity for formal attire, the suit he now wore came from what Kory knew to be a selection reserved for special occasions. Kory had seen his brother dressed this way before and knew he was going on a date.

Kory didn't move out of Damon's way, he simply stood there, a laughable barrier in his brother's shadow.

Damon moved to pass, but Kory sidestepped, trying to run interference.

"Are you going to let me in?" Damon said.

"No."

Damon's eyebrows climbed as he looked down at his brother. "Move."

"Go to hell," Kory said.

"Now, is that any way to speak to your older brother?" Damon walked into the room, brushing easily past Kory, who again tried to make a blockade of his slender body but ended up offering as much resistance as a dangling vine. Damon motioned to a chair.

"Speak? Is that what you're going to do? Since when are you interested in talking? I've read articles about people like you. They start off by torturing animals, and when that no longer provides sufficient thrills, the killing begins. Once they've tasted blood, they become addicted and want more. Then you hooked up with Ken Johnson; now you're in West Point. What a surprise.

"My question is why come back here? What is there here for a man like you? Not quite done torturing me?"

Damon shook his head, looking at Kory like a master watching his dog humping another male. "What the hell has gotten into you, brother?"

"'Brother'? I'd rather believe one of us was adopted."

"Hey—"

"Get out of my room, and while you're at it, get the hell out of my life."

"Watch your manners, young man."

"Okay. *Please*, get out of my life."

Damon gave him a sidelong glance. "May I?"

"No, as a matter of fact, you may not."

Damon squinted, as if Kory were miles away. "Are you objecting to two brothers having a private chat?"

"You didn't knock, ergo this is another one of your stupid surprise inspections. You didn't come here to chat."

"Au contraire," Damon said. "I came to do just that, and we both know you heard me coming."

"Yes, I did, but you never come to chat—your only reason for being in my room has always been to administer an inspection and a beating—"

Damon frowned and waved dismissively. "Ancient history. I don't recall hitting you in years."

"Whether you use your fists or your manipulative cunning, you always end up getting what you want."

"What I wanted was what was best for you. For this family. Unfortunately, you never understood that. If, many years ago, I hit you, it was because of your insensitivity to Mother and her condition."

"Really? I thought it was all about satiating your sadistic needs."

"I'm curious, did you ever care?"

"About Martha?"

"About *Mother.*"

Kory clamped his mouth shut. Heat reached his ears.

Damon studied his brother for a while. "That's pretty much what I thought."

"You didn't answer my question," Kory said. "What are you doing here in Rhodes?"

"You know the answer to that," Damon said. "I explained it to you years ago, when you were in the hospital."

"That doesn't mean I understand it."

"Whether you choose to understand it or not, I certainly don't need your approval, little brother."

Kory laughed. The anger was coming back again and so was his resolve to make his fantasy of having it out with his older brother a reality, regardless of the outcome. "No, you had Martha's approval; that's all you ever needed."

"I really would prefer it if you referred to her as *Mother.*"

"I really don't give a *damn* what you prefer." Kory's mouth twisted into an acidic smile. "Speaking of which: You are twenty-two, and yet for some reason I cannot fathom, you insist on hounding a girl who is still a minor. Now, why is that?"

"First of all, she'll be eighteen soon—"

"In October. That's six months two weeks and four days away, but if memory serves, you were after her from the time she was thirteen."

"Secondly," Damon pressed, "whom I choose to date is none of your business."

Kory stretched his smile as far as it would bear. He had hit on something. If he pushed just a little harder, Damon would snap and Aunt Mary would bear witness to the psychopath he really was. "I remind you that I denied you entry, and yet you forced yourself in. You then ignored my two requests for you to leave. The alleged purpose of this intrusion into my bedroom was to chat. So, since you won't leave, and you insist on having a chat, I am obliging.

"I am inquiring about your pertinacious presence in Rhodes. It's not a question of whom you date—I really don't care what poor soul you choose to victimize—but why do it here? That's what I'm asking. Is there a shortage of adult females that has forced you to return to the small town of Rhodes to chase after a minor? You've been a legal adult for four years; when can I expect you leave this nest of yours and be gone from my life once and for all?"

"Really, Kory, I think I've had enough of your lip." Damon looked at his younger brother. "You go too far. I came here to have a little chat with you about responsibility. You're seventeen. I had hoped you'd be more receptive, but it's obvious you're still not ready to grow up. Sadly, I'm not surprised. You're getting a bit too old for disciplining, and I get this funny feeling that's exactly what you'd like me to do. I have to say, I'm not in the least impressed by this little show you've put on here. Are you trying to make some sort of stand? Prove to me that you're a man or something? Is that what this is all about?"

Damon stood up, and Kory pulled back instinctively. "You're a disappointment. Nothing but a little kid who uses big words. Go impress your aunt, I'm not buying."

Kory held out his hand to stop Damon from leaving the room. "I couldn't care less what you think of me. About my aunt: you might not like Mary, but at least she cared."

"What, now you're saying I didn't care? For your information, I had to take charge of this family. You didn't like it? Tough. That's life. Grow the fuck up."

Kory didn't move, but his knees were shaking. Damon would hit him, of that he was certain, but anticipating the pain was almost worse than the blows themselves. "You hide under the coattails of the military. You can fool them, you can fool your friends at the Academy, you can fool Dorothy, and you can even fool yourself; but you're not fooling me. You're screwed up, deeply disturbed. Get help. Who knows, if you hurry they still might be able to give you a discount lobotomy. It's not like anyone would notice."

Damon looked ready to explode. Kory was expecting to wake up in a hospital like he did after the accident, or perhaps not at all, but instead of beating Kory to a pulp, Damon let out a short burst of laughter. "You had me going there for a moment. You might try a gig on Broadway." Damon's smile vanished as he glanced at his golden watch. "I'd love to continue our little conversation, but I've got a date, and we can't keep a woman waiting, now, can we?"

Damon turned to leave, but Kory grabbed his brother's arm. "We're not finished."

Seizing Kory's wrist, Damon applied pressure with his thumb and his brother's grip lost what little force it had. He squeezed a bit more, and Kory's knees buckled. They both heard footsteps. Kory let out a muffled groan, as the vise clamped down even harder.

Mary passed by. Damon let go and Kory grabbed his reddening wrist.

"Boys, is everything all right?"

"We were just having a little chat," Damon said. "Isn't that right, brother?"

"Are you comfortable?" Damon asked.

Dorothy nodded, but her tight lips and fleeting eyes told a different story. "Yes, I'm fine." She shifted, almost squirming in the leather passenger seat.

Damon knew Dorothy loved him, otherwise she wouldn't have made the effort to lie. It was unusually cool for this late in March; perhaps that was the problem.

He turned up the heat.

The rain drummed softly on the windshield, and after half an hour, the rhythmic pulse of the wiper put Dorothy to sleep.

Damon looked over at her. He had never seen her asleep, and her vulnerability created an intimacy he'd never felt before. Damon watched her breathing gently through her open mouth. Was he in her dreams?

A pressure grew, trying to push out of his pants.

Dinner had not gone well. They had ordered and eaten, and somehow in that time, Damon had not managed to get to the point.

This kind of dance just wasn't his style. But there'd been no alternative. His usual direct approach would have scared her away. He had to play it cool.

So he'd started off talking about Bob, a guy from the Academy, but she'd changed the subject. He had let her finish and then he told her how Bob was in love and had found himself the perfect girl. She'd replied that her friend Nancy was in love too. Damon had said how Bob and his girl were getting married this summer, right after Bob graduated. Damon had told her that a lot of guys were doing that, and he'd offered two more examples. She'd said something like "That's nice." They hadn't exchanged another word until dessert, when Dorothy had surprised Damon by asking where they were going to send him after graduation and when.

That Dorothy was no fool: her question had hit the nail smack on the head. When and where, *indeed*. She knew what he was up to and even understood why.

In a way, Damon was pleased she could see right through him. It meant that he'd been right about her. She was beautiful—anyone could see that—but she was *smart,* too. Oh, yes. Perhaps the company couldn't figure that out, but Damon sure could, and he knew his mother had somehow known as well, otherwise she would have never approved.

Damon had explained that he and the other cadets would graduate West Point as officers in the US Army. As such, they would serve their country wherever and whenever they were needed. They'd been given a choice of assignments, however, and the Army's official decision would come just before graduation, in June.

Damon actually had his assignment—he knew exactly where he'd be going and when—but this wasn't the right time to tell Dorothy. He didn't want to overwhelm her on this date; he merely needed to test the waters in preparation for his formal proposal. He had hoped she would be more encouraging and show some signs of her interest in building a life and a future with him.

Spring break was ending, and Damon would once again have to return to West Point. His next and final hope was summer vacation. Dorothy went to Hawaii with her father each and every summer, and although this time Damon would be graduating, and his friends would be getting married, Dorothy showed no indication she was changing her plans. If he could at least get her to stay, they'd have the whole summer together, and there'd be all the time in the world to get married.

On-screen, Clark Gable was saying something to Marilyn Monroe. It was a good movie, but Damon was not in the mood to see *The Misfits* at that moment. They could have seen *The Absent-Minded Professor,* and after some consideration perhaps they should have, since *The Misfits,* still out in the theaters after more than three months, was monopolizing Dorothy's attention.

Clark Gable was still at it. It was easy to be a smooth talker when you were fed words by the best scriptwriters in Hollywood. Damon whispered in Dorothy's ear, "I think they had the right idea."

"Who? Roslyn and Gay?"

"Well, yes, I suppose," Damon said, "but I wasn't talking about the movie, I meant Bob and Cindy. Remember, my friend Bob from the Academy? The one I was telling you about over dinner?"

"Oh, yes. I remember," Dorothy said, and then she added dreamily, "don't they make a wonderful couple?"

This time he knew she was talking about the movie. No point pushing things any further. She'd dodged each and every attempt he'd made that evening.

Damon had promised himself he'd be patient on this date. That had proven to be a very difficult promise to keep. He still had a few months left before the summer, and if he rushed her, he could end up spoiling years of courtship. It was obvious Dorothy wasn't going to let him be subtle about it, and this wasn't the time to come out with a direct marriage proposal.

When the damned movie was finally over, Damon was one of the first to stand. Dorothy remained seated, and somehow still transfixed, as though she were watching the final climactic scene all over again, and not the credits.

Half the theater had cleared out when Damon finally took her hand. "Shall we?"

She followed him out the narrow exitway.

Some asshole whistled.

Damon tensed as he scanned for the source of the sound.

"Ow!"

Damon released her hand and said, "Sorry, honey." To the guy leaning against the corner: "What is it, buddy—are you blind? Can't you see she's not alone?"

The guy smiled, but when he got a better look at Damon, his cigarette drooped from his mouth. He plucked it out, tapping the ashes and watching them fall. "Just admiring the merchandise."

With his left hand, Damon shielded Dorothy, with his right, he grasped the punk by the collar and smashed him against the wall. The cigarette fell.

"What did you just call my girl?"

"Easy, buddy." The voice came from the right.

Damon had known the punk wasn't alone. Glances had telegraphed their alliance along with their readiness to act.

He'd counted at least three of them and had sized them up in seconds: he could take them all, and quickly, but not without creating an ugly scene, and in these narrow confines, it would be difficult to keep Dorothy from harm. Somebody might even call the police. Not the memorable end to this date Damon had planned. "You might want to tell your friend here to watch what he says to accompanied ladies. Unless, of course, he's looking for a quick ride to the emergency room." Not waiting for a response from the punk's friend, Damon gave the guy one last shove against the wall and let him go.

The punk made a show of straightening out his jacket, but nobody in his group made any aggressive moves.

Satisfied, Damon took Dorothy's hand—gently this time. "Let's go."

Dorothy returned a forced smile. The last time they'd been in a situation like this, the outcome had been quite different.

God, he'd wanted to pummel that bastard. Instead, he'd shown restraint and self-control.

Dorothy was smart. She'd proven it that evening. She had to know how hard it was for him to hold back. She had to know he did it for her. Dorothy knew, all right, she just wasn't showing it. Like all women, she was as hard to read as the Shakespeare nonsense they'd rammed down his throat in high school English.

That's okay, he told himself.

He'd been patient. He'd played her game, danced her dance.

Come graduation he'd make his move in no uncertain terms.

His way.

MARRIAGE PROPOSAL

1961

This phone call would be tapped. There was no point in telling Stavridis not to listen in—that would be like announcing Damon had something to hide.

It really wasn't a secret, anyway. Stavridis had probably figured out Damon was planning on marrying Dorothy, despite the company's persistent attempts to dissuade him.

Absolutely nothing had gone as planned that year.

That last date had been a complete flop. Then Damon heard that Dorothy was leaving for Hawaii earlier than usual, and so there was no opportunity to meet with her again before she left.

Shortly after learning of her plans for a premature departure, Damon had sent her a letter asking for her hand in marriage.

Weeks went by with no response.

Dorothy was soon to leave, and Damon had no choice—he had to call her. By the time she returned from her vacation, his would be over, and he'd already be in Infantry School. Immediately after that, the Army would send him to Airborne Training, followed by Ranger School. All that was left was Christmas break, because after Ranger School, he'd be shipped off to his assignment of choice, Berlin.

Finally someone picked up the phone. "Saunders residence."

"Hello, Mr. Saunders; it's Damon."

"Hello, young man, how are you doing these days?"

"Fine, sir. I hear you're leaving for Hawaii early this year," Damon said. "I just wanted to say good-bye to Dorothy before she leaves."

"We'll only be gone until mid-August," John said. "I'm sure you two will have time to get together after."

"Actually—"

"I'll let you talk with Dorothy. Enjoy your vacation."

The line went quiet for a while.

"Hello." Dorothy's voice sounded childlike over the phone.

"Hello, my dear."

"Hi."

"Did you get my letter?"

Damon heard her sigh over the phone. "Yes."

"And?"

There was no answer for some time, but when Dorothy finally spoke, her words were hurried. "I'm not eighteen yet. So you'd need my father's consent, and he'd never approve—you know how he is."

"No," Damon said, "I'm not sure I do, and I don't think *he's* the problem; consider this"—Damon stopped himself, and just in time—"you have to make your own decisions now, you're a big girl."

"Yes, I know, but you can't get around the law, Damon."

He directed a sigh away from the mouthpiece. "You said you read my letter, right? Listen, I've explained all this: We won't get married this summer, because you'll be in Hawaii, so that leaves Christmas break. I'll have a week off Ranger School. That gives us plenty of time, and you won't have to worry about permission from anyone because by then, you'll be eighteen."

"Give me some time to think about this . . . it's all . . . a bit . . . well . . . I'm kind of overwhelmed right now."

"Okay, I can see that. But since I don't graduate from the Academy until the seventh, when you'll already be in Hawaii, could I at least have your answer before you leave?"

Damon thought he'd lost the phone connection.

"All right," Dorothy said.

"Good. I'll leave you to think about this. I expect to hear from you soon, okay?"

Dorothy stared at the receiver for a while. There was only one person she could think of to talk to. Dorothy ran up to her room and started dialing.

"Okay, okay," Nancy said. "I get it. He's pushing you for an answer and you want to buy time. Remember, men are supposed to wait for women. We pressure *them*, not the other way around."

"But he *does* have a point, I mean he has a right to an answer, and it's been three weeks since I got his proposal in the mail."

"Listen carefully, because you're not getting it: he wants you as his wife. He wants to take you away to Germany."

"Not exactly. He'll be stationed there, but he's got a house in Geneva, where he'll be spending his time off. That's where he wants us to live."

"That's a lifetime sentence. There's no parole and your only get-out-of-jail-free card is divorce. Once he knocks you up, then you're stuck, divorce or not."

"Gee, thanks for the words of encouragement."

"Yeah, well you need to hear it from someone. Don't tell me I didn't tell you so ten years from now, because I am telling you so."

"What exactly *are* you telling me?"

"That this is very serious, and you have a right to take all the time you need to decide, and if he can't understand that, then he's not worth it."

"It sounds like you don't think he's worth it no matter what," Dorothy said.

"Hey, you want to throw your life away the second you turn eighteen? Go ahead, don't let me stop you."

"I won't."

"Fine, but you buy yourself some time, you hear?"

"Yeah, that's what I want, but just how am I supposed to do that?"

"Simple, you tell him you'll write him a letter. He proposed in a letter, so you'll answer in a letter. That's how you have to handle these things."

"Really, and how would you know?"

"Do you want my advice or not?"

"It doesn't sound like I have much choice," Dorothy said. Then, remembering that she was the one who called, she added, "Sorry, I didn't mean that, it's just that I wasn't expecting—"

"You thought I'd be happy for you and I'd tell you to go for it because you'll never get another chance like this."

"I don't know what I thought. To be honest, I feel sorry for him, I mean he's been waiting for all these years . . ."

To Dorothy's surprise, Nancy did not respond.

After a while Dorothy said, "So you were saying? A letter?"

"Uh-huh."

"So I just mail him a letter?"

"No, no. That wouldn't do. You want to keep this a secret, right? Whatever you decide? If you end up accepting, then you want to buy time and wait until you're eighteen. If you're going to dump him, you don't want to give him the opportunity to beg or get bitter on you. So you wait, see? Wait until the end of the summer, just when he has to go on that training thingy you were telling me about."

"Infantry School."

"Yes, that."

"Okay, but where do I mail the letter?"

"You don't. Just leave the letter with me and I'll give it to him."

Dorothy thought for a moment. "That's an interesting idea, let me think about it."

"Cadet van Luden, your telephone call."

"Thank you," Damon said, taking the phone.

"I work for you, but I also work for Van Luden Enterprises." It was Stavridis.

Damon had hoped it would be Dorothy. She had called him before she left, as promised, but it was not the response he'd wanted to hear. In fact, it hadn't been a response at all.

She needed more time to think and had told him she didn't want to be rushed into making such an important decision. She promised he would have a response before he went for training. Damon didn't like the sound of that—as though she was laying down the foundations for rejection.

"I asked you to tell me if you thinking of marriage," Stavridis continued. "The company wants to know this. Is there problem of trust? How come you did not say you were planning on marrying Dorothy?"

Damon had anticipated this reaction and decided to play dumb. "How do you know?"

"I've got her phone tapped. You forget? My men listen to every conversation."

"Right, but you were supposed to be listening to Dorothy, not *me*."

"The company is paying, through your trust fund. Perhaps you don't appreciate their position, the expense?"

"Don't be ridiculous."

"I ask again, why you don't tell us about your intentions to marry Dorothy?"

"Any run-of-the-mill detective should have figured out what my intentions were. If you must know, I didn't say anything because I'm still waiting for her answer. My proposal means nothing until she accepts."

"You don' understand. This is about *trust*, Mr. van Luden. Of course I knew what your intentions were, from the day your mother hired me. In the beginning, I thought maybe you were playing some game with the company. Now I know is no game. But you must keep me informed about *everything*. I cannot do this things for you and work for the company if I cannot trust you hundred percent, understood?"

"The company doesn't have to worry about trusting me, and neither do you. I would have mentioned it, in due course."

"We have monitored a conversation between Dorothy and this friend she has, Nancy. Dorothy is planning to give you her answer by the end of summer. When she does, you must tell me. Understood? I must say, she was not sounding enthusiastic. You must prepare yourself . . . you might have unpleasant surprise.

Also, I really believe you should think about this again. She is too young."

"I've made up my mind, and I know what I want. As soon as I have her answer, I'll let you know."

"Okay, but I still—"

"And in the future, don't call me here unless it's important."

Dorothy sat in the passenger seat as her father drove them home after a day at the chess club. Kory and Charlie were seated in the back. Kory was right behind her, just where she needed him. He had won his third tournament in a row, and her father wouldn't stop talking about his promising future. It took a while before John's attention was sufficiently diverted. She looked back. Charlie was staring right at her, with a big silly smile on his face. Dorothy really loved that guy, but at the moment she needed him to look elsewhere. Charlie was still looking out the front, and to make matters worse, her father started talking again.

They were just half an hour from Rhodes, and Dorothy was wondering if she'd ever get her chance, when Charlie peered out the window and the curving road kept her father's eyes from wandering in her direction. She had her purse rested against her right thigh. She slipped out the letter and poked it between her seat and the door. Kory took it silently and made it disappear like a seasoned spy.

She had called Kory the day she spoke with Nancy. A letter was the way to go; Nancy had been right. But no way was Dorothy going to give it to her. Dorothy only knew Kory through the ritual chess excursions with her father and Charlie, and though in the beginning Kory had been distant, he had recently started opening up. Strangely, his peculiar lack of interest in her made him more trustworthy. Right now, he was clearly her best option.

She didn't tell Kory what was happening, though. There'd been no need to get into all that. All she'd said was she wanted him to give his brother a letter. She told him it was a secret and nobody, absolutely *nobody*, could know. She told him she was leaving for Hawaii and that he had to promise he wouldn't open the envelope and read the letter. On the last day of his brother's vacation, the day before he had to leave for Infantry School, Kory was to hand Damon the letter; not a day earlier. Until that time, he was to keep the letter hidden in his room, so there'd be no chance he'd lose or forget it.

His reaction had been odd. He'd said: "Why would I do this for him?"

Without thinking, she'd replied, "Then don't do it for him, do it for me."

DESPERATE

August 1961

Mary went after him.

"I'm going to have lunch in town," Damon said, shutting her behind the oak door.

He walked briskly toward Route One, bypassing Ken Johnson's place. Normally, when Damon was back home, he visited his mentor on an almost daily basis, but this time he wasn't in a mood to chitchat about his achievements. Damon's career was well on its way. He'd graduated a Starman—top ten percent of his class. After the Academy, most Starmen went to the Corps of Engineers, since that was the most sought-after and prestigious of all corps. Damon had given this careful consideration, and following Ken's advice he'd chosen the Infantry Corps instead. From there Damon could eventually find his way to the Special Forces, following the path Ken had prepared him for.

But his career wasn't what was bothering him.

It was Kory. He was completely out of control. His subtle insults were no longer sounding so subtle; even Mary had been shocked.

What a lunch.

Damon had eaten nothing and said nothing, waiting to see how his aunt would react. It had taken her long enough, probably because she couldn't believe her own ears. Mary ended up scolding Kory, but it had done nothing to stop him. She might as well have tried getting a rabid dog to heel.

It had taken all Damon had to keep himself from belting that smartass brother of his right then and there. He was glad he'd kept his cool; that way Mary could see what a crappy job she had done bringing up Kory for the few years she'd been in charge. *Serves her right for not sending him to Livingsford.*

Family had been everything to his mother. Was the van Luden legacy to be left in the hands of Damon's promiscuous aunt and self-righteous kid brother?

What had come over Kory? He'd never been so aggressive before, and that demonstration had crossed the line and traveled halfway to the moon. Kory was obviously challenging Damon, but to what? A fistfight? That would have been over quickly, and no matter what the hormones were doing to Kory, he still had to have enough presence of mind to realize that much. Kory had mounted several verbal attacks that year, but until that day, at least he'd shown enough sense to do it in private.

At lunch, Mary had been right there, listening to Kory spit out insult after insult. She watched Damon sit there, say nothing, and finally walk off like some fucking coward.

Jesus, had it been any other situation, anybody else . . . It was like Kory had this crazy death wish. Damon wasn't about to give him the satisfaction.

The Academy had taught Damon many things, and one of the greatest lessons he'd learned had been that of self-control. If Kory had tried this shit four years ago, he'd have spent the rest of his life moving his precious chess pieces with his teeth.

"Hi, Damon." It was a girl's voice.

He turned his head to look, not certain the young lady had actually spoken his name.

She was looking right at him.

"Hello," Damon said simply, and when she didn't respond, he added, "do I know you?"

"I'm Nancy." The girl smiled. "I'm a senior. I'm also Dorothy's best friend. Hasn't she mentioned me?"

Dorothy had never spoken of her friends. In fact, after four years, Damon had only managed a handful of dates with the woman he planned to one day call his bride. During those brief encounters their most intimate exchange had been a simple good-bye kiss on the cheek.

"Of course, yes," Damon said. He had heard plenty about Nancy, but the information had come from Stavridis, not Dorothy.

Nancy's smile said she did not believe him. The lie seemed to please her, though, as if cornering him marked a personal victory.

"You've just graduated from West Point?"

"Yes. Well not *just*. Two months ago, actually, July seventh."

"Congratulations. Second Lieutenant, right?"

"That's right," Damon said, the corner of his mouth rising perceptibly.

"I hear you graduated Starman."

"Right again," Damon said. "So Dorothy's been talking about me."

Nancy gave Damon a grave look. "Listen, you're a nice guy." She fidgeted with her fingers, as if the perpetual untangling motion helped her work out a moral dilemma. "I really shouldn't say this but"—Nancy searched his face for hints—"can I speak openly?"

"Certainly, what is it?"

"I didn't learn about any of this from Dorothy. The fact is, you're kind of famous here. I mean, you know how word gets around?"

"I'm not sure I follow," Damon said, suddenly wanting to leave before Nancy could say any more.

Nancy looked at him, her smile strained. "Dorothy doesn't talk about you." Shaking her head in a show of pity, Nancy added, "She doesn't really care about you, Damon, she never did. Not *really*. You know? I guess she figured you were fun . . . for a while . . . but now she's had her fill and she wants to move on. She just doesn't know how to break it to you."

"Really. Why do you say that?"

"I'm her best friend, remember? She tells me *everything*. You guys haven't even made it to first base."

Damon frowned.

"Hey, it's not your fault. The problem isn't you, it's *her*."

"I thought you were supposed to be her best friend."

"I *am*. For most girls, you might be a dream come true, but I don't think you're right for her, and I know she's not right for you. I hate to say all this, but it's for her good and yours."

"How would you know?"

"Like I said, she tells me *everything*." Nancy looked away. "She's told me about your letter; actually, she read it to me over the phone, word for word."

Damon turned red. *Over the phone.* Now Stavridis and his men had a transcript with every detail of his marriage proposal.

Nancy waited for Damon to say something. "She's going to turn you down."

Damon winced, clamping his mouth shut with such force his teeth hurt. He needed to let Nancy spill the beans first, before telling the bitch to go fuck herself. "What exactly did she tell you?"

"It wasn't something she just said; she's been wanting to dump you for over a year now. Haven't you noticed? You may not have realized you're not meant for each other, but she has."

"So *you've* been talking to her," Damon said, his face hot.

Nancy planted her hand on her hip, shaking her head. "If you don't want to hear this, that's fine. You know this hurts me as much as it hurts you."

"I doubt that, but go on."

"Well, as I was saying, she hung out with you out of pity. You were alone at the Academy, and you'd been nice to her . . . she didn't have what it takes to tell you it was over."

"Are you telling me she sent you to talk to me?"

Nancy laughed. "No, no, not at all." She furrowed her eyebrows. "Well . . . actually . . . coming to think of it, you're not far off. She never asked me *directly*, if you know what I mean. She doesn't think you're the right guy for her. I told her that was dumb, but she doesn't want my advice. So anyway—oh, and you're not supposed to know this, so you never heard this from me—she's going to give you a letter."

"I'm leaving in a few days and she's still in Hawaii . . . I thought she was going to call me."

"Dorothy? She doesn't have the guts. She called me to ask for ways to get out of breaking the news to you directly. I was the one who told her she should send your rejection by mail. I hate to be the one to say this, but trust me, you're going to get a Dear John letter."

Damon turned and walked away. Just loud enough for Nancy to hear, he said, "Over my dead, rotting body."

Clarissa was a drab blonde in a gray business dress. She was Brad Chambers's secretary, nothing more. He was a bachelor and could have easily selected a younger lady, one easier on the eyes, but Mr. Chambers didn't seem like the kind of guy who messed around.

This was Damon's second meeting with the man. The first had taken place shortly after his mother died, and at that time Damon didn't have the presence of mind to take in all the information the attorney had tossed his way. This time, Damon had come better prepared, but it had ended up making no difference: discussing the trust had not been on Mr. Chambers's agenda for the day.

Over the years, Stavridis had repeatedly made clear his concerns about the company's position regarding Dorothy. And Mr. Chambers sat at the top of the corporate pyramid, so whenever Stavridis said "Van Luden Enterprises," he really meant Mr. Chambers. The VPs, executive managers, and corporate representatives all took care of the details, while Mr. Bradley Chambers made the big decisions for a company with investments that were approaching half a billion dollars. Thinking the topic of this meeting was going to be the trust, Damon had made a point of coming prepared.

During their first meeting, Mr. Chambers had been very cordial, and he behaved like he had all the time in the world for the young man who had just lost his mother.

This meeting had been primarily symbolic. Bradley Chambers, CEO of Van Luden Enterprises, the van Luden family trustee, Martha's personal attorney and adviser since Nicholas was alive, set up this one-on-one to make clear his disappointment in Damon's choice of bride.

For the time being, Mr. Chambers had full control. Damon had listened and kept his mouth shut. He'd wanted to slam the door so hard it would come off its hinges, but instead he'd closed it gently, quietly. *There'll come a time the high and mighty Bradley Chambers will eat his words.*

After another five minutes, Damon said, "Will Mr. Stavridis be much longer? We have reservations for six o'clock."

"He'll be right along, Mr. van Luden," the secretary said. "A car is waiting for you and the restaurant is not far. You should be there in plenty of time."

She hardly finished her sentence as she looked down the hallway at Stavridis, who was approaching with a hurried skip.

He put out his hand. "Sorry to keep you waiting."

"That's fine," Damon said, crushing the detective's palm.

Chez Louis was candlelit, not a problem for a man as young as Damon—he could probably read fine print in a dark cave. Stavridis was about to pick up his briefcase when a waiter came by, wearing a smile that was simultaneously patient and condescending.

"I recommend the fondue Bourguignon," Damon said.

Stavridis ignored the suggestion and turned to the waiter. "Excuse me. Do you have spaghetti? I cannot eat anything heavy. I have ulcers."

The waiter looked at him as if Stavridis had snot hanging from his nose. "This is a *French* restaurant, Monsieur. We do not have *spaghetti*."

Stavridis felt the urge to spit. "Perhaps, then, you have something with vegetables?"

The waiter nodded. "We do indeed. I can offer you today's special, Monsieur: vegetable ratatouille."

"Is good?"

The waiter flinched. "But of course, Monsieur. Only the best Chez Louis."

Stavridis nodded. "Okay, then."

"Je prendrais un steak tartare, avec des frites," Damon said.

140

The waiter offered a micro-bow. *"Mais bien sûr, monsieur. Voulez-vous aussi un peu de vin?"*

"Oui, du Beaujolais, s'il vous plaît."

The waiter smiled approvingly and left with their order.

Stavridis opened his briefcase, expecting his client to start with the questions at any moment: over the phone, Damon had the patience of a toddler.

Damon said, "Not now. We'll eat, then discuss business."

Stavridis had given up his private-eye business for the promise of a more lucrative future with Van Luden Enterprises. A future that meant early retirement and an opportunity to one day return to Greece. If working with this arrogant American was the price, then so be it.

The waiter came over with a trolley, took Damon's plate from the heater, and plopped a cylindrical slab of pink meat on the side of the dish. Stavridis wrinkled his nose. Only a snob would eat uncooked food.

Finished with Damon, the waiter started filling Stavridis's plate with miserable portions of broccoli, cauliflower, and asparagus. In the center of the plate, he placed something that Stavridis assumed was the main course. That's the French for you. *"Malakes,"* he cursed under his breath. He'd have to find a *real* restaurant if he wanted to go home on a full stomach. Perhaps a gyro on the way back? He knew a place only two blocks away.

They ate in silence. Damon was taking his time.

Noticing the empty plates, the Frenchman cleared the table and asked Damon a question. Damon replied, *"Non."*

As a boy, his French teacher had tried his best to teach Stavridis the language, but *"non"* was the only word he remembered. "I am finished too."

The waiter walked off, not the least bit impressed with Stavridis's interpretive abilities.

"Show me what you have," Damon said.

"Of course." He reached for his briefcase and produced several manila folders, stacked in chronological order, each neatly labeled with dates. "Okay, Mr. van Luden"—he showed Damon the folders—"1957, 1958, 1959; here I have 1960, and this last one is this year. Where should I start?"

"From the first phone taps."

"That would be October 1957, after the party."

"Good, start there. Don't leave out any details—I don't care if I've heard it before."

"Very well." He squinted at the folder, trying to make out the year on the label. Finally, with a gesture of frustration, he pulled out his reading glasses. *They use candles here so people can't take a good look at the garbage they serve.*

Stavridis sifted through some papers. He cursed himself for not sorting them in order. He had done a good job with the folders, but the papers inside were a messy confusion. He had been working on them the night before, when Christina had the desire to play wife.

It took Stavridis twenty minutes to go through the first three years. He made it to August 1960, but couldn't find the papers for September.

Damon was staring.

"Gamo to Christo tou," Stavridis mumbled. In English, he said, "Yes, sorry, here it is. September 1960. Sorry, it was in the folder for the '61. Let me see . . . this is the year you asked me to monitor Kory. Still not much activity to report. Like always, he never misses a day of school. He walks there, and he walks back. Always alone and always at the same time—do you want them? The times?"

"Walks?" Damon asked. Then he remembered: the previous fall, the trust had dismissed Oliver, so Kory and Mary no longer had a chauffeur. "Never mind, go on."

"Where was I? September 1960. Nothing else to report."

"Nothing?"

"Strange, yes? Kory was not going out of the house except to go to school. No visits from boys or girls his age. In fact, for nine months, nobody came over."

"Go on."

"I suppose because his mother died—"

"Don't interpret, just tell me what you have."

Stavridis took a deep breath. "That is all there is for the month September. The activities of his aunt, also not interesting—"

Damon stared.

"But I will tell you. She stay at home, she goes shopping. Nothing more."

"Go on."

"October 1960. Here we have interesting changes. We have one trip—"

"A trip?"

"Yes," Stavridis said. "Yes, but just one. In October."

"*Just* one?"

"Please, let me finish," Stavridis said. "One trip to New York. October 11. It was Saturday." He produced a photograph and handed it to his client. Damon studied the picture. It showed Kory with his aunt outside of the Forty-Second Street Odeon Theater. Block letters on the canopy read ALFRED HITCHCOCK'S THE BIRDS.

"That's it?"

"I have more," Stavridis said, handing him another photograph.

This one showed Mary and Kory entering the "A Taste of Italy" restaurant on Thirty-Eighth Street.

"This was after the movie," Stavridis explained.

"Okay, go on," Damon said.

"I don't mention phone taps because there is nothing important. They rarely used their phone. I have marked four long distance phone calls to San Francisco. Would you like me to read the transcript?"

"Summarize."

"All conversations were to—"

Damon saw the waiter and scribbled something in the air with an imaginary pen, saying something that sounded like "Ladission." The waiter nodded and disappeared.

"A fellow she called Quinn," Stavridis said. "No talk about money or things like that. He is taking care of her house. They were talking about the carpet—"

"Fine, fine, go on, let's not waste time on details."

"But you told me—"

"Your job is to know what details are important."

"Mr. van Luden, what's important to one man is not import-ant to another. I do not read minds. How am I supposed to—"

"Go *on*," Damon snapped.

Stavridis grimaced, sighed, and proceeded to report his findings for November, December, and January. Each month showed increased activities with Mary. Several movies in Rhodes, and numerous weekend outings to New York.

Stavridis was sifting through photos of Kory walking home with a classmate when Damon leaned forward. "Let me see those."

In the pictures stood a tall, scrawny teenager frozen in animation as he spoke with Kory, his hands waving in the air, his hair an unkempt gray mass.

"This kid here, was he a redhead?"

"Yes, very red hair."

"Okay, I know who that is," Damon said. Charlie Patterson—the clown. He remembered seeing him at school, and on that day he'd taken Dorothy to the diner. Damon tossed the photo on the table. "Were they friends?"

"Not exactly . . . not at this point." Stavridis went through the transcripts of the phone calls from Charlie's house to the van Luden residence. Stavridis showed his client photo after photo of Kory walking with his friend to and from school. Pictures taken later on showed Charlie at the van Luden residence itself.

Stavridis told his client about the chess match with Mr. Saunders, the first trip to the Manhattan Chess Club, and the subsequent trips that had made it into a ritual. There were Xeroxes of cancelled monthly checks made out to Grandmaster Schelowitz for lessons given.

Stavridis expected a reaction, but received none. The mention of fees for chess lessons did not hit home as Stavridis anticipated it would. It was his understanding that Kory, Mary, and Mr. Saunders were put under the microscope because of Damon's concern for the trust fund. Damon had never offered an explanation, but why else would he want the surveillance to include anyone other than Dorothy?

"I have more," Stavridis said. "It is about your aunt." He showed Damon evidence of a growing relationship between Mary van Luden and Dorothy's father, Mr. Saunders. "You see, if they marry, this Mr. Saunders might have access to some of the family funds through your aunt." In Greece, talking about money so openly was considered vulgar, but this wasn't home, Stavridis reminded himself for the thousandth time since he'd immigrated to the United States. Here, the rich had no shame when it came to money and inheritance.

Damon examined the bill, produced several twenties, and slid them in the check folder.

"So, Mr. van Luden, up to the moment, my investigation show no other threat to the fund." He held out one of the folders. "The only thing more I have was this friend, this Charlie. And unless your brother prefers the boys, I don't see a problem with this."

"Kory is no fairy, and if he was, he'd be no threat to the fund. You know that as well as I do."

Stavridis cleared his throat.

"Let's get back to Dorothy."

The detective nodded. "No very important changes. Her father finds bottles under her bed, hashish in plastic bags. He believes that her psychologist will help her out of this. This is the information you are wanting, no?"

Damon seemed deep in thought.

"I learn something new, talking with the father," Stavridis said. "Did you know Dorothy tried to commit suicide?"

Damon's eyes opened wide. "When?"

"Years ago. Mr. Saunders told me after a few drinks. It happened before she came to Rhodes, after the death of her mother."

Damon looked quite upset. Stavridis let him stew for a while. "This is no game. Dorothy has *real* psychological problems."

For a long while, Damon sat quietly. "She hasn't answered."

Stavridis nodded and waited for more. He almost felt pity for the man.

"I'm worried," Damon said. "She promised she would answer me, and I'm leaving tomorrow. I just don't think she's going to call." Damon looked at him, gauging his reaction. "You told me you had bad indications, that you thought my chances weren't good. What exactly were those indications?"

"It was just a feeling," Stavridis said.

"Oh, I think it was more than that."

Stavridis shook his head. "What you saying? You think I don' tell you everything? Let us not forget, *you* were not telling me, eh. You never said you were going to propose."

"We've been over that before. I didn't tell you because I wanted to have her answer first. So answer my question: why did you say you thought Dorothy would say no?"

"I told you, I had a feeling."

"Really? Just a feeling?" Damon said. "That's interesting, because I had a chat with Nancy, and she told me she heard about my proposal from Dorothy." Damon eyed him. "So if you've been doing your job and monitoring the calls, you had a transcript of that phone call."

Stavridis frowned and leaned over the table speaking loudly. "Yes, I read the transcript. I told you about the call between Dorothy and her friend and I told you Dorothy would be answering by the end of the summer. So where is the problem?"

"My problem is you didn't tell me what those indications were. You just admitted you read the transcript of that call, therefore you knew Nancy convinced Dorothy to send me a letter with her answer, and yet you never told me."

Stavridis thought for a moment. Finally he nodded and sat back in his seat. "Yes, this is true what you say."

Damon looked at Stavridis for a while. "Until I spoke with Nancy, I was expecting Dorothy would call me. I'm leaving now, and if she were going to send me a letter I'd already have it. She couldn't have timed mailing the letter from Hawaii to have it arrive on the very day I leave."

"Yes, you are right, I don't see how you could get a letter at this point. But if you don't get the letter tomorrow, before you leave, you can have your aunt send it to you while you are in Infantry School."

Damon shook his head. "*If* there is a letter. *If* she even responds. Too many damned *ifs*. I don't like this. Tomorrow I'm leaving, and I'll basically be cut off from her and any hopes of making her my wife."

"You cannot control everything," Stavridis said. "Some things are not meant to be, eh. Even all your money cannot change that. It is for the best. It will hurt now . . . perhaps for a long time, but eventually, you will get over her and find a girl better for you. Take advice from an older man."

"You couldn't possibly understand."

"Have you perhaps considered Nancy?"

"Considered her for what?" Damon said.

"Surely an intelligent man like you can see the girl likes you."

Damon laughed for the first and last time that evening. "Nancy? She's just a confused kid who doesn't know what she wants."

"She does not sound confused to me." Stavridis smiled. "No. She knows *exactly* what she wants. You two have much in common."

"Well, I haven't read the phone taps, and I've only seen Nancy once. All I know about her is what Dorothy has told me, and that wasn't much."

Stavridis nodded. "She did no say word for word, eh. It is my experience and how you say? Reading between the lines? Nancy is very careful, so I believe Dorothy does not know . . . since that party where Dorothy brought the alcohol, I think Nancy has been trying to get her to leave you."

"Really?" Damon said, looking at Stavridis as if he had been the one trying to change Dorothy's mind.

"Dorothy might still answer as you hope. If Nancy believes this, she might be trying to give bad picture of you, so you give up before Dorothy has a chance to give her decision, yes?"

Damon's eyes lit up.

Stavridis said, "Again, I tell you: I just give the information. Who knows, perhaps Dorothy will call tonight?"

Damon said nothing.

They left the restaurant, and still hungry for that gyro, Stavridis declined a ride. As Damon got in the back of the limousine, Stavridis turned to him. "Remember, a man without hope has nothing to lose."

"Yeah, that's true," Damon said, "and nothing to gain."

The drab-green duffel bag lay at the foot of the bed. Damon regarded it for a moment, and he took one last look in the mirror to see that his uniform was pressed and perfect on him. There was no requirement to travel in uniform, but Damon chose to do so anyway. He'd worked hard at the Academy to earn the right to wear the uniform of an officer of the US Army. He grabbed the duffel bag and turned to leave, but his brother was standing at the door. Only Kory could have come so close without Damon hearing him approach.

Damon smiled, but there was no joy in his face. "Come here to insult me one last time?"

Kory merely shook his head. He looked like someone about to break the news of a death in the family.

Damon waited but Kory didn't speak; he stood there for a moment with his head hanging in reflection, as if he were trying to remember the lines from a script.

"I'd love to stand here all day, brother, but as you obviously know, I have to be going."

Kory pulled an envelope from his pocket. "This is for you, from Dorothy." As Damon took the letter, Kory turned to leave.

"Wait," Damon said softly. "Have you read it?"

"No," Kory answered, expecting the question. "Look, as you can see, it's sealed."

"Know what it's about?" Damon asked, testing.

"Not a clue."

"Then how—"

"She gave it to me, with explicit instructions to hand it to you, in person, on the day you leave."

"You know her?" Damon said, half expecting to catch his brother lying.

"Yes, her father takes me to his chess club, and she and Charlie are friends."

Damon nodded. "I get the feeling you didn't want any part in this."

Kory studied Damon. This was the first time his brother had actually read him correctly on anything.

Mary opened her arms. Damon walked past her and his brother.

"Good-bye," Damon said, and marched off, duffel bag in hand.

THE MUSEUM TRIP

September 1961

The door to the school bus creaked open and Mrs. Matthews went in first. Kory was standing fifth in line. Now he was sixth, Kenny Flatstroem just cut in front of him.

The only interest Kory had in a trip to Manhattan was to go to the chess club. Ideally, he'd go alone with Mr. Saunders, but he knew he was lucky to be going at all. Having Charlie and Dorothy with him as part of the package deal had become less and less irritating lately. He was almost used to having them there. At least Charlie knew a little something about chess. Dorothy was hopeless.

And worse, she was Damon's girl.

At first, just the thought of being in the same car with her had bothered him. She was a constant reminder of his older brother. And any reminder of Damon was unwelcome.

He wished he could have opted out of this pointless expedition to the museum, but Mary had insisted he go. She had been very good to him since she took charge. She tried a bit too hard, and he wished he had more privacy, but without her, there'd have been no chess club. No lessons with Grandmaster Schelowitz.

Cindy and three of her friends bumped Kory to the side, forcing their way ahead, while Charlie was being pushed from behind. There was another shove, this one feeling more like a jab.

Kory walked to the back of the bus and took a window seat. He should have waited for Charlie. Charlie could be annoying at times—to say the least—but better the devil you know . . .

The bus was filling up quickly. It amazed Kory how much noise his classmates were making.

Where was Charlie?

Kory stood. He could make out a red crop of hair in the very front of the bus. What was Charlie doing in the back of the line?

There weren't that many places left now. Not a single window seat.

Dorothy was coming down the aisle and Charlie was three kids behind her.

Kory waved at Charlie.

Dorothy waved back.

Kory sat back down in his seat. That was a stupid thing to do. She'd seen him. There was no way to pretend she wasn't there.

Kory stared at the filthy floor and half out loud, he muttered, "Come on, Charlie."

He felt someone sitting beside him, but it wasn't Charlie. Of all people, it was Dorothy.

What was she thinking?

People would see her sitting next to him. People would talk. They always did. Gossip at school spread like current across a phone line.

Kory didn't dislike her the way he used to. He didn't even mind having her tag along all day at the chess club. But this was going too far.

He looked around. Trapped. There was no way out of this. He couldn't get up and look for another seat. That would draw even more attention.

"Hi."

Kory didn't turn to look at her. "Hi, Dorothy."

"Charles, take a seat!" It was the teacher.

Kory looked up and saw his friend appearing both puzzled and betrayed.

"You're blocking the aisle," Mrs. Matthews added. "Charles Patterson!"

"Yes, yes, Mrs. M, I'm sitting, I'm sitting already."

"Did someone say 'shitting'?"

"Aw, can it, Steve," Charlie said to his friend.

Kory looked away, feeling like Benedict Arnold. This mess wasn't his fault, but Charlie wouldn't believe that. Kory was supposed to save a seat for him.

"Have you been to the museum before?"

"What?"

"The museum? The Museum of Natural History?" Dorothy laughed. "The museum we're going to visit today?"

"Oh, right. My aunt took me to the Met, but no, I haven't been to this museum."

The bus took off with a sudden lurch, as if the driver had popped the clutch.

"Atta boy," Steve yelled, "let's smell the rubber."

"I thought you were supposed to wear it, not smell it," someone else added.

"That's some aunt you have," Dorothy continued, ignoring the boys three rows behind.

"Huh?"

"Your aunt? Mary?"

Kory nodded.

"I'll bet you'd rather be going to the chess club, right?"

"There's nothing I'd rather do," Kory said, realizing he might have smiled.

"You van Ludens seem to know exactly what you want."

Kory looked out the window.

"What's the matter?" Dorothy asked.

Kory did not reply.

"Come on," Dorothy pressed, "you can tell me."

"I never asked you about that letter," Kory said, his breath fogging a circle on the window.

"No, you didn't, and I appreciate that."

Kory gazed at his shoes. "It's been bothering me."

"The letter?"

"The whole thing with my brother." What the hell? Too late. He'd said it. It slipped out. Just like that. Keeping quiet came as naturally as breathing to Kory, yet now, when he needed to keep his mouth shut the most, he'd blurted this out with the self-restraint of a three-year-old.

"What do you mean?"

"Nothing, never mind." His hands were suddenly slippery. "So, have *you* been to this museum?"

"What about your brother?" She poked him. "Kory?" She wasn't going to let this go.

Kory turned in his seat and looked her in the eyes. Those damned green eyes. Forbidden eyes. Forbidden, like the conference room.

She was Damon's girl.

His head felt suddenly hot.

Screw Damon.

"You know, I used to think you were just some girl, like all the rest. In the beginning . . . you and Damon . . . it didn't bother me. I didn't care."

Dorothy looked puzzled.

"I didn't even want to be near you. I didn't want you coming to the chess club."

Her mouth was pressed tight.

Now he'd hurt her feelings. Just what did he think would come of this confession? He wasn't thinking. For some inexplicable reason, he was talking, and there was no stopping himself now. "Mary forced me to be nice to you." Kory gave a weak smile. "It was that, or no chess club."

He expected her to say something. To be angry. Instead, she seemed sad. Concerned.

"At first, it wasn't easy. It had nothing to do with you. Honestly. But you were Damon's girl, and . . ."

"And?"

Kory bit his lip. "And . . . nothing."

"Please, Kory?" She said it so softly. So gently.

"Of all the people in Rhodes, why did you go out with *him?*"

Dorothy shrugged. "We just went on a few dates. Nothing happened. It was no big deal."

Kory shook his head. "You two have been dating for years; that amounts to more than just a few dates."

"You're his brother, you two share the same house, how many times has he been in Rhodes since he left for the Academy?"

"Thirteen," Kory said without hesitation.

Dorothy's eyebrows arched. "You sure didn't think about that for long."

"It's hard to forget when he visits."

"Well, we didn't date every time he came over, you know. I go skiing during Christmas and to Hawaii during the summer, so—"

"So that makes five dates, not including your first date before he left for West Point," Kory finished.

Dorothy smiled. "Sometimes I forget who I'm talking to. Yes, we've gone out six times. That's six over a period of four and a half years. So now that we agree on the numbers, let's get this straight too: nothing happened between us. We went out—to eat mostly—sometimes we'd catch a movie, and that was it. He was a gentleman, I'll have you know. Nothing happened, and nothing would have happened because it wasn't what you think. I mean, he's a nice guy and all, but—"

"But what?"

"But not like that . . . not for me, at least."

Kory thought about this for a moment. "Are you sure?" He didn't wait for an answer. "So you go out with him for all these years and it means nothing? Why go out with him at all?"

"I didn't exactly say it meant nothing, I just said nothing happened because I don't think of him that way."

"What way then?" Kory said, sounding more hostile than he intended.

"Look, it was a mistake, okay?"

Kory shook his head. "No, you don't understand. You don't get it at all. It's *not* okay because *he's* not okay."

"What do you mean?"

Kory looked down and sighed. "You don't know him. Nobody does."

Dorothy frowned. She started to speak, but Kory cut in. "He's a lot smarter than people think. He's a master manipulator, Dorothy. And he always gets what he wants. *Always.*"

"What are you saying?"

"I'm telling you that you should steer clear of him. Keep as far away as you possibly can. He's like a bulldog. Once he latches on, he never lets go. Things have to be *his* way."

"Well . . ."

"You still don't get it. He used to beat me up. But nobody knew, because he punched me where it wouldn't show. Am I getting through to you?"

"Kory, Damon's your brother. Should you really be saying things like this about your own family?"

"I knew you wouldn't understand. Nobody does. Everyone thinks he's this great guy. I could tell you things . . . horrible things . . ." He stopped himself. "But there's no point. You wouldn't believe me."

Dorothy didn't speak, and Kory was certain he was losing her. Like everyone else, she would find Kory's accusations distasteful. Inappropriate. Exaggerations stemming from sibling rivalry. He was glad he hadn't mentioned Dollie.

Any bad thing he said about Damon inevitably backfired, making Kory look worse. It always worked that way. With everyone. Why would Dorothy be an exception? Why hadn't he learned his lesson trying to convince Mary about Damon's true nature? He thought he had. For some reason, he felt the need to warn Dorothy. For some reason, he cared.

Dorothy said nothing for a while. "Look, I'm an only child, so I can't speak from experience, but I know from my friends who have sisters that it can get kind of rough at times. I don't know what happened between you two and I don't know much about Damon, either—just what I picked up on those six dates. I can only tell you he was always polite and decent. Always a gentleman. He was—" She stopped herself. "Look, I went out with him once and I thought that was going to be it, but he kept sending letters and flowers, and so I went out with him a few more times."

Kory avoided her gaze.

"It was silly. I just didn't know what to say, I sort of felt sorry for him. I couldn't simply break it off."

Kory looked at her; something changed in his eyes. "Is that what the letter was about?"

Dorothy half-smiled.

Kory felt himself relax. "So the relationship is over now?"

"There never *was* a relationship. That's what I've been trying to tell you. The only person who thought so was Damon . . . and I guess you."

"Dorothy," Kory said, "you know as well as I, the whole town thinks that you and my brother are a couple."

"I really don't care what they think," Dorothy said. "I care what you think."

Charlie watched from the corner of the museum lobby, while peeling the tinfoil from his sandwich. Had this been going on for a while and he just noticed now? He watched Kory and Dorothy sitting down together, munching away at lunch. Mrs. Matthews had told the class there was to be no food or drink in the museum, so everyone had to go out for lunch break. Kory and Dorothy had a whole bench to themselves. They were talking nonstop—about what, he couldn't imagine—they were too far to make anything out.

Charlie stuffed the remainder of his sandwich in his mouth, and as he got up to get a drink from the fountain, he bumped into something. Someone. It was a short guy with white specks all over his coat. "Excuse me," the man said. He had a funny accent. Italian?

When Charlie realized what the white stuff was, he shook his sleeves in vigorous spasms to get rid of the dandruff. "Aw, shit, gross."

The class was huddling around the Neanderthal Man exhibit when Kory noticed Dorothy had fallen behind.

Seeing he was following her, she headed for a hallway. When Kory caught up, he said, "Where are you going?"

"Away from them."

Kory looked puzzled.

"I don't want anybody to see us." She smiled, her lips full of mischief.

"Why?"

She kissed him quickly on the mouth.

An electric feeling climbed his spine, making his head tingle. "We can't do this."

She nodded in agreement, but her smile was telling an entirely different story.

"If somebody sees us and Damon finds out . . ." The tingling in his head had become a buzz. Without a thought in his mind, he embraced her, kissing her full and long on the lips.

This was crazy, but he didn't care. He held her closer, feeling her pressing on him. The old excitement, dormant for eight years, of invading Damon's room suddenly came alive, rekindled in the flame of this reckless act of passion.

She giggled, pulling out a mirror.

Kory looked at the lipstick smear and burst out laughing.

Still giggling, she put her finger to her lips and said, "Shhhhh."

"That's the last thing I thought I'd ever hear: somebody telling me to be quiet."

She dabbed a handkerchief around his mouth, rubbing in places, scratching in others. "There, that looks good."

After reapplying a modest amount of makeup, she said, "You go first. I'll go to the ladies' room and come over in a few minutes."

On the way back, Charlie made sure he got on first and took a seat in the back of the bus—not too far back, just enough to be discreet. If Kory wanted to sit with him, Charlie was saving the seat. If not, big deal, it was a free country, right?

Kim came storming down the aisle and Jessica sat next to her. Then John, followed by Steve and Ben and Dorothy. Kory was right behind her.

Steve ran down the aisle, came to a skidding stop, and plopped himself right next to Charlie. Ben stretched out on the double seat beside them.

"Hey, Charlie!" Steve said.

Charlie didn't answer his buddy. He was watching Kory.

There were several empty rows ahead of Charlie. Kory sat down in the first empty row, and then, *on purpose*, he slid over to the side to make room for Dorothy. They must have planned it. Charlie cursed under his breath. This was stupid. Why did Steve have to sit next to him and ruin everything?

Who was he kidding? Charlie knew that even if the seat next to him had been empty, Kory would still have chosen an unoccupied row for Dorothy. They had obviously already agreed to sit together. Or at this stage, it just went without saying. Shit, maybe they had plans to stop the bus at some town on the way to Rhodes, jump off at some church, and get married. Why wait?

"So did you like the museum?" Dorothy asked.

"I liked the company," Kory said. It was like someone else was doing the talking. As if he were possessed.

The driver cranked the door open, and Mrs. Matthews blocked the aisle, waving her hands high above her head. "Listen to me for a moment!" she shouted, but the volume of chatter didn't go down. "Listen to me! I want those reports in by Monday. Remember, 'Our World Then and Now.'"

Charlie muttered something.

Outside the bus, groups were forming and breaking up. Charlie got off the bus, half running. Kory shot out his arm, blocking his friend's path. "Where are you running off to?"

"I thought—"

"Don't you want to walk home with us?"

Us? Charlie didn't know what to say. He couldn't remember the last time he'd been at a loss for words.

"It would be easier to talk to President Kennedy."

"This had better be important; this isn't a resort."

"You were supposed to get an answer before you left. Did she mail you that letter? Did she call?"

"Have you stopped monitoring her?"

"No. What does that have to do—I'm asking if you have an answer."

"If you're still monitoring her, then you know she didn't call."

"She could have called from another phone. Okay, so she didn't call—did she send that letter?"

There was no answer from the other end of the line. Stavridis raised his voice, partially due to the poor quality of the connection. "Do you have answer, Mr. van Luden?"

Damon hesitated. "Yes."

"Are we going to play games, or are you going to tell me?"

"I don't appreciate your tone," Damon snapped. "Let's not forget; you work for me."

"This I don' forget!" Stavridis shouted. "*You* forget. The company is paying this through your family trust, and you promised you give her answer."

Damon wanted to yell or hang up, but he did neither of these things. Stavridis had a point. Van Luden Enterprises needed an answer, and they had a right to one, as it directly affected the trust.

Damon was cornered: no good would come from telling Stavridis about the letter, but at this point he had little choice. This was not what he had planned.

"Mr. van Luden, are you there? Can you hear me?"

Damon considered hanging up.

"From your silence, I guess the news is no good. She said no, am I right?"

"Why do you assume she won't marry me?" Damon said so loudly Stavridis had to hold the phone away from his ear. "You think I'm not good enough for her?"

"Not at all," Stavridis said slowly. "She is not right for you. This is what I have been saying."

"She accepted. Dorothy is going to be my wife."

The static on the line was still popping, and there was no tone to indicate they'd been cut off, so Damon knew Stavridis was still on the other end.

Finally the detective said, "She wrote you a letter? You have this in writing?"

"Yes and yes."

Stavridis did not reply.

"She wants to elope," Damon said, "in secret. During my Christmas vacation. She wants to go somewhere exotic for a honeymoon. Everything has to be a complete secret; she said she'll contact me for the specifics but she doesn't want me writing or calling because she thinks her father is monitoring her. Have you given her reason to believe she's being watched?"

"Please," Stavridis said, "we are professionals."

"I respect her wishes. That's why I didn't call you when I got the letter. Happy now?"

"Is not me, the company want to know if you have answer from Dorothy. How am I supposed to know she would ask you to keep this secret?"

"I was in the same boat as you, believe me. Anyway, if she wants to elope and not tell anyone, that's fine by me."

"Okay," Stavridis said, "by now you know the company position on this marriage and so I will not mention again, especially since there seems to be no way to change your mind."

Damon did not answer, and it sounded like Stavridis didn't expect him to.

"Now, if the marriage ends in an annulment or divorce, you understand you will get nothing?"

"Yes, Mr. Chambers explained it all when Mother died."

"If, as you say, you plan to elope, please do it here. This way the company can begin the paperwork so you control half of the trust fund."

"I'll mention it to her when she calls."

"Please, it is important."

"All right."

"One more thing. The company did not expect Dorothy to accept to marry you, but they made some condition just in case she did, okay? They say for your good, for her good, and the good of the marriage, when you talk to her next time, she must agree to admit herself to clinic. As you know, this is something her psychologist has suggested. The company believes one month should be enough. There is a good clinic in Geneva.

They want her to go, and they say the sooner the better. If it cannot happen before the marriage, then they want her to go after the honeymoon. Did she say where she wanted the honeymoon?"

"Not specifically. She said she wanted something exotic, and I don't suppose she meant Hawaii, because she goes there with her father all the time. Hold on, though, what is this about a clinic?"

"Do you have objections?"

"Yes and no," Damon said. "It's actually not a bad idea, but I don't like being told what to do and when to do it, especially not by people who work for me."

"First, at the moment, the trust is in the control of Van Luden Enterprises. Second, they make this conditions for your good. Do you understand?"

"Seeing it from their perspective, I suppose it makes sense, but—"

"Mr. van Luden, having half control of the trust is very big responsibility."

"I know that."

"So do you agree on conditions: your wife will be admitted to clinic in Geneva, right after your honeymoon, for one month at least?"

Stavridis just called Dorothy Damon's wife. "I do," Damon said, drawing out the words in the ceremonious fashion of a wedding vow.

"The transfer will take about a month, but the company will still let you enjoy some benefits of your new position." There was a slight moment of silence on the line and then Stavridis added, "Congratulations, I am sure your mother would be proud."

Maybe the Greek detective wasn't such an asshole after all.

"I appreciate that, thank you," Damon said. "Now that we have an understanding, do you think Van Luden Enterprises would help me with arrangements in Geneva?"

Stavridis hesitated. "I suppose. I will have to ask, but I don't see why not."

"If it's a problem . . ."

"No problem," Stavridis said. "It is possible they have already considered arrangements after your honeymoon, I do not know. If Dorothy accepted, I was supposed to tell you she has to go to clinic. That was the most important thing. That was all they told me."

"Fine, look, we'll be needing a cook, at least one maid, groundskeepers, and, of course, someone to look after Dorothy once she returns from the clinic for the times I'm gone in Berlin."

"Yes, I will talk to the company. From what I know, the trust has been taking care of the mansion in Geneva. I believe they have already groundskeepers and cleaners."

"Yes," Damon said, "that is what Mr. Chambers told me when my mother died."

"Then this should not be problem, once the company says okay. I will personally make sure you have everything you need. Maids, a cook . . . and bodyguards for Dorothy; I know two men who might be available to help."

"Great."

Stavridis was surprised at the sudden change in tone; it was as if someone else had come to the phone. "From Berlin to Geneva is long way. Are you planning on finding a place for your family in Berlin eventually?"

"Initially, the property in Geneva will do," Damon replied, "but you're right, it *is* a long commute by train. We'll start off in Geneva and see where the Army wants me. After that, we'll play it by ear."

"I wish you luck," Stavridis said, "and I will call you as soon as I know more about the arrangements."

"You do that," Damon said. "Oh, and thanks for going the extra mile."

"Just doing my job."

VERMONT

December 1, 1961

Mary reached the phone on the fifth ring. "Y-yes?"

"You sound out of breath," John Saunders said.

"I was just packing, actually. What about you, are you ready?"

"*I* am, but not my Dorothy. I tell her it's just a weekend in Stowe, and she's packing like we're moving to some other country. You know how girls are these days."

"You're going to have to stop calling her a girl, John, she's eighteen now."

"Please, don't remind me. How in the world did she grow up so fast? It seems like yesterday when she was just a little girl bouncing on my lap."

"You've got to let go sometime," Mary said, realizing the same would soon apply to her with Kory.

Her comment left them both in silence for a while.

John said, "I hear it's going to be perfect skiing weather. First weekend in December, and there's fresh powder to be had. Season's started nice and early." The weather reports prompted last-minute hopes for a weekend in Vermont, and on the spur of the moment, he had invited Mary and her nephew for two days of skiing.

"Yes, snow and Vermont make for a magical combination," Mary said. "I haven't been in ages."

Kory appeared in front of Mary. "Oh, good gracious, you startled me," Mary said, holding her chest. She still couldn't get used to the way he floated around the house making about as much noise as a butterfly.

"What?" John said.

"Oh, not you, John, it's Kory. He's here, looming over me like a Dickensian apparition," Mary said.

Kory laughed. "I hope you're not planning on spending the weekend on the phone here. You've been talking for a million hours."

"And you're starting to sound more and more like Charlie." Into the phone, Mary said, "I'm being harassed. He's been itching to go—he's been packed since last night. I should be done in half an hour."

"Okay," John said, "I'll be over by three. I don't think Dorothy will be ready any sooner. Bye—oh, wait, she wants to talk to Kory. Well, bye from me—see you in a bit."

"Kory?" Dorothy's voice asked from the phone.

"Oh, no, honey, it's me, Mary. Kory is right here, hold on."

"Kory?"

"Hi."

"Did you bring everything?"

"I have the chess set and all the required accessories," Kory said, in case Mary was still within listening range.

John Saunders pulled up at the van Ludens' in his new '61 Bentley Continental Flying Spur twenty-three minutes late. Mary got in the front seat while John loaded the trunk.

"Get in, Kory," John said.

Dorothy was smiling at Kory from the backseat. Charlie wasn't there this time to sit between them.

Kory hesitated.

"Come on," John said, "the more of this trip we can manage with the sun still up, the better. Off we go, next stop: Stowe Mountain. Kory, I don't think your door is shut, open it and close it again."

John stepped on the gas and his Bentley spewed gravel while he honked a good-bye to the empty mansion.

They headed west into Massachusetts to avoid the Appalachians before turning north toward Vermont. Tall pines were casting an intermittent shade, turning Dorothy's eyes flower-stem green. So much had happened since that trip to the museum.

Kory fought back the urge to kiss her right there. The corners of her mouth lifted just enough for him to notice, as if she'd read his mind.

Mary and John were chattering nonstop throughout the trip.

"He likes the Queen's Gambit," Kory said. "Positional play is his forte, and it's hard to set an aggressive pace."

Dorothy nodded. Kory prompted for more, Dorothy finally understood. "The Queen's Gambit is nice."

It was a good thing Mr. Saunders was too busy talking to Mary to hear. Dorothy's knowledge of chess was conspicuously weak after so many visits to the chess club. "Well that's why he's called the Wall."

"Must be," Dorothy said, pursing her lips.

Kory looked at the rearview mirror. Dorothy was sitting behind her father, so he couldn't have seen, but all Mary had to do was glance a bit more to the left and—

"So what are you thinking of doing about it?" Dorothy said.

"About what?" Kory asked. "Oh, the Queen's Gambit? It's easier to set the stage for an aggressive opening as white."

"Of course," Dorothy said.

There was that smile again. Time to talk about something else. But what? With Charlie in the car, it was easy. He did most of the talking, and Kory could simply look across at Dorothy while pretending to listen to Charlie.

Kory wondered why Dorothy had insisted on the secrecy.

As they headed farther north, the trees were increasingly burdened with snow, their branches bending down like fatigued arms. Sun flashed between the branches, momentarily blemishing his view with floating spots. Their brief discussion had proven to be a technical minefield for Dorothy; she had only succeeded in flaunting her ignorance on even the most fundamental of chess concepts. Fortunately, Mr. Saunders, who normally never missed an opportunity to correct his daughter, was too engrossed in his conversation with Mary to notice.

Kory and Dorothy had spent the previous hour staring out their respective windows. Kory was interested in a much different view.

John and Mary were still at it. Talking about nothing of importance, yet talking nevertheless. Obviously, neither of them were interested in keeping their mutual affection a secret, or even discreet, for that matter. Kory wondered how Dorothy felt about that. She had not spoken of it, and Kory had not asked. Talking had never been top on the agenda during their covert meetings in the park.

John pulled over. He laid down the snow chains, drove a foot forward, and meticulously fit them onto each tire. With the chains on, they couldn't go faster than fifty.

Kory watched Dorothy, wishing he could hold her. Even friends could show more affection—at least friends had nothing to hide. Their relationship had been a secret for only two months, but to Kory it seemed much longer than that. They had agreed to tell no one until it was the right time, although they had never discussed when that time would be.

Kory suspected Dorothy derived a sort of aphrodisiacal charge from their little secrecy game, just as they'd both had when they'd first kissed. Mostly because it acted as a catalyst to their affections, he tolerated it . . . for now at least.

As they approached Brattleboro, it started to snow. A few feather-sized flakes at first, and then it was as if a thousand pillowcases had burst from the heavens.

John turned the wiper on the highest setting. The road narrowed, and the brown tracks left from other cars quickly transformed into white grooves. The road itself was losing definition.

Mary turned and looked back for the first time that trip. Kory was reading a book on chess, and Dorothy was immersed in a hardcover copy of *Gone with the Wind.*

Mary said, "Look, it's so beautiful."

John laughed, pointing to the speedometer. "Look at *this,* we're doing thirty!"

The narrow mountain road slowed them to twenty miles per hour. An eleven-year-old Hudson Super Six struggled two cars ahead of them. It was spewing black exhaust, and the driver didn't have the forethought to use snow chains. "It only takes one," John said bitterly.

"Don't worry, John, we'll make it, we still have plenty of daylight left."

The following morning, John Saunders told his daughter to take on Kory as her first ski pupil and he gave her ten dollars to treat her student to lunch. "Remember: be patient with him, it's the effort that counts."

"You and Mary are taking the advanced slopes?"

"Yes, she started skiing as a little girl, just like you did."

"So, you'll be at the rental place after?"

"Five o' clock, sharp. Have fun!"

Kory managed to do the snowplow immediately, but had difficulties shifting his weight to turn, and ended up skiing straight down the slope, unable to slow down. Dorothy slalomed in front of him, blocking his path. Not wanting to crash into her, and unable to think of any other way to arrest his momentum, he let his knees buckle, inducing a semi-controlled fall. Poles and skis entwined, and Kory's left ski came off. It dangled from his boot-string attachment. With each effort to free themselves from the mesh of poles and skis, both he and Dorothy slid a few feet farther down the slope. Other skiers slalomed past them, some of them asking if they needed help.

"We're fine," Dorothy told them through mouthfuls of snow. Kory was completely covered in powder, his red-and-blue hat was knocked over to one side, with only a few patches of color still showing. Snow was melting over his pink face and inside his ski goggles.

Kory burst out laughing, Dorothy joined and lost her grip, sliding down another yard. One of her ski poles latched itself onto Kory's ski, dragging him down with her. She came to a full stop, but he continued sliding, one ski cartwheeling from tip to tail and the other skidding down, its dangerous path kept in check by a flimsy cord. The free ski collided with one of Dorothy's poles, fixing it there, while Kory kept on rolling. Dorothy put out her hands to stop him, but he milled into her, ending up in her arms.

"Sorry." Kory pulled a hand from her breast.

"Are you, now?" Dorothy said, wiping the snow from his mouth. Before Kory could catch his breath, she kissed him quickly on the lips and rolled away. "Come on, put on your ski."

Kory struggled, but couldn't reach the dangling ski without slipping farther down the slope. She parallel-stepped up to grab his ski, and slid it under his boot.

"Wait," she said, picking off the snow with the point of her pole, "you have to get the snow off the ski first, silly."

Kory popped the toe of his boot in as he had been taught, pulled back the spring, and stepped into the binding.

"Get your skis parallel to the slope and dig in with the edge." Dorothy demonstrated.

Kory managed to stand and get his hands through both pole straps. She was right next to him. Suddenly he started to wobble uncontrollably, and she shot out her arms to keep him from falling. He pulled her to him, kissing her on the mouth. They stayed that way for a while until Dorothy pushed him away, giggling. "You did that on purpose. I'll bet you rolled on me on purpose too."

"No, I can't take credit for that one, but I *am* learning."

"What if they see?" Dorothy beamed.

Did she *want* them to?

"No chance of that, the advanced slopes are on the other side. We're home free."

"Follow me," Dorothy said, "time for a lesson in powder skiing."

She guided him off-slope and through the trees. "Put your skis together . . . like this . . . parallel, see? Good, now lean back."

Kory tried, lost control, and fell on his side.

"Too much for the first lesson, I guess," Dorothy said, looking around. She took off her skis.

"What are you doing?"

Dorothy didn't answer. Kory watched her pat down a large circle in the snow. Dorothy took off Kory's hat, shook off the snow, and threw it up at one of the ski tips. It missed.

Kory plucked her hat from her head and tossed it high in the air, with an exaggerated lack of dexterity, not even aiming for the skis. Dorothy pulled two pins from her hair. A long golden waterfall of hair spilled almost to her hips. The sun was at its apex, shining brightly through the dark towering pines.

She unbuttoned his heavy coat, and he unbuttoned hers. Dorothy giggled, again. Kory felt his desire down to the pit of his stomach.

"Well? Are you going to just sit there? Take it off!" Dorothy was still laughing.

He took off her coat, still facing her, while she kissed his hairless chest. His pants were beginning to hurt him now. They were both topless, kneeling in front of each other, the sun staving off the biting chill. The sight of her breasts alone almost brought him to climax.

"Excuse me," he said, blushing, as he struggled to find room down there. Moving made it worse. To his amazement, instead of scaring her, Dorothy found it funny. Kory's pants came off easily; hers did not. Each wore the other's coat, like capes. They lay naked, nested on top of their clothes, which only partially covered the snow.

He pushed, she gasped. When Kory started to shudder, Dorothy clamped on to him. He waited there briefly before moving again. Dorothy squeezed down and Kory didn't move until she relaxed, and then he continued until it happened again for him. They were both sweating, despite the cold.

"Oh, no! It's all wet!" Dorothy jumped up and out of his coat, standing completely naked except for her socks, which were beginning to soak in the snow.

Kory jumped up too. "Christ, Dorothy, you'll freeze."

"Your *coat.*"

"What about it?"

Dorothy pulled his coat out of the snow and pointed at the lining.

"I don't see—" Kory noticed a dark black stain—her blood. "Nobody will see that."

"But what if they do?" Dorothy said.

Kory detected a trace of panic in her voice.

"Let me see," Kory said, flipping it over. He put his hand between the lining and the inside of the coat. "It didn't go through the lining, so it won't go through the coat."

Dorothy did not appear convinced.

"Look, it's a dark color, and the stain is on *my* coat, not yours."

She thought for a moment and conceded. "I guess."

"Don't worry." Kory gave Dorothy her panties. "You'd better put these on before you get pneumonia."

"Can you imagine if I go skiing with just this on?"

Kory laughed. "Do you think it would arouse suspicion?"

"It might arouse something else."

John and Mary were having hot chocolate at the café next to the rental shop.

"Get enough exercise today, Kory?" John asked.

Kory strained not to laugh. "Yes." He avoided looking at Dorothy to keep her from giggling.

"How's he doing?" Mary asked Dorothy.

"It's as if he's skied many times before," Dorothy said. "He's a natural."

Kory turned away, feeling his cheeks go warm.

"Always modest about his talents," John said, and Mary nodded in agreement.

Dorothy grimaced at the sight of the curry chicken. Indian for dinner had been Mary's idea, a taste she'd acquired in San Francisco.

"Come on, honey, you have to learn to enjoy the new things in life," John said.

Dorothy laughed.

Kory felt something brush against him, then squeeze. Right *there*. Kory looked at Dorothy before he could stop himself. She had her hand under the tablecloth, and her father was looking right at her. She didn't seem the least bit concerned. Kory got up. "Excuse me, I have to go to the bathroom."

"What's so funny?" John asked Mary.

They were back in their respective rooms by nine thirty, as planned. It wasn't until she was in bed that she realized she had nothing to do for the remaining hour and a half until eleven. They had chosen that time to be certain both Mary and John would be sound asleep.

Dorothy slipped out of her nightie, completely naked for a moment, as she felt for the drawer handle. She would be in quite a pickle if she had to explain herself to her father. He'd probably have a heart attack—the last time he'd seen her naked she'd been five.

She angled her watch under the door to read the dial for the fourth time in the past hour. It was ten fifty. Close enough. She was ready; and she couldn't stand waiting in the lodge room listening to her dad snore for another second.

She reached for the doorknob and then stopped herself. She'd almost forgotten.

Her father's coat was hanging on the rack behind the door. Dorothy reached into a pocket and felt around through the change. Nothing. Where else could he have put them? She tried the other pocket and felt the ragged edge of the key.

It was a cold, still night. The moon was nearly full, and it provided more light than she was comfortable with.

Kory appeared from the far corner of the lodge. Looking in all directions, he walked briskly toward her.

"You're early."

"I couldn't wait."

"Did you get it?" Kory asked.

"You bet. Did you?"

From the inside pocket of his coat, Kory pulled out the stem of the bottle of Port he had smuggled from Rhodes, courtesy of

Charlie. "We're going to have to use a pocket knife; I couldn't get a corkscrew."

They ran over to the Bentley, and Dorothy handed him the keys.

"I can't drive," Kory said. "I don't have a license and I've only had a few lessons from Mary, and that was on estate property . . . I've never been on a real road."

"Now you tell me. Oh well, I'll let you in on a secret: I can't drive either."

Kory took the keys and shrugged. "I guess if we get caught, we're dead anyway."

He'd driven Mary's car in the driveway in preparation for his eighteenth birthday, when he'd be getting a car of his own, but that wouldn't be until the twenty-fifth of January.

He put the key in the ignition and winced at the rumble the engine made as it started. "My God, that's loud. I hope he didn't hear."

"Only you would hear such a noise. Besides, my dad is sleeping like a baby."

Kory couldn't see any markings for reverse. "Don't look at me," Dorothy said.

He released the clutch and the car jolted backward, stalling the engine. On the second try, he let the clutch out slowly and managed to maneuver the car out of the lot and into the narrow country road. "Where to?"

"Anywhere but here, and you might try changing gears before Dad's car blows up."

"Right," Kory said, finding second.

There was nobody on the road.

"Faster," Dorothy said.

Kory managed to slip the car into third. The speedometer showed fifty. It felt a lot faster on the dark, curving road.

Dorothy started giggling.

After ten minutes, they found a suitable side road—a snowy path cutting into the forest, leading nowhere Kory could discern. "I hope this road widens at some point, otherwise I'm going to have to drive out in reverse."

"Can you do it at fifty?"

"Doubtful, at least not without plowing down a few trees."

"Dad wouldn't like that."

"I suspect not." Kory drove until they came to a gate with a sign that read:

PRIVATE PROPERTY

NO TRESPASSING

Kory completed a K-turn after stalling the engine twice, and came across a small country road that sprouted out to a clearing with no view. It wasn't Inspiration Point, but for the moment it was perfect.

Kory opened his door and began digging at the cork with his Swiss Army knife. The cork came apart, and bits of it floated in the bottle. After two more frustrating minutes, Kory gave up and showed Dorothy his handiwork.

She inspected the bottle in the moonlight. "It's not completely ruined, but we'll have to drink it through our teeth." Dorothy demonstrated with a long sip.

Kory tried it and was surprised at how sweet it tasted. He had never had more than a glass of wine at a time, and that had been during formal meals. For some reason, Kory couldn't recall his brother ever having as much as a sip. During recent visits, Damon had taken an almost fanatical opposition to alcohol. Probably more conditioning from the Academy.

Kory felt warm inside and slightly dizzy. As they undressed each other silently, he played out the lessons he'd learned on the slopes. They took their time making love, watching each other closely in the glowing light.

He was feeling drowsy and was beginning to fall asleep in her arms. "It's one thirty. We can't stay here any longer. What if one of them gets up at night to pee?"

"I put the pillows under the sheets like we said, didn't you?"

"Yes, but any number of things could still go wrong."

On the way back, he kept it under forty. The wine must have gotten to Dorothy too, because she wasn't pushing him this time. Kory found the same parking spot at the lodge, and inspected the Bentley before getting out. It was just as they had left it.

Dorothy let the door open just enough to squeeze through, to keep the moonlight from waking her father. She closed the door and tiptoed over to the bathroom. Even if he did wake up now, she could say she just had to use the facilities. Of course, hiding her clothes would be a problem, especially if he needed to use the bathroom right after her.

She opened the bathroom door, with the light off, waited for her eyes to adjust to the dark, and felt her way to the commode. She dumped the pile of clothes she'd just removed into her drawer, shutting it with care. Her father grunted something unintelligible, and then he rolled over, falling back into a deep slumber.

"Wake up, sleepyhead, we want to get some skiing in before we have to head back to Rhodes."

Kory moaned. It felt like he could sleep straight through the day. "What time is it?"

Mary didn't answer, and Kory realized his mistake. The wine had messed up his internal clock. "Just testing."

"It's eight o' clock."

"I knew that."

Mary pulled off his bedcovers, Kory rolled over on his stomach just in time. "Okay, okay, I'll get ready, give me a minute."

"I'll meet you where we had breakfast yesterday. John and Dorothy should be there by now. Do you remember where that is?"

"By the lobby, right?"

"Yes, it's the third lodge on the left."

They skied through the early afternoon. Mary, John, and Dorothy watched at the bottom of the slope as Kory carved a prudent path down the mountain.

"You had a good teacher," John said when Kory finally arrived. "Keep that up and you'll be parallel skiing in no time."

Dorothy slept through most of the drive back to Rhodes. Kory played over the weekend in his mind while Mary and John talked for hours without a break.

Kory checked the rearview mirror, and then looked at Dorothy as she slept, wondering when they would have the chance to be together as lovers again.

"When did this happen? What did she say?" Stavridis asked. This was the first time Damon had called him.

"Right after you called me, on Tuesday," Damon said. Stavridis had told Damon about Dorothy's ski trip to Vermont, and the plans his aunt Mary and Mr. Saunders had for yet another trip during Christmas. For once, Stavridis had been right to think it was important enough to warrant a phone call.

Stavridis pulled out his calendar. He was in his tenth-floor Wall Street office, at the Van Luden Enterprises headquarters. It was small, but at least it had a window.

"She called," Damon said, "just as she promised she would. She wants to elope in Vermont, at midnight, so we can be married on Christmas Day."

"Good, so you will have marriage in the States. Now we know where the wedding will be; what about the honeymoon?"

"She said Saint Croix, could you make the arrangements?"

"Of course," Stavridis said, "this is great occasion for you, and very important for the trust and for the company. So when will be the marriage?"

"Christmas."

"We listened to telephone conversation: your aunt invited you to go on trip. You said you had other plans. Now you say you are going?"

"I'm going to Vermont, but not with them. I'm going to get married—I have no interest in skiing."

"You have told them?"

"No, no. Dorothy wants this all kept strictly private; it has to stay a secret until after our honeymoon."

"Surely the father will have to know," Stavridis said. "She cannot just leave in the middle of a Christmas trip."

"He'll know," Damon said. "Once we're married, we'll tell him."

"As a father, I can tell you: Mr. Saunders will be very worried."

Damon didn't answer immediately. "She turned eighteen in October, as you know, so she doesn't need permission—"

"Yes," Stavridis said impatiently, "but he is still her father. Will she leave him a letter?"

"No, nothing like that. We *will* tell him, but after the marriage. It's not how I'd like to handle it, but it is the way she wants it, so that's how it's going to be."

"As you wish. I will call you when the company has made the necessary arrangements."

Damon said good-bye, hung up, and waved at the lieutenant who was waiting out of earshot to use the phone.

BACON

December 17, 1961

The frying pan spat out scorching oil as John Saunders shoveled three strips of bacon. Dorothy approached him for her good-morning kiss. The oversized white dots wandered away from his red apron. She felt her legs buckling and a wave of nausea that grew with alarming intensity.

She turned away, covering her mouth. Once she made it to the bathroom, she was much better, and to her surprise, she didn't vomit.

"Dorothy? Honey? Are you all right?"

"Uh . . . I'll be right out . . . just a moment."

Sitting on the toilet seat, she rested her head between her knees. This had never happened before. Maybe it was because she'd stayed awake late thinking over the plans.

The smell of charred pork from the kitchen found its way through the sides of the door. Could the bacon be making her feel like this?

No. That was silly. She loved bacon, and had been a faithful bacon eater for as long as she could remember. It hadn't bothered her before, why would it bother her now?

"I have news for you!" her father shouted.

"Coming." Dorothy splashed two handfuls of water on her face, dried off, and skipped into the kitchen, circumventing the stove for good measure.

He smiled cautiously. "I spoke with Mary, and she's accepted my invitation to come with us to Stowe this Christmas."

Dorothy already knew that, but was happy to have her father confirm what Kory had previously told her.

Things would go just as planned.

"Oh, Dad, that's wonderful! You know how much I love skiing!" She ran over and hugged him.

He frowned for a moment, but he was smiling too. "Yes, but we go skiing every year, honey."

"I know, but this year it's different." Seeing her father's bewildered look, Dorothy added, "Mary will be with us."

He nodded, but it wasn't convincing. "Mary and Kory, yes."

"Well that's wonderful," Dorothy said, "isn't it?"

"It is," John replied, more doubt in his voice now. "Honey, is everything all right?"

"Better than you know," Dorothy said. She wanted to tell him right then and there, but now wasn't the time. The temptation was almost irresistible.

"There's something you're not telling me," he said gently.

Dorothy nodded. "I'll tell you, but not now, okay?"

John kissed his daughter on the cheek. "Okay," he said, wishing he could know what was on his daughter's mind and, more pressingly, what was in her heart. Whatever it was, it overshadowed any objections she may have had to his dating Mary. He had expected a reaction—it would have been normal for her to defend her monopoly on his affection. John had spent a long time coming up with the right words to explain it all to his daughter: despite the divorce, despite her mother's drug abuse and subsequent suicide, there would always be a place in his heart for her, and no woman could take her place. Nothing would change between him and his Dorothy, no matter whom he dated.

John Saunders hadn't had the occasion to say any of these things, however, and that left him feeling both relieved and concerned.

That evening Dorothy went to bed at ten. She had to count sheep again, but it didn't take as long as it had the night before. She'd been going to bed half an hour earlier, every night, for three nights, but it wasn't helping—in the morning she had the same problem, so it obviously wasn't due to a lack of sleep. It was the bacon.

That day on the slopes had been the third. Her period should have come on the tenth. The problem with the bacon started three days ago. Today was the seventeenth. And she'd been regular since her very first period.

Dorothy decided to find out at school, and just say she was asking on behalf of a friend. She could have tried the library, but she didn't. Dorothy couldn't wait, she just had to know, and before Christmas.

She looked for someone trustworthy, someone who would have the answers she needed and who wasn't friends with Nancy. Dorothy decided on Jenny. That turned out to be a wrong choice.

She never mentioned her bacon problem to Kory; it was probably nothing anyway, and she had special arrangements for Vermont—it was going to be the best time in her life.

Instead, Dorothy and Kory spoke about the trip. Her father said they would be leaving on Saturday, the twenty-third, after the very last day of school. As Kory spoke of dreams for their future, Dorothy thought of what was going to be, of things Kory didn't know yet, of her plans.

Dad wouldn't be pleased. He'd say, "You're too young, Dorothy, you have your whole life ahead of you," or something like that. He'd give in, of course, eventually. He always did. And this time, he would have no choice.

So far, he suspected nothing.

Wednesday, December 20

A week earlier, while Kory was getting his weekly lesson at the Manhattan Chess Club, Dorothy had gone to the corner phone booth on Sixty-Fourth and Central Park West, called the operator, and requested the phone number for the nearest GP. She wasn't about to ask for a gynecologist, and from what she'd learned from Jenny at school, she didn't have to; GPs could do the job just as well as any gynecologist. That was good because that way, if her father found out, all hell wouldn't break loose. Still, even if she went to a plain old doctor, and Dad heard about it, he'd worry, there'd be questions, she'd make excuses, and that would lead to disaster. She just had to make sure nobody found out.

Though the secretary had claimed nothing was available until early January, the desperation in Dorothy's voice had gotten her an appointment for today, the only Wednesday that would work since this was the last trip to the chess club before Christmas.

Dorothy had told her father she had to go see Nancy's older sister, Lauren, who lived on Columbus Avenue, just three blocks south from the Manhattan Chess Club, to pick up a Jerry Lee Lewis album. Dorothy wore her mother's diamond engagement ring that her father had given her for her eighteenth birthday just two months before.

Dr. Battersby's office wasn't that far from the chess club, but getting there would take her six blocks farther from Lauren's apartment. The timing would be very tight.

Before entering the doctor's office, Dorothy twisted her ring, hiding the diamond from view. Now all anyone would see was a gold band on the fourth finger of her left hand. She introduced herself to the lady at the desk as "Mrs. Eyre." The secretary furrowed her brow as she checked the appointment book. "Mrs. Jane Eyre?"

Dorothy nodded, a bit too vigorously. "Yes . . . I have an appointment."

The lady instructed Dorothy to have a seat. Dorothy was eighteen; she could easily have been married, but she didn't seem to be giving that impression.

Her encounter with the doctor was mercifully brief. She needed to be out of there and on her way as soon as possible.

She had to restrain herself from running to Nancy's sister's place. The doctor had been on what was labeled the fourteenth floor but was actually the thirteenth. The chances of anyone looking down at her from thirteen stories up were slim to none, but Dorothy still felt she was being watched as she half trotted, half skipped her way to Sixty-First Street.

Lauren had her own apartment. Her father was renting it on her behalf while she was attending NYU.

"Hi, Dorothy," Lauren said, "won't you come in?"

Dorothy thanked her and entered. As she walked past she saw Lauren looking at her left hand. Dorothy quickly turned the diamond back to the top. "It used to be my mother's."

Lauren gave her a look that said she deserved to hear more. Not surprising, Nancy must have spared no details about Dorothy's relationship with Damon.

"I wear it upside down," Dorothy explained. "It keeps the predators away."

Lauren smiled. "Clever."

Clever for finding a way to keep men from flirting, or clever for coming up with a good lie so quickly?

Nancy had been bugging Dorothy about her decision since the beginning of the fall semester. Dorothy hadn't told her, or anyone else for that matter, and that probably made Nancy suspicious and chances were she'd passed those suspicions on to her sister.

"I don't think you need to worry about predators," Lauren said with a sly smile. "No man in his right mind would dare lay a hand on you—everyone knows about you and Damon."

Bingo. Lauren was already twenty-one, and hadn't been near Rhodes High for three years, so she must have heard it from Nancy.

Dorothy would tell all, but not now, and nobody—not Nancy, not her sister, nobody—was going to force it out of her before the time was right.

"Yes, well, speaking of affairs," Dorothy said, "I have unfinished business at the Manhattan Chess Club."

Lauren smiled knowingly. "Careful, the games you play."

Dorothy turned crimson, furious at herself for her stupid choice of words. "I don't play chess, Kory does. Charlie and I are his managers." Boy, did that sound lame.

"I'm not talking about chess, and you know it. You play a much more dangerous game, young lady."

This was too much to turn away from. Dorothy tried her most indignant voice. "And just what, might I ask, are you talking about?"

Lauren took a deep drag from her cigarette and puffed toward the ceiling. "Let's get something straight: I'm not one of your playground friends. Nancy told me about your little *problem*."

Dorothy was confused and was completely honest when she said, "I really don't have a clue what you mean."

"Oh, please, you can stop the act now."

"What are you talking about?" Dorothy shook her head. More to herself than to Lauren, she said, "I never said anything to Nancy."

Lauren rolled her eyes. "You didn't have to. She heard it from Colleen, who heard it from Jennifer. You were asking if a GP could perform a certain test?"

Dorothy's mouth dropped.

So Lauren didn't know about Kory.

Dorothy turned away, but Lauren walked back into view.

"What happened?" Lauren said. "He just couldn't wait for the wedding night? You couldn't turn down a handsome officer? Afraid you've got a bun in the oven?"

"I don't know what you're talking about," Dorothy said. She should never have trusted Jenny. It was dumb to think she'd fall for that I-have-a-friend-who-has-a-problem trick. Now everyone knew.

No. That wasn't true. Lauren didn't know; she was just fishing. Dorothy just had to keep her mouth shut and stick to her story. Lauren couldn't prove a thing.

"Sure you do. Damon found some time off, the two of you hooked up, and the rest is history."

"No," Dorothy said, wondering if her anger was making her more or less credible. "That *never* happened. I haven't seen him in months."

"Hey," Lauren said, waving the cigarette in a circle, "calm down, it's not like I'm going to tell anyone. Besides, Nancy already knows." Lauren took a deep drag at the remains of her cigarette. "You can't deny it."

"I *can* and I *do*," Dorothy said.

"I see," Lauren said. "So you were at this chess club because you're some guy's manager, and all of a sudden you just *had* to borrow my Jerry Lee Lewis album?"

"If you don't want to lend it to me, that's fine, you could have just said so."

Lauren chuckled, but she wasn't smiling and her eyes narrowed. "Nice try, but it just won't fly. I'm not Nancy."

If Dorothy went back to the chess club without the record, she'd have to explain why she was gone so long. "I'm sorry, I didn't mean to—"

"Right, you didn't, but you did. Things just happened that way," Lauren said. "Hey, it's no skin off my back, but you just turn around and take that apology to my sister."

Dorothy said nothing. She wanted to slap Lauren, but there was a chance she could get her to cool her heels. It was the only way out of this mess. "Fine, I promise I'll tell Nancy I'm sorry for not filling her in"—*on every private, none-of-her-business thing in my life*—"if you promise to keep all this between us, and *never* mention it to anyone."

Lauren gave Dorothy a look and a shrug. "Fine."

She turned to leave but Lauren tapped her on the back with the edge of something. "Don't forget your excuse."

Dorothy grabbed the LP and left, her heart beating hard.

She stared at the receiver, as if to confirm the words she'd just heard had really come from there.

"Hello?" said the voice on the other end.

"S-sorry, I just thought—" The bell rang. Lunchtime was over.

"Is that a school bell?" Dr. Battersby said.

Dorothy put the receiver back on the hook as gently as she could. With any luck, Dr. Battersby would think they'd been cut off.

CHRISTMAS

December 23, 1961

Kory figured this trip to Vermont would be a good two hours shorter than the last one—the roads were dry and Mr. Saunders was driving as if the speed-limit signs were put there for decoration. It was a wonder they hadn't been pulled over yet.

"This is going to be so nice. Finally, a white Christmas," Mary said.

John laughed. "You come from New York, haven't you seen enough snow?"

"Not in California, I didn't," Mary said. "Somehow Christmas never felt right in a short-sleeve shirt. This is the way it was meant to be." Mary motioned at the snow-covered hills. "As a child, I used to take this sort of thing for granted. Sometimes you have to lose something before you really appreciate it." She turned to look at Kory. "It's been so nice these past years here in Rhodes with you, Kory, hasn't it?"

When Mary turned back, Kory tore his gaze away from Dorothy and directed it out the window.

His aunt was still waiting for a reply, to what Kory couldn't remember. It seemed like she was looking for confirmation . . . something about Rhodes being nice? Kory nodded, that satisfied her, and she turned her focus back to John Saunders.

"And with Damon too, of course," Mary added, "when he came to visit."

"So he couldn't join us?" John asked.

Mary sighed. "I did mention it. I don't know . . . he hasn't come down for one single Christmas since I've been here."

"I've been gone with Dorothy skiing every Christmas," John pointed out.

"Well, I did invite him," Mary said again.

"And you told him Dorothy was coming along?"

Mary nodded. "Oh, he knows, but he said he had other plans."

"I've noticed he hasn't sent Dorothy a single letter since this summer, and he's stopped sending flowers, too."

Mary said nothing.

Kory kept his head down. He was turning red. Dorothy wasn't looking at him.

"He hasn't been calling, either, pumpkin, has he?" John said.

"Daaad."

"You were on the phone nonstop since he left for the Academy, and for some months now, I've had the use of my phone for the first time in years."

"I was talking with *Nancy*, Dad, you know that."

"Okay, fine, then what happened with Nancy?" John looked at Mary when he asked the question, as if to say: *See what I deal with?*

Dorothy sat back in her seat. "Nothing."

"Uh-huh. You're on the phone all the time with your best friend, now I've got the phone to myself, and I'm supposed to believe nothing is going on?"

"She's *not* my best friend," Dorothy said.

John turned to Mary. "Once they hit a certain age, it's like the invasion of the body snatchers: same physical appearance, but inside, some alien has taken control."

Mary shook her head, not quite rolling her eyes.

Not taking the hint, John said, "Maybe he's moved on, found somebody his own age?"

"Dad. I'm right back here; it's not like I can't hear you."

John said, "*I'm* not the one trying to keep secrets, darling."

No one said anything for ten miles.

"So there's going to be a lodge party?" Mary tried.

John sighed. "Yes, on the slopes."

"That should be fun. And when are we going to the Mill Inn?" Mary asked.

"That's for tomorrow night. I've made reservations, and it's a good thing I did; we got the last table they had this Christmas Eve. This evening, we go to La Montanino, right before the lodge party. Then tomorrow, we hit the slopes first thing, and . . ."

Kory didn't need to hear the rest. Mary had successfully drawn Mr. Saunders's attention away from his daughter, and now Kory had his opportunity to speak. He eyed the rearview mirror. It was safe. Kory leaned over to Dorothy and whispered, "You didn't tell him?"

Dorothy gave a few rapid shakes of her head. "Not *now*."

Kory pulled back, waited. Mr. Saunders had stopped talking for a while. When Mr. Saunders resumed, Kory whispered, "I don't mean about *us*, I mean about Damon."

"I know what you mean, and no, not yet." Dorothy saw her father glance at the rearview mirror, and she said in a normal voice, "But I did notice those Rossignols. Where'd you get them?"

"Paragon," Kory said, sitting back in his seat. "Mary got me new boots, too."

It was five thirty, and already dark by the time they reached Montpelier. John Saunders was forced to slow at Waterbury, where the road to Stowe and the Mountain View Lodge was covered in patches of ice and snow.

Only a few guests went to the lodge party. The majority chose to spend their Saturday night at the well-heated indoor club rather than freeze on the slopes where the bonfire only provided warmth at close proximity.

Before Mr. Saunders explained the evening's arrangements, Kory had held on to some hope of taking a drive with Dorothy. It would have been a great bonus, but their real plans were for Christmas Eve. Still, Kory had waited for what seemed like an eternity since the last outing, and he didn't know how he would contain himself in the meantime.

The next day Mr. Saunders announced that Kory was going to ski along with everyone else, on the intermediate slopes. That meant the private lessons with Dorothy, the ones Kory had been looking forward to for weeks, had just been cancelled.

"I don't think I could handle intermediate slopes, I can barely snowplow," Kory said.

"Don't worry, we all have confidence in you," John said. "You did so well on the green slopes, we don't want you getting bored, do we?"

Kory didn't answer.

The intermediate slopes were harder than Kory had imagined. All of his five falls, with the exception of the first, were controlled. It was his way of braking before taking on the impossible challenge of the ice-laden moguls ahead. He was turning well, actually managing to lift the inside ski and parallel it with the other.

The chairlift bounced hard as it passed under the bull wheels of the support tower. Kory watched the tiny skiers below. He pushed himself against the seat. *It was his fifth ride on this very lift, why was he suddenly frightened now?* Well, it wasn't fear, not exactly, it was a feeling . . . like something he'd felt before but couldn't quite place. It was probably nothing.

Christmas Eve, leaving the Mill, Kory had that feeling again. He brushed it away like a summer fly.

Kory changed in the bathroom and stacked his clothes in preparation for his evening exodus. He emerged in pajamas and jumped when he saw Mary standing directly over his suitcase.

He had left it open. The two bottles were at the bottom, covered in layers of clothing.

Mary wasn't looking at the suitcase. "You've made a lot of progress."

"Thanks."

"I'm not just talking about your skiing."

This could be a prelude to a long conversation, and he and Dorothy had chosen to meet at eleven, just like last time. If they didn't get to bed soon, there would be no guarantees—Mary could still be awake when the time came for Kory to sneak away.

"I've watched you these past months, and I don't know what it is, but you've really come out of your shell." She looked for a reaction. "You seem happier with your life."

Kory nodded. "I am."

"The chess club, your new friends—things are really happening."

"I have you to thank, you've been so good to me." Kory could tell she needed to hear that.

Mary gave him a loving smile and hugged him. He reciprocated. He'd managed to get out of one of their usual, drawn-out talks; all it had required was a hug and a pat on the back.

"Good night, Kory," Mary said, not knowing this was the last time she would see him happy again for years to come.

"Good night."

Kory got dressed early, slipped out of the room, and ventured into the cold night. He walked over to Dorothy's room and was surprised to see couples walking around in the night. It hadn't been so busy last time. Christmas Eve festivities, no doubt. He didn't like the idea of being seen, but nobody seemed to be paying attention to him, so he proceeded to give the door a tap with his fingernail. He listened, heard movement. The keys to the Bentley appeared from under the door. He'd arranged it this way, so Dorothy didn't have to keep checking the time.

Kory waited inside her father's car, with the engine off, while Dorothy changed. Two cars pulled in, one pulled out. Nobody knew him here, what was he worried about?

That feeling of danger, the same one he had on the slopes, passed over him like a fast-moving thundercloud. It was almost palpable.

In just a few more minutes, Kory would be in her arms. He could think of little else. Not of unseen dangers, of potential witnesses, and not of fears haunting him from the past. He was whisking away Mr. Saunders's daughter; taking his Bentley;

driving without a license . . . not to mention what they planned to do in the car. The risk was exciting and a bit frightening, that was all.

Don't do this.

Kory ignored the voice.

As he turned onto the main road, he handed Dorothy the knife, and she started working on the cork. They passed the bottle back and forth, taking long gulps with each swig.

Kory saw a car in his rearview mirror. It seemed to move slowly, creeping around the tight curves. Somehow, even when Kory pushed the Bentley to fifty, the car behind them was still there.

"I think we're being followed," Kory said.

"Well, *I* think that's the wine talking." Dorothy laughed. "Relax. Don't you start being paranoid."

For a while, Kory thought the car was gone, but then two pinpoints of light appeared in his rearview mirror. Kory took a tight turn to the right as the road corkscrewed up the mountain. Afterward all he could see behind him was a dark snow-covered road.

He looked up several times as they drove to their special spot, adjusting the mirror each time, certain he'd again see lights, but the car was gone. Maybe it made a bad turn and slipped off a cliff. Where could it be? There were no other roads, and not even enough room for a U-turn. Kory took another swig from the bottle. He was just moments away.

Kory drove to the very same spot where they'd parked the last time. Already, more than half of the bottle was gone.

Neither of them noticed a car with its lights off park where the narrow road bent, fewer than three hundred yards away.

Dorothy was finishing the wine when Kory said, "Hey, save some for me."

"I've got something better." She pressed herself against him, and as they became immersed in a deep kiss she worked on removing his clothes.

"What's the matter?" Her words came out in dreamlike plumes.

"This is so embarrassing. It must be the wine. I'm sorry . . . I . . . I really have to go."

She giggled. "Don't stay out there too long or it'll freeze."

Once outside the car, the winter night bit into him as though in his haste he'd forgotten to dress. He walked into the snow-covered thicket, relieved himself behind a tree, and was zipping up before he realized the absurdity of his actions. Who did he think was going to spot him like this in the middle of an alpine forest?

He certainly had nothing to hide from her; they'd been intimate before. Admittedly, she'd never seen him answer this particular call of nature—

Out of nowhere came the sound of softly crunching snow. Before he could turn, something slammed over his face. He struggled frantically, but the crushing force smothering him grew even stronger.

Only one person he knew of could sneak up on him like that.

Though he tried holding his breath, he could not prevent the fumes from making it to his brain, causing him to hemorrhage consciousness with each passing second.

He saw a leather-gloved hand holding the handkerchief. With the last of his energy, from the corner of his eye, he saw a flash of gold. Only half the dial was showing, but there was no mistaking his brother's Patek Philippe.

A second later, Kory was still.

WEDDING NIGHT

Christmas Day, 1961

"Do you have the rings?"

Dorothy felt the wedding band twist its way onto her finger. . . .

"I now pronounce you man and wife. You may kiss the bride."

The Old Spice was making her dizzy.

He kissed her hard and long on the lips.

Dorothy slept through most of the trip in the JetStar. She slept next to Damon, still in her wedding dress, looking so innocent and pure.

Early that morning at the suite, he turned her from girl to woman.

CRY FOR HELP

Kory woke up to find he couldn't move.

It was freezing, but there was more to it, something was restraining him. He was in the backseat of the Bentley, lying on his side. Damon must have tied him up.

Kory tried moving again and winced. This was the mother of all headaches.

He used his legs to slowly push himself upright. At last, he could see himself in the rearview mirror. He'd been wrapped in his overcoat, straightjacket-fashion, the buttons fastened all the way up. The foggy windows were completely shut—there was no telling where he was. The Bentley could be hanging off a cliff for all he knew.

Not likely. If Damon had wanted him dead, he'd have left him outside to freeze in the snow.

Kory looked at the reflection in the mirror. The only way to do this would be to get his hand partially through his collar. That was easy enough, but he couldn't get his finger to the top button. Even if he could, he'd need his thumb to unbutton it. He was starting to choke. Kory retracted the hand.

"Heeelp!" It was pointless, but screaming made him feel better.

He took a deep breath and pushed both fists up his coat and out. The mirror showed the top button straining, but still holding on. Kory screamed again, pushing until he felt a throbbing at his temples. Finally, the stitching gave in, and the button went flying. His hand could then go all the way through the top, and after a few frantic attempts, he unfastened the next button, and then the next.

Kory opened the door. It was even colder outside, the snow pink against the rising sun.

The Bentley hadn't been moved an inch.

"Dorothy?" Kory ran around the car in a large sloppy circle.

He cried out her name several more times, but his voice was muffled by the snow-laden earth, unable to disturb the surrounding tranquility. He continued to run, plowing a path in and out of the trees. He ran down the trail he had driven through the night before and saw tracks coming in at an angle from where Damon's car must have been parked.

He couldn't keep himself from staring at the tracks. Something refused to register. He pushed and pushed, but it wouldn't give, his mind as blank as the snow around him.

"Dorothy?"

There was no reply, just a tomblike silence.

If she had been made unconscious the way he had, Kory doubted she'd ever wake up.

He imagined her lying frozen in the snow as if merged with it, her crystallized golden hair splayed on a white blanket of snow.

Kory was sinking deeper into the powder with every step. He trekked through the trees for another hour, and with each passing minute he grew more certain he'd never find Dorothy anywhere nearby.

There was no shelter for miles, so she couldn't have simply walked her way to salvation. By the time he thought of looking for tracks, it was too late—he had created too many of his own.

What would Damon do to her?

Teach her a lesson? Beat her to a pulp? If he did, what was to prevent her from telling the world what a monster he really is?

And what would he do to her if she did?

He'd kill her. He'd kill her and make it seem like an accident.

Like he did with Dollie.

No. No. That was crazy. Kory wasn't thinking rationally. Damon always had a reason for everything he did. A self-serving reason, stemming from the depths of sociopathic psychosis, but a reason nevertheless.

And beating up his girlfriend only to kill her afterward made no sense whatsoever. Even for a psychopath.

Think.

Damon had knocked Kory out, packed him away like a salami roll, and Dorothy was nowhere to be seen. Damon hardly needed much of an excuse to get mad: misplace a book, speak a decibel too loudly. Exist. This time, Kory had given plenty. Even a normal man might have been ticked off to find his ex-girlfriend engaged in hanky-panky in the back of her father's car. Let's see, Mary invites him over—that's how he knows where everyone would be—and he says he can't make it because he has other plans. Yes indeed, Kory could testify to that. Mary must have told him where they were staying, too. Damon observes Kory leaving the hotel with Dorothy, follows them, sees them kissing in the car.

Wait, had the windows steamed up by then? He couldn't remember. If Damon had seen them at it, he'd have been furious, but it probably made little difference. This had all been carefully planned, of that Kory was certain. It simply couldn't have happened as some spontaneous act of vengeance.

So Kory goes to empty his bladder, and Damon is waiting for him. How could he have known Kory was going to pee? The answer was obvious—he couldn't have. It was just a convenient break for Damon. Or maybe that wasn't what his brother had hoped for; maybe he'd wanted to open the car door and catch them in the act? That made more sense.

After Damon had chloroformed him, then what? Did he stroll over to the Bentley, have a little chat with Dorothy about why he was slightly peeved at his younger brother, and then offer her a lift back to the hotel before he left for wherever he had to go to complete his training? No more damage done?

Sure, that sounded about as likely as winning the lottery without a ticket.

Damon had tracked them down, in the middle of nowhere. He'd come with chloroform. That meant there was no question that Damon had planned it, just like he'd planned everything. Brilliantly. Faultlessly . . . almost. While there was little chance Damon could have foreseen the possibility of his coat sleeve slipping back in the struggle, wearing that rare, hand-made watch had been a gross oversight.

None of this was answering the big question, however: *why?*

Back to square one: If Damon had planned this, which he almost certainly had, he would've come to the conclusion that Dorothy could never be allowed to tell anyone what had happened. Therefore, she would have to die.

Kory shook his head violently as if the act would expel the thought.

It didn't help, and collapsing to his knees, Kory shouted as loudly as his lungs could bear.

Exhausted, he walked back to the car. The keys were still in the ignition. Damon had wanted him to live, and had been kind enough to leave him with means of transportation.

What could Kory do now? Call the police? Tell Mr. Saunders? Mary?

None of those options would yield immediate results, and there'd be a hell of a lot of explaining to do.

Well, Officer, it was like this: we went for a ride in her father's car, and my brother, who'd been following us, chloroformed me. When I woke up, she was gone.

Let's see: driving without a driver's license; taking a car without consent—which would amount to no less than grand theft auto if Mr. Saunders pressed charges, and why wouldn't he when his daughter ended up missing because of their misadventure; and of course there's bullshitting with intent. Who in hell would believe that his brother suddenly appeared out of the blue and chloroformed him?

Kory got into the car and headed back toward the lodge. There was another option, of course, but even though it was the safest bet, he hated himself for even considering the possibility of saying nothing.

He could park the car, sneak into his room, change into his pajamas, and play dumb. The drug had messed up his internal clock, but judging from the sun and the time of year, Kory guessed it to be seven thirty. He could probably still make it there before his aunt woke up. They would then discover that Dorothy was missing.

There'd still be a search, but only after the concern grew sufficiently to warrant involving the police. At first they'd probably assume she'd gone off for an early breakfast, and then maybe a long walk, or who knows what. And wasn't there a minimum time before the cops went hunting for someone unless they had good reason?

Kory had all the reason in the world.

But they wouldn't believe him even if he did tell them. They'd laugh at him. They might even deduce he'd been drinking the night before. So what good would that do anyone?

Seeing the curving arrow he slowed to thirty-five. It wasn't that the Bentley couldn't manage the turn, he just wanted to give himself more time—he remembered that sign; the lodge was less than a mile away.

If Kory said anything, the results would be no better than if he kept his mouth shut. It would be worse, in fact, because there was the matter of Dorothy's virtue. He didn't care about saying that he took Mr. Saunders's car. As far as they knew, he'd never done anything like that before, and in light of Dorothy's absence, it wouldn't be a major concern. But what would he say he was doing with Mr. Saunders's daughter in the night?

We were just drinking, and about to make love. It wasn't like we were stealing or anything . . .

Like grand theft auto.

Either way, Kory would have to lie, so he might as well come up with a credible story. He and Dorothy had done a brilliant job of making everyone believe they were nothing more than friends. A lie would no doubt prove to be more believable. It was essential that they bought his story, true or not. The only truth that mattered was that Dorothy was gone and in grave danger.

The fact that Dorothy was missing would be self-evident; the problem was getting them to accept that she was in danger, and that everything that could be done, had to be done, and as soon as humanly possible.

He made a tight left into the parking lot. A family of five were racking up their skis, getting an early start on the slopes.

It could be later than he thought. Mary could be awake, already looking for him.

His parking space was still available. That was lucky; with all the people out there, it could easily have been taken by now, although most would probably be leaving at this hour. As Kory removed the keys from the ignition, he froze.

Shit, shit, shit!

Of all the stupid things. Dorothy was supposed to put the car keys back in her father's coat pocket. Now Kory would have to find a way to get into Mr. Saunders's room. What if he heard him sneaking in? How in God's good name would Kory explain that?

No. Too risky. He'd go back to his room and if Mary wasn't asleep, he'd just say he went out for a walk, perhaps even an early morning breakfast. That made sense. Wait. What if they didn't offer breakfast at the lodge on Christmas Day? Or what if they served a special Christmas breakfast? What would he say he had? Of course, he could always go over to the lodge, have himself a five-minute breakfast, and then try to sneak back into his room. That was no good either. During that time, Mr. Saunders could easily wake up and notice his keys were missing.

Kory broke into a run. A few heads turned. Some might have wondered how someone his age was driving an expensive Bentley. To hell with them and what they wondered.

He was heading back to his suite. He needed to get back there pronto and make like he'd just woken up. Then he'd go over to Mr. Saunders's place. He'd say he wanted to get a head start on skiing or something. Mr. Saunders would ask if Kory had seen Dorothy this morning, and Kory wouldn't have to lie about that.

Kory grabbed the doorknob to his suite door. He'd spent a lifetime making an art out of turning knobs noiselessly. He twisted halfway. The bolt hesitated in the latch when he heard Mr. Saunders's voice. Kory stiffened.

It was Mr. Saunders's voice all right, and it was coming from *inside*, no doubt about it. Then Kory heard Mary speaking. Why was Mr. Saunders in Mary's room, this early on Christmas Day? They had to know something was wrong. Somehow Mr. Saunders knew his car was missing. He probably woke up early, saw that Dorothy wasn't in her bed, and went out looking for her only to find that his car was missing too.

This was all irrelevant. Dorothy was in danger, that's all that mattered. Time to fess up, time for plan B.

Kory knocked on the door. Somehow, just barging in—even when this was his suite—didn't seem appropriate with Mr. Saunders in there.

"Who is it?" Mary said.

"It's me, Kory."

"Oh." Mary sounded disappointed. "Come in."

Kory pushed the door open. Mary was sitting on the lodge chair. John Saunders had his head bowed.

"Where were you?" Mary asked.

Kory took a deep breath and was about to speak, but his aunt wasn't interested in his reply; she was looking at John.

"I still can't believe it," John said. "This is not at all like her."

A forged suicide note? Too crude for Damon. "What's happened?" Kory wasn't sure he wanted to hear the answer.

"Dorothy has run off," John said without raising his head.

She was alive. They knew she was gone, but somehow they also knew she was alive. "What do you mean *run off?*"

John did not reply.

"Kory," Mary said, "Dorothy has eloped with your brother."

He laughed weakly, but neither Mary nor John cracked a smile. "Excuse me?"

John raised his head but did not speak.

"We're all surprised, as you can see," Mary said.

"Surprised?" Kory shouted. "Are you fucking kidding?"

Mary stared, dumbfounded.

John raised his head, and Kory pulled back reflexively.

Instead of yelling, John gave Mary a puzzled look.

"John," Mary said quickly, "I'm so sorry, I really don't know what got over him. Kory, how could you say—"

"No, no, he's right," John said in an unaffected voice. "I should have seen this coming; she grew into a woman and I never noticed. All those letters, the flowers, the way she avoided talking about Damon. She never hid a thing from me before . . . I should have seen the signs. I didn't want it to be this way; she's so young."

"She's eighteen, John," Mary said in a gentle voice. "You couldn't stop her even if you wanted to."

"Don't you see? I never wanted to stop her; I wanted to give her guidance . . . to be a good father. Why did she have to brush me aside like this? I've given her everything a father can give his daughter. She's my only child; I would have said yes . . . if marriage was what she really wanted. We would have arranged for a nice wedding in Rhodes, invited all her friends. This way is—it's, it's . . ."

"It's romantic," Mary said.

Kory snapped his head in Mary's direction, stared at her for a second, and turned to John Saunders. "Just what makes you think they've eloped?"

"*Kory,*" Mary said. "What's the matter with you?"

"It's okay, he's family now," John said, as if all energy had been sapped from his body. "He called me, that's how I know. He told me he eloped and that my Dorothy had become a van Luden."

"Is that so? Tell me this: did you speak with Dorothy?"

"No," John said sadly, "she's not . . . with him right now."

"Great, and you don't see something wrong with that?"

"I'm not exactly pleased with how this was handled, in case you haven't noticed."

"*Pleased?* Your daughter is gone, *missing.* You listen to me: Damon hasn't eloped with Dorothy, he's taken her."

"She's not a chair, Kory, she's a person," Mary said. "You don't take a person."

"And this is your brother you're talking about," John added.

"Exactly," Kory said. "Neither of you know a thing about him. You think he's some kind of angel, but he's not. He's a monster. He gets whatever he wants, whatever it takes."

"Really, what *has* gotten into you?" John said, anger creeping into his voice. "Nobody should speak about family that way."

"I don't care how people should speak. I don't care what either of you think, for that matter. Dorothy is in danger, that's all I care about. You've got to call the police."

Mary was first to speak. "I've never had to scold you, Kory, but I really don't like your tone."

"I don't like his tone either," John said. "You should respect your elders, young man. And as far as your brother is concerned, he's a good fellow. I trust my instincts." John leaned forward. "I don't know what sibling squabbles you two have, but whatever they may be, you've gone too far."

Kory squeezed his eyes shut. He took a long, deliberate breath, as Schelowitz had once taught him. Kory needed to apply some tactical psychology, keep his cool, and say only what was necessary to get the desired reaction. What he felt like saying and what he should be saying were two different worlds. His anger could directly compromise Dorothy's safety.

John shook his head again. "Dorothy has never run away like this. It's not like her, but she's in love, and love can make us do strange things."

"Why didn't you demand to speak with her?" Kory said.

John shook his head. "I couldn't, for good reason."

Kory drew blood inside his mouth. "Let's say there's a one-in-a-million chance I'm right; shouldn't you do everything you can? Since he won't let you talk to her, why don't you just call the police?"

"I do want to talk to her," John replied, "but, like I said, I can't."

Kory raised his voice and checked himself after the first words, lowering it through clenched teeth. "You keep saying that. Would you mind telling me what lies he's been telling you?"

John didn't speak for a while. "She's on her way to Switzerland . . . to a rehab clinic in Geneva."

"*Rehab?* Why? And why would Damon take her all the way to Geneva to go to a clinic? And how did they have time to get married *and* fly to Switzerland?"

"Actually," John replied, "your brother is in Saint Croix. Dorothy is on her way to Geneva on the company jet."

"This is ludicrous," Kory said, but the energy of his conviction was draining rapidly—the explanation was too fantastic to be a fabrication. Damon wouldn't concoct such an unbelievable story if there weren't at least some truth to it.

"They were married last night," John continued, as if there'd been no interruption, "in a church in Vermont. They went to Saint Croix on a corporate jet for their honeymoon, but last night—"

"You're trying to tell me you actually believe this baloney?" Kory said, raising his voice again.

"Kory," Mary said. *"Please."*

"I had my doubts . . . at first," John said, speaking more to himself than to Kory, "until Damon told me there'd been an incident . . . Dorothy had behaved . . . inappropriately." He sighed. "She had to go to the clinic. Damon told me they'd made an agreement that she would go. She just ended up going earlier than planned."

"What's this about a clinic?" Kory said. "Why in the world would she agree to go for rehab?"

"Dorothy's been having problems," John said to Mary, as if she'd been the one to ask the question. "She's been drinking and"—he stopped for a moment, shaking his head as if even he couldn't believe what he was saying—"and she was involved with drugs as well."

"I had no idea," Mary said.

"This is ridiculous," Kory said. "How can you believe that? Dorothy would *never* take drugs."

"I'm afraid it's true, Kory. She was seeing a psychologist—not just because of the drugs . . . there were other problems. . . . Anyway, he was the one who'd originally suggested a clinic. At the time she didn't want to go, but I guess now . . . now that she's married, she's made the responsible decision."

"You have to speak with her and ask her if she's all right. She'll tell you what really happened. There's no way she would take drugs, or go to some clinic four thousand miles from here, and hell would freeze over before she'd even think of marrying that psycho."

"For *heaven's sake,*" Mary said.

Kory hardly heard her. "Dorothy is missing and all you've got is Damon's story. You think he's some angel? Fine, think what you want. I'm telling you he's kidnapped her. You don't have to believe me, but you cannot deny that I could be right."

"Don't be ridiculous, Kory, why would your brother kidnap his girlfriend?" Mary said.

"*I'm* ridiculous?" Kory turned to John. "Yesterday she's here, with us, today she's on her way to some clinic in Geneva. That makes sense to both of you, and I'm the one who's ridiculous? What if Dorothy really is in danger, shouldn't you be doing something?"

"Yes," John agreed. "Of course, I should. Don't you think I'm concerned? I'm not worried about her being kidnapped, and if you must know why, it's simple: there's no way Damon could have known about the rehab clinic. That's something we've kept very private. It's something I know Dorothy wouldn't share with a kidnapper, only her husband. That said, I do want to talk to her."

"Then let's call the police," Kory said. "They could confirm that there weren't any churches holding services past nine in the evening on Christmas Eve."

John said nothing.

"Please," Kory said in a louder voice, "don't sit around thinking about it. Let me do it."

John glanced at Mary and gave a sigh.

"I don't know, John," she said. "It couldn't hurt. What do you say?"

But Kory was already on the phone.

Hoping Dorothy might call, John went back to his suite, where the three of them waited for the police.

There'd been no opportunity back in Mary's room to slip the keys back into John's coat—Mary had been watching Kory the whole time. Once they'd walked over to John's suite, Kory hung his coat right next to John's, blocking the view with his back as he returned the car keys to their rightful owner.

It took the local authorities fifteen minutes to answer the call. The tall policeman offered his hand. "Deputy MacLeam." Pointing to the shorter man next to him, he said, "And this is Deputy Wallis."

MacLeam pinched his hat visor. "Madam." To John Saunders: "How can we help you today?"

"My daughter is missing, she—"

"How long?" Deputy Wallis asked.

MacLeam gave his partner a sideways look.

"Since last night, sometime after we went to bed . . . that was around nine thirty, ten," John replied. "I know it hasn't been that long, but it's not at all like her to do this."

"Do what, sir?" Deputy MacLeam inquired.

"Run off."

"I see."

"There was a call," Mr. Saunders added with a sigh.

"A call?" Deputy Wallis made no effort to hide his smirk.

"Yes, but I didn't speak with her, I spoke with her boyfriend."

Both policemen looked surprised.

Kory noticed this and said, "He's not her boyfriend." While he still had their attention, and before anyone could interrupt, Kory added, "She's never done something like this, and, as her father just said, this isn't like her. My brother called, but he said she wasn't there to speak on the phone. He said they'd eloped, but that's a lie, he kidnapped her."

"Your daughter eloped?" It was Deputy Wallis.

"That's what I was told, yes," John said. "He said they were married yesterday night. You have to understand, eloping is not like my daughter. Why would she do something like this?"

"My point exactly: she wouldn't," Kory said. "You can check the churches and see—"

"Let me get something straight," Deputy MacLeam asked John, as if Kory wasn't there, "is your daughter a minor or not?"

"She turned eighteen in October, but—"

"So, we're not talking about a minor here . . ." Deputy MacLeam said, looking annoyed.

"Does a person have to be a minor to be considered missing?" Kory asked.

"You say you haven't seen her since last night?" Deputy MacLeam studied his watch. "It's almost ten now, so you're telling me she's been missing for around twelve hours at the most?"

John did not respond.

"When did you know for sure she was gone?"

"I woke up to Damon's —uh, her boyfriend's—call at seven thirty," John said. "I saw the clock, so that makes three hours since I knew she was gone."

"Three," Wallis echoed.

"He's *not* her boyfriend," Kory said again. "He kidnapped her."

The two officers looked at Kory as if they were trying to decide if he had the right to speak.

"Are you saying she's been kidnapped?" Deputy MacLeam asked John.

"No, no. It's not that," John said, "but I didn't get a chance to speak with her, and naturally I'm concerned. We don't have a contact number, you see—"

"Mr. Saunders, it's Christmas Day. Is there a problem here we can help you with?"

"My daughter was dating his brother," John said, pointing to Kory. "Mrs. Thorn's nephew," he said, motioning toward Mary. "Now he called out of the blue to say they've been married."

"Right," Deputy MacLeam said, "but did he make any threats or demands?"

"No, no, I just want to speak with my daughter. I want to know she's all right; this really isn't like her."

Deputy MacLeam shook his head. "If she's eighteen, she's an adult. We can't do a thing unless threats were made, or you had a ransom note or something—anything that would indicate she's been taken against her will. From what you've said, it sounds like your daughter has eloped, and while this might not be like her, it is her right. I'm sorry, but the law cannot interfere in family matters, not without grounds."

John nodded as if he'd expected this outcome. "Could you at least keep an eye out and call me if you hear anything?"

"This was planned, and I realize it has caused you distress, Mr. Saunders, but it's Christmas and we got families and plans of our own. Assuming her boyfriend hadn't called, we'd need twenty-four hours before we could file a missing-persons report."

"Even if we did file a report tomorrow," Deputy Wallis added, "if she wanted to elope and keep you in the dark, she's got the right to do so. And assuming we did find her, we couldn't force her to come back home, you understand?"

Before Deputy MacLeam shut the door, his partner said, "Have a Merry Christmas."

"I was afraid this would happen." Kory brushed his cheek. John didn't notice the tear, but Mary was looking right at him and couldn't have missed it. "This is just the way he planned it. He's duped you all, and Dorothy's going to pay for it."

John had started packing, as if he were alone in the room.

"What about the police? Aren't you going to wait until tomorrow to file the report?" Mary asked.

"No," John said. "The police won't help us. They're right, this is a family matter."

"You can't just give up," Kory said. "You've got to do something."

"I don't understand your behavior, and I certainly don't understand your problem with your brother, but I'll give you this: I don't like how this was handled, not one bit. I deserve better than a phone call from my son-in-law telling me Dorothy just got married. This should have been the most joyous time in her life." John turned to Mary. "It's hard to give away your only child, but I've always known the time would come. All I want is for her to be happy."

"I promise you she is not," Kory said.

"Honey, that's a terrible thing to say. John's really worried."

Kory ignored his aunt and said to John, "You're right about the police; there's no point in pursuing this with them. If we wait until tomorrow and file that report, nothing would come of it, and we'd have wasted a day. They don't really care because they have their own ideas about what happened, and none of us could change their minds. All we'll ever get from them is lip service."

Kory sat still against the dresser.

Nobody said anything. Kory took another deep breath and tugging gently on John's sweater, guided him away from his suitcase. "Sit down. Please. You too, Mary."

His aunt took a seat next to John like a person at gunpoint.

"I think you ought to know something. It wouldn't have changed the police's mind, but it might change yours." Kory stopped himself. He had to be sure he didn't say too much. Dorothy's safety was paramount, but he didn't want to jeopardize her probity unless it was absolutely necessary. "Dorothy and I are in love."

John looked at Mary. "So that's what this has been about."

Mary had nothing to say to that; she was staring at Kory.

"Well that explains a lot," John said. "There's no easy way to break this to you, son, but believe me, I know my daughter, and you were more like a brother to her than anything else."

"So then tell me why she would run off with some stranger she only dated a few times?"

"Damon is hardly a stranger, Kory. You know perfectly well they've been seeing each other for a long time now. They've been on numerous dates, he's sent letters, flowers; they talked on the phone. Your brother has been Dorothy's boyfriend for over four years."

Kory held back his anger, but judging from the way Mary was looking at him, it had to be written all over his face. "I don't doubt you know your daughter. On the other hand, you admitted that this is not at all like her. Can you honestly say you believe she'd just disappear like this and elope?"

"This may be hard for you to accept," Mary said, "but maybe she really does love Damon."

"It is not hard for me to accept; it is *impossible* for me to accept. It's simply not true." Kory eyed John. "Did you give her a reason to fear you?"

"What?"

"If you think that all this makes sense, then surely you must have given her a reason to believe you would disapprove. Were you that strict with her?"

"Of course I wasn't."

"Then why would she run away to get married?" Kory could tell he was getting his point across. "You were a good father; you gave her no reason to fear you. Then why this? Why would she choose to elope? She had to know it would hurt you. Are you saying Dorothy would willfully do something that would cause you pain?"

"Of course not. I don't know why she did this, Kory, that's why I let you call the police."

"I realize that, except the police didn't help, and they're not going to."

"What do you want me to do? Let's say we manage to pinpoint and check every single church in the state of Vermont and we find out Dorothy didn't elope. If that's the case, then there's no reason to believe that she's in a clinic in Switzerland. That means she could be anywhere. Are you suggesting we get in the car and start searching every nook and cranny in the country?"

"Oh, she's not in a clinic, and she's not in Switzerland. That was a lie to throw us off. I couldn't guess where she is, and I agree, driving around aimlessly would not benefit anyone."

"Well, Damon has to report back to Ranger School, somewhere near Eglin Air Force Base," Mary said. "That much I know. He told me when I asked him to join us here."

"When?" Kory asked.

"I think he said the second, the second of January."

Kory shook his head. "We can't wait that long, God knows what Damon will do to her by then."

"Okay," John said, "so what *are* you suggesting?"

"A good detective would have the best chances of locating her in the least amount of time."

John clicked his suitcase shut. "No. Not yet. When Damon called, I was taken by surprise, and I didn't have the presence of mind to ask for the number at the clinic. So the first thing to do is head back home, in case she calls. If she's all right, she'll call."

"What if she doesn't?" Kory said.

"If she doesn't call in a day or so, then I won't hire a detective."

Kory looked at Mary; she was just as surprised as he was.

John stood. "I'll hire an entire team."

Mary and Kory went back to their suite to leave John to his packing.

She was putting away her cosmetics. "Why didn't you tell me?"

"Tell you what?" Kory asked, knowing the answer.

"About your feelings for Dorothy."

"So you don't think she felt the same way about me either, do you?"

"I didn't say—"

"You didn't have to. You phrased the question as if my relationship with her were a one-way thing."

Mary said nothing for a while. "What is it that makes you think she considered you more than a friend?"

"She told me."

"What did she say?"

"That she loves me."

Mary sighed, went over to Kory, cradling him with a hug. "Honey, sometimes girls play games. I'm not saying it's intentional, but girls like that crave attention."

"She's no two-timer."

"Of course she isn't." Mary stroked his hair.

Kory shook his head violently and she withdrew her hand.

"I might as well be talking to a wall," Kory said. "You see Damon, he's older, stronger, and an officer; then you see me. As far as you and Mr. Saunders are concerned, I'm just a kid. So naturally, you come to the simplistic conclusion that she was playing me, while all this time she and I have been together, her heart was with Damon."

"I shouldn't have said anything. I love you very, very much, and I just can't bear seeing you hurt like this. Puppy love can be very intense, Kory. It's your first time, and it takes you by a storm. But there will be other times, other girls. You'll see—"

"I'd rather be dead."

Mary held him tightly, but Kory yanked himself free. "Right now it doesn't really matter if you believe me or not. Both you and Mr. Saunders think that she's eloping with Damon, and that she's with him out of her own free will. I don't care. You can believe what you want, let's just find her and see that she's not hurt. Let her be the one to say she's fine."

"You are a sweetheart; you really do care."

Except for the steady rumble of the Bentley's 3.4-liter engine and the sounds of passing cars, the silence was unbroken for a full hour before anyone spoke. "Trust me," John Saunders said, addressing Kory via the rearview mirror. "She will call. She's okay."

Mary must have had a chat with Mr. Saunders before they'd left Stowe.

Take it easy on the poor boy; he's heartbroken. He really believes Dorothy loved him.

Kory didn't answer Mr. Saunders. He wasn't interested in their pity.

John helped Mary and Kory unload their things, and then he got back in the Bentley. Mary trotted over to his window. "I'll call you tomorrow."

John nodded and the Bentley crawled away.

John's house was cold, and for the first time, looked barren. It was completely dark. He found the switch by feel and turned the hall bright. He went downstairs to the basement to switch on the heater, and then he took his things to his room to unpack. On his way, he noticed Dorothy's door was ajar. His chest tightened. He was about to close her door when the phone rang.

"Hello?"

"Hello? Mr. Saunders?"

John sighed loudly into the phone. "Yes, Kory, what can I do for you?"

"You'll tell me if she calls, right?"

John didn't know whether to be angry or sympathetic with the boy. He was too tired to argue with him; he just wanted to head off to bed. "Yes, I'll call you the moment I hear from her."

"And if she doesn't call, you'll hire a detective, right?"

"Right, now get some sleep, it's really late."

That was easier said than done. John had told Kory, in no uncertain terms, that he was wrong about his brother. The boy was clearly irrational, but suddenly, in his empty house, John wasn't so sure.

You don't have to believe me, but you cannot deny that I could be right.

Dorothy was fine. She would call. If she didn't, he really would hire a detective. Either way, he'd talk with his daughter soon.

In the morning, John woke to the sunlight, which, for that time of year, was late for him. Sleep hadn't come for a long while. He couldn't have had more than a few hours of rest.

He showered quickly, with the door left open in case Dorothy decided to call at the worst time, then made himself two sunny-side-up eggs with bacon and an English muffin.

How Dorothy had changed. She used to love bacon; then, out of the blue, she wouldn't take a nibble. She stopped talking about Damon for some time, and then she runs off and marries him. Leaving for a new life in a foreign country? Why would she even think of living so far away?

Just then the phone rang. His chair crashed back against the kitchen floor as he made a dash for the phone. He got it on the second ring.

"Mr. Saunders?"

"For heaven's sake, Kory, do you know what time it is?"

"Yes," Kory said, "it's three thirty in the afternoon."

This took John by surprise; he stole a look at the kitchen clock. "Try again, Kory, it's nine thirty in the morning."

"Not in Geneva, it isn't," Kory said. "And that's where you believe her to be, right?"

"I see where you're going with this. . . ."

"If she could have called, she certainly would have by now."

"Uh-huh, but she hasn't, so hold your horses."

"Mr. Saunders, I'm very concerned."

John shook his head at the receiver. "Yes, so am I. Listen, I just got three hours of sleep—"

"You weren't sleeping when I called?"

"Well, no . . ."

"Good. I've found several detectives out of New York City who'd be perfect for the job."

"Now, hold on. I said I'd hire a detective if she doesn't call, and I will, Kory, I will; but when it's time. Right now it's the morning after Christmas. Speaking of which, how in heaven's name did you find anyone at this time?"

"There are private eyes who take on emergency cases. They just charge an extra fee."

John said, "I see, but that's not my point, though. It's too early for this. She might still call."

"She might," Kory conceded, "but if she doesn't, we'll at least have someone at the ready. We can't just sit around here and do nothing."

"Right, and we've been speaking for five minutes now, and Dorothy could have called in that time. I'm hanging up. If she calls, I'll call you."

"The nerve," John said out loud as he hung up the receiver. How could Kory imply he didn't care about his daughter when he could think of nothing else? While Kory might be overreacting, they both shared the same deep concern for Dorothy's well-being, and for that he could not harbor bad feelings toward the boy.

For the next two hours, John sat in his easy chair, fumbling with his pipe. He left the television on. He wasn't watching, but it reminded him of Dorothy, and it filled the void in the house.

The phone rang.

He had it right next to him, and he picked it up immediately. "Hello?"

"Did she call?"

"No, Kory, she didn't. I *told* you I'd call you the moment I hear anything."

"Well, if she hasn't called, then I'm calling the detective. I've decided on which of them would be the best. He said he could tell us where she is within a day if she really did elope."

"That's one hell of a claim," John said. "But again, you're jumping the gun. I said *I* would hire a detective, not you. The day is not over."

"Oh, but it is in Geneva."

"Right, but when I said I would give her a day to call, I wasn't talking about Geneva time and you know it."

"We need to give this PI the green light before it's too late."

"Listen to me, Kory. I will call you if I hear anything. If I *don't* hear anything and I decide it's time for a detective, I'll let you know. You are not to call me here again. I want this line clear."

"Yes," Kory said. "I know. So let me come over and wait there with you. Once you've had enough of waiting, we can call the PI together."

"No, Kory, I don't think that's a good idea."

"Please."

"Give me your aunt."

"Will you at least consider it?"

"*Now*, Kory."

"Is he driving you bananas?" Mary said as she got on the line.

"I'm afraid so, but I can't really blame him. Look, I have to stop chatting on the phone with him every five minutes. She could call at any moment."

"Yes, but if the line was busy, she'd try again, would she not?"

"That makes sense, of course. I guess his paranoia is contagious."

"Would you like me to come over?"

"No, that's okay. Just try and calm him down. I'll call if I've got any news."

John went back to his easy chair. *Lassie* was on. He changed the channel. It was just too much for one day. The other program was boring, and he soon fell asleep in his easy chair; his neglected cigar had long since stopped burning.

The phone tore him from his sleep with a jolt. It took him a few seconds to orient himself. He picked it up, fully expecting to hear Kory again. Instead the voice echoing from the other end of the crackly line came in a French accent. The lady asked him if he would accept charges from one Dorothy Saunders. Gripping the receiver tightly, John said he would.

A small voice said, "Dad?" She sounded twelve again.

"Honey? Dorothy?"

"Daddy?"

John thought he heard her crying.

Dorothy Saunders.

She had given the operator her maiden name. John Saunders's heart started pounding heavily. He could hear the fear in her voice, even though she'd only spoken two words. Oh Lord, what have I done? Kory had been right all along.

"Daddy, I can't talk. Please come. Come and get me."

"Okay, honey, you hang in there. Where are you?"

"The *Etienne* Clinic." Dorothy was whispering.

"So you really *are* in the clinic? Pumpkin, what's going on?"

"I . . . I've got to hang up. When can you come?"

"The first flight available, honey."

"I love you," Dorothy said.

"Wait—" But his daughter had already hung up.

The Etienne Clinic. Damon had called it Clinique de Genève.

Purposely misleading? Maybe he'd said Clinique Etienne de Genève?

He could call an international operator, get the number for the clinic, and ask for Dorothy. On the other hand, from the sound of it, she'd called secretly. He wouldn't be helping his daughter any by alerting Damon to the fact that she'd made a distress call.

The grandfather clock, which had actually belonged to his grandfather, was showing it to be almost four in the afternoon. He'd slept for more than two hours. He called the operator and asked to be connected to Swiss Air Reservations. He was informed that it was too late for today's flight to Geneva, so he arranged for a first-class round-trip ticket for himself, and a one-way ticket for his daughter for the following day.

He knew he wouldn't be sleeping that night.

He thought of what Kory had said of his brother. A shudder ran through his spine. It was best not to think of these things. He was doing everything he possibly could.

Now he just had to pray he would get to his daughter in time.

CHASING THE TRUTH

Monday, January 8, 1962

"**W**e've got to get out of here," Charlie said. He was standing with Kory in the southwest corner of the schoolyard. Kory had been acting strangely since the beginning of school that day. Not the usual Kory strange. This was something different. Charlie hadn't seen his friend since he came back from Christmas vacation, and he could tell something was very wrong. But Kory had refused to say much, and nothing in Charlie's usual arsenal of conversation starters had worked.

Kory followed Charlie off the school grounds, via the janitor's entrance, avoiding the school monitors with ease.

They ran a few hundred yards exposed and then found safety behind a cluster of elk. The detour cost them a good ten minutes, but they were in the clear, and only half a mile from Mayward Street.

It was Charlie's idea to cut music class, of course, but he hadn't expected Kory to agree, and certainly not without a word of protest.

"Let's head towards Johnson Street. We've got lunch after this anyway; we can chow at Joey's."

"You know I don't eat there."

"My treat."

"Fine, but not at Joey's. Let's just go to Pappa's Pizza."

Charlie patted his friend on the shoulder. "I pay, you talk. So what the hell is going on?"

"It's Dorothy."

Kory spoke at length before Charlie interrupted him. "Wait. I distinctly remember asking you—back in September . . . after that trip to the museum—and you told me nothing happened between you two. You said you weren't interested in her that way."

"We kept it secret."

"Yeah? Why?"

Kory sighed. "We promised each other we wouldn't tell anyone until the time was right and Damon was gone. We were about to, but we never had the chance."

Charlie thought back on that day at the museum. The way Kory and Dorothy had been all over each other. Then the sudden change. As if it had never happened. "So how far did you get? First base? Second? Third?" When Kory looked away, Charlie said, "Oh come on, *home run?*"

Kory rolled his eyes. "Shut up."

"Even first base means she was cheating on your brother; you know that, right?"

"I already told you, she wasn't his girlfriend."

"Uh-huh, so all those years of dating, what was that?"

Kory gave him a look that could peel an onion. "Are you going to let me finish?"

When Kory was done, Charlie said, "That's completely bonkers."

"Are you saying I made it all up?"

"Not unless you're the world's greatest actor. You really believe this sh—story. That's what worries me. You of all people. Mr. Logic. It makes zero sense, and that doesn't seem to bother you."

"I told you what happened."

"Okay, then give me one reason your brother would kidnap Dorothy. Just one. I mean, you guys are loaded. Why the hell would he need to steal his own girlfriend?"

"This has nothing to do with a ransom. And Dorothy isn't his girlfriend, and she certainly wouldn't run off and marry him. Now, if you would shut up and listen, I'll tell you."

"Damn, you don't have to be so touchy."

They started walking again.

"Charlie, you're my friend. I don't have anyone else to talk to that hasn't already given me the brush-off. You're a loud-mouth, but I trust you. I *can* trust you, right?"

"'Course."

"Because, if you spill any of this—if you so much as utter a solitary word in your sleep, I swear—"

"Spare me the threats. Bambi scares me more than you."

"I don't suppose you'd want people to find out about the *Playboy* magazines?"

"Get serious, Kory, every guy in Rhodes has them."

"I'm referring to your little business."

"Now, wait just one cotton-pickin' minute!"

Kory looked at him. "So do we understand each other?"

"Fine, but I can't believe you'd threaten me with that."

"What I say now is between you and me. Keep it that way, and everything you've ever told me will remain confidential. I keep my word."

"I guess that's fair."

"Come over here." Kory walked toward a tree.

Charlie followed.

Kory leaned forward, staring his friend in the eyes. "We were going to get married."

Charlie's smile disappeared. "Okay, now you've *got* to be pulling my leg."

Kory ignored him. "We were going to wait for Damon to leave for Germany and once we graduated high school in June, we were going to make the announcement."

"Oh God, he's serious," Charlie said, looking skyward. They walked for a while before he spoke again. "If Damon is the psycho you say he is, then didn't it ever dawn on you that taking his girl was asking for trouble?"

"She was never his girl, and, if you remember, I kept away from her for months. Mary said if I wasn't nice to Dorothy, she wouldn't let me go to the chess club."

"*Nice to her,*" Charlie said. "That doesn't mean *marry* her."

"I didn't sit down and say to myself: 'Here's an idea, why don't I fall in love with my brother's girl so that I can make my life miserable and put hers at risk.' It just happened: one day we were friends and the next, we were in love. The more we tried to fight it, the stronger our passion became. Nothing was going to change what we felt. And I wasn't worried about Damon because I knew that once he started his postgraduate training, he would be totally isolated from the rest of the world. And after that, he'd be shipped off to Berlin. There was no window of opportunity."

"Except for Christmas vacation."

Kory nodded. "I know, I know. When Damon turned down Mary's invitation I was certain that was the last I'd see of him for a long time."

"So let's say your brother is this mega-brain, like you, and he's come up with this plot to kidnap Dorothy. Why would he let her talk to her father? Why would he allow Mr. S to go see her?"

"Mr. Saunders has been gone for twelve days. Think about it: *twelve* days and not a single word."

Charlie shrugged. "Maybe he's having a good time there? Maybe he's skiing the Swiss Alps, how should I know? Besides, what obligation does he have to call you, anyway?"

"See, I knew you weren't really listening. Mr. Saunders never called because he *couldn't*. Dorothy never went to Switzerland. Damon must have somehow managed to get her to believe she was in a rehab clinic so that he could trick Mr. Saunders into going to Geneva."

"What would be the point? Buy himself some time?"

"To arrange for Mr. Saunders to have an 'accident' outside US jurisdiction. As far as I know, Mr. Saunders is Dorothy's only living relative, so with him gone, all ties to her would be severed. The last anybody would hear was that Dorothy had eloped and left the country with Damon. With Mr. Saunders out of the picture, Damon could do with her whatever he pleased."

Charlie looked at Kory. "You're scaring me."

"Then you're finally beginning to understand."

John had called Mary the night before, only an hour after he'd returned from the airport. She could have had her talk with

Kory that morning, but it would have been rushed. She needed to give herself more leeway. Boy, was she nervous. Like a little girl auditioning for her first school play. Silly. She was his aunt—his guardian—and she'd been through two marriages. Why would a teenager make her feel that on edge?

He was infatuated, that much was very clear. After years of emotional imprisonment, he finds release in Dorothy but is not yet equipped to handle the disappointments that often go hand in hand with relationships. Mary knew exactly what it felt like to learn that the one you love has been shopping elsewhere. To a certain extent, she could understand her nephew's reaction, but Kory had gone beyond the bounds of the brokenhearted. She wondered if there could be more to it.

The bad news about Dorothy may have triggered some delayed teenage revolt. All teens go through it, right? John had suggested the boy get some help. He'd said it could be handled with discretion, and if she wanted he could even refer Kory to Dorothy's psychologist.

She glanced at the kitchen clock—Kory would be back any moment. She started to make herself some mint tea, and then changed her mind, deciding on chamomile instead—her stomach was feeling a bit off. Butterflies.

Nervous as a seventeen-year-old. She tried to remember what it was like to be that age, and reminded herself that Kory was turning eighteen at the end of the month. Eighteen had been a roller-coaster ride for her—sudden freedom, lost to a sudden marriage. It wasn't until her second divorce that she finally felt like an eighteen-year-old but by then, people had long since stopped looking at her that way.

She finished the rest of her chamomile in one long sip, walking the cup over to the sink to rinse it off. John had barely treated her like she was still desirable. Was she going to lose him, too? After Christmas, he hadn't called once, except to ask her to get Kory off his case, and then the call last night.

Of course, John was in the middle of a family crisis, and it wouldn't have been easy for him to call while he'd been visiting Dorothy in Switzerland.

But he'd sounded so cold and distant when she last spoke to him. All he'd said was Dorothy was fine, that she wasn't being held against her will. She'd called him for help because she wasn't adjusting well to the clinic. He'd said detoxification had that effect on many patients, and her initial reaction was not so unusual after all. Mary had heard an undertone of disappointment in his voice, as if he'd almost hoped Kory had been right.

Mary recalled how her parents had reacted when she had eloped with Rich.

Oh, that's great, dear. We're very proud.

That had been over a long-distance phone call with a crummy connection. She had eloped to spite her parents, and their reaction had been one of unloving indifference. If Kory hadn't gone rabid, perhaps John would have cried on Mary's shoulder for consolation.

Maybe there would still be a chance for that, in time.

At the moment she had a different problem.

The kettle was whistling.

"It's going to spill over." Kory was right behind her.

"Oh!" Mary gasped. "You have to stop sneaking up on me like that. You frightened the daylights out of me."

Kory shrugged. "I don't do it on purpose."

Mary pointed to a selection of teas. "Would you like some?"

"Yes, please. Earl Grey."

She filled Kory's cup and reached for a bowl brimming with sugar cookies. Mary motioned to the table and they sat down in the sunlit kitchen for afternoon tea, a little tradition they'd established over the years.

As usual, Kory said nothing.

Mary took several sips before gathering the courage to speak. "John returned from Switzerland last night."

Kory's cup stopped in midair. He let it down softly, not bothering to taste his tea.

"Honey, Dorothy really did get married. She's in the Geneva rehabilitation clinic for her alcohol and drug problem. She admitted herself there, just as Damon said. Her problem was getting out of control."

Kory remembered Dorothy's easy familiarity with the bottle from the two occasions they'd been to their mountain stop. The color drained out of his face. "*She* told her father this?"

"Yes, honey, she did. Face to face."

Kory looked around as if he had suddenly lost something. "This *can't* be. You must have heard him wrong. He's telling you stories."

Mary regarded her nephew with growing concern. "Honey—" She tried to touch his shoulder, but he pulled away. "I know you have feelings for the girl, but we should be happy when our loved ones are happy. That's what love is all about. It's give and take, but mostly give."

"Let me call her."

Kory appeared calm, but Mary could see the anger in his eyes. "Honey, that wouldn't be a good idea."

"Please."

"I don't have her phone number, Kory. John—Mr. Saunders does."

"Then I'll ask him." Kory went for the phone.

Mary held up her hand. "If you talk to him at this point— especially about Dorothy—you will be ill received."

Mary was right: if Kory called Mr. Saunders he'd be given an immediate brush-off, and he'd have played his very last card. "May I go see Charlie?" he asked, changing tack.

Mary seemed hurt, but she said, "Of course, honey."

Kory left the table, his tea and cookies untouched.

Charlie held the door open for a few seconds before making way for his friend to enter.

This was Kory's first surprise visit ever. Charlie looked his friend over. "You look like shit."

Kory slid past him, peering into the entrance. "Are your folks here?"

"Yeah, why?"

"Tell them you're going out. We need to talk. *Now.*"

Charlie restrained himself from snapping into a Nazi salute. He disappeared into the house, reappearing moments later. "Okay, it's cool. Where are we going?"

Instead of answering, Kory made a beeline for the woods. Charlie had to jog to keep up. Now he was running.

A branch grazed Charlie's orange hair, pulling out a few strands. "Hey, you're killing me here. Slow down!"

But Kory only ran faster, coming to an abrupt halt at the edge overlooking Route One. He crept down the steep hill slowly, looking left and right three times, and crossed the road in several leaping strides. By the time Charlie caught up, Kory was already on top of the white rock.

"Now that . . . we've run . . . the marathon . . . can you please . . . tell me . . . what this is all about?"

Kory was also out of breath, but that was not why he didn't reply.

"How about clueing me in a little here? I think I've earned that—I was almost scraped to death. Look!" Charlie touched his cheek and showed Kory the red smudge on the tip of his finger. *"See?"*

"Impressive."

"What's the matter? Not enough blood for you? Would you like me to cut my arm off, or are you going to tell me what's going on?"

"I need to find Damon." Kory let this sink in for a moment. "Charlie, I need your help."

"So what else is new?"

"Okay, let me put it this way: *Dorothy* needs your help."

"Did you come up with a plan? What do you want me to do?"

"Cover for me. I'm going to find Damon. You just say that I'm going somewhere with you or something."

"Cover for you? Again? I covered for you and Dorothy a million times, and while you two were exchanging body fluids, I was thinking you were talking about chess."

"I told you it *wasn't* like that." Neither of them spoke for a while until Kory said, "Look, we would have told you, in time. You would have been the first to know." Kory shifted to the side. "Come on up."

Charlie jumped up onto the rock backside first, and using his hands as supports and his body as a pendulum, he plopped himself next to Kory.

"We used to sit here, you know. Just like this. Just to talk. We couldn't even risk a kiss. We wanted our relationship kept confidential, and it's hard to keep secrets in Rhodes. The only time anything happened was in Vermont, on that first trip. We never had a chance the second time we were there." Kory's voice tightened. "He kidnapped her before—"

"So what's the deal?" Charlie interrupted. "You're planning on getting on a white horse and rescuing Dorothy from your wicked brother?"

"Actually, I was thinking of taking the bus."

"Then what? How're you going to find him?"

"My aunt said he's somewhere in Florida, near the Eglin Air Force Base. Dorothy has got to be with him, so he couldn't be where Mary and Mr. Saunders think he is. They believe Damon and Dorothy are married, and she's in Geneva, in some clinic, waiting for him to finish his training."

"Okay, so what are you going to do when you get there?"

"I'm going to prove that Damon is not where he claims to be and therefore he's a liar and not to be trusted. Without evidence to substantiate my statements, nobody listens to what I'm saying."

"Yeah, I wonder why. Come on, Kory, I mean it's not like people haven't eloped before. You may not like it, I may not like it, but it makes a hell of a lot more sense than your story."

"Will you cover for me or not?"

"Nope."

"Why?"

"'Cause, if you're going, I'm going too, but I still don't get why we're chasing shadows. You said he's this complete psycho, right? I think we should find out where he is and move to the other side of the planet."

"That's not funny, Charlie. Damon has got Mr. Saunders believing his stories and what's worse, he's forced Dorothy to confirm them." Kory summarized what Mary had just told him.

"Uh, I hate to be the bearer of bad news," Charlie said, "but don't you think it's high time you deal with reality and accept the fact that she's married instead of trying to explain away the obvious with all this talk about kidnapping?"

"My brother attacked me from behind. He chloroformed me. If Dorothy wasn't kidnapped, if she really did marry him, then she was a willing part of all this. Is that the reality you're expecting me to accept?" Kory waited, but his friend had no response. "I'll only concede such a thing if she tells me herself, without Damon behind the scenes holding a gun to her head."

"But you said Damon is in the States, at the air force base."

"No, I said that's what *they* believe."

Charlie shook his head impatiently. "You're making no sense."

"Really? So she calls her father to come and get her, and then she suddenly changes her mind, saying everything is nice and dandy, and Mr. Saunders ends up flying back to the States, alone. *That* makes sense?"

"No," Charlie admitted, "it doesn't. But since when do women make sense?"

"Yeah, I forgot, you're the expert. This is *serious*, Charlie. I need to find Damon. That's the only way to figure out what he's done, and what he plans to do with her."

"Oh, sure, that'll be easy. We'll just waltz over there and say, 'Hey, Mr. Two-Hundred-Pound Motherfucker, tell us what you did to Dorothy to make her lie to her father, and tell us where she is, and why you kidnapped her.'" Charlie shook his head. "Sorry, but I like this life. I kinda want to stay alive."

"He's not there, and even if he is, he's not about to murder us in public, Charlie."

"Oh, great, I feel much better. For a moment there I thought I was going to be killed in front of an audience, but now I can rest easy, knowing he'll accident my sorry butt and everyone will think I died because I'm a klutz. Great."

"Relax, he may be smart and strong, but I'm not about to underestimate him again."

"Wonderful. Do you at least have a gun?"

"Sorry, no, but I'm guessing he does."

Charlie laughed. "That's comforting. You're nuts. You say your brother is crazy, but you're certifiable, do you know that?"

"Hey, it takes one to know one."

"Yeah, yeah, the difference is that I *know* I'm nuts—I'm nuts because I'm actually listening to this shit."

"So you'll still come with me?"

"Hell, Kory, you know I will."

"You're a good friend."

Charlie made no effort to hide his smile. "Remind me again, 'cause apparently I'm a bit slow: why are we going to go all the way to Eglin when you don't believe he's actually there?"

"Because there's no other way to ascertain that fact. The Army keeps its trainees sequestered from friends and family except for matters of extreme urgency."

"You tried calling?"

"Yes, Charlie. I haven't exactly been sitting on my hands all this time."

"And?"

"And they gave me the brush-off. Right off the bat."

"So then how are you planning on contacting him?"

"I'll go over there and personally tell them it's a family emergency."

"And if he's not there?"

Kory smiled. "Then Mr. Saunders would have to concede that something fishy is going on. I'm not about to approach him again without some proof to back up my argument. I'll need Mr. Saunders's help and cooperation if we're going to find her in time."

"And if he *is* there?"

Kory looked down at the trimmed grass as if he were peering from a deadly precipice. "In that case, the only logical conclusion would be that Dorothy is dead."

"Or she's happily married, of course, but I don't think you want to hear me saying that."

Kory did not reply.

"So what were you planning to do if he's there?"

Kory sighed. "I don't know."

"I think you do."

"Believe what you want."

Charlie's eyes widened. "You were going to take him on, weren't you? That's why you didn't plan on bringing me along, right?"

"I never said that."

"You didn't say *anything*, and believe me, that says it all. Maybe you would get a punch in—and I seriously doubt it— but then he'd hammer-fist you on top of your head so hard you'd pop out somewhere in China. Or he'd just whip out his gun and blow your brains out, and it wouldn't matter if there were witnesses, because it would be self-defense."

"If he's there, then Dorothy's dead, so I don't care."

"Uh-huh. Nice plan. I'm sure Schelowitz would be bursting with pride if he could hear you now."

"Can it, Charlie. Damon is not going to be there. She's still alive; I've got to believe that."

Charlie nodded, and tapped his temple. "Love has messed with your mind, my friend."

Kory said nothing.

"Let me be the rational one here, since you seem to have flushed all common sense down the toilet. Have you considered the possibility that he's there and she's still alive?"

"I don't see how that could be."

"Maybe he's got her with him or something, I don't know."

"Are you telling me he ties her against a tree while he trains in the day, and takes her with him to the barracks at night? Gee, that makes sense."

"I don't know, but you have to admit there could easily be another explanation. If you cause a scene there, even if you aren't shot to pieces, your credibility certainly will be. What happens if Dorothy's there and she's not dead? You'd be endangering any chances she might have of coming home safely."

Kory cocked his head to the side as he regarded his friend. "I'm impressed. It seems that underneath that clownish façade lurks the potential for logical thought. You're obviously right; I'm not thinking clearly. I haven't slept properly since I don't know when. Continue, please, I'm all ears."

"If Damon is there, and we manage to trick him into saying something that can be used as evidence against him, you'll need a witness. You'll also need me to make sure you don't lose your cool, because if you do, then you'd be endangering Dorothy."

Kory nodded.

"You were thinking of taking a bus, right?"

Kory nodded again.

"Waaay too slow. It would take at least a day to get there, and a day to get back. And that's from Port Authority. We'd have to take a bus to get to the city first. We'd have to find the timetables, and then we'd have to find a bus going from there to Nowheresville in the Florida Panhandle. I don't know what the closest major city is."

"Tallahassee," Kory said immediately.

"Okay, then how do we get to this air force base from there? A taxi?"

"I suppose, but it's not at the air force base, it's somewhere nearby."

"Oh, perfect. I can just see the bus schedule showing Port Authority to Somewhere-Near-Eglin-Air Force Base. What were you thinking?"

"I was thinking about going to Tallahassee."

"If we just left now, your aunt and my folks would have a search party after us. I'm in the clear, but your birthday isn't until the twenty-fifth, so you're still a minor and if you go missing, the police would be after us in a second. You and I would be in a shitload of trouble."

"Which is precisely why I asked you to cover for me," Kory said. "Once I made it to Eglin, it doesn't matter if I'm caught because at that point I'd have sufficient proof to get Mr. Saunders to do something about Dorothy."

"Yeah? Well if the cops catch us before we get there, then all of this would have been for nothing."

"That's not going to happen."

A furrowed brow suggested Charlie didn't share Kory's optimism. "We need to know exactly where Damon is before we set off, and we need driving directions from Tallahassee."

"A taxi driver would know."

"Yeah, but if it's a hundred miles or something, you don't even know for sure if a taxi would take us that far." Charlie shook his head. "We're not taking a taxi. We're not taking a bus, or anything like that. We're going in my car."

Kory lifted his eyebrows in surprise.

"We'll need an excuse, of course," Charlie continued. "I need to come up with a solid cover story...." He snapped his fingers. "I've got just the thing: Ben and his family are going skiing, and Ben asked if I wanted to join him. I said no, but it's not too late to change my mind. Ben's little brother is only eight, and he doesn't take up much room—I've gone with them before—so I usually fit in the back of the car with Ben and Timmy. I'll let Ben in on this—I'll only tell him what he needs to know. He's a good guy. I know he'll help us out. He'll tell his dad that you and me are going skiing with them."

"Wait, you just said you barely fit in that car, so there wouldn't be enough room for me."

"Exactly." Charlie grinned. "That's why I'll say I'll have to take *my* car. And because I don't want to drive in the night, we'll meet them at the slopes on Saturday. Then, come Saturday, I'll have Ben say that we changed plans and cancelled. By that time, we should be at Eglin."

"Great plan, but what if Ben's parents call your parents to confirm the arrangements?"

"Why would they?" Charlie thought for a moment. "Even if they do, we'll be in Eglin, and we'll still have time to have a one-on-one chat with that maniac brother of yours. Of course, I'd kinda like to get back on Sunday without being chewed out by my folks, but I'd say our chances of making it with my plan are damned good."

"So this weekend?"

"Yeah, this weekend. Friday. This'll work. Don't worry, Kory, I haven't let you down yet, have I?"

"Would you like to grab some lunch?" he'd said, with the forward-ness of a man in too much pain to bother with small talk. Mary had been equally forward, saying she thought he'd never ask. That had been the extent of their phone conversation. He hadn't even said when or where. Mary had just started getting ready, and twenty minutes later he came knocking on the front door.

They ended up at Michelangelo's, an Italian restaurant that had recently opened along with a host of foreign restaurants that were becoming the latest fashion in the new section of Rhodes.

John was taking it harder than she'd expected. After all, his daughter had married; she hadn't been victimized by any of the horrors her nephew had imagined. But Mary didn't say anything. She just listened. Something she'd learned from years of trying to bring Kory out of his shell.

The less she said, the more John talked. She could actually see him unwind as he voiced his hurt. He was sounding a lot more like the John she knew. Things would work out in the end. For Dorothy and Damon, for Mary and John, even for Kory. It was just a matter of time.

John stopped speaking for a while, so Mary tried a change of subject. "Did you know Kory is going skiing with Charlie?"

John put his glass down. "Really? That's odd. Just like that?"

Mary smiled. "Charlie's quite the charmer. He called me saying that Kory wasn't himself and he needed some cheering up. Charlie was going on a ski trip with some friends and he thought of inviting Kory."

"And Kory actually accepted?"

"Yes," Mary said. "I asked him about it, and he said he wanted to go."

"Really?" John said, sounding dubious. "I suppose that's good news."

"I get the impression you're not convinced?"

John shrugged. "It could be good news, Mary; it really could be."

"But?" she asked.

He struggled with himself before answering. "I've just had firsthand experience on how complex teenagers can be. Through her therapy sessions, I've learned a great deal, and yet I was totally unprepared for this move of hers. First she elopes, then she calls me for help, and then after I fly across the Atlantic to take her back home, she says all is well, as if that's all that needed saying. I've told you this before—she's had problems. Alcohol, drugs . . . you know. And there was a time when she tried to hurt herself."

Mary gently took his hand in hers, and she was pleased to see he didn't pull it away.

"Anyway," he continued, "one of the things her psychologist taught me was that positive signs of progress do not necessarily preclude a relapse."

"So you were worried she'd try to hurt herself again."

He nodded. "She didn't, of course, but it was always a concern."

Now it was Mary's turn to nod. "And so you're saying I shouldn't get my hopes up for Kory."

"I don't know the kid as well as I thought I did. Here's this timid guy who's so closed in on himself he never gave himself the opportunity to play chess with another person until Charlie forced him into a game with me. So then he goes from playing chess with himself, to actually looking forward to playing at the club. Then, before you know it, he's got friends for the first time in his life."

"Yes, and a first love."

"He sure had a crush on Dorothy," John agreed. "That first heartbreak is a doozy."

"What cruel girl broke your heart, John Saunders?"

He smiled but his eyes darkened. "My wife. She left me for another man. Before I could deal with the blow, she died of an overdose."

"I'm sorry," Mary said, wishing she'd never asked.

"Hello?"

"Mr. Patterson? It's Jerry Sutherland."

"Oh, hello, Jerry. To what do I owe the pleasure?"

"Sorry to bother you, Mr. Patterson."

"Please, it's Andy."

"Andy. I wasn't sure if you were still on vacation."

"No worries there, Jerry, I've been on vacation for three years now—I'm semi-retired. I pulled out of the political arena; I didn't need the money and I certainly didn't need the aggravation. I still keep in touch, and I let my old colleagues try to badger me into running for Senate, but that's all that keeps me from calling myself fully retired."

"Well, Andy, I was thinking—if your son doesn't catch us at the slopes, have him call the hotel, I'll leave a message at the desk with a rendezvous point and time."

"I'm not sure I follow," Mr. Patterson said. "Why would he meet you at the slopes, aren't you going to the same hotel?"

"Yes, but by the time he gets there, we'll have had ourselves half a day of skiing." Jerry Sutherland didn't hear a reply. "Andy?"

"Yes, I'm still here. But I'm confused; Charlie said he would follow you in his car."

"Uh, we're leaving on Friday night. He said you preferred it if he didn't drive in the dark because he's only had his license for a few months."

"Oh," Mr. Patterson said slowly. "That does make sense, and it certainly sounds like something I'd say, but best I can recall, I never did."

"He might not have had a chance to tell you."

"Could be, though it's not like Charlie to be so concerned about his personal safety; he lets me worry about that."

Jerry laughed politely. "Well, if you decide to have him follow us on Friday, just let me know. Either way works for me."

"Thanks for inviting Charlie to go skiing again. I'd take him myself, but I've got a bad knee from my college days, when a mare decided she had enough of me and kicked the usefulness out of my leg. I play some tennis, but even that's pushing it."

"Ouch," Jerry said.

"Hey," Andy said, "a little higher and there'd never have been a Charlie to worry about!"

Jerry chuckled.

After Andy Patterson hung up the phone, he considered his next move. He could wait for Charlie to come back from school and get his side of the story, or he could call Mary Thorn.

Andy didn't wait. Mary was a very pleasant person, and Andy was glad his friend John had taken an interest in her. The poor guy hadn't been near a member of the opposite sex since his divorce.

Mary said she thought the plan was for Charlie to pick up Kory on Friday, and head off on a skiing trip with Charlie and the Sutherland family. Andy told her that was what he'd thought as well, and he told her about the change in plans, omitting the fact that Charlie had used him in a lie to Mr. Sutherland, claiming it was Andy's idea to have the two boys leave on Saturday instead of Friday night. Andy could see no reason in upsetting Mary; he would clear this up with his son the moment he got back from school.

Two hours after speaking with Mary, Andy received a call from John Saunders. He hadn't expected to hear from his friend so soon after his return from Geneva. He knew the story, and he could only imagine what John had been through. Surprisingly, John didn't say a word about Dorothy. Andy couldn't remember a conversation with John that didn't include some comment about his daughter. That girl was everything to him.

Instead, John asked him for a rather peculiar favor.

THE LAST CALL

The gatekeeper recognized Charlie and, tipping his hat, he pulled open the large iron gates. Charlie had only been driving for two and a half months, but already the old man could spot his Ford from a distance.

He let his car creep slowly up the familiar mile-long pathway to his friend's house. The powerful V-8 grumbled, protesting for a change in gear.

Something just wasn't sitting right. His dad had acted weird that afternoon as he left. He'd said good-bye, and he'd said he wouldn't be around in the evening because he had business to tend to. But what business? Dad didn't work. That should have been warning enough.

When he pulled up to the house, there were three cars parked in the cul-de-sac: Mrs. van Luden's Cadillac, which Kory had told him used to belong to his mother; the only Jag in Rhodes, Mr. S's, of course; and last but definitely not least, his father's Rolls. *Shit.*

What business did his father have at the van Ludens'?

Whatever it was, Charlie had a feeling this wasn't going to turn out well.

He walked up to the door and was about to ring the bell when it opened by itself. Kory had a habit of doing that. It was this weird sixth sense he had, sort of like a dog—he could tell when a person was coming well in advance, even behind a thick wooden door and stone walls.

Only it wasn't Kory who opened the door, it was Mr. S.

Why was Dorothy's father answering the door at the van Ludens', at this time? Charlie tried reading his face for an answer. The usual half-amused, half-annoyed smile had been replaced by an expression Charlie had never seen before, an expression that could only mean bad news.

"Come in, Mr. Patterson," John Saunders said, motioning to the family room.

Mr. Patterson? Mr. S never, ever called him that.

Charlie followed him, trailing a few steps behind, as if he were walking his last steps on death row.

In the living room was a surprise party for the damned. Kory was seated, his head hanging, next to his aunt. The Sutherlands were there too for some reason. Ben and his little brother, Timmy, were sitting with cookies and milk in front of them, but only Timmy seemed to have an appetite. Mr. and Mrs. Sutherland were visibly uncomfortable. Charlie's parents were the only ones standing.

His mother and father didn't fit into any explanation with a favorable outcome. This really was bad news. Acting as if this gathering were both normal and expected, Charlie said, "Mom? Dad? Are you going skiing too?"

Kory shook his head in warning as Charlie's parents stared him down, neither of them saying a word.

Charlie's heart sank. Nobody was going to speak. He held on to his smile, but barely. "Is that a no?"

Ben mouthed the word *sorry*, and that was when Charlie realized what had happened.

"What exactly were you planning on doing, Charlie?" John said.

Charlie was about to speak. He was about to say "What do you mean?" but Mr. Saunders was obviously not interested in his answer.

"Drive down to Florida, with Kory," John continued, "and chase after his twisted fantasy?"

"Actually, we thought we'd go skinny-dipping in the Keys," Charlie said.

Ben chuckled, but his mother gave him a look, and he quickly covered his mouth.

Kory stood. "Leave him out of this."

"Sit down," Mr. Saunders said. "We'll deal with you later."

"I think not," Kory said. "You are neither my father nor my legal guardian."

"Please, honey," Mary said.

Kory gave her a look of pity. "This was *my* idea, not Charlie's," Kory said, speaking to John Saunders. Then he turned to Ben's father. "Mr. Sutherland, I apologize for having involved you in this, and for disrupting your trip. I don't see why you need be inconvenienced further."

"I'm *inconvenienced* because my boy, here," Mr. Sutherland said, grabbing Ben by the shoulder, "lied to me, and that's something we don't tolerate in the Sutherland family. Isn't that so?"

"Yes, sir," Ben said, his smile melting into a frown.

"We misled him," Kory said. "He had no idea we were going to Florida."

Charlie's eyes lit up for a second. "That's right, he had no idea."

"Ben? Son, is this true?"

"I swear, Dad, I didn't know."

"And you didn't know they planned to head elsewhere today?"

Charlie answered, to keep Ben from having to lie. "Like we said, sir, he didn't know."

Jerry Sutherland looked doubtfully at Charlie and then at his son in turn, but he seemed uncertain what to believe. A glance at his wife told him she was ready to forgive, so he said, "I guess the trip is still on, then. I had half a mind to cancel the whole thing, but if you didn't know, son . . . John?"

"Please, Jerry, by all means, go. Have a great trip and I'm sorry I had to drag you into all this."

Kory started walking out of the room.

"One moment," John said. "Just where do you think *you're* going?"

"To my room," Kory said.

John was puzzled for a moment, and Kory answered his question before he had a chance to ask. "I'm gathering my things and going to Florida."

Andy Patterson waved his index finger. "Kory, you and Charlie aren't going anywhere."

"I didn't say anything about Charlie, Mr. Patterson. I didn't want him coming in the first place. He tried to dissuade me from going, and then when he saw that there was no changing my mind, he insisted on driving me there."

Charlie said nothing, but he could see that, like Ben's father, his dad was having trouble deciding how to handle this. "Charlie?"

"No, it was all my idea. Taking my car, driving to Florida, telling Ben we'd leave on Saturday and meet him on the slopes, and then telling you guys we were leaving tonight. That was me, all the way."

Kory regarded Charlie, Mr. Patterson, and John Saunders in turn. "We're wasting valuable time. Mr. Saunders, I'm leaving for Eglin Air Force Base to prove to you, once and for all, that your alleged son-in-law is nothing of the kind. He's a liar and a kidnapper."

Mary covered her face.

Mr. and Mrs. Sutherland, their two kids in hand, stood frozen, all eight eyes searching for an escape route.

"Here we go again," John said, his voice rising. "Did you not hear Mary when she told you that I personally visited my daughter?"

Kory looked like he was on the verge of physical violence. "You're basically a good person at heart, but you're naïve and foolhardy."

John stared at Kory with an open mouth.

"You went there, you spent time with her, and you noticed nothing the least bit peculiar about her behavior?"

"Kory, I've had enough of this."

"Answer me."

Nobody moved.

"Dorothy is fine," John said. Well, that wasn't quite true. The drug problem had gotten way out of hand. She'd seemed so frightened, like an abused child. He'd told himself she was ashamed for causing him this much pain, but who was he kidding? Dorothy was suffering from withdrawal, not guilt.

"Then prove it."

238

"I don't have to prove anything, young man."

"Damon is forcing her to lie," Kory said. "Can't you see that?"

"No, actually, I can't. Damon is in Eglin, as you know."

"It is my contention that he is not. He is nowhere near Eglin, for if he is, then—"

"Then what?" Mary said.

Kory turned to her, shaking his head. His eyes were wet. "Then Dorothy is probably dead."

Mrs. Sutherland gasped. Her husband said, "Okay then, I think we should be going."

John ignored him. "What did you just say?"

"You heard me. I'm sorry, but it had to be said. When I first found out she was gone, it was my immediate conclusion. Look, none of you know Damon, so you think *I'm* crazy. I'm not. Since the moment Mary told me you saw her alive, I've been hoping that Damon plans to keep her that way. I'm *still* hoping. That's why I have to go to Eglin. And that's why I can't waste anymore time explaining my actions; I'm going to get you proof."

"You don't have to prove anything," Mary said. "He's there, Kory."

"How do you know?"

"I heard you calling and asking for your brother. I was concerned, so I called shortly after you did. I didn't get to speak with him, but the Army assured me that he is well, and that is all I needed to hear."

Kory spoke slowly. "He's there? Are you sure?"

Mary nodded.

John felt a sharp sting of guilt. He'd set this all up to put Kory in his place, set him straight, and expose his silly plans for the nonsensical ravings they were. But Kory genuinely believed what he was saying—there was no faking those tears. The kid actually thought that just because Damon was at Eglin, Dorothy was dead.

John grabbed Mary's nephew by the shoulders. "Kory? Look at me."

Kory didn't look up. All nine people in the room were looking at him. He was crying now, not just shedding tears.

John tried again. "Look at me."

This time, Kory obeyed.

"She's fine," John said. "Do you understand me? She's okay. I was just there a few days ago, she's fine."

"Then . . . I . . . I want to talk to her."

"You want to go to Switzerland?"

"No. I just want to talk to her. Even if it's just a phone call. Just let me call her, let me talk to her. If she tells me she's okay, and this is what she wants, I swear I'll never bother you again."

John thought about this and instead of saying no, he looked at his watch. "We can't call her now, it's too early. But I was going to talk to her tomorrow anyway, and—"

Kory shook his head. "I can't wait."

John sighed. "Fine, I'll stay here with you. We'll call her from here."

Kory brightened for a moment and, remembering his tears, he flicked them away violently, as if they were the only proof of his behavior that night. "Thank you."

"But not until midnight, okay?"

Kory nodded.

Charlie punched Kory in the shoulder, giving him a thumbs-up before leaving with his parents.

The Sutherlands took this as their opportunity to leave, and offered hurried good-byes, taking their leave as quickly as a group of lost nuns who'd stumbled into a brothel.

Mary, Kory, and John were alone in the house now. Nobody said anything for a while.

In his room, Kory tried a game of chess, but no chessboard appeared in his mind's eye, and for the first time in his life, he was unable to concentrate on the game he was born to play.

When finally midnight came, Kory found Mary and John huddled over the kitchen table in what was either an intimate or highly secretive discussion.

"Do you have the phone number for the clinic with you?" Kory asked. Obtaining her number would have saved him a lot of time and effort, but an international operator wouldn't have been able to help him without the name of the clinic, and Kory knew then, as he did now, that asking Mr. Saunders for the number wouldn't have proven fruitful either.

"Yes, but she's not at the clinic, Kory," John said.

Kory's eyes widened. "I knew it."

"Oh, she *was* at the clinic all right, but she'd left for her house by the time I got there."

"Her house?"

"Yes, Damon's estate in Geneva. I believe it belonged to your father?"

Kory had heard Martha mention something about property over there. "So you're saying she's there? Alone?"

John nodded. "Yes, Damon had to finish Ranger School and so Dorothy is in Geneva waiting for him at his house. Damon should be back by the end of the month."

As Mary handed John the phone, he said, "I have her number at the château."

Kory said nothing, watching instead, as John dialed.

John put the receiver to his ear. "Uh, yes, may I speak with Dorothy Saun—Dorothy van Luden, please?"

Kory bit down on his lip.

John said, "Uh-huh, that's okay." He looked at Kory and Mary and explained, "She was still asleep, and they're going to wake her."

John listened without speaking for three minutes. "Dorothy? Honey? How are you feeling? They tell me you were sleeping?"

Kory could make out a small voice on the phone, but he couldn't hear the words, nor could he be certain it was really Dorothy Mr. Saunders was speaking to.

"Yes, uh-huh," John continued. "I understand. Like I said, you should have stayed at the clinic." He paused. "I know, I know. Uh, Dorothy? There's someone here who would like to talk to you."

Kory noticed that Mr. Saunders didn't wait for a reply; he was holding the receiver out. Kory put it to his ear. It really was Dorothy. She was saying, "Dad? Wait—Dad?"

"It's me, Kory."

There was no response for a moment, and then Dorothy said, "Oh, no. Oh, dear God."

"Dorothy?"

"Is my father there? I want to speak to my dad."

Kory felt suddenly weak. "He's here. Dorothy? What's going on? It's *me*."

"Please, Kory, don't." It was Dorothy's voice, yet there was something distinctly foreign about it. A side of her he'd never heard before.

"Don't *what*? What have I done?" Kory said.

Mr. Saunders gave him a look that said he was losing patience.

Kory remembered the question he had prepared, which was a good thing, because otherwise he would have stood there, speechless, until Mr. Saunders grabbed the phone from his hand. "Dorothy, if someone is listening, tell me what was the last thing I said to you in Vermont. If not, make something up that sounds logical."

There was a long pause. When she answered, she sounded very tired. "You said it's a perfect night for a walk."

"But—"

"Nobody's listening, Kory." After another period of silence, Dorothy said, "I'm sorry. I don't know what else to say."

Kory was going to ask his follow-up question, but Dorothy had started crying. It no longer mattered; in just two words she had said it all.

John Saunders reached out for the phone, but Kory dropped the receiver before he had a chance.

"Kory?" Mary said. "What did she say, darling?"

John picked the receiver up off the floor. "She hung up."

THE FALL

Late August 1962
Seven Months Later

Mary sat next to John Saunders while her nephew moved his chair to the far end.

"First of all, I would like to congratulate all of you, especially Mr. Saunders, on the birth of Damon and Dorothy's son, Jan van Luden." He offered Kory a polite smile. "You're an uncle now, young man."

Kory stared, said nothing.

John looked at Kory, trying to make eye contact, but Kory turned away. The boy was clearly jealous of his brother, no question there; his behavior since Dorothy eloped had been entirely unacceptable for a young man his age. He'd changed since January, and nothing about him had improved except for his phenomenal game of chess. The news that Kory had become an uncle should have brought him joy; instead, it just inflamed his wounds.

According to Damon, Jan had been born five weeks premature, and John had just enough time to pack a suitcase and fly over to Geneva to meet his daughter at the hospital.

The duty nurse had told him that Damon had sat in the waiting room during the entire six hours it took for his child to be born, reading the paper, not so much as tapping a foot. In this respect—and in John's point of view in this respect only—he was like his younger brother. They could sit like statues,

Damon out of discipline and Kory by drawing from his inner world of chess.

No matter what silly squabbles they'd had in the past, John could find no excuse for Kory not joining him and his aunt on the trip to Geneva for such a momentous occasion. It was summer; he was on vacation. No excuse whatsoever. Kory was an uncle now, and he hadn't even bothered to make a congratulatory telephone call. If he didn't care about becoming an uncle, he should have at least said a nice word to Dorothy, or was that infatuation already a thing of the past? It was certainly conceivable.

"And how have you been doing Kory?" Mr. Chambers said. "I hear you are going to Columbia University."

"That is correct," Kory said.

"Well, then, welcome to the Big Apple," Mr. Chambers said. "And you have moved into the Park Avenue residence?"

"Also correct."

"Mrs. Thorn, do you have a new address?"

"I'm afraid not. Not yet, that is. I'll be moving out—"

"She'll be moving out by the end of this month, as per the terms of our eviction," Kory said coolly.

Mary gave her nephew a disapproving look. Since January, she'd grown reluctantly accustomed to his hostile tone, but it made her uncomfortable when he used it on others. Things could have been worse. Many a teen his age had turned to drugs or alcohol, or even thoughts of suicide, during periods of depression. A good example was Dorothy, after her mother died. Only, Dorothy had pulled through.

Mary played with images of Kory as an alcoholic. There didn't seem to be much of a chance of that, thank God. Neither was he the type to contemplate suicide. Socially, he'd reverted to his old, unsmiling self—a Kory Mary had worked for years to change, and for a brief and wonderful period, with the help of his only two friends, Charlie and Dorothy, had succeeded in changing. She wondered how long it would take him to open up again, if ever.

These past months, Mary had been little more than a physical presence at the van Luden estate. As long as she didn't talk to him, Kory put up with her, and at times even came close to being civil. She and John had been wrong to label Kory's feelings for Dorothy as mere puppy love. Inherently mature and sensitive, he had tried to fill the gaping holes in his emotional life with this one girl, and now that he had lost her, he refused to give relationships another chance. There was a streak of stubbornness there—a determination to latch on to the first love and never let go—that reminded Mary of her sister.

"She'll be staying with me," John Saunders said, eyeing Kory.

Kory gave him a bored look.

"And you are still residing at the Rhodes address, then?"

John nodded.

Mr. Chambers jotted something down. "I have requested your company today to discuss the legal aspects of the will as they pertain to the birth of Martha van Luden's firstborn male grandchild. Damon has already been briefed about the details in her will—we met before he departed for Europe and have been in touch over the phone since then." He pulled out a metal cabinet drawer and withdrew a file fat with documents. "I went over these details when Martha van Luden passed on, and of course, when young Kory here turned eighteen."

Mary nodded uneasily.

"What details?" Kory said.

Mary shifted in her seat.

"The details of your mother's will," Mr. Chambers said.

"I see. Why wasn't I included in this?"

"You were a child, Kory," Mary answered. "You had just lost your mother, and your brother was leaving for the Academy. Even I found it troublesome to listen to this legal talk so soon after my sister's death."

"I was referring to the occasion of my eighteenth birthday," Kory said. "Or did you consider me a child then as well?"

"Your aunt wanted to tell you herself," Mr. Chambers said.

"And I did, remember?" Mary added.

"You mean about the town house?" Kory said.

Mary nodded. "Yes, about what would happen with the home in Rhodes, and the money you'll be getting."

"Uh-huh," Kory said, "but as a legal adult, shouldn't I have been present?"

Mary answered again. "Kory, do you recall the state you were in?" *And still are.* "Besides, I asked if you wanted to come, but you insisted on being dropped off at the chess club instead. Remember?"

Kory nodded. He hadn't been the least bit interested in wasting his time listening to his mother's lawyer ramble about the petty details of her will.

Mr. Chambers found what he was looking for quickly, but he took his time sifting through the papers, as if to make certain nothing was missing. "It was your mother's wish that I make her legacy fully clear to all those affected in her will. Furthermore, whenever there's a major occurrence for which there was a provision in the document, she wanted me to gather everyone involved and to reiterate all the pertinent clauses."

Kory cracked a smile. If Charlie were here, he'd be snoring about now.

"I might point out, that as the senior partner of Chambers, Amherst & Roddwell, I very rarely take on matters such as these. This firm has a growing staff of very capable tax attorneys who would be better suited for this task. It is only because it involves Martha's will that I am handling this directly. Chambers, Amherst & Roddwell owes a lot to the van Ludens, and I am not one to forget."

Mr. Chambers took out a cigar and offered one to John, who politely declined.

"Havana," Mr. Chambers said, sliding the cigar lengthwise under his nose.

John brought out his pouch with his pipe and he motioned at the attorney.

"Of course, feel free," Mr. Chambers said. "Damon's marriage was the second event affecting the trust following Martha's death, and then, of course, we had young Kory's eighteenth birthday." Mr. Chambers browsed his desk calendar. "We discussed both matters in our meeting in January, correct?"

Mary nodded.

"What does Damon's marriage have to do with anything?" Kory asked.

Mr. Chambers said to Mary, "You didn't mention it? I thought you said you spoke to him?"

"I did." Mary nodded. "I told him everything that affected him directly."

"Just what was it she didn't mention?" Kory asked.

Mr. Chambers ignored the question; he was looking straight at Mary through a veil of his own cigar smoke. "Mrs. Thorn, I have learned from experience that family members and any person affected directly or indirectly by the terms of a will should be kept informed as to its contents."

Mary did not like what the attorney was implying. She looked to John for support, but he wasn't offering. "I'm not expecting Mr. Chambers to understand, but I expect *you* to trust my judgment, John."

"Mr. Chambers makes a good point, Aunt Mary. Why don't you explain so that we *all* understand," Kory said.

Mary sighed. There was no telling what he was feeling: anger, vengeance, boredom? Curiosity was probably on the bottom of the list. Mary addressed Mr. Chambers. "Kory was infatuated with Dorothy, and he didn't take well to his brother marrying her. He was very upset, you understand."

Mr. Chambers waited.

Mary turned to John, and this time he nodded. "No question about that."

"His brother had just married Dorothy," Mary continued, "and that was enough for Kory to endure. I couldn't see how telling him what Damon was going to inherit would help."

Mr. Chambers cleared his throat. "Since Kory is here, I must insist that he be informed, albeit late, of every aspect of his mother's will."

"Of course," Mary said in a small voice.

"What I told Mrs. Thorn, Kory, was that when your mother died, Damon was already eighteen. By one week, if memory serves. Under the terms of the will, he inherited the house in Geneva, and when he started his education at West Point, which was only five weeks later—"

"Six weeks, three days, and thirteen hours," Kory said, "assuming the military equivalent to orientation at West Point started at nine in the morning."

"Thank you for that, Mr. van Luden, but the precise time interval between the two events is of no legal import. What was significant, however, was the day that marked the beginning of his education, when, in accordance with your mother's wishes, he began to receive a monthly allowance, just as you will when you start classes at Columbia University. Van Luden Enterprises was given complete control of the trust."

"I know all that," Kory said impatiently. "Mary told me."

"Be that as it may, since I don't know what your aunt has told you and what she hasn't, I'm going over every detail. I trust there are no objections?" Mr. Chambers tapped his cigar and a clump of thick ashes detached and crumbled into his ashtray. Without looking for a response from Kory he said, "Good. According to your mother's will, her first child to marry becomes the fiduciary of fifty percent of the trust, while Van Luden Enterprises continues to control the remaining fifty percent, and the first grandson inherits full control on his eighteenth birthday."

Mary took the opportunity to change the subject, hoping it wouldn't come up again. *"Fiduciary?"*

"Yes, of course—you'll have to forgive the legal jargon. A *fiduciary* is a person who holds the trust or estate property on behalf of the beneficiaries of said property. The fiduciary, Damon van Luden, is legally obligated to follow the terms of the will or trust in which the fiduciary is named. The fiduciary is responsible for marshaling the corpus of the trust or estate, for registering the assets properly, for holding and distributing the property as the will or trust instrument directs, for balancing the needs of the various beneficiaries of the trust or estate property and for fulfilling the accounting and tax reporting and payment obligations of the entity, including the accumulation and distribution of income on the corpus."

"By *corpus* I don't suppose you mean dead body," Mary said.

The lawyer didn't smile.

"The estate or trust property," Mr. Chambers continued, "that is, the body of the trust or estate, is called the *corpus*. The trust or estate exists as a separate legal entity."

"Thank you," Mary said, suddenly wishing this whole thing would come to a quick end.

While the attorney spoke, Kory was already eight moves into a Sicilian favored by his most challenging opponent in this afternoon's match, Joseph Saltz. This was a point in the opening where the branch in the tree of options became challenging. There wasn't enough time to analyze all alternatives, even with Mr. Chambers droning on and on about fiduciaries and the like, but at least he could focus on two or three of the stronger lines, which would set the stage for a possible kingside attack.

Kory heard Mr. Chambers say ". . . Attorney General to be cited on behalf of unknowns, even if preresiduary, unless Public Administrator is being cited, in which event the Attorney General . . ."

Now Kory was analyzing the Pachman-Olafsson Portoroz variation. It was played in 1958, and it gave Black a way out of a closed variation. . . .

"Whereas a family tree and third party affidavit if only one statutory distributee or only distributees more remote than siblings or, as in this case, if distributees are grandchildren, in which case their lineage must be set forth . . ."

And if White were to play Knight to King Two in the twelfth move, Black had the brilliant Pawn to Queen Five! Some other part of Kory's brain was weeding out the meaning behind the legal jargon. He had learned to play chess during class, while still getting the basic drift of whatever point the teacher was trying to make that lesson. He hadn't lost his knack.

"Mr. Chambers," Mary interrupted, "forgive me, but could you kindly summarize? I find all this somehow quite tiresome, and to be honest, a bit disturbing."

"Of course, but I must first feel assured that all present completely understand the terms of your sister's will." Mr. Chambers was looking directly at Kory.

Kory sensed the stare, and for a moment, paused his analysis of the Portoroz variation. "I understood what you said, but if my aunt needs you to summarize, by all means, summarize."

Mr. Chambers again repeated who was to get what. "And since his marriage in January, he's assumed fifty percent of the trust. What I was going to say— "

"In other words," Kory said, looking for a way to conclude the meeting, "Damon is in control of fifty percent, Van Luden Enterprises has control of the rest, and I've got the town house and come September a monthly allowance."

"While he's the fiduciary of the fifty percent of the trust, he is still bound by the conditions of said trust," Mr. Chambers said. "Like you, he receives a generous monthly sum from the interest on the fifty percent of the trust controlled by Van Luden Enterprises. All of this is in accordance with the terms of the trust."

Kory said nothing.

John was looking uncomfortable.

"Yes," Kory said, "but if *he* is the fiduciary, as you chose to call him—I can think of other more appropriate names—then what does this have to do with me, my aunt, or Mr. Saunders for that matter? I can't be the first to marry, since Damon already has, and Mary wasn't even in the will."

Mr. Chambers shook his head. "That's not entirely correct. She was mentioned in her sister's will, as she knows, and there are sections of this trust that indirectly affect Mr. Saunders, since his daughter has married Martha van Luden's first son. There is more you need to hear, Kory—but now, if you don't mind, I would like to proceed with this methodically so that no point is missed. Omission is not something I can allow, not as a professional, nor as a close friend to the van Luden family. I would ask for your patience while I go through all this.

"This is no commonplace trust, Kory; this is the van Luden trust. A trust worth in the neighborhood of four hundred twenty-one million dollars. It consists of companies and investments all over the world. Controlling the trust is a tremendous undertaking, and involves a great deal of experience and expertise, which is why your father hired the services of Chambers, Amherst & Roddwell to handle everything while he was gone. Unfortunately, he ended up passing after the war, and we continued serving your family as best we could. Controlling the vast investments and estates is a full-time job."

"Four hundred and twenty-one million?" Kory asked. "You're saying Damon is going to have fifty-percent charge of over four hundred million dollars?"

"Yes," Mr. Chambers said, "that is what your mother wanted."

Kory was trying to grasp at the implications of what he'd just heard. "And you think he's got the *experience and expertise* to handle that kind of money?"

"While he is in Europe, serving our country, he has asked that this law firm help him with the day-to-day financial matters."

"But he still has fifty-percent control?" Kory pressed.

"He does."

"So he could conceivably liquidate half the assets you were referring to and live like a king for the rest of his life?"

"That would be highly impractical, but theoretically, yes." He took a long drag at his cigar. "As Mr. Saunders here can tell you, Kory, that kind of money is not left under a mattress or even in a savings account. It has to be invested. If you don't look after your funds, like plants, they wither and die. A fool-hardy rich man can turn into a pauper in no time at all, no matter how much wealth he might have. Your brother is a very intelligent and responsible young man, and he knows the diligent attention one has to give to one's assets."

John Saunders was nodding as Mr. Chambers spoke. "That's right, Kory—it grows or it goes. That's what my job is all about: managing money and investments."

Kory said, "Yes, that makes sense, but if Damon wants a million dollars to buy himself an airplane, a chalet on the Swiss Alps, or an apartment in Paris, all he has to do is tap into his fifty percent of the trust, right? I mean, with two-hundred and ten million, five-hundred thousand dollars at his fingertips, he could do all that and more on interest alone, right?"

John Saunders let Mr. Chambers answer that one. "You are right, to a certain extent, but I think you'll find that Damon, like his mother, wants what is best for the van Luden family, and like your father he is very much interested in preserving the van Luden line. Which takes me to the reason for this gathering today—Damon's son, Martha van Luden's grandson."

Mr. Chambers went through some papers, noted something, and said, "Okay, I believe this point is covered. I need to reiterate that since you are now eighteen, and no longer in high school, Mary is no longer needed as your guardian and therefore, in accordance with the terms of the trust, as you already know, the Rhodes estate is being sealed. It will be properly maintained as per Martha van Luden's wishes, and retained as an asset in the van Luden trust."

Finding the document he was searching for, he added, "Here we go. I will paraphrase for the purpose of brevity, and you will each receive Photostat copies of the original document for your reference . . . Mary, I know you have one, but Mr. Saunders and Kory do not.

"The trust states that in the event of Martha van Luden's death, I'm to become the trustee of the van Luden trust. This has already happened, as you all know.

"It further states that in the event of Martha van Luden's death, assuming none of her sons have married by that time, fifty percent of the control of the trust shall go to the son who marries first. This, too, has happened—we just went over it—and so Damon van Luden now controls fifty percent of the trust, no need to belabor the point."

Mr. Chambers read to himself for a while, then he continued: "Ah, this is the pertinent part, and the main reason for today's gathering: It states here that as CEO of Van Luden Enterprises, I shall retain fifty percent control of the trust until Martha's first grandson—that would be Jan van Luden—reaches the age of eighteen. When Jan becomes a legal adult, full control of the trust shall be passed unto him. Any questions on this point?"

Nobody said a word.

Mr. Chambers looked at John Saunders. "I'm not saying this would happen, but it is mentioned in the trust, so it needs to be stated: should the first marriage—that would be the marriage between Damon and Dorothy—end in annulment or divorce, then I, as CEO of Van Luden Enterprises, shall control one-hundred percent of the trust until such time as the first grandson born—Jan van Luden—reaches the age of eighteen, at which point he will again retain full control of the trust."

John looked puzzled. "So either way, my grandson gets the trust when he's eighteen?"

Mr. Chambers smiled. "Precisely." He looked at Kory, who was peering out the window, lost in thought. "Again, there is a provision here in the trust for divorce or annulment of the first marriage, and again, I'm obliged to explain this to you, although, as I've said, nobody expects such a thing will transpire. If your brother's marriage should terminate because of a divorce or annulment, there will be no second chance to retain fifty percent control of the trust, nor will you, Kory, as Martha's second son, be able to marry and claim fifty-percent control."

Kory said, "Clearly Martha covered all bases, making sure there was no chance for me to control her money."

Mr. Chambers said, "I happen to know firsthand that she had only the best in mind for both her sons."

Kory answered, "I never doubted she had the best in mind for *Damon*, and the document you're reading proves my point. Any idiot can see that the trust was written to favor him. He was older than me; therefore, logically, he would marry before me, and also have a child before me. Just in case things didn't turn out as Martha hoped, she made it so that if he messed up his marriage, I don't get a chance. Am I understanding all this?"

"As I recall, her only intention was to vouchsafe the continuation of the van Luden line, in accordance with your father's final wish."

"That was *one* of her intentions, but basically she wanted Damon to have control of everything. With this will, she kills two birds with one stone."

Mr. Chambers turned once more to John Saunders. "Again, this is just another legal point, but I need to mention that should the first son to marry, Damon, or his spouse, Dorothy, die, then this would *not* be interpreted as termination of the marriage for the purposes of this trust. Should the first son to marry, Damon, die, the control of the trust is passed on to Van Luden Enterprises until the first grandson reaches the age of eighteen, at which point the entire trust is passed to him."

"What about Dorothy? It isn't passed on to her?" John Saunders asked, incredulous.

Mr. Chambers hesitated. "I'm afraid not."

Kory smiled humorlessly at Mr. Saunders. "I told you, this trust was written for Damon and his male offspring. You never had the opportunity to meet Martha, now, did you?" Kory didn't wait for an answer. "Based on your judgment of Damon, my bet is that you'd have assumed her to be a fair, loving mother."

Mary said nothing but noticed yet again the hostility Kory harbored toward his mother. He rarely mentioned her, and when he did, he always referred to her coldly as "Martha."

Mary was impressed with how impartial Brad Chambers was to all this family quibbling. She suspected he must be very used to this sort of thing after all his years of experience.

Mr. Chambers turned to Mary. "Finally, as we've discussed, there's a provision for the death of all of Martha's descendants. In this case, Mary Thorn shall inherit one hundred percent of the trust."

Mary pursed her lips. "I cannot imagine a worse fate than to outlive my sister's children."

Mr. Chambers nodded as if this were the appropriate remark. He skimmed through the rest. "All it mentions here is the property distribution, and we all know about that. The property in Geneva goes to Damon, the property in Park Avenue goes to Kory, and the Rhodes property remains in the care of the trust."

"Great, are we done?" Kory asked.

"Not quite," Mr. Chambers said.

Kory waited.

"While the property in Geneva amounts to almost twice the acreage of the Rhodes estate, it is not in the city proper," Mr. Chambers said. "Whereas your town house in Manhattan couldn't be better placed, and in real estate, location is a prime consideration in determining property value.

"Before Mrs. van Luden passed on, I used to visit the van Luden estate in Rhodes, and my return trip to New York City took me two hours in traffic. The drive to the city of Geneva— the Old Town area—is half an hour. You, however, are right in the heart of New York City, and that makes your property the best of the three."

"Why are we talking about commuting distances?"

"Because, young van Luden, you seem to think you've been given less than your due. Both the Manhattan town house and the property in Geneva come from your father's side of the family, and your mother felt that they should be passed on directly to her children, and not assigned as an asset to the trust, as is the property in Rhodes. Because your brother was planning a military career, it was evident he could make more use of a home abroad than you could. Therefore he inherited the house in Geneva."

"Right. I'm supposed to believe he didn't ask for it specifically, that he didn't plan to live in Europe?"

"I am unaware of what your mother and brother discussed regarding her will, Kory, but I know that from the time we drafted the original trust to the very end when a few specific modifications were made, your mother went to great pains to be impartial and fair. Now, back to your question about commuting: the farther from a major city, the lower the property value, as a general rule. The property in Geneva is close enough to the city to make commuting a practical consideration. The Rhodes mansion was never intended to be close to anything, and the property would have been on Millionaire Row by the Hudson had that not been too conspicuous a choice. Your property in Manhattan is worth quite a bit in today's money, and it is the only centrally located property in the van Luden estate."

Kory said nothing.

"In addition, it was your mother's wish that you and your brother be taken care of, so neither of you need work, should either of you choose not to. The trust will be sending you a check for the monthly sum of five thousand dollars, adjusted for inflation, of course."

"And Damon gets the same?" Kory asked.

"He does," Mr. Chambers said.

"That, and access to two hundred and ten million, five hundred thousand dollars." Kory was shaking his head. "It makes perfect sense now."

Mr. Chambers looked at him patiently. "In addition, any education-related expenses you or your brother incur— tuition, tutors, books, transportation, et cetera—are completely covered by the trust, be it for a bachelor's degree or a PhD."

Kory had stopped listening. "I don't care about any of this. Damon can have it *all*. I'm not interested in hundreds of millions of dollars. It sounds like a big headache. I am fortunate that my education is paid for, and that my living expenses are covered. I don't want anyone to think I'm some ingrate; I love the town house, I love the fact that it's in the city, and that it belonged to my father. Furthermore, I'm in no way interested in, or envious of, Damon's financial acquisitions."

Mary nodded her approval. For the first time in a long while, Kory was speaking sensibly.

"I don't care about Damon's money," Kory continued. "I really don't. I care about Damon's *actions*—what he did to *get* that money. This meeting today clarified many things for me. It explains why Damon was in such a rush to marry."

Mary frowned.

"Now, wait a minute," John said, "that's not fair."

"Really," Kory said, "isn't it? Let's see. Out of the blue, Damon runs off with Dorothy and marries her, only a few weeks before I turn eighteen. There was an idiotic race to see who would marry first, a race I was never even aware of, and he beat me to it before I even had a legal right to marry. I wouldn't have cared about the trust money, but Damon didn't know that; he thinks everyone is as heartless and materialistic as he. So naturally, he assumed I, too, would try to be first to marry and get my hands on the trust, and therefore he made sure he married before I turned eighteen."

"With consent from a legal guardian, you could have married; you didn't have to wait for your eighteenth birthday." Mr. Chambers smiled. "Did you have someone in mind?"

"Yes, as a matter of fact, I would have married Dorothy."

John grimaced as if the mere suggestion of such a thing was ludicrous.

"I didn't see that there was any rush, and if Damon wanted control of the trust, I would have gladly handed it over to him. I would have married her, because I *loved* her, not for the money. Since, as you are aware, I had no idea about this marriage race, that in itself proves that money played no part in my interest in marrying Dorothy." Kory sighed. "Damon, however, got to her first. God knows what he did or said to persuade her. I suppose I should be grateful about how things turned out, because if she could be persuaded to marry him for his money, then she's not the Dorothy I was in love with and wanted as a wife in the first place."

John bolted off his chair and shook his index finger inches from Kory's face. "I have a good mind to smack you, young man. Don't *ever* talk about Dorothy like that."

Kory shrugged. "You want to hit me, feel free. You can't do anything to me Damon hasn't done, and you can't take anything from me Dorothy hasn't already taken."

Mary grabbed John by the arm. "Sit down."

He looked at her, bowed his head, and did as she demanded.

Mary looked at Mr. Chambers and at John in turn. "Can you imagine what would have happened had I told Kory back in January how Damon benefited from his marriage? It's been eight months now and he still holds on to misgivings regarding his brother."

"You can't let a boy intimidate you," John said. "Mr. Chambers is right, you should have told him. If he misbehaved, it would have been his own doing. I have to admit he's perfectly justified to feel angry about being left out." He looked at Mary. "You really should have told him, but that said, he has no right to bring Dorothy into this. No right at all."

Mary nodded. "I'm sorry, Kory. I really am. I thought it would be easier hearing it now, after having had some time to distance yourself from your feelings for her. I was wrong."

Kory sighed. "I'm sorry too. It's not your fault, Mary. I don't blame you or Mr. Saunders for any of this. It is entirely my mother's doing. She gave Damon all the reason to be what he is today."

Kory addressed John Saunders. "About Dorothy, I don't know what to think or what to say. If you and Mary are to blame for anything, it is for doubting me."

"Damon didn't kidnap her," John said.

"Perhaps not. At least not in the conventional sense," Kory agreed, "but I wasn't talking about that. I told both of you back in the hotel that Dorothy loved me and I loved her. It was easy for you to believe my feelings for her, but neither of you, for a moment, accepted that she could have loved me."

John said nothing.

"Honey . . ." Mary said.

"But I suppose that's ancient history now," Kory conceded. "I'm sorry, Mr. Saunders. I'm sorry, Mary. And Mr. Chambers, for whatever it's worth, my apologies to you as well—you really didn't have to hear all this; you were just doing your job. If there's nothing else, I have a match at five o' clock."

Kory interpreted Mr. Chambers's expression as consent, and without a farewell, Kory left the three of them alone in the Wall Street office.

"What the devil is he up to?" Schelowitz asked.

Bandini did not reply, instead he walked away from the table where the match was being played.

When they had stepped out of earshot, Bandini said to Schelowitz, "If you think this is my doing, you're wrong."

"You're the one who has been training him for the past six months," Schelowitz said, "and if this isn't your handiwork, I don't know what is."

Bandini coughed up a ball of dark mucus. "I would never teach the boy to delay a win. Hausmann there thinks Kory sees something he doesn't, something that's preventing Kory from going for the kill. So Hausmann is going to burn time on the clock until he finds out what it is. The psychological tactic Kory is using has some merit for defeating an opponent over a series of games in a match, but it serves no purpose in a sudden-death encounter like this, and he knows it."

"One game or a series, Kory would never have treated an opponent like that when I was teaching him." Grandmaster Schelowitz walked back to the table to watch. Sweat droplets were forming on Dave Hausmann's shiny forehead as he studied the board and shot nervous glances at the clock.

Schelowitz was not bothered that Kory had left him to study under Bandini, for he valued his friendship with the young man above all else, and Schelowitz still considered Kory to be a friend, even though Kory rarely confided in him these days.

It took a full hour for Hausmann to finally resign. He would have soon lost on time anyway, and decided to save what little face he had left by conceding his king.

When the tables had cleared, Bandini walked up to his pupil and said, "Next time, quit playing with the prey and make the damned kill."

"I'm impressed, you actually shook his hand," Schelowitz said, but there was more sadness than humor in his voice. He took a deep drag from his cigarette, reducing it to a butt, and crushed it in the ashtray.

"You don't approve? Didn't like the game?" Kory said, sour sarcasm directed at both his current and former mentors.

Schelowitz laughed. "They should put a photo of you next to the definition of overkill."

"I did what I had to do," Kory said in that new flat voice of his.

"Really?" Schelowitz said. "You could have finished that game an hour ago with Rook to Knight Six, gracefully and with tact, but instead you chose to take Hausmann apart the way a child tears off the wings of a bug. You gave him hope for a draw where there was none, then you let him make a fool of himself, allowing him to limp around the chessboard like some amateur."

Kory glanced at Bandini.

The Italian grandmaster said, "Don't look for support from me. I play to *win*."

"Perhaps you weren't in the same room," Kory said evenly, "but I *did* win."

Schelowitz was shaking his head. "You played to torment, not to win."

"Sometimes, winning just isn't good enough. You have to crush your opponent. Ground him to the earth and pulverize his spirit so he'll never have the nerve to challenge you again."

"Nice philosophy," Schelowitz said sadly. "Did Bandini teach you this?"

"No, my brother did."

PART III

VOID

September 1962

This was the day Dorothy had been thinking about for months. She dressed Jan and carried him downstairs. Girard and Jean-Luc were both watching television, but she knew they were aware of her. "Hello," Dorothy said.

"Good morning, Mrs. van Luden," Jean-Luc said. He was a Parisian who had moved to Gex for an easy commute. His Swiss partner, Girard, never had to relocate because he'd always lived in Geneva.

"It's time for his checkup," she announced.

This wasn't news to either of them.

Girard looked at his watch, shrugged, and turned off the television, which, had Damon been home, would never have been on to begin with.

Dorothy waited for them to bring the car to the front entrance, and she got in the backseat, holding her baby carefully in her arms. She wasn't allowed to drive. She wasn't even allowed to leave the grounds without permission and an escort.

Jean-Luc and Girard knew where to go; Dorothy had taken the baby to the pediatrician before. No doubt they'd called to confirm her appointment earlier, probably when she'd been dressing Jan.

It began to drizzle, shading the valley in a coat of depressing gray, but the weather did nothing to dispel her excitement. They drove along Lake Geneva, the Jet d'Eau, parked the car outside Vieille Ville, and escorted Dorothy and her child along the cobbled road that led to the old town.

Satisfied that Dorothy and the baby had entered the building, Jean-Luc and Girard found themselves a window table at a café with a clear view of the entrance to the doctor's office.

Dorothy took the elevator to the second floor. She looked at her watch. Ten minutes to go. She hoped she would not be seen waiting. A passerby would undoubtedly wonder what a young lady with a baby was doing sitting down at the top of a flight of stairs.

Jean-Luc, who took pleasure in poking fun at his colleague's country, loved telling the story of how he'd driven through a red light, and a lady, observing the violation from her window, had immediately called the police. They were like that here. Damon had found the ideal country in which to keep his wife.

When the time was up, Dorothy took the elevator to the basement, walked through a door to the common yard, and entered the back exit of the adjacent building. A flight of stairs led her to the street one block north of where Damon's men were watching from the café. The sun poked through the clouds, exposing her.

A maroon Morgan pulled up right on time, and Dorothy slipped into the passenger seat with her baby. Her friend kissed Dorothy on both cheeks.

Dorothy had met Anna Trouvé at the Clinique Etienne during Dorothy's very brief stay in January. Anna's husband had what she euphemistically referred to as a "little drinking problem," which was nothing of the kind. That had been his second protracted visit to the clinic, and, according to Anna, would most certainly not be his last.

The Morgan took a sharp left down a steep, narrow cobbled road. It was a one-way street going in the wrong direction, but they had to take the detour to avoid being seen, even if that meant valuable minutes lost.

Dorothy grasped her seat belt. "Slow down."

"We're past the bridge, they can't see us."

"Oh, I know," Dorothy said, "but the police can."

"We're not doing anything illegal . . . well, except for going a few kilometers faster than permitted—wait, are you saying Damon controls the Swiss police as well?"

"No, but it's much faster to drive the speed limit and not get stopped than the alternative."

Eight minutes went by and they passed the UN on their right.

"Those two mongrels will start to wonder about you now."

"Well, maybe not," Dorothy said. "The last time I had to wait for fifteen minutes just to get into the doctor's office. I don't see them pounding on his door just yet."

"Yes, but—"

"Please, just keep it at sixty."

At Geneva-Cointrin Airport, Dorothy had to restrain herself from running to the counter. She didn't have any luggage, of course, just the tickets and little Jan.

There were seven people in front of her.

"Don't worry," Anna said, giving her friend a gentle nudge. "You've made it."

"Not until Jan and I are flying away from this place, I haven't."

Anna's smile was doleful. "You poor thing. What you have gone through with this terrible man. But this is all behind you now; you must look forward to your future. You are young and beautiful. You have a lovely child and a wonderful new life to look forward to."

The line moved two steps and came to a stop again.

"Just don't forget your friend in Geneva."

"Don't be silly, I could never forget you. You've saved my life." Dorothy regarded her son. "And his."

Finally it was her turn.

Dorothy handed the lady her passport and the tickets. The lady smiled and opened the passport. Then the smile died.

The Swiss Air representative at the counter couldn't have been more than five years older than Dorothy. The lady looked at Dorothy and at the baby, frowned, and returned the passport along with the ticket. "Is this a joke?"

Dorothy felt a chill down her spine. She looked at her open passport and almost dropped it along with her tickets.

Her picture had been replaced with a photo of Shirley Temple with the word VOID written across her name in large red letters.

Dorothy's passport had been fine when she'd last checked it two days earlier. She hadn't thought to look again. She should have known Damon would notice the passport was missing. Nothing was beyond that man. If she'd waited until the last minute, this wouldn't have happened. On the other hand, if she had put it off until just before she left the house, she might not have had the opportunity to snatch her passport in time. "I'm sorry, I must have left my passport at home." Dorothy walked away, past Anna, out the sliding doors, to the taxi stand.

"Where are you going?"

Dorothy handed her friend the passport. "Obviously nowhere."

As if confirming his mother's statement, Jan gurgled up a saliva bubble.

Anna stopped for a moment to take a look at the document. "This is an atrocity." She ran after Dorothy. "You must go to the police, or to the American embassy; you cannot let this man do this to you."

"Anna, please, just take me back to Vieille Ville."

"No! You've come too far to give up now."

"I'm not giving up anything, Anna, I'm just . . . postponing things. I need time to think, to plan. Getting out of here won't be as easy as I thought."

They drove back to the old city in silence, and when they arrived, Anna made one final plea. Dorothy thanked her for her concern, but said it was best she leave for everyone's sake.

Dorothy made her way back into the doctor's building the same way she'd left an hour earlier. She walked out to the sidewalk, with Jan in her arms, but Jean-Luc and Girard were no longer at the café.

Her chest tightened with the onset of panic. This was the first time she was alone in Switzerland, and she felt strangely helpless. She'd wanted to escape for so long, and now it seemed there was nothing to prevent her from doing just that.

Except for her ruined passport. What if Anna was right? Maybe Dorothy could still make it to the embassy, and have the document renewed. She could say she lost the passport and then found it later on, and someone had defiled it. People stole passports all the time. Especially American passports. True enough, but what purpose would it serve a criminal to stick a picture of Shirley Temple on the photo page and write "VOID" on it, thereby rendering the document as useful as soiled toilet paper.

Dorothy remembered reading something somewhere about a passport being government property. Did it say so on the passport itself? She would be presenting the embassy with mutilated government property and a lousy, stupid excuse. Even if they believed her, they'd want to know why she hadn't reported her passport stolen the very moment it went missing.

Besides, there wasn't any time. Her flight would be long gone before she even made it to the embassy, and she hadn't bothered making another reservation when she'd had the chance.

And she certainly didn't have the money to buy a new ticket. This was plain old stupid. She could never get a passport fast enough, even if she did have the cash for another ticket.

Dorothy walked to a taxi stand and gave the Swiss cab driver the address to Damon's estate.

She was free now. Free as a convict released into the prison courtyard.

There really was no choice. She could try to hide, resolve the passport problem, get money from Anna, and buy herself another ticket, but Damon would find her way before she got through any of that. He had two bodyguards working for him; he knew that she'd taken the passport and placed it in her purse, that the passport was ruined, and that she couldn't cross any border without it. Once he found her, he'd make future attempts impossible, and her life much worse, if that was even conceivable.

She just had to go back now, act as if nothing had happened, and try again—as soon as she could figure out how to get a new passport.

Meanwhile, she'd pretend to be angry at Jean-Luc and Girard. The doctor had made her wait forever, and when, finally, her appointment had come to its belated conclusion, they were both gone. That might work. Unless, of course, they'd already checked on her . . . which they very well may have, assuming Damon had told them about the passport, which he most likely had. No sense losing all hope, just in case.

The taxi pulled into the villa driveway, and the driver asked for ten francs. She gave him fifteen and hurried to the front door. The sun had managed to make its way past the clouds.

Dorothy rushed into the house. Jan was tired and hungry, and he needed his milk.

Okay, one more time: she was worn out from the protracted visit and angry at the bodyguards for abandoning her in the middle of Geneva instead of doing their job and looking after her.

She headed for the kitchen.

Oh, and she'd be *really* mad right now, but they were lucky because she'd been near a taxi stand, otherwise—

Dorothy bumped into something hard and unyielding.

"Careful, now, you really ought to watch where you're going." Damon's emphasis on the last four words sent a chill down her spine.

She gave him a nervous, fleeting glance. "I'm sorry . . . I wasn't expecting you."

"Happy to see you, too," Damon said. "I had some time off." He reached for Jan.

Dorothy twisted away. "He's hungry. I have to feed him."

Damon did not make way for her. "Okay. Feed him and put him to bed. I'll be waiting in the drawing room. You and I need to have a talk."

Tired from the adventure, Jan had fallen asleep during his feeding, and he rested blissfully in his crib. There was no point in Dorothy delaying the inevitable any longer.

Downstairs, Damon was standing next to the fireplace. Jean-Luc and Girard were seated on a couch. There was no doubt what those two were doing there.

"Have a seat," Damon said, pointing at the easy chair by the sofa.

Without speaking a word, she did as she was told.

"I had hoped the birth of our son would have motivated you to take charge of your life and shake off your past vices. Apparently, the alcohol and drugs left you more damaged than I thought. I had wrongly assumed that our child would force you to focus on his needs, not yours."

Dorothy looked directly into Damon's eyes. She had plenty of responses, but none would help her at the moment. "First of all, you're not fooling anyone here—we all know I don't have any problems with drugs or alcohol. Secondly, I will not have you tell me I'm not focused on my baby's needs. You know better than anyone that he's all I've got, and he's the reason I'm here."

"If that's the case," Damon said, "explain why you tried to leave the country today." Dorothy was about to respond, but Damon wasn't done. "Jean-Luc told me all about your little escapade."

She sneered at the Frenchman, but from his reaction, she might as well have been blowing him a kiss.

Damon looked at her from under his lowered brow. "Well?"

The less said, the better. Dorothy had to convince them that she wouldn't try to escape again. Unless they believed that, there'd never be another chance at freedom. None of them were stupid, so reestablishing trust wouldn't happen overnight, but she knew much depended on how she handled herself at that very moment.

They'd obviously followed her—how she'd missed that, she didn't know—so denying the accusation was out.

Damon was waiting for her reply.

"I'm sorry," Dorothy said, hating herself for uttering those words.

"Well, I'm afraid that's not good enough." Damon reflected for a moment and then added, "I really don't understand you. This isn't a prison here, Dorothy."

She clenched her teeth. The bastard was *provoking* her. Maybe Damon had been hoping all along Dorothy would lose her mind if she stayed long enough; that way it would be easier for him to claim she was a drug addict. Tough break. If that's what he thought, he was sorely mistaken. Dorothy had a firm grip on reality, although the events of the past year were surreal enough to send the average Jane to the funny farm.

Dorothy was no average Jane.

Perhaps she needed him to believe she was?

"Okay, then why did you defile my passport?"

Damon furrowed his brow. "I have no idea what you're talking about."

"Of course you don't."

"Actually, Madame," Jean-Luc spoke up, "he does not know. We took the initiative to be sure you wouldn't do something foolish."

"What *initiative* are you referring to?" Damon demanded.

Dorothy crossed her arms, not impressed with his play at innocence. "Putting a picture of Shirley Temple in place of mine, writing 'VOID' across the photo page. That's illegal, by the way."

Girard answered, "Perhaps it was in poor taste," giving Jean-Luc an I-told-you-so look, "but when we saw the passport was not where it normally is, we had to do something. Otherwise your wife would be in an airplane, flying over the Atlantic as we speak."

Damon looked at Dorothy. "I'm protecting you from yourself. I'm protecting our son."

"Are you implying that I would harm my own baby?"

"No," Damon said, "at least not intentionally."

"I've heard enough," Dorothy said, but she made no effort to leave.

"Not quite," Damon said. "You've lived a sheltered, spoiled life. I used to believe you were more mature than your years, but unfortunately you have consistently proven me wrong. It is my duty as a husband to care for you, and as a father to look after the best interests of my son. The day I am thoroughly convinced you have completely rid yourself of your addictions and your psychological problems, I will gladly pay your airfare to any destination you please—be it to visit your father or go on vacation—but for now, you're going to get your life in order and deal with your problems here, at home."

THE GOOD DR. GELERNT

Dorothy woke up the next day, staring at the wall, trying to figure out where she was and what had happened. It took her a few long seconds to find her bearings, then she remembered: yesterday, after dinner, Damon had confined her to her room. As if she'd been some misbehaving little girl.

With any luck, he'd already be back at his base in Berlin.

She turned the knob and pushed, but the bedroom door wouldn't budge. Someone must have locked it as she slept the night before.

Dorothy pounded on the door with both fists. No response.

"Open the door!" She looked around the room. Only her bed had enough mass to break the door down. Were she strong enough to use the bed as a ramming rod, she wouldn't need it to smash the door down in the first place.

There were the bedroom and bathroom windows, but nothing to climb down, and although it was only the second floor, she doubted she could jump without breaking at least one of her legs, if not something else in the bargain.

Damon hadn't said how long she was to remain confined to her room. *For the time being* could mean anything. Especially coming from Damon.

She'd left Jan in his crib. Who was going to take care of him? Had Damon forgotten about the baby? He locks her up, keeps her from her child, and then says *she's* irresponsible?

Dorothy had to get out of the room, and she didn't care if she'd end up breaking all her bones trying. She threw herself at the door like the cops did in the movies, but ended up in a teeth-rattling crash that produced a lot of pain and no positive results. That door might as well have been made of cast iron. Even if she could lift the bed, she doubted strongly it would do any good against a door like that. She would need a battering ram and about five strong men to wield it.

She turned to the window, pulling up the sash as far as it would go, and leaned out, hanging on to the frame with both hands for support. A light puff of wind tickled her nose. Dorothy fought the impulse to sneeze and in the process, almost lost her balance.

The drop was much higher than she'd imagined. She would have to push off very hard indeed to make it onto the grass. If she fell short, she'd hit the marble pavement that surrounded the house and wouldn't get away with just a few broken bones. On the other hand, if she were to try pushing off, she could land any which way. After all, the head was the heaviest part of the body. How could she balance her fall all the way down? There were no opportunities to practice, either.

A metallic sound came from behind her, and Dorothy stood reflexively, bumping her spine on the edge of the raised window sash. The pain knocked her forward and out into the cold. She lost hold of the window with her left hand, but her right remained tightly clenched to the frame.

"Nom de Dieu!" The voice was right behind her. There was a clattering sound followed by a few running steps. Dorothy felt the firm grip of hands around her waist, lifting her backward into the warmth of her room.

It was Girard. "Are you okay?"

Dorothy nodded, relieved that he'd been there, although she was sure she wouldn't have fallen.

He was shaking his head in disbelief. *"Jean-Luc! Viens ici toute de suite. Cette femme est franchement malade! Elle s'est presque jetée par la fenêtre!"*

Dorothy couldn't understand what he was saying, but there was no denying the alarm in his voice. What was the big deal?

Her arm hurt; his grip was cutting off her circulation. "Hey," Dorothy said, trying to pull her arm free, "you can let go now."

Girard shook his head. "We are here for your safety."

"Ease off, big guy," Dorothy said, trying to sound calm. "I'll be fine, thank you very much."

Jean-Luc came running into the room with a toolkit. What in the world did the Frenchman intend to do with that in her room? She listened, but couldn't make sense of a single word they were saying. Whatever it was, the two men were in complete agreement.

Jean-Luc produced some very large nails. Dorothy could feel her pulse trying to fight its way past Girard's tight fingers. She had this image of Girard pulling her to the wall, while Jean-Luc rammed the nails through her palms. Instead of crucifying her, however, he pulled the window sash down and proceeded to nail it to the frame. He then went to the bathroom and nailed the window shut there as well.

"What's going on here?" Her fingers were starting to prickle now.

Neither of them answered. Girard had yanked her away from the window and was now watching Jean-Luc's handiwork. Then Dorothy realized what they'd been thinking. "Oh, come on! I wasn't trying to jump out!"

"It looked like that to me, Madame," Girard said. "You would have been dead if I didn't catch you."

Boy, was he proud of himself.

"Now, wait just a minute there, mister, I was holding on. I just lost my balance; I wasn't going to j—" Well, she *might* have jumped—to be with her son, of course, not to commit suicide—although the end result may have been the same. Either way, she was lying now, and she knew they could tell.

"Of course," Girard said, changing his tone. "We just want to make sure you are safe; this is our job. Okay?"

"No, buster, it's not at *all* okay. I was locked in my room. Did it ever occur to you that I was just trying to get out? I've got a baby, for God's sake. What did you expect me to do after you locked me in my room? Didn't you hear me pounding at the door this morning?"

"No, Madame, we did not."

"Some protection you're offering," Dorothy said.

"I am sorry, Madame," Girard said.

Jean-Luc had finished nailing the bathroom window, and Girard's grip slackened enough for Dorothy to snap her arm free. She lunged for the door, almost stepping on the lunch tray where Girard must have dropped it when he saw her hanging out the window.

Girard grabbed her from behind. "Wait!"

Dorothy tried to shake free. "Do you mind? I want to see my son, let *go*."

Instead, Girard pulled her away from the door, blocking it with the bulk of his body. "I'm afraid not, Madame. I have orders from the Monsieur."

"Are you all totally bonkers? *Orders*? Am I Jan's mother, *yes* or *no*?"

"Yes, but—"

"No buts about it, I'm his mother, and I'm going to see him, and if you know what's good for you, you'll get out of my way."

Girard did not move, and seizing the opportunity, Dorothy took several quick steps backward. Jean-Luc maneuvered behind and grabbed for her, but she lunged forward just in time, leaving Jean-Luc hugging air. Dorothy charged like a Rhodes High quarterback. She rammed Girard in the stomach with her head but was unable to push him back far enough to break past him and out of the room. He lifted her in the air, upside down, in a bear hug. Dorothy kicked as hard as she could, but her legs posed a threat only to the chandelier. Girard carried her over to her bed and, attempting to let her down gently, he instead ended up dropping her on her head. Jean-Luc held her down while Girard moved the plates back to the center of the tray, and brought it over to her desk.

"Your lunch, Madame," Girard said, nodding at his colleague. Jean-Luc let go and backed out of the door along with Girard. Dorothy heard the key turn.

"I demand to see my son!" Dorothy shouted, but they were already walking away.

There was no escaping now. Even if she managed to get out, Dorothy knew they would hear her, and just lock her right back in her room. She wouldn't get an inch closer to Jan.

Just then she heard him crying. He was there, near her, probably still in his room, in his crib, or perhaps his playpen.

Dorothy got out of her bed and started pounding on the door. "He's hungry! Can't you hear? He's hungry—he needs to be fed! Let me out!"

The crying stopped. Were they feeding him, or did they muffle the poor baby's cries with a pillow?

Surely they wouldn't do such a thing. Girard and Jean-Luc were nothing more than thugs for hire, but they didn't seem capable of that kind of cruelty.

At around sunset, there was a knock on the door, and the sound of a key turning.

It was Girard. "Dinner, Madame."

"Please, please don't go."

Girard seemed surprised by the request.

"Where is my son?"

The question relieved Girard, as if he were expecting her to say something else. "He is sleeping, Madame, in his room."

"Please, I beg you, let me see my son."

"I understand how you feel, Madame, believe me, but I cannot oblige. The Monsieur was very clear. You are not to leave your room."

"Then bring him *here*."

"I'm afraid I cannot do that either, Madame."

"He needs his mother, he needs to be fed. Can't you *understand?*"

"But of *course*, Madame. You must not worry. We have someone taking care of his needs."

"Did you hear me? He needs his *mother.*"

"Yes, Madame," Girard said, and closing the door he added, *"bon appétit."*

"Is Damon here?"

Yet again Girard showed surprise at her question. "Why no, Madame, he had to go to Berlin. He will come back soon."

Girard locked the door behind him and didn't return until the next morning.

Dorothy hadn't slept much that night. She'd dozed against the door, listening for Jan's cries. She wanted to believe that his every need was being taken care of just as Girard had claimed.

She needed to believe that in order to go on. He cried three times that night, and that was more or less what he usually did anyway. During the day, he only cried once.

Obviously, he was being fed on time.

Dorothy had a long sleep after lunch, and was up most of the second night as well.

On the third day, she was exhausted, but not sleepy. Her back was sore from lying on the bed. The chair at her vanity table was for putting on makeup, not sitting on for extended periods. She felt like she was back at the clinic. This was a make-shift hospital ward without nurses, visitors, television, books, or magazines.

This was solitary confinement.

A place they put people so they could think about their crimes. But even hardened convicts knew the duration of their sentences.

The thought of escaping out the window played over and over in her mind like a catchy tune. Deriving some practical benefit from the story of Rapunzel, she could tie one bed sheet to another and finally to the bedpost. Then, climbing down her homemade rope, she'd push off the wall of the house, distancing herself from the lethal marble below, and then let go at just the right time. She'd be low enough not to hurt herself from the jump and she'd definitely make the grass that way.

If the knots on the bed sheets held.

If she could pry away the boards, and *if* she could somehow break the window without waking anyone. Well, she could use the sheets or a blanket for that, but then the falling glass would still make a frightful noise. And there was that mystery lady who knew enough about babies to keep Jan from crying all night and day. She'd probably report any suspicious sounds the second she heard them.

It was a lousy plan. But better than nothing. She'd save it as a last resort, for when she really did start going nuts.

Because even if everything worked like a charm and she did find Jan, and somehow managed to sneak out with him, what would she do from there? She didn't have a centime on her. She could take the baby to the American embassy. And do what? Show them the passport with the Shirley Temple photo?

That would go over well. It was a bad idea, one she'd thought over and rejected time and time again.

That evening, Dorothy managed to sleep a full three hours.

On the morning of the sixth day, Girard came in with Jean-Luc. She heard the warning knock, and the ever-familiar sound of the door unlocking. She was in her nightie, in the process of brushing her teeth, when they came in.

She quickly rinsed her mouth in time to tell them what she always did: "I don't want to eat. I want to get out of here. I want to see my son!"

"You will," Girard said.

"I—" Dorothy stopped herself. "I will? When?"

"Later, Madame. Monsieur has returned, and is waiting for you to join him for breakfast. Afterwards, you may see your son." They closed the door, and for the first time in almost a week, they left it unlocked. Dorothy changed as quickly as she could.

Outside the room, Girard took her by the arm as if she didn't know where the dining room was.

They ushered her to the dining-room door and waited outside.

"Sit down; your food will get cold." Damon dressed as he always did for meals—as though he were at some five-star restaurant.

Dorothy had to be careful. If she upset him again, he'd think nothing of locking her back in her room for another long sentence. She had just regained her freedom, or a part of it at least, and she didn't want to risk not seeing Jan.

She stared at her plate. A pair of sunny-side-ups stared back at her with shiny orange irises. She poked at one and it bled over the egg white.

Damon still didn't say a word. She could hear her own breathing, and a barely audible murmur from behind the kitchen door. She couldn't make out what was being said. Not that it made any difference; it was probably in French anyway.

"From now on there will be no need for you to leave the grounds."

Dorothy's fork fell into the egg, some of the yolk splattered, falling mercifully within the confines of her plate.

"A pediatrician will be coming for scheduled visits," Damon continued, "and will be available at all times should the boy need anything. Girard and Jean-Luc are assigned to the house full-time now. Girard will be staying at the end of the hall. Jean-Luc will be in the downstairs guest room. I have also found a full-time nanny and she will be doing everything from cleaning to cooking. She has references from prominent families in Geneva, and, from what I'm told, she's a talented chef and has plenty of experience with children."

"Where is my son?"

"*Our* son is with Madame Fahrny, the nanny I was just telling you about."

"I need to see him."

"He is in his room, Dorothy, sleeping," Damon said in a lowered voice.

"May I *please* see him?"

"Of course, go right ahead." He glanced at his watch. "Be in the drawing room, appropriately dressed, in an hour. Dr. Gelernt will be coming for a visit."

"I don't need . . ." Dorothy started to say, but rushed out of the kitchen before she could finish her own sentence.

Jan was sleeping, just as Damon had said. There was no sign of the mystery lady, Mme. Fahrny. Dorothy stared at her little baby as he breathed lightly through his mouth, his tiny bare chest slowly rising and falling. She kissed her son's tummy, leaving a tearstain on his light-blue gown.

Downstairs, Damon was talking to Dr. Gelernt. About her, no doubt. Dorothy wondered if psychiatrists in Europe were held to the same rules of confidentiality as their American counterparts.

Damon cranked his head in her direction to warn the doctor Dorothy was approaching listening range.

The psychiatrist stood stiffly, offering his hand and a tired smile.

"I'll leave you to it," Damon said, and as he left, he gave Dorothy one of those detestable pity stares. She imagined he would have done very well as an actor.

"Mrs. van Luden," Dr. Gelernt said, pointing to the couch where her husband had been seated just moments before. The doctor sat in the leather chair, as he always did.

Dr. Gelernt was Swiss-German, but he spoke in impeccable English with little trace of an accent. How was it a man of his educational background and upbringing could be such an imbecile?

The psychiatrist didn't merit all the blame; Damon's version of reality always made sense. Damon had the money to make it make sense.

Dr. Gelernt allowed his patients to speak first, and normally they jumped at the opportunity to start their monologues. The young van Luden lady was an exception.

She wore a white virginal dress showing an inappropriate amount of cleavage. On occasion or two, his eyes fell from her face to the sight of those luscious breasts.

Dorothy van Luden was a very special case indeed. He had retrieved her file from her psychologist in New York. And while the fellow probably had a solid reputation, Dr. Gelernt had little respect for psychologists in general. They weren't doctors, and believed that psychotherapy should be left to words, not medicine.

The psychologist's diagnoses had lacked scientific methodology and a concise conclusion. It was as though he'd been afraid to acknowledge her true condition. As if it were too serious a matter for him to handle. Either that, or her severe symptoms did not manifest themselves until after she married. Not impossible, of course, but still, the American psychologist probably missed warning signs that had led to her eventual crisis.

There was, however, a note in her file, stating that should Ms. Saunders continue to drink heavily and take narcotics, serious consideration should be given to sending her to a clinic.

This was the psychologist's only positive contribution to the girl's mental health. Dorothy, confronted with the reality of her condition, had agreed to admit herself to a clinic right after she was married.

Unfortunately, she'd checked out before they'd had a chance to really help her. Mr. van Luden had hired Dr. Gelernt shortly after her return, insisting on house calls only. That worked out fine, since the man was very wealthy, even by Swiss standards, and willing to pay Dr. Gelernt almost three times the standard price for his troubles.

The girl was looking at him, straight in the eyes, in a manner that wasn't the least flirtatious. She was clearly repressing anger. The girl was in denial, refusing to discuss any of her past behavior.

"So how are we feeling?" he said.

"I don't know how *we* are feeling."

"Well, how are *you* feeling?"

"Wonderful, couldn't be better."

"Now, Dorothy, I've said this before—you're going to have to make an effort here so that I can help you."

"I don't want or need your help."

Dr. Gelernt's eyes once again fell down on the creamy skin of her cleavage. She probably wore that dress on purpose, hoping his instincts would undermine his professionalism. "What we want and what we need are often not the same, and while you may not feel you want therapy, I can assure you that at this particular juncture in your life, you very much need it."

"Gee, thanks."

"There's nothing wrong with therapy, Dorothy, as I've told you many times. Think of it as a helping hand."

Dorothy gave him a sour look, but Dr. Gelernt pressed on. "So, tell me about this recent incident."

"What is there to tell? I went to the airport and I tried to leave, but it turns out that my passport had been defiled, so I'm trapped here in this prison, with a shrink who thinks I'm a basket case."

Dr. Gelernt ignored her comment. "I'm more interested in what feelings led you to run away."

"Oh, I don't know . . . the feeling any inmate has: that he could regain some semblance of a life if only he could break away and escape."

"Yes, but there's no escaping. You see that, don't you?"

The girl did not respond, but Dr. Gelernt could see she was surprised, and perhaps even a bit frightened. He let himself relish the moment a while longer and said, "You cannot run from your problems; they follow you wherever you go."

Glowering, Dorothy said, "That's for sure. Jean-Luc and Girard would follow me to hell and back for what Damon must be paying them."

"They're trying to protect you," Dr. Gelernt said, "not cause you further distress. They have your best interest in mind, as does your husband."

Dorothy flinched, but Dr. Gelernt wasn't looking at her. "You're a very lucky young lady—you are surrounded by people who love you."

"Uh-huh."

"Aside from running away, I'm told you are doing better," he said, taking a moment to look at his notes. "No drugs or alcohol since you've been in Switzerland."

"Really," Dorothy said. "That's interesting."

"What makes you say that?"

"I would have expected they'd lie to you about everything. But this time, they've fed you a half-truth."

"Half-truth?"

"Yes. I've told you before, I *never* took any damned drugs, not here in Geneva, not in the States, not in this lifetime."

As if she'd said just the opposite, Dr. Gelernt asked, "So, are you feeling any cravings? Do you feel the need? This cold-turkey approach to recovery can often prove quite taxing on a patient."

Dorothy did not respond.

"It's been ten months." He smiled. "So I should think the worst is over." This wasn't the time to bring up the incident that had brought him to this impromptu meeting in the first place. If he tried a direct approach, she would slip back into denial, and it would take even longer to draw her out. Even a layman could read her body language. The girl was highly agitated, evasive, and defensive. He would have to draw her out slowly, using the subtle hints his patients invariably drop during the course of therapy.

She didn't appear ready to discuss her recent attempted suicide, not in this session at least. There hadn't been sufficient time for her to distance herself from the event.

Dorothy didn't justify the psychiatrist's question with an answer. They just sat there, and he waited, pretending to be patient. Did this imbecile actually think she wouldn't notice him ogling her? She hadn't seen Dr. Gelernt since Jan was born, but after this recent escape attempt she knew Damon would be inviting him over for frequent visits. She could always say the guy was coming on to her. Maybe Damon would arrange for Dr. Gelernt to have an accident, or possibly something less subtle. Unfortunately, there was no chance Damon would believe her. Not anymore.

"And you are taking your medication?"

"Yes," Dorothy lied. How could a man so stupid become a psychiatrist? It occurred to her that Damon chose an idiot on purpose, because only a moron like Dr. Gelernt would so readily believe every one of Damon's lies.

"So then what feelings made you want to run away?"

"I told you. Like most normal, healthy women, I don't like being held captive."

"Yes, so you've said. You feel like you are a prisoner."

"Uh-huh," Dorothy said, wondering what med school he'd graduated from.

"Did you feel this way when you were living with your father?"

"No, I wasn't a prisoner then. Let me ask *you* something: what exactly do you think Jean-Luc and Girard do here?"

"They're here to care for you when your husband is gone."

"And to make sure I don't escape. They *mutilated* my passport. What do they have to do for you to get the picture? Handcuff me to this chair?"

"You feel uncomfortable with our discussions? You feel forced to see me?"

"I don't *feel* forced, I *am* forced. But it's not convenient for you to acknowledge that, now is it? If you open your eyes and admit what's really going on, you'll miss out on your fees."

Dr. Gelernt cracked a smile. "And you think that this is the only reason I am here?"

"I would say it is a sizable reason, yes," she affirmed, maintaining eye contact. That, and an opportunity to look down her shirt.

"I am here to help you, Dorothy. I chose this profession to help people. If I wanted to be rich, I would have become a plastic surgeon." He laughed, but it sounded like a bad cough. "Let's talk about your marriage. Are you happy? Any sexual problems? Couples often have adjustment issues following a pregnancy."

Now, there was a loaded question. Dorothy had lied to Dr. Gelernt from the first time she'd met him. There'd been no choice. She would have to lie again now, even though it sickened her to do so. "No, no problems."

Dr. Gelernt looked puzzled. "That's not what I'm hearing."

"Look, Doctor, I really don't know what you've been hearing. You asked me a question; I answered it, isn't that enough?"

"All I want is a truthful response, Mrs. van Luden. If you continue to hide problems from me, I won't be able to help you effectively." He looked at her, but Dorothy was looking out the window, to the courtyard beyond. "Mr. van Luden says that you haven't had marital relations since your wedding night."

Dorothy shrugged. "Like I said, no problems."

Dr. Gelernt looked at his notes. "When he returned from his military training in the United States, you both knew you were pregnant." He looked up for acknowledgment, but Dorothy offered none. "While sexual relations during early pregnancy may be ill advised, after the third month there would have been no danger to the fetus."

Dorothy bit her lip.

"Some women feel their weight gain makes them unwanted."

"I wasn't one of those women, okay? I hardly showed until the sixth month." He seemed surprised when Dorothy broke the silence. "Doctor, would you agree that human contact—socializing, having friends is a good thing?"

"Why yes," Dr. Gelernt said, "of course."

"Then may I see Anna again?"

"Your friend Anna?" Dr. Gelernt asked. "You're not seeing her? Wasn't she the young lady who drove you to the airport?"

"Yes."

Dr. Gelernt shifted in his seat.

"You could make a recommendation, could you not? As a psychiatrist?"

"Well, yes, I could, but I'm not sure that is the optimal course of action at this time. Again, Mrs. van Luden, I must reiterate: your husband wants to do what's best for you. It might not be wise, at least for now . . ."

"Because she helped me escape?"

"Well, no. No, I wouldn't say that, but I would say she's probably unaware of the gravity of your present situation, and I think that a little alone time at home would be advised until you are feeling better."

"I told you I'm feeling fine," Dorothy snapped.

"That is very good. I would like you to have this prescription filled without delay. Take one pill in the morning, in addition to the pill you are currently taking at night. I have increased the dosage slightly. Remember to take these on a full stomach. You might experience some drowsiness; that would be perfectly normal. I'll be back in a week to check on your progress. In the meantime, should you find yourself needing anything, anything at all, call me at the office or at home. You have the numbers?"

Dorothy nodded and Dr. Gelernt answered with a quick nod and an uneasy smile. Damon had arrived, and it was now obvious the doctor wanted to talk to his boss in private.

She thought of going upstairs to see Jan, but she didn't make a move to leave. Instead she looked at Damon.

"Doctor?" Damon said.

Dr. Gelernt regarded Dorothy, indicating as clearly as he could that her presence was not appropriate.

Damon ignored the psychiatrist's not-so-subtle hint. "I think that she should hear what you have to say."

Dr. Gelernt did not speak for a while. "Very well." He sighed. "Her condition has worsened following childbirth. Physiologically, she appears to be in excellent condition, and although it has been a long time since she has been drinking or taking narcotics, I am concerned that on a neurological level, the waters are still quite turbulent. I believe this, along with the birth of her child, has triggered a crisis, Mr. van Luden, one which must not be taken lightly." He was looking straight at Damon during all this, as if Dorothy had left them to speak alone after all. "I feel she needs to be placed in a clinic. I work out of one in Lausanne. It is a first-class facility, and I can assure you she will receive the best of care."

Dorothy stepped back, almost losing her balance. "*No.* Please. I don't want to go back to a clinic. I don't care how nice it is, don't put me back in there, I beg you."

Dr. Gelernt kept his gaze locked on Damon, as if he could hypnotize him into consenting.

Damon creased his brow. "I find your reaction excessive given the situation and your recent transgressions."

He thought for a while longer, Dorothy and Dr. Gelernt watching like guard dogs behind a fence. "I have your word you'll be good? No alcohol, no drugs, no attempts to hurt yourself or others?"

"When did I do *any* of those things?"

"My dear Dorothy, Jean-Luc told me all about your attempt to hurl yourself from the window."

Dr. Gelernt was not at all surprised, so they must have already told him their version of the story. "That's *not* what happened," Dorothy said. "I was just trying to get away."

Damon shook his head. "I can't have you endangering yourself in this house."

"I promise, I won't," Dorothy said, knowing this simple answer would yield better results than trying to explain what her real intentions had been.

"And you'll be good to Madame Fahrny and help her care for our son?"

Dorothy clenched her teeth. Help her? Some stranger was going to care for Jan, and Dorothy was just supposed to *help*? She had to let that slide; she was in no position to argue, not considering the alternative. "I will, I promise. I love Jan. He's my life, I'd do anything for him."

Dr. Gelernt seemed to be studying Dorothy with a perplexed look, most likely due to her uncharacteristic display of emotion.

"Good," Damon said, "then since you've committed to behaving responsibly, I'll let you stay at home, where you belong, with our son." Damon turned to Dr. Gelernt. "I don't believe it appropriate to separate mother and child." He addressed his wife: "This is on the condition that I get good reports from Jean-Luc, Girard, and Madame Fahrny. One bad comment from any of them, and you're off to the clinic."

Dorothy nodded.

"I don't want you going anywhere off these grounds unless someone knows about it. There will be no more visits with Anna. In fact, until the good doctor says so, I want you confined to the gates of this house. Do we understand one another?"

A tear slipped off her cheek. "Yes, I promise."

Damon nodded and turned to Dr. Gelernt. "We'll continue the therapy from here, then, unless I have good reason to believe it's too risky. Jean-Luc and Girard will take good care of her, and Madame Fahrny came highly recommended."

"Very well," Dr. Gelernt said, clipping his words. "I have given Mrs. van Luden a prescription. It is important that she has it filled as soon as possible, preferably in time for this evening's dose." The psychiatrist left after a good-bye and a curt bow.

FRANÇOISE

Opening her bedroom door, Dorothy said to Girard, "Are you planning on getting in the shower with me as well?"

Girard removed a copy of *Le Monde* from a chair that had recently been placed outside Dorothy's room and took a seat, making little noise as he carefully unfolded the newspaper. Damon had everyone around the house well trained.

The hot shower was relieving, but she could feel the asphyxiating fatigue from the past few days clamping down on her. She dabbed herself dry and fell on her bed with just her robe on. Outside her door, Girard and Jean-Luc were having a conversation in a soft, hypnotic mumble.

She sat on her bed, sandwiching the pillow between her back and the headboard. She needed a few minutes. . . .

Just moments earlier, she'd been downstairs, making promises, begging for Damon's mercy. This was a nightmare from which there was no waking up.

This was her life now. If only she could accept that fact, she could make it through the day. The more she struggled, the tighter the noose became. Dorothy slid back, resting her head on the pillow. She stared at the white ceiling with the bulging chandelier, and soon it was gone, taking the shape of a snow-covered mountain. She fell into a dreamless sleep on the bedcovers.

She was startled awake to the sound of knocking at the door.

"Yes?"

"*Madame, désirez-vous quelque chose de particulier pour votre déjeuner? Le monsieur ne rentrera pas pour vous rejoindre puisqu'il est déjà parti.*" It was a woman's voice but barely discernable as such.

"Sorry, I don't really know more than a few words of French," Dorothy said. "Come in, I don't think the door is locked."

The door opened, revealing a wide-shouldered woman who looked like she could tackle both Girard and Jean-Luc without so much as breaking a sweat. She wore a black dress, flat nurse's shoes—to keep the noise down, no doubt —and a white apron, which looked absurd on her manly frame.

"You don't speak French? We will have to fix that. You are in Genève, Madame, you must learn."

"Well, I suppose you're right."

"There is no *suppose* about it. I am older than you, Madame, and so I may say, also, that it is not right for you to be sleeping at this hour."

The nanny *was* old—fortysomething—but Dorothy didn't want her advice, she already had her hands full with Girard and Jean-Luc, she didn't need a third person policing her about. "You're so right. I should go downtown and see the Jet d'Eau, or go to a café, or perhaps a museum."

The maid shut the bedroom door firmly. "You will go no such place in your condition."

Dorothy wondered if this woman had perhaps been in charge of some medieval European orphanage before taking on a job at the van Luden residence.

"You will learn how to run a household and the duties of a mother and a wife," she said.

"Really, now? Just *who* do you think you are?" Dorothy said, raising her voice.

"For your information, my name is Madame Fahrny. *Je m'appelle Madame Fahrny.*"

"Well, then, Madame *Fahrny*, what gives you the right to say I don't know how to be a mother?"

Mme. Fahrny shrugged. "It is simple—you sleep during the day. Your little baby was crying for food, but you did not go to feed him. I fed him—again."

"I don't know who you are, and frankly I don't care. I've been locked in this room for days and all I wanted was to see my son. I wasn't permitted to see him until yesterday. Now you're telling me I'm not a good mother?"

"You are a young woman," Mme. Fahrny said, almost as if such a thing were regrettable. "You have not met the cruelties of life. I have seen this before many times. The young beauty marries the rich man. The difference is that your husband is more aware than most of the dangers wealth can have on the soul. He cares about you."

Dorothy said nothing.

"Do you know what happens to young wealthy women?"

Again, Dorothy didn't reply. Who cares what happened to young wealthy women? Right at the moment she was wondering if bringing down the chair on Madam Farty's head would slow her down enough for Dorothy to break out of the room.

"I will tell you. They become bored. And boredom leads to very dangerous and evil acts, Madame. Shameful acts, like taking drugs, drinking, and thinking of suicide."

"I'll bring out my cross and the garlic," Dorothy said. "Now get out of my way, I wish to see my son."

Mme. Fahrny moved aside. Dorothy had expected some resistance, at least some words of protest. Instead, the androgynous lady just watched as if Dorothy were a passing fish in an aquarium.

Jan was in his crib, fully awake, and smelling of talcum powder. The room itself was immaculately clean. Dorothy went to her son, smothering the baby with kisses, aware that Mme. Fahrny was standing at the door, watching. Dorothy didn't care.

Jan was happy. He'd been well cared for. Dorothy sighed, expelling what little was left of her anger. With her child cradled tightly to her bosom, she turned to Mme. Fahrny and said, "Thank you."

The big woman smiled and nodded.

"You have children of your own?" Dorothy said, already certain of the answer.

"Yes, Madame, I have two. My youngest, Bertrand, is about your age."

"You don't look that old," Dorothy said, feeling silly for having blurted that out.

Mme. Fahrny laughed. "I'm not that old. I was a foolish girl once—just like you—that is all. *C'est tout.*" And before Dorothy could interject with another question, Mme. Fahrny added, "So now, back to my first question: would you like anything special for lunch?"

"No, thank you, Madame Fahrny, I am not hungry."

The big Swiss woman nodded. "Then come with me to the kitchen. We will make lunch together. I will teach you some special recipes of the canton, and when we are done, I assure you, you will have a great appetite."

Dorothy followed Mme. Fahrny out of the room, and past Girard, who got up from his chair to follow them. She said something to him in French, he shook his head, and she replied with a disapproving huff. Girard tailed behind, giving them more distance this time.

Jan slept in his carry cot while Dorothy and Mme. Fahrny prepared lunch.

"*Allons, allons,* keep stirring!"

"*Oui, oui, Madame Fahrny,*" Dorothy said, remembering how they used to chant "wee-wee" at the French teacher back in Boston, years before she'd ever heard of Rhodes, New York.

Mme. Fahrny laughed.

"I took French back in school, but I've forgotten most of it," Dorothy explained, grateful for the opportunity to talk to a woman after all these days.

"But your husband? His French is very good."

"Well, I doubt he picked it up at Rhodes High." Dorothy thought for a moment. "Maybe he studied French at West Point."

The butter had melted in the frying pan, and Mme. Fahrny nodded. Dorothy poured the batter in while keeping her distance from the spattering goo.

"You will be saying more than '*Oui, oui, Madame Fahrny*' soon, Madame."

"I'm sure I will, and long before I've learnt how to cook, by the looks of my progress here. And you can drop the 'Madame'—I don't run a brothel—my name is Dorothy."

The maid smiled. "*Bon*, Dorothy it is. We will keep 'Madame' for when the Monsieur is here. And my name is Françoise. *Je m'appelle Françoise.*"

"*Bonjour, Françoise.*"

As Dorothy had lunch, with Jan sleeping in a pram beside her, she asked Françoise what she'd said to Girard.

"I told him to leave us women to our business. He would not listen. He is a pig, that one. A typical man."

Dorothy and Françoise giggled, knowing the bodyguards were listening right outside the kitchen door.

BLINDSIDED

March 1967
Four Years and Six Months Later

Twenty-one the last time, it had taken around fifteen minutes.
This time he'd been in there, going over the makeshift report cards, for a good thirty.

Damon had announced his first review back in February of the previous year, immediately following his return from a twelve-month tour in Vietnam.

He'd stayed during his entire leave that March, making it his longest stretch at home ever. Thirty-one consecutive days: an unrelenting nightmare. All of them looking over their shoulders: the tutors, Françoise, even Jean-Luc and Girard. And Jan had to do without piano lessons the entire time. In April, Damon was ordered back to the States for nine months of advanced training. God bless the Army. Too bad they couldn't detain him longer.

This second review was taking much longer than the one in March. Jan had been three and a half back then, and with just over six months of tutoring, there wasn't much for Damon to audit.

This time Damon was expecting a lot, as if ten years had gone by and not just one. As before, Dorothy was not directly involved. She didn't have to write a report or suffer through an interview. She was just the mother. So she sat there, waiting along with her son and his tutors. In Damon's book, a mother's purpose was to rear her child—things like teaching him to tie his shoes, and how to handle a fork at the dinner table. This was her primary function.

Françoise had a different view. She believed men wanted women for sex above all else. According to her, all men were animals. Damon was a beast, no question, but Dorothy knew sex was not on the top of his priority list. Power, control, order; those things resonated far more deeply in his psyche, and his career with the Army gave him plenty of that. In fact, after the first year, he'd stopped coming to her room altogether.

For the first twelve months of their marriage, he'd appear in their bedchambers, dressed only in his robe, not speaking a word—his way of saying he wanted to copulate. Dorothy turned him down every time, but he would still come back the next night, like an actor in a tired play, hoping the script would miraculously change. Until one evening he did not bother with the pathetic ritual, finally conceding to the futility of his advances.

It wouldn't have surprised Dorothy had Damon found another woman for his needs. After all, the wedding night couldn't have been enough to satiate him. Even if lust were not the main focus of that deranged brain of his, and even if Françoise's evaluation of men was a bit extreme, once simply wasn't enough for any man. And yet, oddly enough, he'd never again forced himself on her, not since that night in Saint Croix.

Jan tugged at Dorothy's skirt from under the table; he was smiling, and not the least bit nervous. Dorothy kissed her son on the forehead.

Mr. Curtis, his math tutor, observed the exchange from the corner of his eye.

Before leaving for Vietnam the year before, Damon had interviewed several tutors, selecting three out of ten. They were to start instruction six months later, immediately following Jan's third birthday.

Dorothy had objected, mostly because Damon expected her to, and partly because she thought that math, science, English, French, and history were excessive for Jan, considering that at three, most kids were too young to handle kindergarten.

Damon had said he didn't want Jan waiting a year until his return—the boy would simply have to start while Damon was gone. Making it seem as if Dorothy had objected because

Damon wouldn't be present, not because the whole idea of hiring tutors for a child Jan's age was completely idiotic.

Damon had said that he'd try to get the Army to reassign him to Berlin after serving in Vietnam, but if they granted his request—which they ended up doing—it would be his second tour in Germany, and unquestionably his last. That meant he'd be in Berlin through Jan's sixth birthday, in the summer of '68. After that, the Army could send him anywhere.

Regardless of what happened, Damon decreed that Jan would be tutored for three years, so that by the time he was six, he'd be prepared for one of the best boarding schools in the world. Damon hadn't mentioned any specific details about the school, not even its name or where it was located.

On the matter of a boarding school, Dorothy had protested more, making sure that her reasoning was sound and her tone calm. If she hadn't put up a fight, Damon would have known something was wrong. He might have thought she'd been considering a second escape.

His suspicions would have been well founded.

She was going to get out of this hellhole, but this time she'd do it right. No matter how long it took.

Earlier on, when Jan was just a toddler, escaping had been unrealistic. Now, at four and a half, he was a well-behaved gentleman. Quiet, even when he played piano. And he trusted his mother with unquestioning conviction. Jan was no longer a problem; getting out of there with those two bodyguards constantly underfoot was.

Initially, she'd thought Damon's tour in Vietnam was a gift from God—a clear message that this was the time she'd been waiting for all these years. Unfortunately, instead of slacking off with their boss gone, Jean-Luc and Girard had actually tightened up the rules. They shadowed her everywhere; when they watched television, they kept the volume down so they could hear what was going on around them; every activity in the house, every single lesson, was on a strict to-the-minute schedule in true Swiss tradition.

They acted as if Damon was going to suddenly appear from the Far East for a surprise inspection. The only thing they permitted, which would have otherwise been forbidden had

Damon been home, was Jan's piano playing. And even that was timed.

Poor Dad. How he yearned to see Jan. He called every Sunday, speaking with that resigned, uncharacteristic sadness in his voice—the tone people use with terminal patients. He always asked when he'd see his grandson. Each time, Dorothy replied, "Soon, Dad, soon." If only he could know how much she wanted that to be true.

Of course, there'd always been the distant hope that Damon would get himself killed in the Asian jungle. It was true what they say about only the good dying young. Damon was back, very much alive.

After that nightmarish March, while he was in the States for training, Dorothy had again hoped something would happen to him. She'd heard of people managing to get themselves killed on friendly soil. But seeing that Damon had survived Vietnam, chances were slim to none that he'd come back to Geneva with more than a scratch and a bruise. During Damon's second prolonged absence, Jean-Luc and Girard had left no opportunities whatsoever for escape. They'd probably expected she'd try something while their boss was gone, and so they'd been doubly careful.

If Dorothy were to succeed this time, she'd have to do it when they least expected: while Damon was in Berlin. But she'd need help, and last Dorothy had heard, Anna was back in the States, thousands of miles away and completely out of touch. Dorothy needed someone from the inside. Someone she could trust.

Jan looked at his mother. She was thinking something, but he didn't ask her what. A good boy doesn't speak unless spoken to. That's what Mr. Talbaum said. Not because Jan had asked too many dinosaur questions—Mr. Talbaum meant don't talk when adults were around. Except Mommy. Jan could always talk to her.

She looked worried.

Mommy would be happy soon. Jan had an idea how to make her happy. He'd had this idea for a long, long time. She always talked about the chess man in Rhodes. The chess man was Damon's brother. The man who could play blindfolded.

Mommy taught Jan chess. The horse moved like an "L." The castle went straight. Jan knew most of the moves.

Mommy said he was very good for a boy his age. He really liked that. But he wanted to play blindfold chess, because that would make Mommy happy. That's when he had the idea.

He wouldn't ask *her.* She could teach him, because she was really good at chess—even if she said she wasn't—but Jan wanted to surprise her. So he'd asked Mr. Curtis.

Mr. Curtis had said no, but not like that. With a lot of adult words. Jan knew what he was saying from the way he said it: Chess was an adult game; too hard for Jan; maybe someday. That's what adults always mean when they say "no."

So Jan asked Mr. Talbaum, but Mr. Talbaum only knew about dinosaurs, and he didn't like Jan's question.

Jan asked every one of his tutors. But not Mlle. Chorafas. She didn't count because she wasn't his tutor; she was his piano *teacher.*

The only person left was Mme. Fahrny. Jan liked her and was sure she could help him. She said she didn't know how to play chess, and she didn't think people would play a game blind-folded anyway. She asked Jan why he thought people would do such a silly thing. Jan told her it wasn't silly. Damon's brother could do it. Mme. Fahrny said Jan should ask Damon, then.

That's just what he would do. And Mommy would have a big smile.

"Jan?" Mme. Fahrny said. "Your father would like to see you now."

Dorothy stiffened.

Mr. Talbaum looked apprehensively at his pupil. He wanted to offer last-minute advice, but nobody was speaking, and he didn't appear ready to break the silence.

Mlle. Chorafas was the first to speak. "Jan, remember, *piano.*"

Jan nodded knowingly, hopped off his chair, took Mme. Fahrny's hand, and was guided quietly to Damon's office.

Dorothy said nothing, but her mouth had become a stiff line.

Mlle. Chorafas shook her head. "Why am I here? He didn't ask for me the last time."

Dorothy nodded. "I'm sorry. I do regret all this."

When Damon announced his plan to have tutors for Jan, Dorothy had gotten up the nerve to request a music teacher for her son.

To her surprise, Damon had posed no objections, fully expecting her to place some demand on the bargaining table. His only condition was that there was to be no practicing while he was around. That was a non-issue, since Damon wouldn't be anywhere near home for the first six months of Jan's lessons anyway.

As a matter of principle, Dorothy requested Mlle. Chorafas be present for this second review. Damon didn't consider music lessons important enough to warrant his scrutiny. To him, music was probably akin to noise, and only served to disturb the peace and sanctity of his home.

Mr. Curtis just wouldn't stop picking away at his thumb. He'd wear a hole in it soon. What was he so nervous about? She'd tested Jan—he could add and subtract numbers in his head. How many boys his age could make that claim? And Jan loved science, too, forever proudly reciting facts in exchange for praise.

Dorothy looked at her watch once again.

The sliding doors to the office opened, and Dorothy heard Damon say, "How's that for size?"

The tutors followed her at a cautious distance as she ran out of the conference room to her son.

Jan was stumbling about, his sweater wrapped tightly around his head.

"What's the meaning of this?" Dorothy demanded.

"I was hoping *you* could tell me," Damon said.

The boy tried making his way to his mother using her voice as guidance. "I can't see."

Dorothy unwrapped the sweater, and grabbed her son by the hand.

"Who is this?" Damon asked.

"Maria Chorafas," the piano teacher said.

"Pleasure to meet you," Damon said. "Tell me, if I plug his ears, would that improve his playing?"

The piano teacher frowned.

"My point exactly," Damon said, looking at Jan.

"Just what do you think you are doing?" Dorothy snapped.

"Our son wanted me to teach him blindfold chess. We were just beginning his first lesson."

"That's not funny."

"I quite agree. Now that I've answered your question, would you kindly answer mine?"

Dorothy glared at him.

"Cat got your tongue? Let's see if I can figure this out . . . where would Jan get such an idea?" Damon tugged at his chin. "Kory, perhaps?"

Dorothy froze.

"Uncle Kory is a chessmonster," Jan announced. "He can play chess blindfolded."

"A chess *master*," Damon said, not taking his eyes off Dorothy. "I see. And why do *you* want to learn, Jan?"

"To make Mommy happy."

Jan grinned brightly at his mother. Dorothy lifted the boy into her arms in a big hug.

Damon regarded his wife and son with razor-slash eyes.

Françoise came forth, looking the color of wet sand. *"Monsieur, tout est de ma faute, je suis très désolée."*

As though he'd noticed her presence for the first time, Damon said, "I can't see that it is your fault, Madame Fahrny."

She bowed her head, biting her lip to keep from saying more.

The piano teacher turned to Dorothy, waiting for a cue.

"I apologize for this. Thank you for coming, I'll call to arrange the next lesson."

Mlle. Chorafas gave Damon a cool look. "Monsieur." She turned to Jan. "I want to hear the sonatina next time. All three parts, okay?"

Jan nodded, and put his index finger to his lips. "Someone is sleeping."

The piano teacher smiled. Her first advice to the boy for soft playing had been to imagine someone close by was napping, and when the music was marked "piano," Jan's loudest playing should not wake him.

Damon looked to Dorothy for an interpretation of Jan's words, but Mlle. Chorafas was already walking away.

"You could at least treat *her* with some respect," Dorothy said.

Damon ignored the comment and addressed Mme. Fahrny: "Mr. Curtis is next. Have him come to my study."

Dorothy took Jan to his room while Françoise ushered the nervous mathematics and sciences tutor to his boss's office. She waited outside for twenty minutes before retrieving Mr. Talbaum and showing Mr. Curtis out.

Damon detained Mr. Talbaum for longer. Françoise couldn't hear a word of what was being said. Mr. Galbot was next. When he finally left, she showed Jean-Luc and Girard to the study.

Françoise waited five minutes. She looked around. Dorothy was still upstairs, with Jan. Nobody could see her.

Jean-Luc and Girard weren't tutors; they were there to protect Dorothy. So she had to be the topic of discussion. They probably had a few words to say about Françoise as well. After all, she was around Dorothy and Jan all the time. This thing with the blindfold chess upset the Monsieur very much. Why, Françoise didn't know, and it didn't matter. What did matter was that it had been *her* fault.

What could they still be talking about in there?

She had to find out. One more look around. Still nobody. She would know if Dorothy were coming down the stairs. Jan, however, had his father's light feet, and if he were to come down alone, there was no chance Françoise would hear. Still.

She'd only listen for a short moment . . . just to make sure.

Françoise pressed her ear against the sliding door.

GROUNDS FOR TERMINATION

That morning, Dorothy woke to shouts from downstairs. She ran out of her room wearing nothing but her nightgown.

The face-off between Françoise and Girard was raging out of control. Girard was taller than Françoise, but she was leaning forward, her nose only inches from his, offering no sanctuary from her spittle.

Normally, at times like these, Girard treated Françoise to a sardonic smirk and walked away unperturbed. This time, he wasn't at all amused.

In machine-gun French, she said that if Girard didn't follow her out of the house right now, she would test the new butcher knife on his skull.

He told her to calm down.

That made matters worse.

Dorothy ran into the room; Jean-Luc was right behind her. He said, "What in the devil's name is going on?"

"Ask him," Françoise said, facing both men now, her hands at her hips, and her darkened face staring first at one, and then at the other, as if to challenge either of them to take a step forward.

"*Alors, t'es complètement cinglée?*" Jean-Luc said, asking her if she had lost her marbles.

"*Vous êtes vraiment dégueulasses, tous les deux!*" Françoise said, and to Dorothy's surprise, Françoise stormed up the stairs.

"What is going on?" Dorothy said.

"She is upset about the events of last evening," Girard lied.

Jean-Luc gave him a confused look, but Girard's expression said *Trust me with this*.

Jean-Luc held his tongue.

"I don't understand," Dorothy said. "That was Damon's fault, not yours."

Girard shifted uneasily on his feet. "She feels we should have done something, and since she cannot blame Mr. van Luden, it has somehow become our fault."

Dorothy nodded slowly. They were hiding something, and they knew she knew. So be it; she wasn't going to get any more out of those two.

Jean-Luc waited for Dorothy to disappear up the stairs. "What was going on in that peasant mind of hers? I have never seen Françoise like that."

"She knows."

Jean-Luc didn't respond immediately. "I was afraid of that. How did she find out?"

"She heard the report we gave the Monsieur."

"Putain de merde," Jean-Luc cursed.

Everything unusual had to be reported to Damon. This had been part of their job description since the very beginning of their employment, five years earlier. Their boss had assured them they'd never be reprimanded for making an honest report, no matter how petty or seemingly unimportant.

This was their livelihood: protect Dorothy from herself, report to Damon.

The damage was done. Too late to change anything now.

It was really a pity—they both liked Françoise.

"This must have been the first time she's listened in."

Jean-Luc nodded. If she'd heard any of their previous reports, she would have reacted right away.

"I'm afraid there is no other way," Girard said, feeling the need for nicotine.

Again Jean-Luc nodded. "So that's it?"

Girard shrugged.

"*Putain,*" Jean-Luc muttered. "Why did she have to stick her nose where it didn't belong?"

The forecast had been for bouts of sunshine but instead they were treated to a steady drizzle, light enough not to warrant umbrellas.

For a while Dorothy said nothing as she looked across the expansive grounds of Damon's estate. They were passing by the tennis courts, which had been redone twice since the van Luden family had added them to the estate more than fifty years ago. From there, Dorothy could see the swimming pool. Damon used it regularly when he was home, working his body as if he were training for the Olympics.

Dorothy stopped as she approached the net. Charlie used to come to an abrupt halt like that whenever he had one of his silly bright ideas. Kory would keep walking, pretending not to hear.

Dear, sweet Kory.

Dorothy sighed. "I cannot stay here any longer."

"I can see why," Françoise said. "I did not understand before, but I do now."

Dorothy took Françoise in her arms and they hugged. They were being watched—Dorothy was always being watched—but at the moment, neither of them cared.

"I suspect I won't be here long either," Françoise said, with little apparent regret.

"Why?"

"Because of what I overheard."

"What did you hear?"

Françoise didn't appear ready to answer just yet. "I was snooping, when I had no business doing so. They'll probably use that to get Monsieur van Luden to fire me. The *real* reason they want me gone has less to do with my eavesdropping and more to do with what I actually heard."

Dorothy waited.

"I listened to their report. They were the last ones, as always, and I thought they were talking about me, so . . . anyway, they were not. They were talking about *you*. I could not believe what I was hearing." Françoise continued walking. "I had all night to think about this, and no job is worth our friendship. I will not sit back and allow this injustice.

"They've been lying to Monsieur van Luden, and I would guess for a long time now. In the beginning, most of what they said may have been true—or at least it was based on the truth—but not a single word of what they were saying yesterday came even close."

"But why?"

"They are paid more than they are willing to admit. They would be fortunate to make a quarter of that elsewhere. They were hired for a very specific purpose—to take care of you, and make sure you didn't drink, or take drugs, or hurt yourself. You were quite unwell when you first came here."

"That's true," Dorothy said, "but not for any of the reasons Damon would have you believe."

"In any case, you are well now, and you have been for some time. So you see, you presented them with a problem: If you were well, then the Monsieur wouldn't have to worry about you taking drugs or hurting yourself, and Jean-Luc and Girard would have no purpose here, and therefore no job."

"So you're saying they lied to him; that they made up stories? Is that it?"

Françoise nodded. "Yes. I will not repeat what I heard, there is no point upsetting you even more, especially since you have decided to leave."

"I'm not surprised," Dorothy said. "They're just telling Damon what he wants to hear anyway. You didn't know any better, but you really shouldn't have mentioned this to anyone but me. Damon knows I'm not taking drugs. He knows I never did. And I would never commit suicide. There was a time when my mother died . . . but that was long, long ago. Anyway, Jean-Luc and Girard need not worry about their jobs, there's no way Damon would get rid of those two. He needs them, don't you see?"

Françoise turned her head. "I don't understand, I thought you would be surprised. What are you saying?"

"What I've always been saying, only you never listened: I am a *prisoner.*"

Françoise mulled this over for a while. "They told me you were an alcoholic. Worse, actually: they said you might try to take your life at any time. But I've been watching you closely for over four years. My cousin used to drink heavily, and he developed gout, so he had no choice but to quit. He hasn't had a drop since, but there still is that hunger in his eyes. I saw none of those signs in you."

Françoise's voice dropped to a conciliatory whisper. "And with the suicide: yes, you were sad, but I know how much you loved Jan. I cannot see you deliberately separating yourself from him, no matter how unhappy your life became. I always assumed the doctor and all the medication he's been giving you were the reason you behaved normally."

Dorothy stepped closer to her friend. They were still at the tennis courts, but Jean-Luc and Girard were sitting on a bench, only fifty meters away.

"Françoise, I haven't told a soul what I'm going to tell you now. You are not to repeat this to anyone, understand?"

Françoise frowned as if she wasn't sure she wanted to hear more.

"In Christmas of sixty-one, Damon kidnapped me. He brought me here, to this country, and held me a prisoner in this house."

"Kidnapped?" Françoise said, dragging out the word. "But why did you not leave then? Divorce him . . . or at least call the police?"

"Damon is not who you think. He is an evil man with a lot of money and powerful connections."

"Yes, but no man can keep a woman in his house by force for so many years, Dorothy, it is not possible."

"That's what I would have thought before I got to know Damon. His brother told me these horrible stories about him, but I didn't really listen. I refused to believe what I was hearing."

"The brother—the uncle Jan always talks about? Kory?"

"Yes, Kory," Dorothy said. "The man I will always love."

Françoise showed no surprise. "This is why you have been talking to Jan about Kory."

"We met thanks to a mutual friend, Charlie. My dad played chess and Kory was brilliant at the game, a veritable genius, and—"

"Ah, so that's why Jan wanted to learn blindfold chess."

"Yes, that was my mistake—I never should have filled his mind with those chess stories—but I didn't think it would ever reach Damon's ears. Jan never talks to him . . . except for the reviews, of course, when Damon drills him with questions. So I guess that's why—"

"Dorothy . . . it was my fault. The boy came to me, asking if I would teach him how to play chess blindfolded. I don't even play checkers. So I thought of Mr. van Luden—I thought it would be nice for the boy to make a connection with him . . . I told Jan to ask his daddy. I'm very sorry."

Dorothy put a hand on her friend's shoulder. "It's okay."

"Did Damon know how you felt about Kory?"

"Heavens no."

"But if he *did* know, it would explain why the Monsieur was so angry yesterday."

"The two brothers didn't get along, Françoise, they *hated* each other. Knowing Damon, he thought *I* told Jan to ask him about blindfold chess, just to rub in the fact that Kory can do something Damon can't. Believe me, that was enough to trigger last night's outburst. If he knew about Kory and me, I'd probably be dead now."

"You exaggerate."

"Oh, no, I'm afraid not. He killed his own dog just to spite his brother."

"Okay. You said he was a very powerful man, and the marriage was a bad one—you were in love with his brother. But what could the Monsieur do to keep you here? How could he keep you from going to the police, from getting a divorce?"

Dorothy looked at Jean-Luc and Girard; they stared back, straight at her. She kept her gaze fixed on them as she told Françoise what happened, as if her look had in it the power to keep the two men at bay.

Starting from the beginning, Dorothy explained how she met Damon and why she foolishly conceded to date him. She told Françoise about Kory, and how their friendship had developed into much more. How she thought of him every day.

After Dorothy described the first trip to Vermont, Françoise said, "This is not so unusual in America, two teenagers experimenting physically, too young to consider the consequences."

"No, it was more than that," Dorothy said. "We were going to get married one day."

"I don't understand, what about Damon?"

"There never was a Damon in my life," Dorothy said. "Damon was a bad date that lingered. I should have put an end to it from the very beginning. There was just one man for me, and that man was Kory."

"You and the Monsieur, it could not have been an arranged marriage—these things don't even happen in small villages anymore."

Dorothy looked up and said, "In a way it was just that. Only it was arranged by Damon, not my father."

Françoise shook her head. "I still don't understand."

"Damon and I went on a few dates, that was all. I felt sorry for him. I was stupid; I shouldn't have let things continue at all, but I did. So he got the wrong idea and proposed. I turned him down. He decided he wasn't going to take no for an answer and so he kidnapped me, force-married me, raped me, and then held me hostage here."

"Jan is a child born of a rape?"

"No. Jan was born of love. I was already pregnant when Damon violated me."

Françoise was still.

"Jan is Kory's child."

Françoise covered her mouth. "*Bon Saint. Kory's child.*" She said the words as if they belonged in a spell.

Dorothy nodded.

"And the Monsieur knows this?"

"Absolutely not. *Nobody* knows, not even Kory—I was kidnapped before I had the chance to tell him." Dorothy told her about the second trip to Vermont, the kidnapping, and what happened at the clinic.

"That still does not explain why you did not leave; you have had five years."

Dorothy took a deep breath and told her friend about the man with the message. "Despite the huge risk, I *still* tried to leave this place. Just before you came along, remember?"

Françoise turned in the direction of the two bodyguards on the bench. From the look she was giving them, it seemed she was ready to charge over there and crush their heads together.

"We are leaving this place," Françoise announced after an extended period of silence. "Together."

Dorothy smiled but said nothing.

"I will not work another day for such a man, and I won't wait for him to fire me."

"But you *must* stay," Dorothy said. "I need you. *Jan* needs you."

Françoise ran a hand through Dorothy's hair. "Thank you, my dear. Don't worry, I won't abandon you, but I will not take another penny from that man. For now, he will only *think* I still work for him. I will stay with you and Jan because you are like my family, not because this is my job."

The two women walked in silence to the botanical gardens, Jean-Luc and Girard got off the bench and followed at a distance.

Dorothy caressed a yellow tulip and said, "I don't have a passport." She explained what had happened.

Françoise's brow narrowed. "Jean-Luc, eh?"

"Don't do anything, please. He's a nothing, a nobody. Damon is really the one to blame."

Françoise turned her head, sizing up the Frenchman by the tennis courts. She nodded. "I will see what I can do about your passport."

Dorothy said, "It won't be easy, I'm afraid. But I very much appreciate the thought. Listen, we'd better head back; Mr. Curtis will be finishing his lesson soon."

The rain pelted against their umbrellas, muffling their conversation, providing extra privacy. The tutors had weekends off, so

Dorothy and Françoise had been forced to wait for three days for an opportunity to continue their talk.

Jean-Luc and Girard had to abandon their late-afternoon television show for an unexpected stroll in the wet.

Dorothy looked at the two men and stuck her tongue out.

Girard shook his head in disgust.

"I'm afraid getting your passport here is out of the question," Françoise said.

Dorothy nodded.

"In theory, it could be done," Françoise continued, "but you must have with you a birth certificate. You do not have one here, of course, and even if you did, it would take all morning for them to issue a new passport. It is a serious affair. They even make you swear an oath."

"How did you find out?" Dorothy asked.

"I told them I have an American niece who is ill and wants to go home to see her father. I said you lost your purse, and when you retrieved it, the wallet was gone, and your passport had been vandalized."

"At least some of that is true."

"Yes," Françoise said, "but unfortunately the passport is a useless document now, and in order to get a new one, they need your birth certificate."

"My father has it, and I can't go get it because I need a passport to leave the country, and for that I need a birth certificate."

"Can't he simply send it to you?"

Dorothy shook her head. "I don't want him involved. I wasn't exactly honest with him . . . you know . . . because of Jan. He'll wonder why I'm asking for my birth certificate out of the blue. And if this gets back to Damon . . ."

"Why should he be involved?" Françoise asked. "Just tell your father you lost your passport and you need a birth certificate."

"That'll still make him suspicious."

"Not if you do it cleverly. Just write one of your letters, and then slip in a paragraph somewhere saying that you've misplaced your passport."

"What does 'égarer' mean?"

"To lose, misplace," Françoise replied in English.

Dorothy thought for a while and shook her head. "It wouldn't work; Jean-Luc goes through my mail." A moment later a smile grew on her face. "How about this: I tell him we're moving and I lost my passport in the process—that happens all the time. I'll give him your address, and he'll have no way of knowing it's just a tiny apartment belonging to you and not one of Damon's villas. I'll say it's our new address and I'll tell him not to send me any more mail over here. That should do it. The birth certificate will be safe at your place. They don't go through your mail."

Françoise nodded slowly. "Yes, that is very good."

"So far. But I still have to get the passport."

"Yes. You would have to appear in person, and they said it can take a few hours before they have it ready."

Dorothy sighed. "Damn."

"Don't despair. You have waited five years, we'll think of something. Write that letter, give it to me, and I'll mail it when I go home next week." Françoise had Wednesdays off. "By the time your father sends the birth certificate, we'll have a plan."

BATED BREATH

August
Five Months Later

It was two in the morning, and mercifully cool. Dorothy cuddled around her son.

Thank God the roads were smooth—they were forever repairing them in Geneva.

It was pitch-black, but Jan didn't say a word. Dear brave boy. She rewarded him with a kiss on the back of his head.

The Peugeot started to slow. Dorothy could feel it. She squeezed Jan as they came to a full stop. She had to remind herself to breathe until finally the car moved again. Another red light.

This was insane. Five months of planning and *this* is what they come up with?

They were going to get caught. Oh. Dear. God.

The car slowed again. Stopped.

She could make out a male voice. Then she heard Françoise answer. Then silence.

Dorothy's heart was beating so hard, she was certain the man could hear it.

More silence. The car moved slowly.

Pulling over?

Then they started picking up speed. A few minutes later, the Peugeot stopped again—Dorothy could feel the gravel crunching below.

A door opened. A key stabbed into the car and the trunk opened.

It was Françoise, and she was alone. "Welcome to Gex, France."

Dorothy and Jan had been in the trunk for less than half an hour, but her knees were very stiff and getting out was painful. Jan remained where he was, unmoving.

"You can come out now," Dorothy said. "It's safe."

The boy opened his eyes, peering up at his mother.

"Go ahead, you can talk."

Jan smiled but did not speak. Dorothy lifted her son out of the trunk and started to cry.

Gex was a ghost town at this early morning hour. It was too early even for the bakers to start preparing the new day's baguettes. Françoise drove up to her friend's house and the front door was unlocked, as promised. Without letting the door close behind her, she picked up the two large suitcases and put them in the trunk of the car.

The previous Wednesday, at two in the morning, Dorothy had filled the new suitcases Françoise bought with all the essentials she could think of. She'd had to leave a week's worth of clothing behind. Françoise had left on her own, rehearsing the escape as though Dorothy and Jan had been there with her as they had been today. The Gex border crossing had gone just as she'd expected. She'd been alone that day, so she hadn't been doing anything illegal by driving to her friend's house with two suitcases full of clothing. Normally, people shopped in Gex and brought back the cheaper goods to Geneva, not the other way around. Today, Françoise was transporting two stowaways in the trunk instead of two pieces of luggage, and she'd have had a hell of a time explaining that one to the French border inspector.

On the A36, Jan spoke his first words that day. "Why were you crying, Mommy?"

Dorothy turned back and looked at her son. "Sometimes people cry when they're happy. Go back to sleep, honey."

Jan rested his head once more. With his legs stretched he still had room in the backseat, and eventually he closed his eyes.

"This was crazy," Dorothy said.

"We made it, didn't we?" Françoise replied.

"Yes, but what if they'd asked you to open the trunk?"

"I told you before, I cross the border every Wednesday for shopping, and they never stopped me once on the French side. Entering Switzerland is different, but we don't want to do that, do we?"

"Not for as long as I live."

Françoise glanced at her watch. Ten minutes to seven. "We should get to Paris well before the embassy opens."

"Do you think they're looking for me yet?"

"It is possible. Six is the earliest I've ever seen those lazy men get up, but even if we are unlucky and they're awake now, they won't expect to see you up for another hour."

They wouldn't be missing Françoise, either, because it was Wednesday. The bodyguards knew Dorothy had no passport, so initially they'd confine their search to Switzerland. Even if they figured she could slip across the border, Switzerland had three neighboring countries—it could take them weeks to find her.

The original plan had been to cross over at Gex and take a train from there to Paris, but they'd decided against it because the bodyguards would eventually search all the local airports and train stations, and Dorothy didn't want to make the task of tracking her down any easier.

They would call Françoise at home, of course. But this was her day off; she could be visiting her sons, or shopping—they had no reason to expect her to spend the entire day sitting in her house waiting by the phone. With Jan and Dorothy gone, however, the bodyguards would certainly *suspect* Françoise. It wasn't like she planned on returning to Geneva—she'd already made it quite plain she, too, was embarking on a new life—in Paris.

Dorothy and Jan were gone now. Once they got their passports, Jean-Luc and Girard wouldn't have a chance of tracking them down—not for a long time.

"Will we get there before they open?" Dorothy asked.

"Long before," Françoise said. "In fact, we'll have to wait for at least an hour, maybe more. They don't open until nine."

"Yes, but we don't have an appointment."

"They don't take appointments for passport renewals."

"I know, you told me. I'm just worried we're cutting it too close."

"I couldn't find any flight for New York today that left later than two."

They drove a while longer and Dorothy said, "It's just that I've come this close before, and it all fell apart at the very last moment."

"Not this time, Dorothy, don't worry."

"I *do* worry. They told you it could take several hours to get me a new passport. But we need to get Jan a passport too. That's bound to take them longer."

"You have the birth certificates, and you have airline tickets that prove you are leaving on a flight to America today. Considering the situation—a mother and a child seeking help—they're bound to give you priority."

"A mother with a child," Dorothy repeated. "I hope you're right."

Françoise nodded. A miscommunication had cost them some time in the planning. She'd assumed that Dorothy had no access to Jan's birth certificate, and had tried all the options for getting a new one for the child from the American Hospital in Geneva. She'd also asked her friend in Paris if there was any way the embassy would give the boy a passport without a birth certificate. Before she had a reply, Dorothy had informed her that Damon had the boy's documents in a folder labeled "Family Documents." Jean-Luc and Girard had left Jan's birth certificate untouched and unhidden. They must have assumed that since Dorothy didn't have a passport, or any way of procuring a new one, she wouldn't try to get her son one, since the little boy wouldn't be going anywhere alone.

Fifty minutes later, they passed under a blue exit sign:

VILLEJUIF

PARIS

ARCUEIL

Françoise turned onto the A6A.

"Tell me I'm not dreaming," Dorothy said.

Françoise pinched her and laughed.

"Ouch!"

Jan rubbed his eyes with the knuckles of both hands. "What's the matter, Mommy?"

Dorothy kissed her son. "Look outside, that's Paris."

"It's very big," Jan concluded.

"New York is bigger," Dorothy said.

Jan nodded.

She ruffled his hair. "You'll see for yourself soon."

Once outside the embassy, Dorothy stared at the two passports in her hands. "It's really going to happen." She hugged Françoise. "We did it!"

"We must hurry to the airport, the flight leaves in two hours," Françoise said, heading for the car.

"You'll come to the States, you promise, right?"

Françoise kissed Dorothy and Jan on both cheeks. "Of course, we cannot let your French get rusty, can we?"

In the car, Françoise made a left at the light and two blocks down she turned right following the sign: E15/E50/Boulevard Périphérique.

The Paris-Orly Airport was just twenty minutes from there.

HOME

August 21, 1967
Monday

"Honey, that's way too close." She lifted him onto the edge of the bed. Jan kept his eyes trained on the hotel television.

"That's better." Dorothy turned down the volume. "Mommy's going to make a call right now; can you still hear?"

Jan nodded.

"Cornell Admissions, can you hold?"

Before Dorothy could respond, the line went quiet.

"Admissions, how may I help you?"

"Yes, I'm not sure I have the right department? I'm looking for a friend—he would have been in the class of sixty-six."

"Okay, you would want Alumni Affairs; that's area code 607, 254-7121. Let me see if I can connect you—"

The line went silent again.

"Hello, Undergraduate Admissions."

"Oh, I was supposed to be connected with Alumni Affairs—"

"Hold on—"

How much was this long-distance call going to cost her?

"Alumni Affairs, how may I help you?"

She was Jane Foster. Sounded too much like Jane Doe, but too late to think of another name. She'd gone to Rhodes High, with Kory van Luden. Class of '62. She believed he might have gone to Cornell. Good enough, the lady was waiting—

"I'm looking for Kory van Luden, class of sixty-six?" Nice going, Dorothy.

"Yes?"

"Uh, would you have an address or phone number or something?"

"Are you an alumna?"

"Well, we're from the same high school."

"Miss, are you a *Cornell* alumna?"

"Uh, no, but I just want—"

"I'm afraid we can't give out that information."

Now what?

"If you want, you can mail a letter to my attention, Barbara, at Fifty-Five Brown Road, Ithaca 14850—and we'll forward your information over to him, so he can contact you."

"Thank you." Dorothy repeated the address as a courtesy, thanked Barbara again, and hung up the phone.

She could always call Rhodes High. There was a chance they'd know where Kory had gone to college. They might just give her his number in Rhodes. She didn't need that; she knew it by heart. Nobody would be there to answer. Damon had explained that the house was presently off limits to all, but one day it would belong to Jan.

That was neither here nor there.

Kory wasn't with Mary, either. She was living with Dorothy's father. This Dorothy had learned over a year ago, during one of the Sunday phone conversations with her father. He'd made it sound more like a warning rather than good news.

Mary is living with me now.

In other words: you went ahead and did your own thing, now I'm doing my thing, and if you don't like it, pumpkin, too bad.

Dad had been crestfallen. He'd believed Dorothy had abandoned him for a new life. There'd been anger there too; she was sure of it, but could she blame him?

She reconsidered calling Rhodes High. She didn't want to risk some nosy person answering the phone. Who was she? When did she attend Rhodes? She could use another name—call herself Nancy or something—no, that would just be opening a can of worms. Rhodes High was too close to home.

Dorothy didn't want to chance the word getting out that she was back.

Stick with the plan.

The next Ivy League school on the list was Columbia. Dorothy picked up the phone, looked at it for a second, and then hung up the receiver. If Cornell didn't give out information about their students, why would Columbia? Of course, Columbia was a local call, but Dorothy didn't feel like being humiliated a second time.

On impulse, she dialed Information.

"Yes, would you have a number and an address for a Mr. Kory van Luden?"

"Spell the last name, ma'am?"

"Vee. Aye. Enn. Second word: Ell. Yoo. Dee. Eee. Enn. *van Luden.*"

"Hold on."

This was another waste of time. On the other hand, if Kory had gone to Columbia, he might still be staying in Manhattan—

"I'm showing a van Luden, K, on 333 East Sixty-Seventh. That number is—"

"Hold on." Dorothy looked frantically around, but there was nothing to write on. She tried the drawer, found a Holiday Inn pad and a pencil, and copied the information, repeating it twice.

Now what?

Hi, it's Dorothy. Remember me?

What if a girlfriend, or worse, his wife, answered? What would Dorothy say *then?*

She'd thought about this moment for years, and now that she was living it, she had no clue what to do. She looked over at Jan, who was bewitched by a cartoon. This wasn't just about *her.*

She had to call.

And think before she opened her big mouth.

No. No more rehearsing lines. Not after that bang-up job with Barbara from Cornell.

Call Kory, tell him she has to see him. Tell him it's a matter of life and death. And say no more.

Dorothy picked up the receiver again.

She dialed the number. The phone rang.

She closed her eyes. Her chest tightened, squeezing the air from her lungs.

The phone rang a fourth time.

She looked at Jan again, waited for the sixth ring, and pulled the receiver from her ear.

"Hullo?" Hoarse voice. She recognized it immediately. It wasn't Kory.

Dorothy stared at the phone, opened her mouth to speak, and hung up instead.

On the television, Fred and Barney pulled a car up to their thighs, charging full speed ahead, while kicking up a storm of dust with their flipper-sized bare feet.

"Honey, how would you like to see the tallest buildings in the world?"

"But I saw them last night," Jan said, not taking his eyes off the television. Jean-Luc and Girard always watched boring shows in Geneva. Jan had never seen anything like this before.

"It was dark," Dorothy said, "and we were in a taxi. It'll be different now. You'll have to look straight up to see the tops!"

The TV responded with, "Yabba-dabba doo!"

"Honey? Come on." She switched off the set. "We're going to see Charlie."

Dorothy had quickened her pace, and Jan broke into a trot in order to keep up. "Why are you running, Mommy?"

"I'm sorry, honey, I just don't want Charlie to leave before we get there."

"Why would Charlie leave, Mommy?"

"Because he doesn't know we're coming. It's a surprise."

Printed in shiny brass numbers was *333*, resting on the top of a large cream-colored door flanked by stone columns. The town house was squeezed between a redbrick building with a smaller entrance featuring lamp-housing lanterns on the right, and the Manhattan Library in miniature on the left.

Dorothy rang the doorbell. The city bustle made it impossible to hear if anyone was coming.

A bolt slid, freeing the door to open.

Charlie's flaming red hair was a disheveled mess. He was wearing a maroon robe and matching slippers. His face seemed leaner, and uncharacteristically devoid of humor.

"What in the . . . Dorothy?"

"Aren't you going to invite us in?"

"Mommy, is this your friend Charlie?"

Charlie looked amazed, as if he didn't know children could actually speak.

Realizing he was standing on the doorstep to Sixty-Seventh Street in bathroom attire, he retreated into the house, motioning them in.

The floor and walls were white marble, at least a century old. Antiques decorated the hallway, each tastefully nestled in their appropriate place. Impressive, yet not excessive. She'd imagined Kory in a more Spartan abode, but this place had belonged to his father. Perhaps Kory had left things pretty much as he'd found them.

They walked over a Persian carpet and down the long pathway to the living room. On their right, a wooden staircase corkscrewed its way up to the second floor. The living room overlooked a colorful garden designed around a fountain.

As Jan entered the living room, something caught his eye. "Look, Mommy, Charlie plays chess!"

The living room had a small library, a leather sofa, and a round table with two mahogany chairs. Jan was pointing to the antique chessboard on the table. Several pieces of both colors were already decommissioned from service, and had been placed in two straight columns, to the side of the board.

Dorothy recognized the chess set immediately. It belonged to Kory, and to his father before him. "Yes, honey, he does."

Jan ran to his mother and grabbed on to her waist. He regarded Charlie with newfound awe.

"Please, have a seat," Charlie said, as if something was distracting him. "Can I get you anything?"

"No, no—well, actually, water would be fine."

"What about you . . . uh . . . what is it, Damon Junior?"

Dorothy's jaw tightened. "His name is Jan."

"Jan, then. What would you like, young man?"

"Orange juice, thank you kindly."

"Wow," Charlie said, "first Dorothy appears out of the blue, and now I'm seeing a five-year-old with manners. What else will my eyes behold this day?"

Dorothy and Jan sat on the couch. Charlie came back with the drinks. The town house was air-conditioned, but they were still hot from their muggy trek. Jan finished his orange juice without putting it down once.

Charlie took the glass from the boy. "Hey, buddy, how about another?"

Jan nodded enthusiastically.

Dorothy gave her son a gentle nudge and touched her lip. Jan quickly erased the bright-orange mustache with his napkin, and called after Charlie, "Thank you!"

From the kitchen, Charlie said, "This is New York; you're going to have to quit being so polite."

Charlie reappeared with the orange juice. "Nothing like Tropicana on a humid summer's day."

"Tropicana!" Jan pointed. "I saw it on television."

"Speaking of which . . ." Dorothy said to Charlie. "Do you have a TV set here?"

"We do. Two, actually."

We.

"I'd like to talk, Charlie. I'm sure Jan here wouldn't mind watching television. Would you like that, honey?"

Jan bounced in place, regarded Charlie, and promptly checked his behavior. "Oh, yes, Mother, I'd be most grateful."

Charlie led the way, and Dorothy and Jan followed him up the curved, wall-supported stairs to the master bedroom. Charlie pulled the bedcover over the pillows in a quick effort to make the bed presentable. "Hop on up." On the other side of the room, opposite the king-size bed, was a large television. "Do you know how to use a remote control?"

Jan shook his head. "No, sir."

The boy was fascinated with the buttons on the black box. Charlie pointed to the big red button on the top, and Jan pressed. Soon the television was alive with color. He showed Jan the channel button and the boy pressed it repeatedly, awed by the magical power of the box.

"Will you be all right on your own, honey?" Dorothy asked, but Jan wasn't listening.

"If you'll excuse me just a moment," Charlie said, "I'm going to put on something less comfortable."

In the living room, wearing tennis shorts, a polo shirt, and Adidas with no socks, Charlie asked, "Would you like something stronger than water?"

"No thank you, although if there ever were an occasion that would merit—"

"Oh, uh, sorry, that was insensitive of me. I forgot."

"Your offer wasn't insensitive; your apology was."

Charlie watched his fingers drum against his knee. "Not to sound rude or anything, but what's the deal?" He shook his head turning his palms up.

"What's the deal?" Dorothy said slowly. It was barely audible.

Charlie waited.

His freckled face was growing slightly pink. "You disappear off the face of the earth five years ago, now you're here. So? What do you want?"

Dorothy did not look up. "Is he married? Is there anyone else?"

"What is that supposed to mean? *Is there anyone else?*"

"Is he involved with another woman?"

"*Another* woman? Boy, you've got some nerve, lady. You come waltzing in here with Damon's kid and you ask if Kory is involved with someone else?"

Dorothy kept her eyes down.

Charlie shook his head and sighed. Dorothy wasn't going to answer. Charlie waited and finally said, "You know, I wish for his sake he had been. Any other red-blooded male would have a long history of women after all these years. Not Kory. Not a one. After you, the only lady in his life has been the queen, and I don't think a chess piece constitutes a healthy relationship."

Dorothy closed her eyes, releasing a tear. "And he lives here?"

"Yes, this is his town house. I have been his roommate since college."

"He went to college in New York?"

"Yes, yes, we both did. Now would you please—"

323

"Columbia?"

"Yes, Columbia. I went to NYU."

"Where is he now, Charlie?"

"Right *now?* Probably taking a class."

"He hasn't finished his degree yet?"

"He's working on his doctorate." Charlie leaned forward, grasping his hands as if he were giving himself a handshake. "How about *you* answer some questions now."

"I had to know first," Dorothy said softly, "otherwise there'd be nothing to say."

"You had to know *what?*"

"If there was another woman in his life. If so, this visit would have been over, and my life would have taken a very different path." She looked at her old friend with wet eyes.

"Okay," Charlie said. "You've completely piqued my curiosity and redefined the limits of my patience. Would you please, for the love of God, tell me what the hell is going on here?"

Dorothy looked up at the ceiling. She could hear the sound of the television. "Excuse me." Dorothy ran up the stairs and peeked into the large room. Jan was bouncing on the bed, remote in hand.

"Are you all right in there, darling? Can I get something for you?"

"Mommy, watch this. It's in color. Look!"

"Will you be all right here alone for a short while? My friend Charlie and I need to talk."

Jan frowned. "You're not going to watch with me?"

"There'll be plenty of time for that later, sweetie."

Jan didn't appear convinced, but his attention was again lost to the television, and that was all the reassurance Dorothy needed.

Dorothy closed the bedroom door and found her way back down to the living room. "Sorry, I just had to make sure he was okay. And I don't want him hearing any of this. Not yet, at least."

"Am I going to have to tie you down and start administering torture to get you to talk?"

"After what I've been through, I doubt you could come up with anything that would even get my attention."

"Hmmm. That almost sounds like a challenge." A playful grin slipped across his lips.

She returned a partial smile. It was good to hear Charlie sound more like the friend she remembered. She began by describing the first trip to Vermont, and the secret meetings.

"That's pretty much how Kory described it. Nobody believed him, though. He said you two had this thing going, that you were—"

"Lovers," Dorothy filled in.

"Actually, he said the two of you were *in* love." Charlie looked at her with curiosity and suspicion. "So you guys were *lovers?*"

Dorothy hunted for tissues in her purse. "We were."

"I couldn't get him to admit you guys had done anything more than hold hands."

"He was being a gentleman, Charlie," she said, looking down. "He was protecting me."

"Kory also claimed you were kidnapped. That didn't exactly win him any brownie points with your old man. Those two haven't spoken in ages."

"It's true, Charlie." She nodded. "I *was* kidnapped."

Charlie lifted an eyebrow. "You're shitting me."

"I was kidnapped on our second trip to Vermont," Dorothy said. She took her time describing the details.

"I'm still missing some big pieces here. Like the phone call? That, and the fact that you married Damon, and have lived with him for five years. I mean, he didn't have you locked up in some cellar all that time did he?"

She thought for a while. "It isn't that simple; there's a lot more to this, Charlie."

"Why don't you answer my question first?"

She lifted her finger. "I will, but there's something important I have to say, something I never had the chance to tell Kory. I was going to tell him the night I was kidnapped."

"Tell him what?"

"I was going to tell him I was pregnant."

"Wait. What are you saying?"

"I was pregnant with Kory's child, Jan. The little boy upstairs."

Charlie's jaw dropped. "Walking, talking Jesus. Does Damon know?"

"You and a French maid who's now in Paris are the only people who know. I haven't told Jan yet—I want him to get to know his father first . . ."

Charlie held on to his head as if to prevent it from exploding. "Oh, man. This is *wild*. Way-out-there wild. This has to be the wildest shit I've ever heard."

Dorothy waited.

"I have a million questions," Charlie said, "but that's going to have to wait. Right now we've got a major problem."

Dorothy looked at her friend, prompting him to continue.

"Kory didn't exactly take this whole thing lightly. He wouldn't talk for ages. I mean, he put up with me, of course, but I didn't exactly give him much choice. For a long time, he was like this mute zombie. On a good day, he'd give you a yes or a no. I was seriously worried he was going to off himself or something. Instead, he went to college. Zoned out. Focused that brainpower of his on his studies and chess. He was either home, hitting the books, or at the club, putting some poor bastard to shame. And not much has changed, even after all these years. Sure, he's lightened up a bit. Now he even speaks in full sentences, but"—Charlie scratched his head—"Dorothy, I really don't know how he's going to handle all this."

"Don't worry, Charlie. I'll handle it for the both of us. Just tell me where he is."

"Let me think . . . It's almost lunchtime. I know: we could grab a bite and try and catch him after class. Maybe he's got a class schedule lying around. I could check—"

A voice from the hallway said, "Did I hear you say 'check'? Who are you playing with, Charlie?"

Dorothy was seated on the living-room sofa, which was not visible from the hallway that led to it. Charlie hopped out of his seat and scrambled for Kory, but before he could stop his friend, Kory had made it to the living room and was staring at the woman on the couch.

His leather briefcase fell onto the marble floor with a thud. For a long few seconds, nobody moved.

Kory took a step forward.

Charlie blocked him, his arms spread. "Don't say anything until you hear her out. It's not what you think."

"The former might constitute sound advice. Regarding the latter: how is it you presume to know what I am thinking, especially now?" Kory did not take his eyes off Dorothy.

A tear fell off her cheek. "I didn't think I'd ever see you again."

Charlie stumbled out of the way as Kory advanced on her.

All trepidation gone now, she lurched forward and into Kory's arms. Dorothy buried her head in his chest, staining his shirt as she wept.

Kory pushed her away. "Are you done?"

"It's okay," Charlie said, bringing her a box of tissue. "Don't worry, he'll mellow out."

"Characteristically optimistic, Charlie." Kory turned to Dorothy, who had let the tissues fall to the floor. "To what do I owe the pleasure of this impromptu visit?"

Charlie took hold of Kory's arm. "I'm going upstairs. Do yourself a favor—listen to her before you say or do anything?" Charlie walked away, looking back twice before climbing the stairs.

Dorothy spoke softly. "I've spent years thinking about what I was going to say to you. I . . . I . . . can't seem to speak."

"Why don't you start by telling me why you ended up married to that wretched piece of scum I have the misfortune to call my brother?"

"Kory, I—"

"The two of you have a child, Jan?"

"How do you know about Jan?"

"I first heard of it from Mary. Then they rubbed my nose in it at the family attorney's office. That was the last time I saw your father."

Dorothy was quiet.

"I made quite a spectacle of myself over you."

"You did?"

"I did indeed. I told Mary and your father we were in love, and that you weren't the slightest bit interested in Damon. I even told the police you were kidnapped. I demanded your father hire a detective to retrieve you. I wanted to save you from Damon; and most of all I wanted to bring you back into my life." Kory's voice became hard to hear. "You called your father and asked him for help. He went to get you back and returned alone. He said all was well. Just like that: 'All is well.' I refused to believe him, of course. I was going to go to Florida to confront Damon, but your father stopped me and let me speak with you on the phone instead. I presume you still remember what you told me then."

Dorothy nodded.

Kory wasn't looking at her. "After that, whenever you spoke with your father, you kept assuring him your life was just as you wanted it to be. According to Mary, you were living every woman's dream, rose garden and all. She finally succeeded in bleeding away all hope I had of retrieving the Dorothy I once knew."

"What if you could have her back? Would you want her back?"

He stared at her.

"Kory, do you still love me?"

"I loved a girl from Rhodes, a girl I met in high school. I don't know who the hell you are."

"I am that girl."

Kory turned away and started walking up the stairs.

"Please leave," Kory said. "I'm beginning to feel ill."

Dorothy went after him, and grabbing his arm, she turned him around. "I'll leave if that's what you want. But you'll have to tell me you don't love me first."

"What do you want from me?"

"An *answer.* You tell me you don't love me, and I promise I'll be out of here. You can pretend this never happened."

"You leave me stranded for five fucking years with no explanation. What the hell do you expect me to feel?" Kory surprised himself with the sound of his own yelling.

"Anger," Dorothy said, "for one. A lot of hurt, confusion—*all* of that. I cannot expect you to still love me, I can only pray for it."

Kory walked to the easy chair and sat down, burying his head in his hands. "I don't know what I feel. It *was* love. Now it's this constant, unrelenting pain. If you can call that love still—"

Dorothy pulled his hands from his face. "I needed to hear that. Now, Kory, you need to hear this: you were right—I *was* kidnapped."

Kory looked up, his eyes red. "Why are you doing this?"

"Because I love you. I never stopped loving you."

"Only long enough to run off and marry Damon. I spoke to you on the phone. That was you, right? Saying you were sorry? And all those subsequent phone conversations with your father? Wasn't that you? For a long time I was certain you'd been abducted, but you did everything you could to prove to me and your father that you were not. Now you're saying you were."

"Look at me," Dorothy said. "Remember the story you told me about Dollie?"

Kory was quiet for a moment. "You're saying that I was set up?"

Dorothy nodded slowly.

Kory had that expression he had when he was lost in a chess problem. "What am I missing?"

Dorothy took his wrist. "Follow me and I'll show you."

Jan was still in the huge bed when the two of them entered the room.

Charlie came out of the bathroom, his electric shaver still tethered to the outlet and buzzing. Dorothy was standing next to Kory at the bedroom doorway. Whatever had happened down there, the two of them must have somehow worked things out.

Dorothy pointed at her son and whispered something in Kory's ear.

Charlie turned off the shaver, but he didn't return it to the bathroom—he wouldn't take his eyes off his friend.

Kory stood motionless as he looked at his son for the first time.

It took a long five-count before Kory finally came out of the shock. His eyelids were batting, and before Jan could see the tears, Kory stepped backwards out the door, closing it without a sound.

Jan hopped off the bed. "Mommy, who is that man?"

Kory was on his way to his room when he felt a gentle tug at his pant leg. Two blue eyes peered up at him. Kory turned his head to the side, hurriedly wiping off his wet face with the heel of his hand.

He looked down at his son.

Jan had his head cocked to the side. "Are you the man who plays blindfold chess?"

CENTRAL PARK

Sunday
Six Days Later

The sun was out, the humidity was low, and it seemed as if every young couple and family in Manhattan had come to visit the 843-acre rectangular park that bisected the northern half of the island.

The three of them walked to Conservatory Water, a huge pond inspired by its Parisian counterpart. Jan let go of his mother's hand, running over to the edge of the pond defined now by a wall of children. Several were pushing off their model sailboats, hoping the light breeze would blow the wobbling boats the rest of the way across to the other end.

"I really don't know how you did it," Kory said. "He's so innocent, so trusting."

Dorothy smiled. "He's five."

"Yes, but how many five-year olds have been subjected to . . ." Kory looked at Dorothy. "You were his only line of defense. Without your love and protection, Jan would have been traumatized for life."

Dorothy gave him a pensive smile and kissed him on the cheek.

Kory looked over his shoulder.

"Don't worry," Dorothy said, "he's got his back to us—he can't see or hear a thing."

"He might have, in the buggy. I had the feeling that he saw us holding hands."

"He's perceptive for his age," Dorothy said, "that's for sure." Seeing the look on his face, she added, "Don't be so concerned. We're going to tell him soon anyway, right?"

"I'm not sure he's ready. The news could be quite devastating for the child. He could end up resenting me. You were his only sanctuary over there; you were his life. If he's as perceptive as you say, he'll eventually figure out how we feel about each other. He might see me as a threat."

"I know this is hard—especially for you—but try not to overthink this. He's just a little boy. You were right when you said he's trusting. You've got to have a little faith too, okay? Everything is going to be fine, you'll see. He'll accept you as his father, because you *are* his father, because you love him, because you love me. On some level, I think he already knows."

Kory walked over to the pond and said to Jan, "Did you see the statue?"

"What statue?"

Kory lifted Jan, pointing in a direction just north of the pond. "Can you see it? Over there?"

Jan nodded energetically.

"That's the Alice in Wonderland statue."

Jan ran to the statue as if Alice and the Mad Hatter would gather their mushrooms and stroll off if he didn't get there in the next thirty seconds. After a few games of hide-and-seek where Alice's mushroom proved to be the boy's preferred hiding spot, Dorothy told her son that they had to go. Jan did his best to convince his mother to take him row-boating.

"Central Park will still be here tomorrow," Kory said. "Right now, we're going to meet Uncle Charlie for some Chinese food. Don't worry about the rowboats; you live in the city now. We can come back anytime we want. We can even rent bikes if you like."

Jan's smile returned.

They walked west, toward the Central Park Lake, crossing Bow Bridge, their son between them, his tiny hands in each of theirs. They lifted their arms in unison, and Jan rose, running on air. He laughed as his feet pedaled. On the ground, Jan fell back a few steps, and they lifted him once more. Jan laughed as if it were the first time he'd had the experience, not the seventh.

They passed a Häagen-Dazs ice-cream store and Jan's eyes lit up. "You can have ice cream after lunch," Dorothy said.

"They have an ice-cream store next to the school with the teacher in the yellow dress," Jan said.

"Mrs. Martindale," Kory said. The kindergarten on Seventy-First had been the second of the three schools they'd visited in the past four days. "You seem to like that school."

Jan nodded.

Dorothy smiled at Kory. "He certainly knows what he wants."

Across the street, weaving through the crowd unnoticed, a pedestrian stopped to take a quick photograph.

NIGHT OUT

Six Hours Later

Dorothy wrapped the towel around Jan's head and rubbed vigorously. "Okay, you're all set. Let me just comb that hair." She studied her handiwork in Kory's bathroom mirror. "There, aren't you the handsome one?"

Jan marched to the bed, where his mother had laid out his evening clothes. Completely naked, he crawled onto the mattress and started putting on his socks when Kory came into the room.

"Mommy," Jan said, "isn't he supposed to knock?"

"Well, honey, this is *his* room," Dorothy said from the bathroom.

Kory said, "You're absolutely right; next time I will knock. Do you need any help there, young man?"

Jan shook his head defiantly.

"How about you," Kory said, addressing the half-open bathroom door, "need any help in there?"

"Patience, patience," Dorothy said, appearing in a robe. "You really *haven't* been around women, have you?" She smiled. "I'll be just a few minutes more."

Kory met Charlie halfway down the staircase. "They're not ready yet."

Charlie laughed, changed directions, and headed back down the stairs. "I was just going to check on Jan. Say, are you sure you guys are cool with Jan and me going to that movie?"

"You Only Live Twice?"

"Yeah, the Bond flick. I've been meaning to see it for two months now, and I don't know if it'll be in the theaters much longer."

Kory started down the stairs. "If Dorothy says it's okay, then it's fine with me."

"Right, but I get the feeling she's never been to a Bond movie before," Charlie said.

"Jan will be fine. Don't worry, you're doing *us* the favor, remember?" Over lunch, Charlie had agreed to take care of Jan so that Kory and Dorothy could have the evening to themselves. Kory headed for the living room, and Charlie followed him. "If we ever leave here in *time* for you to see the movie."

"You know," Charlie said, "you're going to have to pad your times a bit when it comes to the ladies getting ready."

Sitting in the living room alone with Charlie, Kory said, "Do you think Jan is ready for the truth?"

"You could tell him right now," Charlie said, "and he'd be ready. He's really taken to you. Before going to the chess club with you, do you know what he did?"

Kory shook his head.

"He asked me if I'd give him chess lessons. He didn't want you knowing, so he could impress you. He even asked me to teach him blindfold chess. I told him he was asking the wrong guy and that you were the best teacher he could have. Know what he said?"

Kory sat still.

"He said, 'But then he won't think I'm smart.'" Charlie leaned forward. "The kid wants your admiration."

"He doesn't know I'm his father, Charlie. Why would you say he seeks my approval?"

"Because I think he senses how Dorothy feels about you."

Kory said nothing for a while. When he heard Dorothy and Jan starting down the stairway, Kory said, "You're a good friend, Charlie, you really are."

He was straddling an Oriental woman when suddenly the bed flipped up into the wall.

Jan gasped.

Three men entered the room with machine guns, blasting holes into the mattress. An Oriental policeman came into the room and said, "At least he died on the job."

Jan stared, wide-eyed.

"Hey, little buddy, you sure you're okay with this? We don't have to watch—"

"What was he doing to her, Uncle Charlie?"

"Because we can always go find some other movie. I just thought that you'd like James Bond. It's a great first movie to see."

"What was he doing to the Chinese lady?"

"He was . . . kissing her."

"But—"

"Look, Jan. See? He's not dead, it was a trick."

Jan stared at the screen, his forehead riddled with furrows of concentration. "A trick?"

"Yeah, see James Bond is the hero and he *never* dies. They just wanted people to *think* he was dead and—"

"Hey, buddy," a deep voice said from the seat behind, "if I wanted narration, I'd buy the fucking book. Give it a rest, will ya?"

"Sorry," Charlie said, not daring to look back. Then to Jan, "I can't talk because people are trying to watch. If there's something you don't get, I'll explain it in the end, okay?"

Jan nodded. He knew the importance of keeping quiet.

Kory and Dorothy were walking with their arms around each other for the first time in five years.

"Charlie is convinced he's ready," Kory said.

"Jan?" She pondered this as they walked arm in arm. "Charlie is right. Jan thinks the world of you. If we wait much longer, he'll feel like we've been hiding something from him."

"Which we have . . ."

"Yes, but he'll understand if we tell him now. He's just a little boy, but at times he can be as wise as an adult."

Kory kissed her. "I wouldn't give adults that much credit."

"This place has particularly well deserved reviews," Kory said, leading the way to the entrance of the restaurant.

They were greeted by a man wearing a solid gray V-neck dhoti with an embroidered button stem. "Welcome to Banjara. Do you have a reservation, sir?"

"Yes," Kory said, "van Luden."

"Of course, sir, just a moment." He went over to a podium and looked at a large ledger. "Yes. Mr. and Mrs. van Luden? Party of two?"

Kory smiled. "Soon, I hope."

"Sir?"

"Just the two of us tonight."

"Very good, sir." The waiter headed off to the dining area. "Please follow me."

They were seated in the corner of the room, at a private, candlelit table.

As they browsed the menus, Kory said, "You don't have to answer this. If you're not ready, I'll understand . . . it's just that the question has plagued me for years. I've thought of every possible explanation, every scenario."

She took his hand.

"What really happened that night?"

"I've wanted to tell you since I got back, but I couldn't find an opportunity. I didn't want you to hear it in bits and pieces whenever I could get a few seconds away from Jan. I planned on telling you tonight."

"But?"

"No 'buts,' really. I *was* going to tell you, only . . . well, I was worried you might not believe me. Sometimes *I* find it hard to believe. I've been living a lie for five years. I had to keep reminding myself of what was true. All I had was the hope that I would one day escape and find you."

Kory gave her hand a squeeze.

"That night is a blur. I remember clearly what happened up to the point that you left the car. The rest is like one of those nightmares you try to remember the next day, but it keeps slipping away? Like that. I don't know how he did it, but he must have drugged me."

Kory nodded. "Yes, as he did me. I was peeing and the next thing I know, Damon grabs me from behind, and puts this handkerchief over my mouth. I'm guessing he used chloroform. It knocked me out for hours. I didn't come to until the next morning, in your father's car."

"Well, I don't remember being drugged. Whatever he gave me was a lot stronger than chloroform. Maybe that's what he gave me at first."

"What do you remember?"

"I remember some guy marrying us. I could barely stand. I had this horrible feeling that I was falling. Damon was holding me from behind. I could smell that Old Spice cologne he wore. I remember hearing Damon say 'I do.'"

"*I* would never say such a thing, Kory, you've got to believe me—no matter what they drugged me with, I wouldn't have betrayed you. But I remember this guy—he wasn't a priest, he was some city official—I remember him clearly, saying, 'Then I pronounce you man and wife.'"

"Can you recall anything else? Every detail helps."

Dorothy nodded. "I know, but I blacked out after that. The next thing I know, I'm smelling Old Spice again. It is dark. I'm in a bed. Damon is on top of me. Gasping at me. Then it all goes dark again."

Kory took in a deep breath. "That fucking piece of shit *raped* you?"

Dorothy nodded.

Kory's next words were barely audible. "He kept you in Geneva as his sex slave?"

Dorothy shook her head. "No, it only happened that one time. He calls what happened that night 'making love.'"

The color drained from Kory's face. "Excuse me." Kory walked off in haste, leaving Dorothy alone at the table.

The bathroom was empty. Kory went into a stall. The kitchen wasn't far; if he screamed, people would hear him. He smashed the stall door until there were bloody marks from his raw knuckles. Kory washed the tears from his face, and the blood from his hands, when a man in a brown two-piece suit walked in. "You all right there, fella?"

"No."

Kory returned to the table.

Dorothy looked worried. "I'm so sorry I upset you."

"You have no reason to feel sorry, but my brother does. . . ."

Dorothy put her hand over his. "Let it go. It was a long time ago, and it's over. I'll never forgive him for the five years of my life he stole, but I don't want to spend the rest of my days angry. I've done that for long enough. It's like slow death. It eats at you from the inside out. I have to let go, for my own health and sanity, I have to. I'm here, with *our* son. I'm free, Kory, and I'm happy for the first time since we were last together. You have to let go too."

Dorothy and Kory didn't speak for a while.

The waiter noticed the menus were closed, and he came over to ask if they were ready to order. Kory had to clear his throat to speak.

"Is everything okay, sir?" the waiter said, noting Kory's pale face.

Kory nodded and placed a hasty order for the both of them. The waiter trotted off.

"What happened after that?" Kory said, staring at his napkin.

"Maybe we should talk about this some other time."

"No, I'm okay, really. I need to know."

Dorothy looked at him and hesitated for a while before she spoke. "The next thing I remember, I'm in a bed again, but it's a different bed, and I'm in a bright room. I'm feeling awful. I have to struggle to think. Like my thoughts are distant echoes."

"The drugs," Kory said to himself.

"I think I must have fallen in and out of sleep several times before I was lucid enough to react." Dorothy caressed the stem of her wineglass. "I started screaming for help. Nothing happened for a while and then this nurse in white comes in and tells me everything is going to be okay. She's speaking in English with a French accent, and she's calling me Mrs. van Luden."

"What did you do?"

"Well, if she wanted to calm me down, she wasn't doing a good job. I lost it. Now I really started screaming. Poor lady didn't know what to do. I said I wanted to go home; I told her

I was kidnapped. I said I wanted to call the police. Somebody came into the room—a doctor—and he said he was going to give me something to make me feel better.

"Whatever it was put me to sleep again, and when I woke up, I tried the phone by my bed and called the operator. I was afraid they wouldn't let me make any calls, but for some reason, they did. I picked up the phone and this operator answered. So I just asked her if I could call my father. She said 'Of course,' like it was nothing. It then occurred to me that I had no idea where I was. She said—I'll never forget this—'You're at the Etienne, a clinic in Geneva.' A minute later I was talking to my father. I didn't know how much time I had to talk. I asked him to come and get me."

"And that's when he left for Geneva."

"Yes."

"Okay, that all makes sense, but I can't figure out the rest: why didn't you come back with him?"

"That was my plan, but it turned out I couldn't take the risk . . . because of Jan."

The waiter came and served six bowls on a platter. Kory thanked him without looking at the food.

When the waiter left, Dorothy said, "After the phone call, I felt much better, like there was going to be an end to the nightmare. I was still not feeling well. I was completely drained; I don't really know how else to describe it. I slept again, and when I woke up the next day, I wasn't alone in the room."

THE CLINIC

December 26, 1962

Nobody had turned off the lights, or if they had, somebody had turned them back on. A man in a dark pinstripe suit was weaving a quarter between his fingers. He looked up and grinned. There was something deeply unsettling about that smile.

"Who are you?" Dorothy said.

"It has come to my attention you are dissatisfied with your stay here. Yesterday, you said you wished to leave the clinic. Is this true?"

"Are you a doctor?" Stupid question. Unlike the doctor who had given her the sedative the day before, this man wasn't dressed in white, he wore no stethoscope, and he had no name tag; instead he was wearing a hat and sunglasses.

"Mrs. van Luden, are you insisting that you are here against your free will?"

"Don't call me Mrs. van Luden, it's *Miss Saunders.* And to answer your question, yes, I am here against my free will. I was kidnapped."

The man showed no surprise.

"You had better be a doctor. I'm calling the police. Whoever is responsible for this is going to jail, and if you're involved you're going to jail too."

The man did not seem concerned by the threat. "You're claiming you never had a conversation with Mr. van Luden over the phone, where you agreed to admit yourself to a clinic?"

"Yes, that's exactly what I'm saying."

The man nodded. "I see."

Dorothy looked at him. "How did I get here?"

"You admitted yourself, remember?"

"I did no such thing."

The man cracked a sickly smile. "I'm sure it'll all come back to you sooner or later."

"I'll ask you again: who are you? Are you or are you not a doctor?"

"Damon van Luden will soon be inheriting fifty percent control of a sizable trust. Van Luden Enterprises extended the courtesy of arranging for your transportation and stay here, at the Etienne Clinic, with the understanding, of course, that you agreed to—"

"So if you're not a doctor, who are you?"

"You can call me Jim."

"Okay then, Jim, just what are you doing here?"

Again, he ignored her question. "You asked to elope, to honeymoon in an exotic place, but now you deny your agreement with your husband to admit yourself to a clinic for what is obviously much-needed detoxification."

"I didn't agree to come here and I certainly never asked to elope with Damon."

"You are wearing a wedding ring," the man pointed out.

Dorothy yanked on the gold ring, but it was half a size too small and refused to slip past her finger joint.

"There's also a marriage certificate," Jim continued. "Are you saying that you did not agree to the marriage as well?"

"Of course I didn't. I was kidnapped and I was raped." As Dorothy spoke, she remembered the man in her dreams saying, "I pronounce you man and wife." That had to have been a dream.

Jim said, "Although your wedding evening may not have gone as expected, being that you were married, technically speaking, you cannot actually call it rape."

"I never married him," Dorothy repeated.

Jim tapped on a pack of Marlboros. A cigarette popped out. "You're saying you don't remember the marriage ceremony?"

Dorothy didn't answer immediately, and Jim raised his eyebrow as if to say, "See, you *do* remember."

"I was drugged . . . I was forced. . . ."

"Mrs. van Luden, when you were admitted to this clinic, they ran blood tests, as is the standard procedure here at Etienne. Your blood alcohol level was .25, and there were other drugs in your system. Do you remember that?"

"He drugged me."

"Are you also denying you have drug and alcohol problems?"

"No! I mean yes, I'm denying it. I've been accused of it. My dad—people—they have the wrong idea, I never . . ."

"You never drank?"

"Stop putting words in my mouth!"

"There's no need to scream, I can hear you fine from where I'm sitting, and you've already caused quite a commotion. There was talk of bringing in the police, but they called me instead, since I admitted you on your husband's behalf."

"Wait. You're in on this?"

"I'm not in on anything; I was sent along as your chaperone, since Damon won't be able to come here until the end of the month when he's finished with Ranger School. Do you remember that evening?"

"You mean the rape?"

"I was referring to your behavior on your wedding night."

"What 'behavior'?"

"Being completely drunk, for one thing—"

"No, I wasn't drunk, I was drugged."

"And then running around yelling in the nude, for another. Mrs. van Luden, you caused quite a fuss there at the resort in Saint Croix."

"Saint Croix?"

"Yes, your honeymoon resort, the one you specifically requested?"

"I'll say it again, I never asked for anything."

"We'll get back to that, but first let's discuss what you did at the resort—running naked and screaming outside the bungalows."

"I never—"

"Right, you never. But the thing is, Mrs. van Luden, you did. At that point Mr. van Luden had no choice but to cut your honeymoon short. The alternative was to suffer the consequences with the local authorities. It was obvious that you needed immediate treatment. I know you originally consented to go to the clinic after your honeymoon, but I'm sure you'll agree with your husband, that coming here a few days early was the only viable solution."

"You're crazy. I don't know what you're talking about. Call the nurse, I want to talk to the police."

Jim shrugged and lit his cigarette. "That's your prerogative, of course, but I think you might choose a different course of action once we have concluded our conversation."

"Just tell me this—are you working for him? Because if you are—"

"Not officially. I'm not exactly a nine-to-five kind of guy. I am self-employed and I'm not an employee at Van Luden Enterprises or anywhere else, and you won't find a paper trail or any supporting evidence whatsoever linking me to any of my clients. That is part of the service I provide, but my principal job is to keep things running smoothly, as they should. And if they don't, I'm there to clean up the mess. As I did in Saint Croix."

Dorothy sat up in her bed. "You *are* working for him."

"In a way, yes, but it's not quite as simple as that. You need to understand: because Mr. van Luden will soon be controlling part of a trust which includes Van Luden Enterprises, I have to make sure your husband's best interests are aligned with those of the company. In this particular case, as far as Van Luden Enterprises is concerned, because the transfer of Mr. van Luden's fifty percent takes a few weeks, and is not yet complete, all the services the company has offered Mr. van Luden, up to now, constituted a wedding gift.

"I helped with the reservations for your suite, I found Mr. van Luden a limousine for the wedding, and the company offered their business jet and their two pilots for the trip to your honeymoon resort. After what you did in Saint Croix, Mr. van Luden requested the pilots fly you over here, under my escort, of course. That is all. The company was assured that you volunteered to admit yourself to this clinic with the understanding that you have a serious problem. If you are not happy, or are experiencing a change of heart, you are a free person. You may simply leave—nobody is keeping you here. Is that perfectly clear?"

"Fine, then that's exactly what I plan to do." Dorothy tried getting out of bed, but the room started spinning and the blood drained from her head. She rested herself back on the pillow and felt immediately better.

Jim was doing a poor job of feigning concern; he seemed almost entertained, as though he'd just witnessed a monkey trying to escape from a glass cage. "Are you all right, Mrs. van Luden? You look rather pale."

"I'm fine. Finish what you have to say and go."

"I have been informed you contacted your father today. My sources tell me he'll be on the first flight over. You can fly back with him commercially, if you want. Or, I can once again request the use of the company JetStar—that's the corporate jet, in case you were too inebriated to remember being on it—for a flight back to New York. Would that meet with your satisfaction?"

"No, you've done enough. We'll find our own way back."

"As you wish, but I'm heading Stateside anyway for business, so it would be no inconvenience to me or Van Luden Enterprises."

"Not so fast," Dorothy said. "There is the matter of kidnapping and rape, and if you think I'm going to let that go, you are sadly mistaken, mister."

"I'm listening."

"Wipe that smug expression off your face, or I'll slap it off!"

Amusement lingered in his smile.

"Now, you listen to me," Dorothy hissed. "By the time you set foot in the US, your boss will be behind bars where he belongs."

"Allegations of kidnapping and rape are quite serious, Mrs. van Luden." He took a deep drag of his cigarette. "In fact, if I'm not mistaken, I believe the punishment for kidnapping in some states is the same as that for murder. Have you had time to give this any thought?"

"There's nothing to think about. I'm going to the police. I'm going to tell them everything, about him and about you. Don't think I won't!" Dorothy stared at him. "If you're guilty, you'll fry with him; if not, then you and your precious company have nothing to worry about."

"Mrs. van Luden, for the record, I'm just here to help. As they say: don't kill the messenger. Regarding Van Luden Enterprises: they simply offered transportation, nothing more."

"Well, I'm still charging Damon with kidnapping and rape. As far as you and the company go, I don't care about this whole clinic thing, assuming that was the only extent of your involvement, and assuming you really do let me out of here."

"I told you, you're free to go anytime, and if you don't want to wait for your father here, you can wait for him at a hotel of your choice, all expenses paid, so long as you agree not to involve Van Luden Enterprises in any of your allegations. I am sorry you had to come here earlier than originally planned, but you were in no condition to make decisions, and a decision had to be made. You would have found yourself behind bars for drug use and indecent exposure had we not intervened."

"I don't care about being admitted to this clinic, although I have no business being here. All I care about is the fact that I was kidnapped and raped. I was *raped*. Can you get that through your thick skull?"

"Please, there's no need to raise your voice. I'm very sorry you feel that way about your wedding night but—"

"There was no wedding night. I was abducted against my will."

"Mrs. van Luden, really. You sent Damon van Luden a letter accepting his marriage proposal, and then you called—"

Dorothy slapped her hand on the mattress. "What? That's a *lie*. I never sent him a letter saying anything of the kind."

Jim sighed. "I'm sure Mr. van Luden has kept your letter, my dear, so save your breath. You asked to elope and honeymoon somewhere exotic—let me finish"—he raised his hand—"you asked him to keep it a secret. You subsequently called him, and he agreed to your wishes on the condition that you admit yourself to this clinic, and after a month here, he was going to meet you at his home in Geneva."

"This is insane. *You're* insane."

"Soon after that phone call, you and Mr. van Luden got married in Vermont—and there are witnesses and a marriage certificate to prove it—you flew to Saint Croix, where at some point after consummating your marriage, you started singing and parading yourself without a stitch on, drunker than a sailor."

"At what point was I supposedly drunk?"

"You showed up to your own wedding plastered. It was downhill from there."

"I don't drink."

"Of course not, and you don't take drugs, either. Mrs. van Luden, before you speak to the police, I suggest you talk to your father. Perhaps then, you'll see the folly of your allegations."

"You want me to wait before I talk to the police? Why? To give you time to run away?"

Jim chuckled, cutting his laughter short with unsettling ease. "I have no reason to run. I'll stay with you here, or at the hotel if you prefer, until your father arrives tomorrow."

"Well, if it's only a matter of one day, I'll wait here."

"Good, I'm sure you'll see things differently once you have the chance to clear your system of these poisons."

"Okay, say you're not involved, as you claim. Why aren't you going after Damon? If you're so innocent, you should be out there hunting him down."

"Mr. van Luden is back in Eglin, where he's completing Ranger School. The plans were for the two of you to meet afterwards in Geneva. I'm guessing that's not going to happen."

"You're damned right it isn't. Damon is not getting away with this."

"That is your affair, not mine. I am merely a facilitator, a messenger. And Van Luden Enterprises has been quite generous, considering the situation. I hope you have no complaints with the company, or their good intentions for the welfare of everyone involved."

"I don't care about the company, and if you're a facilitator, then you can facilitate by having Damon arrested."

"I cannot do that, I'm afraid. Once your father arrives and you're feeling better and not so emotional, you can go back to the States and make your charges if you still want to."

"Why not call the police here?"

"Because you claim to have been kidnapped in the United States, and allegedly raped in Saint Croix, which is also US territory, so you would have to take the matter to the States, and since Mr. van Luden is an officer in the US Army, the case would go to military court."

"Fine, I'll take him to court in Timbuktu if I have to."

"Again, that is your prerogative. So, do I have your assurances that you won't blame Van Luden Enterprises in any way for any of this?"

"Yes, I suppose."

"Then if it isn't too much of an inconvenience, would you be kind enough to sign a release stating as much? Not right now, of course. You are still under the influence, and I'd rather you signed in the presence of your father and a company attorney. Assuming, at that time, you still feel the need to press charges against Mr. van Luden."

"I told you, I don't care about the company. I'll sign the stupid thing."

"Good. Then with that understanding, I would like to say a few words. Van Luden Enterprises has been protecting the van Luden trust for many years now, as you are probably aware. It is not in the company's interest to have the van Luden name slandered. Allegations of kidnapping and rape are very serious, and if you somehow manage to have a case tried, even after he's proven innocent, there will be plenty of collateral damage."

"'If I manage to have the case tried'? 'After he's proven innocent'? What are you talking about?"

"I have been quite patient with you, but I think you need to listen to the hard truth: you are an alcoholic and a drug addict. You father knows it and your psychologist knows it. In point of fact, it was your psychologist who recommended you go to a clinic. You have a history of adolescent alcoholism, drug abuse, depression, and attempted suicide."

"I was a kid when that happened, my mother had just died. I know what the psychologist recommended, but he was wrong about me drinking and taking drugs, I didn't do any of that."

"Right. You didn't get drunk at that party, you didn't steal your father's alcohol, and you didn't take drugs. Let's see, what else: you didn't write Damon that letter, you didn't call him and make arrangements, then you didn't get married, and finally you didn't run around at the crack of dawn, making enough noise to raise the dead. None of that happened, despite all the evidence to the contrary. I don't think even you believe what you're saying. No court, civilian or military, would try your case, and even if they did, you would lose. It would be embarrassing and destructive to everyone."

"I told you, I never—screw this, I'm calling the police."

Jim smiled. "Do you know that you are pregnant?"

Dorothy dropped the phone in her lap, and her face turned white for the second time in five minutes. "What makes you say that?"

She could sense him dissecting her through his sunglasses. "They give their inpatients blood tests here. Standard procedure at clinics such as these. You have elevated levels of HCG in your blood. Do you know what that is?"

"Yes," Dorothy said, "I do."

"Really? Then either you're an avid student of biology or a doctor explained the hormone to you. How else could you know? Did you tell your husband?"

"No. I told you, I don't have a husband."

"You do, whether you wish to admit it or not. Did you tell Mr. van Luden?"

"No, of course not."

"Your husband was quite busy with his post-Academy training, so it must have happened during a surprise visit, am I right? When else could he find time to drop by? The doctor here says you've been pregnant for around a month. So when was it you saw him?"

Dorothy flushed. "I, I—"

"Don't say another word—I can't hear what you don't say."

"I don't know what you're talking about."

"Sure you do. You know exactly what I'm talking about, you bed-hopping cunt." The smile grew. "You've been fucking around, haven't you? Spreading those sweet teen thighs of yours. I know you've been a naughty girl—women don't test positive for pregnancy the day after conception. I couldn't care less what you did before you were married. These are modern times, right? As long as nobody finds out."

Dorothy couldn't put her finger on it, but he almost seemed aroused. The first time he'd shown any trace of emotion. "What the hell are you talking about?"

He inhaled deeply and blew smoke rings at her. "Mr. van Luden would be very disappointed to know what sort of person his wife really is. The company tried to warn him, but he was too stuck on you to listen. Now it's a done deal. If he finds out the child is not his, it would disgrace the van Luden name, and he'll probably decide to terminate this marriage, along with the fetus."

"What?" Dorothy tried to move, but she couldn't.

Jim looked around for an ashtray, and, finding none, he tapped the ashes to the floor. "I see three alternatives here: One, you can keep all these ridiculous allegations to yourself. Never—and I mean *never*—speak of it again. We'll chalk up your recent hysteria to the drugs and the unpleasant aftereffects of your detoxification here at the clinic. Once you are cured, you'll move to Mr. van Luden's residence in Geneva, and await his return from Ranger School. You and your husband will live happily ever after here in Switzerland."

Dorothy looked at him, trying to get a hint of what was going on behind those dark lenses.

"Your pregnancy is a delicate matter. I'm assuming you didn't have relations with Mr. van Luden a month or so ago. If you did, then there's nothing to worry about. If you didn't, we have a problem: the clinic's files show you as pregnant, and if your husband finds out, he'll know in a second the child isn't his.

"That's where I come in. Like I said before, one of my areas of expertise is cleaning up after people. I've already arranged to have the clinic keep this tidbit of information from your father, your husband, and anyone else. For a few weeks, you'll have to behave as though you don't know you're knocked up. He won't be done with Ranger School until the end of the month, so wait until then to tell everyone you're pregnant. That way he'll believe your pregnancy was the result of consummating your marriage on your wedding night. You will never tell anyone that you carry a bastard child. Let everyone believe it's Mr. van Luden's kid.

"And this little chitchat we're having? It'll be a secret you'll take with you to the grave. That's really not asking much, because this way everyone wins." He crushed his cigarette against the arm of his chair. "And if you ask me, you two make a wonderful couple."

"Well, I didn't ask you. You're not changing my mind—I'm going to get a divorce and press charges."

Jim showed no sign of being displeased. "That brings me to the second alternative. If you don't wish to stay married to your husband, I'm going to assume this child does not belong to him. In this case, you'll keep all these silly allegations of kidnapping and the like to yourself.

"You will not press charges, as this will cause everyone, Mr. van Luden and therefore Van Luden Enterprises, an unnecessary and monumental headache.

"You won't even need to divorce your husband. Under New York state law, the marriage would be nullified due to the fact that you were intoxicated at the time. Therefore, your allegations aren't necessary to have the marriage dissolved. You were drunk, you weren't thinking clearly—the clinic, I assure you, will back you up on this—and the marriage will be legally annulled.

"Furthermore, it goes without saying, that you will have to have the fetus aborted. It is an obvious point, but I need to make this perfectly clear. If you end this marriage, and then at the same time people find out—which they will—that you carry someone else's kid, it would be a devastating personal insult to Mr. van Luden. It would irreparably tarnish his public image and, by virtue of his control over the company, that of Van Luden Enterprises.

"Therefore, upon your return to the United States, you'll proceed with the abortion. All related expenses will be covered, you needn't worry about that. Nobody will know about the abortion. It will save you the shame. In addition, you will be compensated generously for your troubles, and for keeping your sexual escapades a secret. I'll personally inform Mr. van Luden of your decision to terminate the marriage. Publicly, you will make no mention of the abortion. You will simply wait for a month, and if for some reason someone asks, you'll just say you had a miscarriage. That will spare us any rumors of pre-marital relations. This is not only to protect Mr. van Luden's reputation, but yours as well."

Dorothy was on her feet. "Who the hell are you to tell me what I'm going to do with my child?"

Jim didn't move; he watched as she stabbed her finger in his direction. "If you choose to dissolve this marriage, the child must go."

"And if I refuse?"

"If you don't cooperate, then I'm afraid you're going to find yourself having a miscarriage. You'll wake up one morning soaked in blood, and you'll never be able to prove it wasn't a natural occurrence.

"If you have a miscarriage, chances are that you will suffer excessive blood loss and die. It would be an unfortunate conclusion to your young life.

"That would be option three, and I don't recommend it. It's very messy and it means extra work for me. But however this goes down, I get paid the same.

"Get some rest now. When you're feeling better, think about this talk of ours, but mention it to no one or the consequences will be . . . well, let's not get into that again. Besides, who is going to take the word of a drug addict?

"I'm confident you'll do what's best for everyone. Just be sure you've made up your mind by tomorrow, when your father arrives, so you can get your story straight."

He stood, and they were just a few feet apart. He reached for his jacket pocket and Dorothy pulled away.

Jim produced a business card. "If you choose to return to the States with your father, call me and I'll arrange for that abortion. It'll be like none of this ever happened. Nobody will know, and you'll end up rich for your troubles. If you choose to stay, then I don't expect we'll be meeting again."

He flipped the quarter, snatching it out of the air. "Best of luck with your life . . . and congratulations."

GONE

Dorothy handed Kory a card.

JIM K. NATTAS

MANHATTAN CLEANING SERVICE

He turned the card over. There was a phone number with a 212 area code scribbled on the back.

"Option two was a death trap," Kory said. "A man like Jim would not risk trusting you to keep your mouth shut, and there would be no assurances that bribery would work on you. More importantly, if the marriage were annulled, Damon would lose his fifty percent. I'll bet that phone number was just a trigger to have you assassinated. Anything other than option one, and both you and Jan would not be alive today."

"If it was only for my life, I would have taken the risk and called the police."

"Well, it's a good thing you didn't, because I know Damon, he'd have no compunctions about green-lighting your murder."

"I wish there were some way I could have Jim arrested."

"So do I, but by the sound of it, he was a pro. This guy had all bases covered. He himself said there were no records of any association between him and Damon. We don't even have a real name to give the police.

"Damon hired this man because he was the best money could buy. Also because Damon couldn't have had you kidnapped, force married, and transported to a clinic in Switzerland without an accomplice. In addition, by using Jim,

355

Damon left himself and the company completely untouchable. He had you branded a drug-using suicidal teen. Like Jim said, nobody would take the word of a drug addict."

Kory thought for a while. "One thing, though, after Jan was born, what kept you there? Why not just divorce Damon and leave? Or just run away as you did now?"

"Once our child was born, and they couldn't pretend I had a miscarriage, I tried to escape, but I was caught and punished. After that, I couldn't see friends or leave the grounds, and his two thugs shadowed me wherever I went."

"Of course. He had to keep you under his thumb because otherwise you would demand a divorce, and he'd immediately lose control of the trust." Kory fiddled with something in his pocket. After a while, he said, "When will we tell John and Mary?"

"As soon as they come back from Hawaii. Right now, they don't even know Jan and I are here. We can get Charlie's father to tell us when they're back home. We'll sneak over to Rhodes and pay them a surprise visit. Lord, I don't know how my dad will react to all this."

"I imagine he'll want retribution."

"No doubt, but deep down he's just another softy like you."

"Softy?" Kory said. "That's not very flattering."

"Men." Dorothy smiled. "Your egos are so big, and yet at the same time, so sensitive. What's wrong with being a softy? You're a gentleman in every sense of the word."

"Thank you . . . I think."

"Oh silly, that's just one of the qualities I love about you."

Kory raked his rice with a limp fork. "I have the feeling your father took my aunt to Hawaii to propose."

Dorothy looked up in surprise.

"They've grown quite close in your absence."

"I guess I knew that might happen. I mean, it does make sense—"

"Is that hard for you?"

"Not really, but I can't imagine calling Mary my mother."

"Just as Jan might find it hard to call me his father."

"No, no. With Jan it's a totally different situation. It's as if he *knows* you're his real father. First off, he was never close with

Damon—he was afraid—we all were. There's no person in the world Jan would rather be his father than you."

"That means a lot." Neither of them spoke for a while. Finally, in a lowered voice, Kory said, "We can't let Damon get away with this, not after what he did to you and to our son."

"He's not worth it. I've wanted revenge for years, but I've learned the price is far too high. Besides, once I get a divorce, he'll lose everything."

Kory nodded, poking at his food. "Did you make an appointment with that lawyer yet?"

"Uh-huh, for next Monday. Don't expect miracles, though. Charlie says divorces can take a very long time, especially when the husband is unwilling to sign the papers."

"Which he'll never do."

"Honey, I am thousands of miles away from Damon. I'm home now, with you. Everything will work out in the end, you'll see."

Kory looked up and tried to smile. "I'm the one who's supposed to be reassuring you."

"Don't forgive him, just forget him. If I can, you can." Dorothy held up her wineglass. "To no more Damon."

"Damon who?"

Dorothy smiled.

Kory tapped his glass gently to hers. "To us, to our child."

Jan got his hand in the popcorn bag just in time. It was almost empty. Uncle Charlie had big hands. He told Jan he should slow down, or else he'd spoil his appetite. Jan wasn't falling for that trick.

Bond looked Japanese now. He was doing judo and karate.

Damon had said he was going to make Jan start taking judo lessons. Jan didn't have to worry about that now.

"I'm thirsty," Jan said.

"Yeah, I'm not surprised—you ate most of the popcorn!"

"*You* did!"

"You believed me!" Charlie laughed. "So what'll it be? Lemonade? Coke?"

"What's Coke?" Jan asked.

"Hmmm, tell you what, I'll get you a lemonade. You can try Coke another time. It might make you hyper."

"Hyper?"

Charlie laughed and ruffled Jan's hair. "I'll be right back. Save my seat."

As Dorothy sipped the wine, Kory felt the velvet box in his pocket. He had planned this evening for days, but it wasn't the night.

He gave Dorothy a sad smile.

"What's on that magnificent mind of yours?"

In response, he took her hand, squeezing it gently.

They had so much to talk about, so much pain to share.

He decided to wait for another day, for that perfect moment to come on its own.

It was all right. They had plenty of time.

Charlie walked down the aisle counting rows. They'd been sitting on two left-most seats halfway down the middle aisle. Jan's head didn't make it over the seatback, so Charlie looked for two empty places. He counted fourteen rows but only found one empty seat. The other seat was occupied. Confused, he started walking a few rows farther. He was stopped by a voice. "Do you think this movie is appropriate for a five-year-old?"

At first, Charlie didn't think the words were directed at him. Why would they be?

Charlie searched, but couldn't find any empty seats. The movie was a box-office hit. Charlie turned back and saw a man looking right at him. He was wearing a business suit that bulged at the waist. Despite the vast belly, the man had the look of someone capable of inflicting a lot of damage with little provocation. The seat next to him was empty.

"Excuse me, was there a little boy sitting there?" Charlie's voice sounded like it came from a broken oboe.

"The seat is no longer occupied," the man said.

"That's not what I asked. Was there a little boy there?"

"Sit down," the man said. "You are blocking the view. People are watching the movie."

This time, Charlie shouted the question.

"Hey, buddy, he's right—either sit down or get the fuck out." It was the same guy who had raised a stink earlier.

The man in the business suit got up and turned to the foulmouthed guy. "I am sorry, Monsieur, we are leaving." He hooked a finger at Charlie and started walking up the aisle. "Follow me."

Charlie's knees no longer wanted to support him, and he was suddenly short of breath.

The door to the theater shut firmly behind them, and Charlie found himself once again by the concession stand.

"Where's the boy?" Charlie said, unable to raise his voice now.

"Jan is on his way back to Geneva."

Charlie's mouth moved, but nothing came out. It was a while before he said, "Gone? Geneva? Who are you? What have you done with Jan?"

"Jean-Luc," the man replied, reaching for his breast pocket. Charlie jumped back an inch. Jean-Luc produced an envelope.

Not a gun. Not a gun. Get a grip, this isn't a movie.

"This is bullshit, I'm calling the police."

Jean-Luc waved the envelope. "It is you who should be worried about the police, not me. Madame van Luden ran away with Mr. van Luden's child. That is kidnapping, and you, Monsieur, are a co-conspirator. This letter I have in my hand is written by Mr. van Luden and it gives me the legal authority to bring his child back home."

Thinking was taking an almost physical effort. If Jan was really on the way to the airport, then maybe there was still a chance Charlie could catch up with him. He could try Swiss Air first. Or the first flight out of JFK. No time to waste. Time to act. Charlie headed for the exit.

"We have unfinished business."

"The hell we do," Charlie shouted as he rammed through the glass doors, and out onto the sidewalk. "Taxi!"

There was no taxi. Still, it felt better yelling for one.

A beefy hand landed on Charlie's shoulder. Charlie did a sloppy twist swinging hard at the night air.

The guy called Jean-Luc laughed. "Mr. Patterson, be careful or you'll hurt yourself."

"Fuck you, Froggie. This is America—you don't just snatch five-year-olds out of movie theaters and get away with it."

"*Alors,*" Jean-Luc said, "now you are being rude and unreasonable. May I suggest, Monsieur, that you try, instead, to think about your situation. Jan is not your boy, and so he is not your responsibility. I, however, have been hired to protect him from the day he was born. If you go to the airport, what will you do? Girard, my colleague, is not as patient as me. He also has a copy of the letter. If you run to the airport, you will end up in jail, and Jan will still be on his way to Geneva."

Charlie stared but didn't speak.

"You and I will go back to Monsieur Kory's home. I will explain the situation."

Realizing Charlie was not going to respond, Jean-Luc shrugged. "In any case, I am going there. You can follow me or not."

"This is such a magical city," Dorothy said as they strolled back to Kory's place. "I've always wanted to live here."

Kory smiled. "Then live here you shall."

They walked up the front stoop. Kory produced the key, then unlocked the door and opened it in one fluid motion.

Charlie was standing in the hallway, facing them. He looked pale, and the front of his shirt was soaked.

A man in a suit was sitting in the hallway chair, his hands interlaced, his feet crossed.

"Dorothy, I'm so sorry," Charlie said. "This guy was following us and he took—"

"*Bonsoir, Madame.*"

Dorothy screamed.

Kory was fairly sure, but he still asked Charlie, "Who is this man?"

"He took Jan," Charlie said. "I mean, the other guy took Jan"—Charlie pointed—"but *he's* behind all this."

"Oh, I think I know who's behind this," Kory said.

"*Cochon!*" Dorothy lunged herself at Jean-Luc, beating him with the sides of her fists. He grabbed both arms, got up, and maneuvered her into his seat. He was still holding her arms, bending to keep his eyes level with hers, when he said, "*Vous allez vous calmer, Madame?*"

As Jean-Luc spoke to Dorothy, Kory appeared from behind him, unnoticed. "Let go of her."

It was almost a whisper, and although there was nothing to relate them physically, the command in his voice sounded like it had come from his brother. Reflexively, Jean-Luc complied, releasing Dorothy. She slapped him hard.

"Now," Kory said, "tell us where Jan is."

"He is on the way back to his home, Monsieur," Jean-Luc said. The left side of his face was turning a dark shade of burgundy. To Dorothy: "*Et vous, Madame. Vous devrez faire la même.*"

"She's not going anywhere," Kory said. "This is her home, not that prison in Switzerland." Kory turned to Charlie. "What happened?"

Glassy-eyed, Charlie said, "They took him, I just went to get a drink for the kid, and they fucking took him."

Jean-Luc produced the envelope.

Kory opened it without saying a word. He squinted to read his brother's compressed, neat script. The letter stated that Girard Lemond and Jean-Luc Garnier were authorized to return Jan van Luden to his home in Geneva, from which he was unwillingly and unlawfully removed by Mr. Damon van Luden's emotionally disturbed spouse.

Jean-Luc waited for Kory to finish reading and then he said, "This is out of your hands. It is not your business anymore."

Dorothy was weeping.

Addressing Kory, Charlie said, "We can't just stand here. Surely the police can do something? Right?"

"Monsieur Patterson, as I explained before, Jan is going *home*. Mr. van Luden was unable to come himself to pick up his son, because he is serving his country in Berlin, after a tour in Vietnam, which is far more than you draft-dodgers have ever done."

"*Hey*. Who are you calling a draft-dodger?" Charlie said. "You can't go to the Army and be in college at the same time."

"Mr. van Luden did," Jean-Luc said. "He went to military college; you used college to hide from your duty."

"Oh, please," Charlie snapped. "Were you in Vietnam when the French were getting reamed? We wouldn't be in this mess if you guys had done the job right in the first place!"

Kory looked at the envelope in his hand. He was about to say something, but he walked over to Dorothy instead, trying to get close enough to be heard while Charlie was distracting the Frenchman. Dorothy pulled away, still crying.

"You were left behind for a reason," Kory said to Dorothy, though her head was turned away. "Possibly to help dissuade Charlie from going to the police." Creases formed in Kory's forehead. "But there's more to it. Redundancy is precaution. If you couldn't stop Charlie from going to the police, or if you and I decided to call for help, there'd still be the problem of Damon's letter."

Jean-Luc was finished with Charlie and listened to the younger van Luden.

"I have no idea if that piece of paper has any legal value," Kory said, "but it would certainly delay the police. They wouldn't stop Jan at passport control unless they were certain that the child was being kidnapped. By the time they could confirm that, he would be on his way to Switzerland."

"You are quite correct, Monsieur," Jean-Luc said.

"But that's not the whole picture, is it?" Kory squinted at Jean-Luc. "You didn't just come here to try and delay us, so why are you really here?"

Jean-Luc smiled. He was fiendishly clever, this Kory. Not to be underestimated. "Simple: to escort Mrs. van Luden back to her home."

"And how do you plan on doing that?" Charlie said. "Are you planning on marching her through JFK at gunpoint?"

Jean-Luc raised his arms halfway. "Monsieur Patterson, I am unarmed. Mrs. van Luden is an adult." To Dorothy: "Monsieur van Luden respects your wishes. You can come or you can stay; it is up to you."

Dorothy's mascara had left black lines on her cheeks, but she'd stopped crying. "I have to go."

"What? You can't be serious!" Charlie said. "Don't listen to this guy—you don't have to go *anywhere*."

Kory kneeled next to Dorothy, wrapping his arm around her shoulder. "There's no choice here, Charlie. Damon knew that when he set this whole thing up." Kory spoke softly. "This is all my fault. I should have known Damon wouldn't just sit back and do nothing as he loses control over Dorothy, Jan, and most importantly, the trust. I didn't just make a mistake; it's worse than that, I forfeited the damned game."

"Wait a sec here," Charlie said, "you're going along with this as well?" He looked at both of them incredulously. "Are you two totally bonkers?"

"Not when the alternative is for her to stay here and leave Jan alone with Damon."

Charlie was about to protest, but Dorothy cut him off. "I'd rather be dead than let that happen."

LESSONS

October 1967

"**D**id he hurt you?"

"No, Madame."

"If he did, you would tell me, yes?"

Jan hesitated, was about to say something, and thought better of it.

"I will talk to your mother again," Mlle. Chorafas said. "We'll see." She stood, stretched her arms out, interlocking her fingers, palms twisted forward.

Jan did the exercise without being told. Piano lessons came after judo, so he had to loosen up before playing.

The Week Before Christmas, 1967

Jan looked up at the big Yugoslavian man and wondered how a grown-up could be so silly. There was no way Jan could sweep that massive foot, but he had no choice but to try. Jan used his forward foot, hooking it around Mirko's heel while pushing and twisting against Mirko's arm.

The big man didn't even quiver, and Jan felt a sharp pain where his foot made contact with Mirko's stone leg.

"Aaaah!" Jan hopped on one foot, grabbing his other foot with both hands.

"I didn't do that, *you* did!" Mirko bent down to examine Jan's foot. There was a small pink patch on the five-year-old's heel, but it wouldn't even develop into a decent bruise. "It is nothing," Mirko said. "Look, I show you again, okay?"

Jan sighed.

Mirko performed the maneuver, against an invisible opponent, exaggerating the sweeping movement of the foot against the mat. "Grab and *lift*, like you're knocking away a heavy stone with rake."

"That's what I did," Jan said. "It didn't work."

"And why is that?"

"Because you're a big fat moose," Jan said, and immediately covered his mouth. "I'm sorry, I'm sorry. I didn't mean that."

Mirko laughed in a loud roar.

Jan smiled despite himself. He didn't want Mirko getting the idea that he was starting to like judo.

Jan suddenly jumped forward, trying the sweep a second time. Amazingly, Mirko's foot came away from the floor, and the Yugoslavian judo master rolled onto his back, slapping his hand on the mat and producing a fat sound. Jan got on top of him trying to manage the pin he had been taught, but the moment Jan grabbed at Mirko's thick gi, the judo master rolled over, pinning him down.

Jan slapped the mat twice, which in judo meant *I give up*. The one trick Jan learned easily.

Dorothy and Mlle. Chorafas were at the door.

Behind them, Mr. Curtis was running after Girard. "Excuse me, may I have a quick word?"

Girard sidestepped, got behind the two women he was looking after, and hooked a thumb downstairs. "If this is about Jan's math syllabus, you can find Jean-Luc downstairs."

"I was just wondering . . . because Mr. van Luden is coming soon . . . is there something—will there be another review?"

Girard shrugged. "I don't know. Ask Jean-Luc."

Mr. Curtis walked away with the hustle of a man about to miss the last train home.

Jan turned to go to his mother.

Mirko stopped him. "What do we do?"

Jan faced Mirko, clicked his bare heels together, and pasted his palms to his thighs. Together they bowed, and then Mirko waved him off.

"Mo-oom, you were *watching*?"

"Oh, honey, you were wonderful," Dorothy said, as she straightened out his gi.

"I was *not.*"

Mlle. Chorafas walked over to Mirko, addressing Girard. "How long must this continue?"

Girard turned his hands up. "Look, if Jean-Luc said Jan has to take judo, he has to take judo. I don't make the decisions around here. You are welcome to talk to him again; leave me out of this."

Dorothy said to Jan, "I saw you trip him. That was very impressive."

But Jan was looking at his piano teacher, who was now taking Mirko by the sleeve of his gi, pulling him away.

"If he gets hurt, he might have to stop practicing for days." Mlle. Chorafas shook her finger at Mirko. "If he receives a serious injury, you could be ending his chances to be a pianist." Her eyes narrowed. "I am warning you, if anything happens to him, you are the one responsible."

Mirko seemed amused.

Jan wondered if anybody could hurt Mirko's feelings.

"He's a boy," Mirko said slowly. "Do you expect him to sit in a chair all day?"

Mlle. Chorafas turned to her young pupil. "I'll be at the piano; your lesson is in ten minutes." She eyed Mirko. "Will I have to learn Slovenian to get through to you?"

Dorothy put her hand on the piano teacher's shoulder. "He's just doing his job."

"Yes, but as I have said many times, judo and piano do not mix."

"I know, but Mr. van Luden has made it clear: no judo, no piano," Dorothy reminded the piano teacher for the seventh time.

Mlle. Chorafas eyed Girard. "Do you mind?"

He moved aside as she brushed past him.

"Mrs. van Luden, may I speak with you?" Mirko said, as Mlle. Chorafas disappeared out the door.

Dorothy gave Jan a look, and the boy obeyed, sitting in the corner.

Mirko looked over at Jan. "Your son is making good progress."

"I'm sorry about Mademoiselle Chorafas," Dorothy said. "She just doesn't understand."

Mirko shrugged. "I know. But it is hard to teach him when he is worried about hurting his hands."

Dorothy said nothing.

"I understand it might be difficult," Mirko said, "but really it is important for the child to practice with other boys."

"I'm sure it is." Dorothy nodded. "Did you mention this to Jean-Luc?"

"I was hoping you—"

Dorothy looked the judo instructor in his kind brown eyes. "Damon is in the States. Jean-Luc is the only one who has contact with him right now. I'm sorry."

Mirko knew not to press the matter further. He'd said what had to be said, and he shouldn't have been talking to her about it in the first place. The Frenchman, Jean-Luc, had made it clear when he'd hired Mirko two months ago: he was the one in charge. He'd told Mirko he might not meet with his employer, Mr. van Luden, for some time, and that he was to address any concerns he might have to Jean-Luc and no one else.

With this understanding in mind, Mirko had told Jean-Luc about his idea of getting Jan to spar with other children. The Frenchman didn't seem interested in listening to Mirko, saying that Mrs. van Luden and her boy were not to leave the premises for reasons that were none of Mirko's concern.

Isabeau, the new governess, came into the gym and grabbed Jan by the arm, lifting him to his feet. Speaking to him in French, she said, "Jan, you must clean up. Quickly now."

"Wait just a moment!" Dorothy said. *"Laisse le! Il est fatigué."*

Isabeau started taking Jan out of the gym room, but Dorothy stepped in her way. "I *said*, leave him."

"Ah, ça c'est impossible, alors!" Isabeau said. *"On peut pas jouer comme ça chaque fois qu'il faut faire du travaille ici!"*

Dorothy snapped back in French, "I'm not the one playing games." Her eyes darted at Girard and then back at Isabeau. "I don't need either of you in this house. Why don't you find your-selves employment at some concentration camp in Siberia?"

"I will go change now," Mirko said, looking away from both women.

"I'm sorry," Dorothy said to Mirko, "this has nothing to do with you. Thank you for thinking about what's best for Jan." She looked at Isabeau, still speaking to Mirko. "At least *someone* here genuinely cares what happens to the boy."

Mirko nodded at Dorothy, tried smiling at Jan, and slipped away between Isabeau and Girard.

He heard Dorothy saying, "I'll take care of *my* son if you don't mind—in fact, I'm taking him anyway, even if you *do* mind. Come on, honey, let's get you changed."

Dorothy looked down the hall. Mirko was gone. She said to Isabeau, *"Il est parti."*

Isabeau nodded and took Jan's other hand, gently this time. Together the two women took Jan to his room to clean him up for his piano lesson. Girard turned away at the staircase, head-ing for the conference room where Jean-Luc was speaking with Mr. Curtis and Mr. Talbaum.

THE VISIT

January 1968

Damon arrived at the station at precisely 17:32. Girard chauffeured him home in the Mercedes. He'd greeted his boss with a *"Bonsoir"* and formal tug of his hat, and those were the only words he spoke the rest of the evening.

It wasn't quite cold enough for snow, and the rain was coming down hard against the windshield. Some Christmas Jan must have had. Damon had instructed Jean-Luc to buy the boy a train set and put it in a big red box. He would have to remember to ask about that.

He'd called several times from the States, when he had a break from Advanced Training. They'd managed to recover Dorothy and Jan. They were both okay, according to Jean-Luc and he'd vowed something like this would never happen again.

If Damon had been at home, they could have made all the promises they could dream up, he'd have fired them all. He didn't care if it had been primarily Françoise's fault. Yes, they did eventually return his family back to their home, but they should never have let things get that far in the first place.

But Damon hadn't been at home, nor would he be for much longer, his second tour in Berlin would end in August. He had no idea where he'd be after that. He'd put in a request for Special Forces. Damon would go where they needed him. That was the nature of the job. The needs of the Army come before the needs of the individual.

371

So he was stuck with Jean-Luc and Girard for the time being. He could have had them replaced, but it was hard finding civilians Damon could trust. In eight months, Damon wouldn't have to worry about Jan anymore.

And Dorothy. It wasn't as if she was going to suddenly become a halfway decent wife, or wake up one morning and turn into a responsible mother. He'd hoped she'd eventually see the light, but that dream was burning thin.

Jan, on the other hand, was still young. There was hope for him.

"Monsieur? I trust you've had a good meal?"

Damon eyed Jean-Luc, waiting for a real question.

"If you like, I could brief you now, or we could arrange it for tomorrow, if you are still tired from your trip."

Damon frowned. "You set up a debriefing with the tutors for this evening?"

"No, no—"

"Well, good, because I'm going to hit the sack. I'll talk to them tomorrow."

"No need to talk with them, Monsieur. I have already been briefed by all Jan's instructors. I can give you all the information you need at your convenience. Tomorrow morning?"

"I need to sleep, we'll talk about this later."

Damon listened to Jean-Luc as he went through the list of tutors and the progress Jan was making with each. It was a comprehensive report, well articulated and presented. Still, it hardly made up for the mess last summer.

"Monsieur Galbot is pleased with Jan's French, on the whole, but Jan is weak in some areas of grammar and needs to study more."

"It sounds like he's not studying enough in most of the subjects," Damon said.

"He does not make sufficient time for his studies, Monsieur. He is all day at the piano." Jean-Luc looked for a reaction. "When you are not here, of course."

"Which is most of the time," Damon said. "What else goes on during my absence?"

Jean-Luc cleared his throat before spending the next twenty minutes talking about Dorothy. The Frenchman didn't seem to care for her much, though he was doing his best to cover for it. Damon couldn't blame him; the guy came close to losing his job because of her, and from the sound of it, she was making sure he earned his keep, day and night.

Jean-Luc held the door of the conference room open as Damon walked out.

Mirko stepped up to Damon, extending his hand. "Mr. van Luden."

Jean-Luc walked around Damon and said to Mirko, "You shouldn't be here. I have already spoken with him. I told you, as I have all the other instructors, *I* will be doing the briefings from now on."

Mirko didn't move or even bother looking in Jean-Luc's direction. Instead, he addressed Damon. "I haven't had the privilege of meeting you. I am Mirkoslav Gorišek, Jan's sensei."

Jean-Luc said, "Monsieur van Luden is a very busy man. He does not have time to meet with each instructor individually. You are no exception."

Damon raised his hand halfway. "That's okay, Jean-Luc, I'd like to speak with the man."

Jean-Luc stepped back, but did not leave.

Damon introduced himself to Mirko and shot Jean-Luc a warning glare. "It is a pleasure to meet you." Motioning to the door Damon added, "If you don't mind."

The Frenchman gave Mirko the evil eye, nodded at his boss, and walked off reluctantly.

"Who did you study under?" Damon asked.

Mirko told him.

"What dan are you?"

Mirko cocked his head to the side. "Fourth. You know much about judo?"

Damon shrugged. "Not really, I've seen demonstrations."

Mirko nodded. "I have a feeling you are being modest, sir." He locked eyes with his employer. Cool American blue. Yet surprisingly passionate for a military man. A dangerous combination. "Forgive me for saying this. Mrs. van Luden has told me that you chose judo for your son."

"That is correct," Damon said. "Is there a problem?"

"I think that he would make much better progress if he could train with boys his age."

"That makes sense."

Mirko's mouth opened, then became a stern line. "I was told otherwise, sir."

"Really?" Damon said. "By whom?"

"Jean-Luc," Mirko said. "He told me it was not possible. He said the boy was not to leave the premises."

Damon nodded. "Oh, I see. I get what is happening here."

Mirko waited for more, but instead of offering an explanation, Damon asked, "Where's your dojo?"

"La Route Brochard."

"That's in Vieille Ville, is it not?"

"Yes," Mirko said. "I have lessons for boys Monday, Wednesday, and Friday. Also Saturday at ten in the morning."

Damon thought for a moment. "Could they come here?"

"The boys?"

"Just a few of them. I was thinking along the lines of some of your more motivated and disciplined students."

"I know of two boys who live in this area," Mirko said. "I will suggest this to their parents."

"Perfect. I'll have Girard drive them over if transportation is an issue."

WILL POWER

May 1968

Dorothy held the pole tightly. All seats were taken, and she was only one of three standing in the tram. She rummaged through her purse and found Roger Samuel's address, one of the few American attorneys on the list the embassy had given her.

The tram rocked gently as it headed up la Route de Chêne. The gray buildings seemed to melt through the rain-assaulted windows.

Dorothy wore her yellow raincoat and, expecting the weather, she'd brought a matching plastic purse.

Girard was seated one car behind, reading *Le Monde*. The newspaper constituted his only effort at concealment.

Dorothy hopped off the tram the moment it came to a stop, stepping into a shallow puddle on the island in the middle of the road. The rain drummed against her hood. She wondered if she'd ever see the bright sun again.

Dr. Gelernt once told her that Geneva had one of the highest suicide rates in Europe. Some attributed it to the ionization of the air, while others blamed it on the depressing weather. Dorothy could think of much better reasons.

Girard stood on the other side of the street, under the cover of a tobacco store tent. He did not bother pretending. He was facing her now.

Dorothy waved; Girard shook his head. Underutilized and overpaid. *Way* overpaid. Dorothy laughed humorlessly and walked into the modern office building. A concierge greeted her disapprovingly. Her raincoat was dripping puddles onto the clean marble floor.

"I'm here to see Monsieur Samuel?"

"Fifth floor, on the right, at the end of the hallway."

"The boy's name is Jan?"

Dorothy nodded.

"Do you have any other children Mrs. van Luden?"

"No, just the one. It's really quite simple—"

"Simple? Perhaps. But it is an important document. Of course, you are very young, and have a long life ahead of you, but one can never be sure of what misfortunes life might bring. You are wise to do this now. Most people procrastinate."

"Like I said on the phone, this cannot wait, and I'd like to take this home with me."

"Ah, yes, about that"—Mr. Samuel leaned back in his executive chair—"my secretary has a stack of other documents to prepare. Could you come back and sign? We could have it ready by tomorrow evening."

"That's *not* what we agreed. I hope you haven't just wasted my time, Mr. Samuel. I was very clear about this over the phone: I want to finish today. Not tomorrow, not the day after. And if you can't, I'll go elsewhere."

Mr. Samuel regarded the young lady a moment. "I think you'll find there aren't that many US attorneys in Geneva. The other two are my friends, and I can assure you they are as busy as I. That said, since you must have this now, I'll see what can be done."

He leaned forward and pressed a button on the interphone. "Deb, would you come here for a moment?"

A tall brunette appeared at the door. She smiled at Mr. Samuel and looked at Dorothy as if she had just offered herself to the man.

"Yes, Mr. Samuel?"

He held out some typed pages. "Standard form, I've penciled in the names and crossed out the sections we don't need. Could you do me the favor of whipping this one up for me now?"

"Legal size?"

"A4 is fine," he said. "Sorry about this." He looked at Dorothy with accusing eyes. "I realize I've given you a pile of other things to do, but I'm afraid the young lady here insists she have this today."

Dorothy bit her lip. She was about to say something, but the secretary snatched the papers and walked out the room before Dorothy had a chance.

It took Mr. Samuel's secretary half an hour to stamp out the five-page document.

Dorothy read it over carefully. She signed, he witnessed and stamped, and then Dorothy said, "If some fellow comes over and asks what I was doing here, you have my permission to answer his questions."

Mr. Samuel did not seem sure he'd heard correctly, but eventually gave a hesitant nod.

As Dorothy waited for the next tram, she looked for Girard. He was nowhere to be seen, but she knew he was bound to show up at the lawyer's office sooner or later.

"Thank you," Dorothy said, as the cook placed the roast beef and vegetables in front of her.

"Thank you," Jan said, ever wary of Damon's watchful eyes.

Dorothy and Jan waited for Damon to start before they took their forks. "How are things coming along with math?" Damon said, looking straight at Jan.

"Very well, thank you."

Damon nodded. Jean-Luc had given him a detailed report. The boy was doing exceptionally well with all his tutors, and since they'd started bringing over some of the boys from the dojo, Jan had actually taken a liking to his judo classes.

"And if things were not going 'very well,' you would tell me?" Damon said.

Jan looked at his mother and said, "Yes."

Damon waited for a moment. "Are you sure?"

"Yes sir, I am sure."

"Good, good," Damon said, "because trust is very important. If we don't have trust, what do we have? Isn't that right, Dorothy?"

She was looking away, but her mouth was pursed into a narrow gash.

Damon raised his eyebrows as if to demonstrate to Jan how unreasonable his mother was being. "One day, Jan, when you become a leader, you'll learn the importance of trust. Every single man under my command has trusted me with his life," Damon said, dabbing his mouth with the napkin. "Every one of them." He turned to the cook and asked for some Bordeaux. A glass of wine a day with a meal was his limit. "That trust has to be *earned*, Jan. It doesn't just come with rank. You have to work for it, and once you have it, you must hold on to it. Do we understand each other?"

"Yes, sir."

"Good, because you have to realize that while trust can be gained, it can also be lost. We are given things in life. Some of us are luckier than others. You have a good body, a sound mind, a home to live in." Damon regarded Jan. The boy looked back attentively. "Our parents and their parents before them have handed down their good genes, their culture, their knowledge. Wisdom and culture their parents gave them, and their parents before them. You are at the end of a very long, special chain, Jan. You come from a great family, you know."

Jan had heard all this before. Over and over again.

Jan nodded, but Damon's frown suggested a more affirmative response was needed. "Yes, sir," Jan offered, a bit too loudly.

Damon relaxed. "Good, good. So you must take care of your mind. You have to take your studies very seriously. But you must also work your body. Understand?"

"Yes, sir."

"So how are things with your sensei?" Damon tested.

"He says I am progressing well, sir."

"Do you like judo?"

"I like Mirko, and judo too, of course." Jan stopped himself. He could tell from Damon's reaction he'd said something wrong.

"Mirko is your teacher, not your playmate. You are to refer to him as *Sensei*, not *Mirko*."

"Sorry sir, I won't do it again."

Damon stared at the tears that so easily came to the child's eyes. "You had better not."

Damon turned to Dorothy but spoke to his son. "So tell me, Jan, what made you think that you can address any adult, especially your sensei, by his first name?"

Dorothy returned his look, her eyes shining with rage. He was taunting her, and she knew better than to play this game. Dorothy looked away, said nothing. She wasn't going to argue with him, especially not with Jan around.

Damon tossed his napkin on the table. "It doesn't really matter. Jan will go to one of the best boarding schools in the States, and one of the few that accepts six-year-olds: the Livingsford School for Boys. There he'll be made into a man of character. He needs to go where he will forge his body and mind to a state of excellence." He was looking at Jan now.

A tear slipped off the boy's eyelash, grazed his cheek, and made a gray spot on the white tablecloth. The lines on Damon's forehead deepened as he watched the stain expand. "So it works out perfectly. School starts in September. You'll be old enough and ready both physically and scholastically to start your journey to becoming a man."

Dorothy tossed her fork onto her plate. It clattered with appalling force.

Damon winced.

"He's just a *boy*." Dorothy raised her voice. "Can't you see you're upsetting him?"

Damon took a deep breath through clenched teeth. "He can't fall apart at the first challenge and expect to excel in boarding school."

"*You* are the only one who expects him to excel. I expect him to be a child, something you're making very difficult for him."

"Pampered kids have it harder in life." Damon gave her a look that insinuated who he was talking about. "To be frank, I'm not sure you really know what it's really like out there."

"Well, I wonder why that is?"

"You think that you're far from the world because you're confined to the gates of this home? You know what the real world is to you? A cushy life in upstate New York, where Daddy takes care of you and you don't have a single thing to worry about. The *real* world is a nasty place with people who don't think twice about killing to spread Communism. Do you know what Communism is? I'll tell you what it is—it's just another word for Fascism. You don't know what they do to their minds. They brainwash them from childhood—teach them to hate freedom, to hate America and all it stands for. They will lie under a tank just to slow it down. These are the maniacs that are killing my men in the battlefield, the nut cases that are trying to ruin the world. If you had it your way, Jan would be raised a spoiled sap. I'm giving him a chance."

Dorothy laughed.

Damon smashed the table with his fist. "Don't you *dare* mock me."

Jan recoiled.

"Okay, then let me understand this. What's the idea here, to prepare Jan to be a soldier? So he can die in some place like Vietnam? Is that your master plan?"

"Jan," Damon snapped, "go to your room."

The boy looked at his mother. She was glaring at Damon. Jan slipped out of his chair, walked quickly out of the dining room, and once the door closed behind him, he broke into a run.

"You have serious problems, lady. First it was drugs, then you become paranoid and start making outlandish accusations; and then, last year, your idea of being a good mother and wife amounted to running off with Jan to New York without a word to anyone."

"Oh forgive me. It must have slipped my mind to tell you about my plans to escape from this prison of yours."

Damon shook his head. "You are overdue for a meeting with Dr. Gelernt."

"I don't need Dr. Gelernt," Dorothy snarled. "I need you to leave me and Jan alone. I need you to be gone and out of our lives."

Dorothy expected Damon would strike her, but instead he just sat unmoving in his chair. In a soft, almost conspiratorial tone, he said, "Jean-Luc and Girard say that you've been quite rude to Isabeau."

He waited for a response, and when none came, he allowed the silence to linger for a while before adding, "It's not just them. I've spoken with Mirko and the rest of the tutors, and they all confirm your behavior toward her has been abysmal since the day she arrived. This sets a very bad example for Jan."

"Forgive me for not liking one of my prison guards. She's a bitch. I suppose that's just what you were looking for when you hired her. I don't care about me, but I won't have her around Jan."

"That is part of her job, Dorothy."

"Yes, that and to make sure I don't escape, right?"

Damon ignored that. "She's Jean-Luc's cousin, and he's assured me that she's the best woman for Jan."

Dorothy leaned forward. "I'm Jan's mother, and I assure you, mister, that I and no one else am the best thing for Jan. He's a child, and he needs his mother, not some Nazi house servant Jean-Luc brought in. And how does her being his cousin in any way qualify her for the job?"

"It's not that," Damon said. "You misunderstand. Jean-Luc has worked for me for many years, and I have the utmost confidence in him."

Dorothy laughed with a genuine touch of amusement. "Then you're a fool. He's just after your money. Get that through your thick skull. He doesn't care about you, me, or Jan—just his wallet."

"I'd say that your opinion only serves to solidify mine." Damon sighed. "Dorothy, you need help." Damon paused for a reaction, and he seemed pleased that Dorothy said nothing for once. "The day you disappeared, I called Dr. Gelernt for his professional assessment."

"Let me guess," Dorothy said, "he told you to sic your two French dogs on me, so you did."

"He said nothing of the sort, but he felt that you should have been admitted to a clinic long ago. Given your actions these past years, your behavior towards others, your erratic mood swings, Dr. Gelernt is concerned that, left alone, you could overdose, or purposefully try to cause yourself harm. If something were to happen to you, Jan would be left without a mother."

"Sell that bullshit to someone else. I'm not some dumb blonde who's going to believe for one minute that what you had those thugs do in New York was out of concern for me or Jan. As for Dr. Gelernt, he wants me here. Of course he'll say I'm unstable and I need help. You're a gold mine to him."

"Really, Dorothy, that kind of cynicism is quite unbecoming, even for you."

"So sorry to offend your heightened sensibilities."

"You will be resuming your sessions with Dr. Gelernt, and that's final."

"I don't need a doctor," Dorothy said in a subdued voice. "I need a vacation."

"A vacation?" Damon's tone was lighter, on uncertain footing. He thought for a moment. "So you can take Jan and run off again? Do you think I'm a fool?"

"I didn't say anything about taking Jan along."

Damon stared at her, too confused to harbor anger. Dorothy never left Jan alone, not for a second. The tutors had to battle her for time with the child.

Dr. Gelernt had warned him about the onset of erratic contradictory behavior; it was typical for alcoholics, whether they were currently drinking or not. Damon had been very troubled by her sudden trip to New York, by the fact that she chose to stay with his brother instead of her father. That John Saunders wasn't home was an explanation but not a very good one.

Dr. Gelernt, however, had not been surprised, explaining that *Dr. Jekyll and Mr. Hyde* was a psychological essay about a pathology not dissimilar to the one affecting Dorothy. Now Damon was seeing a demonstration of this very pendulous tendency. Her condition was degenerating; Damon had never seen it this bad. A minute earlier, she was hissing like a venomous snake, then, suddenly, she turns all sweet and submissive.

As if they were a normal couple planning their summer vacation.

Damon frowned. "The idea is absurd, and knowing you, there's something you're not telling me. I just can't see what that might be right now, but I promise you, I intend to find out."

"Fine, you figure it out," Dorothy said. "In the meantime, I'd like your permission to vacation in Vallais."

"At the chalet?"

"Why not? It's yours and nobody uses it."

"It's for skiing, Dorothy, what do you expect to do there now the snow has melted?"

"You know, go for walks, pick flowers . . . collect my thoughts? Most of all, get away from you."

Damon looked at her with resignation and with something Dorothy almost believed to be sadness. For a brief moment, she pitied him, for only the most deluded of men could actually expect a woman to feel anything but hate after what he had done to her and to her child.

He wasn't going to hit her, he wasn't going to give her the excuse she wanted, but it didn't matter much anyway; Dorothy was going to do what had to be done whether Damon made it easy or not. She just had to hang on for a little while longer.

Girard glanced at his longtime colleague and friend. Jean-Luc pursed his lips and gave a short nod.

This was not going to be easy.

Jean-Luc took a deep breath and knocked on the study door.

At first, there was no answer. The sliding wooden doors were closed and they both knew that meant Mr. van Luden was inside. They also knew Damon had heard them. That man could almost hear thoughts.

"Come in."

Jean-Luc pulled one of the sliding sections to the side and peered in. "Forgive us, Monsieur, but it is imperative that we speak with you."

Damon put his gold Montblanc pen back in its marble holder, and laced his fingers together, making a single massive fist.

"Come in then, and close the door behind you."

Girard said, "Madame van Luden is out walking in the garden and young Jan is with Monsieur Curtis."

Damon leaned forward. "Thank you, but I am aware of where everyone is."

Girard looked at Jean-Luc and then said, "Monsieur, I am afraid we have some unpleasant news."

"Go on," Damon said stiffly. "I have to be back at the base this evening, so I don't have all day. The train for Berlin leaves at 14:31."

"Of course, Monsieur," Jean-Luc said. "We will be brief." He took a step closer and eyed the chair in front of the desk, but Damon made no gesture for him to sit down. Jean-Luc took a second step forward and lowered his voice. "I will get to the point, then. Madame is behaving in a manner which is causing us concern. We believe—"

Girard took over, assuming his friend's low voice. "We have seen indications that—"

Damon frowned. "I thought you just said you would get to the point."

"We have reason to believe Madame is contemplating taking her life," Jean-Luc said.

Damon took a long breath. "I'm confused. Did I not hire you both to protect her from herself? Because she's an alcoholic, because she took drugs *and* because she's suicidal? Over the years, the reports you've been giving me confirm this, so why the sudden urgency to restate the obvious?"

"This is different, Monsieur, I assure you. You see, Madame has availed herself of the services of an attorney, for the sole purpose of drawing a will."

Damon's eyebrows floated high in his forehead. "A will?" He clenched his fist. It hovered over the table and came down with spectacular force. "Let me get this straight. My wife left the grounds, found an attorney, and had time to draw up a will? What the hell were you two doing? Sleeping? How did she get off the grounds?"

Jean-Luc had been prepared for this question. "Madame made no attempts to hide herself. She simply left the house. We followed her all the way. We were going to stop her, but she wasn't running. It was obvious, Monsieur, that she was not trying to escape. If we had the slightest suspicion of that, we would have, of course, returned her immediately home."

"Yes," Girard said, nodding, "it was certain she was not trying to escape. And she did not seem to mind that we were following her. We did not lose sight of her for an instant. She went to the lawyer and brought back the will. We found it in her purse after she returned. She did not hide it. These are not actions of a person who wants to escape."

"It is comforting that you have now become experts in that area at my expense, both literally and figuratively."

Jean-Luc and Girard eyed each other.

Damon cocked his head. "How did you know to look in her purse for a will?"

"We just went into the office and asked the lawyer, Monsieur."

"And the attorney in question simply told you?" Damon said. "That doesn't sound right."

"He did not even ask who I was—it was as if he was expecting me. And there is more, Monsieur," Jean-Luc said. "She has been behaving strangely. More so than usual. One moment she says nothing, and then the next, she is angry at everyone. For no reason."

"Is this over Jan?" Damon said.

"Yes, Monsieur," Jean-Luc said. "Always about the boy."

Damon nodded to himself as he removed the pen from its holder. "Did she take Jan with her to the lawyer?"

"No sir, she left the boy behind."

The study was quiet for a few minutes while Damon thought. His pen balanced between his fingers, he rocked it noiselessly in a tapping motion, somehow managing to pull it back just before the tip made contact with the desk.

"Yet at home, she's stuck to his side, right?" Damon said.

"She never leaves him alone. She gets angry when Isabeau or the tutors try to separate Jan from her. Madame makes it very difficult for them to do their work."

"You were right to be concerned," Damon said. "She's kept Jan under her skirt from the day he was born, and since she came back from New York, her overprotective tendencies have bordered on paranoia, while her attitude to everyone in the household has become increasingly hostile. Yet she leaves the grounds, makes no attempt to hide it, and has no compunctions about going without Jan."

Damon let his weight carry him back in his chair as he pondered for a moment more, and then he leaned forward. "This could have something to do with her request to vacation alone in Vallais."

"A *vacation?*" Girard said. "Without Monsieur and little Jan?"

"That's precisely what she asked for," Damon said. "A vacation *alone.*"

"This is very bad," Jean-Luc said. "If we are right, and she is having thoughts about taking her life, this could be a part of her plan to do so. Letting her go alone would be a mistake, sir."

Damon's pen arced over the paper, not quite grazing it. He continued this trick for a minute then he put the pen back in its holder. Girard and Jean-Luc waited in silence for over six minutes before Damon spoke again. "I was going to confer with Dr. Gelernt."

"Yes sir. But we thought this was important and we should tell you immediately."

Damon nodded. "You did the right thing."

"If she wants to go on vacation," Jean-Luc said, "we must be there to watch over her."

"That wouldn't make for much of a vacation," Damon pointed out. "But you are right, she cannot be left alone in her present state, and there's no practical way you could keep her from causing herself harm from a distance." Damon stood and walked past the two men. He opened the sliding door to his study and caught Isabeau's attention. He asked her to bring Mrs. van Luden over.

Jean-Luc and Girard looked at each other, perplexed.

Damon returned to his seat. "I think it is time we talk to her about this."

Dorothy walked into the study in the choppy gait of a hostage. The last time she'd been there was to take Jan from Damon after he'd blindfolded the boy. "You asked for me?"

"Please, Dorothy, have a seat."

Dorothy looked at Jean-Luc and Girard for explanation, but they appeared equally unprepared for her presence there.

"We were just discussing your vacation," Damon said, with the even tone of a CEO at a board meeting.

"Really?"

"Yes," Damon continued, ignoring the sarcasm in her voice. "I would like to grant your wish, but it must be on one condition."

"I'm listening," Dorothy said.

"Jean-Luc and Girard must accompany you. They'll keep out of your way as much as possible, but a certain amount of privacy will have to be compromised to ensure your safety."

"Really, I hardly believe anyone would set out to harm me in the Swiss countryside."

"Actually, we are not worried about others harming you. We think you might do something to hurt yourself."

"Your concern is touching," Dorothy said coldly, "but I don't want anyone with me. I said I wanted a vacation *alone*. If they come along, there'd be no point."

"It saddens me that on two occasions in our marriage you found it necessary to run off. You are unhappy. That is obvious. But I think—and Dr. Gelernt agrees—that this unhappiness is rooted in your internal world, not—as you would have others think—in the world you live in.

"You are very fortunate—you have everything a woman could want. Yet you are not content. And I want you to be happy—believe me. I don't want you to feel you are a prisoner here, and so I'd like you to go on vacation. Then again, as your husband and one who loves you, I cannot risk anything bad happening to you."

Dorothy was caught off guard by his gently placed words, but she found her composure and tried another tack. "If what you say is true, and you do care, then you must let me go."

Her words planted themselves in his being, in a place he wouldn't visit for some years to come. "You can go, but not uncharoned. I could arrange for some time off next month and come with you. We could go as husband and wife."

Dorothy shook her head in disbelief. "And you say *I'm* the one who doesn't have a grasp of reality? Who's living in their own little world here? What would make you think I'd leave prison to vacation with the warden?"

Damon looked away. "Fine. If that is your attitude, unless Dr. Gelernt says it is okay, or you agree to be chaperoned, there will be no vacation."

Dorothy changed the subject abruptly, as if the matter of her vacation was suddenly of little importance. "What about Jan?"

Damon appeared mildly surprised. "Jan?"

"Jan's only contact with other boys his age has been on Fridays, during his judo lessons. He's made a friend who has invited him to a sleepover for the weekend. Would this be okay with you, or is he a prisoner as well?"

"The family Destant are very respectable, Monsieur," Girard said. "Claude is a very nice little boy, I'm sure Jan would be fine for a weekend there. And they are only a few kilometers from here."

Jean-Luc nodded his consent.

Damon said, "Yes, yes, of course, I suppose there's no harm in that."

"Well," Dorothy said, "at least someone will get a vacation from this place."

MEANS TO AN END

August 16, 1968

"Come on, let's see some smiles. You're in the movies." Damon sidestepped, the Brownie 8 movie camera pressed tightly against one eye.

Jan let go of his balloon. It shot straight up, exploding like a small firecracker as it hit the chandelier.

Damon pointed at Isabeau and then at a dozen multicolored balloons tethered to a chair. She removed one and walked into the sights of the camera as she handed a big red balloon to Jan.

"Don't let this one get away," Damon said.

Jan stared at the camera.

"Smile."

Jan tried doing as he was told, but it looked more as if he was going to cry than smile.

"Someday, you'll be showing this movie to your kids. You don't want them to see you like this, do you?"

Jan's eyes became huge.

Dorothy kissed her son. Jan lowered his chin to his chest and now all Damon could see in the viewfinder was the light brown hair on the boy's head.

Damon stopped filming.

"He's camera shy," Isabeau said, becoming nervous herself.

Jan slipped out from under his mother's arm and ran to the other side of the room, where his three friends were congregating next to a stack of unopened presents.

Damon walked over to Dorothy and said, "Is he always like this?"

She offered no reply.

"It's his birthday. What's his problem?"

"You're here; *that's* his problem. In fact, it's everyone's problem."

"Don't you start now. This is hardly the time."

Dorothy snickered. "Do you think throwing this party is going to atone for what you've done to him all these years?"

"All I've done is provide for the boy. For some reason, you never could see that."

"In case you haven't heard, boys don't like prisons any more than adults."

"I can't stand it when you call our home a prison. In two weeks, he'll be going to one of the best schools in America. Full of kids his own age. He's not a prisoner any more than you are."

"You're just transferring him from one prison to another," Dorothy said, lowering her voice as Jan's friend Jacques approached within earshot.

"Mrs. van Luden," Jacques said, "can Jan open his presents now?"

"Hold on," Damon answered. "Wait for me."

Jacques ran back to Jan. "He said no."

"I didn't say 'no,'" Damon called out as he approached the children. He lifted the camera. "I just want to get this on film."

All four boys stared at Damon, unmoving, as if he were holding a pistol and not a movie camera.

"Well? Go on!" The movie camera hummed. "I only have a minute or so left."

None of the kids budged.

Dorothy ran over to Jan, kneeling next to him. He grasped her in a tight hug and she whispered something in his ear.

"That's just *great.*" Damon stopped filming.

Jan was wiping his eyes red with his sleeve as Dorothy carried him away. She looked over her shoulder. "Come on, boys, let's go play outside."

The three children followed her. Jacques shot Damon a frightened look and cut in front of Dorothy, pressing for first place out the front door.

Damon cursed under his lips. Dr. Gelernt had told him he needed to try harder, both as a husband and a father, but what more could a man do that Damon hadn't already done? God knew there was no pleasing Dorothy. And Jan. A spoiled mother's boy. If there was a cure for him, it was Livingsford. They'd straighten him out, if anyone could. Jan wouldn't be weaseling himself out of a good future the way Kory had.

Damon looked at the untouched pile of presents. He had another minute of film. He went outside, examined the sky, and twisted the f-stop ring over the lens. The boys were playing a sloppy game of soccer. Dorothy hand-passed the ball to Jan.

Truly pathetic.

He was out of film now and Damon wondered if it was even worth sending the reel to Germany to be developed.

Damon didn't have to be at the base for a long while. The Army had been pretty good to him—they'd given him ten days. After that, he was to report to Fort Bragg for Special Forces training. With time to spare, Damon had offered to take Dorothy and Jan to the chalet.

She'd taken his gesture and spat it back in his face, saying that Jan was going to spend the weekend with Jacques and his family.

Arrangements had already been made.

Friday

Damon heard the words now, but it was the screaming that had broken his sleep.

He wondered, for a moment, why he was still lying down. In Vietnam, if as much as a twig were to crack, he'd wake up and have his M16 trained on the source of the sound within two seconds. Despite the dreamy mist clogging his mind, he knew it was Dorothy he was hearing. She was screaming, *"Au secours!"* Help.

Strange. Normally people screamed in their native tongue. *"Ne tire pas, s'il te plaît."*

That explained the French—she was asking someone not to shoot her. There was a brief silence, and then her voice pierced the night once again: *"Aide-moi, il va me tuer."* Help me, he's going to kill me.

Who was *he?*

Including him, there were only three men in the house, and since Dorothy only spoke French with Jean-Luc and Girard, one of those two must be trying to kill her.

Move, goddammit.

He tried to focus, but both his body and mind were paralyzed. He'd had wine that evening. Hours before going to bed; just one glass, with dinner. Not a drop more.

Damon commanded his body once again, and this time, with great effort, he managed to get his legs over the bed.

A loud pop echoed through the house, followed a second later by the sound of crashing glass. Silence. Then there was a distant thump. The sound came from below, from outside the house.

Isabeau was screaming.

Damon had heard many a man scream, their limbs severed, their guts spilling. It never got to him. Even when there was no machine-gun fire to muffle the pitiful wails, Damon had been steady as a boulder. This was completely different.

Stop screaming.

Isabeau wasn't listening to his thoughts. She was shrieking out her cousin's name, stretching the last vowel like an opera singer on Quaaludes. Damon could hear no reply from Jean-Luc.

Damon leaned forward, shifting his weight to his feet. They barely supported him. Numb sticks, dead as prosthetics.

For the love of God, stop screaming.

His heart was speeding out of control, and his mind had lost the capacity for coherent thought. Damon tried to run, but managed a hurried wobble instead. Outside his bedroom,

Girard was rushing down the hallway, his face ashen, his hands stretched out in readiness.

Somebody was running down the stairs. It was Jean-Luc. He was talking to someone, possibly himself, repeating the words, *"Oh mon Dieu, oh mon Dieu."*

The door to Dorothy's room was open. Girard was looking out her shattered window. The remaining glass was speckled in red.

A warm summer breeze gently filled the curtains and blew them into the room in thick, lazy waves. The curtain to the right was sagging with the weight of blood.

Dorothy's bed was empty. She hadn't slept in it that evening. Damon struggled to the window, as if the breeze were a relentless gale.

Girard stepped in front of him. "Please, Monsieur, don't look."

Damon ignored him, pushing himself forward.

Girard moved out of his way at the last moment.

Two stories below, Dorothy lay sprawled on the marble, in a slowly spreading puddle of black ooze. The blood made its way around several islands of bone and brain matter.

Jean-Luc was kneeling beside her, checking for a pulse. He sensed someone watching him and tilted his head up at Damon. The Frenchman shook his head, and let her limp arm fall back on the marble.

Damon saw Girard appear next to his colleague. He was carrying a blanket.

Damon hadn't noticed Girard leave Dorothy's room.

Walking was easier now—he was in the hallway, out the bedroom door—but Damon still could not command his feet to run. He considered taking the stairs two steps at a time. That wasn't a good idea. He could fall. Then it would take him much longer to get to her.

The front door had been left open. That was a good thing; he wasn't sure he'd have the strength to open it. It took ages to make it around the house to where Dorothy lay.

Girard was placing a blanket over her. Damon noticed some vomit.

One of those two obviously couldn't handle what they'd seen. Girard looked the palest of the two. He ran to Damon. From the smell there was no question it was Girard who had vomited.

He grabbed Damon by the shoulders from the front: "You cannot see this, Monsieur. It is too terrible. Go . . . go back to the house."

Reflexively, Damon grabbed his wrist with both hands and twisted. Girard winced and lost his grip, letting out a short gasp. Damon let go, and Girard crumbled against the wall.

Jean-Luc was bigger and a great deal stronger than Girard. He stood in front of Dorothy's body, bracing himself like a linebacker. "Monsieur, go back in to the house. There is nothing you can do."

His body had become more responsive. Fueled by instinct and training, Damon threw himself at the Frenchman. The grappling lasted a few seconds longer than it had with Girard. Jean-Luc had wrestling experience from his days with the French Legion. Damon stabbed him in the throat with his fingers, and for a brief moment Jean-Luc lost his grasp. Damon knocked him aside but Girard rejoined the fight, giving his colleague the few seconds he needed to recover.

Still trying to break free, Damon yelled at the form under the brown woolen blanket. "Dorothy?"

Jean-Luc grabbed his arm from behind.

In his haste, Girard had not covered the body completely. As Damon struggled against his bodyguards, he could see the back of Dorothy's head. It was soaked, her blond hair matted against her skull. There was barely enough light to make out any color, but there was no question what Damon was seeing.

Damon's mind went foggy again, and the momentary energy he'd had to fight off the two men was suddenly gone.

Jean-Luc and Girard each held one of Damon's arms, pulling him farther away from his wife. Damon would not take his eyes off of the mutilated remains of her head.

"Monsieur, there is nothing to be done for her. She's gone."

Damon tried to yell, but his throat had turned into a silencer. "No."

He made an effort to pull his arms together, a maneuver that, if he'd had any energy left, would have broken their hold over him. He wondered if they even felt his attempt to break free.

Jean-Luc spoke softly. "Monsieur? You are going to come inside now. I will take you. Girard will stay here, with her."

Damon did not move.

"There is little time, Monsieur." With help from Girard, Jean-Luc tugged Damon for a few steps. "Come with me now. We will take care of this."

Jean-Luc nodded at Girard.

Girard let go, tentatively at first, but seeing Damon was going to offer no further resistance, he went back over to the body and covered Dorothy's head with the blanket.

Jean-Luc took Damon's arm and wrapped it around his shoulder, towing him for the remainder of the distance to the front of the house.

Outside the main entrance, Jean-Luc said, "Monsieur, you are in shock, but you must listen to me. If we do nothing, the police genevoise will arrive and find a woman dead by your pistol."

Damon looked at him dumbly. "Police?"

Jean-Luc nodded. "Can you manage, Monsieur? I'm going to open the door." Damon followed him into the house. "Madame has done what she has been threatening to do, and it seems she planned on taking you down with her."

Damon said nothing, collapsing into a squatting position, where he wobbled for a moment before finding himself sitting cross-legged in the entrance to his mansion.

Jean-Luc pulled him up. "You must get a hold of yourself, if there's going to be any hope for you."

"Hope?" Damon said, as if it were a new word.

He found a chair and helped his boss take a seat. "She called the police. Girard and I, we were not asleep. We heard her making the call."

Louder this time, Jean-Luc said, "Monsieur, do you understand? She called the *police*."

Damon showed no signs of comprehending.

"She told the police you were attacking her. She then left the phone unhooked and started to scream so the police could still hear her, even when she was in the other room. I hung up the phone and then chased after her. I was too late. She already had your gun to her head. She was holding the gun with the curtains, maybe so her fingerprints wouldn't be on it; and she had it pointed to the front of her head, this way it would look like you shot her. When she fired the gun, she fell back, out the window. She was dead long before she hit the ground."

Damon stared at Jean-Luc, his bloodshot eyes half open.

"I ran downstairs to see if perhaps she was still alive, but I knew there was little hope."

"Dorothy—" Damon's mouth remained agape, but he said no more.

Jean-Luc tried a louder voice. "If I hadn't hung up the phone, sir, the police would have heard her screaming that you were going to shoot her and kill her. As it is, they only heard her yelling for help."

"This cannot be happening. . . ."

"Monsieur, if we do nothing, the police will come and there will be an investigation. If she had just jumped out . . . it would be different now. But she didn't—she used *your* gun to kill herself. And the only fingerprints on the weapon are yours. We could wipe off your prints and then hide it, but they'll see the real cause of death no matter what we do. Even if they didn't, they have her screaming over the phone. After her escape last year, it is no secret that she would have tried to divorce you. If she hadn't come back with Jan, you would have lost fifty percent of the trust." Jean-Luc frowned and added a disgusted nod. "Madame said many things about you when she returned from New York —not always the usual kidnapping and so on—this was very specific information. It seems with her dead, you are now guaranteed control over the money. She made certain we know this. Why do you think that is?" Jean-Luc did not receive a response, so he answered his own question. "To point the police in your direction. As far as the authorities will know, you had motive, opportunity, and ability."

After a minute, Jean-Luc thought Damon had not been listening, but Damon surprised him with the first coherent sentence that evening. "What are you saying?"

"We must clean up this mess immediately. There is no time to talk. You must decide. She is dead; she cannot be saved, but you still have a chance."

"She killed herself to frame me?"

"Dorothy wanted revenge. All these stories about kidnapping, rape, being a prisoner here; she must have believed them." Jean-Luc tapped the side of his head. "She was sick. We all know that, but it is a weak defense. It won't work. Monsieur, really, there is no time to talk—the police will surely come."

"Do what you want." Damon shrugged. "I don't care."

Girard came through the door, saw his boss slouched in the chair, and turned to Jean-Luc for direction.

"Girard and I will clean up," Jean-Luc announced. "We'll hide the body in the trunk of the car." To his colleague he said, *"Allez, vite. Dites-Isabeau ce qu'elle doit faire."*

Girard nodded, looked once again at Damon, and ran off to tell Isabeau what she had to do.

Jean-Luc yelled after him, "Isabeau, from now until la police du lac arrive, will be Madame van Luden."

Damon had his head in his hands, but this made him look up. "What?"

"Don't worry, she'll do it. I am confident she can be persuaded, but it will be expensive, Monsieur." Jean-Luc gave Damon a side glance. "You understand, of course, we can only help with the same understanding."

"I can't believe I'm hearing this."

"It is okay: you are in shock," Jean-Luc said in a matter-of-fact voice. "It will take you a while to accept what has happened. For now, concentrate on calming yourself, and get away from here. You must appear to be in control of yourself when the police arrive. Explain to them your wife is drunk and you had a fight because once again, she has had one too many. You apologize for her behavior. We'll instruct her to make a fuss. She'll tell them you always say she's drunk. We'll give her some bourbon to drink, and we'll pour some on her nightgown so she will stink of alcohol. Girard and I will, of course, take your side. We'll say she has had an unusually bad night, but she is often like this. It will be okay, Monsieur, I'm sure the police have seen many similar cases before."

"And what am I supposed to tell her father? What about Jan?"

"I have an idea, but there is no time to talk about it now. It is fortunate Jan wasn't here tonight. Let us clean. You go have a coffee. We'll take care of everything. Calm yourself, Monsieur, for the police, calm yourself. They could arrive any moment."

Damon didn't move.

"Go!" Jean-Luc barked.

Jean-Luc's voice had the effect of a hard slap. Damon looked up at the Frenchman, raised himself from his chair, and walked off, obeying the order like a plebe.

Girard was talking to Isabeau; she looked back at him.

Damon joined them in the morning room. She asked her boss what was going on.

Damon replied in French, "Honestly, I have no idea."

As instructed, with the best American accent she could muster, Isabeau apologized sloppily for her outburst, insisting all was well now. The man answering the phone at the police station explained that a car had already been dispatched, and even if it hadn't, they still required an officer to confirm her statement in person.

Girard guided the Mercedes as slowly down the driveway as his nerves would allow.

Hopefully, Jean-Luc would manage to clean up the mess in time. There must be nothing left to arouse suspicion. Jean-Luc would have to clean up *and* change. There was so little time. If they didn't pull this off, they would be in serious trouble.

As the navy-blue Mercedes rolled past the gates, Girard pressed gently on the gas, keeping the speed at a steady forty kilometers per hour.

Not too fast, not too slow. But there was nothing to be done about the late hour. Who was out driving in this neighborhood at this time?

A blue light flashed in his rearview mirror.

"Mais merde," Girard cursed. The fucking gendarmes could smell guilt a kilometer away.

The policeman made a circling motion with his fist, and Girard rolled down his window.

"Bonsoir, monsieur," the policeman said in a formal voice. *"Vous habitez par ici?"*

Girard answered that he did indeed live around here.

The gendarme looked him over with pointed skepticism, and asked if he knew where he could find the van Luden residence.

Had Girard left a minute earlier, he might have avoided the police car entirely. A minute later, and he'd have been found leaving the grounds. That might have been worse, but not by much.

Girard said that as a matter of fact, he happened to be employed at the van Luden residence.

The policeman asked if Girard would be kind enough to show him the way. Simple directions weren't going to do the trick; the fucking cop wanted Girard to escort him all the way to the house.

At least he hadn't asked him to open the trunk. But then, why would he? Still, Girard wanted to be driving in the opposite direction, doing about 120, not driving back to the scene of the crime.

Girard was nervous, and he knew the pig would sense this, but instead of asking questions, the police officer returned to his car and followed the Mercedes to the van Luden house. Most people were a little uneasy talking with the police, especially the Swiss police. Maybe the gendarme was used to seeing this and thought nothing of it.

Jean-Luc opened the door, and seeing Girard there with the police officer, he pulled back for a second, correcting himself with a plastic smile.

Girard spoke before the policeman had a chance. "I met the police officer on the road, and he asked me if I could direct him here."

Jean-Luc relaxed a notch but was still struggling to maintain his smile. "How may I help you, Officer?"

"Are you Mr. van Luden?"

"I'm Mr. van Luden," Damon said, brushing past Jean-Luc. Damon was dressed in his robe; he looked tired, but otherwise calmer than both Jean-Luc and Girard.

"We had a phone call, Monsieur. There seemed to be some domestic disturbance. Is your wife in?"

Damon nodded. "Yes, just one moment. *Dorothy!* Would you come to the door, please?"

Isabeau appeared in one of Dorothy's maroon robes. Her blond hair was a mess, there were bags under her eyes, and even from four feet away, Girard could smell the alcohol on her breath. The young police officer standing next to him would surely smell it too.

Damon turned to her and in English said, "Honey, would you explain to the good officer what happened?"

Isabeau nodded. "I am so sorry to have disturbed you, Officer. I called the precinct to tell them everything was okay. It was not necessary for you to come all this way."

Damon gave her a *you-have-said-enough* look. "Officer, my wife sometimes drinks more than she should. I told her that she'd had enough; she got angry. I'm afraid we ended up having a bit of a tiff. I was not aware she'd called the police."

"Are you certain you are okay, Madame?" The policeman said, ignoring Damon as if he'd said nothing.

"Yes, yes, I'm fine. I'm so sorry for the inconvenience, Officer."

The young officer gave them both a curt nod and headed for his police car.

Ten minutes later, satisfied that the policeman was not about to return, Jean-Luc left Damon alone in the study and drove off with the body.

Saturday

"Isabeau is about the same height as Dorothy, and she also has blond hair."

"Right, only her eyes are brown," Damon pointed out.

Jean-Luc nodded. "Yes, but this is a problem easily solved with sunglasses."

They were walking along the garden, approaching the tennis courts when Damon said, "The police think Isabeau is Dorothy, and that officer had a good look at her."

"Perhaps, but if so, that is to our advantage," Jean-Luc said. "I strongly doubt, however, that he would have noted the color of Isabeau's eyes, Monsieur. Not in the night, especially since he had no reason to believe she was anyone other than your wife."

The sun shot down at them from across the trees, an uncharacteristically beautiful day in Geneva, even for late August.

"What happens now?"

"Tomorrow, Monsieur, Isabeau leaves for Barbados," Jean-Luc explained. "The story will be that Dorothy is making a vacation stop, that Jan will later join her there, before she takes him to the Livingsford school in America."

"You speak as if she's still alive," Damon said.

"And that is precisely what you must believe. It is what everyone must believe."

"This is madness."

"Not at all," Jean-Luc said, his smile unperturbed. "We simply replace Dorothy's photo with Isabeau's, and she leaves Switzerland as Madame van Luden. Once she arrives at the hotel, Dorothy's photo will be put back in the passport. Then Isabeau, with her hat and sunglasses, will check in as Dorothy van Luden, with Dorothy's picture. They never check the passport photo at the desk, so there will be no worry about that."

"Even if this all wasn't completely insane," Damon said, "you can't just cut out a photo and replace it with another. They'd notice that sort of thing at the border."

Jean-Luc nodded. "Yes, Monsieur, at most borders they do, but we are talking about the Barbados Islands. Even so, the man we are using is very good. If she wanted to, Isabeau could get into Germany as Mrs. Mickey Mouse on one of his passports."

"Wait. What do you mean '*are* using'?"

"Monsieur, as I have explained, there is very little time. I had no choice but to take the liberty of requesting his services. The passport will be ready by tomorrow, when Isabeau leaves for Barbados. I assure you, this man is both discreet and a master at his trade. He cannot betray us without betraying himself."

"What gives you the right to hire someone without my permission? Especially a criminal?"

"I apologize for this, Monsieur. We assumed you were sleeping and there was no time to wait and see. I made contact with the gentleman in question early this morning to be sure he would have time to prepare the passport by tomorrow."

Damon shook his head, and after a pause he gave a heavy sigh. "So he's good at what he does. But what about Isabeau? How is she supposed to put in the original photo before she checks in?"

"That is a good question. While we don't care about the hotel receptionist, we *do* have to concern ourselves with the police, who will later retrieve Dorothy's passport from the hotel. So to be certain the photo is replaced, and the passport is just as it was when it was originally issued, my acquaintance will be on the same flight to Barbados, traveling as a lone tourist. He will take Dorothy's passport to his room in the hotel, where he'll replace Isabeau's photo with the one of Dorothy. Then he'll meet Isabeau in the lobby and give her the passport just before she checks in. He'll spend the night at the same hotel."

"This scheme of yours is completely insane. It won't work."

"Not at all, Monsieur. In fact, it is the only way you have to save yourself. But listen, because there is more." Jean-Luc plucked a petal from a rose, crushing it between his fingers. "Isabeau checks in to the hotel as Mademoiselle van Luden. At the front desk, they'll have her passport, and the next day she will purchase a boat, where she'll be met at sea by my friend the passport-maker, who will rent a boat from a different part of the island. Isabeau will follow his boat until they are at a suitable location to arrange for her boat to meet unhappily with some rocks. They'll sail back to shore in his boat, where he'll let her off. Then he'll take his boat back to the harbor he rented it from, and he and Isabeau leave for Switzerland. Of course, this time, she will return with her own passport and without the hat and glasses.

"Once she's here, she'll pick up Jan and fly back to Barbados. She will wait at the airport for Madame van Luden, but Dorothy won't show up, of course."

"What about Jan?"

"He'll be there too."

"No, goddammit, that's not what I meant. He's too young to be involved."

"Monsieur, his mother is dead. At the very least, he's going to wonder where she is. He can never know about what has really happened. Isabeau can play her part for the authorities. Jan, however, must believe the story that his mother has gone missing at sea."

"This is simply wrong."

"There is no other way, Monsieur. Madame van Luden is dead, by her own hand, and we cannot protect Jan from that fact. It is better for a child to think she is missing. This way he still lives with some hope. Would you rather he knows the truth? That his mother took her own life?"

Damon just stared.

"And if we do nothing? If you tell the authorities what really happened, not only will Jan be crushed, but your life will be ruined as well. This is terrible for you, Monsieur, I know, but the truth be told, she intended to do you harm, and I cannot allow that. Even if you prefer to spend the rest of your life in prison, would you have Jan suffer as well?"

"No," Damon conceded, "of course not."

"Very good, Monsieur," Jean-Luc said, cracking a smile. "So Isabeau will take a taxi and she will tell Jan that perhaps his mother misunderstood their arrival time. At the hotel, Isabeau will ask reception if a Dorothy van Luden has checked in. They will confirm that she has. Isabeau will explain the situation to them, saying that she has arrived with Madame van Luden's son. She'll say that Madame van Luden was supposed to meet them at the airport but for some reason did not show. We will let a day pass, during which time Isabeau will do everything expected of a good nanny, doing her utmost to find the whereabouts of Madame van Luden. Then, she'll do the logical thing and call you."

"Why? What's the point? She knows I know."

"Yes, but the phone records, Monsieur, will show an international collect call, and you will accept the charges. You see, when Isabeau returns to Geneva to collect Jan, after her first trip as Dorothy van Luden, she will wipe her mind of all that has transpired until then. This way she will make herself believe that she is taking Jan to meet his mother and that she will find Madame van Luden there."

"Method acting," Damon said.

Jean-Luc smiled. "As a matter of fact, it has always been a dream of hers to become an actress. She has helped very much with this idea."

"Sounds way too complicated. Too messy. What do you expect me to do in all this?"

"The same, Monsieur, you must believe the story. Dorothy left for Barbados for a vacation, Jan and Isabeau left to meet her, and that is *all* you know. Your role is simple: you listen. You must sound concerned but reassuring. You will tell her not to worry, that you'll take care of everything. Have her call the authorities. Then you call Mr. Saunders and ask him if Dorothy is there. He'll say no, of course, and then you inform him she's missing."

"And where is she? I mean really," Damon said, "what have you done with her body?"

Jean-Luc regarded the flower. "It is best you do not know, Monsieur. That way you can truthfully tell the police you have no idea where Dorothy is should there be an investigation."

Damon clamped Jean-Luc's arm in a vise grip. "Listen here, Jean-Luc, if I'm not mistaken, you still work for me." Damon squeezed a bit more. "Now, I asked you a simple question and I want an answer."

His hand was going numb, but Jean-Luc managed a patient nod. This was more like the Damon van Luden he was accustomed to. "Very well, Monsieur. I burned the body in a kiln and spread Madame van Luden's ashes across the countryside. There isn't a trace of her to be found."

"A kiln?" Damon spat the words out of his mouth as if he'd just chewed on a bar of soap.

"I am sorry, Monsieur, but one cannot simply go to a funeral home with a body and ask to have it cremated. There is a process for these things. This is Switzerland, Monsieur. I have a—"

"A friend?" Damon finished for him. "You have some really fucking shady friends, Jean-Luc," Damon said, releasing his grip.

Jean-Luc discreetly retracted his arm, rubbing the life back into his veins. "There will be an investigation, but they'll have no body. Not in Barbados and not here. There will be one missing boat, but it won't be a rented one. This way the police will not show immediate interest. They will be dealing with a case of one missing lady. These things happen, and this way nobody can find you at fault for anything."

Damon frowned. "You seem to be enjoying all this."

Jean-Luc said nothing.

"That's what I thought," Damon said, watching closely for a reaction. The Frenchman had a good poker face. "That's a discussion for another time. Tell me, how in God's name did you come up with this plan?"

"When I returned, I spent the remainder of the night discussing alternatives with Girard and Isabeau."

Damon nodded. "I heard you come back."

"Then you have not slept either?"

"You expect me to sleep after what happened?"

Jean-Luc shrugged. "Monsieur, I'm afraid there is one more thing that I need to bring to your attention."

Damon looked at him warily. "Money, right? Well, that makes sense. Dorothy warned me about you." Damon frowned. "I should have listened."

"As I said, I have had to ask some friends for some rather costly favors."

Without as much as clearing his throat, Jean-Luc recited a list of expenses, explaining that for obvious reasons it wouldn't be prudent to write any of this down.

When Jean-Luc was finished with his account, Damon wrote three checks. One was made out to Jean-Luc, for sixty thousand dollars—fifty for him, ten to cover expenses—the second check was for Isabeau, and the third to Girard, each for fifty thousand for their respective services.

If there was ever any doubt before, there was none anymore. Damon signed his name, three times confirming his complicity in a conspiracy to cover up his wife's death.

Three times.

Like Judas.

Friday, August 25

"Have you called the police?"

"No, Monsieur, I wanted to tell you first."

"Okay. Call the authorities right away. I'm going to make some phone calls. Maybe my father-in-law knows where his daughter is. Call the police now, Isabeau." Damon hung up.

Isabeau's phone call came exactly as scheduled: six days after Damon spoke in the garden with Jean-Luc.

Damon was astonished by her performance; if he hadn't known any better he'd have been certain she believed her every word. This helped him play his part almost equally well. He spoke sparingly, like a shocked husband might. She told him that Dorothy was missing. There was genuine panic in her voice, and for an absurd moment, Damon wanted to believe her, allowing himself a second to luxuriate in the duplicitous arms of hope.

He forced himself to concentrate. So far he'd done well.

All he needed in his mind was the knowledge that Dorothy went on vacation and Isabeau just called.

That was all that happened. Isabeau called because Dorothy didn't show up. They don't know where she is. No big deal, but better to be safe than sorry, right? She'll certainly turn up, Mr. Saunders, we're only calling the authorities to be on the safe side. . . .

Damon took a deep breath and was about to dial when he stopped himself for the third time. Jean-Luc had been quite clever to have Isabeau call Damon first. He was in the perfect frame of mind now. He was a man who couldn't find his wife and was trying to sound calm, even though anyone listening to him could tell he was panicking inside, just like a good husband.

John Saunders picked up on the second ring. "Hello?"

"Mr. Saunders, this is Damon van Luden."

There was a long pause on the line, as if Mr. Saunders's answer had to travel at the speed of sound across the Atlantic instead of at the speed of light.

"To what, may I ask, do I owe the pleasure of this phone call?" the voice said finally, not sounding in the least bit pleased to hear from his son-in-law.

"Mr. Saunders, is Dorothy there with you?"

"Why? Should she be?"

"No, no. I don't want to alarm you—"

"*Alarm* me?"

"Dorothy left on a vacation a couple of days ago, Jan and Isabeau arrived yesterday to join her, and . . . well . . . Dorothy wasn't there. I was just wondering if she might be with you."

"What is this? You call out of the blue to tell me you can't find Dorothy? What's going on?"

"If you'll just let me explain," Damon said. "Dorothy left on a vacation. She wanted a few days to herself in Barbados— before Jan joined her—and she was going to go to the States from there, to take Jan to boarding school at Livingsford."

"Damon, what happened? Is everyone okay? Just tell me that."

"Yes, yes, Jan and Isabeau are fine, but Dorothy was supposed to meet them at the Seawell Airport yesterday, and she didn't show."

"Dorothy? Alone? Why would she leave on vacation alone, without Jan? Has anything happened to her?"

"I'm sure she's fine," Damon said, wishing he could believe the lie, "but they can't find her. She checked in to the hotel and she hasn't checked out. She's not in her room, and she hasn't left any messages."

"Let me get this straight. I haven't heard a peep out of you since you called to tell me you ran off with my daughter and eloped. Now, six years later, you tell me you don't know where she is?"

"Again, Mr. Saunders, I don't think there's any cause for worry, but with her history of alcoholism and depression . . . well, it might be best if you pick up Jan earlier than planned. Just in case she's managed to get herself in trouble . . . we wouldn't want Jan being a witness to any of that. I'll take care of things."

"You've taken care of quite enough, thank you. I'm catching the next flight out. Just tell me where she is. Give me the hotel and a phone number."

Damon complied, resisting the urge to snap back.

"Okay, now that I've got the number, you listen here," Mr. Saunders said. "You assured me you would take care of her, and I'm no idiot—despite what you might think—I know my daughter hasn't been happy with you. She never admitted as much over the phone, but she didn't have to, I know my Dorothy. You stole her away from me when she was just a kid. She knew little about life, and less about men. So I've seen how well you've taken care of things."

"Mr. Saunders, please calm down, I'm only trying to help."

"You want to help? Is that what you *really* want? Because if it is, you can start by staying the hell out of this. Let me take care of this mess you've made, and you do what you do best and take care of yourself."

"Now, *you* see here," Damon said, feeling the part now. "I understand that you're upset, but my *wife* has just gone missing, and I'm just as worried as you." Damon listened to silence on the other end, and added in a more gentle tone, "We can find a solution together."

"There's going to be no *together* about this," Mr. Saunders fumed.

"You know what I think?" Damon said, in a cool, almost soothing voice. "I think she's there with you, and you're in on this."

"I've heard enough of your nonsense."

"Oh, I'm not finished," Damon said, even more quietly. "She ran away once, and I think she's just decided to do it again. What's more, I think you're hiding her."

"If she's run away, then she's finally come to her senses. I wish she were here, but she's not. Don't worry, though, I'll find her and bring her home."

"You'll fly her back to Geneva?"

"Her home is *here*, in Rhodes, not in Geneva. She needs to come back, and you need to stay away."

"I'm not just going to conveniently disappear," Damon said. "She's my wife and—"

"Not for long. Not if I can help it," John Saunders said. "You're probably right, she has run away—from *you*. So I'm going to say this one last time: keep away from my daughter. Understand?"

"Mr. Sau—"

Damon's father-in-law had already hung up.

PART IV

BRAGG

June 1969
Nine Months Later

Damon slipped his thick arms through the shoulder harness of the T-10 parachute and bounced it on his back. Hooking up to the release box, he verified his leg straps were not crossed. Crouching, he pulled on the adjustment ties to ensure a secure fit. The rest of his team was doing the same. They removed their berets and donned their helmets.

Damon felt for the telegram. It was still there, in his pocket. On its own it was little more than a petty distraction, but enough to warrant an unscheduled call to his aunt. Just one day before he was about to embark on the single most important final event in Special Forces training, where everything they had learned up till then came into play. Almost thirty-three percent of the men ended up dropping out. This was Damon's opportunity to shine and the only remaining hurdle between him and leading his handpicked A-team into Vietnam.

He hadn't been prepared, but how could he have been? Every call to Mary for the past eight and a half months had been both unremarkable and predictable.

Except for this one.

Sergeant Kjellqvist laid Damon's static line over his shoulder as Sergeant Kelly, the assigned jumpmaster, inspected every trooper on the airplane. Kelly slapped Damon on the shoulder, indicating he was ready to jump.

413

Sergeant Kelly turned to the men. "Stand up!"

Damon and his team turned to face the jumpmaster.

Kelly yelled, "Hook up!"

Damon fastened the snaps to the anchor line and inserted the safety wire through the small hole. The rest of the team did likewise.

"Check your static lines!" Kelly shouted.

The men complied in unison.

In the beginning, maintaining focus had been a constant struggle. Special Forces training required one hundred percent dedication. There could be no room in a soldier's mind for family problems, and this was why the Army kept its trainees in virtual isolation. If anybody understood the reasoning, it was Damon. He'd left for Fort Bragg only ten days after Dorothy's death and subsequent "vacation" in Barbados.

While Mr. Saunders had still been on the island getting in the way of his team as they continued their futile search for his daughter, Damon had been going through specialty training, completely cut off from the investigation.

The local authorities had shown little interest in the case. Dorothy was just another lost tourist, and since her boat had been purchased, there was no rental company attempting to push through an insurance claim for lost property. John Saunders had been the only one seeking the attention of the police. He'd ended up hiring a team of private detectives to do the job. Everything had happened just as Jean-Luc had said it would, with the exception of recent events—events that nobody could have foreseen.

"Check equipment! Sound off equipment check!"

The team shouted their reply in sequence.

Hoyle was standing behind Kjellqvist. "Five okay!"

"Four okay!" Kjellqvist shouted.

Damon felt the slap. "Three okay!"

The C-46 tilted abruptly skyward, and the red light next to the door started flashing.

Initially, his only contact with the outside world had been the occasional phone call to Jean-Luc. That had helped him stay on target during the training raids and ambushes, the briefings on strategic villages, the immediate-action drills, the psychological operations, and, finally, escape and evasion training. Damon had excelled in all of these. Not bad for a guy whose wife had just tried framing him for her death.

"Stand in the door!"

Bronson was first in line. He approached the door, using the frame for support.

"Go!"

Bronson jumped, and Furmann took his place at the door, bracing against the chilling wind.

"Go!"

Conrad was next.

"Go!"

Three seconds later it was Damon's turn.

Sergeant Kelly slapped Damon, shouting, "Go!"

In what felt like the same moment, Damon was airborne, his feet clamped together, his elbows fastened at his sides, his chin boring a hole in his chest. He started a mental count-down, and then he felt the pull followed by a whooshing sound and a violent jolt. He was floating to the ground below. Damon landed softly. With no one to see, he permitted himself a smile.

Nothing like a jump to clear the mind.

Once his men were assembled, Damon said, "Welcome to Uwharrie National Forest."

They all looked at the challenge surrounding them, as if they'd been waiting for their team leader's permission to do so.

"It's a hundred-mile trek back to Smoke Bomb Hill," Damon continued, "and we've got one week. Let's get cracking."

He set the pace; the rest followed. This was Permission Training, and there were two buffer teams that went through the same rigorous challenge. But they merely served as backup. His was the "go team" destined for Vietnam.

Damon's smile widened, but then suddenly died as he thought of his brother. Everything had been going so smoothly until Kory started putting his fucking nose where it didn't belong.

Retaining the services of the bodyguards had proven to be one of his better decisions. Despite his lack of official training, Jean-Luc had proven himself to be a highly effective investigator. The Frenchman knew how to give quick, to-the-point reports, and, unlike Stavridis, had the ability to determine what was important and what was not. With Dorothy dead, their job was to monitor Jan's progress, in and out of boarding school, and to keep a vigilant eye on the investigation.

Mary was Damon's only other source of information, but whatever she said had to be balanced against her substantial personal involvement.

She'd repeatedly informed Damon that her husband was not one to give up. At first, John had hoped for good news. But eight months later, he hoped for any news.

While Mr. Saunders took charge of the investigation, Damon had never once been called upon by the police or by any of John's detectives to offer information or assistance of any kind. Nobody seemed interested in what Damon had to say about his missing wife. Which was for the better, of course, although it didn't feel that way.

John and Mary were Jan's legal guardians for the time being, since Damon wouldn't be available to be a father to his son—at least not until he finished his second tour in Nam. Though the boy was in boarding school, he still needed to have legal guardians close by to watch after him, and a home to go to during holidays.

Apparently, Jan was doing quite well at Livingsford. Initially, there had been some adjustment issues, but Jean-Luc had assured Damon that his son was managing better than most in his classes, and there were no serious problems to report.

Mary had also mentioned the difficulty the boy was having living with other children. Her version had not varied from Jean-Luc's to an extent that would cause Damon concern. It had taken Jan a few months to warm up to his new environment, but Livingsford had eventually become his home away from home; he had friends, and was beginning to speak fondly of the school.

Mary had not told Jan his mother was dead. According to her, even John Saunders couldn't bring himself to admit what she and all his detectives perceived as the only logical explanation at this point in the investigation. The boy had been told Dorothy had left for an extended trip and that she would one day return.

Damon didn't particularly like this tactic. It was better to tell the kid the hard truth early on, but he'd never voiced his disapproval, since there was some merit to Mary's approach: the more time passed, the easier it would be for Jan to accept his mother's death. The cost was trust, but Damon wouldn't be paying the price; his aunt would.

If Jan still didn't know by the time Damon got back from Nam, he'd tell him. At some point, the kid was going to have to face the facts of life.

Day Three

They had made several stops so that Kjellqvist, the team medic, could work on Furmann, Bronson, and Hoyle. All three had developed blisters that were keeping them from maintaining pace. Damon wanted his team to get back to Bragg first, but that wasn't going to happen with any of his men injured.

"How're they doing?" Damon asked.

"No problem, Captain," Kjellqvist said. "They'll all be fine."

"Excellent, then we can make good time."

Damon lengthened his strides through the forest, and his team followed closely behind, talking softly as their team leader had told them to.

Bronson was in the back with Furmann. "It's fucking weird, man."

Furmann didn't have to ask what he was talking about. It had already become a worn topic. "That's why he's called Ghost."

"Yeah, I know," Bronson said, "but all that muscle's got to be weighing him down. How's it physically possible to walk through the forest at that speed and not make a single fucking sound?"

Furmann shrugged. "How should I know? You think if you keep asking me the same question, I'm going to come up with an answer?"

Conrad hadn't spoken in over an hour. He looked over his shoulder back at the two men. "Give it a rest. He didn't pick his code name, you know."

They walked for another klick before Bronson said, "What's so bad about *Ghost?*"

"That's what we call Charlie in Nam."

"Yeah? And why's that?" Bronson asked.

Conrad returned a warped smile. "You'll find out soon enough."

Day Five

With useful daylight gone, Damon had his team set up camp. They made a small fire, and sat back to the soothing crackling sound.

Damon felt for the telegram in his pocket. He wasn't about to read it again—not in front of the team.

The only prior communication with Mr. Saunders in the past year had been that phone call, a week after Dorothy died.

John Saunders's telegram was clear, to the point, and despite the telex prose, managed not to be rude:

> TRIP TO HAWAII POSTPONED. LEAVING FOR BARBADOS. POSSIBLE
> BREAKTHROUGH. JAN STAYING WITH MARY. IF I DON'T SEE YOU,
> GOOD LUCK IN VIETNAM. STOP.

Reading between the lines, it would appear this was an invitation for Damon to go to Barbados to see if they'd found Dorothy. The telegram had been crafted that way, but John had to have known Damon wouldn't abandon his career for a possible "breakthrough" in the investigation. This way, Mr. Saunders could claim that he'd invited Damon to participate in the most critical phase of uncovering the mystery of Dorothy's disappearance, and Damon had chosen career over family. It would make for another good excuse for John to stay mad at him.

Mr. Saunders blamed Damon for Dorothy's disappearance—there was no question about that. His initial reaction over the phone may have been considered normal, given the circumstances, but his continued silence in the months Damon had spent at Fort Bragg made it clear that he wasn't about to forgive Damon, despite what Mary had tried to make Damon believe. John Saunders was convinced that Damon had failed to protect his wife from herself and now Dorothy was gone.

Ironically, for all he and Jean-Luc had done to keep the ugly truth about Dorothy's death from her father, Mr. Saunders had still come to the conclusion that Damon, and Damon alone, was responsible for everything that had happened to her.

Mr. Saunders's name was at the bottom of the telegram, but Mary was undoubtedly the one behind its amicable tone. She'd fought Jane Johnson for guardianship of Kory, but Damon's brother could not have brought much satisfaction to a woman so desperate to play mommy. Now that she had another opportunity with Jan, she'd say or do anything to keep him for as long as she possibly could.

She was a classy lady, but Damon would never have left his son with her if not for the fact that Jan would be spending most of his time at a boarding school where instilling proper values was the number-one priority. Growing up with Mary and John, Jan would turn into mush, and never attain the standard required to enter the Academy.

Damon was not overly concerned. This was just a temporary solution. Jan would only be with them during the holidays. It wasn't as if he'd had any alternatives—there'd been fewer than two weeks between Dorothy's death and the time Damon had to report for training.

The "breakthrough" was obviously anything but. In all likelihood, it was nothing more than a short path to nowhere, so John's detectives could justify their bills. Damon had felt obligated to answer the telegram with a phone call to politely state the obvious. The conversation had started with him patiently explaining to his aunt that he had just over a week left to complete the most important training in his military career, and he would not be able to join her husband in Barbados.

Rather than questioning his motives, without offering anything concrete, she'd attempted to convince him that unlike the previous times where the clues had proven fruitless, the detectives were really onto something. "They've found parts of a boat."

"Right, but that could be from any boat."

"The local authorities have found a body."

He hadn't replied immediately. "I see. So John is going to Barbados to see if he can identify the body?"

"We all hope it isn't her. Naturally, we want her to be alive . . . but after all this time it seems unlikely . . . anyway, they're going to see—"

"Hold on. They? You're not telling me Jan is going with John, because—"

"*Heavens* no. We'd never subject the child to such a thing. Jan will stay here with me."

"The detectives are in Barbados, doing their job, right?"

"Of course."

"So then, who's *they*?"

"Your brother and John."

"What does Kory have to do with any of this?"

"Well, I have to be here with Jan, and John is going through a frightful ordeal, so we thought it would be nice if Kory kept him company."

Damon had waited a while before saying, "I've trusted you to care for my only son. Tell me I haven't made a mistake."

"What do you mean? Of course you haven't—"

"Then don't lie to me, and tell me what's really going on. I know Kory, and he wouldn't agree to go all the way to Barbados just to hold Mr. Saunders's hand."

"Your brother has his own theories about what might have happened."

"Like what?"

"Well, he's convinced you are somehow involved. Listen, Damon, this situation has been difficult for all of us. John and I understand if you cannot come, but—"

"'Involved'? What are you talking about? Of course I'm involved; she's my *wife*."

Mary had preceded her explanation with a sigh. "He thinks you are somehow responsible for her disappearance."

Damon had not been prepared for that one. There was no way Kory could possibly have known. Sounding almost bored, but not going so far as to laugh, he'd said, "What else is new?"

"I'm afraid it isn't new."

"How so?"

"Damon, I don't want to say anything that would infringe on your relationship with your brother . . . and I fear I've over-stepped my bounds already."

"There's more?"

"For some time now, he's been saying that you forced this marriage on Dorothy, somehow . . . that you—"

"Held her captive, right?"

Mary did not reply.

"When did he start saying all this?"

"Shortly after she came home to visit."

"You mean two years ago? When you and John were in Hawaii?"

"Yes."

"That makes sense. I happen to know she visited my brother. She must have filled that oversized head of his with her garbage."

"There's more to this."

"Like what?"

"He says there's a letter . . ."

"A letter?"

"Well . . . yes . . . It's nothing really, but before she left for Geneva, Dorothy had mentioned something to him about giving an attorney a letter for her father should something happen to her."

"What does that have to do with Kory going to Barbados?"

"Well, according to your brother, should anything suspect happen to her, this document implicates you . . . so he thinks—"

"He thinks this is all my fault and he wants to try and prove it, but the attorney probably needs a death certificate to enact her will and release the letter to her father. I'll bet Kory is spring-loaded to call Dorothy's lawyer in Geneva the moment John identifies his daughter's body. Have I got all this right so far?"

"Damon, please, try to understand . . ."

"Trust me on this one: I do understand. I understand that Kory has been blaming me for everything his entire life, and his little meeting with Dorothy two years ago gave him the excuse he needed to take this to the next level. Like most addicts, she refused to face the truth. Kory believed her because it was always easier for him to hate me than own up to his own failure."

"Damon, Kory doesn't hate you, he's confused . . ."

"I'll be done with training in ten days, will you and Jan still be in Rhodes?"

"We don't know. We've put off the trip to Hawaii for now. It all depends on what the detectives tell John."

"What about Kory? Will he be staying in Barbados?"

"No. He's only there on a short visit. He'll be back in New York in a week."

"Good. You say he's confused? I say it's high time someone cleared things up for him."

Furmann stabbed the fire with a stick, jolting Damon back to the present. Conrad was skinning one of the rabbits they'd caught. Orange sparks came alive, floated for a second like fireflies, and settled back into the crackling bed of smoldering branches.

Bronson peeled a section of skewered rabbit from the makeshift barbecue.

The telegram and ensuing phone call to Mary had nearly thrown Damon off his game. After speaking with his aunt, he had contacted Jean-Luc to have him find out everything he could about that letter. And Damon needed to get on the horn with the Frenchman again, to see what he'd discovered so that they could come up with a solution before the situation spiraled out of control. The nearest telephone was back in Smoke Bomb Hill, which also served as the finish line for this last race in his Special Forces training.

Damon gnawed the flesh off a rabbit leg. "Gentlemen, eat all you can. Tomorrow we'll be making record time."

THE MANHATTAN CHESS CLUB

Early July, 1969

They were in the GM Room. "GM Room" was a bit of a misnomer, since it wasn't so much a room as a small, doorless area, on an elevated platform, set apart from the rest of the club by a wooden partition. Additionally, though the name suggested this exclusive space was for grandmasters only, often, when the place was not bustling with players, regular club members played there, hoping the platform would somehow elevate their status if not their game as well.

Kory had decided on his move even before Bandini had advanced the pawn, but he needed to play it out in his mind one last time. With all the material on the board, the tactical permutations were staggering. His plan was solid, and the risk to his position was outweighed by opening channels for a kingside assault, and if Bandini were to—

"Excuse me, sir?" It sounded like Sam, but Sam wasn't one to leave his post by the door. "Can I help you?" *Definitely* Sam, and he was actually raising his voice.

"Hey, you can't go there!" Someone else. A club member. And he was s*houting.*

Then a chorus of voices joined in, abruptly spoiling the library quiet.

Heads were turning, games abandoned throughout the club.

Sam, Donald, Brown, and Epstein shadowed the man from a safe distance.

"See here, that's the GM Room!" Sam yelled.

Two other club members joined the group, but contributed nothing to building a more threatening force.

Kory stood. "It's okay, Sam."

The club secretary hesitated.

"He's my brother."

Carefully studying the intruder for a moment, Sam regarded Kory with a sour frown that suggested he thought this to be a practical joke in poor taste. "You should have told us we were having a special guest today."

Without taking his eyes off his brother, Kory said, "Unfortunately my prognostic ability is as nonexistent as our uninvited visitor's regard for protocol."

Standing with his hand extended, Bandini said, "Damon, I presume."

"Mr. Schelowitz?"

Bandini hacked.

"Grandmaster Schelowitz is not here today. That's Grandmaster Bandini," Sam corrected.

Damon turned slowly. "I've come to have a word with my brother. Does anyone have a problem with that?"

"This is a chess club," Sam muttered at the floor, "not a café."

Damon waited, still as a coiled snake.

"All you had to do is stop at the desk . . ."

Turning his head slowly, Damon locked his eyes on Sam.

With an irresolute step, Donald initiated the retreat; the others cowered behind him. Sam, however, stood his ground.

"Consider him my guest, if that makes you feel better," Bandini said. "Now, give us some privacy."

Reluctantly, Sam returned to his station at the reception area.

Grandmaster Bandini waited until the other club members had retreated out of earshot before saying, "I have heard much about you."

"All bad, I'm sure," Damon said, unsmiling.

"I've heard you are the devil himself." Bandini grinned. "I'm a big fan." He looked at Kory. "This game was going nowhere anyway. I'll leave you two alone." Bandini cleared his throat. "Much as I'd love to stay, I came to play chess, not watch a dogfight." He looked around, found what he was seeking, and walked over to a table.

Kory couldn't hear what was being said, but one of the players left and Bandini took his place.

"What brings you here?" Kory said, glaring at his brother.

"Apparently, this is the only place you're sure to be found on a weekend. I'm told you're something of a permanent fixture at this club."

"I mean, what do you want?" Kory snapped.

"She didn't tell you?"

"Who didn't tell me what?"

"Mary." Damon smiled. "Everything."

Kory opened his mouth to speak, but the words had formed a dam in his airway.

The club was quiet again, with the exception of the occasional slapping of a timer switch and the sound of Bandini hacking into his handkerchief.

Damon leaned back in his seat.

The Saturday-afternoon traffic seeped through the poorly sealed windows.

"I've had a rather enlightening chat with Mary about you."

"Mary wouldn't—"

"She would and she has," Damon said. "Women like Aunt Mary who've never had children have waged war against nature. And that's a lost cause. Right now, Jan is her last chance to satisfy her instinct for motherhood, and all I have to do is make a phone call, and I can terminate the guardianship agreement. It's only natural she'd do anything in her power to gain my goodwill."

"I see," Kory said, "and what precisely are you claiming she's done to that end?"

"She was simply being honest. You shouldn't fault her for that."

Kory was silent.

"Aunt Mary told me about this crap you've been saying."

"You can't stop me from telling people the truth. Unless, of course, you're planning on doing away with me the way you disposed of Dorothy."

425

"Truth? What truth, Kory? You've had your head so far up your ass you couldn't see reality if it stared you right in the face. You've been badmouthing me all your life, and that's nothing new, but now I find out that you're infecting my father-in-law with your lies. And that, my little brother, is where I draw the line."

"He's her father and has the right to know who is responsible for her death."

"Her death? I have been told the investigation is still ongoing."

"They've found the remains of a boat."

Damon waited.

"They have good reason to believe the wreckage is from her boat, the *Tropic Sea*."

"And you discovered this on your last trip to Barbados?"

"Mary told you about that as well?"

"According to her, once the word got out they might have found a body, you wanted to be in on the investigation."

Kory said nothing.

"Just like that."

Still, Kory remained silent.

"Out of the blue."

In the distance, police sirens whined out of sync.

Eyeing a fissure in the ceiling, Damon said, "I'm curious: is that when you decided to fabricate this story of yours about a letter?"

Kory exhaled slowly, with the deliberation of a smoker.

"Surprised?" Damon eyed his brother closely. "I thought I'd made it clear: Mary told me *everything*."

"It's not a story," Kory said.

"Is that so?"

"You assumed that by hiring someone to kill her and by not doing the deed yourself, you'd have nothing to worry about. While it does complicate the investigation, once we find the body, you will be the first person the police will hunt down, because you're the only one with motive. Everyone knows that with her dead, there can be no divorce, and therefore nobody can ever challenge your claim of the trust."

Damon studied the chessboard as though he were thinking of a good move. "If Dorothy is dead, and it wasn't an accident, then it would have to be suicide. And to continue with this hypothetical, if this letter existed—which I assure you it does not—then said letter would have been written for the purpose of framing me for a murder I did not commit."

"Really? Then why would she kill herself thousands of miles away from you and in a manner in which her body may not be immediately discovered?"

"That we'll never know, Kory. What I do know is that like you, Dorothy chose to blame others rather than own up to her own actions."

"We'll never know? *That's* your explanation?" Kory looked at his brother in disbelief. "Dorothy would never kill herself. Someone killed her for you, and you arranged for it to be done in Barbados in order to give yourself an incontrovertible alibi. You made it seem like an accident, just as you did with Dollie."

"You've got some nerve bringing that up—"

Kory continued despite the interruption, "You didn't think Dorothy would take measures to protect herself from you. It never occurred to you that she'd write a letter. There's something else you did not foresee: even if Dorothy's body is never discovered, considering the circumstances, her father can have her declared legally dead. At which time, her lawyer will give John Saunders the letter, and you will go to prison for murder."

"If Dorothy is declared dead, then considering her past, they are more likely to attribute the cause to suicide than to an accident," Damon pointed out. "She was not a well person."

"Dorothy told me what you did: you paid a psychiatrist to diagnose her as unstable and suicidal."

Damon plucked Kory's queen off the chessboard, dangling it carelessly between his fingers. "With your head full of Dorothy's lies, I can see how you concocted this fairy tale to blame me for her death."

"The investigation will reveal the truth."

"I doubt it. If they were really on to something, then why did Mr. Saunders leave Barbados and go to Hawaii with Mary and Jan?"

"They were planning the trip all along."

"Maybe, but Mr. Saunders would have cancelled his vacation in a heartbeat if there were any real developments in the investigation."

"I don't know exactly what you did, or how you did it, but there's no doubt you're the man responsible for her death."

"I didn't come here to argue your insanities."

"Argue this, then: I don't give a damn about the trust. You do. That's why you kidnapped Dorothy, that's why you force-married her, and that's why when you saw she was leaving you, you had her killed."

Damon shook his head. "You need serious help."

"Is that what you came here to tell me?"

"No. I came here to tell you to back off. I'll be leaving for Vietnam soon, and I need to know that you're going to stop badgering Mr. Saunders with your crazy accusations and your stories about a letter."

"It isn't a story."

"It is now. When Dorothy was telling you all about the terrible ordeals she'd endured living the luxurious, protected life, with chefs, maids, and private tutors for our son, did she also mention that I'd hired bodyguards to make sure she didn't fall back on her drug habit and that she didn't hurt herself?"

"Yes, the prison guards."

"Which is more likely? An addict calling two men hired to protect her 'prison guards' because she views them as such since they keep her from her drugs, or because they really are prison guards?"

"As always, you've set everything up so that your explanation happens to be the simplest and therefore the most credible."

"Fine," Damon said, "since you refuse to live in the world of reality, here's one for your world of imagination: Let's say Dorothy does commit suicide, but she wants to drag me down with her, so she writes this letter. Assuming such a scenario, I would have to protect myself, so I'd have one of the bodyguards slip into Dorothy's lawyer's office in Geneva during the night. He finds your imaginary envelope marked 'For Dad' and replaces your equally imaginary letter with Dorothy's bracelet."

"How could they have her bracelet?"

"They could have her pink Lamborghini. This is fantasy world, remember? I thought of a bracelet because you prefer your fairy tales to sound believable, right? So humor me, if you would, with my little story, as I have done with yours. Let's suppose John Saunders decides to have his daughter declared dead, as you say he might, and suppose further that the lawyer hands him this envelope. John Saunders would discover his wife's bracelet. The very bracelet she'd given to her daughter before she'd chosen suicide to escape her problems. The message Dorothy would be giving her father would be unmistakable: there'd be no question in his mind that his daughter had chosen the same cowardly path as her mother before her."

Kory did not speak.

"So taking your story about a letter one step further, in this imaginary scenario, the bodyguard flies all the way back from Switzerland, gives me Dorothy's letter, which I read"—Damon smiled—"and subsequently burn." Damon opened the palm of his hand and the queen fell to the ground. "Now, isn't that the perfect fairy-tale ending?"

"What do you want?" Kory asked, his eyes focused on oblivion.

"I think I've already said what I want. I don't care what you think or believe, as long as you keep your crap to yourself. If I ever hear you badmouthing me again, to *anyone*, I'll come up with another story like the one I just told you, but this time, it won't have such a happy ending."

"Is that a threat?" Kory sat up in his seat.

"No more of your lies. Am I making myself clear?"

"The problem is, you see them as lies, I don't."

"You're exactly right: *that's* the problem." Damon got up. "Dorothy also believed her own fiction, and look at what happened to her."

"You have the audacity to admit you killed her?"

"Her addiction killed her." Before walking off, Damon turned and said, "Don't think that because I'll be gone in Vietnam, I won't know what you're up to. You start spreading more rumors and lies, and those two bodyguards will be all over you like flies on shit."

Damon walked out of the building feeling like a million bucks.

Served Kory right. Little shithead. Always causing trouble.

He had to set his little brother straight before leaving for Vietnam, because if at any point things were to go south for Damon, Jan would be completely on his own. The kid had had a tough break, losing his mother like that. He certainly didn't need his father being dragged through the mud just because Dorothy had been irresponsible enough to commit the ultimate act of selfishness.

Jan was on the straight and narrow. Going to boarding school, preparing for the Academy. Eventually, Damon thought, he will inherit his grandmother's fortune and the entire van Luden legacy, fully able and qualified to carry the torch and, in turn, one day pass it on to *his* son, preserving the family line for generations to come.

Damon looked up at what blue sky could be seen beyond the skyscrapers.

Soon, he would be leading his own A-team to war, making history and raising the bar for Jan as Nicholas had done for him.

PART V

BRIGHT LIGHT

1970
Fourteen Months Later

Damon glanced at Sergeant First Class Tom "Snakebite" Dalton. The SFC was shaking his head, but Damon was going to give it a try anyway. What the hell.

The commander of Command and Control Central, CCC, Lieutenant Colonel Fernandez, was a hard nut to crack. You had to give the man credit, however. He'd accrued an assortment of medals, including the Distinguished Service Cross and the Silver Star, and he was currently on his fourth tour in Vietnam—by choice, no less. He did it for his men, and they all knew it.

Damon knocked on the door eliciting the response of a tired voice. "Come."

Letting himself in, Damon gave the colonel his sharpest West Point salute.

Colonel Fernandez said, "What is it now, Captain?"

Damon looked behind him and silently closed the door. "Sir, it's about the POW camp."

"Captain, we've been over this before—"

"Sir, I know sir, but I really think that RT New York is the team for this one. I've got my boys tuned like a concert violin. We can do this, we're ready."

Colonel Fernandez looked up from a stack of papers. "I'm sure you are, but the decision has been made."

Damon said nothing.

The colonel was going gray, and probably had ulcers to boot. Command and Control South had launched several bomb-damage-assessment (BDA) missions from Quan Loi right after the new Nixon administration started secret bombings of the Fishhook sanctuary in Cambodia. They'd lost many good men, including "Mad Dog" Shriver, a legend among the elite SOG. The acronym once stood for special operations group, but this was far too conspicuous, so they came up with studies and observations group, making it sound more like a society for geriatric birdwatchers than a team of elite soldiers.

Only a select few knew the SOG existed. Fewer still knew what they actually did.

Just three months into the New Year, under Colonel Fernandez's command, CCC had six men dead and another twenty-two wounded on recon missions. Then Nixon started a third secret B-52 bombing raid on northeastern Cambodia dropping more than ten thousand Mark 82 five-hundred-pound bombs. Reconnaissance Team Kansas had gone in on a BDA mission with only Cobra gunships for cover. No fighters were allowed into Cambodia due to dated State Department rules. They had landed in an ambush and the entire team simply vanished. A Bright Light rescue team had been dispatched from Dak To, but there wasn't a trace to be found of the missing men. The North Vietnamese Army, the NVA, had taken everything, sparing only their empty shell casings.

Due to Vietnamization—the gradual handing over of the war to the South Vietnamese—the headquarters in Saigon had to be informed of every mission the SOG undertook. A senior South Vietnamese officer in Saigon, a mole code named Françoise, informed Hanoi of the exact times and coordinates of each of these missions. When a SOG team was inserted onto a landing zone, they often met with their demise in an ambush, outnumbered many times over by the NVA.

Colonel Fernandez hadn't cracked a smile in months. He was sending eager young men to almost certain death. Now his most senior One-Zero, the team-leader, wanted to end his life at the very end of his tour.

"RT California was assigned this one, Damon."

Damon was about to protest, but the colonel held up his hand. "They're not going—nobody's going."

"But Colonel," Damon said, feeling blood pushing hard into his head, "we've got positive results on a polygraph from the informant, and we've got OV-10 recon photos; what more proof do you need?"

"It isn't me," the colonel said, too tired to raise his voice. "A Bright Light mission like this needs approval from the Joint Chiefs, from the ambassador to Laos, and from Saigon." He shook his head impatiently. "Goddammit, Ghost, you've been on twenty fucking missions—you know this shit is out of my hands."

Twenty-one, but who's counting? "Colonel, for Christ's sake, there are *Americans* in that camp."

The colonel pounded on his table. Papers slid off the top of the pile, floating to the floor. "You think I don't *care*? What the fuck do you think this is?" he said, pointing at the stack. "My men are dying like flies out there—most of the time, we can't even get their bodies back."

"I'm sorry, sir, it's just that—"

"Look, you're up for promotion, you're at the end of your tour here; why don't you think of your family and leave this fucking country while you're still in one piece? Let me do my job here and decide who does what, all right?"

Damon studied the colonel for a moment, decided there was no changing his mind, snapped a salute, and left.

Snakebite was waiting outside when Damon stormed out of the building. "He told you to get fucked, right?"

Damon gave him a bitter look.

"Told you," Snakebite said. "I fucking told you, but when do you ever listen to me?"

"Yeah, well, thanks for rubbing it in."

"Hey, man, don't take it so bad. The guy does have a point."

"What point?" Damon said, spinning as if he were about to launch a punch.

Snakebite didn't even flinch. "You're too old for this fucking shit, and besides, we don't even know if there really is a POW camp out there."

"We do," Damon said, "and there is. And who the hell are you calling old?"

Snakebite spat in the dirt. "So why aren't we going in, then?"

"Because the fuckers in Washington want to leave our men out there to rot."

Snakebite thought about this and spat once more, this time in agreement. *"Fuckers."*

"Yeah, it's in the sensitive area. As if all of Laos isn't a sensitive area. We're not supposed to be there, but the same goes for the NVA. So what's the big deal now? It's all a fucking crock— politicians jerking each other off at the negotiating tables in Paris. It's fucking bullshit."

"Fucking bullshit," Snakebite agreed, nudging his One-Zero roughly in the small of his back. "Let's go to Fat Albert's and get shit-faced."

When Colonel Fernandez was rotated back home to his family, he was replaced by Lt. Col. Brad Shackelford, a man rumored to be a pencil-pushing bureaucrat from Washington who'd never even been part of the Special Forces and hadn't seen a single day of action in his cushy life. He was a gift to CCC from General Abrams, whose personal mission apparently was to dismantle the Special Forces in Vietnam. Lt. Col. Brad Shackelford was the perfect man to help with the general's plan, for wherever the colonel ventured he left a trail of mediocrity and mismanagement.

As of the end of June, Nixon had ordered all SOG forces out of Cambodia. And so Command and Control South, CCS, was dismantled, and their men were distributed among Command and Control Central, CCC, and Command and Control North, CCN.

With the extra men, some recon teams were now using four Americans. Damon had three: He was the team leader, the One-Zero; Snakebite was the assistant team leader, the One-One; and Ronnie "Razor" Argenzio, the recon team's radio operator, was the One-Two. These were the Americans of Reconnaissance Team New York. Recon teams, RTs, were named after states, and Damon had been RT New York's

One-Zero through numerous successful missions. None had earned him any medals worthy of mention, however, and as far as Damon was concerned, he didn't care about the Bronze Star, or the Silver Star, or even the Distinguished Service Cross, for that matter. There was only one medal that counted.

Damon never shared his aspirations for the Medal of Honor with anyone—he knew the rest of the guys didn't think that way, and they would have considered him an asshole for even bringing up the subject. The SOG was the most highly decorated unit in the US military, but few of the recipients ever made mention of that fact.

Like the other One-Zeros at CCC, Damon wanted to come back from his mission a success, with his team intact. It was a simple goal and the driving force for all recon men.

To this end, he trained his team rigorously before each and every mission. He had them repeat immediate-action drills, using live ammunition every day until they worked together as harmoniously as the patterns in a kaleidoscope. IA drills were used to get recon teams out of tight spots when they were vastly outnumbered by the enemy. These drills involved short periods of highly concentrated fire followed by a vanishing act, which, when done correctly, left the NVA stunned and with just smoke for a target. Damon's team welcomed these relentless exercises; they knew from experience there was no such thing as too much training.

Damon had a week to prepare for this wiretap mission but four days into the training, Colonel Shackelford had one of his sergeants fetch him. The sergeant was a young gofer Damon had never seen around CCC. RT New York was in the middle of an exercise and Damon knew this unusual interruption could only mean something important.

"Snakebite," Damon said, "you're the One-Zero for this one."

Snakebite responded with a brief salute and in seconds, they had resumed the drill. Machine-gun fire crackled once again.

"Captain van Luden," the sergeant announced, and then closed the door behind him.

Damon had seen Colonel Shackelford once before, when the commander had assembled the men on his arrival. Up close, the impression was far worse. If he wasn't going to lay off the food—and from the looks of him there seemed to be little chance of that—he could at least have a new uniform fitted. This one was bloated like an open parachute. Thinning gray strands held on feebly to his bald pink head like dying weeds. He looked at Damon with watery eyes. A bead of sweat lingered on the tip of his cauliflower nose and below that, three inches of cigar protruded from a sagging lower lip. The sides of his jacket were soaked from the armpits down.

Damon wondered how the man in civvies sitting opposite the colonel could stand the smell. Damon had heard from other One-Zeros who had the misfortune of standing in close proximity to the colonel that his body odor was enough to make a rat puke.

The slim man in civvies was wearing a light blue denim shirt, faded jeans, a thick leather belt with an oversized gold buckle displaying a jumping horse, and full-quill two-tone ostrich boots to match. All that was missing was the hat.

Colonel Shackelford looked at the cowboy in blue as he addressed Damon. "This is Jabber, with the NSA."

Damon glanced at the man without as much as turning his head.

Jabber moved his chair so he could see the colonel while facing Damon. "We've got a few changes for you, Ghost."

Damon resented a civilian using his code name, even if he was NSA. He glanced over at his commanding officer, but His Disgracefulness just nodded indifferently.

"We'd like to have you try out the TLA-100. You'll proceed with the wiretap mission. Installing it is just as easy—"

"TLA?"

"Telephone line analyzer," Jabber said, pulling a black device the size and shape of a cereal box from his leather bag. Damon wondered what other surprises the man had in there. He pointed at two lead wires that dangled freely. "Just scrape a small patch off the copper wire and attach these babies the way you would a standard wiretap." He rotated the box, showing Damon two gauges. "This over here reads distance from your location to the first enemy commo device on your right; and this shows you the distance to the first enemy commo device to your left. As soon as they start chitchatting, you'll have your distance to the enemy. After that, hunting the fuckers down is easy."

"Nice," Damon said, "but what if there is no commo traffic? I'm sitting out there with my team hoping someone will talk on the line? Those lines are constantly patrolled by maintenance personnel, you know. You expect us to sit around waiting for commo traffic while some maintenance man spots us and calls for infantry support?"

"We're working on adding a button that would allow you to send an electronic impulse down the lines in each direction giving you guys the meter readings you need without the wait."

"What about battery drain?" Damon said.

Jabber cleared his throat. "Uh, that's a little problem we still haven't ironed out."

Damon nodded. "Okay, but that's it? Just swap the TLA-100 for a standard wiretap? Everything remains the same?"

"Officially," Colonel Shackelford said, blowing a cloud of cigar smoke in front of him, "yes, that's all there is to this mission."

Damon waited, but the colonel said no more.

The NSA agent was the one to speak. "It has come to our attention that the son of one of our senators was recently downed."

"Who?"

"Right now, that's need-to-know . . . until the press get their hands on it, that is," Jabber said with a lupine smile. "Anyway, we have reason to believe that he's still alive in a POW camp in Laos."

Damon's eyes came alive. "You mean *the* POW camp? The one in area Whiskey Seven?"

"The very same," Jabber said, showing his white teeth. "You've been itching for this mission for some time, am I right?"

"That you are!" Damon looked at the colonel, whose expression now conveyed more annoyance than boredom.

"So I'm authorized to do this?" Damon asked.

"Do what?" Colonel Shackelford said, seeming so convincingly confused, Damon didn't get it at first. "You are officially authorized to install this TLA-100 device, Captain van Luden. Washington has already made it clear we are to stay away from that part of Laos. Whiskey Seven is off-limits, do we understand each other?"

Damon hesitated, but when Jabber nodded it registered. "Yes. Yes, sir."

"Good," Colonel Shackelford said, attempting to relight his remaining inch of cigar.

"You will be launching out of the Udorn airbase, with a Jolly Green." Jabber grinned. "As you are aware, teams have been known to miss their LZ, especially out of Udorn."

"Miss their LZ?" Damon said. It wasn't really a question—he knew what Jabber was thinking: they were going to have him miss the landing zone for the official mission, intentionally inserting his team near the POW camp, while making it appear like a mistaken drop.

"Hey, mistakes happen, right?" Jabber said. "And if you, as the One-Zero, should find yourself somewhere other than your LZ, then you could decide to order a general recon. The team will do as you say. Right, Colonel Shackelford?"

The colonel sucked on his cigar; the tip glowed bright orange.

"Okay, but what about the reports to Covey? We have to check in periodically," Damon said. The Forward Air Controller, FAC, flying the Prairie Fire ops area was code named Covey. It was a recon team's only link to the outside world.

"That you do, but Army equipment is not always reliable—made by the lowest bidder and all—so should your radios have transmission troubles; say, for instance, carrier only? You get the picture . . ."

Damon didn't. This was way beyond unconventional.

He belonged to the SOG, top-secret commandos in a branch that didn't officially exist and was never officially acknowledged. They went behind enemy lines, to places in Laos and Cambodia through which Hanoi's National Vietnamese Army had diverted the Ho Chi Minh Trail all the way to South Vietnam. Hanoi denied any NVA presence in Cambodia and Laos, and so the United States had no official business there. The SOG were created to provide the Army, the CIA, and the

NSA with intel about the enemy's actions in those countries, to disrupt their progress and, sometimes, to rescue prisoners of war. Deniability was the key to the operation—so much so that teams went in without dog tags or any identification whatsoever. Nevertheless, despite all the secrecy, Washington and Saigon still had to approve missions.

Except in this particular case.

The spook was suggesting that Damon should lead his men in an unapproved mission disguised as a top-secret assignment gone wrong.

This was completely insane.

Damon wasn't ready to simply leave it at that. "I don't get it: If a senator's son is out there, why doesn't Washington just let me do this without all the cloak-and-dagger? I've been asking for this mission since the first reports came in about a POW camp—"

Jabber shook his head. "Again, this is *not* your official mission. Your mission is to install the TLA. The administration cannot openly sanction a Bright Light mission because, first of all, our ambassador to Laos has given it a thumbs-down. Secondly we've got Kissinger at the negotiating tables with Hanoi, working on a peace treaty and so an officially sanctioned mission could spell disaster if anything went wrong out there."

"I still don't get it. I'm *accidentally* dropped west of the LZ, I order a general recon, and my radios go on the fritz; what happens when I show up with American POWs?"

Jabber smiled. "That's the beauty of all this. You come back with American POWs and Hanoi won't be able to say a damned thing. They're not supposed to be in Laos, let alone have a POW camp there. *They* deny it, *we* deny it. If you come back with American POWs, we'll take care of the rest."

The colonel cut in before Damon could think of more questions. "Be clear on this: if you decide to launch a general recon and you do end up stumbling on this POW camp, you'd better bring us some live Americans. Understand, soldier?"

Damon nodded.

The colonel smashed his cigar in the ashtray. "Dismissed."

At 0400 hours, Damon walked into the Vietnamese team room. "Let's go! We launch tomorrow and I need *everyone* ready!"

The Vietnamese team sergeant, the Zero-One, called his men to attention and Damon knew immediately something was wrong.

"Where's Huong?" Damon said, addressing Nghiem Chinh, the Zero-One.

"Huong is sick," the sergeant said. "Sorry."

"Sick?" Damon said, incredulous. "*Sick?* He looked just fine to me yesterday."

"Amoebic dysentery," Bui, one of the scouts, said, but the team sergeant gave him an angry stare and Bui retreated back to the group.

"Okay," Damon said, "there isn't much time; I want to see five replacement candidates on the double. I'll do the interview for a new interpreter right here, right now."

Nghiem lowered his head. "So sorry, sir, you already have replacement . . . he is an excellent interpreter." He pointed at the stranger Damon had seen when he came in. "He speaks English and he speaks French."

"Okay, fine, include him with the rest of the bunch to be interviewed."

"You misunderstand, sir. He is already . . . selected."

The Vietnamese team sergeant realized he had angered his team leader. "He is very good."

"Maybe I'm confused here, but since when has a One-Zero lost the right to select his team members?"

"No! No!" the Vietnamese team sergeant said. "He is—"

"Very good, yes, you told me. Look, this is *bullshit.* I want to see five men right now and I don't want any more talk—"

Everyone in the room suddenly snapped into a salute. Damon turned around just in time to inhale a cloud of cigar smoke along with the stink of sweat and cologne.

"At ease, Captain," the colonel said.

Damon stepped back, glaring at the man in front of him. It was just two weeks since the colonel's arrival, and already just about everyone at CCC hated his guts. He changed procedures that worked, just for the sake of effecting change.

Marking his territory at the expense of the legacy left by his worthy predecessors.

"I replaced your interpreter," the colonel said.

"With all due respect, Colonel, a One-Zero has the right—"

"*Outside,*" the colonel snapped, his normally pink face now deep crimson.

"Sir?"

The colonel was already marching out; Damon followed.

When they were out of earshot, the colonel said, "Don't you *ever* talk down to me in front of our men, especially Vietnamese mercs. Do I make myself perfectly clear, Captain?"

"Yes sir!" Damon said, wishing he could catch the colonel alone in a dark alley.

"Good. Now, get out of my face or I'll—" But Colonel Shackelford had no audience—Damon had already turned away, and was heading back to the Vietnamese team room.

The weather was marginal. The ceiling was low—three hundred feet lower and it would qualify as fog. Normally there would be no hope of inserting a team under these conditions. The broken cloud layer left gaps appropriately referred to as "sucker holes." You might get in, but the hole could close, leaving you stranded in hostile territory with no air support. Usually, a SOG commander would wait for improving conditions, but for this mission, the weather was just right.

Damon's team stepped into the gaping cavern of the Hercules through the tailgate. Bisecting the belly of the giant aircraft was a roller system used for heavy drops. The floor décor included a layer of sand and blotches of tar, while the rest of the fuselage interior was draped in dark olive canvas. Lining both sides was a long bench made up of pull-down aluminum strap seats.

The crew chief pointed at the jump seats to the left. "Get your collective asses in there, boys, we don't have all day!" He had to yell because all four engines were running, and even at idle they were deafening.

As the team settled in, the crew chief said, "Who's the team leader here?"

"I am," Damon said.

"You sure you want to go to Thailand in this shit?"

"That's what we're here for."

"Okay, then; strap in and let's leave this crap hole while we still have a chance."

"I want to watch," Damon said, pointing at the small window at the exit door.

"You'd better strap in for now, 'cause we're leaving the tailgate open for takeoff. Gets rid of the fuel stink and lets this can cool down."

Damon strapped in with the rest of his men while the crew chief walked over to the rear opening. He took position with an M-60 to deal with potential attack from snipers or rocket bases during their initial takeoff climb.

A few minutes after the gear was raised into the belly, the metallic jaw of the aircraft closed, and the crew master walked past Damon's team, up the narrow stairway to the cockpit.

At cruise, Damon got out of his seat, faced his men, and shouted, "Remember, I want you guys to slip into that Jolly Green quickly and quietly. Don't let any weapons show." Damon was looking directly at Ho. "Thailand is neutral ground, and there aren't supposed to be armed soldiers there."

The aircraft descended through embedded cumulus, jolting Damon into the air and ending his briefing prematurely. He cursed as he strapped himself in along with the rest of his team.

The wheels of the C-130 met the hot asphalt at Udorn Air Force Base in a puff of smoking rubber. The propellers were put into reverse, and the soldiers of RT New York were pressed hard against their seat belts. Once Damon determined they'd slowed to taxi speed, he ordered his team ready at the door. The tarmac steamed like dry ice, and as they jumped off the C-130, they were welcomed by a rush of hot air so wet most average Americans would have trouble breathing.

The sky was bloated with moisture; it was going to rain soon, long and hard—no question about it.

The Hercules had dispatched them next to a hangar. Damon motioned his men to follow him and they slipped inside, putting on their gear in the shadows of the hangar. Ponchos donned, they ran to the Jolly Green Giant; closely grouped as one unit, not one of them could be identified under the cover of olive drab nylon.

In the helicopter, the crew chief shoved a helmet at Damon and mimed the act of putting it on.

"Are you the leader?" a voice said from inside a helmet.

Damon could see the pilot waving at him from the front. He was seated on the right. "Yes. And you're Hawk?"

"That's me. I'm the AC. We've got to boogie, this weather won't be doable for much longer. You copy?"

"Roger," Damon said, giving the pilot a thumbs-up.

The Jolly Green lifted off the ground, lurching forward into the humid day. In just moments, the helicopter was engulfed in cloud, and suddenly there was nothing to see out the windows except for gloomy murk. As they ascended, the clouds radiated more light, and the gray gave in to a blinding white; just seconds later, RT New York was lifted up into blue sky.

Damon stood by a mini-gun mounted on the left of the fuselage and from the window he could see a thick blanket of bright-white cloud sinking below them. They had risen to just a few hundred feet above the cloud layer and Damon wondered how the pilot could navigate in this. As they continued east into Laos, Damon searched for ground references.

Occasionally, bits of forest, propped up by mountainous terrain, peeped out of the thick cloud. In this weather, a pilot, even a good one, could easily mistake his position. Nobody would question the team for ending up so far from their designated landing zone. A mistaken LZ was not what was worrying Damon. The pilot—the aircraft commander—was instructed to drop them at Whiskey Seven, making it look like a navigational error, and he and Damon were the only ones aboard who knew. If the aircraft commander really did make a mistake, they would probably end up in Nowheresville, Laos—far from the POW camp, far from the LZ, and it would all be for nothing.

This was Damon's one and only chance.

"Five minutes," the crew chief shouted.

The team rechecked their weapons and donned their web gear; nobody exchanged a single word.

Damon watched Ho carefully. Colonel Shackelford had rammed this guy down his throat, probably just to make sure Damon knew exactly who was boss.

What a prick.

The day before, Damon had been forced to squeeze one week's worth of training into a single day. Despite Nghiem's assurances that the new interpreter was experienced and would fit right in, Damon, as One-Zero, had to make sure for himself. First on the list was rappelling. With no helicopters available on short notice, Damon had his team hike almost four kilometers to the Dak Bla River, where Ho, along with the others on the team, rappelled off the Kontum Bridge. Then Damon had him demonstrate his target skills with an AK. Ho was the interpreter, but he was also a scout, and everyone on the team was a vital asset, especially when the time came to fight off NVA. This guy obviously had a few missions under his belt, but it took him a while to get in sync with the team during the IA drills.

He would do. He'd simply have to—it wasn't as if Damon had a choice. The colonel had sat there and let Jabber squeeze Damon into accepting an illegal mission disguised as a covert assignment. Had this been any other mission, and other time, Damon would have told them both to go fuck themselves. But this was the only way Damon was going anywhere near that POW camp. He knew it, and they knew it.

After this last mission, his tour would end, and even if he tried for an extension, it wouldn't help. Despite what most civilians thought, taking the Special Forces route was not the fast track for career advancement in the military. Chances were you'd end up coming home in a box, if they could even find your body. When all that was left of you were a few framed photos over your parents' fireplace, career prospects tended to be grim.

And even if you managed to survive, advancing to a higher rank took longer. Damon couldn't care less—in fact, he didn't even want to be promoted. As long as he wasn't ranked any higher than captain, he could avoid being turned into a desk jockey, and he'd still see action along with the rest of his men.

He was long overdue, however. Damon had heard that a good number of his classmates had been promoted to major several years earlier. Soon, he too would be forced to sit behind a desk and push paper, in which case there'd be no point staying a day longer in Vietnam. So Damon didn't extend his tour, and that decision made this his one and only chance at finding that POW camp. Colonel Shackelford and Jabber knew Damon was desperate, and as was typical of the scum that they were, they took full advantage of that fact.

"Go!" a voice called.

It didn't matter that he was being used. He alone shouldered the burden on this one, and that was okay, because his team would get the Americans back home. That's all that mattered . . . that and a shot at the only medal that really meant something . . . the one with the pale blue ribbon.

The one they'd given his father.

Damon dismissed the thought, grabbing at the rope, and with a few quick movements, he tied it into a Swiss seat around his waist. He snapped the metal carabiner link to the line and slid down into the jungle, grazed by a dozen branches on his way. His teammates followed closely, one by one.

They all made it to the ground safely, including Ho, which was a great relief to Damon. He didn't like accidents; they jeopardized the mission and were a bad reflection on him. As a One-Zero, he knew accidents were no mistake. Damon spent every chance he had training each and every one of his men so that they couldn't screw up if they wanted to. With Ho, he'd had just one day. That was the first time in twenty-one missions he'd ever attempted training a guy to meet his team standards in less than twenty-four hours. So far, things were going well.

As quickly as the Jolly Green had emerged from the opening in the sky, it was suddenly gone, sucked into a small blue fissure in the cloud, the sound of its powerful engine fading in a rapid decrescendo.

Masked by trees, the team lay down, listening for any suspicious sounds. All at once, a branch overhead shook in a blurry frenzy; leaves jerked free, parasailing to the ground. Razor aimed his CAR-15 at the source and a black shadow stormed upward, shaking more branches before leaping through the damp air to another tree.

Razor cursed softly under his breath—it was just a monkey. He stole a glance at Nghiem. The Vietnamese team leader pretended not to notice. Ho scoped the area, and then Damon signaled Snakebite, who said two words into his mike, only audible to Forward Air Control: "Team okay."

The team was alone now, each man with his face charcoal black, the whites of his eyes a glaring contrast. The hungry mosquitoes circled their prey, darting within earshot but never closer. All the men had covered their exposed skin with repellant—experience had taught them the consequences of going without.

When he could see Snakebite and Razor were looking, Damon took out his map. This was the tricky part: Damon had to pretend he believed they were at the official landing zone. The POW camp was just fifteen hundred meters due west. As planned, the wiretap was also due west of the official LZ, so he glanced at his compass, made a mark on his map, and motioned his men to follow him.

Damon pushed a vine carefully out of his way, the muzzle of his CAR-15 always tracking the movement of his eyes. He paused, checked the surface of the soil for anything that could make a sound: a twig, a branch, stones. Satisfied, he delicately planted his foot on the ground and then shifted his weight forward. On jungle recon missions, his team usually moved no more than five hundred meters per day.

For this mission, Damon needed his team to pick up the pace: eight hundred to a thousand meters per day. Forward Air Control received a report every twelve hours. On normal missions he would simply send Covey an encrypted message on the new PRC 77 with the ANGR 10 coder burst transmitter.

He'd thought of setting up a rally point where one of his men would send pre-coded messages to Covey every twelve hours. He needed every single man for this mission, however, and the idea of leaving anyone behind rubbed him the wrong way. Setting up a rally point while sending Covey bogus position reports would mean Damon would be forced to let his entire team in on what he was really planning. He would be on an unauthorized mission, providing false information to Forward Air Control, while using his power as One-Zero to oblige his team members to knowingly participate.

On the other hand, if he had understood Jabber correctly, Damon was to purposely botch the position reports, keeping Covey in the dark. If Damon were to go along with Jabber's plan, carrier-only transmissions would probably be the way to go, simulating a faulty transmitter. But even that would be hard to do without directly involving his team, and he didn't want any of them mixed up in this. It also left him hanging if things didn't go right in the end. Convenient for CCC, but not for his team, and a potential disaster for him. To make things worse, if two transmissions were missed in a row, CCC would order a Bright Light team to search for RT New York. That would be a big mess, because they'd be looking in the wrong area, and putting more good men in harm's way.

No, Damon had a much better idea.

For his plan to work, however, they'd have to move faster. Damon had advanced a third step when he heard a cracking noise from behind him. He spun around to find his CAR-15 trained on the interpreter. Ho must have stepped on a branch.

Jesus, they had just arrived an hour ago and already Ho was fucking up. Suddenly, Damon began to wonder if Ho was as good as Nghiem had claimed.

Just over the summit, they could make out the valley below. Damon had studied the OV-10 observation aircraft photographs; he estimated he was around five hundred feet above the valley, looking down at an angle from the east. The OV-10 had taken pictures of the general area at fifteen hundred feet above ground level before descending down, just skimming over the trees, when it photographed the POW camp hooches camouflaged under triple-canopy jungle. From this distance, and from this angle, Damon couldn't make out the hooches, but that was to be expected; they were camouflaged. This was, however, the right valley, and Damon knew exactly where to head to "stumble upon" the camp.

Damon made a big show of looking at the valley and then back at his map. He glanced at his One-One and shook his head. Most of their communication was through hand signals, but when they absolutely had to speak, as Damon did, they lisp-whispered—a trick he had learned during Special Forces training back in Fort Bragg.

"We're not going to find a phone line here," he said.

"Not our LZ?" Snakebite said.

"Not by a long shot. This is the wrong valley. I'm guessing we've been inserted five, maybe ten klicks short of the LZ," Damon said, knowing that the Jolly Green pilot really placed them a full *forty* kilometers west of their landing zone.

"That's some fuck-up. This is bullshit, man."

"Yeah, my sentiments too," Damon lied. Then to his One-Two: "Razor, radio Covey, I'm ordering a general recon, advise them of our estimated position."

This idea was better than his original one of sending pre-coded messages from a rally point, or Jabber's plan of having them pretend they had a faulty transmitter, because now the ball would be in *their* court. S3 wasn't about to deny them a general recon. On the ground, the One-Zero was the field commander, and since they'd encountered no NVA, ordering a general recon made perfect sense. Being dropped at the wrong LZ from Thailand was not so uncommon, as Jabber had mentioned, and ordering a general recon was a perfectly logical decision for a One-Zero. Damon was fully aware of his position, this was unauthorized territory—fucking Whiskey Seven, for Christ's sake—but as far as Forward Air Control could tell, RT New York was dropped just five shy of the LZ. Officially, it would stand on record that was all anyone knew at the time Damon ordered the general recon. The weather was on his side—an O-2 or an OV-10 wouldn't be able to make visual contact, and when the Jolly Green had dropped them off, it was assumed they were at the designated LZ. Covey had no reason to question Razor when he reported their position as a mere five kilometers west of where they should have been.

If the rescue took too long, however, Covey would eventually make their position, and S3 would have to order an abort—they wouldn't be able to officially sanction the POW rescue, and Damon wondered if S3 was even in on this anyway. For all he knew, this was something the colonel and Jabber had stewed up entirely on their own.

"We're not going to extract?" Razor said.

"We're here, so we'll do what we've been trained to do: recon," Damon said.

The One-One gave his thumbs-up, making it clear they were back to hand signals now while also showing his support for the team leader's decision. While the One-Two busied himself with Covey on the radio, Damon looked at his map and confirmed what he already knew. The POW camp was sitting in the center of the valley, approximately fifteen hundred meters from their current position. Damon took the lead, carefully creeping down the mountainside in the direction of the valley below.

The SOG was primarily sent "over the fence" to detect, while remaining incognito. To this end, they moved slower than any other military unit around. For regular troopers, a kilometer and a half wouldn't take more than forty minutes. Damon calculated that even at this accelerated pace it would take RT New York almost two days.

Only two hours after their arrival, it had already begun to pour, and instead of draining, the clouds seemed to darken with each passing hour. The opening in the sky had disappeared. If there was another sucker hole, Damon couldn't see it. He knew there would be no support for his team anymore— no emergency extractions, no gunships to help fight off the NVA. If they found trouble, they were completely on their own until Mother Nature decided otherwise.

The logical action, at this point, would be to stay put and cover-and-conceal until the weather improved, so that if enemy contact was made, Damon could rely on air support. This was a far cry from a normal situation; they were cut off because of the weather and worse, they were in area Whiskey Seven. Even if Damon could have talked about this with other One-Zeros during the days he had to prep for this mission, hunting for tips and advice would have been pointless, since no one in CCC had ever ventured this far west into Laos.

What light remained was dwindling while the downpour had mercifully subsided to a mere drizzle. The mosquitoes were unrelenting now, but even wet, the repellant was still doing its job. Damon showed them an open palm, and his men quietly halted where they stood. He made a circle motion with his finger, indicating it was time to find their remain-over-night area, which in Army-speak was referred to by its acronym, RON. They doubled back, losing some distance to make sure there were no trackers, and then the team followed Damon to the north, where he uncovered a huge, semihollow tree trunk. Damon drew two half-circles in the air with his fingers in a wide arc. His One-One and One-Two were already on it, planting C-4 mines with steel balls that would have the effect of an omnidirectional shotgun blast at point-blank range. Snakebite planted these claymore mines in a fifty-foot circle around the RON while Razor concealed the control wires with dirt and leaves.

As the men ate their prepackaged dehydrated food, LRRP—long range recon patrol rations—Damon wondered how much closer they were to the POW camp. It couldn't be that far; he just hoped his team was ready—this was not the mission he'd prepared them for. They carefully gathered all their dinner remnants and once this was done, the eight of them huddled together in a tight mass to reduce the chances of being spotted. They were soon asleep.

At 0400 hours, Damon woke his men. His One-One gathered the claymore mines and then worked the forest floor, shuffling leaves and removing any trace of human presence. The men followed him the rest of the way down to the valley.

There would be no dawn where they were; instead, it would become suddenly bright because the thick forest blocked most of the light that didn't come from directly above. In Damon's estimation, they would be at the camp in time to still benefit from the cover of darkness, but by then the NVA would probably be awake. It would be foolish to assume otherwise.

Three hours later, his Vietnamese point man, Bui, put his hands together at the fingertips in an upside-down "V," followed by a sawing motion with the edge of his hand against his throat, and then he showed the other men ten spread fingers: *Hooches . . . enemy in sight . . . ten men visible.*

The team snaked over painstakingly to Bui's position.

Adrenaline was the SOG's drug of choice. At the moment it was making Damon's heart pound so hard it felt as though it would break free from his chest. He had waited a lifetime for this moment, and in that instant he saw his father, a wounded man under each arm, running from Nazi fire. The picture changed and now his father was bowing so that Roosevelt could reach over his head with the Medal of Honor . . .

They had been much closer than he'd originally thought, but there was no question in his mind—Bui had found the camp.

They had finally reached a point where Damon could see an abrupt clearing in the forest, but the foliage above had been woven together in a man-made tapestry to camouflage the camp from aerial observers. This must have happened after the photos were taken; there was no way the OV-10 could have managed to take any useful pictures otherwise.

A group of eight NVA was huddled around a small patch. Breakfast, Damon guessed. Two were at the other end of the hooch engaged in casual conversation. More would undoubtedly be inside. He had taken on odds far worse than these—this just might work. He pointed at his eyes with forked fingers and then at the hooch. Nobody moved. Damon waited for them to observe their target before he signaled for them to fall back.

They secured a perimeter in the forest, where they huddled together in a tight semicircle with Damon in the center. It was time to tell them what they were looking at and what he planned to do about it.

"You positive, Ghost?" Snakebite asked, once Damon finished saying they'd just stumbled upon the POW camp.

Damon nodded, thinking of the fewest words to answer the question. Speech on recon missions, especially so close to the enemy, had to be kept to an absolute minimum. "Seen the photos," Damon lisp-whispered. "This is it. No doubt."

Then to everyone: "I'll take the NVA on the left side, forward entrance. I'll kill as many as I can without drawing attention." Damon pointed at his Swedish K suppressed submachine gun. "The second they're alerted to our presence, you join in. Same trigger as in an IA drill, but different procedures here. Kill the men outside and we'll storm the hooch from both sides at once. I need Nghiem and Ho, through the front door following Razor and me. Snakebite, you're with Bui. Take out the two in the back; come in through the rear. Vuong and Phan, you guys take cover at a distance. I want Vuong covering the front entrance from the south; and Phan, you'll be on the other side, covering the rear, from the north. Position yourselves at an angle so you're not facing each other. Nobody fires until they hear gunshots. We'll maintain the element of surprise as long as we can." Damon paused as Ho translated.

Ho was speaking quickly, panic in his eyes, as if he'd swallowed a grenade and was counting the seconds he had left in this world. There was a short exchange with his team leader, then Ho turned to Damon. "How do we know who not to shoot?"

"Don't kill any prisoners. Don't kill any Americans. It's simple."

Ho looked at Nghiem, but he wouldn't speak. His Vietnamese team leader nodded angrily. Ho said, "He says not simple. What if Vietnamese POW?"

"Don't kill any prisoners," Damon said, pissed off by the question.

Ho didn't have to turn to Nghiem; he already understood where his Vietnamese team leader was going with this. "How we know they not *pretend*-POW?"

"If they're bad guys, they'll probably be fat and happy," Damon said, clearly impatient. He didn't like all this chatter, especially so near the NVA. He'd never had this happen on any mission before. Briefings were always done days in advance, but, of course, Damon couldn't have briefed them beforehand—not until they reached the camp, thanks to Colonel Shackelford and his NSA buddy. "If they look abused and underfed, they're POWs: *don't kill them.* No grenades, no mortars. And be conservative with your fire. I don't want a single friendly scratched. Clear?"

Once Ho finished translating, Snakebite and Razor nodded, and Nghiem, Bui, Phan and Vuong added their silent acknowledgment with a bow.

"Ho?" Damon said, noticing the translator's discomfort. "Understood?"

Ho nodded reluctantly.

"Ghost, why not smoke 'em out?" Snakebite said.

"Can't," Damon said. "It'll give them time to think, turn the POWs into hostages. We'll just be left with dead bodies to bring back."

Snakebite nodded, admiring how quickly Ghost had come up with a plan: Bang, right on the spot, as if he'd had all day to think about it.

Damon put his finger to his lips, indicating they were back to hand signals. He motioned them to follow as he inched back toward the camp.

There were only five NVA in the front the next time Damon looked; the two in the rear were still engrossed in conversation. The rest must have gone inside or were out for a stroll.

Damon held up three fingers, then he made a "V" with his forefinger and thumb, rotating it in the air. *Three unaccounted for.* Damon stabbed two fingers toward his eyes. *Keep a lookout for them.*

That received nods all around.

When Damon was close enough to the clearing, he pumped the air with his palm facing down and his team straddled the earth. He pointed at Vuong and then at a tree to his left. Vuong crept slowly to the position the One-Zero had indicated in his briefing. There he nestled down with his AK pointed at the five men and the entrance to the POW camp. Damon pointed at Phan and at a tree in the distance to his right. Phan made his way there. The team waited until he was in position. Both Vuong and Phan were facing the hooch at the angle Damon wanted.

Satisfied that they understood, it was Damon's turn.

Snakebite and Razor watched their One-Zero move. It was as if every step had been carefully planned—a dance rehearsed over and over again.

Damon was only a few meters from the five NVA. They were indeed eating. One of them laughed at something; rice spilled off his chopsticks. He could not single them out—they were huddled together. Flat on the ground, Damon took aim. The Swedish K shook silently as he squeezed off the rounds. Some shells made a *ting* sound as they hit the ground, but that was all that was heard.

The target was chewing on a mouthful of rice and was about to help himself to more when a tight grouping of black dots appeared on his forehead. Three shots, one dead and in that split second, nobody had even noticed. Damon dropped another guy; the bullet went through the second NVA's neck at a slight angle, barely evident there, but the exit wound obliterated most of his ear and everything in between. Blood shot out in a stream. The first NVA he killed was collapsing into his bowl, and the other three turned to look. The element of surprise was lost in that instant. Damon killed another before one of the two remaining men started screaming. Damon charged.

Snakebite watched in amazement: despite all six feet of muscle, bone, and guts, Ghost moved like a puck in an air-hockey game. The two stunned NVA were looking for a target to shoot.

Damon emptied his magazine into one of them while he dove at the other. By the time the NVA fired, Damon was already out of harm's way, too close to be shot; he engulfed the shocked Vietnamese soldier with what looked like an embrace, but Damon pulled away and the small man collapsed backwards onto the ground. Damon's Randall combat knife came into view, bright red.

Damon was on his feet immediately and he charged the door. Using his peripheral vision, he saw Snakebite and Bui running toward the rear, just as planned. Trampling sounds came from behind. No time to turn and look, Damon had to assume it was Razor, Nghiem, and Ho.

Rat-tat-tat-tat-tat-tat. The unmistakable sound of an AK; probably Phan trying to take out the two in the back. Damon hoped the little guy didn't end up shooting Razor in the process. The Swedish K was of little use at this point—every NVA and his uncle within a mile knew about the attack. He slid the small automatic to his other shoulder and readied his favorite assault weapon, the light, sniper-gun accurate CAR-15.

Before Damon could kick in the door, it opened. A line of three NVA were rushing toward the screams coming from outside.

Masked against the morning light, Damon opened fire, downing the two to the right almost instantly. He fired again and lead ripped into the remaining NVA's shoulder. The NVA tried returning fire, but without time to level the muzzle of his AK, the bullets just hit the floor. Damon rammed into him, crushing his rib cage, and the NVA lieutenant was dead before he hit the ground.

Three eliminated, Damon counted. Hopefully the ones he had seen outside, but none of the bodies were recognizable, so he had to assume these were different men.

Damon had his CAR trained on a dark figure—no, two— that were charging from the other end of the corridor. He recognized them and held his fire—it was Snakebite with Bui right behind him. Damon raised an open palm, as if he was ready to swear an oath. His team stood still in the corridor. Damon looked back and saw Razor, Ho, and Nghiem.

He pointed to the corridor on his left, indicating his intended path. Damon signed for Nghiem and Bui to cover from the ends of the corridor. He needed Ho with him; Snakebite and Razor were assigned to investigate the two closed doors on this corridor.

Damon edged his way to the left, keeping as close to the corridor wall as he could without brushing against it. Three steps and Ho's foot went through a rotten plank of wood, snapping it in two like a gnawed pencil. Seeing Damon's reaction, Ho recoiled, giving him an abused-dog look. Damon didn't hit him—although for a moment he was tempted—this was the second time Ho had screwed up. He gave him a long stare and motioned to the first room.

Damon walked past the door, keeping his back just an inch from the corridor. With an extended arm he turned the knob and pushed the door open. Three grimy men in what looked like black pajamas were sitting in the far corner of the room, embracing their knees. There was a tin bowl of water on the floor to the left of the door. A few dirty leaves and a fat water bug floated across the surface. The bug struggled to upright itself with little success. The smell of urine burned into Damon's nostrils, making him wince. There were no traces, olfactory or otherwise, of fecal matter. The NVA had wanted them alive, for the time being at least. They would have probably been tortured or killed once the questioning was over.

Damon had heard stories where the NVA tied up Americans, slit their bellies, and fed their entrails to wild pigs while they watched, laughing.

It was better to be dead; that way your men didn't risk their lives coming in after you.

The prisoners suddenly recoiled in horror. One of them grimaced while another pointed at Damon. The skeletal man persisted, jabbing his finger at the air, and then Damon realized he wasn't pointing at him, but *behind* him. He turned around and saw what was scaring them.

Ho was standing there, in full NVA uniform, with chest style web-gear and a pith helmet, pointing his AK at the men in the room. Damon had all the Vietnamese on his team dress this way to confuse the NVA just enough to get them to hesitate or otherwise risk shooting one of their own. That delayed response was sufficient to give their team a lethal edge over the enemy. Everyone in RT New York, Damon included, had special soles on their shoes to leave tracks identical to NVA Bata boots.

The Vietnamese POWs must have figured Ho for the enemy, ready to shoot them any second.

"Explain," Damon commanded. "Tell them we're the good guys."

Ho started speaking in Vietnamese. Damon couldn't understand a word, but he could clearly tell they weren't buying it.

"I'm American," Damon said, pointing at himself, *"A-mer-i-can."* He pointed at Ho. *"Friend."* Their expressions had not changed. They seemed even more afraid than before.

Snakebite came in from the hallway. "All clear."

"What do you mean, *all clear*? Did you check everywhere?"

Snakebite shrugged. "Yep."

"No NVA anywhere?"

"That's right. Just bodies. That's it."

"Okay, what about the *rest*?"

"The rest? I'm pretty sure we got all the NVA—they're deader than a door stop."

"No, no!" Damon said. "I'm not talking about the fucking NVA, where are the *rest* of the POWs? Where are the *Americans*?"

"We didn't see nobody. No NVA, no POWs. Just what's left of the guys we took out."

Damon looked at him.

"There's nobody else here," Snakebite said slowly, in a calm voice. "All the rooms and bunkers are empty. They've either moved them out of here or there were none to begin with."

"*Fuck!*" Damon screamed, and the three Vietnamese prisoners recoiled in unison, pushing against the floor with their sandals, as if they were trying to burrow their way out through the corner of the room.

"You sure this is the same POW camp you were talking about?" Snakebite said, keeping his voice low.

"I studied the photos . . . I know the area . . . it's fucking got to be!"

"I don't know . . . we could be anywhere, this could be some other place."

Damon ignored him and turned to Ho. "Ask them where the rest of the POWs are."

When Ho didn't respond, Snakebite said, "Ask them where—"

Damon cut him off, yelling just inches from the interpreter's face, "Listen to me, you little pile of shit: when I give you an order, you follow it. You don't sit there and philosophize. You do as I fucking say."

"Very bad situation," Ho muttered.

Damon grabbed Ho by the collar and lifted him off the ground, smashing his back against the wall. "What did I just say?"

Ho could barely breathe. "Yes, sir. Yes, sir. Sorry, sir."

Snakebite shook his head. "Can the *sir* shit."

Ho nodded and Damon let go. The interpreter landed on the floor, wobbling on his feet.

Out of breath, Ho said something to the POWs. One of the three men answered. "They . . . say . . . they gone," Ho said.

"Gone? Where?" Damon demanded.

Ho asked the man who had offered the information. "They . . . don't know. They say . . . many more . . . VC . . . here before . . . now all gone. POW also gone."

"*Where*, goddammit?" Damon said, shouting again. "Where in fuck's name did they go?"

Ho shook his head. "They gone, sir. They say they moved, Truong, sir."

"He's not a sergeant, he's a *captain*," Snakebite said. Although it was common for Vietnamese to call every American on the team Truong, Damon had the feeling the little bastard did it intentionally to insult him.

"And what did I just say about using the word *sir*?" Snakebite added. "No rank, no *sir*. Got it?"

Damon could have had Ho press the POWs for more information, but they'd probably said all they knew—they had no reason to lie. Damon cursed.

Nobody spoke; all eyes in the room were fixed uneasily on Damon.

Snakebite hooked a thumb at the three trembling POWs and he broke the silence, asking, "What do we do with them?"

"Give them some rations—they look like they're about to die of starvation—then we've got to get the fuck out of here."

Ho returned a distracted nod. He obviously did not like the idea of giving the POWs any of their precious food. Recon teams preferred carrying extra ammo to rations. There was nothing worse than being caught short of ammo—it was better to go without food for a few days or live off the land like the NVA.

He complied, making his reluctance obvious to all. Damon wondered if his interpreter had a death wish. Ho looked at Damon one last time, as if he hoped his One-Zero would somehow change his mind, and then he cut them loose. He handed them a foil pouch containing freeze-dried lamb jerky with the enthusiasm of a man at gunpoint. They tore the pouch from Ho's grip and emptied its contents with their bare hands, finishing it off in less than a minute.

Ho looked away in disgust, but there was more to his expression, Damon saw. The interpreter was nervous, almost afraid. Afraid of the POWs? Damon couldn't tell, but he had a feeling that Ho's odd behavior had little or nothing to do with being admonished for insubordination.

Damon turned to Ho. "Are these guys ARVN?"

"Yes, ARVN." The way Ho said *ARVN* made it sound as if being a soldier for the good guys in the South was the lowest form of prostitution.

"Tell them to change into NVA uniforms. Then have them take all the AKs, ammo, and food supplies they can get their hands on around here, and once they're done have them follow us to the LZ. They're not to shoot unless we do, and they're not to speak unless spoken to."

Nghiem entered the room as Ho translated Damon's words. Nghiem didn't seem to find the situation at all unusual.

Damon motioned to his Zero-One. "This is Nghiem, the Vietnamese team leader. You listen to him."

Nghiem barked something in Vietnamese, and the three of them hustled out of the room. Then he exchanged what had to be hostile words with Ho.

The POWs finished changing into NVA uniforms just when Damon heard a sound in the distance. He cupped his ear, made a circle in the air with his index finger and his team slipped into the forest with the three emaciated POWs a few meters behind.

Damon held up his fist; the team stopped where they were. Everyone on the team strained to listen, but there was nothing to hear except for the occasional chattering of monkeys in the distance. He nodded at his One-One and Snakebite went to the back, behind the POWs, and started covering their tracks.

Damon knew he had heard something back at the POW camp. He had to assume the worst: Vietnamese anti-recon sappers. These were the elite soldiers of the North Vietnamese Army—Hanoi's answer to the SOG—trained specifically to take out American recon teams. They were every SOG's nightmare. As stealthy and lethal as they came. The scariest thing was their fanatical devotion to their cause; they would give their lives without blinking if it meant taking a few Americans along for the ride. Or it could also be an entire platoon of NVA. That wouldn't be a piece of cake either, especially if Damon had any hopes of bringing the POWs back alive. He would leave them to their own fate in a heartbeat if at any point they ended up posing a risk to his team. If they'd been American POWs, it would have been a different story.

You'd better bring us some live Americans.

Colonel Shackelford hadn't added an *or else*. He had left that to Damon's imagination. *My last fucking mission and it's going to end with me doing the goddamned rug dance for Commander Shackelfuck.*

Damon pushed the thought from his mind. He had to focus on getting his team back safely. If he could at least get everyone back in one piece, maybe the commander would cut him some slack. Yeah, right.

Whoever was pursuing them, RT New York would have to be extremely careful. Damon would treat this as an escape and evade, E&E. There would be no air cover for them here—the valley was sealed in by a solid layer of thick cloud. He would have to get his team all the way up the ridge to the summit where they had started off before he could hope to find a clearing in the skies.

His team crept eastward until Damon found a suitable area to settle for lunch. He pointed at his watch. It was noon—Pok time—the Vietnamese siesta, which the NVA honored religiously, and any human-generated noise would be precariously conspicuous. Snakebite laid out claymore mines for their two-hour break. Nghiem was not offering the POWs any of the food. They had found time to stuff their pockets with leftovers from the NVA's breakfast. Damon wondered how they managed to separate the food from the blood. They probably hadn't bothered.

Once Pok time was over, they pressed on. Snakebite collected every fallen grain of rice—anything that could signal their presence there. They hooked to the south while Snakebite seeded the ground across a trail with CS tear-gas powder. Once he was finished, they backtracked and headed north. If the NVA were using dogs, they would find the trail to the south and run into the pepper spray. That would mislead the NVA into thinking the team had continued farther south, using the pepper spray to put the dogs off the scent. By this point, Snakebite must have been really sore from constantly bending over to cover their tracks. Every three paces he lagged behind the team to listen for trackers.

It was a steep uphill climb and Damon ordered his men to set up the RON before the last of the sunlight was spent. They were expecting the enemy to come from below and so they planted the mines accordingly: claymores in a fifty-foot outer perimeter and M-14 toe poppers in a thirty-foot ring. The toe poppers were more to alert the team to intruders than to cause any mortal damage. Razor was up for the watch, while the rest fell into an immediate slumber.

Damon heard Razor wake up Snakebite to hand over the watch. Assured that everything was as it should be, Damon allowed himself to fall back to sleep.

His eyes opened suddenly. It was as dark as the inside of a vault; even starlight couldn't find a way through the dense forest canopy. Damon strained to hear what might have awakened him. He looked over and saw Snakebite propped up against a tree, his head limp against his chest. Damon went over to his One-One and tapped him gently on the shoulder. He had to make sure he didn't shock him awake because Snakebite could react with an involuntarily sound or worse. He looked confused for a moment, and then he mimed *I fucked up,* slapping his forehead without actually making contact.

Damon cupped his ear and pointed into the blackness.

They listened for fifteen minutes. They heard nothing. Damon looked at his watch. It was 0330 hours. He could wake the rest of the team, but he thought better of it. Instead he ordered Snakebite to get some shut-eye while he took over the watch. They had headed east for a full day without encountering a single NVA. One more day, and Damon would have RT New York back at the LZ, hopefully high enough to find a clearing in the sky and extract out of this nightmare. Sitting out there in the humid night, Damon knew full well the nightmare, for him, had just begun. Even if they made it back to CCC without a scratch, there would be hell to pay, and he would be the only one to blame.

Damon couldn't remember ever feeling so alone.

Half an hour before he planned to wake his team, thick droplets fell from the leaves above. All at once, water hammered down with such intensity the entire team was immediately awakened. They set off for the landing zone, a solid day's trek in the deepening mud. Sheltered from outside viewing from within his web gear, Damon turned on his flashlight and aimed it at his wrist. The red lens allowed him to retain his night vision for the few seconds it took to read the compass bearing. He wouldn't have to consult his compass for some time; he knew where the team was heading—up, over the ridge, north by northeast—and there was no further need for confirmation. Once they got there, the mission would come to its conclusion one way or the other.

By late afternoon, Damon could see they were close. Close enough to call Covey. Fortune had changed for Damon, because despite the unrelenting downpour, he could see several openings in the sky. If the weather remained precisely as it was at the moment, the breaks in the cloud cover should prove sufficient for an extraction. Damon knew his luck wouldn't last for much longer—if they didn't get out of Dodge soon, his team would be socked in, possibly for days.

Damon shaped his hand like a phone and placed it by his head, signing that he was going to make a radio call.

With his lips directly over the microphone, Damon said, "Covey. Covey, come in, Covey."

Nothing.

Damon tried again, growing uneasy: "Covey, Ghost. Come in, Covey."

"Go ahead, Ghost," a voice only Damon could hear answered.

"Requesting an extraction. We're nearing the LZ."

"Roger, Ghost. What is your team designation? Over."

"New York. Over."

"Roger that."

"We'll need air support, gunships, Sandies—we're being tracked," Damon said, although the suspicion that they were being followed was only a feeling. Experience had taught him it was better to go on instinct and err on the side of caution than ignore his gut sense and risk death.

They were just a few hundred meters from the landing zone clearing in the plateau. Damon had called in early to give Covey adequate time to locate them, given the meteorological conditions and, more important, the fact that Covey probably still believed the LZ was many miles east of where they were actually dropped.

They made slow progress in the cold rain; they were all completely drenched. Every few steps Damon looked up through the trees, as if the break in the clouds would vanish if he didn't keep watching. It was getting much darker; the thick charcoal clouds appeared to be sinking with their load. The sun would set in a few hours, and what little light was left would soon fade away. Damon stepped up the pace.

He had the feeling they were being watched again. This time it was much stronger, and before it had a chance to manifest itself as a coherent thought, a loud, androgynous voice crackled over a megaphone. It couldn't have been more than three hundred meters away. It was a message of some kind, repeated in Vietnamese.

Damon found Ho. The translator was moving toward the clearing when Damon blocked his way. Ho tried to sidestep. Damon grabbed his arm firmly enough to cause the little man to flail, but not hard enough to elicit a scream.

Ho would not speak. Damon dug his thumb into Ho's bicep.

Ho said, "They say *'Give us Yankees, you go free.'* They say we surrounded."

Razor appeared, looking very worried, and as he was about to speak, a loud burst of AK fire cut him off. "Jesus, that was fucking close!"

Damon didn't have time to wonder how the NVA had managed to sneak right up to their position.

There was an explosion in the distance, followed by screams. It must have been one of the claymores going off.

More machine-gun blasts cut into the tranquility of the forest and a split second later, Damon felt a stinging pain as bark from the tree next to him tore through the air and cut into his arm. There was muzzle fire coming from behind and from both flanks. The clearing was their only escape, and that's when Damon realized it had to be a trap.

By this time all sides of the jungle had lit up with AK fire.

One of the POWs walked over to Razor; he was saying something in Vietnamese and Ho wasn't there to translate. His helmet was missing, along with most of his left skull. Blood pumped out in even flushes, some of his brain was clearly visible, shining gray in the heavy rain.

Razor couldn't speak—shock had frozen him where he stood. Razor must have seen a lot of shit in his day, but probably nothing quite as horrific as this. All at once, the POW stopped speaking, his eyes rolled all the way up showing only solid white, and he collapsed into a heap on the ground.

Right then, a round tore through Razor's arm, ungluing his muscle and most of his armpit. The force knocked him sideways and made him squeeze the trigger of his CAR-15. Some of the rounds blasted off bark on a tree just twenty meters in front of him. As soon as he regained his footing, he adjusted his aim, hitting a charging NVA dead mass center. Blood and water puffed off his chest; three NVA in khakis jumped over their comrade's collapsing body, firing as they charged.

Damon had to make a decision immediately or his team would be wiped out in a matter of minutes. The clearing was out—it was more like suicide than a viable option. They were being charged from the north, and there was plenty of enemy fire from the west. Nobody was shooting at them from the south—the NVA were probably avoiding friendly crossfire. Despite the lack of observable enemy due south, Damon had to assume an NVA presence there as well; either that or it was another setup: mines, another platoon . . . God knew.

Damon signaled for an IA drill. It was time to put all their practice to the test.

He emptied his CAR-15 at the charging enemy. The recon team had their first magazine filled with tracer rounds to give the illusion that they had more firepower. The US Army standard-issue tracer round was red, while the NVA used green tracers. Recon teams were not bound by convention, however. The Vietnamese on the team were dressed as NVA and fired AKs, and every team member fired green tracers. They used any advantage they could to confuse the enemy.

Once his magazine was empty, Damon reloaded as he slipped behind his men, while Razor took his place, firing at what must have been at least twenty charging NVA. As he brushed by him, Damon noted that Razor's entire left side was soaked in blood. They would have to do something about that quickly or his One-Two would soon lose consciousness.

Snakebite took over for Razor, who was reloading with his good arm while he rushed back, joining Damon in the rear. As they raced north, NVA appeared from behind the cover of trees. One of them had his AK trained at Damon's head. He was only a few meters away, but Damon killed him before he could pull the trigger. Razor got to within two meters of his One-Zero when he was intercepted by an NVA who jumped out of nowhere, yelling and firing like a man in need of an exorcist. None of his bullets met their mark. Damon shot the teenager between the eyes. A young recruit. Obviously inexperienced, but Damon gave him an "A" for enthusiasm.

Razor's CAR appeared to be jammed, and he struggled with the weapon before finally dropping it.

Two more NVA came at Razor; Damon shot one, but the other was already on top of the One-Two. Damon couldn't fire because with the two of them stuck together, he'd end up killing them both. He rushed at the NVA to try to tear him away from his teammate, but then he saw there was no need. Blood emptied out of the NVA's mouth as he went limp against Razor like a drunk in a slow dance. The One-Two stepped back and the NVA fell on his face into a puddle. Razor wiped the blood off his Wakizashi and sheathed the weapon that had earned him his code name.

Incoming mortar shells blasted mud and crippled a few trees, but for the moment, the team was still a safe distance away.

Behind them, Bui and Phan were keeping the enemy at bay with M-79 40mm grenade launchers, and Nghiem, firing his AK, was the last one to retreat. Damon lobbed a phosphorus grenade. Five seconds later the explosion was answered with screams.

Mortar craters crept closer. The heavens rained down while the forest climbed up in violent jolts as mud, water, and vegetation were blasted skyward.

Damon grabbed the radio off Razor's shoulder, as Snakebite strapped the tourniquet belt from the first-aid kit tightly around the One-Two's arm to keep him from bleeding to death.

"Prairie Fire! Prairie Fire!" Damon yelled into the microphone.

"Prairie Fire" was the code for an emergency—without air assistance, RT New York would not be able to hold out—eventually they would all be slaughtered.

A voice came back, "Covey, Roger."

"I need an air strike fifty meters southwest of my smoke," Damon said.

"Roger," the voice said.

Damon threw his last phosphorous grenade. "Smoke's out." The explosion shot a thick white mushroom cloud vertically past the treetops.

There was a pause and a crackle over the radio. "Ghost? Standing by . . ."

Then Damon understood. Covey was still many kilometers east of their position—probably too far to see the smoke—with no way of knowing RT New York was this far west.

"Look west," Damon shouted into the microphone while he fired his CAR at three NVA behind the trees.

"Negative contact, Ghost: it's all cloud—weather's getting worse."

"Head due west from the LZ, we're *west* of the LZ; you'll see a small opening there. Just fly due west until you see it."

There was a pause, then: "Ghost, are you positive? We're heading west, but we don't see any breaks in the cloud cover."

Damon knew his position, but he couldn't give Covey the coordinates because he wasn't supposed to know where he was, or even that he was this far west of the LZ. On the other hand, his entire team would soon be wiped out if he didn't act immediately. Damon yelled louder, "Covey, head west as fast as you can. You *will* see an opening. When you get here—"

A muzzle flashed thirty meters from Damon's position, mud spat up in front of him, and before he could move out of the way, his radio was ripped from his shoulders, landing on the ground a broken mess. Damon cursed, too involved to care how close that had been to the conclusion of his life. He saw who had destroyed his radio the moment the NVA peeped out of the trees trying to see if he could hit the American with a second volley. Damon fired his CAR, and a necklace of holes marked the NVA from one shoulder to the other. A bullet had sheared the man's trachea, filling his lungs with blood. He dropped his AK as his hand instinctively went to cover his throat. Another group of bullets followed, nesting in his chest, one puncturing his pulmonary artery.

Five NVA were shooting from the other direction. Nghiem fired his AK, cutting down one of them while Bui and Phan joined in. The remaining NVA charged with a small platoon following closely behind. One of them triggered a claymore.

Someone's leg bounced off a tree trunk. Even after the blast, there were still two of them alive. One was on his knees, blood spurting out of his stomach; the other was missing an arm with just enough remaining life energy to empty his magazine. One of the bullets hit Vuong at an angle as the young Vietnamese scout was kneeling toward Damon trying to cover the assault from the other direction. The 7.65mm bullet entered the small of his back and shattered inside, ripping a wound the size of a tennis ball through his abdomen. He screamed in terror as his small intestine burst through his belly. He tried to push his slippery innards back. Without thinking, Damon leaped into the air, landing on his scout. AK slugs buzzed over their heads, slamming into the trees behind them. He covered Vuong like an octopus, shooting at six NVA that were running toward them from the south. He managed to stop three of them, while Snakebite got another two. One of them was rushing Razor, who was struggling to remain conscious. The rain pounded even harder against the leaves, almost drowning out the sounds of war.

Damon fired the last of his rounds, and two of the bullets caught the NVA in the chest but they couldn't have been well placed because he was still coming. Damon reloaded, Vuong motionless under him. The NVA fired a burst before his knees buckled, and although he was aiming at Damon, one of the bullets hit Razor, knocking him to the mud.

"Radio!" Damon yelled. Snakebite made a dash for Razor. The One-Two had the only radio left. Somebody was shooting at him, but Damon had loaded a fresh magazine and was now able to give his One-One cover. Firing at the NVA, he rolled over to offer Vuong a chance to breathe. Damon was covered

in mud, but his weapon fired without jamming. He killed seven men before Snakebite made it to Razor. The One-Two was hit in the chest, his right lung had collapsed, and blood was filling his mouth, choking him. Snakebite lifted him up, and Razor coughed blood and water. His chin and neck were bright red and in the rainy evening he looked like a vampire after a feeding.

Vuong was on the ground, facedown. When Damon rolled him over on his back, Vuong was clutching onto his mud-covered intestines. Vuong wasn't conscious, but Damon could see his chest was still moving.

No matter how many of them RT New York killed, the NVA kept coming in greater numbers. Snakebite fired frantically, trying to find a free second between volleys to turn up the transceiver volume.

"Ghost, come in? Ghost? Over," Covey was saying.

"Covey? Prairie Fire! Prairie Fire!" Snakebite yelled. He had to handle the communications now; there was no time for Damon to make it over to the radio.

Bullets buzzed just inches from Damon's head, but he hardly paid attention—he had to hold off the enemy until Covey could bring air support. That was all that mattered. It was up to Snakebite, and the One-One had no clue what their true position was. Would they fly far west enough to see the small opening in the sky? The smoke from the phosphorous grenade had dissipated already and Damon had no more left to throw.

Rat-tat-tat-tat-tat.

"Ghost, we see an opening, negative smoke."

"Roger, Covey," Snakebite shouted into the radio—there was no time to explain that he wasn't Ghost. "It's coming now. When you see it, give it all you have."

"Ghost, will that give you enough distance?"

"They're right on us, just inside the forest, southwest of the clearing. We'll get to the LZ, you just lay in fire on the mark."

"We'll hit you."

"If you don't do something right now, we're dead anyway," Snakebite said. "Smoke's out."

The smoke grenade was inferior to the phosphorous grenade. Smoke grenades didn't provide the same vertical blast and the smoke was susceptible to winds, often confusing the blast point and making it much harder for Covey to find the mark. Damon had pointed that out countless times, but Snakebite didn't have a phosphorous grenade, so he lobbed the grenade into the forest and grabbed hold of Razor, who was too weak to stand on his own.

When the red smoke billowed beyond the treetops, Covey came back with, "Got your red, Ghost."

Moments later, Damon could hear the sound of an approaching O-2. It was 17:32 hours.

That was a full thirty minutes after the first Prairie Fire call. Damon knew he could have avoided this delay if he'd been willing to give away knowledge of his position. If anyone died as a consequence, he would never forgive himself.

Damon pointed at Snakebite, then at the clearing. "Get Razor to the LZ! I'll cover you! Go!"

Snakebite lifted the One-Two and tried running, but Razor was too heavy, and all Snakebite could manage was a slow jog. As he entered the clearing, his leg was knocked out from under him. He bumped heads with Razor as they both fell to the ground.

His tibia stuck out of his pants. Raindrops were making indentations in his bone marrow. Snakebite tried to prop himself up, but he just managed to scoop up handfuls of wet soil. As he tried rolling over, Damon finally got to him and lifted him easily.

"Fuck!" Snakebite said.

"You're welcome." Damon hauled Snakebite through the elephant grass under one arm and Razor under the other.

"My fucking *leeeg!*" Snakebite yelled.

Damon figured he was probably dragging his One-One's leg, but that couldn't be helped. This was no time for lesser considerations. Snakebite's shattered leg must have hurt like hell, but on the other hand, if Razor didn't get immediate medical attention he would die.

Damon planted the men down in the middle of the clearing. He waved at an approaching Jolly Green, and the helicopter turned, clearly marking their position.

"You guys will be fine, they're coming for you," Damon said.

"Where're you going?" Snakebite called after his One-Zero, but Damon was already running back through the forest.

Nghiem and Ho ran to Damon.

"Get out there to the LZ," Damon ordered. "The forest is hot—gunships. Get out, I'll cover."

Close by, another mortar exploded. The blast showered Damon with mud, rock, and shrapnel. He fired at the figures behind the trees and then he relieved Vuong of his grenade launcher. There was no time to check for wounds; from what Damon could tell, all he had were a few scrapes and nicks, as if he'd been shaving with a bad case of the shakes, and that was the extent of it. Nghiem ran to Damon offering help.

The Vietnamese team leader had a piece of shrapnel sticking out of his cheek that hadn't been there a minute earlier, but Damon ignored this. "Go! Take Vuong! He needs help. Go! Now!"

Nghiem took a last look at Damon with admiration. He yelled something at Bui and Phan, and the two scouts started running for the field.

Vuong had regained consciousness, cradling his intestines and whimpering like a mother at the sight of her stillborn child. Nghiem scooped him up and ran after his two men.

Damon fired the grenade launcher at a group of NVA, finished off another magazine, and performed an emergency reload in record time. It seemed there were as many bullets in the air as there were raindrops. Damon wondered how he could still be alive. He should be dead. In point of fact, he should have been dead many missions ago. So much for statistics.

Damon was surviving on reaction born of experience and continuous training. There was no time to think.

He jumped to a better position just as somebody shot at him from behind. Damon snapped around and saw an NVA with an AK pointed at his head.

Damon fired first. The enemy's right shoulder exploded and in that same instant, Damon realized he just shot his interpreter.

Ho's AK dangled from a useless arm. The rain drained his blood pink, exposing raw bone and cartilage. Ho's screams were muffled by the approaching A-1, and seconds later, 20mm cannons strafed the forest from above. Branches, leaves, and NVA were cut down dead in just one pass. The enemy lobbed a grenade before directing all their firepower at the treetops in a desperate attempt to hit one of the gunships. The grenade was a partial dud. It blew up and sent a body flying. Had it functioned properly, it would have taken Ho and Damon as well.

Ho raised his AK with his left hand, taking aim at Damon for a second time. Damon did a forward roll using the momentum to ram his foot into the translator, splashing him down into the mud. Before Ho could draw a breath, Damon had him pinned with a knee burrowed in his sternum. Damon grabbed at the wet mass of bone and flesh that used to be Ho's shoulder. "Before I kill you, you're going to tell me why the fuck you were shooting at me."

Ho whimpered an unintelligible answer. Damon squeezed harder and Ho started yelling hysterically, three feet from Damon's face. Damon released more weight to his knee, crushing the air from Ho's lungs.

The strafing had silenced the NVA for the moment, but Damon knew he only had a few seconds left before they would crawl out of their defensive positions to attack again. Damon took out his knife and held it against Ho's neck.

The translator was apparently attempting to speak, so Damon shifted his weight just enough. Ho gasped for air.

"Please, Truong . . ." But Damon squeezed before Ho realized what he'd said. "Captain! Please," Ho yelled. "Don't kill me, Captain. Please! I have four children. Please!"

Damon leaned into Ho's face. "I'll ask once more. If you don't answer, I start cutting. One last time: Why did you shoot at me?"

"If I tell you, you don't kill me?"

The Jolly Green couldn't wait much longer. Time to get the hell out of here, Damon thought, and then he said, "That was a question, not an answer. Prepare to meet Buddha." He pressed the knife deeper into the skin of Ho's neck.

"An American paid me," Ho said.

"Bullshit," Damon said, but he was curious to see if there was more. The blade had cut into Ho's skin, but it was a superficial wound. For the moment.

The sound of twin engines grew louder as the A-1s approached.

"He tell me to kill you, make it look like NVA killed you—"

"Bullshit—"

"If you no bring back live American POW."

The knife almost dropped out of Damon's hand.

You'd better bring us some live Americans.

Damon holstered the knife and got off his translator. Ho didn't wait for permission: he shook off his AK and dropped his rucksack and then he ran as fast as he could toward the clearing and the awaiting helicopter. The gunships were coming in for a second pass while machine-gun fire tracked Ho. Damon fired his CAR-15, covering for his translator. It was a reaction, just as natural as a kick of the leg when the doctor tapped that magic place under the kneecap.

Just what the fuck am I doing giving a traitor cover?

The thought took but two seconds, but it was already too late for Damon. Twenty-five NVA—a small platoon—came out of their cover. They came from the south. Damon had been right about that. This was one of those times it didn't feel good being right.

Damon stole a quick glance at the Jolly Green. He couldn't see the helicopter, just a dangling ladder. Three men were climbing up—probably the last of his team to leave. He hoped Snakebite and Razor were on board getting treatment. They would be gone any moment now.

There was no running anymore—Damon could not make it to the helicopter in time, and even if he could, he'd be gunned down trying.

As he fought off the NVA, he noticed a cylinder drop from the sky. He knew immediately what that was, but he kept shooting anyway. Damon's CAR-15 was steaming; the raindrops evaporated on contact, like water on frying oil.

The NVA started shooting at the A-1 and the departing Jolly Green. The helicopter and Damon's entire team were in serious jeopardy.

Damon fired back while the enemy was focusing their fire skyward. Time came to a standstill—a sensation Damon was accustomed to when the odds were outrageous. He'd certainly lose this gunfight: Twenty-five to one and he only had two magazines left. No grenades.

"Come to Daddy—I'm your one-way ticket to Commie hell!" Damon yelled.

He knocked down five of them with his CAR-15, injuring a sixth. Damon would be dead soon. He treated himself to the thought of his team in the Jolly Green, flying away to safety. Who knew, maybe some would make it to the States someday . . .

Then he remembered the falling cylinder.

He dove behind a tree for cover, thinking it was probably too late anyway. The NVA continued firing, their AKs rattling as the rain beat against the thick forest leaves. There was a muffled explosion and the sharp smell of petrol. Damon covered his head, knowing full well it would do nothing against the napalm. This was followed by a blast of heat, and air was instantly sucked from his lungs. Damon didn't move.

A few seconds went by—seconds that lasted forever—and Damon could breathe again. All he could hear was the downpour against the forest leaves. No AK fire. No screams. No sounds. All gone. Something else was missing too . . . the Jolly Green.

They had made it, and Damon was breathing and unscathed. If his team had tried waiting for him, they would have all died.

Damon breathed through his mouth, but it did little to avoid the stink of burning flesh. The sight around him was eerily like his vision of hell. Flames everywhere—the napalm burned on trees, on the mud, on bodies, and the rain was powerless against it.

The A-1 made a final pass, strafing the forest. This time there was no return fire, and the gunship followed the Jolly Green through the closing gap in the clouds.

That pilot—a wizard as far as Damon was concerned—couldn't have dropped the napalm canister to a better position had he walked over and planted it there with his bare hands. Were it to have landed a few meters closer, Damon would have been a charbroiled mess like the rest of the bodies farther into the forest. But something *was* burning, and when he realized what it was, he ripped off his rucksack and threw it in the mud. It kept burning there.

Damon looked around once more and then he salvaged what he could from his rucksack before the napalm burned its way through. Damon continued his search; none of the bodies showed any signs of life. Mounds of mud-caked NVA littered the forest ground.

One was leaking brains and blood into a growing puddle. It wasn't an NVA, Damon saw. The rain poured into the open eyes, making it look like the corpse was crying. His cheeks were sucked in—a skin-coated skull Damon now recognized as having belonged to the ARVN POW who had been the first to speak to Ho back in the camp.

A strange weakness came over Damon, one he'd felt before in the distant past, but never out here. Never in the battlefield. The sickness was gone as quickly as it had come.

Damon examined another body. Most of the clothes had been blown off this dead NVA. Probably a result of a nearby grenade or 81 mortar. Something stuck out of the mud and Damon wiped it off. It was a disintegrating *Playboy* magazine. Back home an issue this old would almost be a collector's item, but in its current condition it wouldn't even serve as kindling. He threw it back to its dead owner.

Damon glanced left at a third corpse. This NVA looked clean. No guts or blood to be seen, probably because of all the mud, and the rain could have drained—

Suddenly the arm moved, pushing the body it was attached to out of the mud. Startled, Damon almost fired his weapon, but he managed to stop himself just in time. He wouldn't have recognized the mud-caked face but for its skeletal features, which told Damon this was one of his POWs. The ARVN had apparently played possum during the shootout. Clever. Not very admirable, but *definitely* clever; the guy was alive, and that was quite an accomplishment, Damon had to admit.

Damon put his finger to his lips, apparently an unnecessary gesture because the little fellow hardly seemed eager to speak.

Damon fanned the air with his palm down and the ARVN understood, and crawled back down in the mud to take cover by a tree. A flaming branch went limp and then broke off. The guy dodged it with less than a second to spare.

Damon pushed his open hand in the fellow's direction, and the ARVN nodded. *Wait.*

The POW went limp, reverting to his convincing imitation of a corpse. Good idea, Damon thought, there still could be NVA out there watching. The guy was Army, but Damon had to assume he was very poorly trained; as far as he was concerned, the entire South Vietnamese Army was a joke. Their biggest talent was getting themselves killed. Americans were dying for these dumb fools. Go figure.

Damon eyed him once more from a distance, noting his position. He hadn't moved an inch, and from where Damon was standing, he looked as dead as the rest of them.

Damon had one magazine left for his CAR-15. He collected two AK-47s and as much ammo as he could before he headed back toward the ARVN, stepping over heaps of bodies. On his way, he noticed another rucksack. This one was probably Razor's. It made sense: Snakebite had enough weight to carry with the One-Two over his shoulder, why carry his rucksack, too? Damon counted three foil packs of LRRP rations, two CAR-15 magazines. Extras—most SOG carried all their ammo in their web gear, but some kept additional supplies in their rucksacks. This was good news for Damon.

No radio, though.

Without a radio, Damon was stranded.

He couldn't stay near the LZ for long; the NVA would certainly return, especially if they knew that an American had been left behind. There would be another extraction attempt and the NVA would want to throw a reception party. Most of the enemy, who had seen Damon left behind, were burned or shot dead by the A-1. But it would only take one of them to get away and report an American alive and all hell would break loose again. Even if they thought all the Americans had gone, they would be back to collect their dead and look for any American weapons they might get their hands on.

Damon had to move.

There was one last piece of hope, his ELT. He felt for his emergency locator transmitter inside his web gear—it still seemed to be in one piece. He flipped the switch. Nothing. The light didn't come on. He tried again, but it was no use. It was supposedly waterproof and shockproof, and Damon had tested it just before leaving on this mission. Now the fucking thing wouldn't work. He remembered what Jabber had said:

Army equipment is not always that reliable, made by the lowest bidder and all, so should your radios have transmission troubles . . .

Now he was really screwed. What the hell could he do? They would send a Bright Light team after him—no doubt about that. *If they could.* The rain was coming down even harder, and the opening in the sky—that small jagged cut in the clouds—had healed and there was nothing but gray to be seen.

It was already getting dark; soon it would be nighttime. There would be no Bright Light team that night, and if the weather stayed like this, they wouldn't be able to make it through tomorrow either. It could be days before the weather cleared. Damon was alone, except for the skeletal ARVN, who probably didn't speak a word of English, and would only serve to consume the remaining rations that much faster.

Damon cursed softly and split up the supplies between the two rucksacks. He walked over to the ARVN, handed him an AK—the POW had apparently decided to lose his during the fight—and the lighter rucksack.

Ironically, despite the presence of water everywhere, Damon was completely parched. He took a long swig of purified water from his canteen. He offered it to the ARVN, who finished it off as if he'd been stranded in the desert for a week.

Again Damon put his finger to his lips and made a "follow-me" motion with his hand.

It was already too dark for the NVA to be able to track them; they would probably wait for the daytime and that meant that Damon had to distance himself as much as he could from the LZ while there still was time.

From their present position, Vietnam was much farther away than Thailand. Also, unless he could get back to CCC somehow, Vietnam was no safer than Laos and he would have to make his way across the Laotian mountains just to get there.

If there were to be no Bright Light rescue, Damon would have to move. He decided to head west, in the direction of Thailand, and as far from the NVA as he could get in one night. Not all of Laos was crawling with NVA, Damon knew, but he didn't have intel about areas this far west, so all he had to go on were his map and compass. Knowing he would be dropped west, Damon had a 1:50,000 map of midwestern Laos; without that, he wouldn't even have the sun to guide him.

Damon had no delusions; it would take a miracle to get him out of there alive; with no radio, no team, stuck in western Laos. A fucking miracle, nothing less.

Damon was walking quickly. There was mud everywhere and at first he tried to step on tree stumps to avoid leaving footprints, but they were too far apart and there was no time to waste—if it stopped raining, they would find his muddy trail immediately. The Bata boot soles would do little to confuse the trackers at this stage, since his team had already been spotted impersonating NVA. The rain was cold, and although it had been refreshing for the first half hour, Damon had no change of clothes and no opportunities to dry what he was wearing.

What a great last mission, Damon van Luden. Nice fucking job.

Damon cursed himself some more and then he stepped up the pace. The two of them walked the forest for two hours without even pausing. Surprisingly, the POW kept right behind him, showing no signs of protest or even discomfort, and unlike Damon's treacherous translator, he walked silently, like a seasoned recon soldier.

During the trek, Damon had time to think about what had happened with Ho. Was there even a remote possibility the translator just so happened to repeat what the colonel had said, almost word for word?

You'd better bring us some live Americans.

If it wasn't a coincidence, though, what was Damon to believe? That the colonel or Jabber, or possibly both of them, had plotted to kill him? Why the hell would they do that? Pay some Vietnamese translator to kill him? Not likely. Not a fucking chance. There's no way the Army would do that to him. Not after all the sacrifices and the years of service he had put in.

Damon finally stopped and took a swig from his canteen. Normally, it was a bad idea to leave your canteen half full; the water sloshing around would make too much noise, but right then it would have taken a hell of a lot for any sound to be heard against the unrelenting downpour. He motioned at his canteen, but the POW didn't seem to understand. Damon took a canteen from the POW's rucksack and handed it to him, making a drinking motion. "Drink," Damon said, "or you'll dehydrate."

"Comprends-pas," the guy answered.

Damon didn't pay attention at first, brushing it off as Vietnamese. The POW's speech was so accented, it *sounded* like Vietnamese, but then Damon wondered if he could have meant "Don't understand" in French.

"Tu parles français?" Damon said, doubting there would be a response.

The Vietnamese smiled and nodded. *"Moi, Hiep,"* the POW said.

"Je te comprends pas." I don't understand you, Damon said, now sure the POW had just nodded as they all did when they didn't comprehend what you were saying.

"Je m'appelle Hiep. Moi, Hiep."

Now, *that* Damon understood. The guy really did speak French. Damon nodded and offered his English code name in return.

Hiep made a few attempts at pronouncing it, but it ended up sounded more like *Gust.* Close enough for government work. *"T'as faim?"* Damon asked, wanting to know if Hiep was hungry.

"Oui."

Not surprising. Damon looked around and this seemed like as good a place as any for dinner.

"Bon, on va manger, mais il faut faire vite," Damon explained.

Hiep nodded, and it seemed to Damon that he really did understand how important it was that they keep on moving as soon as possible.

Damon got out the rations and they downed their food like a pair of street dogs. Damon just swallowed; he didn't want to think about it much. This particular food was not a good thing to put your attention on. It compared with vomit and mucus, and other things that would make it hard to keep down if he gave it any thought. Hiep apparently didn't mind the culinary selection at all. Starvation did that to a man.

Damon couldn't hope to bury the foil packs in the muddy soil, so he put them in his rucksack instead.

He started walking again, even faster, with Hiep quietly in tow. Damon couldn't rid himself of the image of Ho's AK muzzle pointed at his face. He should have killed the fucker. Jesus, why did he let him go?

That fucking traitor.

Thinking about it was generating a headache.

That little piece of fucking shit.

Damon had gotten a bad feeling about that guy from the beginning. He didn't even pick him, for God's sake.

Damon stopped, and the POW stopped behind him, not making a noise, probably thinking Damon had heard something. But it was a sudden realization that had frozen Damon in his tracks. Huong, his previous translator and friend, had all of a sudden become too sick for the mission. Damon hadn't given it a second thought before—lots of guys got sick, especially if they drank bad water without purifying it. But the Vietnamese were usually smarter than that. They lived in this country, after all, and knew better than to eat or drink anything that would get them sick. It happened just before the mission, and that, too, wasn't unheard-of. But to have a Vietnamese team member picked for you by the CCC commander himself? That *never* happened. Damon remembered how angry that pitiful excuse for a colonel had been when Damon had tried to question his decision.

Damon shook the thought from his mind. It was too much. The CCC commander was an asshole, no doubt about that, but even assholes didn't pay assassins to kill one of their own. No *way* would he do that. The guy was a prick to be sure: a brown-nosing political piece of shit with no field experience. Then there was the NSA agent. Jabber had seemed nice enough. Typical spook, though. Could he have been the American Ho was referring to?

Damon pressed on. He wasn't about to take the word of a traitor, not even given the evidence. It was coincidence. Fucking had to be.

Three hours later, Hiep tapped Damon on the shoulder. *"Gust, où allons-nous?"*

"We're going west," Damon answered in French. "Thailand."

Hiep asked how far. Damon got up against a tree and pointed on the soaked map, indicating their position. Then he pointed to the border. "Thailand."

"Trop loin," Hiep protested, saying it was too far.

Damon answered that they had no choice.

"Huey?"

Damon shook his head, pointed at the black clouds above, and explained their predicament. He left out the details about Ho and his faulty ELT, but he did mention he had no radio.

Hiep looked suddenly frightened.

Where did Hiep think he was going, Disneyland? How could he imagine anything could come save them in all this shit?

"Pas par là." Not that way. Hiep pointed at the map then he pointed in the direction they were walking. "VC, VC!"

Damon nodded his gratitude. Hiep apparently knew where the enemy might be, and they were heading straight for them. Hiep showed Damon a slight detour to the southwest in the direction of a village, right across the Mekong River. His finger pointed to a position on the map between Champasak and Pakxé.

"Ici, on peut nous aider," Hiep said, believing they could find help in that village. Damon nodded, for the first time realizing that Hiep was actually a great asset and, judging from his stamina, despite his weakened physical condition, a decent soldier to boot.

They made it to the river in just two days. The relentless rain had frozen them both to the bone, although Hiep was obviously suffering more, shivering uncontrollably all through the day and night. They took short naps, but it was impossible to get much sleep in the heavy rain. They had run out of C-rations the previous night, even with the extra supply Damon had gathered from the two rucksacks he'd managed to salvage. Hiep wouldn't make it far in these conditions—his bodily resistance was already pushed beyond its limits. That, combined with the cold rain and lack of sleep and food would eventually do him in.

Over the previous two days, Damon had learned much about Hiep. He had four brothers and two sisters, all of them living in Saigon. He had been with the Army of the Republic of Vietnam for some years before becoming a mercenary. He had been working with SOG, on a recon mission with RT Idaho, when he was captured in Laos. That happened in the spring. The NVA had killed most of the POWs there, but for reasons beyond his comprehension, they had spared him. He had been there the longest of them all. Two other prisoners had simply died of malnutrition and abuse.

Hiep was young when the NVA captured him. It had been only three weeks after his nineteenth birthday, and by that time he had worked with the SOG for a full year. Consequently, he had been stronger and better fed than most of his Vietnamese peers. He told Damon that toward the end, he had lost hope of being saved, and he wouldn't have survived more than a few weeks longer if RT New York hadn't come along. He said he owed Damon his life.

Damon found himself trusting the little fellow, and he told him part of what had really gone down. Damon mentioned the informant and the polygraph test, and that there were supposed to be Americans held at the POW camp. That, Damon said, was the real reason RT New York ended up saving Hiep and his friends.

Hiep was neither surprised nor offended that the team hadn't come all that way just to save him. He told Damon there could have been Americans there, he just never saw any. The valuable POWs—ranking officers and Americans—were usually transported to Hanoi, he said, so if there were any Americans at the POW camp, they wouldn't have stayed for long.

When they reached the Mekong riverbank, Damon could immediately see the vast body of water was far too wide for Hiep to swim across. Damon consulted his map. They were about ten kilometers north of Champasak. He pointed and told Hiep they would walk the riverbank northbound until it bottlenecked just due south of Pakxé. Hiep answered something sounding like "Whatever you say, boss," but at this point the heavily accented words were difficult to decipher coming through chattering teeth.

They could see the river narrow up ahead, and forty-five minutes later Damon figured it was just about as good as it would get. Still a healthy swim, even for an athlete, but Damon knew he could manage the crossing. He wasn't that sure about Hiep, however.

Damon didn't know the political orientation of the people they would meet on the other side. They were both still wearing NVA uniforms, and Damon decided at this point, it was best to appear like tourists. Damon would be Scandinavian, he didn't speak Swedish or Norwegian, but he doubted any villager they might encounter would either. He was tall and had blue eyes. That would have to suffice.

Time to bury the weapons; they wouldn't get the kind of cooperation they needed from villagers using force, so Damon started digging a wide hole in the mud. He made a notation on his map just in case they needed to come back and dig something up. There was no harm in being thorough, although if they really needed anything, they probably wouldn't have time to retrieve it anyway. Even with weapons two men couldn't maintain a defense for long without air support. Damon put his CAR-15 and Hiep's AK, along with the web gear, in the rucksacks and buried them. The innocuous necessities he kept: two flashlights, one compass, and his blood chit. The latter would save their lives—he kept more money and gold in his blood chit than any SOG he knew, just for good measure. At least he had done *something* right on this mission.

He asked Hiep if he thought he could manage the swim. Hiep's knees wobbled uncontrollably. The little man was hugging himself as if this act could somehow stop the shaking. Damon could see Hiep's ribs protruding through his wet T-shirt. Not a confidence-inspiring sight, Damon thought. Hiep tried to nod, but the gesture was hard to discern from the battle with his body and the earthquake from within.

At this point there wasn't much of a choice anyway.

They walked into the cold river and began to swim. Damon had only made it across a quarter of the river when he noticed Hiep was already far behind. On closer inspection, Hiep didn't seem to be swimming in any particular direction; he was expending all his energy just to remain afloat. Damon wondered if he could swim back to him before Hiep drowned. He gave it his best crawl. Hiep had stopped flailing against the water—at this point his exhausted body staged a mutiny, no longer taking orders from his brain. Damon focused on his swimming, pushing as hard as he could. He reached Hiep before he started swallowing water. Hiep immediately wrapped his arms around Damon's neck from behind. He was about as heavy as a nine-year-old, but in his panic he was cutting off Damon's air supply. Damon unlocked Hiep's hands and put them on his shoulders. *"Ici, comme ça,"* Damon said, *like this.* Hiep dug into Damon's shoulders painfully, but at least now Damon could swim.

And he wasn't going to turn back. Hiep wouldn't last if he didn't get to some food and warm shelter on the double.

Although Damon was extraordinarily fit—even for a SOG—having Hiep on his back was more than he could handle. When they reached the halfway point, Damon was suddenly unsure they'd make it. He focused on his breathing. The rain rammed into the river water, creating thousands of hypnotic micro-splashes on the river surface for as far as the eye could see. Damon tried not to drink the water as he inhaled, but it would make little difference. If it was contaminated, he'd get sick—there was just no way around that. A river would probably be a safer bet than a stream, but it didn't matter anyway, it wasn't like he had much choice. Every time he pushed back at the river doing his breaststroke, Hiep's fingers seemed to dig in even deeper into his shoulders. A witch's massage.

The current was carrying them back toward Champasak, where the river widened impossibly. Damon hadn't thought about that, but it wasn't a factor at this stage—he could see the riverbank clearly, and he would make it, even if the fucking current took him all the way back to the opening, he would make it. He hadn't survived twenty-one missions to end up drowning in a Laotian river.

Damon could hear Hiep's teeth rattling, even over the mesmerizing sound of the rain against the water. *"Je peux pas! Pas plus! Je peux pas!"*

"Hold on!" Damon yelled back at Hiep, forgetting himself and speaking in English. "Hold on! We're almost there." But Hiep let go and Damon bounced to the surface as Hiep slid off his back. Damon would not let him die—they were almost at the bank now. He had to submerge to retrieve Hiep, who had gone completely limp.

Damon surfaced, holding Hiep in a vise grip under one arm, the other arm desperately trying to keep two bodies afloat in a makeshift sidestroke.

Soon Damon felt the riverbed under his feet and he was just able to stand with his toes extended. He walked through the remaining river to the shore, and when he got there he lifted Hiep to the grassy bank.

They had finally made it, but Hiep was not breathing. Damon pushed the heel of his hand into Hiep's sternum while using his other hand for support. Hiep was so thin, it felt to Damon as if he would push through his chest and into the grass if he wasn't careful.

It wasn't helping.

Damon lifted Hiep's head from behind the neck, arching his chin to the sky, and he started breathing air into his lungs, following this with more quick pumps on Hiep's chest. "Come on, don't die on me now!"

As if in response, Hiep coughed up river water in Damon's face.

Damon laughed. "You see? You do understand English!"

Hiep choked and heaved for a while and then after a few minutes he started breathing normally again.

Hiep said something, but Damon could barely hear him. *"Merci, mon ami, c'est la deuxième fois."*

Damon was still laughing. "Okay, so you don't owe me one, you owe me two. I'm just glad you're still with me, little buddy."

Hiep managed a weak but genuine smile, not understanding the English, but getting the message anyway.

Damon lifted Hiep up effortlessly and started walking. Still speaking in English, for his own benefit, he said, "Time to find this village you were talking about."

Damon carried Hiep in his arms, cradling the man as if he were a child. Walking was a relief, but Damon's arms felt drained after the long swim. He carried Hiep half a kilometer along the river—the current had indeed carried them farther than Damon had originally thought—to the position

Hiep had pointed to on the map. From where they were, Damon could make out twenty or so straw houses. It had to be the village. Soon he saw women and children scurrying around everywhere. When they saw Damon with Hiep in his arms, they froze where they stood, as if they'd just seen Medusa.

Now the question in Damon's mind was what language should he choose to ask for help? In Laos, they spoke English, French and, of course, Lao. Damon didn't expect anybody in this tiny village would understand English, or French for that matter. Besides, they may not have the best memories of the French, so he decided French was out.

Hiep started talking.

Damon put the young Vietnamese soldier down. Hiep could barely stand on his own.

Damon had no clue what Hiep was saying, and in what language, but they seemed to listen to him.

Hiep tried to walk, and did a poor job of it. Two women came to his aid and he put one arm around each. They guided him into a hut, where he was immediately stripped naked. Damon stood outside, not knowing what he was expected to do next.

They wiped Hiep down vigorously and then they wrapped him in dry cloths. He kept repeating a phrase. Damon guessed it was probably something like "Thank you."

Damon was surrounded by giggling village children; four of them were pulling at his soaking pants. A woman came over and said something to the children and in response, they let her pass, laughing at the delightful scandal that had walked into their lives.

She motioned shyly for Damon to follow her. They did not attempt to strip him down; instead, they left him alone in the hut with cloths to dry himself and a change of clothing. Damon peeled off his clothes and left them in a dripping heap. He rubbed himself raw with the makeshift towels. His skin had become water-wrinkled, especially his hands and feet. He'd never realized it could feel so good to be dry. He tried to dress, but the pants came up to his knees, reminding him of a 1920s photo of his grandfather in a bathing suit. His arm got caught in a sleeve when it reached his biceps. He gave up trying to fit into the shirt and wrapped the sleeves around his neck instead, turning it into a shawl.

The clothes they had given him just weren't working. Damon needed something else. Cloth would do. Anything to cover up with. He poked his head outside the door—with any luck, one of the ladies who had escorted him to the hut would be around to offer assistance. There was nobody in sight and he stepped out, hoping to get someone's attention when suddenly it seemed like the entire village was there watching him. The children laughed hysterically, pointing at Damon. The women giggled and the men smiled. Damon started laughing too. It felt like he was blasting away six days of stress in one happy moment.

He was alive and his team was safe. Life wasn't all bad.

Incredibly, Hiep did not develop pneumonia, although it did take him three days before he was back to his usual self. The two were well fed on sticky rice, fish sauce, and chili and for the first time in what felt like months, Damon had hot food. He didn't care what the hell he was eating, as long as it was warm and it didn't taste like regurgitated freeze-dried meat.

On the second day, the weather finally moved east, and with the sun shining, Damon noticed how beautiful this country was—he never had the luxury of making such subjective observations while on recon.

During Hiep's recovery, Damon found time to ask his friend how it was he could communicate with the villagers. Hiep said he had a fiancée in Saigon whose mother was from Laos. He knew of this village because her mother was raised here. Hiep said he didn't speak much of their language, just what he picked up after three years of courting. They were to be married this summer, and he wondered if she was still waiting for him or if she thought he had abandoned her or died. Damon assured him that if she was worth marrying, she would be there waiting.

When Hiep was better, Damon told him they had to leave. The village would not be a safe haven forever, and Damon had to find a way to contact CCC as soon as possible, hopefully before Bright Light teams jeopardized their own lives searching for survivors.

He asked Hiep if there was any way they could get from the village to Thailand and from there to Bangkok. Hiep answered by rubbing his thumb against his forefinger. Damon told him he had gold and US dollars. Hiep nodded and without a word, he left Damon alone to wonder what solution his money would buy him. Hiep came back with two villagers, introducing the older man—the one in charge—as Lu Tán. They spoke without taking a breath and the exchange ended as abruptly as it had begun.

Hiep said they wanted fifty US dollars per person. Damon had a hell of a lot more than that in dollars alone, but he kept his poker face and shook his head. He offered thirty, lifting three fingers. If he'd simply accepted their offer, they would know he had more money, and getting to Thailand would suddenly cost a fortune. Bargaining was part of the culture here; to try and bypass the protocols would be to flaunt ignorance.

They pretended to be offended and shook their heads.

Hiep said, *"Ils pourraient nous emmener au terminal de bus a Pakxé, mais pour nous en faire passer par la douane, pour éviter le NVA qu' on peut rencontrer jusque là, et ensuite nous emmener à Bangkok, ils demandent cinquante dollars chacun."*

The villagers were offering to take them to Pakxé, but no farther, not past the NVA and the border to Thailand and then to Bangkok. For that, they would need fifty dollars each. A clever negotiation technique: instead of arguing the price, they accept the counteroffer, but with unacceptably inferior service.

Damon started walking away, and there were shouts. Hiep said, *"Quarante-cinq! Ils disent quarante-cinq!"* Damon ignored their counteroffer for forty-five.

"Quarante!" Hiep shouted after him.

Damon stopped walking and pretended to think. *"Trente-cinq, mais pas une centime plus!"*

Hiep translated. The two Laotians engaged in a brief heated exchange and then, finally, one of them nodded.

They set off the next day. The villagers either walked or used bicycles; there wasn't a single motorcycle there, not even a moped. Thirty-five bucks per person was damned steep for three bikes and a tour guide, but these people knew where the NVA were, what route to take to cross into Thailand, and how to avoid the border patrol. It was better than nothing, and nothing is precisely what Damon would have ended up with had it not been for Hiep.

A quick glance at the map showed that Highway 217 would have been the fastest route to Thailand—a short bike ride into Pakxé, and from there it was asphalt all the way across the border. Instead, the villager had chosen to take them into Thailand, leading them along a trail well south of the highway. Lu Tán agreed that a man of Damon's size could probably be identified as a foreigner from as far as the naked eye could see. Two guys and a giant riding bikes on unmarked trails would not go unnoticed, and that sort of attention was the last thing Damon needed at the moment.

The seat on Damon's bike was missing its left spring, but most of the leather was still there. The other two were not as lucky, but neither complained.

The trail was a tortuous ride, ramming the leathery stump into his backside with every bump. The guys at SOG would have a long laugh at this one. If he ever got back there to tell them. As they approached Thailand, Damon grew increasingly confident he might actually live through this mess, but beyond mere survival, his future was far from certain.

Hiep and Lu Tán rode ahead, chatting happily through most of the day. After five and a half hours of biking, Lu Tán dismounted and opened his arms in a welcoming gesture. Hiep translated. They had arrived in Thailand, just southeast of Chong Mek.

Damon looked around as if he expected to find some tell tale change in scenery that signaled their arrival in neutral Thailand. He asked if they were sure they were in Thailand—it seemed too easy.

Hiep translated that they were most definitely in Thailand now; few people, Lu Tán had asserted, knew of this trail. It was one of the special secrets the Laotian natives kept to themselves.

Damon figured this for an after-sale pitch—he doubted the borders were so heavily patrolled. They were in Thailand however, and they had managed to get there without running into NVA. For that Damon was genuinely grateful. He thanked Lu Tán for his invaluable help getting them there, by way of apology for suggesting it had been a simple task.

They biked a northwesterly arc around the Sirindhorn Reservoir, arriving at Chong Mek just before Damon decided that his derrière had taken all the abuse any human could handle, even a SOG. His ass would be purple in the morning.

They parked their bikes and he waited while Hiep and Lu Tán bought three tickets at the bus station. The next bus for Warin Chamrap didn't leave for another hour. Damon waited for half an hour at a safe distance from Chong Mek before returning to the station on his bike.

Damon found the last seat in the aft of the bus, and sat crunched low. It wasn't a very long ride, but it certainly felt like it.

As they approached Warin Chamrap, the streets began to swell with traffic. There were no hiding spots, so when Damon got out of the sardine can they called a bus, his only recourse was a stroll around the general area, hoping he could lose himself within the crowd. But no matter where he turned, people seemed to be watching. Damon gave them his best doofus smile without stepping up his lazy pace. It took him longer than anticipated, and when he had come full circle, Hiep was already outside the train station, waiting. Damon and Hiep said good-bye to Lu Tán, who was in a hurry to catch the next bus to Chong Mek.

Damon reached into his blood chit and pulled out a hundred-dollar bill. Lu Tán stared at it incredulously. Damon told Hiep to tell him the extra cash was for the two bikes Lu Tán would have to leave behind in Chong Mek, although anyone could tell you all three bikes together weren't worth more than ten dollars at the most, and Lu Tán would probably have hawked the bicycles in the village before leaving for Laos anyway. Damon didn't even feel the bill slip out of his hand.

Lu Tán departed a happy man.

Hiep handed Damon the ticket the station teller had assumed was for Lu Tán. Getting them to buy the tickets was probably an act bordering on paranoia, but excessive precaution—an oxymoron, any good soldier would tell you—had got him through two tours and twenty-one recon missions—twenty-two, counting this one. If anybody were to ask the teller, he would say he didn't remember selling any train tickets to an American and most certainly not a man fitting Damon's description.

He recalled the saying he'd heard as a West Point plebe: *Why did the paranoid man die? He wasn't paranoid enough.*

They shared a first-class cabin, with two bunk beds. Damon never left the compartment as the train carried them across Thailand through Si Sa Ket, Surin, Buri Ram, Nakhon Ratchasima, Saraburi, Ayutthaya, and to the last stop, Bangkok. Hiep brought him food, but Damon slept most of the trip away. The train was like a mile-long cradle, rumbling and rocking Damon in his soft mattress into a twenty-four-hour slumber.

Bangkok was Disneyland to the men-in-arms, and after two tours it had become Damon's home away from home. As usual, the city was bustling with activity. Mopeds and bicycles weaved through buses. Three- and four-wheeled taxis trailed clouds even Pig-Pen from *Peanuts* couldn't rival.

Their first stop was at a clothing store. Damon was looking for something simple and inconspicuous. Hiep located a pair of pants and a matching-color shirt almost immediately. However, nothing in the store would fit Damon, so they went elsewhere until, at the third establishment, Damon found a gray pair of pants with a shirt that felt more like pajamas than anything one should be seen wearing in the streets.

This sort of attire was appropriate for a native, but on Damon it was laughable. Less ridiculous, however, than the makeshift outfit they had sewn for him at the village—that would have worked for Halloween, if he were going as a cross between Casper the Friendly Ghost and the Incredible Hulk. It took another two hours to find him a pair of decent shoes; then they went to a tailor Damon knew worked fast and produced quality clothes for a bargain, even by Thai standards. It usually took three days to have a suit tailored. Damon fished into his blood chit and, seeing what the American was offering him, the tailor said it would be ready by the next morning.

Hiep got two rooms at the Royal Thai Hotel while Damon waited for him three buildings away. He came back fifteen minutes later and handed Damon his key. As instructed, he had told the registration attendant he needed two rooms, and if asked, he would have said the second room was for his brother. He prepaid for both rooms for one night—cash. No questions were asked.

They had dinner in Damon's room. He had ordered enough room service for five men.

They ate quietly for half an hour without exchanging a word.

Finally Hiep spoke, asking the question Damon had anticipated since they arrived at Chong Mek: there was no threat in Thailand, no NVA, no enemy, so why was Damon still hiding?

There had been plenty of time for Damon to come up with a creative answer, but he found himself hesitating. He sensed he wouldn't see Hiep in a very long time—in all likelihood, ever again—and he didn't want to leave his newfound friend with a lie, yet at the same time Damon didn't really have much to offer except questions of his own.

He could choose to say nothing or he could just say little, but before he arrived at a compromise, Hiep said, *"Les choses sont compliquées?"* Things were indeed complicated, and it was obviously a rhetorical question.

Damon realized Hiep knew far more than he was letting on, so he pretended not to fully understand the question, hoping it would prompt Hiep to say more, and it did just that.

Hiep had witnessed the brief conflict between Damon and Ho, just before an NVA grenade exploded, knocking Hiep to the ground, unconscious. Fortunately for Hiep, it was another defective weapon made in China. Had it functioned properly, he would have been killed. As it happened, he hadn't even sustained a concussion.

Damon decided to tell him everything, and he did, starting from the first rumors he had heard about someone in Saigon claiming he knew of a POW camp holding Americans, back when Fernandez was still the CCC commander. This time he didn't leave out any details.

Hiep nodded when Damon mentioned the Vietnamese informant in Saigon; he told Damon he had heard one of the other POWs, Trung Anh Dung, say his fellow ARVN would not abandon him and that they would get the word out to someone in Saigon who had connections with the US Army there. Trung had tried for months to convince them they would be rescued. Damon asked what had happened to Trung. Hiep said he was the one who had been shot in the head and had died before the team was extracted.

Damon's cake was suddenly tasteless. He asked if there were ever any Americans there or did the guy in Saigon just make that up to get a recon team to rescue Trung. Hiep said he didn't know, but it wasn't impossible.

Hiep then asked the next most obvious question: why had Damon been left behind?

Weather, Damon said immediately, that and the fact that the chopper was taking heavy fire. Hiep was not satisfied, but he didn't press the point. Instead, he helped himself to more rice. Damon had already finished his dessert.

Hiep looked at Damon, taking a short break on his third helping of rice. Damon knew what he was thinking, so he said it for him. It could have been weather, it could have been. It could have also been the fact that they were taking heavy fire. The SOG wouldn't just leave someone behind, though, no matter what the conditions, especially not their One-Zero. *Not unless he was dead.* So there had to be some other explanation—right now things just weren't adding up. It was because of this inexplicable abandonment coupled with Ho's words— words that so closely echoed those of the commander—that Damon had decided to be extra cautious. Until he could get some answers.

Hiep asked Damon what his next step was.

Good question, Damon thought. He needed to know what was going on. He needed to know where he stood. He had to report back as soon as possible; otherwise the Army would consider him AWOL. On the other hand, if this really was a setup, Damon would need some cover and a back door so he could slip away undetected.

The next morning, after a long shower and a careful shave, he put on his brand-new suit that Hiep had fetched for him just an hour before.

The plan was to meet Hiep back in the hotel when it was over. Damon had no identification, no dog tag, nothing whatsoever to show he was a United States citizen. He needed to get past the guards and into the embassy. The guards wouldn't believe he was with the Army. Every soldier has a dog tag, at the very minimum. And why hadn't he simply rejoined his company? What would he want with the embassy, where was his identification? Of course, there was no way Damon could tell those fools the truth. He couldn't mention the words "Observation and Surveillance Group." Any story would be more believable than the truth.

The embassy took up an entire block with a gate and guardhouse at three sides. It was set apart, semi-secluded in the big city, with one of the main roads leading to a dead end.

Damon had the taxi wait for him outside the embassy.

"Citizen?" the Thai guard asked.

"Yeah, I'm on leave and somebody stole my suitcase right out of the hotel room. I've lost my passport, my military ID, and my driver's license. I need to talk to someone in the embassy about it."

The guard waved him through, not paying attention to the explanation. Damon walked past the guardhouse to the embassy. There was nothing for the metal detector to detect; Damon didn't even have any coins on him—Hiep was handling all the transactions and was the only one of the two who had any local currency. He walked through a door flanked by two Marines in dress uniform who were as tall as he was, and into the embassy offices marked UNITED STATES CITIZEN AND PERMANENT RESIDENTS SERVICES.

A receptionist asked Damon what she could do for him today.

"I would like to see the consul, madam," he replied.

She looked him over, examining his suit and his incongruous crew cut. "And your name is?"

"Damon van Luden."

"Would you spell that for me?"

"Damon. Damon van Luden. *Van* like a minibus and *Luden*: Lima-Uniform-Delta-Echo-November."

"Van Luden?" she asked, looking at the large college-ruled appointment book.

Damon nodded impatiently. "Yes, *Damon van Luden.*"

"Well, I don't have you here. Do you have an appointment?"

"No, madam, I need to speak with the consul now, if you please."

Her expression changed with that, and at once Damon saw she took his tone as a direct challenge to her authority.

"I'm sure it's important, but there are plenty of other people with important business, and they *do* have appointments." She looked up, as if she expected him to recoil in apology.

"There's no time for an appointment; this is an emergency."

"What is the nature of this emergency?" she said, stretching out *emergency.* "Military," Damon said, "and that's all I'm authorized to tell you. If you please, madam, this really is an urgent matter. I'm not saying this to try and cut in line here, I need to talk to the consul."

"Well then, since you put it that way, have a seat along with the rest, and I'll call your name when the consul is ready to see you."

Damon turned away and took a seat among a group of Asians and Americans without offering a thank-you or even a conciliatory smile. It was forty-five minutes before he heard a female voice over the speakers calling for him.

The consul was a bony man in his early thirties with delicate fingers and a cultured manner. His hair was already thinning, but there was enough to manage a neat part. No traces of gray, yet.

"Have a seat, Mr. van Luden, and tell me what I can do for you today—what is this emergency?"

"I am a captain with the Fifth Special Forces Group at Command Control Central in Vietnam. I was detached from my unit and I need to contact Lieutenant Colonel Shackelford, the CCC commander, immediately."

The consul was taking notes. "In Vietnam, you say? Why come to the consul here?"

"I was detached from my unit," Damon said, not able to think of anything better.

The consul pondered this for a moment. "Okay, then, Captain van Luden, I will see what I can do for you."

He was gone for twenty minutes. When he returned, he didn't sit down; instead, he stayed right at the door, as if he needed the exit proximity for an easy escape. He was speaking slowly, trying to sound calm. "Mr. van Luden, there's a slight problem: there's no record of a Captain van Luden with the Fifth Special Forces group in Command Control Central. Uh . . . they can't seem to find your name in *any* Army records. Would you please wait here while I try and resolve this . . . uh . . . confusion?"

"Of course," Damon lied. There was no way they'd checked the entire Army records in just twenty minutes. It would have taken the consul that long just to get through to the right person at CCC. That much he had managed, Damon was convinced. For the first time he had no doubts: this mission had been a setup from the outset. Ho had told him the truth. They didn't want him around. He had failed his mission—a mission that should never have been started in the first place—and they needed the deniability.

That deniability was Damon.

He pushed away the thought, along with the welling emotion and unthinkable implications that came with it. Right now he had to get the fuck out of there, and on the double. He opened the door and the hallway was clear except for a secretary carrying a stack of papers. She looked at him with the corners of her mouth raised hopefully. Damon returned a platonic smile—if she thought he was coming on to her, he would stand out more clearly in her memory.

Damon no longer wanted to be remembered.

He was in the waiting area, walking briskly toward the exit. From the corner of his eye, he could see the receptionist almost leaning out of her cubbyhole.

Her head tracked his movements like the muzzle of a gun. By the time she managed to get her mouth to work again, Damon was already walking past the Marines, taking the final steps to the main floor two at a time, but quietly, the way he used to at home. These stairs were marble; it would have been difficult for Damon to even try making a noise. Damon could hear her shouting at the guards. They turned but couldn't make out what she was saying. She was out of her booth now, running in high heels.

Voices rose from within the building when he turned the corner, and now *he* was running. His taxi hadn't waited for him. Big fucking surprise. He ran another block and found a three-wheeler *tuk-tuk*. "Royal Thai Hotel. *Fast!*" He showed the driver a twenty-dollar bill and as if this sort of thing happened every day the driver popped the clutch and the small two-stroke engine managed an impressive streak mark as it sped away from the embassy and lost itself in heavy traffic only moments later. Somehow the traffic didn't seem to slow the driver much. He accelerated, came to a screeching stop, and blasted off again like he was trying out for stuntman in a James Bond flick. Fortunately for Damon, this kind of driving was hardly conspicuous in Bangkok.

Back at the hotel, Damon told Hiep what had happened. His Vietnamese friend was not surprised.

"Il t'a dit la vérité," Hiep said.

Damon knew he was talking about Ho. Yes, Ho must have been telling the truth. The Army no longer wanted Damon around. To them, he no longer existed.

Hiep said the police would be after him. Damon nodded, still not able to believe what was happening to him.

He looked at Hiep for a moment and then, to both men's amazement he pulled him into a crushing bear hug. It occurred to Damon that Hiep was the only real friend he'd ever had. They'd have to part ways now, as Hiep would not be safe at his side. Damon told him to go back to Saigon and marry his fiancée.

Hiep said he would never forget Damon and, with that, Damon left the hotel and found himself a taxi.

It was only a few blocks, but Damon didn't want to be seen walking the streets; he stood out too much. By about a foot in most cases.

Fred Stoke's Cellar Bar was a well-known SOG and Special Forces hangout, second only to the Center. The Center couldn't have been more appropriately named, although RTs California and Idaho started calling it Herpes Haven, and for good reason. There was no lack of business in Bangkok for bar owners, which was a good thing for Fred, because otherwise he would have lost most of his clientele to the Center a long time ago. You could actually walk from the Center to the Cellar Bar, but usually it worked the other way around.

Damon knew the owner well. Fred had been the region's CIA bureau chief for many years. If there was anybody in the business Damon could trust, it was Fred. Damon cursed himself for not going to him in the first place. The US embassy had not exactly been the best of ideas. *Everyone* would be after him, and he was out of time.

Fred was the owner, so Damon could expect to find him there at almost any hour on any given day. It was early evening; the sun hadn't retired just yet, and although the bar was open, with the exception of a GI and a local girl huddled at a corner table, the place was devoid of clientele.

Damon walked up to the bartender.

"What'll it be?"

"Nothing, I'm looking for Fred, is he in?"

"Mr. Stoke?" The bartender sounded suspicious.

"Yeah, is he in?"

"Let me see. Just wait a moment."

Damon knew Fred was in. Fred was *always* in. The bartender was merely going through the necessary motions, making sure Damon wasn't some undesirable.

Fred appeared three minutes later. He was in his fifties and looked thirty-five. The only giveaway was a full head of silver hair and a matching gray mustache. He was a runner. Five miles a day, sometimes more. It was unusual to see a bar owner without some testimony to his trade in the waist region.

"Ghost? Haven't seen much of you."

"Yeah, and I haven't heard *that* joke before."

"How the fuck are you, man?"

Damon smiled and clamped down on the hand he was offered. "I've been better, Fred."

Fred initially returned the smile but as he digested what Damon just said, his mouth tightened into a small dash.

"So, what's going on?"

Damon looked at the bartender and Fred took the hint, saying, "Why don't you come in back, I've got a few bottles of the good stuff I'd like to show you."

Damon followed him.

They walked down a flight of stairs and Fred flipped a switch, giving dimension to what, just a second before, had been solid darkness. There were several kegs of beer against the wall in front of them and two racks of wine on the wall to the left.

"I have a '64 Bordeaux. It's a Château Haut-Brion that must be worth a hundred bucks," Fred said, "but I don't suppose you came here to discuss my wine collection. Here, have a seat." Fred pointed at the chair by a small square wooden table.

Damon sat down. "I don't know how it happened, but somehow I've gone from having a promising career in the Army to being a fugitive."

Fred said nothing.

Damon started from the beginning, stopping only to make clarifications. Fred was a man of details. When Damon finished, Fred sat back, reflected for a while, then said, "I guess it was *you* they were talking about."

"Who?"

"Some of your boys out of CCC."

"No shit! Who? What did they say?"

"Lurch was here on R&R."

"Joe? Joe Adams?"

When people looked at Joe, they figured him for a basketball pro. His six feet and seven inches didn't add up to much on the court, however.

"Yep."

"What did he say?"

"That RT New York lost its One-Zero."

"That's it?"

"No. Their commander, Colonel Shackelforth?"

"Shackelford."

"Right, that's the guy, Shackelford. Anyways, he has this camp formation and he reads the promotion orders—oh, by the way, congratulations Damon, I guess you're now a major.

So anyways, he reads these promotion orders and tops it off with a citation for a Silver Star. Congrats on that too," Fred added, the irony very sharp in his voice now. "Then he says a few more words, you know, almost like a eulogy? All this bullshit about what a dedicated trooper you were. Not that you weren't, but—well—you know what I mean. Working the old nose up the ass of public opinion. Then he says he will never rest until you're found, dead or alive . . . from what you told me, I'm guessing dead."

Damon was shaking his head, hot blood rushing up his neck. "That cock-sucking bastard."

Fred didn't respond.

"How can they do this? *Can* they do this? I mean they can't just do this, right? They *can't.* I've fucking given my *life* to them: West Point, two tours in Berlin, two in Vietnam. I volunteered for suicide missions and this is how they repay me?"

"They had bad intel. They thought you'd come back with Americans. That's all I can think of. I doubt they expected you'd come back empty-handed."

"So now it's *my* fault?"

"No, of course not. Nobody's at fault, Damon, because there was no mission to fail in the first place. The only mission was the wiretap mission, and that failed because of a bad drop. Then you ordered a recon. Then you went MIA. That's it. That's the official story—that's what the guys are saying over here. That's how it went down."

"Yeah but why did they just leave me there? I wasn't MIA, I was right there. I was there, holding off the fucking NVA!"

"They figured you for dead. They were told you took some heavy AK fire and you were completely motionless. Ho must have been the one who told them you were shot."

Damon nodded, stunned by the brilliance of it. "Yeah, and Ho knew we don't go risking lives to bring back bodies."

"Did you see anyone following you?"

"Huh?"

"When you left the embassy, were you followed?"

"No."

"You sure?"

"Certain. It would have taken a chopper to follow that crazy taxi driver. I was looking back all the way. I wasn't in the hotel for more than ten minutes, then I came straight to you."

"Okay, look, this is what has to happen: you need to disappear before they give your code name literal meaning."

"You're suggesting they're going to hunt me down and kill me?"

"They obviously wanted to detain you at the embassy. I don't know what level security breach you would present at the moment. Washington turned down the mission and you went ahead and took out the POW camp in W7. That can't be good. I may be out of touch, but I'd say heads would roll over something like this, and I know the brass would rather it be your head than theirs. If you disappear? Don't make any waves? They'd probably let it go. Eventually."

"Define *eventually*," Damon said.

"Depends on how serious this is to them. Worst case would be until the Nixon administration comes to a conclusion: either in January '73 or, if he's reelected and makes it to a second term, then you won't be off the hook until January '77. But that's taking this to an extreme."

"And trying to have me assassinated is not?"

"Well, yes, you do have a point there." Fred offered a crooked smile. "Getting some merc to off you in the field is one thing, hunting you down is quite another. If your translator had taken you out with his AK, and nobody saw him do it? It would be a cinch to say you died in the line of fire while taking on NVA. Now that you've slipped out of hostile country, it's not going to be that easy for them."

"I can't just act as if nothing has happened."

Fred shook his head. "I'm not saying that. Not at *all*. In fact, you have to act. You have to disappear. The sooner the better."

"So you don't think I'm safe in Thailand?"

Fred shook his head. "They know you're here, and I don't recommend you push your luck. Not after what happened to you in Laos and the way you were handled at the embassy."

Damon followed Fred upstairs and out of the Cellar Bar. They went to the adjacent building, where they climbed three flights of stairs to a small room that barely fit a bed. "You'll stay here. I keep this place for the twenty-minute specials, but you can use this room until I get you a passport. Try to keep out of the Center; you could get recognized."

"Yes, I figured that out already."

"Good." Fred looked him over. "Yeah, you could pass for Norwegian."

"Or a Swede."

"Same thing as far as I'm concerned, only don't tell them that, they have this weird thing going, those two countries. Do you speak any Norwegian?"

"I can say *hey san*—that's *hello* in Swedish."

Fred waved at him dismissively. "Good enough. Where you're going, the immigrations inspector couldn't smell a rat if it crawled up his bony ass and out his nose."

"Okay. So where *am* I going? And for how long?"

"One of our guys got involved with a Norwegian gal over here—she really turned his head—the guy actually proposed! Can you believe that shit? Jesus, when will they learn? Anyway, it turns out she says she's not the marrying type—which is funny, because she *is* married—and he ends up brokenhearted, which is great for business, but I felt sorry for the guy. He won't let go, right? He starts following her around, and he finds her screwing this *other* guy. After he gives this guy a new face, he finds out he's her husband. So this guy goes ballistic and almost has this kid dragged off by the MPs. So I get involved, and with a little forgive-me money from the GI, I had the whole mess smoothed out in a jiffy. She's been visiting the East—temples, historical sights; you know, the kind of shit wealthy liberals like to blow their money on. But we all know what she's really after here in *Bang! Cock!*" Fred laughed.

"Anyway, she's learned her lesson. Now she tells guys at the bar she's married and it just makes the hunt more interesting for them while keeping the husband from turning into a punching bag again. Oh, and in case you care, he's no better; while she's out there satisfying her hunger on young fresh GI meat, he's getting the Thai sandwich massage at the Center. Item sixteen on the menu, if memory serves. Anyway, they have an arrangement, see? They call it a modern marriage. That kind of shit can never work if you ask me, but she's great for business, so what the fuck do I care, right?"

"Right," Damon said, becoming impatient, "but what does this have to do with me?"

"I was just getting to that. She and her husband are leaving for India in a few days. I don't think she'd object to having a replacement husband for the trip; she owes me big-time. Her name is Madeleine Knutson. If she's game, you could be Karl Knutson, her husband. It's safer to have you travel as a couple anyway. The day after you leave, her husband, the real Karl, calls his embassy and reports his passport is lost. He'll get a new passport and fly over to India, where he can join his wife and continue living in marital bliss. These two are a real number, and I'm pretty sure they'll do almost anything if the price is right."

Damon thought about it a while and said, "Okay, let's do this."

The very next day, Fred came back with a Brownie camera. He pinned a blue bed cover on the wall and took several headshots of Damon before disappearing again. He came over on a few more occasions to chat and keep Damon company, but most of the time he was at the Cellar watching over his business.

It took another day for Fred to have Damon's photo transplanted in place of Mr. Knutson's. The whole affair, including tickets, had set Damon back $1,400. It didn't help that Fred knew he was from one of the wealthiest families in America. Damon only had a hundred dollars left; Fred had taken all his gold as well. He didn't bother asking what Fred's cut was. He didn't want to put a friend in an awkward position, but he doubted Fred would do anything for less than thirty percent.

You could find anything in Bangkok if you knew where to look, and Fred admitted that the "documentation expert" who had made the necessary alterations had been quite reasonable. The first-class tickets were already paid for and the reservations were in the correct names: Mr. and Mrs. Knutson. What was left was the cost of the ticket for the real Mr. Knutson, and that ticket couldn't be purchased until he notified the embassy of his lost passport once Damon was safely gone. Mr. Knutson would receive that money in cash. According to Fred, the rest of it, and by far the highest percentage, had gone to help persuade Mr. and Mrs. Knutson to alter their vacation plans for a few days and accommodate an American in need of a little assistance. As a bonus, Fred gave Damon a fake New York driver's license. They were easy to do, he explained—much easier than passports—and it could prove useful should Damon have any plans of someday returning to the States through Canada.

Damon let the taxi driver put his duffel bag in the trunk and he quickly slipped in through the back door, feeling as exposed as a nudist on Park Avenue. Mrs. Knutson was sitting on the left, with her bare legs crossed. She was dressed to give the pope a hard-on. Her breasts were barely contained, her cleavage a long deep line. Too much lipstick, the miniskirt and the high heels made her look like a common whore. It bothered Damon that he would be traveling as her husband—she made heads turn. He'd really prefer someone bland. Mrs. Jane Average. Of course, beggars couldn't be choosers, and Mrs. Jane Average probably wouldn't agree to do any of this in the first place.

As the taxi sped off to the airport, Madeleine gave Damon a *Hi, loverboy* smile.

"We're supposed to be married," Damon said softly so the driver couldn't hear. "So it won't look right if you smile."

But she did. "On this trip, baby, we're going to be newlyweds."

PART VI

RISHIKESH REFUGEE

1970

The stewardess offered him a steaming towelette. "Would you like a cocktail before dinner?" Her smile insinuated mischief.

Damon turned down the offer.

"Have you had a chance to look at our menu?"

Madeleine asked for an Indian curry dish, but only after the stewardess had assured her it was one hundred percent vegetarian. Damon ordered a sirloin with wild rice.

According to Madeleine, cows were sacred in India. That meant Damon wouldn't have much hope of eating a decent steak for a very long time. He was going to enjoy his meal, whether she approved or not. Madeleine had given him what she'd claimed to be the best guidebook on India. What she hadn't given him was an opportunity to read the damned thing.

The stewardess addressed the couple. "We have soufflé au chocolat, apple pie with whipped cream, and ice cream of your choice. We also have a nice New York cheesecake. The purser will be over with the dessert trolley so you can make your selection."

It was the best meal Damon could remember eating since he left the States, and he still had room for more. He told Madeleine he thought the soufflé was tempting. She ignored him and said to the stewardess, "Thank you, maybe later. We have something else in mind for dessert."

There was barely room in that tiny lavatory for the two of them, but Madeleine maneuvered herself on top of Damon with ease and economy of movement.

That one time with Dorothy, on their wedding night, had been Damon's first, and for years thereafter, only experience with a woman. During the last year of his marriage, a stint with a young Fräulein had offered sporadic relief from the intolerable abstinence to which Dorothy had so cruelly subjugated him, but that had been his only transgression. And Dorothy had pushed him to it. Only a saint could pay no heed to his needs forever.

On his first tour, his men, both married and single, had thrown themselves into the arms of the local prostitutes without as much as a second thought. They'd explained it simply: "It's war, man."

Still, it had bothered Damon. Who would give himself to a *whore?*

Certainly not his father. If ever there was a man faithful to his wife, it was Nicholas van Luden.

But then Dorothy died that vulgar insult of a death that spat in the face of Damon as a man, as a husband, and as the eldest surviving van Luden. This, more than anything, had made his hunger unbearable.

Nim had been his personal favorite in Vietnam. He had to remind himself she was putting on an act. *Don't ever let it be more than about getting your rocks off.* Snakebite's words of wisdom.

But Damon found he couldn't go with anyone else. He'd visited Nim on ten occasions. Each time, he'd promised himself, would be the last. The moral issues that had plagued him when Dorothy was still living were no longer a concern. What had bothered him was the grinding knowledge that Nim gave herself to other men, *dozens* of them, some his friends. Snakebite had said she was the greatest lay he'd ever had. Damon had told him to shut up. But that had cured Damon of any desire to go back. Snakebite was no fool, and he was a loyal friend. He'd known exactly what had to be said.

Since then, matters of the flesh had been of little concern. Damon was in Vietnam as a soldier, and his missions had become the be-all and end-all.

In those passionate minutes in the tiny cubicle that had constituted a bathroom, Madeleine had entirely rekindled his fire. She had in her this feral ferocity that left Damon feeling simultaneously aroused and confused. The dormant emotion was revitalizing; it was something he could get used to.

That set off warning bells.

This was no vacation. Damon was on the mission of his life.

The flight west to Delhi was scheduled for four hours, but they'd arrive in three and a half. According to the captain, the summer headwinds were unusually light. First class made the journey seem even shorter.

This was going to be Damon's last taste of luxury for God only knew how long. Back in his leather seat, he said, "I'm not sure I get this. Meat is supposed to stunt your spiritual growth, but it's okay to fornicate like there's no tomorrow?"

"And why not?" Madeleine said. "Some people consider it a path to enlightenment."

"I see."

"It's called the *Kama Sutra*," Madeleine explained. "There's an entire book of fun positions—it is all part of a spiritual path."

"Wow, that's convenient." Damon laughed. "So is this why you're going to India, this Karma Sutra thing?"

Madeleine smiled. "*Kama* Sutra. Karma is another story. Actually, I'm going to Rishikesh to be with Maharishi."

"Rishikesh?" Damon said, reaching for his tour book. "Where's that?"

Madeleine looked at a large-scale map of the country and pointed to a small dot near the intersection of the Chandrabhaga Hadi and Ganga Rivers. "Here."

"North, eh? I take it the weather's cool there?"

"Comparatively. Why, would you like to join me?"

Damon considered this. "I'm not sure that would be safe for either of us."

"Why?" Madeleine said, resting her head on his muscular arm. "We're married, remember?"

"They're looking for me," Damon explained.

"Yeah," Madeleine said, "I know. So what did you do?"

"Nothing . . . look, it doesn't matter. What matters is that they're after me."

"Well you must have done *something*. I can imagine a man like you is capable of doing a *lot* of things."

Damon laughed. "Yes, but right now what I have to do is disappear."

"Okay, but since you are traveling as Mr. Knutson, and I am Mrs. Knutson, and they're looking for a single man, not two newlyweds, wouldn't it make sense if we went to Rishikesh together? As a tourist couple?"

Damon admitted that did indeed make sense but added, "I don't want to put you in any danger."

Madeleine kissed him. "That's sweet of you loverboy, but I have handled men in uniform before."

"Not *these* men. And I doubt very much they'll be in uniform."

"Oh," she said pinching him, "I do even better when they're not in uniform."

Damon smiled. "So I've seen. What's your idea? We go to Rishikesh, then what?"

Madeleine shrugged. "We find Maharishi."

"Right, so who is this guy?"

"You haven't heard of him?"

"Should I have?"

"Well, have you heard of Lennon?"

"The *Russian* Lenin or the singer?"

"The Beatle, of course. Maharishi is his guru."

"Oh," Damon said, "and that's supposed to mean something to me?"

"He's his guru, his *teacher*, his spiritual guide along the path? The *Beatles* go there, *Lennon* goes there. Maharishi is famous."

"Well, in that case, I'm definitely *not* going there. If he's as famous as you say he is, then going to Rishikesh to see this Maharishi fellow would be the equivalent of advertising my whereabouts. That's the *last* place I'd want to be."

Madeleine shook her head. "No, think about it: you didn't even know who Maharishi was, so the people who are after you won't either."

"Information is their game; it wouldn't be healthy to assume there's something they don't know."

"Okay, so say they *do* know. The last place they'd think a soldier like you would go would be a spiritual retreat. It's for the very open-minded; the spiritual . . . the liberal."

"Okay, I get it. . . ."

"No, no—it's not political—I didn't mean to say that, but—"

"But it *is* a hangout for flower children," Damon cut in. He'd heard about the antiwar movement in the States. Back home college kids were calling the soldiers in Vietnam baby killers. Almost all of America's youth had gone down the shithole, infected by extreme-left ideals that had no value but to undermine everything America stood for. From what Snakebite had told him, and from the little Damon had seen during his time in the States on Special Forces training, this was more than a passing fad, it was the beginnings of a revolution, of anarchy.

The government kept playing the middle road on foreign policy to fight the Communists, pussyfooting to please the voters. Snakebite had been right: that's why America was losing the war in Vietnam. Guided by the one-sided media and Ho Chi Minh psychological warfare, the hippies were bringing their government to its knees and to the brink of Communism.

"So this Rishikesh place is going to be full of hippies holding hands and chanting 'Make love, not war'?" Damon asked.

"It isn't political. Maharishi doesn't stoop to the level of politics. It is a sanctuary for spiritual growth."

"Well, I'm not sure what it's a sanctuary for, but you're right about one thing: they'd never expect to find *me* there."

"So you'll come with me?" Madeleine asked.

"This Maharishi guy, are there others like him there? Gurus? Not as well known?"

"Yes, Rishikesh is the home of gurus."

"So you think I could find a place to stay there that people haven't heard about?"

"Oh, yes, there are many such places."

"Then I'll go with you to Rishikesh and we'll part ways there. Once we get to the airport, we need to change into something less conspicuous. We'll travel as two average middle-class tourists."

Madeleine offered her hand and Damon shook it. "Okay, it's a deal," she said. "But you have to promise you'll let me teach you some Kama Sutra positions."

"And you'd be a great teacher, I'm sure, but isn't your husband supposed to meet you somewhere?"

"Yes, in Rishikesh, but not for a few more days, and besides, he's a bore in the sack."

The fan on the bus from the airplane to the main terminal was broken. There was no air-conditioning in the terminal either, but they made it through immigration and customs with no trouble at all. Fred had been right about that as well.

In the men's room, Damon changed into cheap khaki shorts, a plain white T-shirt, and sandals. He had considered throwing his dress pants, shoes, shirt, and tie in the garbage, but someone would most likely pick it up, and that could arouse unwanted attention. He might one day need the clothing anyway.

Had he and Madeleine remained in first-class attire, they'd have stuck out like a steaming pile of elephant shit on the hood of a Rolls-Royce.

Madeleine got them their Ambassador from a nondescript rental place. The car was a small blue four-seater that looked like a '55 Morris Oxford, with the steering wheel on the right, but the tanklike feel of a Citroën Deux Chevaux.

It took a long while just to get out of Delhi. Cows walked the busy streets, redefining traffic flow with their every lazy step. Countless people and antiquated vehicles moved in all directions. A monkey used a dog as a springboard to jump onto a moving cart.

The road to Rishikesh was mercifully empty. They passed several slow cars and had to stop for a herd of sheep, but otherwise the only thing holding them back were the endless potholes. Damon wondered if the car would survive the journey. Madeleine pulled over twice to demonstrate some of those special positions she'd been talking about.

Rishikesh was beautiful beyond any of Damon's expectations. The lush green reminded him of Vietnam, but it was very different, very tranquil. He took in the view of the three large hills and, of course, the river he'd read about in the guidebook.

A bald man in an orange robe walked by the car and as he did so he put his palms together against his chest as if in prayer and he smiled and bowed. Madeleine bowed back, copying the man's gesture.

Friendly little buggers. Gullible, borderline naïve. Until they pull out a knife and try to slice off your head.

No. This wasn't Nam. These people weren't at war with anyone. They were just a bunch of peace-loving, cow-worshiping vegetarians. Still, they were not to be underestimated. Underestimate *anyone* and you were setting yourself up for trouble.

Madeleine parked the car and they set out to find lodging on foot. There they were, under the guise of being two lost foreigners, which wasn't much of a stretch, despite Madeleine's assertions to the contrary.

They walked along the Ganges, where people everywhere were brightly clothed in native garb. Many had dots on their foreheads. It was either a religious thing or some sort of decorative custom. Damon suspected the former. From what Madeleine had told him, these were extremely religious people, and Rishikesh was monk central.

More men in bright-orange robes crossed their paths, and Madeleine bowed, pressing her hands together.

Damon imitated the gesture and asked, "Excuse me, do any of you speak English?"

The men returned the greeting in tandem, smiling easily. One of them pointed. Damon followed his finger. In the distance, he could vaguely make out what looked like a group of people. The other man nodded energetically and said, "English." He looked at Madeleine, who in turn looked at Damon.

Damon nodded and thanked them. The two monks waited for the young couple to head in the right direction before they continued on their way.

The "English" group was far larger than Damon had initially estimated, and as he approached, he could tell from the way they dressed all of them were unquestionably foreigners but not the least bit English. These folks were tourists—some Japanese, the rest, for the most part, American.

It made sense to try to blend in with this group. A bunch of loud senior citizens had dressed themselves in sneakers and shorts as if they were going to some luau; some of them were actually wearing sandals and socks, as well as bright shirts in outrageous yellows, greens, and blues. It all said, Look at us, we're from Florida.

There were others in the group, some in their thirties and forties, and a few younger couples, probably Europeans, but nobody whom Damon thought could be of any help.

If this was a tour group, and it certainly looked like one—what else could it be?—that meant there had to be a guide. Damon searched for the leader, but missed him at first because the Indian stood no more than five-four and was at the far end of the group, leading the way.

"Is everyone finished taking pictures? Yes? Yes? Good, please follow me, we have much more to see before sun-fall." The guide spoke with an accent that suggested an expensive English education.

Damon waited for the right opportunity, took Madeleine by the hand, and together they slipped into the group unnoticed.

"What are we doing?" Madeleine whispered.

"Being tourists," Damon whispered back.

"The Ganga has been a source of purification for millennia. The Ganges, in India, is considered holy. The name Rishikesh is loosely applied to an association of five distinct sections encompassing not only the town, but also hamlets and settlements on both sides of the river. These include Rishikesh itself, the commercial and communication hub; the sprawling, suburban Muni Ki Reti, or the 'Sands of the Sages.' Rishikesh is the birthplace of yoga. Through the practice of yoga—the physical practice of hatha yoga combined with meditation—is, for many, a path to enlightenment."

The guide stopped for a moment and pointed. "North of here is Shivananda Nagar. Still farther north and you will see the temple section of Lakshman Jhula. There are temples and shrines all along the holy Ganga, and you will find ashrams there as well. This is where people follow a guru on a path to enlightenment."

Damon had weaved his way nearer to the guide. He was surprisingly young up close.

"Are all the followers natives?" It was one of the Japanese tourists.

"No, we have many foreigners who come to Rishikesh during all seasons of the year to study with a famous guru."

"How do they know the guru will accept them?" the lady holding the Japanese fellow's hand asked.

"Ah." The guide smiled. "They do not know. They may travel for thousands of miles only to be turned down. Not just anybody can be admitted to an ashram."

"What are the requirements?" the same Japanese tourist asked.

"It depends, really, on the guru. There are so many here in Rishikesh." The guide started to walk again. "Okay, we must continue; follow me, please! This time of year the sun is abundant and persists to the late hours, but we must continue because there is much to see. Speaking of the sun, in Rishikesh, the winters last from November to March, when temperatures fall below zero centigrade. The monsoons are generally experienced in the months of July and August."

Damon and Madeleine kept with the group, listening to the guide's untiring stream of facts while Madeleine waited for the opportunity to ask one of the English-speaking tourists about a hotel.

A minute later, she poked Damon in the ribs. She was nodding to her left, indicating a small hotel in a cluster of two-story buildings. Damon and Madeleine gradually slowed their pace, letting the people overtake them until they were in the back of the group. They lagged behind and, assured that nobody was looking at them, darted to the hotel.

Their room was hot, there was no air-conditioning, and despite the fact that they registered as a married couple, all they got was a tiny cot. Madeleine didn't seem to mind. They spent most of the night on the Kama Sutras. She was remarkably fit, and had a stamina that could and actually *did* put a Green Beret to the test. Damon pitied the other hotel guests; the springs moaned loudly at his every movement, and so did Madeleine.

While it was still dark, Damon retrieved the car and upon his return they slept most of the day away. They resumed their Kama Sutra studies after Madeleine brought in a late lunch she'd picked up from the town. Damon told her this would have to be their last night together. She asked him where he planned on going and he replied that he had no idea, and even if he did know, it was best she didn't. "It wouldn't be wise for you to stay here once I'm gone," Damon said. "You should check out in the morning." He told her to carry on as if her husband had been there all along. Damon warned her never to seek him out, for to do so would be to point the enemy in his direction.

She kissed him softly and said she would never do anything to harm him. "I never asked, and don't feel you have to answer, but is there someone in your life?"

Damon shook his head. "Not anymore."

She sensed the heaviness in his words and pressed the subject no further. Instead, she said she'd had a wonderful time and had rejoiced in her body, and now it was time for the soul. She'd meet up with her husband after her spiritual retreat with His Divinity, Maharishi. Madeleine said Karl should be there the next day or the day after.

"And you'll be okay with this Maharishi fellow?"

"Oh, yes. I'm going to be purified."

You're going to have to be with him for a long time. No sooner had the thought entered Damon's mind than she went at him like this was going to be her last chance at her favorite pastime.

Although he only slept for three hours, Damon got up to the bright morning, about an hour after sunrise.

Madeleine was still sleeping. He covered her with the sheet.

What a woman.

Thankfully the tiny bathroom down the hall was not occupied—it wouldn't serve him well arriving at an ashram smelling of lovemaking. The tools of ablution consisted of a hardened slab of soap, what amounted to a modified hose that spewed cold water, and a partially clogged drain in a warped cement floor. Still, better than the accommodations in Vietnam. Damon bathed quickly.

Breakfast consisted of a buffet in an open room at the far end of the lobby. The sun was already dousing the room with dusty bright rays. A man in his late fifties sat at one of the small tables. He had several helpings of a bread loaf, a half-finished bar of butter, and two jars of marmalade that he was working on greedily when Damon came to join him. "May I?" Damon said.

The man looked surprised but not annoyed. There were several more tables there and they were all empty.

"But of course," the man said, pointing at a linoleum chair.

Like the Indian tour guide, this man was obviously educated. He was also obviously not Indian. Blue eyes nested like two marbles in a doughy face. He carried at least forty excess pounds in the gut.

"Are you here on business?" Damon asked.

"Research."

"Scientific research?"

"I'm with the Department of Philosophy at Yale."

"You chose not to teach in England, say . . . Oxford?"

The professor smiled. "Yale offered first. Cambridge has the Dharam Hinduja Institute of Indic Research, and that was, of course, intriguing, but still, I found myself gravitating to the Philosophy Department at Yale." The professor washed down the bread with some tea. "Dreadful stuff, this," he said, pointing to the teapot, "but a man must make do with the resources available to him."

"What kind of research?" Damon asked.

"Nothing funded by Yale, I'm afraid. I'm working on a book, and I'm taking advantage of the summer break to finish it off."

"Interesting," Damon said. "A book on Indian philosophy?"

"East Asian religion, actually. Philosophy and religion are inseparable in these parts." The professor scooted his chair back to make way for his belly and he trotted over to the buffet to help himself to some more bread.

Damon joined him. He got a slice of bread, some marmalade, and an apple. He wasn't particularly hungry, but he had to stuff himself until he was too full to eat any more. There was no telling where his next meal would be coming from, or more important, when it would be.

When they sat back down at the table, the professor said, "And what, if I may be so bold as to ask, is your quest here?"

Interesting choice of words. An insightfully formulated question. The man actually resembled Hercule Poirot. They both wore outdated white suits, and they both had hats. Everything was there, with the exception of the color of his eyes and hair, and the fact that the professor had no mustache.

Damon chose his words carefully. It was no fun demeaning himself by pretending to be a flower child from the land of the bleeding-heart liberals. He'd have to get used to swallowing his pride for a while.

"My wife and I are here to find a guru."

"Really?" the professor said, half frowning. "You hardly seem the sort."

"Oh, and what sort is that?"

"No offense, I hope. One has an idea of the stereotypical Caucasian who comes here hoping for salvation and sanctuary."

"And you don't believe in either of those two things?"

"Well, I didn't quite say that—that's a subject in itself." The professor's face became solemn, almost sorrowful. Damon noticed that he had suddenly stopped eating. "I presume you've thought about this?"

Damon nodded.

"Whom are you seeking?"

"I don't know; perhaps you could be of assistance," Damon said, using a gentle, respectful voice.

"Well, you've happened upon the right person, if ever there was one," the professor said. "This place is a treasure house of sages, sadhus, yogis, and ashrams. Rishikesh is the perfect location to find a guru—a teacher—of yoga."

"Please, go on," Damon said, trying to extract as much information as possible while in turn giving none.

"You would have to do some very careful research on all of them," the professor said.

"Who's the best?" Damon said, going for gullible and impulsive.

"I don't know, really, that is hard to say. There's Sri Sri Srimat Swami Tirthaji Prajnanpad, Swami Niranjanananda Saraswati, Sri La Sri Swami Balasai Saraswati, Swami Anirudhha Akhandanand Dev or simply Guru Dev, Bhagawan Sri Radhamadhavananda Baba, and, of course the well-known Maharishi Mahesh Yogi and his Shankaracharya Nagar ashram. That's just for starters, I could name a host more."

"I do not recognize any of these names, except for Maharishi. Everyone knows the Beatles have come to him for spiritual guidance. How would one determine who is the best guru?" Damon said.

"That's highly subjective, I'm afraid. As an *advaitas*—a devoted one—it would be quite difficult to hazard a guess as to the state of exaltation or enlightenment of the guru in question. And even if one could determine the guru's spiritual status, it wouldn't necessarily mean he was a great teacher. A yogi once said of Krisnamurti—a famous Indian philosopher—that he was enlightened from birth, and being the spiritual prodigy he was, he found it impossible to relate to the ignorant masses who could not understand his words. To them, this was a man pushing them off the cliff, commanding, 'Fly!' when they had no wings. He was once called the guru's guru."

"Really," Damon said, intrigued. "And is this guru here in Rishikesh?"

"No, no," the professor said with a laugh. "He's not the man for you. This man thinks along similar lines with Friedrich Nietzsche, although Krisnamurti has openly denied any ties with nihilism and any other -ism, philosophy, or religion, for that matter. This is a man who rejects all teachers, himself notwithstanding. He would hardly be teaching yoga in Rishikesh.

"I've had several 'discussions' with Krisnamurti in the past. He was meeting with groups. I doubt he would ever frequent such a place." The professor said, surprising Damon with the disdain in his voice when he said "such a place."

The professor pasted a wad of marmalade over the melting butter. "Don't get me wrong, I have nothing against any guru here in Rishikesh. It's that I find it sad to think of fine young men and women such as yourself blindly committing themselves to the whim and words of some self-proclaimed teacher. Instead of simply accepting answers like chicks taking worms straight from their mothers' mouths, why not learn to ask *questions*?"

"From what you've said, I gather you hold Krisnamurti in the highest regard."

The professor looked up from his mouthful of breakfast. "You are indeed an astute young man." The professor took some tea. "Mr.—I didn't catch your name, forgive me—"

"Karl. Karl Knutson," Damon said, offering his hand. The conversation had gone on long enough for Damon to hope the professor might forget to ask his name. No such luck.

"Pleasure to make your acquaintance, sir. Professor Andrew Hardings at your service."

"What of Guru Dev?" Damon said.

The professor looked up as if the falling plaster would offer an answer. "He is famous here but few people know of him abroad. He followed a saint until the saint in question died, and then Guru Dev became a recluse in the mountains."

"You say he's not well known in the States?" Damon asked.

"No. Few people know of him there. A few academics, some serious seekers, that's about it. In India, however, his name is synonymous with yoga, especially amongst serious students."

"Then why didn't the Beatles go to him?"

The professor smiled. "I strongly doubt they knew of him. Besides, their fame and money would mean nothing to Guru Dev."

"But it did with Maharishi?" Made sense, wealthy people like the Knutsons following in the Beatles' footsteps.

"No," Hardings said. "Maharishi does not discriminate in any way; he even accepts women. His initiation process involves a simple ceremony, if I'm not mistaken. I believe he's trying to marry Western science with Eastern philosophy. It will be interesting to see how his movement develops. Maharishi believes his Transcendental Meditation technique is a path to the various stages of enlightenment as he's defined them. Whereas Maharishi is an openhearted man who would gladly take on students, only a select few make it into Guru Dev's ashram. Only the purest of heart and purpose would ever be considered. Guru Dev's initiation process is for the most committed of devotees."

The professor looked at his tea. With a hint of melancholy, he said, "Anyone who has been his student is considered blessed."

And well sheltered. Damon pretended to ponder the professor's words. He asked questions about another three of the gurus the professor had mentioned. He probed deeply while maintaining a window shopper's distance.

In the same casual tone, he brought up the topic of ashrams, asking about all of them. That way, the professor would have no way of knowing which, if any, Damon had chosen. Still, it felt like he was divulging too much. It was a tricky business trying to get information without giving any away.

By the time their conversation had died down to a trickle of pleasantries between bites, Damon had finished off three helpings. The good professor had outdone him by two, and that was since Damon had joined him.

Damon thanked the man for his company and valuable advice and was about to leave the hotel when a thought occurred to him. Damon ran up the stairs to find Madeleine still asleep. He considered leaving a note, but he didn't want to leave anything in writing.

The sheet snaked around her naked body. To Damon's surprise, despite the very active evening and a huge breakfast, he experienced a fresh jolt of lust.

Madeleine sensed him and stirred. She squinted as her eyes adjusted to the sun-filled room. A smile grew on her face. "I thought you would be gone."

"I had breakfast with Hercule Poirot—the English version. He thinks I'm your husband and we're here guru shopping. I wanted to give you a heads-up just in case you bumped into him."

Madeleine smiled. "I don't think I'll run into your English friend because I wasn't planning on having breakfast"—she tapped the cot—"but I *do* have a strong appetite for something else."

Damon didn't need more coaxing. They were together for another two hours before Damon took his second shower and left, this time for good.

Guru Dev, like many other gurus, had his ashram by the Ganges River. It was a five-kilometer walk from the hotel. Still morning and already humid, but not like Vietnam. Not by a long cry.

It would be recon day minus the proper preparation and equipment. A camera was to a tourist what a gun was to a soldier. Damon didn't have either. It would be nice to cover all the territory, research the ashrams one at a time, and see just why the professor believed Guru Dev's was so special, but the more Damon roamed around alone, the more likely someone would remember him.

The first ashram Damon came to was the Shankaracharya ashram. He gave it a wide berth and arrived at a long footbridge, which to the untrained eye would have appeared flimsy, but Damon knew better, they had many like it in Vietnam.

Most of the other ashrams were located on the other side of the Ganges. Maharishi's ashram had no gates. It consisted of a multitude of small, domelike structures, packed together on hilly terrain. Madeleine and Karl would soon be in one of those buildings.

It still didn't seem right, Madeleine holding on to a marriage with a little-minded fool like Karl Knutson.

It was a long walk from there to Guru Dev's ashram. It was set apart, isolated from the rest. It *did* have gates, and a wall around the entire compound. The ashram had been constructed on a huge plot of land, starting at the Ganges and chewing its way up an incline. Men in orange worked on the fields. Manual labor for room and board. Damon laughed.

This was certainly the right place. Just as Damon had hoped it would be: exclusive and reclusive. The last place anyone would expect to find a white man, especially a soldier.

There was nobody at the gate.

Damon looked in. More men in orange working the fields. Eventually, one of them looked in his direction and Damon waved. The man turned to another guy in orange and pointed. The man walked in the other direction, probably to summon his superior.

A few minutes later, a bald Indian with a dot painted on his forehead came to the gate. He was also dressed in an orange robe. If it was a sort of uniform, then this guy was no higher up the food chain than the man who had called for him. Damon offered the bald man the greeting he had learned just the day before.

The bald fellow responded with, *"Jai Guru Dev."* To Damon this sounded like a question: *Are you looking for Guru Dev?*

Damon nodded. His assumption seemed to be correct, because the bald man let Damon through the gate.

Damon had passed his first test.

Monks in yellow-orange garb everywhere. Not a woman around. They were probably in a compound sewing and weaving. The men seemed quite content raking and plowing, as if the act fueled their smiles.

Somewhere, a group of men were chanting, *"Agnim ile puruhitam, ya stana Veda kurushati . . . OOOOmmmmmmmm."* It came out as one deep voice. He was being guided in the direction of the chanting; the smell of incense was getting stronger.

They walked into the one-floor structure and through several rooms. A man was facing a rug that hung from ceiling to floor depicting blue-faced Indians wearing gold and beaming down at the mortals below with devious grins.

The man sat cross-legged, unmoving and perfectly straight. Damon only had a view of the man's back, his long hair.

This could only be one man.

Damon and the guide in orange waited for what must have been a full hour before the master spoke. He did not turn or move his body in the slightest, but somehow the disciple knew he was needed and ran over, kneeling beside Guru Dev. The master spoke too softly for Damon to hear. He could have been ordering pizza take-out, for all Damon could tell. Not that Damon could speak a solitary word of Hindi, of course, but tone mattered in any language. The bald disciple got up and motioned at Damon for him to leave.

This came as no surprise. This was clearly part of the initiation process. Both Madeleine and the professor had mentioned something about being initiated. Damon would play their game and he would play it well.

Damon bowed, his hands together against his chest, and followed the man in orange all the way back to the gate.

There, Damon tried to communicate his determination solely by means of facial expression. It was of no use. It wouldn't matter if Damon suddenly broke out into poetic verses in Hindi. The man was obeying orders from his master.

The monk waited, perhaps to make sure Damon was on his way. Instead of leaving, Damon planted himself by the left pillar, in the exact posture he saw the master use for more than an hour. Damon closed his eyes. The pillar was shading him for the time being.

For a few seconds, there was no sound. Hopefully the monk was watching him. All he had to do was see that Damon had sat down. The monk would tell his master. They'd get the picture. The gate closed with a loud clang.

The Army had put him through test after test. Damon had been through initiations aplenty: from the Beast Barracks when he was still just eighteen, to the Airborne and Ranger schools. Then there was advanced training and Special Forces training. He'd made it through sleepless nights, endless treks, and physical challenges so great most guys simply gave up, even the most athletic. Because the Army tested a lot more than physical endurance and ability. They tested a man's *will*. Not everybody had what it takes. Plain and simple.

And after all that training, he'd been assigned to a SOG team as a One-Two. With no political pull like some dipshits who thought being with the SOG would be a fucking joyride. Most lasted for a mission or two. Three tops. They either got themselves killed or they dropped out on their own. SOG was for the best soldiers on this planet. Special Forces men, Navy SEALs. All volunteers.

These Indian monks had no clue what they were up against, but it wouldn't be wise to underestimate them either.

Evening came and not a single person had entered or left the ashram.

Damon had his duffel bag with him. Time to set up camp.

He was hungry, but it was bearable. The triple servings of breakfast had been a damned good idea. He slid into his sleeping bag. It had cooled down enough to where this was bearable. He covered his head to keep away bugs and flesh-eating rats, like he used to in Vietnam. They probably had their own special variety of nightmare creatures in Rishikesh.

Damon woke up early the next morning to the sound of slapping sandals. He reached for his weapon, but by this point he was used to not finding one.

Damon was wide-awake and out of his sleeping bag in five seconds. Too slow. Probably residual fatigue from the trip. By the time the footfalls approached the gate, Damon had already packed in the duffel bag and was seated, eyes closed, in the exact same position the disciple had left him in the previous evening.

The sandals slapped away and the gate closed. They'd come to see if he was still there, just as he had hoped they would. Damon waited for fifteen minutes before he let his eyelids crack open enough to see what the disciple had left for him.

It was just as he had hoped: a full bowl of rice and a bowl of water.

Without water, a man dies very quickly, and so Damon drank every drop they'd left for him. The rice he left to the ants.

There was no offering of lunch.

After two hours Damon carefully got up and stretched his legs. He did some rudimentary exercises to keep the blood flowing, but he had to be careful not to overtax his body. He needed to conserve his energy for the hardship to come. It could last days, maybe even weeks. He wondered how long it would be before he would be with a woman again.

He took out the book on India that Madeleine had given him and started reading while keeping his attention on the perimeter. He could see anyone approaching the ashram from the outside for a good klick ahead of him, half a klick to his right, at least, and on the left was the Ganges.

That *slap-slap* sound their sandals made would give him plenty of warning. Assuming they all walked like that one monk, of course. It would be foolish to make any assumptions. The next monk could be barefoot, for all Damon knew.

They could very well try catching him off guard. Just to see if he was really meditating or if he was doing something else when he thought they weren't watching.

Of course, there had to be a careful balance. Damon was in hiding until he could assume his next cover as a student at the ashram. But if he avoided contact, he'd never become a student.

The threat was from the outside. If Damon were to observe anyone approaching in the distance, he'd have to clean up camp, take his stuff with him to the tree that stood sentry in the direction of the Ganges—the tree he would use to hide behind when it was time to answer nature's call—and wait until the threat was completely gone.

Once the coast was clear, he'd have to run back to the gate pillar, set up camp again, and wait for another approach.

Now, if the approach was from within, that was a totally different story. It would be an opportunity, not a threat. Damon would have to assume the seated meditation position, and hopefully they'd think he'd never moved, except, of course, to drink the water. There was nothing Damon could do about that, and they knew he had to hydrate himself.

The day grew longer and the Seiko watch they'd given him for capturing an NVA seemed to have slowed to a complete stop. The sun, overhead, was a serious concern. Damon couldn't abandon his position every time he lost the shade.

The sleeping bag was the first thing he thought of. He could use it to make a tent, but while it would protect him from the sun's rays, the sleeping bag was a dark blue, and dark colors absorbed heat. There had to be something else.

His T-shirts. He found a white one and wrapped it around his head. He was wearing the other.

Evening would not come. He imagined the cool water against his skin. *God, it would be nice to dive into the Ganges.*

Damon read the guidebook for the fourth time.

When finally the sun started to settle into the horizon, Damon removed his makeshift head covering and took off his shirt. They were both soaked with sweat.

Slap-slap.

Damon put the book back in his duffel bag, made sure there weren't any telltale stories of his restless day to be found marked on the dry soil, and, satisfied, he looked for the marked spot, angled himself to face the sunrise, just as he had been the last two times, and he sat still, eyes closed.

The footfalls were almost upon him. The gate opened, and the soft padding on the ground stopped for a while. Damon figured it was the same person. He had the same sort of walk and he paused for the same amount of time. One hollow wooden sound followed by another. The gate was again shut. Damon listened as the sounds diminished, waiting a full half hour before opening his eyes.

Damon drank the water in seconds, it seemed. This time, leaving the rice to the ants was not as easy.

He was famished.

No matter. It was all part of the test. He noted the position of the bowl, ventured ten meters away and left it there. He could get to the bowl and return it to its exact position in plenty of time. He had to move it, there was no way he could sleep with that food within smelling range. Sure, he could drown the steaming rice in soil, but that would show the enemy he was weak, and that he couldn't resist the temptation.

The *enemy?*

No. These guys weren't the enemy. They were the means to an end. The means by which he could accomplish his mission. They were his *allies*. And he'd have to see it that way from then on—he'd have to believe this to the core, because if he didn't, they would eventually sense the hypocrisy, and the entire mission would be jeopardized.

They were the allies.

The image of steaming rice found its way back into his mind.

They were the allies.

Hunger was the enemy. That and the fucking sun.

This whole thing would have been a lot easier in the winter. Tough. It wasn't like Damon had a choice. *Hey, Colonel, next time you hang me out to dry and hunt me down, could you please do it in the winter?*

It was way too early for sleep, but still cool enough for Damon to slide into his sleeping bag. He closed his eyes.

He woke up six times before daybreak, and only once to urinate. That wasn't good. He wasn't hydrating enough. Two bowls of water was not going to cut it. He would have to find a solution quickly or he would be in serious trouble very soon. Dead, he was of no use to anyone.

He kept his eyes closed and his breathing shallow. This technique worked the first four times. It took half an hour to fall back asleep the fifth time and Damon had no clue how long it had taken him the last time, but the sky had already started showing signs of life.

Damon was up a full hour before the approaching foot-falls. In his meditative posture, he listened as the gate opened. *SLAP-slap.* Something had changed. The now-ceremonial pause before the gate shut was the same. Well, *similar.*

It was easier to sit comfortably. The sun had just begun its long climb and it was still relatively cool. He sat for forty-five minutes.

No point rushing it. They could be watching. He couldn't hear anything, he couldn't even sense anything, but they could be watching. From a distance.

No way. He was positioned behind the gate pillar; they'd have to come right up to the gate and pop their heads through the bars to see him. Unless they had spies outside the com-pound—*ashram*—and communicated via radio or telephone. Not likely. These people weren't characters from a James Bond movie—they wouldn't exactly have spies. It was a silly notion, but Damon had learned that it was never silly to overestimate the enemy.

They're not the enemy.

It was hard to keep focused—his knees were killing him.

What a stupid way to sit.

After what felt like forty-five minutes, Damon slowly lifted his eyelids. The rice was there, just as he knew it would be. The smell had been driving him crazy since that weirdo left. *Not a weirdo. Not the enemy.* What, then? Friend?

Better than weirdo or enemy. These guys would pick up on the negativity and as he became weaker—and this was bound to happen, of that he had no delusions—his ability to fabricate a lie would diminish exponentially. He would have to embrace the lie until he believed it completely. It was the only way to withstand questioning, to withstand this torture. This is what this was. Torture. Self-imposed, of course, but torture nevertheless. He was trained for this. He'd pull through. He would never have put himself in this position if failure were even a remote possibility.

Lying next to the clay jug was the usual bowl of rice. He opened his eyes further and then checked the perimeter. All clear. He double-checked and then ran the rice bowl over to its waiting spot. His stomach tightened as he gripped the bowl. He held his breath, but the angelic scent somehow found its way into his nostrils. He held the bowl as far away as he could, but with every step he advanced onto the rising steam. This was easily the hardest part of the day.

Back at his location by the pillar. Now what?

Boredom was dangerous. He knew that from his training. He could find himself losing, running to the rice bowl, finishing off every last grain, and before he realized what he'd done, it would be mission over. He'd read the guide so many times he could recite the damned thing word for stupid, boring word.

The sun reached its apex and Damon had already wrapped himself up like a mummy when he was surprised by something that just appeared at the peak of the hill, half a kilometer away. Damon looked around. He'd finished half the jug, but the bowl was still out of place. He looked around. No one else was approaching so he gathered his things into his rucksack and made a dash for the tree. From that distance, they wouldn't be able to identify him unless they had binoculars. From behind the tree, Damon watched as three men approached the gate. One had a round tubular black hat with no rim; the other two wore orange robes, just like his enemy-friend. They were all Indian, and they certainly weren't wearing any uniforms.

He could barely hear them speaking quickly in their funny-sounding tongue. The chattering continued until, finally, the gate was opened. He heard a few words in rapid-fire staccato, and the gate closed behind them.

They weren't police, and they didn't seem like undercover investigators—if they even had such a thing out there—so what were they? More Guru Dev disciples? Visitors? Did they allow visitors at this ashram? That would be a serious concern. If the professor had been right, then this place should be pretty much prospective disciple and visitor–free. Whoever the hell those guys were, it confirmed that threats could come from the outside as well as from within the ashram. No, that was wrong. Approaches from within the ashram were *friendly*, not threats. It was outsiders Damon had to worry about. He had to be on his toes all the time, especially during the day. He doubted there would be anyone to worry about in the night.

They wouldn't come for him here in Rishikesh, and certainly not to this ashram.

Nighttime in Vietnam was a totally different story. When the sun went down, the beasts hunted. It was time for death, and death crept up on you in the dark and tried to seize you before you had a chance to react.

Let them try. Bring it on. He'd wake up, he was programmed to. No doubt about it. Gun in hand in three seconds. Yeah, but he had no gun. Didn't need one. This wasn't Nam.

Jesus, man, get back in the game.

Damon scanned the area for as far as he could see. They seemed to be the last of the visitors for the moment. He ran back to the gate and quickly set up camp, placing everything back exactly where it had been, not forgetting the untouched bowl of rice.

Damon assumed his seated stone-stiff position, but instead of meditating, he listened for sounds. An hour later, he carefully opened his eyes and when he was certain it was safe, he finished off the remaining water in the jug—all of it. He thought it wiser to store the water in his belly rather than risk something happening to it before he had the chance to finish it off. There could be more visitors, his enemy-friend could come, anything could happen, and the water and the opportunity to drink it unnoticed were far too precious to risk to chance.

He thought about the man who had dutifully provided him with food and drink for several days now, probably on his master's orders.

Not friend, not enemy, a bit of both.

Frenemy.

Damon spent another hour unmoving. He stretched afterward. Slowly, carefully. If he pulled a muscle, that would mess everything up.

He heard footsteps from behind the gates. It wasn't time for dinner.

What was going on? Was this some special day at the ashram? He stopped stretching and forced himself back to his sitting position. The gate opened, and a group of people, three or four of them, stopped next to him. They could have been the same people who came in, except there seemed to be more this time. There was no telling, since he had his eyes firmly shut. They were silent for a while and suddenly they broke out in rapid Hindi, followed by another pause, and then one of them approached Damon.

Something climbed on Damon's leg; it paused and then darted up his thigh and toward his groin. Damon had seen cockroaches longer than a stick of gum and nasty-looking spiders the size of a teacup saucer. From the weight, he guessed it was a roach, but it could also have been a small spider. No way of telling without opening his eyes. He figured the Indians watching him would brush off a deadly spider from a man deep in meditation. Unless they wanted him dead, and Damon had already established that was unlikely.

The Indian stopped, perhaps just a meter away, and he said a few words. It sounded like he was attempting to communicate with Damon, but Damon managed to maintain a frozen body and an expressionless face. The creature on his thigh did an about-face and crawled off in a hurry. Maybe the Indian had scared it off.

Damon shallowed his breathing to where his chest was barely moving. The man took a step forward but someone else said something; the voice came from behind the opened gate and he halted abruptly. He said something back, there was a brief exchange, and the man walked away from Damon.

They could watch, but if they got close enough to touch him, Damon would be forced to react. There was no telling what they could do, and Damon did not relish the prospect of being physically probed while he played statue. He suspected that touching him was precisely what the approaching man had in mind, and he was greatly relieved when the voice called the Indian away.

He did not know who they were and what they wanted, and he didn't want to risk opening his eyes, even slightly, to find out. By this point, he was certain they weren't after him. They were Indians, *all* of them. The group didn't move; they were engaged in some discussion, although it seemed like a rather calm exchange at this point. No doubt they were talking about him—probably trying to figure out what to do with him—or whether to report this back to their master.

They talked just outside the gate for about ten minutes and then they left, and the gate shut with an unfriendly rattle.

Damon found it quite hard to wait, but he forced himself to suffer through another fifteen minutes of motionlessness before he opened his eyes. His jug was there, and so was the bowl of rice. He knew they hadn't refilled the jug, for he'd heard no telltale sounds of water.

On the one hand, Damon needed the students within, especially Frenemy, to see him fasting and always meditating. On the other, Damon couldn't risk bringing himself to the attention of people *outside* the ashram. It was a delicate juggling act, and Damon wondered how long he'd have to remain in this precarious situation.

Damon resumed his stretching. He took his time focusing primarily on his legs and back.

He could trim off a small layer of rice. Nobody would notice. Right?

Damon cursed.

There was no fighting these thoughts; they were par for the course. It would be too easy if he didn't have to fight himself every minute of the day. That was the whole point: to prove resolve.

Damon no longer thought of Madeleine and her Kama Sutra lessons. The body had its priorities. Drink, sleep, food, in that order. Sex was not a priority when the body was in trouble. Made sense.

An ultrathin layer? The Indians weren't that observant. Two thin layers of rice a day along with a full jug of water and he could endure for weeks.

Damon forced to mind the image of Colonel Shackelford's fat, sweaty face with a wet stinking cigar dangling from those loose lips.

He would find that motherfucker.

The colonel had wanted the glory of being in command when Damon's recon team brought back the senator's son. And just in case it all went to shit—and God knows it did—he had a patsy ready. Damon.

The thought of slowly crushing Colonel Shackelford's throat would not stave off the image of steaming rice plaguing Damon's mind.

The hunger came in waves. There were short periods where he felt he could go on like this forever, and then, suddenly, just when he was convinced he could make it another hour, the squeezing, suffocating hunger would come alive, bringing with it the desperate plea for relief.

It's just a few grains of rice. Just to taste. Nobody will ever know.

Withstanding torture was all about mind control. Sleep deprivation was worse, and Damon had managed to survive through that test too. The force of his determination was far greater than his body's cry for sustenance. Soon his body would accept the reality that it was starving. Once the fat stores were consumed—and there hadn't been much of that to begin with—his system would begin devouring his own muscle mass. And there was plenty of *that* to go around. True, but that wasn't respecting the body. And without the body, you can accomplish nothing. You are nothing.

Damon slept a shallow, restless sleep, drifting in and out of consciousness.

By the tenth day, Damon was barely able to sit when Frenemy arrived with the jug. He had this new habit—it had started three days earlier—of dropping the jug from a height so that it would land with a thud. Frenemy's attempt to get Damon to flinch, no doubt. Damon lived for those daily visits. Each brought with it some hope that the man would invite him in and Guru Dev would reward him by accepting him as a student, and Damon could finally put food in his mouth.

Frenemy left. There was no invitation to see his guru. It came as no surprise, yet somehow Damon couldn't fight off the feeling that this was all for nothing.

And Damon was not respecting his body, his most treasured possession.

By risking the body, you are endangering the mission. You cannot possibly complete the mission if you die.

Damon hadn't planned this out well while he was still strong and could think clearly. After all this time, logical, sequential cogitation came with great effort, and Damon could not come up with something to refute the argument.

This was just fucked-up self-torture. The enemy was defeating him without having to lift a finger. All this was getting him nowhere; the Indians didn't care if he lived or died.

There would be no invitation for Damon to pass through the gates. His plan was failing. He was starving himself, eating away at the muscle he had spent years to build, destroying a perfectly good body—

The gate opened. Damon could tell it was Frenemy.

Damon hadn't moved from his seated position.

"Is there something wrong with the rice?" he said. "Why you are not accepting the food we offer you?"

Damon was too exhausted to come up with a worthy answer. He thought of saying nothing, but that wouldn't do either: he'd waited for ten days and suddenly, finally, he was getting their attention. It wasn't exactly the question he wanted to hear, but this was his opportunity, and silence could possibly be taken as another insult.

"Good sir, the last thing I intended is to offend you," Damon said, slowly letting the sunlight slice into his eyes. "I am deeply grateful for your daily generosity."

Frenemy gave a simple smile. He wasn't the man whom Damon had met on the first day. This little fellow had long flowing gray hair and a mustache and beard that still retained visible traces of its original dark brown. It occurred to Damon that Frenemy was smiling whereas the other man, the bald guy, hadn't shared Frenemy's enthusiasm with Damon.

Damon said, "I would like to see your master."

"Why?"

"I want to be a student here at the ashram. I want to be Guru Dev's student."

Frenemy started walking away. "Come with me."

Damon had difficulties standing, and despite his painstaking efforts to hide it, Frenemy took notice. "Do you need help?"

Damon shook his head, gaining his balance. "Thank you, I'll be fine."

As they walked, Damon looked very closely at the ashram. He focused on each step, making sure he wouldn't lose his footing. Frenemy walked slowly. Damon was at pains to keep up.

Damon had seen it once already, but this time, starved for food and visual stimulation for ten days, it felt as if he were in the Louvre, observing masterpieces for the very first time. Several of the men in orange were talking, apparently unbound by a sacred code of silence as were their counterparts in the West. Damon smelled incense. Oddly, it made him even hungrier, as if he could eat sandalwood. At that point, he could eat anything.

Frenemy walked him through the ashram, observing Damon as he looked at the many students and devotees performing their daily tasks.

Frenemy just stood there, in the middle of the ashram compound, while Damon waited. Did Frenemy expect Damon to guide him to Guru Dev?

"I thought I would see Guru Dev," Damon said.

"You see all these gentlemen here? They all are being here for a reason. Not because 'I want to be Guru Dev's student.'"

Frenemy was clearly displeased with Damon's answer. What did he want to hear?

Damon did not move. If he had more time, he could think of something better to say. Something that would force Frenemy to take him to Guru Dev.

Damon sensed there was little he could do at this point. He had already offended them by not eating their rice.

Shit.

Why hadn't he thought of that?

Frenemy headed back. Damon followed.

They walked in silence.

Damon was being escorted out of the ashram for a second time.

When they reached the gates, Damon slowly managed to sit down outside his pillar.

"You will eat." It wasn't clear if Frenemy was asking a question or making a statement.

Damon nodded. "I shall. Thank you." There was no rice to eat, since on this unscheduled midday visit, Frenemy had delivered neither the jug of water nor the bowl of rice. It was understood the monk had been referring to dinner.

Instead of leaving, Frenemy walked up to Damon and pointed. "This is a most uncomfortable position, sir."

"But Guru Dev sits this way."

Frenemy laughed. "Most certainly not, sir!" He shook his head energetically. "No, no." He sat down next to Damon with a deliberation that made it plain this was a demonstration. Frenemy used a hand to assist his right foot *over* his left bent knee, and then the other foot over the right knee. It was the inverse of what Damon had been doing all this time. Damon watched and carefully repeated the Indian's moves.

"Very good. This is the *lotus* position." Without warning or ceremony, Frenemy unlocked himself from his seated position, hopped up, and left.

It looked painful, but strangely Damon found this new position more comfortable. Maybe he could sit this way for longer. He would find out, eventually, but there was no point in trying the experiment now that Frenemy was gone.

Why bother? Sitting still for forty-five minutes was pointless. Frenemy and his buddies had never stood outside the gate watching him for more than fifteen minutes, and Damon was sure he could sit for that long on nails if he had to. What he needed to do was practice getting *into* the position. That could take up valuable seconds. Damon tried releasing his legs from the pressure lock and he found that he needed to use his hands to assist. He got in and out of the Lotus position three times seated. That was easy, but it wasn't the real test. He needed to be able to snap from lying down into the Frenemy's yoga posture in seconds.

He practiced over and over, each time focusing on shaving a second from his previous try. The Seiko had proven very useful these past days. Keeping track of the passing hours helped Damon maintain order in his mind. He had a goal, and he could measure how much closer he was to attaining it every passing day. He kept the timepiece fastened over the strap of his rucksack. He wasn't about to wear the watch; even though it was nothing fancy, the Indians would probably see the Seiko as a sign of wealth and materialism. It certainly didn't fit in well with their whole spiritual outlook, not according to the book Madeleine had given him.

Well, from now on, Damon resolved, he would keep the watch *inside* the duffel bag. That way, there was no chance they'd see it unless they violated his privacy by searching through his personal belongings. Highly unlikely in a place like this.

The walk had exhausted him, but Damon had relished the brief change of scenery.

Still, they'd rejected him a second time. That wasn't necessarily a bad thing, of course. If Frenemy had showed him to Guru Dev and the master had taken him under his wing, it would have been too easy. No guru worth his salt would accept a disciple without a real challenge. According to the professor, a man accepted by Guru Dev was considered *blessed*. No, this was just the beginning. There'd be a lot more of these tests. It was the way it had to be, and if Damon wanted to avail himself of the security of hiding in the ultimate shelter, he was going to have to pay for it. Big-time.

Damon wrapped himself in his threads and waited. He wished there was some way he could go over to the river and wash his clothes. They were beginning to smell, and he hadn't worn a clean pair of underwear in ages. It reminded him of SF training, when he'd been out in the woods on prolonged hikes.

Ten days had gone by and nobody had come through the gates after sunset. He woke up a dozen times every night, anyway, so why not sneak out to the Ganges to bathe and soak his filthy clothes? He didn't have any soap, of course. He could have grabbed a bar of soap from the hotel. But he hadn't thought of that. Damon was on a mission to restore his life, his honor, and his career, and there he was without a bar of fucking soap. Well, too bad. The river water alone would just have to be enough.

He wasn't about to disappoint Frenemy this time. He'd eat all his food. Hell, if he could, he'd eat the fucking bowl.

The sun slipped down the sky, and right on cue, Damon heard Frenemy walking over with dinner. He came at the same times every day, but Damon gauged his arrival by the position of the sun, not the time on his watch, because he might find himself without his Seiko one day, and he had to be prepared. Damon went to his spot—now a clear depression in the soil—and once in the newly learned lotus position, he closed his eyes.

The jug landed with the ritualistic thud, followed by the hollow sound of the bowl of rice. God, it smelled good.

"Eat!" Frenemy said, leaving without waiting for a reply.

Damon's eyes popped open. There it was, the bowl of rice. Only now he could finally eat it.

This wasn't his mind playing more of its tricks; he didn't have to starve himself anymore. That part of the test was over. But he had to be careful: if he ate his food too quickly, his stomach would toss it out and it would all go to waste. There was another small problem. His hands were filthy.

How was he supposed to eat the rice? Nobody was watching. Damon took a small bite out of the mound.

All at once, his brain came alive in an explosion of neural fireworks. His body tried forcing him to swallow. Damon fought back, chewing until the rice had become a liquid paste.

He counted to twenty before allowing himself the pleasure of the second bite.

Eating like this was an entirely new kind of torture. He had waited twenty seconds between bites. He used his watch. He was *sure* he'd waited. Yet the bowl was suddenly empty. He licked off the last remaining grains from the side and regarded the empty bowl in disbelief.

He wanted more. He had managed all this time with nothing and now he couldn't stand another second without.

Go in there. Ask. Screw asking, beg.

That would compromise the mission.

Please, for Christ's sake, before it's too late, before Frenemy is out of rice for the evening.

There was a much better idea: drown the hunger with half the jug of water.

Under normal circumstances, that probably wouldn't be a bad idea, but with his body starved for ten days, Damon figured he needed to give his stomach a chance to digest the rice before throwing anything else in there, even water.

He wasn't thirsty anyway. He imagined he could devour all that rice he'd left to the ants for the past week and a half in just a few minutes. Yeah, and then puke his guts outs, ants and all. A lot of good that would do. And the rice was gone, anyway.

He was playing with fantasies. While he was at it, why not just find a pay phone and order a pizza?

The rice had made things much worse. He'd never been so hungry in his entire life.

If he didn't preoccupy himself with something, and damned soon, he'd lose the last of his self-control and his mission would be compromised. All he needed to buy was twenty minutes or so, and then he'd be home free. The stomach would finally stop sending that maddening hunger signal to the brain. After ten days on a diet of water, a bowl of rice was surely all his shrunken stomach could handle.

Damon forced himself to read through the now tattered *Guide to India*. He hadn't opened it in a while. By page twenty, the hunger pains were subsiding to the level of nagging white noise.

One full day and two bowls of rice later, Damon was a new man. That evening he felt he had the energy to go and wash his smelly clothes and body in the Ganges. The night before, despite having dinner for the first time in ten days, he'd still been unable to manage more than a string of restless naps under the starlit sky. That night, he expected things would be different.

Despite the regular meals, however, Damon woke up at three. It was time to take advantage of his insomnia. This was the perfect opportunity.

All was quiet, except for the sounds of nature. Damon gathered his rucksack and headed for the Ganges.

It seemed like a long walk. Either Damon had miscalculated the distance, or lack of food and exercise for more than ten days had weakened him to the point where even such a minor trek felt like an endless hike.

The water was surprisingly cool. What a delight. He rubbed himself clean then he started washing his clothes. Everything except for one change of clothing, which he'd need to wear until the rest had dried.

Shit. How was he going to dry his clothes? There wasn't much to worry about—underwear, shorts, and a couple of T-shirts he hadn't torn—but he couldn't just hang them over the gate. The thought of it made him laugh.

Christ, what was the deal? Had he taken a blow to the head in Vietnam he couldn't remember? Had he lost his ability to make even the most elementary plan? It wasn't as if he hadn't had time to think things out. Plenty of time, but until the day before, he'd had no energy to think. He'd grown accustomed to a lazy, haphazard mind, and as a result he wasn't even trying to plan anymore.

Well, that would have to change. This was just a temporary setback. He'd be his old self again soon enough.

So, back to the small matter of the wet clothes . . .

Come on, this was easy. He'd just stuff them in the duffel bag when Frenemy came along. He'd leave them to dry on the open mouth of the bag, so he could just push them in and zip the bag shut in a few seconds if he had a visitor. He'd leave them in for the morning meal—it wasn't hot enough to dry them out at that hour anyway—and then once Frenemy was gone, he'd dry one piece of clothing at a time. It wouldn't take long—just a few hours at most. That way, nobody would see and there'd be no reason for anyone to suspect he had gone to the river and left his post.

For the following weeks, when it was dark and all of Rishikesh was asleep, Damon went to visit his new friend, the Ganges. Moonlit nights were the best, for when the moon was gone and the stars filled the sky, the Ganges was as dark as crude oil.

Every night before his ablutions, Damon exercised by the Ganges. It was the perfect time—it was cool, so he sweated less and didn't expel the precious water from his body. He had become much thinner, although he had been able to regain a lot of the muscle mass he had lost during the first ten days when he was fasting. He looked like a wrestler trying to make it several weight classes below the norm for his height.

He liked his new body; it was lighter, faster. All that extra muscle wasn't of any use to him anymore anyway. This mission would be successful only by virtue of exercising his wits. These Indians were into mind games. That was their thing. That's what they did in the eastern part of the world. Damon thought of Ho Chi Minh and all the mind-fuck ploys he had used to seduce the American youth back home while he killed American soldiers in Vietnam. For a fleeting second, he felt a familiar rage. The feeling vanished without as much as an aftertaste. Odd. There was something definitely weird about this place, as though many of his usual emotions were not welcome there and had gone on an extended vacation.

Maybe it was the Ganges. It was as if the river had a consciousness of its own. Damon imagined he could feel the river's presence just as palpably as he could sense Frenemy's approach before he could hear his footfalls.

He was beginning to plan and think ahead. That was a relief, but with it came a loss, and he hadn't noticed it until he started eating again—what had it been, three weeks? There was a subtle layer of thought that had been available to him back then that he no longer had access to—nothing tangible, more like starvation-induced sparks of understanding that came alive in his brain when he least expected it.

Damon waited another two weeks, but still there were no offers. He was eating every grain of rice Frenemy gave him, and there wasn't a drop of water left in the jug by the end of the day. Surely Frenemy could not be offended. Damon wasn't doing anything to offend anyone.

Then again, he wasn't exactly doing anything to *impress* Frenemy either.

It was definitely possible that Frenemy somehow knew Damon assumed the seated position just before Frenemy arrived at the gate and that Damon was merely trying to make himself appear like one of the pious followers, God-seekers, disciples, devotees, or whateverthefucktheycallthemselves.

Frenemy could know all this, but he would have also known that Damon had remained put, outside the gate, for a full month and a half. That had to be worth something. How long was long enough? Months? Half a year? When would this hazing finally end?

Madeleine had referred to it as an *initiation*.

He wondered what she was doing. She was probably back in Norway with her boring, unappreciative husband. It occurred to him that he hadn't lusted for her since the fasting. Oddly, he found the realization neither disturbing nor surprising.

Each time Damon thought of seeking Guru Dev's audience, he convinced himself he needed to wait a bit longer. He needed an *invitation*.

Frenemy came forth with no invitations, no offers; not even a spoken word. If Damon fasted again, it would only serve to offend Frenemy, and, God forbid, Guru Dev, so that was out of the question. He needed to prompt an invitation, since what he was doing was obviously not enough. He could end up sitting out there for the rest of his life, for all he knew, and they still wouldn't accept him.

He had to think of something. *Anything.*

An offering? What could he offer?

He had nothing. A duffel bag, tattered clothes and a Seiko watch. That was about it. They certainly wouldn't want his clothes, and they probably couldn't care less about his watch. It couldn't be anything material. These people did not appreciate that sort of thing. It had to be some kind of gesture. A *symbolic* gesture.

Damon could construct an offering.

That's it. He would build something. What, though? With what? He had time, and that was one thing on his side. If they were still hunting for him at this stage, they weren't doing it at the ashram.

The only tool Damon had at his disposal was his army knife. It wouldn't be easy, but he would come up with an idea.

Only, he didn't. He spent all day searching for inspiration, for something that might propel his mission one step further toward success.

While he was reasonably safe in the little camp outside the ashram, especially with more than a month of time on his side, Damon knew he was still exposed. Anything could happen. Inside the ashram he'd be untouchable. He could hide until they gave up on him and then he'd emerge, ready, and with the element of surprise.

By the end of the third day, he was starting to get discouraged. Perhaps there was no solution. He pushed away the thought like he used to push back the waves of hunger.

That night, he exercised vigorously, and sleek with sweat he plunged into the Ganges.

The cool shock of the river water on his skin gave him that familiar exhilaration he cherished so much. Only this time, it didn't dissipate so quickly.

A branch floated by. It was an odd branch with four twigs fanning out of one side like arms. The arms had a few leaves on them, reminding Damon of something. Something he'd seen over and over again but for some reason he couldn't quite remember.

Then, finally, the Ganges told him.

THE CARVING OF KALI

1970

Eight and a half weeks of sitting by the gatepost hadn't gotten Damon one iota closer to becoming Guru Dev's disciple.

He looked at the branch over which he'd performed delicate surgery for a period of nine days. The wood was now a work of art.

Frenemy delivered meals like clockwork. Breakfast at 0700 hours, dinner at 1800 hours. It could have been boot camp. *Everything* ran on a schedule, Damon had no complaints on that score. It went quiet at the same times every day, and not a single person was outside farming when it was time for meditation. They all performed their daily functions as a group. Thanks to the rigid routine, Damon could afford certain liberties. The periods of silence gave him a cumulative total of six hours to work each day.

Until his first tour in Vietnam, and with the exception of art class in high school, Damon hadn't done any carving in his life, and he definitely didn't expect to go to war and spend hours cutting figures out of branches, but there you have it. Most of the time, life in the jungle was painfully boring.

It was a waiting game. A game that went from endless stretches of dreary sleepiness to bursts of gut-spilling mayhem. You had to stay alert, though, or you'd end up dead. At the same time, you couldn't talk or make any kind of noise, otherwise you'd be killed even faster.

Damon had seen Snakebite carving, so he'd tried it too, and pretty soon most of the guys on the team had taken it up. They all had to bury the shavings and destroy the end product—you couldn't leave anything behind for the enemy to trace your whereabouts, and every pocket was filled with precious ammunition. So there was no alternative but to kiss your hard work good-bye. After two tours, Damon had created a few interesting pieces, but their only value had been to keep boredom at bay and his mind alert.

This current work was destined for more than an unceremonious burial. This would serve as his ticket into the ashram.

The branches he'd collected that evening by the Ganges were small enough to fit in his duffel bag, and yet the finished work would be sufficiently large to make an impressive offering.

Damon had one piece of wood around two feet long and just thick enough to form her twisted body. Finding the right wood for the rest of her had kept him hunting all night.

There hadn't been any blueberries around; he didn't know if they even grew in this country. He'd worry about that later.

For although their basic shape was ideal, the eight branches still needed a great deal of delicate work.

Carving at night was impractical unless there was a full moon, and more important, nighttime was Damon's only opportunity to leave the ashram and bathe in the Ganges.

Nine full days. He could have done it in five, but he wanted to take his time with this project.

Looking it over, he was glad he had. Although, while the carving was complete, the artwork was not. A few crucial final touches were needed. He looked at it and rolled it over, examining every crevice. He referred to the photo in the book.

His statue was better.

The light wood, about the length from his elbow to his fingertips, looked nothing like the small log it once had been. The woman twisted in a provocative wooden pose, her many wavy arms fanning out from her shoulders almost down to her hips. The result reminded Damon of Popeye's girl. This mutant Olive Oyl, however, was grim and humorless. There was something ominous and alluring about her, creating a feeling of impropriety and forbidden fascination when he looked at her inhuman form.

The weather had cooled since he first arrived in Rishikesh. He was able to hold out on drinking water until just before sleeping, when he downed the entire jug.

It was an old trick the Native Americans used to make sure they'd wake early before battle. That night, it worked like a charm.

He was up twice to urinate. The second time was still a little early, but better that than late. Damon walked off the ashram grounds; this time he didn't head for the Ganges.

This was a risk, no question about it, but nothing he had tried so far had worked, and if the offering were anything less than perfect, it would all be for nothing. It was imperative Guru Dev understood the depth of Damon's commitment.

They had seen Damon out there, every day, without fail, sitting in the lotus position. They would know the carving was a handmade artwork that had taken Damon many hours to complete. They'd know just by glancing at it.

Leaving the area was to risk his present safety in order to secure it later, and for the rest of his stay in India.

Arriving at central Rishikesh, Damon located the hotel where he and Madeleine had stayed.

He could use the main entrance, but the front desk was probably manned, even at this early hour, and Damon was in tattered clothes, looking more like a street bum than a tourist or a student of yoga.

He had enough facial hair to qualify as a hermit, were that sufficient in and of itself. But even with a head of hair that hadn't been shampooed or properly trimmed in months and clothing that looked like Elmer Fudd had worn it through a trip across a minefield, Damon was unmistakably a foreigner.

Fine, and if someone were to see him, then big deal, what would they remember? A hippie in Rishikesh, India? They were as common as roaches in a sleazy New York apartment.

Damon slid into the alleyway that led to the back entrance. Nobody had seen him; the streets were deserted at that hour.

The back door was not locked. There was no reason for it to be. Damon had checked every exit to this hotel very carefully during his brief stay almost two months earlier.

He examined the knob and found no signs of rusting. He gave it a test squeeze and then, very cautiously, he twisted. In seconds, he was in the dining room, and from there he could make out the reception area.

Nobody at the front desk. Good. With the receptionist probably fast asleep in his office, he could find what he needed at the front desk, unless they were modern enough to favor ballpoint pens, of course.

When they find it missing they'll probably think the monkeys were to blame.

During a Kama Sutra lesson, Damon had witnessed a monkey trying to steal his clothes right out of his duffel bag. He had tried to scare the animal but the monkey had pulled back his gums in a yellow-toothed sneer. It had sat there, challenging him for a while, jeering with mischief, and then, losing interest, had jumped out the window, making its escape by way of a branch. In the hotel garden, sprawled out in a pile, were various bits of stolen attire. The manager had explained to Madeleine that if the other guests wanted to retrieve their clothing, they would have to offer the monkeys food in exchange.

Behind the desk, in a drawer, Damon found what he was looking for. He held it up trying to get some light to shine through the glass, but discerning the difference between black and dark blue was not going to be easy. He rolled it in his hand and let the liquid paint a thin coat on the inner surface of the glass. Blue. Definitely blue.

He returned to the dining area. He couldn't find any drawers at first. They didn't have anything out for breakfast yet. Too early for that. Which was both good and bad. Good because since nobody was up yet, nobody would see him; bad because it was going to make finding what he needed harder—

Damon saw something promising in the kitchen. Second drawer from the top. Perfect.

He was out of the hotel in seconds, and had made it back to his camp outside the ashram with time to spare. After carefully hiding his two acquisitions in his duffel bag, Damon dozed for two hours, awaking just before Frenemy arrived with breakfast.

Rice and water. These people really didn't care much for variety, but when Frenemy left, Damon ate his food with gusto.

It was a very special day. Damon waited for the second period of silence, when the sun was at its apex, before he cleared a shallow area three feet in diameter. He opened the inkwell and poured a third of the contents into the bowl he'd taken from the hotel. Plan B had called for finding blueberry jam, but since he'd found the ink—*blue* ink—there was no need for the jam, which certainly would not have worked as well, if at all. The only snag to using ink was that whatever bowl he used would be ruined, and destroying a bowl from the ashram, even for the purpose of creating an offering, was out of the question. Left with no alternative, he'd taken one from the hotel.

He poured some water from his precious supply, stirring carefully with a twig. Satisfied with the consistency of the diluted mixture, it was now time to put his idea to the test.

He left the twig in the bowl for a few minutes and pulled it out. The wood had a faint blue hue. Perfect. He placed the sculpture in the area he'd cleared and slowly poured the ink water until it was completely covered. By the time the period of silence was over, it was dry and the color was ideal. Just a faint hint of blue. He scooped earth over the tainted soil until the ink stains could no longer be seen.

He'd found two tar-black stones, and while neither was a perfect sphere, they were about the same size, and had a glossy surface similar to living eyes. Damon had carved the sockets to accommodate each stone, and this had proved to be one of the most delicate feats in the carving. The stones had to be forced in so they would remain in the recessed wood and never pop out. Damon couldn't push them in with his thumb, so he covered their surface with cloth and gently tapped with a heavy stone until, one after the other, they both finally popped in. Removing the cloth he drew a quick breath.

Damon had created a statue of the goddess Kali, and in his estimation, his work was significantly more impressive than the photo on page 47 of Madeleine's *Guide to India*. This was a magnificent piece of art. The best sculpture Damon had ever made, and unlike his other creations, this one he would not destroy.

Frenemy arrived just a minute later than seven. He set the jug and bowl of rice down, but he did not retrieve the old jug.

Damon was in the lotus position, as always, but this time his eyes were completely open and he was staring right at Frenemy. "Would Guru Dev honor me with his presence? I have something for him."

Frenemy looked at him for a short while, clearly surprised to hear him speak after such a long time. "What is it?"

"I must show him in *person*."

Frenemy shook his head and left. Damon had held on to some hope that Frenemy would consult his master, but that hope soon died away.

Frenemy didn't return until the next morning.

Damon was in the lotus position, his eyes closed this time. "Please, sir, I would like to give Guru Dev something."

Frenemy did not leave. He took a few seconds before he spoke. "Show me."

Damon opened his black duffel bag and pulled out a large object wrapped in sheets of cloth.

It was clear now that Damon wasn't going to be allowed to see Guru Dev with his offering covered. Frenemy might consider it a potential threat. Normally, that would make sense, but they didn't have guards; they didn't even have locks on the gates or any kind of security measures anywhere in the ashram.

Damon unraveled the cloth strips. "This is my gift to Guru Dev."

Frenemy stared expressionless for a moment before he burst into laughter.

Who the hell does this gofer think he is? Damon looked away so Frenemy wouldn't see his anger.

This little guy was keeping him from seeing Guru Dev, the one and only person who could admit him to the ashram. And only in the ashram would Damon be completely safe.

Frenemy was *jeopardizing* the mission.

It was imperative Damon manage to control himself and pretend not to notice the insult. If he could remain respectful, he might still be able to turn things in his favor.

Damon drew in a slow, deliberate breath. "Forgive me, I thought you would approve."

"Kali has no place in this ashram, we have made our peace with her." Frenemy smiled with gravity.

There was no time to waste with protocol. Damon had to come straight to the point or Frenemy would leave again. "I want to present this as an offering, to honor Guru Dev."

"What does Kali represent to you?"

"Kali is a Goddess."

"Kali is the Goddess of desire, of death, of the material. What you might perceive as evil."

In the *Guide to India* under the photo, a caption read simply "The Hindu Goddess Kali."

"I had no idea. . . ."

"You acted from your level of understanding."

There was nothing condescending in Frenemy's smile, but still Damon felt a second welling of anger. He swallowed it back. "Please believe me, I did not wish to offend you with this, I only hoped—"

"Keep Kali here, with you, until you, too, are done with her," Frenemy said, and was about to walk off.

"Please, I want to be a student here."

Frenemy's smile was gone. "Why?"

Was this guy kidding?

"I believe I've answered that question, sir." Damon couldn't help himself, it just slipped out.

"You certainly have not."

"Guru Dev's reputation is known around the world—"

"That is not what I am asking," Frenemy said patiently.

Okay. Clearly missing the mark here. What the *hell* does Frenemy want to hear? He's obviously not into brown-nosing bullshit, and he doesn't take well to the idea of Damon wanting to be a student here. Fucking useless book. What did Damon expect to find, the Hindi equivalent to "Open Sesame"?

Frenemy cut into Damon's thoughts. "You must answer this question."

Damon was out of time. It was all or nothing, now or never. "I want to be his student because—"

Frenemy cut him off with a wave and shake of the head. "Be silent. Answer from within."

The gate closed.

Frenemy was gone.

FOLLOWING JAN

1970

"**C**ome on, fatso, *do* it!"

Bobby was about to cry.

"I *double* dare you." Jason rammed the blue carbon sheet in Bobby's face, but Bobby wasn't about to lick it, double-dare or not.

The kids at UNIS were kind of weird. And for some reason, they were *really* weird on the school bus. The traffic was making the morning's ride longer than usual and Jan doubted Bobby would make it all the way to school without crying. And that was just what bullies like Jason counted on.

Bobby wasn't Jan's friend, but Jan felt sorry for him just the same. He was really fat and sweaty, even in the winter. But Jason and his gang called him a fag and picked on him for no reason all the time. That made Jan really want to show those dorks some of what Mirko had taught him.

Livingsford would have been ten times worse, for sure. He didn't want to imagine what it would have been like if he'd had to actually go. They'd shown him photos of the place and talked to him about it, but that had just been to get him ready in case Damon came to visit. Jan had never even been there to see the boarding school.

It was raining hard again.

Bobby was crying and Jason was poking at him like a campfire marshmallow.

Two more stops and they'd finally be at school.

Jean-Luc watched Jan from across the street. It was recess and children were running about; some screaming, some laughing. No matter what the country, what the language, playgrounds sounded the same the world over. The United Nations International School was located in an old stone building with a fenced-in yard for the kids to run around during recess. Truck tires were hoisted on chains making crude swings. UNIS was going to be relocated to a nice modern building by the East River one day, but in the meantime it wasn't much to look at, especially for an expensive private school.

The rain had stopped when the beginnings of a playground brawl came suddenly to life.

The children were ganging up on a kid who either must have done or said something wrong, or he was simply one of those boys who made himself into the ideal victim. There was no telling.

The doughnut hole in the circle of children was filled and, as one, they pounced on the kid, stacking themselves on top of him, like something Jean-Luc had seen in American football. The hill of bodies came to life and the kid, held by two boys on each side, was dragged to the swings, where his face was forced into a tire until he started choking on the filthy rainwater.

A lady in her forties ran out of the building, into the yard. She pulled the boys away from the kid. From this angle, Jean-Luc could see the boy was even more overweight than he first appeared. The kid was completely soaked from the neck up and crying loudly enough for Jean-Luc to hear him.

The crowd quickly dispersed, every child there most likely proclaiming themselves witnesses not participants.

Jan had been with another, much smaller group, playing peacefully when the trouble had started. They'd stopped what they'd been doing and watched from a safe distance while Jean-Luc, in turn, watched them.

At no time did Jan look in Jean-Luc's direction, and if he had, he would have only been able to observe a car with dark, tinted windows parked on the opposite side of the street.

Jean-Luc and Girard were never to be seen. That had always been part of the agreement.

Damon was after the trust and there were two people in his way: Kory and Jan. That was where Jean-Luc and Girard came in, but neither of them knew when they would have to take action. It depended on whether Damon returned from the war.

Either way, they were guaranteed their money.

ARJUNA

Early 1971

Damon wasn't going to let it go. Not after all the months he'd invested in getting himself into what amounted to the best hideout in India. Frenemy was obviously the ashram henchman. He kept guard on the place, making sure no unworthy wannabes bothered Guru Dev. He was probably a high-ranking senior student, too. He certainly acted like it.

Enough was enough. Damon wasn't even going to wait for Frenemy to come with breakfast.

Damon entered the ashram, opening the gate carefully—past thirty degrees, it squeaked.

"What am I doing wrong?" Damon said in a low voice, from right behind Frenemy.

The old Indian turned around, smiling as if he'd just seen a friend after a very long absence.

What dope is this guy on?

Damon locked eyes with the yogi.

"There is no right or wrong," Frenemy said.

Then why the fuck am I still camped out here and not in there with the rest of Guru Dev's smiley students?

"I have obviously done something wrong," Damon said, "something to offend you."

The Indian kept his smile as he shook his head. "You have not done anything wrong."

"You mean to say that everyone goes through this to become Guru Dev's pupil?"

Frenemy's smile widened, and Damon expected him to laugh but instead he said, "Heavens no! Everyone has his own path. This is your path. You have chosen it; you are walking it. It is as unique as you are, my Kshatriya friend."

Friend.

First ray of hope since he came to this place. His efforts had not been in vain—now he had an ally. Frenemy was indeed going to prove useful to the mission.

"My name is Damon."

"Is that an American name?"

Damon laughed. "I'm American, of Dutch descent. There are no real Americans, unless, of course, you're talking about the Indians."

Frenemy's eyebrows climbed an inch.

It was Damon's turn to smile. "I mean the *American* Indians."

Frenemy nodded. "And my name is Anirudhha."

That rang a bell, but the memory slipped from Damon's mind. "Well, that name doesn't sound very American either."

Anirudhha laughed. "And we thought you had no sense of humor!"

We. So they've been talking about me. More good news.

Damon tried to come up with a way to redirect the conversation back to his original question, but Anirudhha had already turned around. Another Indian disciple was approaching, they chatted as if Damon didn't exist. They were laughing happily at something.

Probably laughing at me.

Damon returned to his camp, not once glancing back.

The water was nice and cool.

There is no right or wrong.

"Bullshit," Damon said out loud as he waded naked in the river. "The little fucker just doesn't want to tell me the secret to being accepted here."

Stop talking to yourself.

Damon never used to do that before. It was a very danger-ous habit, and in Nam it could get you killed. Damon won-dered if these months had taken a toll on his mind.

Too much fucking time on my hands, that's the problem.

Too much time, too little action.

A wind stirred the branches of the trees on the embankment. Action.

Damon was giving birth to a plan; he could feel it rising within, but he'd learned not to push his mind when thoughts were at the prenatal phase. If he did, nine times out of ten, he'd end up drawing a blank.

He closed his eyes, floating on the river, his arms and legs spread like Da Vinci's *Vitruvian Man*, making tiny circles in the water to keep himself on the surface.

So quiet here.

They liked their quiet almost as much as Damon did. During the periods of silence there were absolutely no human-made sounds that Damon's trained ears could discern. Then there were the periods of activity. A lot of hustle and bustle. Plenty of action.

Action.

Damon was a strong man and a damned good soldier. They obviously had no need for his military expertise. He doubted any of these people even knew what the word "enemy" meant. They lived in complete trust and simplicity. The gate was sym-bolic more than anything else, except, perhaps to keep animals out. They couldn't use him as a soldier but . . .

The next morning, when Anirudhha came with his food, he found Damon sitting in the lotus position and for the second time, his eyes were open. "Anirudhha, would it offend anyone if I were to go into the ashram and—"

"Have you carved another god?" Anirudhha grinned.

Damon remained composed. "No sir, I wish to help."

"Help?"

"Yes, with all the work you do in there every day. I receive food and I offer nothing in return. So I would like to help."

Anirudhha shrugged. "If you wish, but it is not necessary."

Damon nodded, careful not to say anything offensive. "I understand. Then allow me to help—not in repayment for the food—but simply because I wish to. Would that be all right?"

Anirudhha studied Damon for a while. "Follow me."

Damon jumped up, landing on his feet straight as a broomstick. He followed Anirudhha for a while, and just when it seemed they were walking toward Guru Dev's residence, Anirudhha pointed to a small hut.

"Over here," Anirudhha said, and once they were inside, he looked Damon over from head to toe. He did this twice, quickly, and then scuffled off to a small room. A moment later, he reappeared, holding a neatly folded orange cloth with two sandals on top.

"We have never had anyone of your size before."

Damon stared at Anirudhha in disbelief. "But should *I* be wearing this?"

Anirudhha chuckled. "It isn't a uniform, we don't have costumes here. If you insist on helping, I think you will be more comfortable wearing this rather than the torn rags you have on now."

"Thank you, Anirudhha, you have been very kind."

Anirudhha smiled and then left Damon alone, presumably to change.

Damon shed his tattered rags and had donned the robe in less than thirty seconds. It was a wonderful feeling to wear something resembling clothing again. The robe left Damon with a bare shoulder, like all the other men in the ashram. Even wearing the sari, Damon stood out like lightning against a black sky. He was at least half a foot taller than any man there, and although his skin had darkened following months of exposure to the hot sun, his eyes blazed the blue of his Dutch ancestry and there was no hiding that.

Damon emerged from the small hut fully robed, wearing the sandals that fit his size-thirteen feet perfectly. For a second, Damon wondered if they'd made the sandals especially for him.

Anirudhha was gone once again. The guy didn't seem to like hanging around for very long.

Damon examined his surroundings. There were plenty of things to do; that much was obvious. Everyone in the ashram was involved in some activity. Carrying buckets of water, cooking, plowing the land, trimming the small trees, picking fruit.

It was time to get busy.

After working the fields for three weeks, Damon started to feel concerned again. He had expected someone would invite him to see Guru Dev. He could always go back and ask Anirudhha to see the master, but what would he say?

I've labored on your land for almost a month, I've paid my dues, take me as your student?

It was beyond stupid.

Anirudhha was really starting to piss him off. Why was the stubborn Indian so determined to keep him from seeing Guru Dev?

Damon started working harder. Harder than anyone else in the entire ashram. He didn't walk, he ran. If he was carrying something especially heavy, it would only slow him to a jog.

But nobody was impressed. He did the work of ten men and his labors went unnoticed.

Hey guys, over here? See?

Four months of this shit and not one of them gave a flying fuck.

It occurred to Damon for the first time that it was already 1971.

What the hell else could he do? Fred had warned him he would have to stay in hiding for a long time. If Damon wasn't accepted as a student—and soon—they would most likely expel him from the ashram. He would have to either try another ashram, starting from scratch, or live like a scavenger hiding in the mountains where he'd probably freeze to death. Neither option was particularly appealing.

At first, none of the students approached Damon. That was not surprising—monks the world over did not have much of a reputation for being conversationalists. But in time, some came to him, polite and curious.

The few who spoke would talk of Vishnu, Krishna, and a long list of other gods. Damon learned it was best to keep his mouth shut and nod.

It wasn't easy listening to stories about Krishna as a baby and endless tales from something called the *Bhagavad Gita*. Despite everything, Damon had made a good show of being interested in what the monks were saying. He had to get on their good side. These guys were all Guru Dev's students, and as Damon had been finding out these past months, that honor didn't come easily.

Damon played dumb and became the student's student. It reminded him of the early days at the Academy, where he'd been less than a nobody.

The smiling, the well-timed nods, and the equally well-placed questions went over with increasing success. Conversations were lasting longer, and he felt the layer of resentment toward him fade, at least to some small degree.

Damon didn't give a damn if they liked him or not; he hadn't come to make friends, but if this was his only way in, then so be it—he had a mission to accomplish.

Of all those who approached him, an exceptionally emaciated Indian named Vadu had seemed to take a special, if peculiar, interest in Damon.

This one was different. Like Frenemy, he smiled easily, and didn't seem offended that a foreigner was parading on his turf uninvited. Vadu made a habit of approaching him as Damon worked the fields or carried large buckets of water to the various dormitories.

He would walk right up to his face, only a foot or two away, and smile, peering at him like a tourist watching a tiger behind thick glass. Damon soon grew accustomed to this odd fellow. It was a wonder the little guy could do any chores at all. He didn't seem to have any muscles, only tendons.

But Damon soon found Vadu to be a great resource. He had answers to important questions, and although, like all his comrades in the ashram, there was never a short response to anything—each question earned itself a short story or three—unlike Anirudhha and the rest of them, he did eventually get to the point.

Damon endeavored to take advantage of the situation as best he could. He was working, and working hard. Information from Vadu was payback. He intended to get every penny's worth.

Damon had asked him how he ended up at the ashram and had been shocked to hear that Vadu once had a large family. His wife had blessed him with five boys and two girls. His children were married with kids of their own, and all but one lived the modern big-city life in Delhi.

Grandchildren seemed impossible for one as young as Vadu. The Indian had reacted to the comment with a proud smile, proclaiming that he was actually sixty-three.

Damon had looked at him doubtfully, but he'd let the improbable statement slide. After all, why would a middle-aged man want to appear older than he actually was?

Vadu was a Brahman, and in Indian society that meant he was born into a privileged class back in a time before Gandhi had publicly denounced the arcane caste system. He would talk about the British rule, about a life of sweetmeats, many servants, and all the privileges his stature had afforded him. Damon sensed Vadu had been more than a Brahman. A statesman, perhaps? Vadu wouldn't say. To the Indian, it was another lifetime. His dharma, or *purpose* as he'd explained it, was elsewhere, in pursuit of the Void.

For a long while, Damon had been careful not to spoil his growing relationship with Vadu by asking him the one question that mattered.

But the time had grown ripe. Damon knew from experience, however, that in his surroundings, direct questions rarely earned direct answers. He'd learned a lot about Vadu over the weeks he'd spoken with him, and he used this information to develop a line of questioning that would hopefully reward him with the information he desperately needed.

"How is it that so many of the disciples here speak English?" Damon had posed this question before to some monk whose name he'd long since forgotten.

Vadu smiled, revealing his missing front tooth. "India was under British rule since 1776, and for most of my youth. All of us here remember it."

"Yes," Damon said. Vadu had spoken about this on more than one occasion. It was a topic Vadu liked, so to keep the Indian talking, Damon indulged him. "Difficult times?"

"Yes, for some. But Gandhi-ji set us free, and now the land has been returned to the people."

"I could not help but notice that you have a better command of the English language than anyone I've spoken with here at the ashram."

Vadu barely nodded. "I studied political science at Oxford." He said it as if he had spent four shameful years in Leavenworth.

Political science made sense. It confirmed Damon's theory about Vadu's background. His family had probably been grooming him for some high-level government position. Damon wondered what they must think of Vadu now.

"How did a Brahman Oxford grad like you end up here?" Damon asked, pleased with how artfully he'd slipped in the precursor to his vital question.

Vadu shrugged, but his expression was anything but indifferent. "It was my dharma. I lived the material life: I was blessed with a wonderful family. I was very wealthy, and I wanted for nothing. For a while, I believed I had it all. But I was not living my dharma, and I was very unhappy because of it. Once I discovered my dharma, I found my path and I went to the mountains to be with Guru Dev, the great master." He looked at Damon and seemed unsatisfied with the reaction he was getting. "Do you have doubts?"

Odd question.

Doubts? Damon wouldn't call it that. "You said you had to go to the mountains?"

"Yes." Vadu nodded. "There was no ashram back then. So I became Guru Dev's student in the mountains."

"It was that easy for you?" Damon said, bewildered. Didn't the professor say Guru Dev was one of the most selective Gurus in all of Rishikesh?

"Oh yes," Vadu said. "It was my dharma. Guru Dev knew this immediately. It was very easy."

Why the hell would Guru Dev accept some rich family guy with no trial or tribulation whatsoever and then refuse Damon the same privilege not once but five times?

"It's not so easy for me, though," Damon remarked, and when Vadu did not reply, he added, "because I'm a foreigner."

Vadu smiled with that childlike ease, shaking his head. "Is that what you think?"

They all seemed to have that nasty habit of answering a question with another question. "It is. Anirudhha called me a Suh-tria or something like that. That means foreigner, right?"

"Satria?" Vadu thought for a moment. "You mean *Kshatriya?*"

"Yes, that was the word."

"It doesn't mean foreigner, it means *warrior.*"

"*Kshatriya,*" Damon said slowly. "But still a foreigner, right?"

"You are our brother; we are all part of the same thing."

"Maybe *you* consider me your brother. But what about the rest of the students here? I get a sense that they don't welcome me the way you do."

"We are part of the same thing," Vadu repeated.

It was clear the Indian didn't want the subject pressed further. "But you mention Kshatriya, that's a caste, right?"

Vadu nodded.

"So we are *not* all the same," Damon pointed out. "You are a Brahman, I am a Kshatriya."

Vadu smiled. "It is interesting to see how you attach yourself to ancient values that are completely alien to you."

Damon frowned. Vadu did not understand the military.

"Gandhi-ji was a great soul. A true seer. There was no caste system in his eyes, but not all of us have risen to such divine clarity. We still see things from where we stand. And I am quite a short man." Vadu giggled.

"Forgive me, sir, but I am still confused. You claim we are all the same, yet you say that they think of me as a Kshatriya."

"There are many layers of truth," Vadu said, suddenly without a smile. "We may say such things, even though we know they are true only on the very surface. Words lie. It is the folly of Kali. It is illusion. Like ego. The Ultimate Truth is that we are all one." Vadu made big gestures with his arm, pointing.

"This. You. Me. The earth under our feet. The glorious sun over our heads. All of this is part of the same thing."

"Okay. So on the very surface then, is that why I'm not Guru Dev's student? Because I'm a foreigner, a Kshatriya?"

Vadu said nothing.

Damon must have pushed too hard and offended the Indian. He should have waited for a better time; it was another mistake and he couldn't afford—

"You are under the impression that the question you ask has a simple answer?"

"Well, no, but—"

"It does."

Damon waited.

Vadu shook his head as if to refute Damon's unspoken words. "It is not the simplicity that you are thinking of, however. It is the simplicity of *truth,* and to the ignorant, nothing is more complicated."

More riddles. Pity. Damon had grown to like the little man—Vadu had been the only one who really answered his questions. Except for the most crucial question.

Vadu sighed—Damon's disappointment was plain. "If you are thinking Guru Dev is not taking you as his student because you are a foreigner, or because you are a Kshatriya, you are quite mistaken."

"Then what must I do?"

"Search deep—search within. And then answer the question."

The same line Anirudhha had given him. Had all the students agreed on what to say when Damon cornered them for an answer?

Ironic. Telling these guys the truth would get him into the ashram, and yet unless he believed they were completely trustworthy—which he most certainly did not—to do so would defeat the entire purpose of his mission.

I'm on the run. It's a secret, see. They're after me. Who, you ask? The Army, the CIA, the NSA, hell, I don't know. I need a place to hide for a few years until I'm forgotten. Then I'll go find the fuckers who ruined my life and when I do, I'm going to ruin theirs.

Yeah, maybe they'd all have a good laugh before they kicked him out on his ass and told the local authorities that the blue-eyed foreigner everyone was wondering about is actually a fugitive hell-bent on revenge.

Damon said, "I want to be like you, accepted here, in the ashram, as Guru Dev's student."

Vadu nodded shortly.

Was that impatience? Couldn't be. These were the most patient people he had ever seen. They had their very own definition of time.

"That is obvious, Arjuna."

Arjuna? Another caste? Damon wasn't given the opportunity to ask.

"What is not obvious is why a warrior such as you would travel a great distance all the way to Rishikesh to end up here, at Guru Dev's ashram."

"I've explained that," Damon started, but was cut off when Vadu gave him that same quick nod.

"Explanations are not answers, and they often have little to do with the truth." Vadu waited for that to sink in. It didn't seem to, so he said, "What is your dharma?"

"My life purpose?"

"Purpose," Vadu said, looking eager, as if he suspected Damon might give him the answer.

And it slipped out, surprising Damon more than Vadu: "My mission?"

Vadu leaned back, his hands locked in front of him, looking deeply at Damon. "Arjuna, the question is for *you*. Guru Dev already knows the answer. When you discover it for yourself, you will be ready."

Damon's face was expressionless, but his mind was racing.

No fucking way. *Impossible.*

Damon had said nothing to anyone here. This mission was unlike any other in his life. They couldn't possibly know unless they had ESP and could read minds.

That was simply dumb. A lot of Hollywood yoga hokey-pokey. Capital *B*, capital *S.* They didn't read minds. They weren't even trained to read expressions. These were men who believed in blue gods.

Damon couldn't let this sit for very long; it would appear like he was hiding something or even worse, that he actually bought into what Vadu had just said. "What is Arjuna? A subcaste?"

Vadu laughed. "Arjuna was a great warrior from the *Bhagavad Gita*. 'Damon' does not become you. It is a name from your past life."

Damon's last mission had indeed separated him from another world—another life. Although it was inconceivable that they had somehow found out about it. They didn't have some intel team investigating his past. This wasn't the Army, after all, this was a small, harmless ashram in the middle of nowhere.

Damon figured they used the past-life expression quite freely there. These people were keen observers, not by virtue of any training, but as a by-product of years of introspection. They weren't his enemy, but he had to be very careful—if they discovered the truth, he'd be hounded off the ashram in the blink of an eye. The only way they'd ever find out is if Damon made the mistake of underestimating them.

And if they already knew, then it was game-over anyway.

He hadn't underestimated Kory, his aunt Mary, or even John Saunders. He wasn't about to underestimate anyone here, either. As outlandish as it was, Damon had to assume that they were somehow able to get a read or perhaps just a scent of his thoughts, or his intentions.

Nothing was lost, not yet. There was time. Damon had to believe that. They may have gathered a few hints, or developed an uneasy feeling in the back of their oversensitive minds, but nothing more.

Fred knew Damon was in India, and Madeleine knew he was in Rishikesh. Even if one of those two had suddenly developed an urge to betray him—and that was a crazy stretch—the snitch would have to come in person or send someone to alert the ashram of his presence, because there were no telephones there. And nobody came through the gate without Damon knowing first.

Besides, Vadu wouldn't be smiling at him at the moment if he had the slightest hint of the truth.

FORETHOUGHT

1971

Arthur, acting as arbiter, announced, "Board Four: Queen to King's Bishop Three."

Kory didn't say anything for the full two minutes allowed. "Rook to Queen Two."

The arbiter nodded and left the room to move on Kory's behalf. He was playing twenty boards in a blindfold session where anybody with up to an expert rating was allowed to challenge Kory, a grandmaster for three years.

He had eighteen opponents still remaining.

Board Four was his biggest headache. He was either unrated, an undiscovered talent, or a master who'd chosen to bypass the rules. If he was a master, he wasn't known in New York, otherwise the organizers would never have permitted him to participate.

The strategy for any simul, *especially* a blindfold event, was to eliminate the opponents as soon as possible. The more boards Kory had to play, the less time he had to think per opponent.

The other seventeen boards were not going to be a problem. The best of them, Board Seven, was an expert Kory knew well because Hugo Dobrowski was his student.

Arthur returned with Board Five's move. It took Kory six seconds to announce mate-in-three.

The arbiter smiled.

In the next fifteen minutes five more contestants resigned, lightening the load. Usually the weaker players held out to the bitter end so they could tell their friends they lasted for more than twenty moves against a grandmaster.

Soon after, Board One was escorted over to Kory for a conciliatory handshake.

"It really was an honor," Board One said, pushing his glasses up the bridge of his nose with his free hand. "That was amazing! Bishop to Queen Four came out of nowhere!"

Kory thanked him, wondering if the guy was ever going to let go.

With some prodding on Arthur's part, the man was finally ushered out of the room, and Kory could focus on a strategy for Board Four. Win or offer a draw?

His old mentor would have crucified Kory for even pondering the question.

Very well then: win.

Kory didn't have much riding on this, and it wasn't as if a loss or two in a blindfold simul against twenty opponents—when few grandmasters these days would even consider such a thing—would in any way affect his reputation or his rating.

This was his first year as a professor of philosophy at Columbia University. It had long since become obvious that chess was going to be his passion, not his career.

If he lost to Board Four, it would at least be interesting. As Bandini always used to say: challenge yourself at all times or watch your talent slowly bleed to death.

There was only one opponent Kory was truly concerned about—one man who had always managed to remain a step ahead.

Nobody had heard from Damon for almost a year. He could be dead or a prisoner of war, and there was no way to confirm or deny either possibility. People like him didn't simply vanish from the face of the earth. He was charged with purpose: to wreak havoc, disaster, and misery on anybody close to him.

In all likelihood, Damon was setting the stage for a surprise visit. He had most likely stopped writing Mary to have everyone believe he was dead or a prisoner so that he could someday come over and do whatever his devious mind pleased.

And while Kory had taken the obvious precautionary steps, it simply wasn't enough.

When you have Damon as your opponent and decide on a draw, you condemn yourself to doom. Kory had to come up with a definitive attack.

Four months after her nephew's last letter to her, Mary received official notice from the Army that Maj. Damon van Luden was missing in action, and that was the last anyone had heard of him. Surely, if the Army knew he was dead, they'd have sent notice by now.

Damon was keeping everyone in the dark. Logically, he'd want to return to the States and take advantage of his fifty-percent control of the trust. But this wasn't chess; this was Damon's game. A game without pure logic and definitive rules; a game where each time Damon captured a piece, a life is destroyed.

The arbiter was waiting, Board Four had moved.

Kory saw his opportunity to attack.

INITIATION

Damon had told Anirudhha, months earlier—sometime in the fall of the previous year—there was no reason for him to bring water and rice twice a day. The Indian had explained that it was his duty to feed a guest. Damon had insisted. Without protest Anirudhha had told him to help himself.

Since then, Damon had been making his own meals, mostly during his brief breaks from working the land. As a result of adding lunch to his diet, and following a rigorous exercise regimen, Damon had regained much of his muscle mass, making him almost as fit as he'd been after Special Forces training.

On several occasions, Vadu had invited him to eat in the dining area with the rest of the devotees, but he'd politely and firmly declined the offer.

He had no right to eat with the others. He was not a student yet. It would be like some NCO just waltzing into the Officers' Mess. Every man had his place. At the ashram he wasn't even a student. He was the Army equivalent of a candidate cadet. Way lower than an NCO. He was nothing, a nobody. And despite what Vadu had repeatedly said, despite how friendly they'd all been to him, he remained a foreigner.

The idea of helping with the daily chores had been a partial success. He had complete access to most of the ashram, he was learning their routine, and most important, he was making contact with the students on a daily basis. They were his only source of information.

For all of them, with the confusing exception of Vadu, becoming Guru Dev's student had not been easy. They each had a very different tale, and Damon could find no common link.

Even Anirudhha had gone through hell and back in order to win over the great guru. The story had become a legend in Rishikesh. Not surprising, of course, considering the fact that Anirudhha was his first student. Simply locating the legendary yogi known to the villagers as the Mountain Saint had been quite difficult back then. There was no ashram. The Mountain Saint lived in a tiny cave in the Himalayas, where he spent his time from sunrise to sunset practicing yoga, most of which consisted of meditation. He'd been living in that cave for ten years when Anirudhha, still a teenager at the time, had set out for the cold, distant mountains, hoping to become his first disciple.

Anirudhha had taken over the villagers' task of bringing the master rice. He'd done this for months.

Damon had asked Anirudhha, since he had performed this chore for his master, why would he then do the same for Damon who was neither master nor student? Anirudhha had explained that it was his duty to feed a seeker. People in India did not think like Americans. There was no shame in begging, no matter who you were; a seeker of Truth was respected and fed.

That had still made no sense. Why would Anirudhha, the first and most senior of all the students there, be the one to bring Damon the rice and water twice a day?

Was Anirudhha under orders? Some kind of penance?

"Heavens no!" Anirudhha had laughed. "What we do, we do voluntarily."

"But you said it was your *duty* to bring me the rice."

"*Duty,* yes. But this has to do with karma, my American friend, not with orders."

Damon had nodded. "Yeah, I've heard of karma. You do something bad, and it comes around to get you in the future. So what did you do to deserve the rice run?"

"No, no, this is an American interpretation. *Karma,* Arjuna, means *action.* Nothing more, nothing less. And every action affects everything everywhere, no matter how small the action."

"Okay, so it has nothing to do with penance."

"Right, nothing to do with penance," Anirudhha echoed. "It has nothing to do with anything. Pure action has no purpose. One simply acts. One does not act expecting anything. Any action with purpose and expectation is a selfish act because it benefits the self. Action without purpose and expectation, action not born of desire, my American friend, is that which benefits the *big* Self: you, me, Rishikesh, America, this planet, this universe. God."

"You guys have a knack for turning a conversation, even one on rice, into a discussion about God."

"Rice is God. Everything everywhere is God."

No matter what angle he'd tried, he couldn't get closer to Anirudhha. Certainly not close enough to get the Indian to stop with the philosophy and actually say something useful. Like how to be accepted as a student there, for starters.

Damon's rapport with Vadu had developed into something akin to a friendship. They were all friendly there, so it was hard to pinpoint the difference, but for whatever reason, Vadu had always seemed to be fascinated by Damon.

Damon was uprooting some weeds when Vadu came along and greeted him with the customary "Jai Guru Dev."

Vadu was staring again.

"What are you looking at?" Damon asked with an amused smile.

"Oh, it isn't just me. We all feel it. Your dharma is very strong. You carry it over your head like a burning aura." Vadu walked up to him. "It is strange that you have so much purpose, and yet you know not what it is."

The hell I don't. But instead, Damon said, "My purpose is to be Guru Dev's student." If he just left it at that, he'd get the same old lecture about looking deeper to find the real answer. He added, "So since you say this is *not* the answer, and since the answer is the key to becoming his student—which is my purpose—would you teach me how to find the answer Guru Dev is seeking, so that I *will* become his student?"

Vadu laughed. "Your logic is very academic. You take me back to my Oxford years. But this place is not Oxford, and it is not America, so leave your logic at the gate when you come in, and stop listening to the rubbish in your brain."

Damon reddened.

Vadu watched him gleefully, as if anger were an alien and therefore completely novel emotion.

"My thoughts may be garbage, but surely yours are not. Would you please help me find the answer to Guru Dev's question?"

Vadu waved at him as if what Damon was saying was complete nonsense. "You take things personally. Thought itself is insignificant. Your thoughts, my thoughts, they are born of the ego, and they serve the ego. In reality, they *are* the ego."

Damon resisted rolling his eyes. Vadu just wouldn't give him the answer. Had they all been forbidden to help Damon out with this?

Damon wasn't about to let it go. "Please, sir, do me the honor of guiding me to my purpose."

"Yes, of course," Vadu said, beaming. "Why didn't you ask in the first place?"

Vadu emptied his baskets and he motioned to Damon to do the same. Leaving things in order, and the baskets in the stock house, they proceeded to the Hatha Yoga area at the far end of the compound.

Vadu removed his sari, and was now wearing what looked like a white loincloth.

Yoga diapers. Damon swallowed a laugh. Vadu was waiting. It was Damon's turn to undress. Silently, Vadu walked up to Damon and wrapped a cloth around his underwear. Damon watched carefully—he didn't want this particular lesson repeated.

Vadu motioned to the mat, and Damon walked over and faced him. Vadu taught him several elementary stances. All of it was done in mime. Vadu went from over talkative to mute. Damon was amazed at how limber the man was. He had never seen a sixty-three-year-old maneuver his body with such ease.

"Very good. You are very flexible for a man with your musculature." Vadu added, "I have noticed, you never make any sound when you move. You know this?" It didn't sound like a question. Vadu stopped talking again as he moved on to more complex exercises.

Damon learned all the asanas in just two weeks, and rumors of his uncanny ability quickly spread throughout the ashram.

He had finished his lesson for the day and was changing in the food supply hut when Anirudhha came by and said, "Good evening."

Damon bowed. "Jai Guru Dev."

"Vadu is very pleased with your progress in Hatha Yoga."

"I am honored to have him teach me."

Anirudhha nodded. "You take good care of your body. This is the first step in yoga. The body is the temple of the soul. It must be purified and strengthened so that it can withstand the energy of enlightenment."

"I have always taken good care of my body," Damon said simply. "I take care of everything that is mine."

Anirudhha looked at him carefully. Something Damon just said had sparked his interest. As if he'd caught a mistake. But the number two in command said nothing.

"Practice your asanas along with your Western exercises on your own. Vadu has guided you along a path, and now it is time for the next step—to look at the universe from behind your eyes."

"This is the time of silence," Damon said. "I must go before—"

Anirudhha made a *follow-me* motion and walked Damon over to a place where all the other students were gathering. Most were carrying straw mats. Some of them were already sitting down, cradling their noses with their hand. It looked like controlled sneezing, but it was actually the breathing exercise Vadu had taught Damon called *pranayama.*

They went into a smaller, separate room. Anirudhha sat, slipping easily into the lotus position, where Damon had seen Guru Dev more than half a year ago.

"There are four paths to yoga. Yoga is the union of the soul with the Universal Soul—the self with the Divine Self. Yoga occurs when the illusion of duality—small self and big Self—is cast away and one lives in Unity. This is the state of Samadhi.

"The first path is Jnana yoga, the path of the mind. The mind inquires into its own nature and frees itself of itself, leaving pure consciousness, unadulterated by thought. You will be initiated to this now."

Damon said nothing. What was happening, exactly? Was this some sort of ceremony? What did he mean by *initiated?* Could this mean he was going to be accepted as a student? He fought the urge to believe it. Silence was safest. He was making headway—to what end, Damon wasn't sure, but he was making headway, no question about it. He kept his eyes fixed on Anirudhha.

"The second path is that of Raja yoga, and you have already been practicing a small part of Raja yoga through Hatha yoga, which includes pranayama and asanas. There are eight limbs in the practice of Raja yoga. You have covered them all in these months.

"First there is Ahimsa, which means nonviolence. You are clearly a warrior, Arjuna, but the tiger within you has been fast asleep since your stay with us.

"Then there is Satyam, which means truthfulness. This is the one you had problems with. You could not answer the question because you could not be truthful." He searched for signs of protest, but Damon's blue eyes did not waver. "You could not be truthful to *yourself.* You made a small step with Vadu, and it is now time you go beyond. A man cannot be truthful to anyone unless he is truthful to himself. He cannot be truthful to himself unless he knows the truth. You are as truthful to yourself as your knowledge of truth will allow."

Damon nodded, trying to appear convincing.

"Thirdly there is Brahmacharya. This is moderation and control of everything. Your senses and your desires. And, of course, it requires celibacy. You have no problems with control or discipline. It is a gift from your past life.

"Fourth is Asteya or non-stealing. You haven't been stealing, have you?" Anirudhha giggled.

He spoke for half an hour, patiently elaborating on the remaining of the eight limbs, their meaning, and their significance to Damon.

"There is Bhakti yoga, which is the path of devotion. And finally, the fourth path is Karma yoga—the path of action."

Damon sat still. "Which path have you chosen for me?"

Anirudhha turned toward Damon with closed eyes. "*Yogasta Kuru Karmani*—through action you attain Yoga."

Was Anirudhha answering his question by saying Karma yoga was the path for Damon, or was he simply continuing his discourse on the four paths?

Anirudhha got up and left Damon seated. He made no motion for Damon to follow.

Damon waited.

A few moments later, Anirudhha asked Damon to follow him into a second, even smaller, room. The first thing he saw was a black-and-white photo of a man. One of those photos taken with a box camera that left a light brown background, as if it had been overexposed and then subsequently left to bake in the sun. It looked like it might have been a very old photo of Guru Dev. A reef necklace hung on the frame, and to the left and right of the centerpiece burned a stick of sandalwood incense. These items had been laid out on a small table covered in white cloth. Anirudhha sat kneeling in front of the frame. Damon joined him, feeling awkward.

"You are quite skilled at maintaining external silence. I am going to give you a mantra and teach you to meditate. Where I will take you, there will be no thoughts. You will become one with the source of thought. You will learn the silence from within. You will be in a state of stillness. You will be one with the Void. The source of all that is, was, and will always be."

Anirudhha began to sing softly.

Damon had never heard anything like it. Most of the Indian chants seemed more like a variation on Byzantine drone and had a sleepy, hypnotic effect that was unappealing, on the verge of being irritating.

This was different. It had melody, like a lullaby.

The numbness started at the limbs. It was painless, as if his body was gradually fading away. The room appeared projected in his mind as clearly as if his eyes had been open. The man in the photo was suddenly in full color, and he was the one singing, not Anirudhha.

And then the last threads of thought slipped away and Damon was still.

GURU DEV

An eternity had been packaged into what felt like a second. When Damon opened his eyes, he realized he was alone in the room. His extremities buzzed with a pleasant, serene energy.

Anirudhha walked in and said quietly, "Please, come join us."

They walked through a hallway, into the room where Damon had once seen Guru Dev. Anirudhha opened a door that led to an open patio. The sunlight was painful and his eyes weren't adjusting quickly enough. Against the blinding sun, he saw two people seated in the lotus position, a few feet from where he stood, on the patio. Damon could only see their backs. There was a third mat in the middle. This one had no occupant.

Not ten feet away, the entire population of the ashram was seated in the lotus position, facing the patio.

The two Indians on the mats got up. One of them was Vadu, who, upon seeing Damon, gave him a knowing, conspiratorial smile. The other looked much like the disciple who had escorted Damon to Guru Dev that very first time.

Anirudhha and the other disciple went back into the room, returned with an extra mat, and placed it on the ground, extending the row of mats. They motioned to Damon to be seated on the mat adjacent to Vadu.

Damon was facing a large crowd. They waited with silent intensity.

Anirudhha and Vadu were talking. The other disciple was quiet.

For a while, nobody spoke. Anirudhha suddenly cut into the silence in Hindi in a voice that carried with surprising efficiency. Vadu translated softly, "Arjuna, would you tell us what happened?"

Damon gave Vadu and Anirudhha a puzzled look. Anirudhha nodded encouragingly.

Me? What?

"Tell me, I will translate," Vadu said. "They all want to hear."

Damon didn't know what to say. They waited. More than a hundred of them.

Damon looked at Vadu. "I don't get it, what's going on?"

Vadu said, "Don't be nervous, we're all your friends. Just tell me what you experienced and I will translate in Hindi."

"I don't really know."

Vadu turned and spoke to the crowd in Hindi, using an orator's voice.

The crowd broke into laughter and smiles.

Anirudhha said something, looking at Damon and then at the seated group below.

Vadu turned to Damon and smiled. "Try starting from the beginning; go slowly, we will understand."

"I can't really remember . . . anything. I felt numb. But in a good way. It was like I was floating and then . . . I don't know. I just felt this . . . this energy?"

Anirudhha smiled. "What did you expect would happen?"

Vadu was translating quickly now, taking ready advantage of every pause.

Damon looked confused. "Expect? I didn't have a clue what to expect. Like now, I don't really understand this. What's going on here?"

Anirudhha seemed not to hear. "You didn't expect anything?"

Damon nodded, still confused.

Anirudhha turned to the large audience and once again he addressed them in Hindi.

Vadu turned to Damon, spontaneously translating just loudly enough for Damon to hear over Anirudhha's words: "He expected nothing, and was given everything. This man experienced the Void for forty minutes and until today he didn't even know what Samadhi was."

Someone in the audience spoke. Despite the rapid Hindi, Damon could make out the words "Guru Dev."

Vadu said, "Chandra asks you if you felt like this before."

Damon hesitated. He *had* heard the name Guru Dev, right? He'd probably missed the *Jai* part of the greeting. They often started off saying things with *Jai Guru Dev.* Sort of like *Hello.*

"Arjuna?" Vadu said.

Damon knew he had to answer the question. He could tell them, he just wouldn't give them any details.

"I'm not sure," Damon said. "Maybe . . . in a way. Last year, I was in comb—in the middle of a fight. It was like this but not. For a few seconds, I felt I was watching from a distance."

Vadu directed his translation to Chandra, who was in the third row, but in a voice for all to hear.

This time, when Chandra spoke, there was no doubt in Damon's mind he'd heard the name Guru Dev, and there was no *Jai Guru Dev* greeting.

Vadu said, "He is asking—"

Damon's mouth dropped open. He stared wide-eyed at Vadu. "Wait a minute. He called *you* Guru Dev! *You're* Guru Dev?"

Vadu and Anirudhha burst into laughter. A few of the men in the very front row had managed to hear what Damon had said, and they too were laughing. It took Vadu a while to recover to the point where he could shout out what Damon had said.

Suddenly everyone was laughing.

What the—?

Vadu had *clearly* said he had gone to the mountain to meet Guru Dev, and Anirudhha had said he was the master's first student. So who was Chandra calling Guru Dev? The bald guy?

"So you're not Guru Dev?" Damon said, when Vadu's laughter had subsided to giggles.

"Goodness no!" Vadu leaned back, affording a clear view of the two men to his right. "That, Arjuna, is Guru Dev."

The man who had led Damon to Guru Dev on the first day was also leaning back.

Anirudhha looked back at Damon, smiling his usual simple smile.

"Impossible," Damon said. "He was serving me meals for months and he said he was Guru Dev's first student."

"I was *Sri Visnurama's* first student. You saw his photo." Anirudhha was pointing behind him, at the room where Damon had just been initiated. "That was a photo of my teacher—the Mountain Saint. He had only had one student before he gave up the body."

Damon stared at Anirudhha. All this time he had wanted to speak with Guru Dev, and the master was appearing to him twice a day, every day, for months, and Damon never had a clue.

He thought back to that first day, the day when the disciple—who was now standing silently behind and to the left of the patio, almost like a guard—had taken him to Guru Dev. Damon had only seen the master's back, but he never thought to compare it with anyone else's. Damon had assumed Guru Dev would never mingle with his disciples.

How wrong he had been.

Anirudhha—Guru Dev—had started talking to the crowd again, and there was a sudden heavy silence.

Vadu translated for Damon, "Chandra, let us have your question and then let us eat. It is time for dinner."

"Guru Dev," Vadu said, translating Chandra's words, "I have spent my life seeking the Void. I have given up all desires and pleasures in life. How can this man, barely beginning on the path, suddenly experience Samadhi?"

"You have given up everything you say? What about the Void?" Guru Dev replied.

Vadu spoke more softly now, leaning closer so only Damon could hear.

There was a long silence.

Damon had already forgotten what Guru Dev had asked Chandra.

Still, there was no response, so it must have been one of those questions for which there was no answer that would satisfy.

Damon could sense the uncertainty in the questioner's voice, and hardly needed Vadu's translation. "Master?"

Guru Dev waited, said something.

"Did you give up your desire to seek the Void?" Vadu translated.

Chandra bowed his head, speechless.

"If you desire the Void," Vadu translated, "then you have not given up everything. In order to have nothing, you must give up the *desire* to have nothing."

Chandra pointed an accusatory finger at Damon as he spoke.

"He speaks of you," Vadu said. "He says you are a man plagued by the material, plagued by desires, and a man who has never even heard of the Void."

Guru Dev smiled at Chandra, and so that Damon could understand without need of translation he replied in English, "Desire infects the mind, anchoring it to thought. Arjuna had no desire for the Void, no expectations of experiencing the Void, and so his mind was completely open to the Void."

A reverent silence ensued.

"Beginner's luck," Damon mumbled, and Vadu burst into laughter.

THE DREAM

March 1973
Two Years Later

As Vadu had instructed, Damon practiced yoga every day, twice a day, before his meals. This included Hatha yoga asanas, pranayama, and twenty minutes of meditation. He did this alone and outside the ashram, keeping time with his Seiko. His yoga mentor did not have a problem with this, although nobody else in the ashram used any mechanical timepiece—watch, clock, or otherwise.

Two years of yoga and Guru Dev's advice not withstanding, the magic answer that was supposed to reveal itself never did.

While once all-important, the answer had long since lost significance. It was Damon's only key to becoming a student at the ashram, but the fact remained that he'd received more one-on-one attention from Vadu than any properly ordained student could have ever expected.

At this point, Damon couldn't imagine anyone at the ashram ratting him out. It wasn't in their makeup, and had it been, they'd have long since done so.

Therefore, for all intents and purposes, he might as well have been a student.

He let these thoughts play in his mind.

Two more minutes.

Damon called it the meditation cool-down period. Vadu always laughed at that: "The *coool-down period*," blowing the words with relish.

Meditation had an undeniable appeal, but Damon's passion, likely born of natural ability, remained unwaveringly with Hatha yoga.

He'd never felt as strong and flexible in his life.

December 1973

Damon kept walking, propelled by a current of curiosity even his paralyzing fear would not impede.

Last chance.

Run. Don't look back. Run.

But he was already heading for the light.

His throat was on fire; his body, top to bottom, cold and wet.

He opened his eyes.

Cassiopeia looked down at him from an ancient distance.

You couldn't see the sky in the forest, so this wasn't Nam. Or Laos.

The stars waited patiently, but revealed no further clues.

He was awake. He could feel his body. His pounding heart, his raw throat. The freezing dampness.

He jumped out of his sleeping bag and into a fighting stance, scanning for whatever it was that had torn him from his sleep.

Screaming.

His knee had almost made contact with Guru Dev's ribs. The old master was in the lotus position, his eyes closed, looking like a frozen corpse in the monochromatic night.

Had they finally come for Damon?

Idiotic question.

Guru Dev was the only one there.

True enough, but the screams *had* been real.

It was night. The ashram leader was there, right next to him, apparently either meditating or dead.

Damon was either very sick or he'd just woken up from a nightmare. Or into one.

It was no nightmare.

That familiar voice. He'd just heard it. The Grim Reaper, basking in the cruelty of his savage pragmatism.

Not a solitary image or detail came to mind. Only the rotten aftertaste of fear.

It couldn't have been a nightmare, because he *always* remembered his nightmares.

What was important was to get back to reality. And *pronto.* He'd trained himself over the years to be fully alert and ready to take on command decisions within seconds after waking. Even from the deepest sleep or the darkest nightmare.

He must be sick. Hallucinating.

Guru Dev sitting there in the middle of the night? Waking up to find the queen of England sleeping by his side made about as much sense.

Guru Dev spoke without opening his eyes. "What are you afraid of?"

Afraid?

The question: simultaneously insulting and disturbing.

Because he really was afraid. He couldn't recall feeling so debilitated by fear in his life.

Not even when he'd been on a recon, certain this time a bullet would finally find its way through his forehead. Most men wondered what it would be like to have their bodies ripped to pieces by enemy fire. Would there be time to feel pain or experience the transition from life to whatever happened or did not happen thereafter?

Damon had never found himself tormented by that kind of thinking. He was well accustomed to death. Most didn't live long enough to get used to it, but then again, most didn't survive twenty-two missions.

Not that he hadn't been afraid to some degree. Everybody was. But that just kept the adrenaline flowing. What Snakebite used to call the "kill buzz."

He was standing there, with this little Indian guru sitting before him, and no one else around for as far as the eye could see in the fluorescent full moon.

And yet, despite the utter tranquility, Damon was trembling and could not stop.

"I don't know," Damon said. It came out like the voice of some quivering namby-pamby.

Guru Dev appeared to be deep in thought.

"Do *you* know?" Damon asked.

"You were shouting in your sleep," Guru Dev said, as if this were a normal occurrence.

"But how did you end up out here, sitting next to me?"

"Swapnil said he heard someone screaming," Guru Dev said simply.

"For how long?" Blood pushed into his head. How could he have put himself in this intolerable situation?

"It is not important. I took myself to where I could help."

"You should have woken me."

"One mustn't disturb the body as it expels karma."

"I am very sorry to have troubled you."

In the moonlight, Damon could make out a smile. He'd never seen the Indian show a trace of anger, or even frustration, in the three years he'd known him. "Are you feeling better, my American friend?"

Friend. Anirudhha had once called Damon *friend*, before Damon knew who the man really was. And there he was, saying it again, and this time as Guru Dev.

Damon had not compromised the mission, just his ego. Despite the embarrassment, he was greatly relieved to still be referred to as a friend. "I am fine; please go back to sleep. I apologize for waking you."

"Is the fear gone, Arjuna?"

Surprised at his own directness, Damon said, "No, I can't say that it is. I'm still shaking."

"Do you remember this happening before?" Guru Dev said.

"Never. No."

"Are you sure?"

"Positive," Damon said. "This . . . this just isn't me."

Guru Dev cocked his head. "Isn't it?"

"No."

"Because you are a warrior? Because you think you cannot be touched by fear?"

"No. I've known fear . . . within limits. This went *way* beyond the rational."

"It was not rational? Is fear rational?"

Damon wasn't interested in more mind-melting philosophy. "Look, I'm really sorry about all this. I'll be fine. I just need to rest. I appreciate your coming out here, but if you don't mind—"

"This was not the first time."

Damon looked at the Guru. The old man clearly wasn't intentionally insulting. He had that expression on his face, like he was explaining to a child how trees have deep roots, even though one can't see how far under the ground they actually reach.

"No, I can assure you, sir, I've never—"

"You have, Arjuna, you just do not remember."

For a second, a vacuum sapped his energy, and Damon thought he was going to puke. That's all he needed: to get sick all over this guy. "If something like this had happened to me before, how could I not remember it? And how would you know such a thing anyway?"

"It is your karma," Guru Dev said. Damon expected him to continue, but the guru seemed to think the explanation was sufficient.

"Sorry, but I still don't understand why you think I've been in this state before."

"It is the process of purification. You have prepared the body with Hatha yoga. Meditation touches the self more deeply even. What karma the body absorbs must be released for the body to be cleansed. You let go some very deep karma tonight. In order for karma to come out, at some point it had to come in. That is how I know you have experienced this before."

This time, it wasn't so easy to dismiss Guru Dev's words as more philosophical gobbledygook.

At least stop fucking shaking!

"I uh . . . I don't feel well."

Shut up and get your fucking act together, soldier!

"When the arrow of karma is plucked from the body, it is often more painful than when the wound was first created." Guru Dev waited for a minute or so. "Can you remember now? Your dream?"

"It's all blacked out. I don't have the slightest clue. I'm . . . I'm trying."

Guru Dev nodded. "Don't force yourself. You've had your answer, but your mind is not yet ready to deal with what your heart knows to be true."

"Answer," Damon said, "what answer?"

"Why you came here, Arjuna."

Damon stared, not believing he'd heard correctly. "Was I talking in my sleep?"

"No. You were communicating, but not with words." Guru Dev stood, rolled up Damon's duffel bag, and handed it to him. "Now, please, will you come inside with the rest of the students?"

The *rest* of the students. He had not misheard.

The fasting, the little statue nobody wanted, the years of yoga, and what this guy was waiting for—the answer to his impossible question—was a disgraceful night terror?

What kind of a place was this?

Guru Dev was walking away, toting the duffel bag.

"Let me carry that," Damon said, trying to get his weakened body to keep up. "Please."

The Indian laughed. "I need the exercise, Arjuna, you do not."

Damon was relieved despite himself. Though the shaking had begun to subside, and he no longer felt like he was falling down a well, he barely had the strength to walk, never mind carry anything.

They walked to the dormitory without exchanging words. Damon decided it was best to hold off on his question until the morning.

Guru Dev handed over Damon's duffel bag and pointed to a small chamber, where a cot had been made. "We've had this room ready for you for two years."

To hell with waiting for tomorrow. "What was the answer?"

"You came here to be freed, Arjuna."

Damon was about to speak, but Guru Dev had already turned to leave. "Sleep well."

Damon lay in his cot, unable to comply with the old man's request. He could not sleep, well or otherwise. The cot was best suited for a Hobbit, not a Special Forces heavyweight. He removed the sheets and the pillow, and made his bed on the stone floor. It felt like he was lying down in an elevator. The night sky was blocked by a low ceiling, and the air had a slightly stagnant flavor. The hard, cold floor was no big deal, but those walls . . .

They had prepared a room especially for him. To turn it down would be an unthinkable insult.

He closed his eyes, but the walls pressed in. He couldn't stand another minute of imprisonment.

Imprisonment. Dorothy had used that word many times—

He shook off the thought, grabbing his pillow and sleeping bag as he left the dormitory, making about as much noise as a leaf on water.

He found the ideal place to set up for the night, out in the fields, by the gate. Now, and for the very first time, within the ashram compound. Like a sentry post.

It felt like home.

He'd have to wake extra early and find his way to his room before any of them were up.

The dream-induced infirmity was almost completely gone.

But Damon would not allow himself to forget, not now, not ever. When shit goes wrong, you don't just pretend it never happened. That kind of wishful thinking got men killed.

What an exhibition: the screaming, the shaking, the shit-my-pants utter pusillanimity, all right in front of Guru Dev himself. And instead of telling Damon to fuck off and find some other place to whine and moan—and you can bet your sweet ass that's what Damon would have done had he been in Guru Dev's shoes—the guy gives him the greatest gift this ashram can offer. Damon was now officially a student, and for what? For reacting to a nightmare like a two-year-old?

It simply wasn't right.

It was like getting the Medal of Honor for desertion. Not that similar things never happened. He'd heard of one instance during his second tour. The captain in question was given the Distinguished Service Cross. He deserved to be shot. Damon would have happily obliged had he been given the opportunity to meet the dipshit up close.

Damon opened his eyes to the stars.

You came here to be set free.

For all his insightfulness and cunning, the old Indian master was way off this time.

Free. Obviously a reference to spiritual freedom, not freedom from those hounding after him. Damon was no seeker; he was a refugee, and Arjuna was merely a character in a Hindu myth.

They liked seeing him as this Arjuna incarnation; a man seeking enlightenment. One day, Damon would have no choice but to disappoint them.

He had completed a major part of his mission. Phase two was to confirm his suspicions about who had set him up, and then make things right. That would take some time. And if the first phase had been harder than expected, the second would come within kissing distance of impossible.

Not a problem. Impossible was what he did best.

All said and done, Damon owed his Indian hosts. No question. After all, he was not an ingrate. They liked him as Arjuna? Then Arjuna they'd get. Until the day he was fully satisfied the Army had called off the hunt. Then it would be time for Phase Two, when *he* would become the hunter.

How could they honor him with student status after what happened? *Because* of what happened? How did that live up to his mythological namesake?

And what the fuck happened back there, soldier?

The most tempting answer was some sort of food poisoning. Or a stomach flu. Something, *anything*, that had never happened to him before and could explain his behavior. It was no excuse, but at least it was an explanation.

Only, there was nothing wrong with his stomach, or anything else as far as he could tell.

He wasn't about to lie to himself. He'd just discovered his own Achilles' heel.

Guru Dev did not mind, but what about the others? What if someone else besides the master and Swapnil had heard the screams? What would *they* think? This foreigner, going by the name of an ancient Hindu hero, screams at night like the world's biggest pussy, and the very next day they find out he's now one of them?

Damon would be the first to rise. He'd make it back to his room, leave his things in a neat pile, and then wait for Guru Dev to wake. He'd then have a talk with him. He'd get him to understand the importance of keeping what happened quiet. At this point, with his new student status, Damon should be able to ask this one small, but crucial, favor of Guru Dev. That would take care of the problem. If Guru Dev were to tell Swapnil and anyone else who might know of the evening's disgrace to erase it from their minds, they would most surely obey.

That was only a temporary salve to a potentially chronic problem. And it didn't explain what happened.

Damon had his eyes closed, and he struggled to remember what it was that had reduced him from One-Zero to sniveling wimp. Sleep was starting to cloud his mind when suddenly he had an image of a baby in his crib.

A screaming crybaby.

Damon's eyes shot open.

The crybaby was *Kory*.

The little shit was screaming. Why couldn't he just shut up?

Damon's heart jumped as if he'd downshifted from fourth to first gear.

His snot-nosed, crybaby brother? *That's* his Achilles' heel?

Damon laughed at the absurdity, but a voice inside him wasn't laughing at all; it was telling him he was getting warmer.

He had taken on hordes of NVA.

Kory, stop that screaming.

Red hot.

Snakebite was yelling now, grabbing his butchered arm.

He fell. Only the forest remained, and soon even that slipped away, leaving Damon in a deep, dreamless sleep.

Screaming in the night . . .

"Huh . . ." The sun flooded into Damon's eyes.

The Spartans put babies to death for less.

Unworthy.

He blinked, trying to force his eyes to adjust.

Got to wake up from this ridiculous dream.

I am a soldier. I led a team into the jungle . . .

"You did not like the room?"

Damon stirred, then bolted upright. "What the—"

It was Guru Dev.

Jesus! Not again!

The old Indian could have taken him out while Damon had been in oblivious sleep. How the hell did the old guy manage that trick? No creature, man or otherwise, had ever come within ten meters without waking Damon.

Yet this little guru had done it twice within a span of hours.

"You are not the only master of silence, Arjuna."

"You really shouldn't sneak up on a guy like that," Damon said, but it came out more like an apology than a warning.

"You prefer it outside," Guru Dev said, looking around as if this were the first time he had seen the outdoors. "I know how it is. I remember when my guru died and I left the mountains to come to Rishikesh. I felt like a caged tiger."

Damon nodded. "I couldn't have put it better myself."

"You may sleep here if you wish, but now it is time for breakfast."

"Christ," Damon said, "I must have been out of it for hours."

"You needed to rest." He bent down to roll up the sleeping bag, but Damon beat him to it, swooping up the bundle, compressing it into a strudel. "I'll take this."

"As you wish, but come and eat. After what you have been through, you must be famished."

598

It came to Damon just in time. "One thing. What happened was very private. If I could make a request: I would appreciate it if we could keep what happened last night, in fact, my very presence here—"

Guru Dev turned.

Vadu was trotting over, waving cheerily. "Welcome to the ashram, Arjuna!"

Damon forced a smile destined to appear as strained as it felt. He should have made his request last night.

Now it was too late.

Vadu walked him into the group of students who'd already started their asanas. He nodded, indicating Damon was on his own now.

Damon knew what to do. Some of the students were already doing the utthita kurmasana. He had some catching up to do if he was going to complete his asanas along with the rest of them, in time for pranayama. The last thing he needed was to have everyone there waiting on him to finish.

Damon caught sight of Swapnil, who acknowledged him with a kind smile as he slipped into the purna-shalabhasana. There was no cynicism there, no irony or ill will. He was the very man who'd notified Guru Dev that someone was screaming in the night. None of his buddies in the Army would have ever let Damon live something like that down. But this was India. If there ever was a place to get away with going yellow, this was it.

Guru Dev came out to the patio and sat down beside Vadu and Gangadutt, the other disciple who had been there after Damon's initiation.

The students softly echoed each verse that Guru Dev sang.

Rig Veda, if Damon had to conjecture.

He sat there and listened. He had a one-in-four chance of guessing right.

According to Vadu, the Sanskrit sent good vibrations into the atmosphere. If a mistake was made, it was spontaneously corrected by a group specially designated to the task.

At the conclusion of the ritual, Guru Dev spoke a few words, after which everyone closed their eyes. It was time for meditation.

It seemed like only an instant later, the old master was talking again.

Damon waited the required two minutes, and when he opened his eyes, he could see he'd been the last to do so.

Guru Dev gestured toward Damon, speaking with slow deliberation.

"Welcome . . . Arjuna . . . " then something else Damon couldn't translate, and finally: "student of the ashram."

Still seated, the students shifted in his direction, their hands reverently clamped in front of them.

Damon returned the gesture.

Guru Dev was speaking faster, possibly narrating the shameful events of the previous night.

"Arjuna . . ." Seven.

". . . Arjuna . . ." Eight.

". . . *Arjuna* . . ." Nine times—and that didn't include adjectives and nicknames Damon couldn't understand. He wondered what was Hindi for "pussy."

Instead of looks of disdain, Guru Dev's words were earning Damon enthusiastic nods all around.

The group turned back to their master, and after a few minutes, with no mention of his Indian name, it was clear to Damon the talk had moved on to a different topic.

Damon did his best to keep up, but when later that day, they walked en masse to the Ganges, he found himself at a complete loss.

All his prior visits to the sacred river had always been alone, and at night. This time, in the daylight, the feeling was as completely alien as the rituals his fellow students were currently performing.

Damon watched from a respectful distance, not trying to imitate their actions and mimic their words. This was the correct thing to do, Vadu explained later. He would learn in due time.

He'd been very wrong about these people. They'd accepted him like a brother. Why, Damon couldn't imagine.

That evening, instead of his usual greeting, when Vadu came to Damon he said, "Your past and your secrets are safe here."

Receiving no response, Vadu added, "Guru Dev has requested I relay his assurance that nobody speaks of you outside this ashram."

"That was precisely my wish. I knew that man was a mind-reader."

Vadu laughed. "Actually, you asked him this morning."

"I didn't think he'd heard me, and I don't remember finishing the request."

"He heard you. Not everything is spoken with words."

Damon smiled.

He was now one of them.

BEST FRIENDS

1977
Four Years Later

They went to the late showing, since the previous two were sold out. The line wrapped around the block. Definitely worth it though. Jan and Vio (pronounced *Veeo*, only his mom called him Octavio) had waited for months for the premiere of *Star Wars*.

For Christmas, Jan got a Eumig super-8 sound movie camera, Walt Disney's *Escape from Atlantis*—trimmed into a twenty-minute film (which was really cool anyway)—and a projector to view it on.

Vio was a Trekkie. Big-time. He was going to be a director one day so he could make *Star Trek* movies and be a part of the legend.

Between school and practicing, Jan didn't have much time for TV. But Vio had been his best friend since forever, so Jan went to conventions and Vio went to recitals. Each committed to convincing the other he was equally enthusiastic about his friend's life's passion.

The Eumig was great. But although the camera belonged to Jan, he'd barely touched it since he'd unpacked the gift four months ago. Vio, on the other hand, had broken in almost every feature the Eumig had to offer.

Jan performed, Vio filmed. To date, they'd produced four movies. The first three were easy. One Chopin etude per reel.

No splicing necessary, just a bit of creative filler in the beginning and the end, because the reel was three minutes long, and most etudes ran a minute shy of that. In the fourth, Jan played Beethoven's "Appassionata," and that had required loads of editing. Vio pulled it off, making about as good a film as any professional limited to super-eight.

The next project would be a full-feature sci-fi movie. Jan owed him. Vio would have to come up with a plot and a script. Jan could memorize some lines, play a few characters, but no more. That was the deal, and Vio was completely cool with it.

He'd wanted Jan to bring the Eumig to the movie theater so they could film excerpts of the coolest parts. Vio thought it would give him ideas for their next movie. Jan could have said no right off, but instead he told his friend that movie cameras were probably not allowed in the theater, and what would happen if they ended up waiting for hours to get tickets, only to be sent away? To which Vio had responded, "Good thinking, man. Getting kicked out would have sucked. We'd have been royally screwed."

"I wouldn't have minded being royally screwed," Jan had said, without missing a beat, "if the royalty in question were Princess Leia."

Jan was going to stay over at Vio's again, so they walked back home, talking about the mind-blowing, ultracool movie they'd just seen. Jan hadn't really expected much, but even Jan had to admit that was the best flick ever. Of course, when the *Star Trek* movie came out, it would be *way* better. Vio had responded with "Duh!"

"Got a match?" The voice came from behind.

You walk in the middle of the sidewalk, never to one side. If you were too close to the curb, a car could pick you up or run you over; too close to a building, and they could pull you in. Vio and Jan were smack in the middle of the sidewalk.

You walk at a pace just fast enough to show you know exactly where you're going and that you're in a rush to get there. If you walked too fast, they'd think you were scared, and then it was game-over. Vio and Jan were moving along at just the right speed.

You never look a guy in the eyes; you look past him, like he didn't exist. There wasn't anyone in front of them to not look at.

You avoid the dark, if you can, but if you do go out in the night, you walk with another guy, never alone. Well, they had that one covered too.

Jan and Vio hadn't broken any of the cardinal rules, but for some reason, this time, it didn't matter.

Maybe the guy behind them really wanted a light?

Yeah, and maybe Jan could use the Force, and plant the mental suggestion for the guy to go home and start a new life as a law-abiding citizen.

Shit, this was really bad.

The two boys didn't break pace, but they could tell the guy was catching up.

Another man, sitting on the steps two apartment buildings ahead, got up and walked toward them.

No doubt about it anymore: they were screwed.

"Then how about your wallets, muthafuckas?"

Good thing they didn't have the Eumig with them.

The man in front of them had something in his hand. He pressed a button and a long blade flashed into view. "*Now*, honkey, I ain't got all fucking night!"

The toss-and-run would be their best option. Jan reached for his money clip. It was the last defense in a situation like this. A wallet was no good, because the muggers couldn't see the money. Filled with ones and wrapped with a twenty, the gold money clip would catch the mugger's eye for sure. Jan would throw it in one direction, and run like a jackrabbit on fire in the other. Hopefully, Vio would catch on. Ninety percent of the time, the mugger will go for the money rather than run after you. No time to think, time to a—

Two figures came running at them in the dark. Big middle-aged men, revolvers drawn.

The mugger behind them said, "Fuck this," and started to run, but Jean-Luc tackled him before he could make an escape.

Girard chased after the other man. He was trying to close the gap, maybe to get within firing range, but the guy had already turned the corner a block away.

Jean-Luc slammed the mugger against a building, knocking the wind from his lungs and the switchblade from his hand.

"Are you young men okay?" Jean-Luc asked, giving them a quick glance over his shoulder.

"Yes," Jan answered, but his shaky voice told a different story.

Jean-Luc couldn't see any immediate physical trauma on either of the two boys. He directed his attention to the assailant squirming in his grip.

"Who sent you?" Jean-Luc asked.

"The fuck you talking about, asshole? Ain't nobody sent me."

Jean-Luc pressed his revolver against the mugger's temple while crushing him against the brick wall with his shoulder. "I won't ask again."

The squirming came to a sudden stop. "Hey man, I don't know what shit you're tripping on. I tol' you, ain't nobody sent me."

Jean-Luc pulled back the hammer on his gun. "Do I look stupid to you?"

"Man, I can't even see yo ass."

Vio gave a short, nervous laugh.

Girard came running back, his face shining with sweat. He shook his head, the message clear: *Lost him.*

Jean-Luc tilted his head at the mugger: *Doesn't matter, I've got this one.*

"What was the job? Kill them, make it look like a mugging?" Jean-Luc said as Girard went to the boys.

"I ain't killed no one. This wasn't no *job.* I wanted the motherfucker's *wallet,* dig?"

"Has the city no more helpless old ladies?"

The mugger said nothing.

"Eh! I'm talking to you!" Jean-Luc gave the revolver a jolt, almost breaking the mugger's skin. "You expect me to believe you picked these young men out of the blue?"

"Ol' ladies or two white-assed pussy motherfuckers, same shit."

"*Appelez la police,*" Jean-Luc said.

Without responding, Girard looked for a pay phone to dial 911.

DHARMA

1977

It seemed nothing he said surprised Guru Dev. Maybe that would change this time.

"*Dil Chahata Hai* . . . ah . . . ostensibly," Damon couldn't remember that last word in Hindi.

In seven years, he'd only ventured from the ashram once, to get ink to color his unfortunate statue project. He got all his information on world events from Kush, a seeker who had been there for slightly over two decades, and was almost as good at Hatha yoga as Damon. Unlike the others, Kush liked to read the newspaper, and would often bring one over from the village while trading apples for sugar and ghee.

Ford had taken office on August 9, 1974, following Nixon's resignation. The new president had offered amnesty for all draft dodgers, but out of the 100,000, only a fifth had come forward.

Still, it meant that the political climate had changed. And that had been three years ago. America had new problems to worry about.

The politicians who had to cover their asses over certain questionable events that had taken place in Vietnam, Laos, and Cambodia were no longer in power. That meant the Pentagon, the NSA, the CIA, or whatever organization had once cared about Damon had probably long since put his paperwork in a file labeled "Good Riddance."

A year or so ago, Vadu had asked Damon why he continued to show interest in foreign affairs.

It was time to give him his answer.

It was just the three of them. Damon, Vadu, and Guru Dev. They spoke like this every week, a habit that had become ritual, and eventually tradition.

"I had to keep something from you, for my protection and yours."

Guru Dev smiled. One of his thousand smiles. This one prompted by the word "protection."

"By 'you,' I mean the entire ashram," Damon added.

Guru Dev did not react.

That was the way it went ninety percent of the time; Damon spoke, Guru Dev listened. Vadu was somewhere in between, playing spiritual referee.

"So we are talking about what you believe brought you here?" Vadu said.

"Yes and no." Damon had learned a thing or two: their questions often had many layers.

"The source of your stress?" Vadu asked, referring to conversations they'd had about Damon's family.

"Not exactly. We've pretty much talked that subject to death. I'm referring to something else." Damon looked Guru Dev in the eyes. "What I'm trying to say is that, at the time, there were people—bad people—looking for me."

Guru Dev was waiting for more.

"I came here seeking asylum. I'm sorry, but that is the truth." He told them about the colonel and the man from the NSA. How his last mission turned him from a man with a promising career to a fugitive from those who had set him up. "I chose this place because I thought it would serve as my best cover."

"No," Guru Dev said.

Damon knew where the master was going with this. "It was the reason I came here, but it wasn't the reason I've stayed all these years."

Guru Dev continued as if Damon hadn't interrupted. "It is a truth, a shallow truth, but it is not the real reason you are here."

"I agree, it is not the reason I am here. *Now.*"

"It is not the reason now, it wasn't the reason then. It was *a* reason, but not *the* reason. It was a product of your logic, an excuse you created so that you could come here and fulfill your real dharma, Arjuna."

"Why can't the reason be something petty, something non-spiritual? I am not proud of it, I admit it freely."

"This is an interesting question you ask. We all had our reasons to start on the path, and even if we thought our intentions were noble and spiritual, they were just as petty and earthly as yours."

"Think about what Guru Dev said," Vadu prompted. "You will understand."

Damon followed his friend's advice. "You're saying that an ignorant mind cannot—"

"Precisely!" Guru Dev said with a smile. "You see? How can an ignorant man want enlightenment when he doesn't know what freedom is? He may have explanations—things he has read, things he has heard, fantasy creations of the mind. But these all amount to ambition of the ego. So whether you came thinking you would protect yourself from those who would wish you harm, or you came believing you would attain spiritual enlightenment, as an ignorant man, any reasoning or explanation for your being here would be equally petty."

Damon was quiet for a while. "It was the action of coming here that was not petty."

Guru Dev nodded.

Having nothing more to offer, Damon did not speak.

"That you were hiding from something or someone was obvious," the old master said. "What is it you have not told us, Arjuna? What is this karma that made you scream?"

"More? About my family? I've already told you."

Guru Dev was silent.

"I turned my back on my brother, and I effectively abandoned my son, all for a career that ended up destroying my life. And I may not have caused my wife's death, but I *was* responsible for her unhappiness, which eventually led to it."

"Karma affects the environment, this is true, but you were affected by karma just as she was. We each have our own path, though your karma may have been deeply intertwined. While you may blame yourself for these things, this is not what caused you to scream in the night."

"It isn't? Are you saying there is no such thing as free will?"

Guru Dev and Vadu exchanged a quick glance.

"Are you saying my actions didn't constitute sufficient bad karma to have caused the nightmare?"

"Do not say this is *good* or *bad*. Be the observer, Arjuna, not a judge."

"I have had years to think about that night. How is it that what I have told you could not be the source of karma that caused the nightmare?"

"You were frightened when you screamed?"

"I have to say yes. I still can't believe I yelled like that. I've never done that before or since."

"So this happened before you were a warrior, when it was okay to scream."

"There was never such a time."

"You were born a warrior?" Guru Dev said, not intending it to be a joke, but Damon laughed anyway.

"Of course not. But you have to understand, that sort of thing—screaming—just didn't happen in my household. For as long as I can remember, and way before I joined the Academy."

"And before that?"

"A past life?" Damon asked.

Guru Dev ignored the question, although Vadu seemed to consider it. "Do you remember your actions with your brother?" the old master asked.

Damon nodded.

"Your son?"

Damon nodded again.

"Your wife, her death, and hiding the truth from the police to protect yourself?"

"Yes, of course, I remember everything."

"And you just told us about your last battle where your superiors turned out to be your enemies. So none of what you have told us today could be at the root of your stress, Arjuna."

Simple logic, hard to refute.

Years of spiritual ablution and Damon still could not come face to face with this damned thing. No event in his life could justify the hysterics of that evening.

"I have felt this burden in you from the day you came here, and it remains with you now. The karma hides within, waiting for the right moment to reveal itself to your conscious mind, as it did to your heart."

After an enduring silence, Damon said, "What must I do for the truth to reveal itself?"

"You must fulfill your dharma," Vadu said.

"My dharma has always been to be a soldier."

Guru Dev opened his eyes, and aimed them directly at Damon. "Is that so?"

"For as long as I can recall."

Guru Dev's eyes opened slightly more. A knowing smile grew on his face, but he didn't speak.

"That's the key isn't it?"

Nobody replied.

"Are you telling me my dharma *wasn't* to be a soldier?"

Guru Dev didn't say anything.

"Could this be linked to my dream?"

Vadu couldn't resist. "Everything is linked."

"I made a bad career choice; *that* made me scream?"

"You believe you had a choice," Vadu said.

They'd already had a long discussion on the subject of choice, and Damon hadn't been able to wrap his mind around that one before, so he wasn't about to try again. He could sense he was finally getting close to a revelation, and didn't want to be sidetracked. "It wasn't a choice, so it *was* my dharma." Damon looked at both men, couldn't get a read, and tried another answer to Vadu's question. "At the time, yes. In the beginning."

Still nothing.

Damon looked at Guru Dev, but all he received in turn was that ever-patient smile.

"Being a soldier is all I know, but I can't go back to the Army. So what else is there for me?"

"Home," Guru Dev said.

"Right now, this is the only place that feels like home."

"Then you are where you should be, Arjuna."

THE ONE-SEVEN

1977

"Yes," Jean-Luc repeated, "they are both fine."

Jean-Luc looked over at Girard, who was waiting on a bench along with Jan and Vio. The two boys were chatting and Jean-Luc was able to roll his eyes at Girard without them noticing.

"No, no, nothing like that. They are a bit shaken, that is all." He listened some more, giving this answer special attention, speaking slowly into the phone, his voice lowered. "Yes, this was my initial thinking. I have never heard of this happening to two people, especially young men. . . . Yes . . . If he had been alone, maybe . . . yes . . . of course. I questioned the mugger about this . . . no, he was clueless . . . Oh yes, he would have to be a very good actor . . . right, okay."

The desk sergeant was talking to a police officer, but every so often his eyes darted in Jean-Luc's direction, as if to warn him to keep his distance.

"No, we are still waiting to speak with someone . . . yes, at the police station. Let me give you the address . . . do you have a pen? . . . Okay. . . . It is the Seventeenth Precinct, on Fifty-First Street between Third and Lexington—Hold on, Girard is waving at me. Okay, someone has finally come to see us . . . no, not yet . . . we've been waiting all this time . . . I am not sure how long . . . yes, we'll be here . . . yes . . . okay . . . good-bye."

Jean-Luc thanked the telephone switchboard operator, met the sergeant's challenging eyes one last time, and walked over to Girard and the boys, who were being led to a corner desk by a man in civilian clothing.

The detective in charge acknowledged their presence with a brief nod. "Detective Miller. My department is actually upstairs, but we're really busy tonight. We've got a drug deal gone bad with three DOAs, a jumper, and arson we're pretty sure is linked to two other insurance-scam cases. All within two hours and the confines of the One-Seven." He took out his notebook. "So if you don't mind, we'll do this here."

After jotting down their names and listening to a synopsis of the attempted mugging, Detective Miller said, "So you're saying you'd be able to pick this other guy out in a lineup?"

In unison, Jan and Vio said, "Definitely."

The sergeant looked up at Girard, who replied, "I only saw his face for one second, before he ran, but I am also confident I could recognize him."

Jean-Luc said, "I was preoccupied with the other man, so I did not have the occasion to see the one who ran away."

The detective nodded. "Well, you boys are lucky. Nobody's hurt and we've got one of the perps in lockup. It won't take long to get him to rat his buddy out. They're not loyal; not when it comes to saving themselves time in the slammer, especially if they've got a record." He looked at Jan and Vio, cocking his head in Jean-Luc and Girard's direction. "You owe these friends of yours. If they hadn't stepped in, we might be looking at a double homicide here. All too often, these muggers figure they're better off killing their victims rather than risk leaving witnesses around."

"We are the boy's bodyguards," Jean-Luc said. "We were just doing our job."

"Bodyguards? You armed?"

"Yes, and we have shown the arresting officer our gun permits," Girard said.

"We were hired to protect him from his uncle," Jean-Luc added.

Without even asking why they considered such measures necessary, Detective Miller said, "What's this uncle's name?"

"Damon van Luden," Jean-Luc said.

The detective frowned, pecked on the notepad with his finger, and flicked it across the table to Jean-Luc. "You mind spelling that?" He tossed him a gnawed pencil. It had been chewed almost to the lead.

Jean-Luc pulled a fountain pen from his breast pocket and started writing, pushing away the pencil with the edge of the notebook. "He's kidnapped before."

"A custody battle?"

"Something of that nature," Jean-Luc replied, avoiding Jan's look.

"Where is this van Luden guy now?" The detective asked.

"Nobody knows. He's MIA."

"MIA?" the detective said, as if he'd misheard.

"Vietnam," Girard said. "He could be a POW, or he could be dead. He could also be right here, in this city, looking for the boy."

"So that's how you ended up at the scene and were able to stop the mugging?"

Girard was ready to reply, but Jean-Luc hushed him with a look. "May I have a word with you in private?"

"Private?" the detective said, as if he'd never heard the word before. "Uh . . . Look, I'm sorry but I'm really busy—"

Jean-Luc leaned over to the detective, speaking in his ear. "I don't want to frighten the boys. We think it might have been an attempt at murder which was supposed to appear like a mugging."

Vio and Jan exchanged the same he-thinks-we're-too-young-to-hear-this look.

Either Jean-Luc smelled bad, or what he'd just said had given the detective an equivalent reaction.

When the Frenchman receded into his seat, the detective dropped his notebook on the desk. "I've got to tell you, the way I see it we're just looking at a couple of junkies after some cash to fund their next fix."

Jean-Luc said, "Perhaps, yes. But the one I stopped seemed quite coherent to me. Enough so that he would not risk stealing from two young men unless he had more incentive than what he could expect to find in their wallets."

"You're saying they were hired help." The tedium in his voice made it impossible to tell if this was a question or an assertion.

Jean-Luc leaned forward. "Precisely."

The detective looked at his watch. "Well, unless you have something else you'd like to add, I really have to get back to—"

"Hey, where are you going?" The TS could be heard across the floor.

The uniformed officer who'd been talking with the sergeant chased after them. "Sir? Ma'am? Just a minute!"

Jean-Luc said something to the detective, who responded by waving the couple to his desk. Addressing the uniformed officer, Detective Miller said, "It's okay, they're with me."

The police officer reluctantly stopped his pursuit, mumbling something like "Procedure in this damned place."

She held Jan tightly in her arms, then pulled back enough to examine him top to bottom. "Are you all right, honey?"

Jan blushed. "Ma, they're looking at us."

"Let them," Dorothy said.

Kory put his hand on Jan's shoulder. "Are you okay?"

"Yeah, Dad, I'm fine."

"Vio? How about you?" Without waiting for a reply, Dorothy turned to Jean-Luc. "Did you contact his parents too?"

He shook his head. "I—"

"I thought it would be better if you called them, Mrs. van Luden," Vio said.

In all the excitement, she'd almost ignored her own rules. Vio knew about the bodyguards; his parents did not. Letting him in on a few family secrets had been unavoidable—after all, the boy was like a brother to Jan.

"Oh, of course, honey. I'll do that right now." Addressing the detective: "May I?"

"You can't get an outside line on this," the detective said, then pointed at the sergeant's desk, "but there's a phone over there you can use."

Dorothy hesitated, looking back at her son. At this moment, more than ever, she didn't want to leave him alone. Not even for a second.

PART VII

RESURRECTION

1980
Three Years Later

Damon watched himself leave the ashram, and say good-bye
to the students—his friends, all. He observed as Guru Dev
had taught him—without the interference of thought. He'd
expected to take his time with Kush, Vadu, and certainly Guru
Dev. Like sipping extraordinary wine. That was not to be.

Good-byes aside, there had been no special ceremony;
nothing that would distinguish that day from any other. What
would have taken hours with words was spoken instead with
one cameraless snapshot. The image of his three friends standing together, smiling, became a framed photograph on permanent display in the office that was Damon's mind.

Kush, Vadu, and Guru Dev. Smiling as if to say good night
instead of good-bye.

Like the separation would never take place.

For them, it never would.

The man sitting next to Damon on the Air Canada flight, currently tracking a great circle path to Toronto, was eager for
conversation. He was a businessman returning from a two-
week annual conference in Paris. He had a three-year-old

daughter. Not receiving Damon's admiring approval the first time, he mentioned again how his company would cover the hotel phone bill. He spoke with his daughter every day from the hotel. Now he would see her.

Damon nodded politely. When the man stopped talking, Damon closed his eyes and meditated.

The man next to him spoke as if there'd been no interruption to his entirely one-sided conversation. "We should be there in under an hour."

As if to save face from Damon's lack of response, the businessman pulled out an issue of *Time*, cracking it open as though it were a newspaper. Damon was able to take in most of the cover at a glance. It showed a charging faceless soldier in basic fighting greens with his bayonet in place for hand-to-hand combat. In yellow letters it asked, WHO'LL FIGHT FOR AMERICA? Under the soldier's M16 was the qualifier "The Manpower Crisis."

Apparently, the military was having staffing problems. Which made sense. After the way soldiers were treated during and after the war, this crisis didn't surprise Damon in the least. Maybe politicians would one day figure it out, but he had serious doubts—the Republican nominee was a Hollywood actor.

The world had changed a lot in ten years.

And Damon's passport, the one Fred had given him almost a decade earlier, was soon to expire. Getting another fake on his own, one made in Delhi, would have been too expensive, too risky, and far too difficult. He was out of touch with all his contacts now and had no assurances they could be trusted even if he could locate them. Like his driver's license, his passport expired in '81, and that gave him just six months' use out of both. He barely had enough money for his ticket. He would need to show the Canadian authorities a return ticket, and procuring one had been an additional cost he hadn't anticipated—a cost the ashram had covered at Guru Dev's insistence. While he could try showing up in Canada as Damon van Luden, the Army might still be looking for him, as unlikely as that was, and there was no point in throwing ten years of precaution out the window.

That had been the practical explanation for leaving the ashram. It had come more by way of habit than to fulfill any genuine need to understand what were ultimately the workings beyond the control of the thinking mind. Returning home was not about expiration dates on documents any more than going to the ashram had been about seeking asylum. This was about dharma. It had always been so.

"You travel much?"

Damon offered the man a smile. It was a kind smile. A smile foreign to the Damon of ten years ago. "Not by airplane."

"I figured you for a frequent flier. Usually people need a few thousand miles under their belt before they can sleep so soundly on a flight."

"Actually, I haven't been on an airplane in ten years."

"You've been gone from Canada for ten years?"

"This will be my first time in Canada."

"Really? Where are you from?"

"Good question."

That piqued the man's interest.

That was not what Damon was after, so he served a truth-lie cocktail. "I'm originally from Norway, but raised in New York. Can't speak a lick of Norwegian, though that never seemed to bother my mother."

"When you say 'New York,' you mean the city?"

"No, a small town you've probably never heard of."

"So you haven't been back to the States in ten years?"

Damon nodded, not liking where this was going.

"If you don't mind my asking, where were you all this time?"

"Vie—ah—here and there. India. Mostly, India," Damon said, making a mental note to spend more time thinking before he spoke. The spontaneous honesty he'd been used to at the ashram was tripping him up.

The businessman thought about this. "That's a very long time. I've been gone sixteen days and it feels like an eternity. It really is a long time when they are that young. They grow like crazy at that age. You can almost see the difference overnight."

"Yes, I can relate. I'm going home to see my son. I imagine he's done his share of growing up too."

As Damon handed over his passport and ticket, the Canadian immigration inspector asked, "Purpose of your visit?"

"Pleasure." They only gave you two choices, and "business" could prompt more questions. "Pleasure" was the safer bet.

The inspector looked at the photo, then up at Damon, and back down at the passport. He did this three times. Damon must have appeared deflated in his ten-year-old suit, and although he had shaved before leaving for Delhi, he had changed from the likeness in the antiquated passport photo. Yoga didn't maintain bulk, and he had given up on Western forms of exercise many years ago.

"How long will you be staying, Mr. Knutson?"

With a return ticket, the Canadian embassy had informed him, there was no need for a visa. Which was good, because Damon wasn't about to try putting a visa on a doctored Norwegian passport.

The inspector would check his response with the date of return indicated on the ticket. The Canadians needed reassurance that he wouldn't end up becoming a burden to their country—they had plenty of illegal immigrants to worry about as it was.

"Two weeks," Damon said.

The inspector nodded as he handed Damon the passport and the ticket. "Enjoy your stay in Canada."

There wasn't much of a line, and when it became Damon's turn, customs took all of twenty seconds. He had purchased a modestly sized suitcase before his trip, one that would not look incongruous with his suit. He'd transferred the few remaining earthly possessions he'd kept from his past life minus the drab green duffel bag.

The next day Damon took the bus from Toronto to Niagara Falls.

He had been to Niagara Falls before, as a child. When had that been? Thirty-five years ago?

He'd been a little boy of no more than six. Had his father taken him? No, he would have been in a wheelchair, and Nicholas hadn't left home after returning from the war. Was it his mother? Couldn't have been. She would not have left her husband's side.

He remembered someone smiling down at him—a woman—but her face refused to take shape. It felt like he was even younger than six.

Five? Four?

Four.

If that were the case, it had to have been sometime at the end of 1943, when his father was in Europe, fighting the Nazis.

Damon would have remembered Kory, had he been with him, so his little brother couldn't have been born yet. That meant his mother was pregnant, and therefore wouldn't have been gallivanting around upstate New York.

Then it came to him: his aunt Mary had come over to help her sister.

So *Mary* had taken him to Niagara Falls.

He pictured himself eating cotton candy. Was that here or in Coney Island? He was sure he'd been there, too. Damon couldn't remember, although he could almost taste the sticky pink goo on his lips.

A stream of images unleashed themselves. She was holding a book. She'd been reading to him: a Dr. Seuss book. It was large, with a red cover, and a bright color illustration of green eggs and ham. He remembered laughing . . . such a simple joy.

Damon watched the children with their parents as they played in the grass with the rushing sound of the falls in the backdrop. The children here were laughing too, as effortlessly as drawing a breath.

He realized just then that this was the first childhood memory he had of himself laughing.

Did Kory ever laugh? Or Jan, for that matter? He couldn't recall one instance.

And the only memories he had of his wife laughing were in sardonic retribution.

He waited for a while, spotted what he was looking for, and joined a group as they crossed Rainbow Bridge to America.

As he made his way across, he looked over at the falls. The beauty of it mesmerized him. He lost track of time as he stood there watching.

The US immigration inspector let most of the people through without even bothering with IDs. "Americans?"

A man holding what appeared to be a miniature movie camera in one hand answered in the affirmative on behalf of what must have been a group of at least three families. The immigration inspector waved them all through.

He stopped Damon, who didn't have Madeleine to help give him that tourist look.

"Good afternoon, sir," Damon said, offering him his phony New York driver's license. Fred had decided to keep the driver's license under the same name as the passport, explaining that it was safer that way. "Busy day?"

The inspector glanced at the driver's license and handed it back. "Yeah, it's always like this in the tourist season."

Damon smiled and walked past the inspector into the United States of America and his home state of New York.

He found himself drawn to the water again. This time his view was of the Canadian falls.

He watched the falls for a while longer, gathering his thoughts while he eyed a pay phone.

There was a fistful of quarters in his right pocket. He had exchanged all the money he had into US dollars. The hotel accepted American currency, so there was no point in getting both Canadian and US dollars. His rupees hadn't gone very far—just two hundred dollars' worth. He had been out of touch for a very long time, but he knew that after an oil crisis and double-digit inflation, his two Benjamins wouldn't get him far.

He called Information, got the number for Livingsford, and spoke with a lady at the Office of the Registrar. Her response had been unexpected. Something wasn't right.

Time to call home.

Someone picked up on the second ring.

"Hello?"

It was Mary. There was no doubt in Damon's mind. She had this way of speaking, as if she'd been trained as an actress during the Hollywood '40s.

"Mary? Aunt Mary?"

After a moment's hesitation: "Who is this?"

"Mary? It's me, Damon."

If not for the slight background hiss, he would have thought they'd been disconnected.

"Mary?"

"What do you want?" Her voice was small, tight with shock.

"Mary? It's me, Damon."

She did not answer.

He should have been better prepared for her hostility. He hadn't prepared for anything in a very long time.

There hadn't been a need. It didn't seem to come naturally anymore.

The war was over.

Only the war in Vietnam.

Out loud, Damon said, "I'd like to see my son."

More silence.

"When can I see him?"

No answer.

"Mary?"

"I don't think that would be a good idea."

It was time to play his card. "I called the school. They don't have Jan van Luden on the graduation list. Not this year, not the last."

"The graduation ceremony isn't until next week."

"That's not what they told me; they said it was tomorrow. I had them check—they don't have any record of Jan at their school."

"Which school did you call?"

"*Which* school? Livingsford, of course."

"He doesn't go to Livingsford."

It was Damon's turn to be silent. "Where *does* he go to school?"

"UNIS," Mary said. "It's a school in lower Manhattan."

"Why Manhattan? What was wrong with Livingsford?"

"UNIS is an international school; it was the right choice for Jan—" Her voice sharpened. "I don't have to explain myself to you—" Now she was speaking quickly. "You haven't bothered calling or even writing. You don't show any signs of life in over a decade, and *now* you're concerned about Jan's well-being?"

"I'm his father, for Christ's sake—"

The line went dead.

Damon hung up the phone, walking slowly toward the beckoning falls.

The steady rumble—thousands of gallons of water crushing in on itself—lured him to the railing, where a child was on his toes peering through big binoculars planted into the cement balcony on the precipice.

Damon watched the water, the light dancing on its surface as it fell and fell.

Mary reading *Green Eggs and Ham*.

Smiling.

You don't show any signs of life, and now you're concerned about Jan's well-being?

Damon laughing.

Cotton candy.

A seagull landed on the thick railing just a foot away, its orange feet almost too bright to be real. For a moment, it seemed to be staring at Damon, and then it flew away, as if to deliver some message.

GENERAL ASSEMBLY

June 1980

She tried to speak, but as it turned out, one look from her was sufficient.

John had thought it strange that his wife had been standing throughout the conversation, but unable to see her expression, let alone make out what she'd been saying from across the way, there hadn't been any initial cause for alarm.

"What is it?"

Mary didn't turn to him. Instead, she sat down with care, as if the sofa would not otherwise support her weight. "He's back."

He had to strain to hear, but there was no mistaking what she'd said. While impossible to believe, he knew immediately to whom she was referring.

It took him a while to articulate his next question. "Where is he?"

Mary did not reply.

John let the question linger, for he suddenly lacked the resources to speak. This couldn't be happening. Mr. Chambers had told them Damon was MIA. And while that didn't necessarily mean he was dead—he could have been detained at a prison camp—after ten years, it had been a fair assumption. John barely heard himself speak. "What did he say?"

When she was through, John said, "I can't believe you told him Jan goes to UNIS."

She regarded him closely. There was no malice written into his face, only concern. "I wasn't thinking. I should have hung up sooner."

"He knows where Jan is. He's going to go after him; you realize that, right?"

Mary looked away.

He wanted his pipe, a craving he hadn't felt since he'd given up smoking.

Mary said, "I was taken by surprise. I couldn't think. When I realized what was happening, I hung up."

"He's come for the money," John said, ignoring his wife for fear that he might otherwise lose his train of thought. The lawyer had explained the details of the trust. Once Jan became a legal adult, Damon would have no claim over any of his mother's estate—the boy would have full control of the entire fortune. "It's no coincidence he shows up just two months before Jan's eighteenth birthday."

Mary appeared to be studying the shiny surface of the leather armrest. She knew exactly where he was going with this, but nonetheless offered, "Perhaps he's planning on returning as the war hero, hoping Jan will be impressed or possibly even take pity."

John shook his head, though he couldn't really fault her for clinging to hope. Besides, it went along with Kory's original theory: Damon had wanted Jan in boarding school—far from his grandparents—so that as soon as the Army would allow, he could return to America and once again exert his influence. Winning over the boy, he could control the entire trust by proxy.

It had been along this line of thinking that Kory had the French bodyguards demand that they continue working for Damon. A tactically brilliant move that unfortunately had no effect. In all the years Damon was gone, he hadn't once made contact with the bodyguards to inquire about Jan. Whether he was unable or unwilling to do so, nobody knew. He might have sensed they could not be trusted and hired outside help.

In half a day's work, any dimestore detective could easily have come up with devastating information. And given the time and money, a first-rate investigator might even have discovered that Jan wasn't Damon's son.

In arguing his case for having the bodyguards watch over Jan, Kory had warned that were his brother to feel betrayed, he could kill Jan just as easily as he had killed Dollie. He said that even assuming Damon had somehow outgrown his murderous jealousy, his chances for influencing Jan, and thereby controlling the trust, were diminishing with each passing year.

Whether he was motivated by jealous vengefulness or just money, there was no doubt what Damon was here to do.

"Ten years ago, he might have come back for that reason," John said. "But at this point, it would make no sense."

"Could he have discovered a loophole somewhere, something Mr. Chambers may have overlooked?"

"He hasn't found any loopholes. There aren't any. Your sister had the trust written by one of the best tax attorneys in New York." John Saunders stretched out a sigh. "Kory has been right all along. I should have listened to him from the beginning. There might have been time to stop Damon right there in Vermont. I could have saved my daughter from—"

Mary put her hand on his. "He was a child; we thought he was jealous."

"When Jan was born, Kory said Damon married for the money. We didn't listen then, either. And again with the bodyguards, remember?—after all that had happened up to that point—I still thought he was overreacting. God, I'm glad I kept my mouth shut."

"That was three years ago, and the police said it was a mugging," Mary reminded him.

"Yes, but if Kory hadn't hired those men, who knows what would have become of the two boys?"

Mary said nothing.

"I've been such a damned fool."

"So you think Kory was right? If Damon returns after all this time it's to hurt Jan?"

"Oh, yes," John said, anger coloring over his voice, "and Damon's not here to hurt Jan, he's come to kill him."

Mary squeezed his hands, her nails almost drawing blood. "What are we to do?"

John grabbed for the receiver. "We're going to call Kory, that's what we're going to do."

As he waited for someone to pick up, Mary said, "I'm his aunt, I should be the one to tell him."

John considered this, drew a sigh, and handed her the phone.

"May I speak with Professor van Luden, please? Yes, I'm his aunt, Mary Thorn . . . Oh . . . When will it be over? . . . I see . . . No, this is urgent. Please have him call me the moment he comes out."

When she hung up, John said, "Not there?"

"Lecturing." Mary consulted her wristwatch. "Class should be over soon. She promised she'd get the word over to him immediately."

"I just hope *immediately* is soon enough."

Kory left class, thinking he'd bypass his office after this last lecture. It had been a long day, and he really wanted to beat rush hour and take the subway home.

He walked through a stream of college kids, squeezing past the double doors to Philosophy Hall. A bony hand grabbed his arm, pulling him to the side. It was Sandy, his secretary.

"I wasn't sure I'd catch you. You need to call your aunt."

"I'll call her once I get home."

"Call her now."

Kory frowned. Sandy was a good assistant, but she could get bossy when she thought he was fogging out. That was her expression for it, he—

"Professor? She said it was urgent."

Still holding on to his arm, Sandy guided him to his office, as if he wouldn't otherwise know where to find it.

"What's this about?" Kory asked once they'd arrived.

Sandy held out the phone at an angle that seemed to promise she'd whack him over the head with it unless he did as instructed. When he started dialing she said, "I'll close the door to give you some privacy."

"Hi, John, it's Kory. Mary called, my secretary said it was important—"

Kory heard his aunt asking her husband to give her the phone. There was a rustle as the receiver changed hands.

"Kory, honey?"

Dread squeezed the breath from his lungs—he'd heard that tone before. The conciliatory voice that tells you someone you love is dead.

That morning, Jan had left earlier than usual, and Kory had some special time with his wife. Afterward, Dorothy had jokingly said they should do this more often so that the primitive part of his brain would be less susceptible to the cute teenagers in his Philosophy of Science class. They'd had a great breakfast, his favorite: french toast, an omelet with Swiss cheese, and freshly baked baguette. He'd almost told the chauffeur he was going to walk all the way to Columbia University.

Suddenly his life felt as though it were being held at gunpoint, and Mary, the unwilling messenger, would at any moment pull the trig—

"Honey, Damon called."

Kory shut his eyes.

She might as well have really killed him. That way his last memories would have been of his morning with Dorothy.

"Kory, darling? Did you hear me? It sounds like he's in the States, I don't know where, but he wants to see Jan. He asked me where I could find him. Kory, are you there?"

"I'm here," Kory said, his voice twenty years heavier. "Tell me precisely what he said—word for word."

There was no question what Damon's intentions were now. He'd waited just long enough to almost be forgotten. Like the earthquake destined to one day devastate San Francisco, but delaying until complacency soaked into the core of everyone living there. That way their shock, just moments before their final moments on this earth, would make the agony of death absolute.

How can San Franciscans live like that, lying to themselves every single day? Worrying about root canals or making the next mortgage payment instead of facing the prospect of being swallowed alive down a throat of rock and asphalt. Unlike the

inhabitants of Northern California who passively faced a growing risk, Kory had both acknowledged the danger to his family
and had taken every prophylactic action he could conceive,
the ever-decreasing likelihood of Damon's return notwithstanding. But no matter how forcefully he'd resisted, with time,
hope had grown stronger and his convictions weaker . . .

"And then I finally hung up. John and I are worried Jan
might be in danger."

"How long has it been since he called?"

"An hour or so?" Mary said. "Why, do you think he could
find Jan right now?"

"I doubt it. This was the first he'd heard about UNIS, so it is
unlikely he's in the city. Knowing how he thinks, he's probably
in New Hampshire. His original plan may have been to find
Jan there, kill him, and make it look like an accident. Putting
Jan in another school may have saved my son's life. Damon was
MIA for ten years, and officially presumed dead, so the police
could never suspect him for murder. He would have slipped
out of the country before any of us could have claimed him as
a potential suspect. Not finding Jan where he expected him to
be foiled his plans, forcing him to call."

"But—"

"Yes, I know," Kory interrupted. "It doesn't make sense to
give up such a powerful advantage. By calling you, he forfeited
the element of surprise. That wouldn't make sense. Good
point. I have to think about this."

"It *is* a good point, but I must admit that wasn't what I was
thinking. As I told you before, I cannot remember for certain,
but I think he said he'd *called* Livingsford rather than inquiring
in person."

"Yes, and he could have simply said that to throw you off."

"But you're right, why give away his presence?"

"That worries me, however we must not lose sight of the
greatest threat: Damon somehow getting to Jan before we can
protect him."

"Do you think he could find him so quickly?"

"On one hand, Damon would have no reason to assume Jan
was in Manhattan. On the other, we have no way of knowing
where he called you from. We also don't know how long he's

been back in the States. It could be one day, it could be a week. If he's in the country, and just arrived, he probably came in through JFK, and that's just a forty-five-minute cab ride into Manhattan."

"Oh dear Lord. Honey, you must call Jan."

"Jan has finished his final exams, and the only thing left is the commencement ceremony next week. He's either at home practicing, or he's with Vio."

"You don't know?"

"I'll find him, don't worry. Again—and trust me when I say I am not in any way underestimating my brother's ability at deception and planning for every contingency—it seems highly unlikely Damon could get to Jan before I can. Assuming Damon did call you from JFK and then immediately grabbed a cab to UNIS, he'd still be on his way, even in light traffic. The only way to get to UNIS sooner would be to charter a helicopter to the Thirty-Fourth Street heliport. From there, it's a five-minute walk. And even if he's there, the remaining staff would tell him Jan was not presently in school, and I doubt they'd just give him Jan's home address. He'd have to do some investigating to find him, and even *I* am not sure where Jan is now."

"What can I do?"

"Stay by the phone. I'm going to hang up now and call home, and if he's not there, my next call will be to Vio's place. If I still can't locate him then, one of the two bodyguards will know where he is. Either way, I'm going to need their help now more than ever."

"Kory?"

"Don't worry, Aunt Mary. I give you my word: my brother is not going to hurt another person again."

Damon slipped through one of the double doors.

UNIS held their graduation ceremony in the UN General Assembly building. Invitations were given, but it was more for notification purposes—anybody who knew about it could attend. Half a year earlier, the pope had come on a visit, and security measures had been very high. Today was just another graduation ceremony for the UN school, and so one only had to say where one was going in order to gain admittance.

As planned, the ceremony had commenced. Unless they'd changed Jan's last name, he wouldn't be up on the podium until the very end, so there'd been no reason for Damon to show up earlier.

The auditorium was almost filled to capacity. The high school principal was introducing Kurt Waldheim, who had been the first to notice Damon's tardy arrival.

The UN Secretary General, still seated, had looked up for a moment drawing his attention away from the principal at the podium. Heads followed his gaze. This was Damon's chance to identify his son.

But he couldn't spot Jan. He would be taller, of course, already a young man. If Jan wasn't among those for whom curiosity had played the better hand, Damon would be hard pressed to single him out, especially from behind.

There was a commotion in row three, just left of center. A man stood.

Kory looked different at first, but in a matter of seconds the man Damon saw was reconciled with the teenager Damon remembered. This was no adolescent, but he didn't look anything like someone in his thirties, either. No potbelly lurking under his suit jacket. No bald patch or even receding hair. He wore what looked like the very same round, rimless glasses. After all these years, however, they had to be a different pair. At thirty-six, Kory van Luden looked like a healthy man in his mid-twenties. Damon wondered how he must appear to his brother.

He smiled, but Kory did not reciprocate.

At that moment, two men stood. It made no sense whatsoever for them to be there, but there was no questioning what Damon was seeing.

Both of them had changed, and in their case, the years had not been kind. Pregnant with blubber, Girard appeared to have lost his chin.

Damon was pleasantly surprised to see his brother appear at his nephew's graduation. Damon scanned the crowd but couldn't locate his aunt Mary or John. Jan could very well have been seated elsewhere along with the other graduates.

The two bodyguards were slowly jogging up the aisles on opposite sides of the auditorium. Both wore expressions that said they meant business.

They walked up to him at a calculated distance, just shy of kicking range.

Damon could no longer see his brother.

"Get out, now. We don't want a scene." It was Jean-Luc, his French accent no less intense, even after all this time.

Damon's eyebrows lifted a full inch, but the rest of him did not move.

"And this new year brings on a new decade and a new promise for the youth . . ." the principal said, continuing his speech, but he was pausing at the wrong times, watching the developing scene at the exit with jittery eyes.

"Who's *we?*" Damon said softly.

Girard edged back half a step, his eyes darting nervously between Damon and Jean-Luc.

"Please," Jean-Luc said, "let us talk outside."

Damon considered this for a moment, and held the door open. Neither of them moved, so he exited the auditorium first.

Once all three men were outside with the door closed, Damon said, "So *now* are you going to answer my question?"

Jean-Luc obliged. "Mr. van Luden and his family do not want you here."

"*I* am Mr. van Luden, and that's *my* family in there," Damon said, his voice low.

Jean-Luc's eyes became narrow slits. "Do not make this hard for us. I strongly urge you to leave."

"Is there some law against me seeing my son on his graduation day?"

"Do not talk to us about the law, Mr. van Luden," Girard sneered. "Not to *us.*"

"Need I remind you, gentlemen, that cover-up was your idea? The last time we spoke, you blackmailed me for continued employment. There's a standing order for monthly payments to your account. Are you not receiving the money?"

"We are. Not to appear ungracious, Monsieur, but we no longer work for you."

"Fine by me," Damon said.

"We work for your brother."

"And why—"

Jean-Luc smiled. "Because he pays better."

Damon looked at the Frenchman. "I can see how that would motivate you, but that's not what I was asking. I want to know what use my brother could possibly have of your services."

"That does not concern you," Girard cut in.

"Fine. Listen, I don't want to make anything difficult for anybody. I just want to see my son. If Kory doesn't wish to see me, that's his prerogative. I'm here to see Jan."

"Then come to Rhodes, you can see him there. Tomorrow at eleven hundred."

"You can say *eleven a.m.*—I'm not in the military anymore."

"So we've heard."

"Okay, let me get this straight. I want to attend my son's graduation, and you two want to prevent me?"

"No. We want you to leave."

"And if I don't? If I just go in?"

Girard took a full step back, one hand slipping into his breast pocket.

Damon was still, but completely at ease.

Girard had his gun out as Jean-Luc drew his. "I'm warning you, keep away. Do not attack us or we will shoot."

"Attack you?"

"Yes, we saw you reaching for a knife."

Damon smiled, amused. "I don't have a knife, Girard."

"If you force us to shoot," Girard said, "we'll put one in your dead hands."

"We have character witnesses," Jean-Luc added, "and you, Monsieur, have motive, opportunity, and as a Special Forces veteran, more than sufficient ability. But killing you would mean we are inconvenienced by the New York legal system. So please come over tomorrow and save everyone the trouble."

"You are not on US territory," Damon pointed out, "and therefore you are not within the confines of New York jurisdiction. There are UN guards everywhere." Damon pointed to a figure in the distance. "See?"

"Should we be forced to defend ourselves, UN jurisdiction, New York jurisdiction, it makes no difference—you will be dead."

Damon considered his options.

A decade earlier, in this situation, these two would be on the ground.

"Very well," Damon said, "tomorrow at eleven."

THE VAN LUDEN TRUST

1980

To Damon's surprise, he realized the bus was already approaching the outskirts of Rhodes.

Now there was barely enough time to go over his situation, an imperative he'd for some reason been avoiding since the day before. He had enough money to get him through another two weeks, three tops. The two detectives who used to work for him had become turncoats. Obviously, his brother no longer wanted to see him, and from the sound of his aunt Mary's voice the other day, he probably wasn't the only one who felt that way. What had happened over the years to turn him from lamentable kinsman to leprous stranger? Thus far he was unable to come up with a reasonable answer. Time was supposed to heal old wounds, not infect them.

Damon watched the passing trees. Emerald clouds perched on stems, blended together in a dreamlike blur, like a sea of green cotton candy raised in a toast by a battalion of children.

The Army had taught him to plan, assess, and then reassess; but he could neither muster the enthusiasm to think and behave as he once did nor convince himself the old approach held any value for him in the here and now.

How intensely beautiful this country was. Each time he looked, he seemed to notice for the first time.

New England houses floated past his window with increasing frequency. There had been plenty of development in the decade that had passed: colossal shopping centers with expansive parking lots appeared where there once had been nothing but New England pine. This new world superimposed itself on his memory like a transparency over a map. The disorienting and the familiar joined in a bizarre and disquieting union.

The ashram had been sheltered from the anguish and tension of what was by some—especially Americans—considered a normal life. Introspection had brought forth the karma-induced stress of his past, in a long process of release and cleansing. While one day had not been outwardly distinguishable from the next, cushioned under a blanket of simplicity and routine, his life there had been anything but dull—the journey through the world within an exploration more intense than any found on this earth or beyond.

Back home the workings of nature were quite different than those found in Rishikesh, but no less of a delight to the eye. As he plodded south through gorgeous upstate New York, he felt no different than he had the day before when confronted at gunpoint by his former employees.

Damon warned himself of the dangers of underestimating Kali, for to do so would be to fight her. And that's just what the goddess wanted. A hopeless battle. Like fighting thought in order to be free from it. The best course of action is to allow her to do as she pleases, accept her as a guest, and wait until she is ready to leave of her own volition. He shouldn't attempt to coax her into leaving, and neither should she be wooed. Both tactics would invariably fail.

The bus arrived at a completely remodeled station. It was exactly where it had always been—the northeast corner of Main and Crescent—but only its location remained the same. It now looked more like an embellished log cabin than a bus station. There was a little gift shop, two ticket counters, and a desk with an elegantly engraved sign proclaiming INFORMATION.

Those who lived there, in the new part of town, drove; those living in the old section were chauffeured. At least, that was how it used to be. Not anymore. The station was clearly a hive for less well-to-do tourists, no longer serving primarily as transportation for the non-live-in help.

Damon glanced at his wristwatch. He had half an hour. The walk home took fifteen minutes, just ten with the shortcut. There was no rush, so he chose a route that would take him through town.

At the Hallmark store, he queried a young lady working there about the changes he'd observed in his hometown. Happy to oblige, she explained that Rhodes, built by reclusive upper-class New Yorkers, had grown to become a hot spot for the nouveaux riches. Everyone with plenty of cash to spare who wished to avoid the madness of the city came to this town. The past ten years had been a gold rush for real estate in the area. Damon asked about the van Luden estate, but she hadn't heard of it and was quick to add that this was just her second month. She was a junior at Middlebury, making some summer vacation money. Though he hadn't inquired, she went on to mention that she was staying with a boyfriend from college, and they were seriously involved. Damon offered his congratulations and thanked her for graciously reciting the history of Rhodes, the learning of which, by her own admission, had been one of the requirements for her getting the job.

He walked up past Route One. They had built a convex mirror the size of Roman shields on both sides of the winding road. Where Dollie had died, caution signs warned of pedestrians crossing.

Three hundred meters from his mother's estate, Damon stopped to gather his bearings. This was the right place—he'd come from this very path thousands of times before—but from this point on there was little to recognize. The gate had been completely redone and had grown to three times its original size. A well-thought-out combination of classical design combined with highly advanced gadgetry, including two camouflaged cameras perched on each pillar. They moved by remote control. He hadn't expected the technology to become so quickly available to civilians.

Two sentries manned each pillar. They were dressed in dark suits and shades, and held walkie-talkies. At this time of year, sunglasses may have been warranted, but these two seemed the type to never remove them, even indoors. The Pentagon should have such security.

"My name is Damon van Luden. My son is expecting me."

One of them pulled out a radio. "He's here."

From the radio, a voice said, "Check him, then send him through."

"If you don't mind," one of them said, approaching.

"Don't mind what?" Before Damon could finish his question, one of the guys raised his arms to the side in pantomime.

Damon complied with an amused smile as one of them patted him down.

The gates swung leisurely open on their own, further demonstrating the modernization that had taken place during Damon's long absence. On the other side, a chauffeur motioned him into the back of the limo.

"I can walk," Damon said, demonstrating his point.

There were two men in the back of the stretch Mercedes; one got out. It was Girard. "Good morning, glad you could come. Please allow us to escort you."

"Why, did they move the house?"

Nobody laughed.

Girard and Jean-Luc sat in the back, and despite the cavernous space available, they sandwiched Damon between them.

Silly, really: if Damon wanted to disable them, he'd have no problems given that they were both within elbow's range.

It began to make sense when, without speaking, the guards he'd seen outside took seats facing Damon on the other side of the expansive interior.

Still, not good enough.

They had to be thinking the same thing—once the limousine started through the gates, the sentries drew their revolvers, resting them on their laps.

Friendly bunch.

A half-mile drive later, the chauffeur opened the door and Jean-Luc and Girard flanked Damon all the way to the main entrance.

"As much as I love you guys, enough is enough. Do you mind? I'd like to be alone with my son."

"I'm afraid we *do* mind. You come with us or you leave. Take your pick," Girard said.

An Asian, possibly a Korean, answered the door. Dressed in a black suit with a bowtie, he flashed a hospitable smile. "Good morning. Welcome to the van Luden estate."

"And good morning to you, good sir," Damon said. "I've come to see my son, Jan van Luden."

The butler seemed confused. Girard answered for him. "That's okay, he's with us." Then to Damon: "Follow me."

"Thanks. How delightful—a personal guided tour of my own house."

"This never was your house."

"I see. I was born in Fort Bragg, a readymade twenty-five-year-old soldier."

"You've become a regular comedian," Girard said, as though the prospect made Damon an even greater threat.

Damon was led to the conference room. When Nicholas died, Martha had sealed it off, the curtains shut with orders never to open them again, and she'd left her nine-foot grand piano covered in black, like Goliath's coffin, a standing metaphor for the death of her husband, her career, and along with it, her love for life.

Now every curtain was drawn, and the chandelier was ablaze with diamond bulbs so bright they made a difference even with the morning sun pouring in from each of the six ten-foot windows.

Martha's grand was uncovered, its lid fully open like the sail of a majestic schooner. The ebony lid reflected the golden glow from the harp within the piano case. She had once played there, and for a large, devoted audience. Back when this was the music room. One of Damon's earliest recollections, from when he was only three, was of his mother playing the most beautiful music he had ever heard. His father was there, and in this version of the memory, he was looking at Damon with pride, as if he had been playing, not his mother. It was the only image he retained of his father and his mother together before Nicholas had been crippled in the war.

This had always been a very special room. A room reserved for special occasions. It felt wrong to barge in on its sanctity; worse still, escorted by two foreigners and a pair of armed strangers with the cumulative self-importance of a dozen Secret Service agents.

There they were, only seconds ago talking, now all of them mute. They were seated at the conference table.

Mary was sitting in his mother's chair. Mr. Chambers was seated next to her, at the head of the table. John, looking aged, was by his wife, clearly uncomfortable with the approaching armed men. Next to Kory was an empty seat, presumably for Damon.

Jan was not there.

Everyone at the table followed Damon's approach with suspicious, watchful eyes. He was guided to a chair on the opposite side of the table from his brother. The closest person to Damon was Mr. Chambers, and he wasn't even at a body-length's distance. Jean-Luc and Girard stood behind Damon, and it soon became apparent they weren't about to leave. The other two bodyguards, the guys with the sunglasses, stood at opposing corners of the room, their pistols in hand, but pointing at the ground.

"Hello, everyone," Damon said with cheer and a grin.

He was favored by three icy stares from his family and an acknowledging nod from Mr. Chambers.

"What a lovely reception you've arranged," Damon said, "but we seem to be missing someone."

Kory looked behind Damon. "Is it safe now?" It must have been, because Kory added, "Okay, you can come in now."

Evidently, they wanted to have Damon encaged by body-guards before they allowed Jan to enter.

The door opened, but Jan wasn't behind it.

In his place stood a woman who'd been dead for twelve years.

Mary and John were the first to react. They looked positively stunned. Mr. Chambers regarded Kory with befuddled eyes, but was not to be rewarded with an explanation. Kory was directing his complete focus on Damon.

His body shocked frozen, Damon was watching the scene from above.

An illusion? Of course it was an illusion.

Finally, the body managed to link three syllables into a meaningful word-question: "Do-ro-thy?"

Agitated conversation escalated to an argument in seconds.

Watching from above, despite his sudden ability to see from all angles at once, the sound was muffled from up there, as if he were hoisted in a parachute, slowly descending on a suddenly roofless mansion with only the ground floor visible.

Mr. Saunders karate-chopped the air with both hands like a spastic conductor with each word he shouted at Kory.

Damon caught the tail end of the silent-movie yelling: "—is she doing here?"

Expecting the verbal onslaught, Kory had a ready reply, but Mr. Saunders was not to be easily calmed.

If, in fact, John had asked what his daughter was doing there, Damon wondered how that question had made any sense to Kory, and even more incredibly, how his brother could have possibly *anticipated* such a thing. That John had asked this reasonable question in anger rather than shock had also not surprised Damon's little brother. Not in the least.

The older, living version of his wife began talking to her father. The tone was apologetic but firm and determined. Like Kory, she wasn't shouting, and Damon could derive meaning from her dampened speech only from her body language and the effect she had on John Saunders, who had redirected his charged emotion at his daughter, but his anger was completely gone, and had turned into grave apprehension.

The Dorothy apparition approached the table and said something that also made no sense. "He didn't want me here, believe me."

Kory was talking to John now. "I've hired extra guards, as you can see . . . he can't hurt her . . . better knowing where he is and having the upper hand . . . yes, but consider . . . rather than guessing, getting caught by surprise . . . we're in control now . . ."

John had calmed down somewhat, and for some reason this allowed Damon to hear every word he said to his daughter: "Okay, but even if it is safe, why would you expose yourself to him?"

The parachute was drawing closer. The scene below was beginning to come into focus.

"To watch his reaction when he sees I'm not dead." She glared at Damon. "Is it dawning on you? Do you get it yet?" She looked at Kory. "Oh, I'm not sure he does . . . not yet." To Damon again: "But by the time you leave here, everything will become clear; then you'll wish you were the one to kill yourself."

Damon was just a few feet above, barely hovering, slowly succumbing to gravity.

Mr. Chambers cut in, speaking to Kory. "What is going on here? You told me we were here to sign an agree—"

"Everything in due course," Kory said. "We'll get to that."

"But how . . . ?" It was a stupid thing for his body to say, but Damon wasn't disturbed that those were his first words to his wife after all these years. After all, his mouth was doing the talking, not him.

Best not to confuse detachment with indifference. If Damon were to leave the body to its own devices for too long, the results would not be favorable.

Suddenly cut from his parachute, Damon crashed into his physical shell. No longer witnessing, he tried regulating his breathing, but despite all those years of yoga he could not. "I saw you . . . you were dead . . . I saw your . . . your . . ."

A voice behind him said, "Those were cow brains. We heated them so they would give off steam, just the way we heated the pig's blood."

"No, no," Damon said, his voice sounding miles away. "I saw her . . ."

"I'm happy to disappoint you. I can assure you I'm very much alive."

He regarded the talking apparition before him, seeing her from his body for the first time. This was an older Dorothy, her facial bones more pronounced now, giving her an air of maturity and sophistication.

"You are too beautiful to be real."

At this, she recoiled, as if he had delivered a blow, not a heartfelt compliment.

She wore a royal-blue dress with a golden lapel pin he'd never before seen.

No longer the little girl at Rhodes High, the one with the white dress and gloves, she was lovelier than she'd ever been.

The expression "dressed to kill" came to mind, for if he wanted to believe she'd worn that clothing to please him, her expression dispelled all hope. Then why had she come? Even her own father had been perplexed by this. What had she said? He couldn't recall. The body, left to its own means, had a lousy memory.

A voice from the past, Capt. Damon van Luden, a man with twenty-two recon missions under his belt, said this was shock. The Damon of the present was surprised to find he hadn't lost his wartime instincts.

Captain van Luden, aka Ghost, was not finished, however. The Damon of 1980 might not have been foolish enough to hope for a pleasant family welcome, but he certainly had not prepared himself for this.

You've just been hand-delivered to the enemy. A trophy for the killing. All guns are on you, mister, and you are unarmed.

He ignored his past self. If true, his point was of little value anyway. This was Kali's world, and Damon wasn't going to put up a fight.

Silly though it was, he couldn't help but look for scars on her head. There was no evidence of a gunshot wound; her skin was unscathed, her head completely intact.

Dorothy took her life in 1968, and Damon had borne witness to the resulting gore.

Surprising himself with the ability to speak, Damon asked, "Where's my son?"

Kory answered, "You don't have a son."

Very Guru Dev. Damon didn't realize his younger brother was also fond of riddles. There was another possibility, and it caught him like a sucker punch. "Is Jan okay?"

"Yes," Kory said, "Jan is fine."

Relieved and puzzled, Damon said, "I was told I'd see my son. I don't see Jan here."

"You cannot see your son, because you don't have one."

"Yes," Damon said, "and Dorothy—that *is* you? Right? Because I've never been one to take drugs."

Nobody answered, nobody smiled.

"Is that Dorothy seated over there?" Damon said, noticing for the first time his voice was shaky.

"Yes, that is Dorothy van Luden," Kory said.

"So my wife is sitting over there, still alive."

"She's alive," Kory said, "but she's not your wife."

Damon looked at Mary, but her face was tight and expressionless. Dorothy kept staring at him. Damon turned to Mr. Chambers. "Would someone tell me what's going on?"

"Mr. van Luden," Mr. Chambers said, looking at Damon but realizing there could be confusion. "Uh—Damon, I'm just as surprised as you—I was not informed Mrs. van Luden would be attending. I have come to discuss a proposal—an agreement, if you will—and so without further ado—"

"That might be why *you* are here, but I didn't come here to see you—nothing personal—I came here to see my son." Damon looked over his shoulder at his unfaithful bodyguards. "That *is* what you promised yesterday."

Girard smiled. "Like Mr. van Luden says, you don't have a—"

Mr. Chambers cut in. "Am I to understand you brought him here on false pretexts?"

Kory raised his index finger. *Not now.*

"Mary? Will you tell me what's going on?" Damon said.

His aunt looked at him with all the compassion of the undead.

"Dorothy, where's our son?"

"You want to know what's going on? You want the truth? I'll tell you, which is more than you ever did for me. Without knowing it, what you did to me, what you did to Jan, you did to Kory. You messed with the wrong man, buddy. Everything you've done has backfired, and I mean *everything.* You're going to rot; first here on earth, then in hell, all the while knowing that your brother got the better of you."

"Mrs. van Luden," Mr. Chambers protested, "I must say, I find this most distasteful." He addressed Kory: "I've come here to draw an amicable and legally binding agreement. If I am to bear witness to a family feud, I want no part of it."

"You didn't seem surprised to see Dorothy alive," Damon said flatly, "so my guess is that you are very much a part of this little ploy to lure me here."

"I assure you—"

Kory cut Mr. Chambers off and said to Damon, "He never knew about the faked suicide. Her being dead or alive had no bearing on your control over the trust, and therefore there was no point in telling him. Leave Mr. Chambers out of this. What he's saying is true—he's here to administer the signing of a legal and binding document. Nothing more, nothing less." To Mr. Chambers Kory said: "I apologize for this, but Dorothy insisted she be present, and despite my fervent attempts, I was unable to dissuade her. I didn't advise you of this because I correctly assumed both you and her father would object and that might have placed this meeting, and therefore the signing of the agreement you've authored, in jeopardy."

"Don't *stare* at me," Dorothy said to Damon. Addressing the two men behind him, she added, "Make him stop looking at me."

Jean-Luc and Girard looked to their new employer for more specific instructions. Kory fanned the air in a calming motion. They removed their hands from their weapons.

Damon remembered warmer receptions from the NVA. He stood. "I may never have qualified for husband-of-the-year. I was a lousy brother, and a lousier father. I wish I had done things differently, but there you have it—I didn't. I came back here to sort things out with my family. To patch old wounds—"

Mr. Chambers raised his hand, indicating he was going to interrupt.

"Excuse me," Damon cut in, "I'd like to finish speaking if you don't mind. So I understand there might be some bitterness toward me. I want this all resolved. I will not stand here, however, and be treated like some third-class criminal."

"That's *exactly* what you are," Kory said.

"Come on, what's gotten into you, little brother?"

"Spare us the Mr. Nice Guy routine. You've never tried it in the past and for good reason. You want to try that angle, you'll need to polish your act." Kory looked at Mr. Chambers. "May I proceed?"

Mr. Chambers said, "Unless he acknowledges and accepts the recording of this conversation, it's not admissible."

Damon noticed the black machine for the first time. It was smaller than his *Guide to India* and had no electrical cord, so it had to be running on a micro-battery source. "I really don't care what you record," Damon said. "Now, would you please tell me where our son is, Dorothy? Why isn't he here? What is this charade all about?"

Kory pressed down the black Play and the red Record levers, and the miniature reel-to-reel tape device started to operate noiselessly.

"I didn't want this meeting," Dorothy said.

"But then—"

"I wanted to be there when you heard how everything you schemed for, all the hurt you've caused so many of us, has finally boomeranged back to its source," Dorothy said. "You don't deserve a second chance, and I hate that we're here talking about a possible binding agreement that would give you just that. I'm doing this for Jan."

"What are you talking about?" Damon asked.

"I'm talking about protecting my son. Otherwise I'd have you thrown in jail. Or better still, in an institution for the criminally insane."

"The only insanity is this current situation," Damon said. "I was MIA for ten years, I come back to my family and these two"—he pointed at Girard and Jean-Luc—"keep me from attending my son's graduation. They say I'm not welcome and threaten to shoot me." Mr. Chambers shot a nervous glance at Girard, but Girard was unperturbed by the accusation. "They tell me to come here this morning, and I'll see Jan. Well, I kept my end of the bargain." To no one in particular, Damon said, "So why did you lie to me?"

"I'll answer that," Kory said. "You were told Jan would be here because it was our only assurance you would attend this meeting."

"Fine, I'm here. So why is it that Jan is not?"

Dorothy said, "You'll *never* see Jan."

"I won't let you within ten miles of him," Kory added.

"Really? May I ask why?"

"You want to continue playing Mr. Innocent? I don't know where to begin. How about killing your own dog to spite me?"

Damon sighed. "That was an accident, Kory. A horrible accident. I loved that dog. How could you ever believe I would do anything to hurt Dollie?"

Kory glared at his brother.

"We were both responsible for her death," Damon said. "You for taking her without permission, me for trying to find you. That's all it was. Plain and simple."

"So then why did you run?" Kory said.

"At the time, I believed you needed to learn responsibility. I believed you needed to grow up and learn about things like honor. I was hoping you would come home and take responsibility for what happened to Dollie. Instead, you blamed me. Accused me of actually murdering my own dog. After what you said, I didn't feel like owning up to my part in what happened. I'm sorry it caused you so much pain. I'm sorry you couldn't see it for what it was, and you instead chose to turn against your very own brother."

"Just shut up for once," Kory said, his voice not nearly as harsh as his words. "Martha believed your lies, but she would have believed anything that came out of your mouth. You convinced everyone you were innocent regarding what you did to Dollie and all your subsequent psychopathic acts. I assure you, that is over now. Spin away, you will no longer find any of us caught in the web of your morose fiction. After *one* date, you claimed Dorothy as yours, by right. So when you couldn't have her, you took her by force."

"Little brother, we didn't go on just one date, you know that, right? We were going out for years, in point of fact, and then we got married. We were in love."

Kory rose from his seat. "Why, you psycho pile of shit . . ."

Mr. Chambers said, "Now, see here! Your mother would turn over in her grave if she could hear her only two children arguing like this. I owe a great debt to the van Luden family, but I'm not going sit here—"

"Don't provoke him," Mary said to Kory, looking uneasily at her older nephew.

Kory vacillated, finally taking his chair.

"What's he going to do," John said to his wife, regarding Damon with a smirk, "kill us all with his bare hands? He'll have a bullet in his head before he can get out of his seat."

To Mr. Chambers, Damon said, "That's okay, if this is the only way I'm going to get answers, I'll listen." To John: "I'm not here to hurt any of you."

"You've always been a smooth liar," Kory said. "It's hard to blame anyone for not heeding my warnings. Dorothy never did, so how could I? You created evidence to support your lies and make me out to be a bumbling fool."

Damon shook his head. "What evidence? What on earth are you talking about?"

"You had just *one* date with Dorothy before you left for the Academy," Kory said.

"Yes, that's true, but—"

"The other encounters you call dates only took place because she *pitied* you."

"Now, just a minute—"

"You went from that to asking for her hand in marriage. She wanted to let you down gently, so she said you'd have your answer by letter—a letter I hand-delivered."

"Right," Damon said, "and in it, she said she accepted my proposal—"

"Liar!" Dorothy shouted, slapping her hand on the table.

"Okay, show us," Kory said. "Where is this letter?"

"Well, I left for Infantry School that summer. Then Jump School, followed by Ranger School. There was Berlin, my first tour in Vietnam, then Berlin again, then my second tour in Nam, and finally ten years in India." Kory and Mr. Chambers exchanged looks of surprise. "And after almost twenty years you expect me to have that letter? Let me see," Damon shoved a hand in his pocket, and in response Girard pulled out his .38 Special. "I guess I don't have it on me right now, imagine that."

Girard's .38 found its way slowly back to its shoulder holster.

"Of course you don't," Kory said. "You destroyed it the moment you read she was rejecting you. Why leave incriminating evidence?"

John said, "You set everything up from the very beginning. You made it seem like she had a drug and alcohol problem."

Mary nodded her agreement.

Damon looked at Dorothy. "What the hell is he talking about?"

To Kory, Dorothy said, "He's not going to admit it, he'll keep playing dumb."

Kory nodded. "He'll pretend to be innocent until he knows the game is up." To Damon: "And believe me, the game *is* up. It's over. You go with your little act all you want. It won't make a difference to anyone in present company."

"You forced my daughter into that clinic," John said, while Mary continued to support him with more nods.

"Why? Dorothy had serious problems; why would I force her to do something she already agreed on doing?"

"Dorothy agreed to nothing," John said, "until you threatened to kill her and her unborn child."

"I did *what?*" Damon said, raising his voice. "Are you people completely insane?"

Dorothy shook her head, anger gripping her as it had Kory.

Damon stood. "I've had enough of this. Dorothy, all I wanted was for you to be happy, and it saddens me to see that you have yet to find inner peace." Damon turned to his brother. "Kory, you are far too intelligent to be making such ridiculous accusations. I'm sorry to discover you've been the primary instigator of this lunacy. I'm leaving."

Mr. Chambers said, "Son, please, as a favor to me, sit down and hear me out. I was the one who originally suggested you and your brother should come to a written agreement. Kory wanted to take matters directly to the police, but subsequently agreed with my idea, and set up this meeting. I've had a very long relationship with your family. Your mother confided in me. She was very proud of you and loved you very much. It would break her heart to know her son was sent to prison. She trusted me. I urge you to do the same."

"That's all very well, but you're the family lawyer, and last I looked, I'm still a van Luden. I don't see you representing me, I see you here to persecute me."

"On the contrary, I am seeking a viable solution for all. One where you don't end up in prison."

"Brad, I haven't done anything wrong, and you know it. And if you're not here to convict me, why bother with this idiotic recording device? Sorry, but I'm out of here."

"Then I'll be on the phone to 911 before you make it out of this room," Kory said.

"Do what you want," Damon said. "I haven't done anything illegal."

"Do you take us for fools?"

"No," Damon said. "Certainly not you, little brother."

"Then why the grand act? Mr. Chambers is right: *He's* the only reason you're here now and not in prison. He's the only reason you're getting this chance."

"I'm not acting." Damon stood. "Watch: this is me leaving."

"Wait," Kory commanded. "This is my final warning, I'm not messing around; I *will* call the police."

"And? What will you tell them?"

"There are a host of charges we could press."

Damon laughed. "Have you lost your marbles?"

Kory did not respond.

Damon asked Mr. Chambers, "What is he talking about?"

"I'm not a criminal lawyer, Damon, and I must reiterate: I'm not here to make threats or accusations. I believe it would be mutually beneficial to resolve this conflict, and so to that end, would you just listen to—"

Dorothy said, "Don't bother, he belongs in prison or a nuthouse."

"What charges could you possibly make? Being a crummy husband in the first degree?"

"You kidnapped me, faked our marriage, and raped me! You threatened to kill me and Jan if I didn't stay as your wife-slave!" Dorothy screamed.

"This is all news to me. I'm not sure I'm the one who needs to go to the nuthouse, it seems all of you are suffering some collective delusion," Damon said. "The kidnapping story is old and worn, but this business about a fake marriage? That's new. When did you come up with that one?"

Kory answered for Dorothy. "Okay, pretend you don't know what you did, but I assure you that tactic won't help your case. There are other events, however, about which you are genuinely ignorant, but at this point need to know."

"By all means, compound the things I've allegedly done and supposedly know I have done with those that I have done but know nothing about. I'm eager to hear the conclusion to your little fairy tale."

"By the time you kidnapped Dorothy, she and I had been secretly dating for approximately three months."

"Did you say *dating?*" Damon gawked at Dorothy. "You were dating *Kory?*"

Dorothy nodded. "It started shortly after he gave you my letter rejecting your proposal. Kory and I were in love."

"If that is so, and you'd turned me down in that letter—which you didn't—then why did you marry me?"

"You know damned well. You *forced* me. But that marriage is over and done with."

"That's odd, I thought I heard Mr. Chambers refer to you as Mrs. van Luden."

"He did. That's my name. I married Kory soon after you left for Vietnam—the second time."

"Then you've committed bigamy," Damon said flatly.

Mr. Chambers sighed. "According to the law, once you were absent for seven years, she was free to remarry. I handled the paperwork personally. This has no bearing on your status with the trust, however, since merely being absent, no matter for what duration, cannot, under the terms, revoke your privileges."

Kory turned sharply, directing blazing eyes at Mr. Chambers. "You thought it necessary to *remind* him?"

"I am duty-bound to do so, Kory."

"We're talking about a *criminal,* and you're treating him like the emperor of the estate."

"He's not a criminal until proven so in a court of law. As the main executor of the trust, my primary interest is to serve Martha van Luden's wishes. That entails doing what is best for those in her family who have survived her, not putting her first-born in prison. The estate has grown to over one billion—"

Damon paid no attention to the attorney. To Dorothy, he said: "Let me get this straight, you fake your suicide, and then wait for me to be legally dead so you can marry my little brother?"

"Just like you faked our marriage, I faked my suicide."

"Your suicide obviously never happened," Damon said, "but I can assure you our marriage most certainly did."

Jean-Luc said, "You're not the only one who can play games. The only thing real that night was the police. We were only worried in the beginning, until we could get you to agree to fool the authorities. It must be said, you played your part unusually well. I'd say very much like a man accustomed to chicanery."

Damon looked at his brother sadly. "I can understand those two, but why in God's name would you partake in such a scheme?"

Kory smiled for the first time. "Deception hurts, doesn't it? It was high time you got a dose of your own medicine."

"Faking her death was the only way for her to escape," Jean-Luc said. "She'd tried leaving you twice before, but she failed because of us."

"Jean-Luc," Damon said, "you knew she had drug problems, I didn't want her hurting herself."

"Yes, that is what Girard and I believed for years, but then when I went to New York to retrieve Jan, Dorothy and Kory told me the truth. How you planted the drugs in her house to make her father believe she was an addict. How you staged the marriage, and forced her to admit herself to a clinic, then threatened her life."

"I did none of those things and you know it," Damon said. "Tell me, though, why a suicide? Why not fake an accident? Do you have any idea what that did to me?"

Kory answered, "I don't believe you were born with the human qualities to be affected by such sentiment, so don't tire us with your displays now. We faked a suicide so that you would lock yourself in a cover-up. This kept you from going to a funeral. We couldn't stage a bogus funeral, and we didn't want you asking the authorities about an accident which never took place. This way you thought the body had been destroyed and that everyone believed her to be missing at sea. It was therefore to your advantage to remain uninvolved. Just to make sure, however, I had my father-in-law pressure you to keep your distance."

Damon's mouth dropped as he looked at Mary. "You made him play along too?"

Mary glared at Damon with a peculiar mixture of ambivalence and contempt but did not speak.

"Wait," Damon said, remembering something. "I saw the tickets and I remember paying for them. The first was in Dorothy's name, and it was from Geneva to Seawell Airport in Barbados. Isabeau left using Dorothy's altered passport and she was disguised as Dorothy."

"The tickets were real," Kory said, "but Isabeau didn't go to Barbados as Dorothy. Dorothy went there as herself. She checked into the hotel, took a boat, and left for the States. That was backup in case you'd chosen to ignore Mr. Saunders's wishes and investigate matters to see how well Jean-Luc had managed to create the cover-up scenario."

"Why would I do that? I had to go to Special Forces training, and I didn't want to get more involved in the mess than I had to be."

"Yes, that was the plan, and the timing was no coincidence. But there remained the remote possibility you'd instigate your own personal investigation, hoping that this display of concern would make you appear less suspect."

"So you instructed Dorothy and Jean-Luc on how to pull this off and used them as pawns in your chess game against me. You turned my plan to have Jan attend boarding school to your advantage. That's why you let Dorothy return to Geneva, right?"

Rather than respond, Kory listened as his brother put the pieces together.

"You sent her back to me so that she could convincingly fake her own death, and so that Jan could return to the States and live with you, while simultaneously guaranteeing I would be out of the picture." Damon thought for a while more. "I still don't understand it, though: I'm supposed to be this kidnapping rapist whose motivation is not really a relationship with Dorothy, it's control of the trust, have I got this right?"

Kory looked at the tape recorder. "We all know what you did."

"So you've mentioned," Damon said. "Back to what I was saying. Even from this point of view, it doesn't make sense. Why send her back? Why not keep her in the States? Have her simply divorce me? Why have her stay with me for six months if things were really so terrible for her?"

Kory frowned. "You answered your own question a minute ago. We needed you out of the picture."

"Yes," Damon said, "I know. What I don't understand is why. Why didn't Dorothy simply tell me she no longer wanted to be my wife?"

Dorothy said, "Can you believe this guy? You held me hostage! I tried escaping twice and you sent people to get me back—by force. Wasn't that a clear enough message I wanted out? When you kidnap someone, you can't expect that person to subject themselves to you willingly. That's why you hired men to keep me imprisoned. You needed me there so you could have your hand in the trust."

Damon shook his head. "No, I kept you there for your own protection. And I've already said I was wrong for doing that. I'm not going to get into a circular argument with any of you, since you've all made up your minds about me and aren't interested in listening to reason. My question is why didn't you just go back to the States and why fake your death?"

Kory started to speak but Damon cut him off. "Why, when you had already convinced Jean-Luc and Girard of all these crazy allegations about me?"

Kory said, "For one, while I'd convinced Jean-Luc, he had yet to convince his partner. Also, Jan was in Geneva with Girard, so Dorothy had to go back to retrieve him."

"Why not just send Jean-Luc back to get him? He could have gone back to Geneva, told Girard the same lies you told him, and come back to the States with Jan. Why the elaborate plan? I keep saying this, and nobody seems to care: do you realize what this did to me?"

"You're right," Kory said. "Nobody cares. Your actions over the years have rendered you unworthy of our solicitude. We're not answering the question because you ask it only to illustrate your ignorance of the answer, and thereby lay the grounds for your innocence for the benefit of the recording. You know what the answer is: you've always had others at your disposal. And even if you didn't, you could always come up with replacements. You created a very convincing story, and had both the money and resources to effectively eliminate any doubts. It would have taken you a simple phone call to get more men—assuming you didn't already have them readily available—convince them that your wife is going to harm herself or her son, and have Dorothy and Jan returned to you the next day. You would have fired Jean-Luc and Girard, and held Dorothy and Jan in a prison from which there would never have been another escape."

"Wow," Damon said, "I would have done all that? Not everyone is quite as brilliant as you are, young brother. I'm afraid you overestimate me, I'm actually a simple man."

"Spare us," Kory said, "you're anything but simple."

"That was true in the past. I had my priorities screwed up." He looked Dorothy in the eyes. "You were unhappy, and I was largely responsible for that. I messed up—I should have let go, but at the time, I couldn't. But we had Saint Croix. How can you say all these things after what happened there?"

Kory looked at Dorothy. "What's he on about now?"

"That's where he took me after he kidnapped me and staged the marriage."

"I never faked anything," Damon said, "and you know it. We *eloped*. We flew to Saint Croix where we made sweet love."

"I'm going to be sick," Dorothy said.

"Honey," Kory said to his wife, "his sociopathic mind is incapable of distinguishing between lovemaking and rape."

"I never raped anyone," Damon said. "That night was the only time Dorothy and I were together as man and wife—she wouldn't have me after the pregnancy."

"I wouldn't have had you at *any* time, mister," Dorothy spat. "But for your information, I was pregnant the evening you forced yourself on me."

"No, we never made love on any of our dates, and so the evening of our marriage was the only possible time of conception. You couldn't have been pregnant—" Damon froze mid-speech.

Everyone except the attorney was looking at him now. "Are you telling me you were carrying someone *else's* child?"

"The child of the only man I have ever loved," Dorothy said as she eyed Kory.

Mary said, "The Christmas Dorothy disappeared, Kory told us about their relationship, but neither John nor I believed him. What we didn't know at that time was that a doctor in New York had examined her, confirming her suspicions that she was pregnant."

"She didn't tell us until she came back to the States," John said, giving his daughter a brief look of disappointment.

"You yourself admit the only time was that wedding night," Mary said, "and we have medical records showing she was already pregnant by then, so you see, there's no doubt that Kory is the father."

"If you believe all this, why would you want proof from a doctor?" Damon asked his aunt.

Kory said, "I know what you're going to say: It won't stand up in court. And you're probably right. But that's not why we've kept the medical records. They're for Jan, so that he knows, without question, the monster he once thought was his father was never anything more than his oppressor."

"I was going to tell Kory that Christmas," Dorothy said, "but you kidnapped and raped me before I had the chance."

Damon shook his head. "If you loved him and were carrying his child, then why didn't you marry *him* instead of me?" Dorothy tried to answer when Damon said, "And it wasn't *rape*. I'll not sit here and listen to you saying that word over and over again. It was everything but—you were all over me that night."

"Sure I was. And we lived happily ever after."

Damon said, "You know as well as I our marriage was not a happy one. I'm not saying it wasn't my fault, but after that night you wouldn't let me touch you, and I never did. I *never* forced myself on you."

"Liar!"

"I wasn't the one who was dating one brother while secretly having a relationship with the other. What was with you? Couldn't decide between us? You thought you could have your cake and eat it too? What made you choose me? Did you flip a coin? And why me if you knew you were pregnant with *his* child?"

"I *never* chose you. You kidnapped me. You had everything faked and now this fake world has become your personal delusion. I have the feeling you really believe your own lies. You're a very sick man."

Damon regarded Kory and then Mr. Chambers. "What I don't understand is why all the games?"

Nobody responded.

"Kory? Was this your idea too? Is this about the trust? What, are you trying to prove Jan is your son so you get fifty percent?"

Mr. Chambers said, "It doesn't work that way."

"He knows the provisions of the trust," Kory said, addressing Mr. Chambers. "He's known them from the time Martha died. That's why he kidnapped Dorothy, and why he threatened to kill her and the child if she didn't comply. Because the kid was of no use to him, only the marriage."

Damon turned to his former wife. "I really don't care what anyone says. I loved you, and at one time, the feeling was more than mutual. You said so in the letter—I can't prove it because I no longer have it—but you *did* accept my proposal. And after the letter, you called me and asked to elope. You even told me where you wanted the honeymoon to be."

Dorothy said, "You're either the world's best liar or an incurable nut case. Maybe both."

"I can see how this is going to go," Damon continued, "but I don't care, it's high time this subject is put to rest. You wrote me that letter, you called me. I could tell you were drunk, but I still took you seriously. I was in love and I wasn't thinking. I asked you to go to the clinic for your own good. I loved you. I cared for you. I had you *protected*, in Geneva. These men know what I'm talking about, even if they've decided to change their story now to gain favor with their new employer. I know what went down. I know what the psychiatrist said. You were suicidal. We got married your way. It was a quick drunken ceremony. I may not recall most of it, but I *do* remember the wedding night." Damon looked at the recorder and said, "I don't think you'll want what I'm going to say on tape."

Nobody made a move to shut the contraption off.

"Okay, have it your way. I don't want to be coarse, here, but you're leaving me with no choice. You couldn't have been raped: You were on *top*, remember? I was almost too drunk to move. You were doing most of it. You even woke me up to have sex. Are you denying that too?"

"*Shut up!*" Dorothy screamed. "Make this liar shut up!"

"I'll shut up, and I'll leave," Damon said, "but not until this matter has been cleared up."

Mr. Chambers shifted uneasily in his chair. "Wait. Don't leave, we haven't—"

Damon ignored him and continued talking to Dorothy. "After the lovemaking and the streaking incident, I left for training. I was in the States, so I *couldn't* have threatened you at the clinic."

"You had your thugs do that for you," Kory answered.

Damon frowned and looked at Jean-Luc and Girard. "Who, them?"

Jean-Luc laughed. "More of your humor?"

"*Who* then?"

"Someone like you wouldn't put all his eggs in one basket," Kory said. "There were others, and that is precisely why I couldn't simply have Dorothy come back to the States, and why there was no choice but to have her disappear. Why she had to suffer through six more months with you until the timing was right to fake a suicide in order to assure her safety and that of our child."

"The only people working for me were those two," Damon said, hooking a thumb over his shoulder. "Unless 'others' includes maids and groundskeepers."

"Really?" Kory said. "What about Stavridis? Are you saying you didn't hire him?"

"Stavridis threatened you?" Damon asked Dorothy.

She turned to Kory. "He's *really* mad."

"That depends on your point of view," Kory said. "Is evil necessarily mad, or is it merely cunning and ruthless? Is it all of these things?"

"You think of me as evil?" Damon asked his brother.

"Your actions speak for themselves."

"They do indeed, brother," Damon said with a smile that made Kory shudder. He addressed his former wife: "I didn't have Stavridis or anyone threaten you. If you'd like, we can have him over and he'll confirm that."

"That won't be possible. Mr. Stavridis no longer works for Van Luden Enterprises, and has long since returned to his country," Mr. Chambers said.

"Well, I'm sure you can at least vouch for him during the time he did work for you," Damon said.

Mr. Chambers nodded. "Yes, I'm quite certain he wouldn't threaten Dorothy, or anyone for that matter."

"I mentioned Stavridis not to implicate him necessarily," Kory said, "but to prove that you did indeed have others working for you and you know it."

"I was in training, in the States. I didn't have anyone do anything you are accusing me of." Damon said to Dorothy, "When I arrived in Geneva you gave me the cold shoulder, as if I were a stranger and not a loving husband ready to embark on a new life with you. No matter how hard I tried, nothing between us changed."

Dorothy turned away, as if this would prevent her from hearing him.

Damon said to the Frenchmen, "I apologize for having you go after her when she tried to escape. At the time, I honestly believed I was doing what was best for her, but I have since realized, after many years of thought, that this was not the right thing to do."

"You sent them to get Jan," Dorothy said.

"Well, yes, but—"

"So you admit it!" Dorothy said. "You used me for the trust and you wanted Jan so you could mold him into another version of yourself."

"Look, if you want to discuss—"

"I'm not here to *discuss* anything. You can't come here and apologize away what you've done. You *used* me. And you were planning on using Jan too. You were going to brainwash my baby. After boarding school, and the Academy, and whatever else you had in store for him, he would have turned out to be a mindless soldier at your beck and call. The trust would be his on paper only. You would control it all through him."

"It seems you've got me all figured out," Damon said. Then, eyeing his brother: "I'm afraid someone else in this room has been doing the brainwashing, not me."

"She didn't need my influence to despise you," Kory said.

Ignoring this, Damon turned once again to his former wife. "Dorothy, I did try to hold on to you, but I thought it was for your own good. I am sorry for that. I'm also sorry I wasn't a better father to our son. I should have been at home more. There are a lot of things I should have done, but didn't." Damon sighed. "Now I'm back, and you're married to my brother. He's obviously filled your head with nonsense, and you've completely distorted the past. Sounds like a match made in heaven. I wish you both the best of happiness."

"If I may," Mr. Chambers said, "we haven't finished yet."

"This is pointless," Damon said, sounding tired.

Mr. Chambers motioned to Girard to stop the device.

"No longer on record?" Damon said with surprise.

When Girard pressed the Stop button, the attorney said, "This part of our discussion cannot be."

"Really," Damon said with a scornful smile, "but all that personal stuff before, that was okay?"

"We can't have evidence on record that we're knowingly aiding and abetting a fugitive." Kory looked squarely at his older brother. "We know all about your little escapade in Laos."

At that, Damon lost his smile. "What did you just say?"

"You heard me."

"I don't know what you are talking about," Damon said, wearing the lie like a toddler in high heels. "I was stationed in Vietnam, with the Fifth Special Forces Division."

"You were with the SOG," Kory corrected.

Damon lost some of his color. If he tried, he could probably cut through Jean-Luc, Girard, and the two kids with the sunglasses, but he would never reach Canada. He was almost broke, and the police would be all over him before he made it two miles. Why run anyway? "I was with the Fifth Special Forces Division," he repeated.

"There is no record of that," Kory pointed out, "as you saw for yourself at the embassy in Bangkok."

"How the hell do you know about that?" Damon said. "This is no joke. You're playing with fire. That's information you have no business having. You—*all of you*—can get in serious trouble."

"We already know about your mission, your visit to the embassy, your escape from the authorities."

"I went—" Damon was about to say he went to the embassy and attempted to report to his commanding officer, but that was classified information. Everything he did with the SOG was classified. *Especially* his last mission. Instead, Damon said, "I did not go AWOL. I served my country."

"That is correct," Mr. Chambers said. "You are not officially AWOL."

Damon went back to his seat. "Okay. How can you possibly know my current military status?"

"You are—and continue to be—a major trustee. It was my duty to dispatch investigators to determine your status. That is how we happened to come by certain sensitive information."

"And you thought it necessary to let them all know?" Damon said, motioning around the table.

"As your family, I felt they had the right to know. You were officially missing in action, and that has not changed."

Damon eyed the machine on the desk to make sure it was still switched off. "What are you saying, then?"

"He's saying that if you do show up," Kory said, "there will be an official inquiry to determine if you were MIA or AWOL. After that last mission of yours in Laos—that unauthorized, *illegal* mission—you went missing. While it is true you went to the embassy, it cannot be construed as a mitigating factor being that you subsequently ran away before they could apprehend you and impose charges."

"Charge me for what?"

"I'm sure they have a formidable list. Enough for a court-martial, no doubt. Why else would they try and detain you? And more importantly, why else would you run and vanish from the face of the earth for ten years?"

"I am not at liberty to discuss—"

"And while we're on the subject of your absence, why did you come back here? Did you think we wouldn't figure it out? You suddenly appear here just a few months before Jan's eighteenth birthday. When the trust becomes his."

"*Whoa*," Damon said, raising his hand. "Just a minute. Is *that* what this is all about?"

"It's what it has always been about, Damon, and you know it. It's about threatening Dorothy's life and that of her unborn child to preserve your control of the trust. That's what it's all about, whether you wish to admit it or not."

"I'm not admitting anything. This is insanity."

"If that's the way you want to play it, fine," Kory said. "You'll be looking at a court-martial for desertion, and who knows how many other military crimes they'll charge you with."

Mr. Chambers motioned Kory to calm down. "There is an alternative, Damon, as I said before. I have a proposition which I believe benefits all, if you would allow me—"

Frustrated, John said, "You don't need his permission to speak, for heaven's sake. Just tell him what you're offering and if he accepts, he signs. If not, we call the police."

"Very well," the attorney conceded, taking obvious displeasure in John Saunders's unmannerly tone. "We know your current financial predicament. You cannot access your bank accounts because you are presently operating incognito. I am unaware of how you entered the country, but it is my understanding that leaving should present no problems. We will give you a generous sum of money, along with tickets in any name you please, to any destination of your choosing, as long as it is not US territory. Additionally, should you agree to our terms, and, of course, abide by them, when Jan becomes eighteen and has full control of the trust, he has acceded to letting you have the house in Switzerland, should you wish to retain the property. While your brother and former spouse wanted you gone immediately, they have agreed, at the request of Van Luden Enterprises, to allow you one week more in the United States."

Mr. Chambers said to Kory, "I am fully cognizant of your objections to what I must now say, but I ask that you see this from my perspective, and understand that I am acting out of responsibility to the trust, and in the interest of the van Luden family as a whole."

"Damon," the lawyer continued, "this agreement, should you accept it, like your wife's decision to marry your brother, has no bearing whatsoever on the provisions of the trust, or your current status both as benefactor and executor. During the time you are here in the United States, I have made arrangements for you to review all the financial ledgers of the estate, all the investments made, in addition to our short-term strategies and plans for transfer of the trust to Jan in August." He handed over his business card. "My secretary will be contacting you to arrange an appointment at your convenience."

"What fun. Another family gathering? With these morons here pointing guns at my head?"

"It will be a private meeting. Just you and me, I assure you—"

"Can we talk about the important points?" Kory said, disgusted.

"Yes," Mr. Chambers said, "I'm getting to that. The agreement will require that you are never, from this day forward, to come within ten miles of Dorothy, Kory, Jan van Luden, or Mary and John Saunders."

"Hold on," Damon said, looking at everyone seated, "a restraining order? Is this what you all want?"

The attorney answered when nobody else would. "Restraining orders are issued by courts. Violation of a restraining order would amount to contempt of court. The offender could be taken into custody and to jail, and could be charged with a misdemeanor or a felony crime. However, this is not a court of law, and I am most certainly not a judge. What we are talking about in this case is merely one of the terms of what we hope will be a mutually agreed-upon contract. May I proceed?"

Damon did not reply, but the attorney continued anyway. "You are to leave the United States no later than seven days from the signing of this contract, and you may return no earlier than August 16 of this year, when Jan will be awarded complete control of the trust. In return, the sum of ten million US dollars will be deposited in a bank account of your choosing once you have departed the United States, followed by an additional ten million on August 16 of this year on the condition that you have not reentered the United States before then. This financial compensation serves a threefold purpose—"

"Let me get this straight, you guys are trying to buy me out of your lives?"

"It guarantees your financial security," Mr. Chambers said, "and I know your mother would have wanted this for you."

"And you think that's what *I* want?" Damon said, raising his voice. "I don't care about the damned money."

"That is your prerogative, Damon. Your objection, however, ties in nicely with my next point: These two very substantial payments serve as legal compensation for the purposes of this contract. Allow me to elaborate, because this point is of great import. You have our word we will not disclose your whereabouts to the military, any governmental organization, or prosecuting agency—federal, state or otherwise. However, we could not include this in the contract because doing so would amount to aiding and abetting a fugitive, and a court will not uphold a contract requiring any illegal act. We were therefore obligated to create some other form of compensation for you in order to validate the contract. This is because, in order for any contract to be binding and legally enforceable, in addition to the offer and the acceptance of said offer, each party to the contract must provide consideration, which is a legal term for something of value." Mr. Chambers waited but got no reaction. "Do you have any questions? Is there something you would like me to clarify?"

Damon did not reply.

"If you're thinking this doesn't guarantee we won't turn you in the moment you sign," Kory said, "you're right, it doesn't. But think about it: If we were going to call the authorities, we would have done so already. Either way, whether you sign and leave the country or don't sign and go to jail, Dorothy and I want you as far away from Jan as possible until the trust is in his hands. Once that happens, he'll have *full control*, which means he can and will make it so that in the event of his death, you will not be entitled to a penny of his estate. That way, you will no longer have any incentive to harm him."

"I wouldn't dream of—"

"At first, it seemed the simplest way to protect him would have been to call the police. Even if you were cleared of all

charges, you'd still be incarcerated and tied up in legal pro-
ceedings for months. We were under absolutely no obligation to come to any agreement with you, but as Mr. Chambers
explained to us, if you decide to go to prison, none of the
charges against you would keep you there indefinitely. One day,
you would come out. And when you did, nothing would stop
you from once again ruining our lives. On the other hand, if
you sign, everyone benefits: In two months, you'll have twenty
million dollars, and Dorothy, Jan, his grandparents, and I will
not have to worry about seeing your face ever again. If you come
within fifty-one thousand, seven-hundred and ninety-nine feet
and eleven inches of any of us, you'll be in breach of contract.
The court will force you to return all the money, and you'll be
as penniless as you are now."

"I *told* you," Damon said, slicing the air with the edge of his
hand. "I don't care about the money. I don't care about any of
this crap. I just came here to see Jan." He paused before giving
a sigh of resignation. "Does he know about all this?"

Kory did not answer immediately. "Not the details, no.
We've just told him you've returned."

"And *you* are his father?"

"Yes I am," Kory replied, looking straight into Damon's eyes.

"Does *he* know?"

"He has known for a long time. Dorothy and I told him
shortly after we were married."

"Has he asked about me?"

Kory sighed. "On rare occasions."

"Does he want to see me?"

"Certainly not," Kory said, his voice as warm as a winter's
night in Stockholm.

"I'll want to hear him say that."

"Not a chance," Dorothy said.

Kory shook his head. "That's not going to happen."

Damon looked at Mr. Chambers. "Then I'm not signing
your document."

Kory broke the long silence. "Would you sign if you talked
to him?"

"If I talk to him *and* he says he never wants to see me again;
then yes, I'll sign your silly agreement."

Kory looked at his wife and she nodded. "You can't see him, but you can talk to him on the phone."

"When?"

Kory motioned with his finger, and one of the young bodyguards fetched a telephone with the longest cord Damon had ever seen. It had buttons instead of a dial. Kory put the phone on his lap, under the table so Damon couldn't see the numbers as he pecked them out. He handed the phone to Dorothy.

"Hi, honey . . . No, we're still having our meeting . . . Yes, he's here and he wants to speak with you . . . You just tell him how you feel . . . tell him—"

"No coaching, if you don't mind," Damon said, "or the deal is off."

She handed the phone to Damon. "Jan? Yes, it's me, Damon. Look, I realize this is hard for you—"

A small voice answered, "What do you want?"

"I just want to see you, to talk to you—"

"I'm really busy, I've got to go. Sorry."

The dial tone filled the conference room with the tenacity of a fire alarm.

Kory said, "You can't expect us to force him to speak with you."

"What have you told him about me?" Damon said.

"Not much," Kory replied. "Certainly not everything."

"What, exactly?" Damon said.

"He knows only what he's seen for himself."

"What is that supposed to mean?"

"We've spared him the details about what you've done to his mother."

"What about me?" Damon insisted.

"Nothing he doesn't know. You treated him the way you used to treat me. And, of course, he remembers the horrors of Geneva. He remembers escaping. He remembers being kidnapped. And he knows you might do it again."

"This gets crazier by the minute. First you say I kidnapped Dorothy. Now you're telling me I kidnapped my own son, too?"

"The one fact does not negate the other," Kory said.

"Dorothy kidnapped Jan. That's a fact. Dorothy faked her own death. That's another fact."

"She was running away from you; she had no other recourse."

"Right, but that doesn't change what she did," Damon said. "I want to know what kind of spin you put on this to get Jan to hang up on me."

"I've already told you," Kory said.

"You said he *knows* I might kidnap him again," Damon pointed out. "First of all, that makes no sense. Secondly, it isn't something he would conclude from what he's seen firsthand."

"True on both counts," Kory admitted. "Dorothy and I don't believe you have any motive to kidnap him at this stage, but when he was younger, you did. We didn't think we should terrorize the boy with the possibility that you might want to kill him for the trust. So we've justified the bodyguards using the old explanation that you might want to kidnap him as you've done before."

Shaking his head as he regarded the receiver he still held in his hand, Damon said, "I've heard enough. Just tell me this: is he happy?"

"Ever since you've been out of the picture."

"Very well. You let me speak with Jan, and he obviously doesn't want anything to do with me, so I'll be gone within a week. Just so you know, I'm not signing because of your threats. I'm not afraid of the Army and I'm certainly not afraid of your cockamamie accusations. Furthermore, I couldn't care less about the money. I've worked hard all my life when I could have lived like a playboy. I went and fought for this country you are kicking me out of, while you and others like you became professors or did whatever it took to dodge the draft. I've made it on my own for a decade; I don't need anybody to take care of me now."

Mr. Chambers said, "Then you agree to the terms?"

"Agree? No. But I'll sign the stupid thing because Kory kept his side of the bargain, so I'll keep mine. Besides, this piece of paper, this document of yours you all want me to sign, is meaningless to me."

"What is the problem?" John said, with a snort of derision. "Twenty million not enough? Not really satisfied unless you get your money by destroying people's lives in the process?"

Damon shook his head sadly.

"You can sign right here," Mr. Chambers pointed. "Mrs. Saunders and I shall act as witnesses."

After speed-reading the one-page contract, Damon looked over at the woman who'd once been his wife, and the man who no longer considered him a brother. "Is this really what you want?"

Their expressions were answer enough.

Damon scribbled his name three times, once for each copy.

"Dorothy," he said when the contract was signed, "could I at least see him one last time? I only want to say good-bye to my son—" When Dorothy winced, he corrected himself: "To Jan."

"Out of the question. You keep away from him."

"As you wish. He's lived under your influence all these years, so I'm not surprised he doesn't want to see me. None of you want me here." Damon got up and offered Mr. Chambers his hand, the attorney hesitated, as if a handshake was as appropriate at this point as a French kiss. "Good-bye, Mr. Chambers, I never really had a chance to know you, but I trust you will continue to care for my family as you have in the past."

"You have my word," Mr. Chambers said. "And as I said, regarding the trust, I'll be at your disposal for the duration of your stay."

As Damon walked over to Kory, Jean-Luc and Girard positioned themselves to block him, but Kory told them to stand aside. Rigid, Kory stood his ground, like a man before a firing squad.

Damon hugged him. "I love you, little brother, no matter what you think of me."

Kory stared as Damon walked over to Dorothy. John Saunders tried to find his way around the Frenchmen, but Damon got to his daughter first, taking his former wife's hand, brushing it with a kiss. "You will always have a place in my heart, Dorothy. And despite how you chose to remember it, I'll always cherish the memory of our wedding night together. I'm at peace knowing you, Kory, and Jan are happy together, and I hope one day you manage to liberate yourselves from the past."

John had joined his wife's side, puffing out his chest. Damon kissed his aunt on the cheek, not taking the slightest notice of Mr. Saunders.

As Damon walked out of the room, he stopped at the doorway. "I noticed the piano is uncovered."

Dorothy almost smiled. "Jan is a pianist."

"Just like his grandmother," Damon said with a hint of melancholy.

As he left his childhood home, he heard his brother say, "I want him out of this country in one-hundred and sixty-eight hours, and not a second later. While he's here, you two keep a close eye on him. Don't let him near Jan."

The bodyguards offered their assurances they'd do exactly as Kory wished.

Damon did not intend to be as accommodating.

ZUGZWANG

1980

"We're going to the Waldorf," Jean-Luc said to the driver as Girard and Damon followed him into the limousine.

"Is that where you guys are staying these days?" Damon said. "Living it up?"

Girard gave him a blank stare; Jean-Luc offered a grunt.

"Well, you can drop me off at the bus station," Damon said. "Actually, just leave me outside the gate."

Jean-Luc said, "Your accommodations are courtesy of Mr. Chambers. Everything is paid for. A suite, Monsieur, with room service compris."

"Maybe you guys didn't hear me back there," Damon said, "but I didn't come asking for a handout."

"Look at it this way," Jean-Luc said, "you are not invited at the van Luden residence, so by consequence, you have no place to stay. Accept Monsieur Chambers's generosity, he is the only one who has stood up for you. To refuse would not be polite."

"Yes, it was so nice of him to have me kicked out of my country and keep me from seeing my family again."

"That is your doing, Monsieur."

Damon shrugged. "Whatever you say, asshole."

Girard leaned forward in his seat, but Jean-Luc was not so easily riled. "I say you go to the Waldorf and we go home."

"If you insist," Damon said. "At this point, I really don't give a shit."

Jean-Luc nodded and the limo started on its way.

"Out of curiosity, what name did you use to make the reservation?" Damon asked as they left Rhodes on Route One.

"We used mine," Girard said, handing Damon a key. "You are in Suite 2021. If someone asks for Mr. Lemond, they're calling for you, Monsieur."

"Is that how I'm supposed to leave the country, as Girard Lemond?"

"Certainly no," Jean-Luc said. "We did not think there would be a problem for you to leave the country, since you managed so effectively to come in. But we had to make a reservation at the hotel, and using your actual name would naturally have posed difficulties for you, Monsieur. Mr. Chambers will provide you with everything you need—as long as it is legal—an airline ticket, travel money, special accommodation requests during your stay. You have only to ask."

"There aren't many people who get a red carpet on the plank," Damon said.

"*Qu'est-ce qu'il dit là?*" Girard asked his French companion.

"Forget it," Damon said.

Half an hour south on the New York State Thruway, Jean-Luc gave Damon a metal box. "This is for you. Affairs of your parents. You left before you could receive them."

"Affairs? You mean belongings?"

"Yes, some small items from the will," Jean-Luc replied. "Mr. Chambers has kept this for you."

"What's in it?"

"I don't know," Jean-Luc said. "Mr. Chambers simply asked me to give this to you. He did not tell me what it contained. In fact, he has told me that you must view the contents in private. Oh," he added, fishing for something in his pocket, "you will be needing this key as well."

Jean-Luc handed Damon a pen and a piece of paper.

"What's this for?" Damon said, glancing at the document with the Van Luden Enterprises letterhead.

"Sign that you have received this," Jean-Luc explained. "That way, it is no longer my responsibility."

"What is it, a bomb?"

"I do not know," Jean-Luc said, "but one can only hope."

Traffic was unusually light, even for this hour. Another thirty minutes or so and Damon would be at the hotel.

While Jean-Luc maintained a weary eye on Damon, Girard slouched in his seat, taking his rest from siesta to slumber.

Strangely, of all the untruths and allegations, the one about the rape bothered him the most. It was nothing he hadn't heard from Dorothy before, of course, yet it nagged at him relentlessly from the moment the bodyguards had stopped talking.

Looking at it in context, he had discussed intimate sexual details in front of his ex-wife's husband who happened to be his brother, the family attorney, his former father-in-law, and his aunt. His wedding night, of all things.

The one and only sexual experience he had with the woman he loved, and she called it rape. In front of *everyone*. He would have been better off saying nothing instead of exposing the details of the sexual positions they'd used that night. And for what? To stage his pathetic defense? He couldn't have remained silent, on the other hand. Not about being called a rapist.

They were entering Manhattan.

She was on top.

Damon shook his head, but not enough for Jean-Luc to take notice.

How could he have said such a thing?

It had been his only defense.

Why was this rape thing grating at him when there were so many other lies he could be upsetting himself over?

It wasn't the humiliation. It played a role, certainly, but that wasn't the answer. Most of the other things they'd said were pure fabrication. This was truth twisted into a horrendous lie—lovemaking being called rape. That had to be what was eating at him.

Nobody listened when he'd said she was the one on top. They didn't care what he had to say. And it was his word against hers—

Damon sat up in his seat, startling Jean-Luc.

The *blood*.

That's why he couldn't get it out of his mind: he'd been trying to tell himself something.

He'd completely forgotten about it, but the evidence was irrefutable: there'd been blood on the sheets.

Dorothy had been a virgin.

That confirmed what he always knew to be true: Jan *was* his son.

Damon's heart was beating quickly, trying to keep up with his racing thoughts.

Girard was still asleep, but in less than ten minutes, they would arrive at the Waldorf and it would be too late.

Damon leaned forward, about to speak.

"Yes?" Jean-Luc said.

Don't. Not this way.

He had to think this through first. Carefully.

"Can you give me your phone number?" Damon said. "Just in case I have one of those special requests you were talking about."

Two spoonfuls before he could finish off his crème brûlée, the phone rang.

Expecting the call was from Room Service to ascertain if the lunch had been prepared to his satisfaction, Damon answered with, *"Allô? Oui?"* That was pushing the Lemond identity to its limits, but Damon was in a mood for fun. He'd accomplished more than he imagined possible in just a few days. And all without Jean-Luc's help.

In the end, all he'd needed was the *idea*, the *suggestion*. On some level, what had really worked for him had been his genuine intention to carry this through.

"Mr. van Luden?" a young unfamiliar female voice said.

"Who is this?" Damon said, not comfortable conceding his true name to a stranger, even one with a sweet voice like hers.

"I'm calling from Van Luden Enterprises. I'm Mr. Chambers's secretary."

"Oh," Damon said, no longer in such a fun mood.

"Mr. Chambers is quite booked this week, but he's asked me to make an appointment for you this Friday at three. Would that work for you?"

"Actually—"

"He has an appointment with Kory van Luden right after you. And before then he's got a board meeting—"

"I appreciate all this, ma'am, but I'm afraid I'm not interested. I've already told—"

"Excuse me," she interrupted, "do you mind if I put you on hold?"

A few bars of the "Für Elise" started playing before Damon could tell her he did actually mind. He could always hang up, but he didn't have anything against the lawyer except for the fact that he took the word "boring" to a new level.

"Sorry about that, Damon," Mr. Chambers said on the other end. "I told her to call you about the meeting, but I suppose she didn't understand that I actually wanted to discuss it with you before she put it in the calendar."

"Yeah, about the meeting—"

"I've cleared my schedule for two hours."

"That's very nice of you, but like I said last week, I'm not up for another family gathering."

"Yes, I know, and if I recall I assured you it would be just the two of us."

"So why is Kory coming?"

"Kory?"

"Yeah, that's what your secretary said: he's got an appointment too."

"Oh dear," Mr. Chambers sighed. "I'm going to have to have a word with her. I do hope she told you that your brother's meeting does not coincide with yours. Please allow me to explain: As I've said, I've set aside two hours exclusively for you. Between three and five p.m. this Friday. We can be finished as soon as half an hour, if you're pressed for time. And if you have questions, I'll be happy to spend all two hours with you. Kory won't be arriving until five."

Damon laughed. "If we cross paths in the hallway, I'll be in violation of your restraining order—"

"It isn't a . . . Look, I apologize for last week's family unpleasantness, but I do believe I've made my position quite plain. I'm on your side, Damon."

"And I thank you for that, but—"

"But you don't want to come if Kory's bodyguards will be there watching you. Is that it?"

"Yes, but—"

"After our last meeting, I took the liberty of speaking with your brother about our private appointment. I have his personal assurance that no family member or employee— detective, bodyguard, or otherwise—for the duration of our engagement, will be present, following, or otherwise harassing you in any way, shape, or form."

Damon was about to say something, but he stopped himself. After a while he asked, "So he's going to have them wait for me in the lobby?"

"Nothing of the sort. I have defined our engagement period as being from two thirty, when a company car will be dispatched to retrieve you, through six, which, accounting for a two-hour meeting and possible rush-hour traffic, is the most conservative estimate for your return to the hotel."

"I didn't know you had that kind of clout over my brother," Damon said.

"Your brother is actually quite a reasonable man."

"Well, I can't say I agree with that, but as far as Friday goes, we're on. Keep those two hours open, would you? Like you said, I might need the time, I might not."

Friday, 4:30 p.m.

"I have an appointment with Mr. Chambers," Kory said.

Before the secretary could check the calendar, Kory added, "I'm early. My appointment was for five."

"Oh, yes. Mr. Kory van Luden?"

Kory nodded.

"Please have a seat, Mr. van Luden."

"I don't remember—is that Mr. Chambers's office right there?"

"Yes."

"Oh, then I'll come back later when his other meeting is over."

"His three o'clock left early. Mr. Chambers should be available now. Would you like me to see?"

"Early? When?"

"Almost an hour ago."

He'd walked as quickly as he could up Park Avenue without drawing attention. It wasn't hard to do— at this hour, everyone walked like his pants were on fire.

He was on Sixtieth. Just seven more blocks.

Damon hadn't been to his father's townhouse since he was a little boy.

He was behind schedule. He'd tried to appear interested in the presentation, but had only just managed to keep his eyes open. On the positive side, Mr. Chambers had been good to his word and had concluded in thirty minutes. Damon had to ask at least a few questions; after all, the family attorney had gone out of his way to make arrangements. More important, just rushing off once the slideshow was over would have seemed suspicious. The three questions had taken about five minutes each.

Still, Damon had time. The Frenchmen weren't supposed to start looking for Damon until 1800 hours.

Once this was over, Damon would have plenty of time to get back to his hotel and into his room undetected by his brother's bodyguards.

"I wish I'd been informed earlier about this," Kory said. "You told me the meeting would last two hours."

"Please do sit down," Mr. Chambers said. "Would you like a beverage?"

Kory ignored the offer. "I need to call Jean-Luc."

Mr. Chambers sighed. Not addressing Kory's request, he said, "I did try calling you. To see if you were interested in moving up your appointment time, but you were at the chess club—"

"I need to call Jean-Luc," Kory repeated.

"I have tried both bodyguards," Mr. Chambers said patiently. "Neither of them is at his residence."

"Then I have to call Jan," Kory pressed. "I need to know he's okay."

"Why wouldn't he be?" Mr. Chambers said. "Your bodyguards are probably out enjoying some personal time. Remember, you agreed—"

"Please call Jan," Kory said.

Mr. Chambers looked at the younger van Luden, dialed his Manhattan number from memory, and handed Kory the phone.

"Jan? Is everything okay there? . . . Listen, I'm coming right over. In the meantime keep the door locked . . . No, it will have to wait for another time. . . . You can still practice while I'm there, I won't get in your way, I promise. . . . I don't know . . . at this hour. Maybe fifty minutes . . . Love you."

"Is everything all right?" Mr. Chambers asked.

"I'm going to have to cut this short I'm afraid," Kory said.

"But we haven't even started," Mr. Chambers protested.

"We'll do this some other time."

"Very well," Mr. Chambers said with an injured look, "but I'm leaving for Chile the day after tomorrow." He pressed the intercom button and spoke into the box. "Darla, do we have an opening for next week, after my trip?"

The intercom went silent for a moment as she checked into his query. Mr. Chambers brightened. "Never mind, I have a better idea. Have my car ready. Mr. van Luden and I will be leaving for his residence on Sixty-Seventh immediately."

"Oh, you don't need to do that," Kory protested. "I'll take a cab."

"This is an opportunity: I can summarize what I would have told you on our way to your place, and then I'll have a quick chat with young master van Luden." He lifted his hand as if it could prevent interruption. "Oh, I realize your son has a recital this evening, but I'd only need a few minutes of his time. Half an hour, say? A quick house call, if you will. That way I will have briefed everyone before I leave."

"I suppose that would be okay," Kory said, not wanting to hurt the old man's feelings. "But we really must keep it short, otherwise Jan might lose his groove."

Jan picked up the phone on the fifth ring. "Hi, Dad. . . . Yeah I'm fine. What's up? . . . I always do, you know that . . . Your meeting is over already? . . . But Dad, I've got my recital tonight. . . . Okay, so when will you be here? . . . See you soon." Jan hung up the phone.

"He's coming now?"

"He said fifty minutes with the traffic."

"We still have time," Damon said.

Kory fidgeted in the back of his limousine as Mr. Chambers poured himself a brandy. "I'm afraid there's really not much we can do about the traffic. It is a Friday, you know."

Kory did not reply. He'd already pestered the driver three times, asking if he was certain there wasn't a better, faster route.

Mr. Chambers wouldn't stop talking about the specifics of the transition, and how important it was that *young master van Luden* understand the scope and implications of taking charge of such a significant and financially complex trust fund.

Though listening to the lawyer must have been as excruciating for his brother as it was for Kory, he had a gut feeling that it hadn't been Damon's primary motivation for leaving so soon.

"That looks like a new addition," Damon said, looking at the impressive grand piano.

"Dad bought it for me when I moved here."

"When was that?"

Jan hesitated, clearly unsure as to whether he should answer.

"Is it like your grandmother's?" Damon asked, quickly cutting into the brief silence.

"You mean like the one in Rhodes?"

"Yes, like your grandmother Martha's piano."

Comfortable with the subject, Jan relaxed. "No, this is a *B*."

"A *B*?"

"Uh-huh, a Steinway B. Dad got it for me new. It's a '68. Grandma Martha's was made in 1916 and it's a Steinway D—a full concert grand. It wasn't tuned, so it needed some work. It's a great piano, though."

"Which one?" Damon asked, realizing Jan had inadvertently told him when he'd moved in with Kory.

"Well, Grandma Martha's was never tuned—I don't know why—at least not until Dad had a technician service the piano regularly so I could play it when I was staying with Grandma and Grandpa. They're both great pianos, but the *D* is a classic," Jan said, the tension completely gone from his voice, "and after the second tuning, it held on just as well as my new *B* did."

"She didn't tune the piano," Damon explained. "Not after your grandfather died."

Jan looked at him doubtfully. "Why?"

Good question. "As you already know, my mother, your grandmother, was a pianist and—"

"Well, I don't know about that. Dad said she used to play a long time ago—before he was even born. That doesn't make her a pianist, however."

"No, but she was. A concert pianist, in fact. And she could have continued to perform if she'd wanted to. She had a great gift, you know. But she fell in love with Grandpa, then she had me and Kory, and we became her main focus in life. I still remember her playing, though. It was quite something."

"What did she play?"

"I don't remember exactly. I was just a little boy."

"I heard she died when you left," Jan said, almost as if he'd caught Damon in a lie.

"Prior to that, actually. Just one month before I went to the Academy. But she stopped the piano altogether when Grandpa died, that's why I don't recall what she played." Damon touched the smooth surface of the Steinway's lid. "It's a really beautiful piano; Kory must love you very much."

The comment seemed to make Jan uncomfortable.

Damon was quick to change the subject. "Since I can't go to your recital, would you play for me now?"

Jan made a move toward the piano and then stopped himself. "I don't know . . . you really shouldn't be here."

"Just one piece?"

Jan stared at the piano, conflicted. "I don't think we have time."

Damon smiled. Jan was almost eighteen, but still just a kid in many ways. "Your mom is in Rhodes with Aunt—Grandma and Grandpa, right? You said they won't be coming until after the recital, which is at nine. Your dad is stuck in traffic. It took me almost forty minutes to get to my hotel, and that's twenty blocks closer than your house. So I think fifty minutes in rush hour traffic is optimistic."

"Yeah, but he called twenty-five minutes ago."

"Okay, then don't play the *Hammerklavier* Sonata, and we should be golden."

Jan's mouth dropped. "How do you know the *Hammerkalvier* Sonata?"

"Like I told you on the phone," Damon said with a smile, "there are a lot of things about me you don't know."

At first, Damon had expected he'd end up asking Jean-Luc for help, but trying to bribe the Frenchman into allowing a harmless phone call to Jan was dicey, even though it wouldn't have constituted a breach of contract. In all probability, the pocket money Damon had been given wouldn't amount to a sufficient payoff, and the Frenchman would end up telling everyone what Damon was up to.

Taking it a step further, Damon would have been willing to offer the Frenchman a promissory note for millions in exchange for a few minutes with his son. Jean-Luc was not a trusting man, and recently he'd made no secret of his contempt for Damon, but using the threat of telling Mr. Chambers that the agreement had been violated, the bodyguard would have had all the assurance he needed to believe Damon could be held to his word.

Damon had put a stop to both his ideas. Thank God.

Knowing Kory and Dorothy were in Rhodes, Damon had tried calling the townhouse residence without involving the Frenchman and without exposing his plan.

Finding the number had been easy; it wasn't unlisted and there were very few van Ludens in the directory. The hard part, the part that had worried him, was getting Jan on the line. Harder still was getting Jan to stay on the line. Luck had been on his side and after just two rings, Damon had heard his son's voice once again that day. This time Damon had been thoroughly prepared.

Most seventeen-year-olds want to believe they know who they are and what they're all about, but only a handful really do. They're struggling for an identity, looking desperately to the outside for something stable within. To top it all off, his mother and the man he thought of as his father had no compunctions about sandwiching him in the middle of a family dispute, making him the centerpiece of their argument to outcast Damon. Even if they were right and Damon was nothing more than a tyrannical uncle, he'd still played an undeniable role in Jan's life, especially during the first six years.

This time, Damon hadn't given Jan a chance to hang up. Speaking quickly, but at the same time managing not to sound rushed and therefore desperate, he'd told Jan he wanted to see him. And why. With a second breath, he'd finished with, "This is for us both. Give me one chance. Just a few minutes with you alone. After that, if you never want to see me again, I promise I'll be out of your life."

Jan hadn't hung up the phone as he'd done earlier that day. Instead, he'd asked the question Damon had been hoping for: "How is this for both of us?"

"It's your chance to make up your own mind about what is true and what isn't. You must have wondered all these years, right? Unless you're the kind of person who just accepts everything they hear. I don't think you are. I think you're your own man."

Jan had remained on the phone, and it had been at that junction Damon knew he had a shot at a first step along the path to winning over his son. "Why do you want to see me in private?"

"It doesn't have to be in private. If it makes you feel better, we can have Jean-Luc and Girard there too. Why don't you ask your parents? If you tell them you want to see me, they might let you."

"Are you saying I need their permission?"

"I'm only saying you have options. You decide what you want."

Jan had called Damon twice since then. Not only had the kid warmed up to a private meeting, he'd actually come up with ideas on how to arrange their sub-rosa tête-à-tête. His first thought had been to have Damon give the detectives the slip in a crowded department store, after which time Jan could meet him in some public place. After due consideration, however, they'd both agreed a more solid plan was called for. Their final idea was born when Jan had told Damon about his piano recitals. He'd been giving performances regularly, at least one or two per month, in preparation for the Juilliard entrance exams. On a recital day, he always had the town house to himself so he could practice undisturbed. The last time Jan had called, Damon had given him the great news. As luck would have it, Mr. Chambers had arranged a meeting with Damon on the very same day as Jan's recital. Damon could leave early, giving them a window to finally meet in private.

Upon seeing his son face-to-face, however, Damon couldn't help but feel disappointment at the boy's trepidation. Jan had kept his distance, stipulating it as a condition, as if he'd suddenly changed his mind and regretted not having the body-guards there. And despite all the initial enthusiasm, despite the painstaking planning, Jan had added another stipulation, insisting they speak alone for no longer than five minutes.

Jan had cold feet. That was to be expected. Damon had seen many young men, men not much older than his son, priming with fire and spirit until the moment of truth—in the battlefield, where death was not a remote conversation topic but a stark, pungent reality.

After all the lies they'd fed the kid over the years, it was a miracle Damon was there alone with his son at all.

"Just one piece?" Jan said, his five-minute limit now long since forgotten.

"Just one." Damon smiled.

Jan didn't need further encouragement. The boy clearly wanted to play, as if he were drawn to the piano by force of addiction.

"Rachmaninoff Prelude in G Minor," Jan announced, clos-ing his eyes to open them a moment later wearing a face with all the gravity of a village elder. He sat with his back perfectly straight, yet relaxed, reminding Damon of how he had been taught to meditate.

The music started off sounding like a military march. Damon was awestruck by the intensity and power his son evoked.

Not wanting to trivialize the music, Damon refrained from clapping. Instead, he said, "That was beautiful. Your grand-mother would have been proud."

Jan smiled fully for the first time that evening. A kid once more, he looked at the clock, at the piano, and back at the clock once again. Visibly fighting the temptation to play some more, using the village elder's voice, Jan said, "It's late. I'm afraid you have to go now. Dad will be here soon."

"Okay," Damon said, a sudden weight pressing on his chest, "I'll let myself out."

Jan walked beside him, breaking his previously man-dated five-foot separation limit. A gesture of forgiveness and reconciliation.

Damon fought the growing lump in his throat. "Good-bye, Jan."

"Bye, Uncle Damon," Jan said, closing the front door.

Damon stood with his back to the door, closed his eyes, taking it in.

A lady passed by, walking her pedigree toy dog. Figuring him for a loiterer, she gave Damon a disapproving tilt of her head and hastily trotted away.

The prelude kept playing in his head. His son had talent. Just like his mother.

He made it down ten blocks to Fifty-Seventh Street and was stopped by a red light.

He stood there at the corner. The light said WALK.

Damon didn't want to.

He had no clue what he wanted, but returning to his fancy hotel room, though a required and crucial element to his plan, was the last thing he could see himself doing.

Did his family really expect him to sit around watching television and eating room service, wasting away the last remaining days before leaving home and country?

This whole thing was stupid: He didn't care about the fucking money, and he wasn't afraid of the Army.

The light turned red. Damon did an about-face.

He loved Jan. At the very least, Damon owed it to himself and to his son to tell him so. At the very least, Jan would acknowledge Damon's sincerity. And that would count for something. If not today, one day.

Damon would not attempt to prove he was Jan's father. There would be no point in trying to do so after Kory and Dorothy had convinced the boy otherwise. Even if Damon could come up with hard evidence, the aftereffects of such a revelation could prove traumatic.

There was a way to do this without hurting the boy and without lying to him. Damon would tell him that in his *heart*, Jan always had been and always will be, his son.

Damon was walking faster now. He looked at his watch: 1720 hours.

Kory was on his way.

He started to run.

Damon stood at the town house entrance and was about to knock, but it wouldn't have been of any use over Beethoven's Fifth Symphony.

Why would a musician such as Jan blast any music, especially *classical* music, like some Led Zeppelin groupie playing hard rock? The sheer volume of it was so great, it reduced the great work to noise pollution. Damon was certain none of the nearby residents could be pleased. He caught the sound of shouting during brief, quieter sections in the music.

Kory must have returned. Jan probably mentioned the visit and got his father riled up. But why would Jan break his word, especially since doing so could only be unpleasant for him? And why in God's name was the volume to that music set to "deafen"?

Damon had heard this piece many times before. He anticipated the next musical pause. He heard spurts of shouting. Jan's voice. Damon could not hear anyone else. His heart stood still.

Jan wasn't shouting anymore, he was screaming.

The music was playing full blast, and yet still, through the deep bass of the cellos, Damon could make out the word "please."

Damon turned the knob. The door was unlocked. There was no splintered wood, no visible damage whatsoever.

He slipped in, hiding behind a pillar. There were two people in the living room. Neither had spotted him.

Jan was kneeling, as if in prayer. Someone was standing, and even at this distance Damon could make out what he was holding.

The gun was pointed at Jan's head. The boy was pleading, his voice surfacing from the ocean of music like a minor instrument in the orchestra.

"Please . . . my dad has money . . ."

The thought that Jan was being robbed at gunpoint was interrupted by another quiet passage, and this time, Damon heard Jan's every word.

"He can get you anything you want. He's got money."

A burglar would be in a big hurry. Five minutes from breaking in to slipping out.

"Sorry, kid."

Damon's spinal fluid was replaced with ice water. He still managed to move, sliding down the open hallway with feline grace and speed.

He kept to the side, but there was no cover and no time to lose. Not a second. Breathing through his nose, he tried to slow his pounding heart, but the effect of the adrenaline coursing through his bloodstream could not be so easily reconciled.

The music was deafening again.

There was no way Damon could get to the man before the assailant pulled the trigger, ending Jan's short, innocent life.

"Over here!" Damon yelled at the top of his lungs.

It worked.

The man turned, aiming at Damon.

He charged, pinballing from side to side, toward his son. The adrenaline and the newfound hope of saving Jan transformed Damon from man to missile.

The Colt M1911 flashed in rapid succession, but the explosions were reduced to mere pops in the wake of the blaring music. The killer had used Beethoven in lieu of a silencer. Not the actions of a professional.

Damon pushed himself harder, his feet barely touching the marble floor. The NVA had never managed to shoot him, and this guy wasn't about to have better luck.

Running this jagged lightning course, he got a snapshot of his enemy. He was tall, had blue eyes, fine hair—completely gray now—and just as thin and fit as Damon remembered him from a decade before.

Damon had been wrong about Jan's attacker.

He was a pro if there ever was one.

Jabber recognized Damon at that same moment and ceased firing. *"Stop!"*

A man like Jabber wouldn't hesitate to kill. Killing, therefore, wasn't his plan. At least, not for the time being.

Damon jumped. Airborne and almost completely horizontal, he used Jabber to cushion the landing.

A silly question entered Damon's mind as he knocked the semiautomatic from Jabber's gloved hand and watched it spin across the marble floor: why that gun when NSA agents could get whatever suppressed weapon they wanted?

Damon lay on top of him for a moment.

There was no movement. He got his hand around Jabber's throat, pressing his thumb on the man's Adam's apple. He felt a pulse. Damon was relieved Jabber wasn't dead, but it would have been better had he been conscious to answer questions.

While he had motive to set Damon up in Vietnam, what was Jabber doing *there*? And what could he possibly gain by killing a seventeen-year-old?

The chauffeur drove away, leaving Kory and Mr. Chambers in front of the Manhattan town house.

Mr. Chambers seemed quite alarmed when he heard the intolerably loud music.

Kory walked hesitantly up the steps to the door. His eyebrows were furrowed in confusion. "What in the world?"

Kory was fishing for his keys when he noticed the light coming from within the partially open door.

He gave it a push.

Sensing their approach, Damon turned his head to see his brother and the family attorney stampeding in his direction. Kory was shouting something, but there was no making sense of it over the music.

The speakers emitted a nerve-shattering screech as Mr. Chambers plucked the needle from the record one last time. Beethoven's famous symphony was replaced by a loud hum.

The remainder of his sentence was a yell in the relative silence: "—shots!" Standing a few feet from Damon, Kory said, "What are *you* doing here?" Pointing to the man on the floor he added, "And who is that?"

Before Damon could answer, Kory saw Jan crouched beside his prized Steinway.

The attorney's face appeared to have acquired a thick coat of flour glue. He stood there observing the scene before him as if not just his face but his entire body were cemented by the very same epoxy.

Kory ran to Jan, holding him. "Son? Are you all right?"

Jan stared dumbly at his father, wanting to speak, but seemingly having forgotten how.

Still grasping on to the boy, Kory snapped his head in his brother's direction. Damon remained in an unsettling embrace with the body beneath him like a necrophiliac caught in the act. "What is going on?" Kory's anger and confusion graduated abruptly to terror. "Oh, God! Blood!"

For a second, his brother's observation seemed absurd. But Kory was right: a pool of blood was spreading on the marble floor. All Damon could say was, "I didn't have a gun, he did."

Kory and Mr. Chambers saw the weapon Damon was referring to. Kory remained with Jan, Mr. Chambers went for the gun but hesitated to retrieve it from the floor. Quickly and with a trembling hand, he plucked a handkerchief from his breast pocket using it to handle the weapon.

"No," Damon said, "leave it! He can't get to it from—"

Mr. Chambers pointed the gun at Damon. "Don't move."

"Hey! That's loaded, don't point it at me."

"What have you done?" Mr. Chambers said. "What have you done to this man?"

"Damon came for Jan," Kory said.

Mr. Chambers seemed not to hear. "Get off that man," he repeated, the gun a trembling extension of his hand.

"That wouldn't be a good idea," Damon said, pausing between words.

"I . . . I will use this," Mr. Chambers said.

"Brad, listen to me: I know this guy," Damon said, "and he's bad news."

"Get off him . . . get off him . . . get off that man."

When faced with a lawyer on the verge of hysteria and pointing a loaded 1911 at your face, the first step, Damon decided, would be to calm him down. To that end, Damon inched his way off Jabber, and with exaggerated care. As he moved aside, however, Damon kept his hand on the NSA agent's throat.

Kory looked at Mr. Chambers. "Do you know how to use that thing?"

The attorney gave Kory a nervous glance but did not reply. To Damon he said: "Now, stand up. Move away from him. And . . . and put your hands behind your head."

Wanting to appease by way of demonstrating his cooperation, Damon raised his arms with deliberation. Arrested by a sudden pain, he caught his left arm mid-fall with his right.

Mr. Chambers jumped where he stood. "Hands up!"

"I can't," Damon said. "I've been shot." A glance told him no major arteries had been hit. Only one wound out of five shots, but Jabber had done better than all the NVA Damon had encountered in his two tours in Vietnam. Still, Damon had been lucky. A few inches to the right and he wouldn't be alive to assess the injury. The bullet had gone straight through, penetrating the muscle and cartilage of the left armpit. Nevertheless, it was bleeding noticeably. He pointed at the wound with his right hand. "See?"

His repository of commands exhausted, Mr. Chambers was silent.

"Kory? Look. That's *my* blood on the floor. I didn't shoot him, he shot *me*." Not getting a response from his brother, Damon appealed once more to Mr. Chambers. "That's his gun."

"Okay . . . okay then. If that's true, you have nothing to worry about," the attorney said, grasping the gun more tightly then before. "The police will find the fingerprints."

"No. He's wearing gloves, can't you see?" Damon said, pointing at Jabber.

"I'm calling the police," Kory announced, and facing no objections, he made for the phone. As he came closer to Damon, he noticed the wound. "He really *is* bleeding."

Mr. Chambers squinted at Damon, staring at him with mortification.

Jan spoke for the first time. "The guy on the floor was going to shoot me. Damon came in and knocked him down. He saved my life."

Trying to steady his voice, Mr. Chambers said, "This is terrible. A terrible experience. This must be so hard for you. But we have to be careful. Damon may have been trying to save your life. But . . . but what if he was trying to make it *appear* that way? It's not safe to trust him. Kory is right. We need to call the police."

"What was Damon doing here in the first place?" Kory asked.

Jan avoided his father's gaze. "He came to see me—I . . . I . . . he left, but he came back. If it weren't for him, I'd be dead now."

"We'll talk about that later," Kory said. "Who is that other man?"

"He's ex-NSA," Damon answered for Jan. "That illegal mission you were talking about the other day? Well, this is the guy who set me up. He's the one you need to worry about, not me."

The man on the floor groaned.

"He's alive?" Mr. Chambers exclaimed, his eyes wide with amazement.

"You thought I *killed* him?" Damon said. "I told you, that's my blood on the floor."

The man started to gag.

Damon moved in Jabber's direction, but Mr. Chambers waved the gun, and yelled, "Step away!"

"I was just going to pin him down before he comes to."

"Don't you move," Mr. Chambers said with renewed determination.

"This guy is dangerous. How many times do I have to say this: that's his gun. He shot me. He came here to shoot Jan."

The barrel of the gun dropped half an inch.

"He's a killer," Damon added. "You don't want him unleashed. Trust me."

"I'm not sure whom to trust," Mr. Chambers admitted, gradually winning the battle to steady his voice. "Can you speak?" he said, addressing the man on the floor. "Who are you? What are you doing here? Are you associated with this man? Is it true you were trying to harm the boy?"

Jabber looked up, coughed, and got to his feet. He looked around, studying the scene as he massaged his head.

Damon was at the ready.

"You were, weren't you?" Mr. Chambers said. "You can speak but you don't want to. It is as the boy says, isn't it? You tried to kill him. Damon saved Jan."

Jabber scrutinized the weapon in the attorney's hand.

"Don't you get any ideas. You stay precisely where you are!" To Damon, Mr. Chambers said, "You're right. I believe you. Jan wouldn't lie. He has no reason to lie. And I can't accept that you'd want to harm your own nephew. But we still have to call the police. You have to leave immediately."

"What are you talking about?" Kory said. "We can't just assume he's innocent."

"If the police find him here, they'll arrest him," Mr. Chambers said. "This stranger has no obvious motive, but Damon does. If it is true—if he is an NSA agent—then he's not going to speak. Are you? . . . No, he isn't. . . . See? He's not going to say a word."

"No way am I leaving you with him," Damon said. "He'll kill you all."

"I have a gun," Mr. Chambers said, waving the weapon as if Damon wouldn't otherwise notice it. "And I'll use it if I must."

"I don't care if you have a bazooka, you're no match for him."

"Forget it," the man said, still rubbing his temple. "It won't work."

"See, even he agrees with me," Damon said.

"Jan, this is very important," the attorney said. "Did this man try to shoot you?"

"I told you, he was going to kill me."

"And as far as you could tell," Mr. Chambers said, "Damon had nothing to do with this, right?"

Kory interrupted, "No, no, no. You were right before. This was probably an act. I mean, look: the man isn't dead, Damon just knocked him out. They could have been a team. Damon must have heard us coming, and took his partner down to make Jan think he's innocent."

"Is that what happened, Jan?" Mr. Chambers said.

"No way!"

"How could he possibly know?" Kory said.

"It wasn't like that, Dad. Damon stopped him *before* you and Mr. Chambers came."

"If he's innocent, the police will sort it out," Kory said. "If these two are a team, and Damon leaves, you'll be letting a murderer run free."

"I realize you two have had your differences, but he's still your brother," Mr. Chambers said. "Damon, I implore you to leave. Don't worry—I can handle this man until the police arrive. Jean-Luc gave you your ticket, right? Hurry! We must call the police and you have to leave! Go!"

"If you really think I'm innocent," Damon said, "then why are you still pointing that gun at me?"

"I am?" Mr. Chambers said in a thin voice. "I'm sorry. I'm not accustomed to these things."

"I told you it won't work," Jabber said.

"Why were you trying to hurt the boy?" Mr. Chambers said, regaining some of the basso of an older man.

"Because you told me to," Jabber said. "Game's up. Give me the gun and let me finish this."

Mr. Chambers avoided Jabber's eyes. "I don't know what you're talking about."

"For a lawyer, you really suck at lying." The NSA agent smiled.

"Don't listen to him!" Mr. Chambers said. "He's trying to trick you."

"*Bra-ad,*" Jabber said.

Damon lunged at the NSA agent.

"Don't move!" Mr. Chambers said to Damon.

"He's going to take your gun," Damon said. "Give it to me before it's too late!"

"I *said* don't move." Something had definitively changed in the attorney's voice.

Damon advanced slowly, despite the warning. "Hand it over before you do something you'll regret."

Instead of giving Damon the gun, the attorney pointed the 1911 at Jan.

"Have you gone mad?" Kory shouted.

"Stand back," Mr. Chambers said, still addressing Damon. "You may not care about your life, but are you willing to jeopardize his?"

Damon took a small step away from the attorney.

To Jan, Mr. Chambers said, "You stay on your knees. Come over here on all fours." When the young man had come within two yards, Mr. Chambers added, "That's far enough. Lie down on your face, spread your arms." Addressing Damon: "Take two steps back. That's it. Now, get down on the floor, just as Jan did."

Keeping his eyes on the attorney, Damon stepped diagonally backward, trying to get between Jan and the gun. There was too much distance to cover, and Mr. Chambers made him lie down in spread-eagle fashion before Damon had a chance to make it half that distance.

Speaking now to Kory, Mr. Chambers said, "You too. On the floor. Hurry."

With all three of them lying on their stomachs, the attorney regained some composure, his expression shifting down from panic to disbelief and annoyance. "He's been out of commission for a decade and you couldn't stop him?"

"He's a SOG," Jabber replied. "They don't go soft. And for fuck's sake, I told you: if the music is playing, don't come in. The job wasn't finished."

"Right, but you were supposed to be done before we arrived. You *assured* me—"

"Don't try pinning this fuck-up on my ass. Who would have thought five minutes would turn into a forty-minute trip down memory lane and a private fucking piano recital?"

"In that case, you should have aborted," Mr. Chambers said.

"We weren't going to get another opportunity like this and you know it. After this, Jan would have told everyone what a nice, misunderstood guy Damon is, so you could forget him being convicted of anything except getting me sick to my stomach."

Lying down, his face to one side with a view of Mr. Chambers, Damon could see the weapon was still aimed at Jan. He was holding it with one hand, his arm fully extended, like a man who'd never fired a pistol in his life.

Soon he would tire, bend his arm, and lose aim. That might present a window of opportunity. A fraction of a second during which Damon would have to bolt up and position himself for the attack. It was a long shot, but a lame plan was better than no plan; something to work with until he could come up with a better idea.

Jabber was the real problem. Damon didn't have time for problems; he needed solutions.

The first step would be identifying the weakest link. His was Jan. Theirs was Mr. Chambers.

Kory cut in. "What the hell is going on?"

"Good question," Damon said. "Why don't you explain, Jabber."

"Roger's the name nowadays."

Damon said, "Listen, Brad, I don't know how you fit into all this, but Jabber here—whatever he is to you—is the bad guy, not me, and certainly not Jan."

"I'm his cousin, asshole," Jabber said.

"Don't say any more," Mr. Chambers snapped.

"What does it matter?" Jabber said. "He's history anyway."

"No," Mr. Chambers said, "that's *not* the plan."

Jabber shrugged. "He knows. He's seen you here. It's too late to do this your way. He's dumb, not retarded. He leaves us here, they die, and you think he won't connect the dots? You're hoping he won't blame you? That's it, isn't it? What were you thinking of saying? That I overpowered you, took the gun, killed these two, and somehow left you alive?"

"I wasn't going to mention you."

"Oh, I get it. He's seen me, but you'll claim I wasn't here. What will you tell the cops? Damon kills them, leaves you? No? What then? You let yourself in later, then discover the mess? That's plain fucking stupid."

"The police won't believe a word out of his mouth," Mr. Chambers said. "He'd be better off arguing temporary insanity or crime of passion. I won't allow a penny of the trust to be spent defending a criminal, so with a court-appointed attorney on his side, he'll end up in prison. It works."

"It doesn't," Jabber said, shaking his head. "You're not thinking straight. All these years you've been able to work the unexpected in your favor. This isn't the time to cling to a plan out of stubbornness."

"This has nothing to do with stubbornness," Mr. Chambers said.

"Come on, Brad, you never got over your obsession with Martha and her fucking family. You just want to draw it out, watch him fester."

"I'm not giving up a lifetime of work because of a hiccup."

"He goes to the cops, we've got trouble, even just with what he knows now."

Mr. Chambers said, "He signed for the box, and his finger-prints are on the gun, and all over this house." He hesitated for a moment. "They *are* on the gun, right?"

"Yes, yes," Jabber said. "I took care of—"

"I've never seen that 1911 before," Damon said.

"Oh, yes you have," Mr. Chambers said, still looking at his cousin. "It was your father's gun."

Jabber added, "The one he used to blow his brains out, remember?"

"That's a load of—"

"My father died of complications," Kory interrupted, look-ing for support from his brother.

"You wouldn't know," Mr. Chambers said, "but Damon here does."

"What makes you think I wouldn't know?" Kory said. "He was my father too."

"Tell him, Damon," Jabber said.

Damon did not answer. He wasn't moving.

"One gun for all van Luden men," Mr. Chambers said. "And Damon gets to watch now, as he did then."

"He can watch," Jabber said, "but that's got to be the end of it. We can't afford to let this guy go. He kills his brother and nephew, then he vanishes. It's sloppy, but at this stage it's our only option. I can work the scene. The police will go for an easy solve."

"No," Mr. Chambers snapped, "I'm not going to let you ruin this."

"You have any better ideas?"

"Yes. Drug him. Then you kill these two. He won't remember—just like before."

Jabber shook his head, but Kory interrupted before he could speak. "Like before what?"

"Shut the fuck up," Jabber said. He motioned at the weapon in his cousin's hand. "We're wasting time. Give me the gun, Brad."

"No," Mr. Chambers said, "you'll kill him."

Surprised by his cousin's refusal to relinquish the weapon, the former NSA agent thought for a moment before speaking. "He survived the Vietnam setup, he dodged the government for over a decade, and he almost took me out a moment ago. Let's say you're right: his family points the finger at him, they go along with your story, and the cops end up believing you. What if they don't catch him? Think about it. Alive and free, he'd be a major pain in our ass."

Mr. Chambers did not speak, but the gun remained tightly clamped in his hand.

"Either shoot him or tie him up," Jabber said, eyeing Damon.

"Okay . . . you're probably right. Restrain him."

Jabber put out his hand. "Give me the gun first."

"No. Not until you convince me you'll leave him for the police."

Jabber shrugged.

Mr. Chambers spoke to Kory: "Get some rope and tie Damon's hands."

"I don't have rope," Kory said.

"Then use masking tape," Jabber said. "Move it!"

A few minutes later, tearing off the surplus tape, Kory announced that he was done.

"That won't hold a baby," Jabber said. *Tighter.*

Reluctantly, Kory added a second layer, trying to do so without cutting off his brother's circulation. His limp arms suggested he had lost consciousness, yet he was breathing rapidly, his eyes squeezed shut. Pain from the wound? Could be, but from what Kory could discern, Damon wasn't bleeding that badly.

"Those two I can leave here for the police. This one," Jabber said, pointing at Damon, "I need to dispose of, and that's going to take some time, so—"

"I don't want him dead, I want him in prison."

"Why? Dead worked for you before."

"Nonsense," Mr. Chambers said uneasily.

"Nonsense? What about Martha? With her alive, the trust was worthless—"

"You killed my mother?" Damon said in a bewildered, distant voice, as if he were speaking in his sleep.

"Now, did I say that? It was her time to die, and she did." Jabber kicked Damon in the ribs. "Interrupt me again, and I'll slice and dice the boy, and feed him to you like cheap sushi."

Speaking once again to his cousin, Jabber said, "And what about Damon and Dorothy? You seem to forget your little plan for them if things went sour. And Jasmine? You wanted her gone whether she'd performed or not."

"That was different," Mr. Chambers mumbled.

"Okay, I'll buy that. Back to Damon, then. What about that mission you had me set up? Dead was okay then, but it's not good enough now?"

"I've waited a lifetime—"

"Right, like you ever stick with one idea."

"I always do."

"Really? Let's see: First, you don't want Damon married, so Stavridis makes Dorothy into a junkie. Then when Damon doesn't give her up, you have the detective fix the marriage so that she dumps him just like Martha dumped you. Is that what you call sticking to your decisions?"

"If I didn't change the plan, they could have been happily married, that would have spelled disaster."

"Yeah, it would have, but despite everything you had me do, they did stay married. So much for your new plan."

"It still worked out," Mr. Chambers said.

"Until you thought he might return to the States and start meddling with the trust."

"It was a reasonable concern."

"I agree. That's my point. There was a reasonable concern, and you came up with a reasonable solution: have him killed in action. So why was it reasonable then and not now?"

"The van Ludens have always been unpredictable. I had to be flexible."

"Then be flexible now. You came up with this prison idea just a few days ago, so cut the 'I've-waited-a-lifetime' bullshit."

"It *has* been a lifetime. I had the perfect opportunity, don't you see? From the day those two were at one another's throats over—"

"Give it a rest. A fucking dog died and you take it as some message from God. You are so full of shit. Let's just do this and get the fuck out of Dodge."

"You touch my boy," Damon said, glaring at Jabber, "and I'll rip your fucking heart out."

The fact that Damon held on to his belief that he was Jan's father wasn't what surprised Kory. It was the nature and timing of his threat to Jabber. Former SOG or not, Damon's hands were securely tied behind his back. And if Damon really wanted to attack Jabber, why eliminate the element of surprise?

Of course, it might not have been a calculated reaction. It could very well have been a belated reaction to numerous things, not the least of which was the possibility that Martha had been murdered. But Kory never understood his brother, and unraveling the inner workings of his psyche remained as impossible a task as it had ever been before, especially considering the fact that the playing field was changing minute by minute.

The only helpful conclusion Kory could draw was that provoking the NSA agent in this manner had been part of his brother's plan. From a layman's perspective, angering the enemy seemed counterintuitive in any hostage situation. Perhaps the Army trained SOGs for such a contingency, perhaps not. Either way, if anyone could get them out of this, it was Damon. A war-hardened man such as he would be fully capable of repressing emotion. For Jan's sake, and for the first time in his life, Kory would have to trust his brother.

Jabber gripped Damon's bleeding shoulder, giving it a sharp twist.

"Is that all you got?" Damon said, wincing but not crying out despite the excruciating pain. Damon looked for an opening to attack, but Jabber had already let go, distancing himself once again.

At first, Damon's disappointment at seeing his tormentor leave seemed confusing, but then Kory understood. Not all of it—not the details most certainly—but enough to work with. Damon had a plan. Why wouldn't he? He'd never allow emotion to get the better of him. Why had Kory even entertained such a possibility? He sensed the answer, but probing deeper would lead him astray, and couldn't possibly prove beneficial in the current predicament. Kory had to devise some way to get Jabber to remain next to Damon. Evidently, Jabber was aware of the danger of lingering near one of the Army's elite. That explained why he wanted Damon tied up, and why he wouldn't perform the task himself.

"He's pissed now. You still want to keep this guy alive?" Jabber said to his cousin. "If you don't let me eliminate him, he'll hunt you down. He might not get to me, but he'll certainly get to you. If he's feeling charitable, he'll finish you off quick and simple. But if I'd have to guess, I'd say he'll torture you first, make you beg to be killed."

Mr. Chambers said nothing.

"Every minute you waste thinking about this makes my job harder. Damon has seen you. He knows what you've done, and if he lives, he'll go after you."

"I haven't done anything."

"Of course not. You're not the hands-on type. Me and Stavridis did most of your dirty work, but I don't think that's going to matter much to Damon here, because you thought of all this, not me. He's going to want your hide, and if you let him live, I guarantee he'll get it."

"You have all the money, so don't play innocent."

"I don't do innocent; that's your deal. But he's not buying it, Brad. He knows what you had me do."

"I don't recall asking you to violate the girl on her wedding night," Mr. Chambers said.

"I had to be sure."

"There were other ways."

"Mine was more fun."

It took a moment for Damon to realize what they were talking about. "That's impossible. Dorothy was with me. There was blood on the sheets. She was a virgin—"

"You screwed a whore-actress and that wasn't human blood," Jabber said without taking his eyes off his cousin. "I got to fuck Dorothy. I can tell you, she was no virgin, but she was the tightest piece of pussy I've had since high school."

As difficult as it was, Kory managed not to scream. This was Damon's opportunity to act, and there might not be another. Like his younger brother, Damon did not yell. He remained quiet, his face twisted and growing darker with each passing second.

"He's right, you haven't thought this through, have you?" Kory said, shocked to hear how calm he sounded.

"What?" Jabber said.

"I'm talking to Mr. Chambers," Kory said, lifting his head off the ground to get a better look at the family attorney. "You've placed a lot of faith in your cousin. I hope for your sake you have a solid basis for this loyalty. From my perspective, if you take away the trust fund, Jabber will have all the reason, and equal lack of compunction, to dispose of you as he would us."

Jabber's smile disappeared. "You don't know what the fuck you're saying. Without Brad, I'd have nothing."

Still addressing Mr. Chambers, Kory said, "You said before that he had all the money."

The attorney did not reply.

Jabber spoke in his place. "What I have now is nothing compared to what we could have after another two decades."

"Did you hear that?" Kory asked. "He said: 'What *I* have.' So tell me, has the trust always been in his charge?"

"It never was," Mr. Chambers said.

"I just help trim a bit off the top," Jabber added.

"I have nothing to do with that," Mr. Chambers said. "He does."

"Yeah, you have nothing to do with *anything*," Jabber snapped. "Grow a fucking spine! Why do you care what a dead man thinks?"

"If you have nothing to do with it," Kory said, answering Mr. Chambers, "then logically he should kill you."

"You know why he trusts me, you dumb fuck?" Jabber said. "Because I've *never* once let him down. And because one hundred percent of what we have now doesn't come close to my cut on our present stash plus what I could get over the next twenty years."

"But according to your cousin, you haven't given him a dime of the embezzled money, so how does he know you ever will?"

Instead of answering, Jabber kicked Kory.

"Is that really necessary?" Mr. Chambers said. "Or does his question trouble you?"

Jabber regarded his watch. "Use it or lose it."

Mr. Chambers stiffened in response to the threatening tone.

"Come on, Brad," Jabber said, trying a friendly voice, "it's not like you'd ever use the thing."

"You give me your word Damon goes to prison?" Mr. Chambers said, sounding like a schoolboy.

"We've told him everything. With all the details he has, the police are bound to listen to his story and start investigating us. My way, he'll be dead, but he'll still be the number-one suspect. That'll taint the shit out of the van Luden name."

"What good is that? All van Ludens would be dead," Mr. Chambers said. "Listen, we don't have to do this. He won't remember anything after you give him the drug."

"Sorry, I'm not a walking pharmacy, I don't carry a syringe in my back pocket. And even if I had the drug, I couldn't do anything with it. The old dose calculations were for succinyl-choline and based on what he weighed back then."

"I'm not talking about the '60s," Mr. Chambers shouted. "I mean *today*."

"That wasn't even a plan. I just said I'd look into it. Leaving him here drugged next to Jan's body isn't anywhere near as good as the setup we have right now."

"But you said—"

"I didn't *say* anything," Jabber snapped, pointing a finger as if he had the pistol.

"You tricked me! You could have told me this earlier! You gave Damon incriminating information to force me to have him killed."

Jabber shrugged. "It was for your own good."

"For my own good?" Mr. Chambers yelled. "You idiot! You know Martha was too cunning to allow me to draft loopholes. If you kill Damon along with these two, I'll lose control of the trust, and Mary van Luden will get everything."

"Don't get your panties in a wad," Jabber said, his affable voice betrayed by a condescending smile. "So he dies? I'll just make the body disappear."

Mr. Chambers frowned but did not make a counterargument.

Jabber's smile did not abate. "Everyone, including the cops, will suspect Damon. Do this my way, and you'll never have to worry about him repeating any of this. He'll be dead, and his body will be as easy to find as the Ark of the Covenant. Good enough for you?"

Mr. Chambers shook his head. "I can't believe this is happening."

Jabber walked over to the record player.

"What are you doing?" Mr. Chambers said.

"Time to give me the gun."

Instead of handing it over, Mr. Chambers pointed the weapon at his cousin.

Jabber's eyes widened in a brief moment of disbelief. An equally fleeting prideful grin became a mocking flash in his eyes. "Come on, Brad, we both know you don't have the balls to shoot a tin can."

The weapon was still pointed at him, but Jabber laughed as if he were looking down the barrel of a water pistol.

"Ever since Martha dumped you, I've had to do your fucking dirty work. " Ignoring the threat of the gun, Jabber walked over to the record player, and placed the needle back on the moving turntable. Once again, the walls shook with eardrum-rupturing music.

"You haven't given me your word!" Mr. Chambers shouted.

Jabber may have replied, but Damon couldn't hear.

Kory had succeeded in getting Mr. Chambers to point the gun at his cousin. This was as good as it was going to get.

Not anticipating the attorney would ever take his aim off Jan, Damon's initial plan had been to get Jabber in the line of fire, and use him to ram Mr. Chambers. The rest he would have figured out on the fly.

In preparation for Jan's murder, the former NSA agent would have used a low-energy hollow-point. Possibly a magnesium and lead Black Talon, which would slice the fingers of any surgeon attempting an extraction. In all likelihood, a 230-grain hollow-point would come apart in Jabber's innards and not make it through Damon. The .45s were subsonic, but even if the 1911 had been loaded with full-metal jacket rounds, they would probably go straight through Jabber and stop in Damon, killing them both but sparing the boy. Either way, for a few seconds, Mr. Chambers's weapon could not harm Jan. Now the gun wasn't even pointed at the boy. That was all the assurance Damon needed, the rest was reflex.

He rolled onto his back, curling his knees over his head in a modified yoga maneuver while using all his might to throw his straightened arms over his knees. Pain lit up his left arm. It was extreme, but not paralytic. The momentum carried Damon into a forward roll, propelling him to his feet, his tied hands now out in front of him.

In the second it took Damon to complete this maneuver, Jabber had gone for Mr. Chambers's weapon, probably hoping to take over control before Damon could. The NSA agent was fast. Mr. Chambers leaned back, losing both his footing and his aim. Jabber grabbed the 1911 by the top of the slide with his right hand, and Mr. Chambers's hand with the other, and twisted. The single-action semiautomatic had already been fired, leaving the hammer cocked, requiring only a few pounds of pressure on the trigger to release its next load. The barrel of the .45 spewed flame and smoke in a string of blasts.

At almost the same instant, as Damon was about to ram into the cousins, headfirst, Jabber sidestepped, the weapon in his hand. Mr. Chambers lay facedown, his life essence mixing with the coagulating puddle Damon had left before.

Damon attempted to hook his foot, but Jabber pulled away as he raised the 1911. Damon charged him, trying to get up inside Jabber's arms, where there'd be no room to use the gun. Two more shots fired. Damon attacked with his knee but only found air. With his hands tied, his best hope was to keep Jabber on the defensive. He was too late.

Raising his arms and slipping downward, the NSA agent had freed himself from Damon's lock hold. A judo technique Damon had used himself in training. The next move was to disable with a kick to the groin. Jabber didn't have to do this, however. He had the gun out and ready.

Damon tried to spin out of the way, but Jabber had already squeezed the trigger. There was no sound, no flash. The soft *click* of the firing pin could not be heard, but Damon could see the slide was locked back. The gun was empty.

Damon went for a frontal attack.

Still holding the weapon, Jabber was only able to partially deflect Damon's double-punch. One fist made contact with ribs, but the force was mostly absorbed by Jabber's arm. Using the pistol as a hammer, he came down on Damon's head. Damon caught it easily between his hands. Twisting in a wide arc, he tried to grab hold of an arm to throw Jabber over his shoulder, but there was no give in the tape that bound Damon's hands. The NSA agent retreated, kneeling slightly as he did so. He was going for an ankle knife.

Before he could grasp it, Kory came charging, beet-faced, a chair held high over his head, Jan close behind. Jabber reacted as any sensible man would when outnumbered three-to-one. He ran.

Jabber must have studied the layout of the house, because he took a back exit Damon was unfamiliar with. Probably the very same escape route he'd planned to use after he'd killed Jan.

In the unlit garden, Damon looked around for an exit but couldn't find one.

"This way," Kory said, running past him to a door.

Bolting out through the front door, Jan who had been in the back of the three, was suddenly in the lead. They made it to Sixty-Seventh Street in time to see Jabber in full sprint, disappearing around the corner, heading south on Fifth Avenue.

Damon gave chase, but he was wounded and his hands were tied. Jabber was lean, fit, and running for his life.

"Stay right here," Damon told Jan.

Holding out his hands, he called after his brother, "Hurry, help me get this off!"

"There's no time," Kory said, starting on the task anyway. "We'll lose sight of him."

Seconds felt like minutes as Kory tried to scratch off enough tape to grip. The first strip came off. The second seemed to have no end. More scratching at the surface, more precious seconds gone. Finally Damon's hands were free.

He was a fast runner, but it was an obstacle course slaloming between the pedestrian hordes. And that was just on Sixty-Seventh Street.

Fifth Avenue was jam-packed with bumper-to-bumper southbound traffic and the sidewalks were flooded with people.

Shit. Fifth Avenue. Rush hour. A Friday night.

If Jabber had been parading around on stilts, wearing a psychedelic clown outfit, Damon might have had a chance at spotting him, but as things were, it was hopeless.

And Kory and Jan were standing outside the town house unprotected.

Damon ran back to the town house; his brother and nephew stood outside, looking apprehensive.

Damon shook his head, answering their question before they could ask. "He's gone." The town house door was still ajar. "I'm going in first. I'll just be a moment. You two stay behind."

"Do you think he's alive?" Jan said.

"I doubt it, but I'm not taking any chances."

Inside, the phone had just stopped ringing.

Damon searched for something to use as a weapon. A sterling silver candlestick in hand, he made his advance to the living room, visually clearing the area every five meters.

The attorney lay precisely where he had fallen.

Damon rolled him onto his back.

Three bullet holes, all center mass.

The one through the heart had been fatal.

EN PRISE

June 1980
Friday, 6:00 p.m.

"**H**and me that balloon."

"Honey, you shouldn't be standing on that ladder if you're not feeling well."

"I'm just . . . very tired."

"Come here, let me feel your forehead . . . I think you might have a slight fever. You'd best lie down."

"But John is coming to pick us up now. We have to get going."

"You've been to all the others. This isn't his first and it won't be his last. Take a nap. You'll feel much better, and we'll be back before midnight."

"Would you call them for me?"

"Of course, you just get your rest."

"I couldn't reach Kory about the change in plans. . . ."

"I know. I'll take care of everything. Don't you worry."

Some fuckers have all the luck.

If cats have nine lives, that asshole had a thousand.

Jabber could have gone for the gun. His car had been right across the street, and he'd left the .38 in the glove

711

compartment. It was fully loaded, but that meant just six rounds, and though he might have been able to nail all three of them, there would have been dozens of witnesses. Disappearing Damon and pinning the murders on him would have been out of the question.

First the call.

Then back to the car. Then wait and listen, wait and see.

A man in a Wall Street pinstripe suit tapped on the glass phone booth.

Jabber pushed the folding door enough to shout through the crack, "Fuck off, jackass!"

The guy flipped Jabber the finger but didn't budge. Without taking his eyes off him, Jabber started picking his fingernails with his hunting knife.

The guy walked off.

"Is he dead?" Jan asked.

"Very," Damon said. He looked at his brother. "This wasn't an accident. Cousin or no cousin, the moment Brad became a liability to Jabber, his fate was sealed."

"So I'm responsible for this?" Kory asked.

Damon walked away. "You didn't pull the trigger, Kory, Jabber did."

"What are you looking for?" Kory asked.

Damon did not seem to hear; he was making a beeline for the piano.

The phone rang, and for a moment, nobody moved to answer it.

"That's got to be Dorothy," Kory explained as he picked up the receiver. "They must be getting ready to leave."

A man's voice spoke on the other end of the line. "Hi, asshole."

Kory looked to Damon and mouthed *Jabber*.

As Damon sifted through Jan's sheet music, he motioned for the phone with his free hand, but Jabber started talking and Kory decided he could handle this himself.

"If you're thinking about calling the cops, think again. The police find out? The feds? You let anyone know—I mean fucking *anyone*—and Dorothy dies. Do I make myself clear?"

"Yes."

"That didn't sound convincing."

"Nobody will tell anyone anything."

"I'll fuck her long and hard first."

"I get the picture—"

"Maybe you do, maybe you don't. I don't give a shit. She dies, it's on your head. On the other hand, do this right, you all get to live. All I need is a little off the top. Like the arrangement I had with Brad. The kid won't be involved. But if he or anybody else ever gets in my way—runs any kind of interference— you're all dead, Dorothy is fish food, and your brother gets the credit."

"What are we supposed to do with the body, then?"

"That's your problem now," Jabber said. "You can keep it in the house for all I care. If you do, put it in a refrigerator or find a taxidermist, because a New York summer will make a stiff go ripe really fast. That might get you some unwanted attention. And unwanted attention will get you more bodies to worry about."

The line went dead.

It took him three minutes to get back to his car. Three minutes he could not afford to lose.

From the sides, there wasn't much to see, thanks to the tinted windows, but the descending sun blazed straight through the windshield. Any pedestrian approaching the car head-on would have a clear view, in which case his cover was limited to sunglasses and a Yankees cap.

But these were New Yorkers. The worst witnesses on earth. They minded their own business. The way it should be.

The earpiece and the wire were well hidden, and even a cop wouldn't see the equipment under the passenger seat.

Jabber listened. Nothing.

He turned up the volume. Nada.

This wasn't good.

Jabber looked at his watch again.

His gaze wandered to the glove compartment. Too fucking sloppy. Too damned risky. No element of surprise. Five minutes more, then—

Footsteps.

Then: "You think he'll be okay alone upstairs?" *Barely audible.*

"Don't worry, most guys puke the first time they see a killing." *Definitely the SOG talking here.* "Hey, I'm surprised you managed to hold your lunch. Don't worry, he just needs to lie down. Give him a few minutes and he'll be as good as new."

"Will you?"

"I'll be fine."

"I'm not so sure. That wound is still bleeding." *The professor, talking to his brother.*

"I know."

"When they made me tie you up, I thought I'd lost you for a minute. I thought you'd passed out or worse."

No reply.

"It wasn't the wound, was it?"

Silence.

"Was it what he'd said about our father?" *The professor again.*

"We'll get there, little brother. We've got lots to talk about, but first things first: like I said upstairs, if we're going to call the police we've got to do it now."

"So you think he'll go through with his promise?"

Some jerk in a Fiat was leaning on the horn. Jabber pushed the mini-receiver deeper into his ear.

"If the police come, he'll know." *The SOG.*

Jabber cracked a smile.

"Dorothy, John, and Mary must be on their way by now, so he won't be able to get near my wife. At least, not for a couple of hours."

"I wouldn't be so sure. Remember, this is the guy who outsmarted both of us."

Jabber's smile grew.

"Why wouldn't he call the police himself?" *Good question, Kory.* "He could make an anonymous call. I answered the phone, so he must know we're here. We wouldn't have had time to hide the body, and all three of us knew Mr. Chambers. That would make us all prime suspects. At some point we'd be cleared, but that would give Jabber the time he needed to escape."

"He's not planning on escaping."

No response from the professor.

"He's a spook. There's no file on him, it would be close to impossible to track him down. He doesn't want anybody mentioning him at all. If he let us call the police, he'd have to go under deep cover for a long time. He'd probably have to leave the country."

"All these years, I've been trying to think like you, to figure out your next move. I was playing the wrong opponent."

"At least now you know who's on the other side of the board."

Four seconds of silence.

"Jabber said he was the one with access to all the money, right? And if Mr. Chambers was working with him but didn't want to get his hands dirty, there might have been a third person in the company. A bookkeeper. Someone corruptible yet sufficiently naïve to play middleman in the dark for a sizeable commission or fee. Under those circumstances, if Jabber were forced into deep cover, he might not be in a position to obtain any of the funds he has stolen."

"That's an interesting theory." *Damon, coming in loud and clear.* "The other possibility is that Jabber wants us to keep quiet so that he can kill us, eliminating all witnesses, and then place the blame on me. He threatened to do so if we contacted the police, but killing us would be beneficial to him regardless of whether or not we keep quiet. More beneficial, actually, if we do keep our mouths shut."

"Are you saying we *should* call the police?"

"No. At least not now. There's nothing linking Jabber to this. All the evidence points at me. We could wipe the prints he planted off the gun, we could go over this entire house with a rag, and that would still do very little to help my case. You were right, we'd be detained for questioning as prime suspects with me on the top of the list. All we'd have for our defense is a story about an ex-NSA agent who is supposedly Mr. Chambers's cousin. First, second, or third cousin? We don't know; we don't even know if he really is his cousin. And we think Jabber's first name might be Roger, but we can't be sure of that, either. And while we're trying to convince the police of the truth, Jabber would have all the time in the world to attack anyone who isn't in custody. They'll probably lock me up, so that would leave you, Jan, and Dorothy at his mercy. It wouldn't be in his interest to go after her, but he might be crazy enough to do it anyway."

"So we follow his instructions, then?"

"As far as he'll ever know. We get rid of the body, and that shouldn't take us more than one to two hours at the most. Then you and Jan need to get out of here. Somewhere safe. Rhodes. Go to Rhodes, but not to John's house, Jabber might think of that. Go to Martha's place."

"Then what?"

"We'll find a way to send Dorothy and her parents back home. Somebody can tell them what's going on when they get to the recital hall. You and Jan wait for them to return. If the recital is at nine, they should be arriving earlier, so let's say eight thirty. A two-hour drive to Rhodes and they'll be there by ten thirty, eleven at the latest. If you and Jan leave here by eight, you won't be alone at Mother's for more than an hour, tops."

"What about you?"

"I'll meet up with you when all of this blows over. Right now, I'm the prime suspect. You get over to Rhodes. Get everyone there. Get your bodyguards there."

"Sounds logical. Regrouping your pieces. Mounting an attack disguised as a defense." *The professor.* "And that's when you're thinking we should call the police?"

"Exactly. With me out of the picture, they're more likely to believe you. And even if you're detained for questioning, you'll be under their protection and the bodyguards will be with Dorothy, so she'll be safe from Jabber."

"So that means we have to clean up this mess."

"If we agree to it this way, yes. He could be watching the area, and we can't leave a dead body lying around on your living-room floor. But once we disturb the evidence, there's no turning back."

"I know."

"And people are going to be looking for Mr. Chambers. When is his driver coming for him?"

"He was dismissed for the night. I'd thought that was odd, but at the time, I was distracted by the music. Thinking about it now, it makes sense: Mr. Chambers was expecting us to discover Jan's body. We'd call the police and would most likely be escorted to the station for statements. So he must have been anticipating a busy night."

"Yes, but there are people other than his driver who are bound to notice he's gone."

"He's supposed to be leaving on a trip. He won't be missed until Monday or Tuesday. We'll have to worry about that later, but first you really have to do something about that arm."

"Do you have a sewing kit?"

"Don't tell me you're planning on stitching yourself . . . Okay, okay, fine. As long as I don't have to watch. I've seen enough blood for one day. You'll need a painkiller—I think we have some from when Jan had his upper molars removed, and I know Dorothy has needles and thread upstairs."

"No drugs. I need to have a clear head tonight."

"Are you sure? Personally, my mind shuts down when I'm in pain."

"I've handled worse."

"Have it your way, then. While you play surgeon, I'll check up on Jan."

Footsteps, then nothing out of the earpiece.

That was fine, Jabber needed the time to think.

He cracked a smile. *By ten thirty, the professor and his son will end up like Brad. By tomorrow, the SOG will be on the run or in jail. Just the way good old Brad would have wanted it.*

Twenty-three minutes passed before he could hear them again.

As they walked down the staircase, Kory said, "He doesn't know what we're planning. That's our main advantage."

Jan glanced at the body. "All that blood . . ."

"There'd be a lot more if Jabber hadn't shot him through the pump," Damon explained.

"Don't look," Kory said. "You'll get sick again. Maybe you should go back to your room."

"No. He's safer staying where I can see him," Damon said. "And I need to be here to watch both entry points."

This idea his brother had of involving Jan was potentially precarious, and undoubtedly burdened the already trauma- tized boy with pressures Kory was unsure he could withstand.

Jan sat on the piano bench, studying the keys. Without lift- ing his gaze, he sensed his father looking at him. "Don't worry, I couldn't play even if I wanted to."

Kory offered his son a conciliatory smile. They'd explained to him why it was imperative he remain quiet while they spoke. But it had felt like they were pushing the boy away at a time when they should be embracing him.

Never before had a van Luden been painted in so dark a manner, and yet somehow, without the benefit of Jabber's self-incriminating revelations, Jan had found it in his heart to entrust his uncle, inviting him into his house and back into his life.

The boy was all heart.

In contrast to his son, Kory was feeling nothing. Neither remorse nor the beginnings of fraternal love reborn. His mind took charge instead, mapping the disorderly insanity of life onto a chessboard whereupon the moves were limited and emotion unwelcome. Perhaps feeling would one day return, filling his numbed heart once again. Perhaps. In time.

Jan did not have to wait for hours, days, or weeks for shock to subside. He reacted immediately, as his mother would. She was as quick in temper as she was in forgiveness. He was sen- sitive in a way even his mother was not. Jan had no temper, only compassion, and this left him neither lame nor delicate. He brimmed with passion. One could hear it in every note he played. Jan spoke through the piano, through its limitless shades of emotion.

Kory had no such gift. His focus was the chessboard, the logic center of the mind. And maybe that wasn't such a bad thing. Especially at a time such as this.

Appraising the body of the family attorney, Kory said, "If we remove the body in a sufficiently inconspicuous manner, Jabber won't be able to make an anonymous call without lending credibility to our story, and doubt to his. Unless he can definitively lay blame on us, police involvement would not be to his benefit. In fact, if the police found out the truth, he'd have to go into hiding."

"I told you, he's not going to call the cops," Damon said. "If he did, he'd have to know that we'd tell the police our side of the story."

"Right, and he wouldn't be able to do anything to any of us with you in custody because that would give further credence to our statements."

Damon nodded. "Like I said, Jabber is not a runner. He's not the type to become a recluse and retire in defeat. He was the real brains behind Mr. Chambers's plans. After all this work, after everything he's invested and risked, he's not about to go until he's got his money. He'll have enough to buy himself freedom, without having to live in some non–extradition treaty country."

"Are you guys going to do anything about the blood?" Jan said without taking his eyes off the piano.

"Well?" Damon said to Kory. "Are we in agreement, then?"

"Yes. We'll play his game for now, and tonight we'll force him to play ours. It's the most logical course of action for now."

"Do you have garbage bags?"

Kory gave his brother a nod.

"Good, bring them all."

"It's decided, then," Kory affirmed. To Jan, he said, "Cancel the recital. Call everyone you've invited."

"What do I tell them?"

"Keep it simple, believable, and temporary. Like a sprained wrist."

"That hurts just thinking about it. If you don't mind, I'll tell them I've got the stomach flu. Or cancer. Anything as long as it doesn't involve my hands."

Kory laughed as he ran to the kitchen and returned with an armful of supplies. "I didn't have much for rags, but I've got a bunch of towels, garbage bags, and I brought scissors."

"That should do the trick," Damon said.

Kory danced around the puddle, tossing towels in his wake, creating a cloth dam around the attorney.

With his brother's help, Kory pushed the towels toward the body, constricting the circle.

Damon took the two remaining towels and cut them both in half lengthwise. He wrapped the cloth strips around Mr. Chambers's chest as tightly as he could, keeping it in place with duct tape.

"That won't hold it," Kory pointed out.

"That's what the garbage bags are for." Damon cut the garbage bags open to form rectangular sheets that he used as a final layer in the mummification of the attorney's midsection. He examined his handiwork. "This will do."

"Now what?" Kory asked.

"I was hoping you could tell me that," Damon said. "After all, you were the one who masterminded Dorothy's fake death and the cover-up."

"The key word here is *fake,* Damon. And you have to remember, I didn't just come up with this idea in five minutes, I had months to think."

"I always found it strange that someone like Jean-Luc came up with such a detailed plan before Dorothy's body even had a chance to cool," Damon said.

"Speaking of which, we need to determine how much time we've got to work with here."

"Before we figure out how we're going to get rid of this body? Very little," Damon said. "Everything we do leaves an evidence trail."

Kory nodded. "Let's see. The recital is at nine."

Damon looked at his Seiko.

"It's six," Kory said.

Damon turned to Jan. "What else did you have going on for tonight?"

"There's going to be . . . *was* going to be . . . a short reception outside the concert hall for everyone, and Mom was planning a private reception for friends and family . . ." Jan looked at Damon. "But that was cancelled because I have to get up early tomorrow to go to Rhodes for a matinée Charlie arranged."

"Matinée?" Kory said, surprised.

"Yeah, Mom said she tried calling you, but you were at the club and you had that meeting with . . . him." Jan couldn't keep himself from looking at the body this time.

This change of plans concerned Kory. "Do the caterers know? Did she cancel?"

Jan shrugged. "I guess. I mean she must have, right?"

Damon said, "If she didn't, when would they be coming over?"

"They were supposed to come at seven thirty."

"That's less than an hour and a half from now," Kory said.

"We don't have much time," Damon said. "So, Dorothy is coming down here with John and Mary, and then what?"

"We were going to spend the night here, as we normally do," Jan said. "And head for Rhodes tomorrow morning."

"Okay," Kory said, "we have yet to determine precisely how much time we have."

"For starters, we've got until the caterers arrive," Jan offered, not certain he should be answering a question he hadn't been asked. "If Mom forgot to cancel . . ."

"We cannot calculate how long we have until we come up with a plan," Kory said.

Damon said, "What are our options?"

Kory was thinking. "We can use my old plan. Make it work for us now."

"What plan?"

"The one I had Jean-Luc sell you on after Dorothy's fake suicide."

"Yes," Damon said, "but in this case we have a real dead person."

Kory smiled. "He's not dead, he's *missing*. That was the premise for the fake cover-up. Nobody's dead until a body is found."

Damon nodded. "So, are you telling me that Jean-Luc has a cousin here in the States with a kiln?"

"He didn't even have a cousin in Geneva," Kory said. "And a kiln wouldn't have been the best method anyway. I did a lot of research on this."

"So why did you have Jean-Luc tell me you were going to put her body in a kiln if it wasn't the best way to get rid of it?"

"Because, if he told you the best way to get rid of a body, you would have wondered how he knew so fast. A kiln was the first idea that came to my mind, so it was the first solution I had him suggest to you. When you asked him how he ended up getting rid of the body, he told you it was best you didn't know. If you'd pressed the matter, he'd have explained the better solution he'd come up with, telling you that his original idea had flaws and the new idea did not."

"You thought of everything."

"Like I said, I was only able to do so because I had the luxury of time on my side."

"So what's the better idea?"

"I'll explain once we figure out how to get the body out of this house."

"Can't apply the old plan to this?"

Kory shook his head. "In Geneva, we had a house with a driveway and all the privacy we needed. While Girard was taking care of you, Dorothy got into the trunk."

"You mean she was in the trunk when the police were questioning me?"

"She was used to hiding in the trunks of cars by then," Kory said. "That's how she managed her first escape. Anyway, this is clearly different. This is the city on a Friday night."

"Can't we wrap him up in a carpet?" Damon said.

Kory was thinking. "First we have to determine if we should hide the body, or take it out now. If we wait, it could be a problem. Any nighttime activity will attract attention."

"Yes, but there'd be fewer people paying attention," Damon noted.

"True, but who takes out carpets in the middle of the night? No, we need something better."

"It isn't that late right now," Jan said, defending Damon. "What about a refrigerator box?"

Kory nodded. "Not a bad idea. Presumably we're replacing an old refrigerator with a new one. So we'd have to bring in a box. No. The box would go in, the old refrigerator would be removed for disposal. It wouldn't be in a box, and you can't put a body in a refrigerator." Kory looked around and pointed at the piano.

"You can't fit a body in that; the top wouldn't close," Damon said.

"You're going to put a dead body in my piano?" Jan said, going a shade paler.

"No, of course not. I was thinking of the crate Steinway & Sons uses to move their grands," Kory said.

"You could fit him in one of those easily," Jan said, relieved his father wasn't considering ruining his most precious possession. "It's just a wooden crate that houses the main body, the legs are removed and transported separately, along with the bench. They pack it tightly in cloth; it comes out without a scratch, which is kinda the point when you're moving one of the most expensive musical instruments in the world."

"So they carried this crate in?" Damon asked.

"It's fifteen hundred pounds," Jan said. "They used dollies and they had three men."

"How does this help?" Damon said. "You'd still have the same kind of problem—you'd be pretending to remove an old piano and replace it with a new one. But the grand would still be there. Unless you want to make it seem like a move, in which case you'd have to move everything else in the town house."

"It helps," Kory said, "because though a refrigerator box could fit a body, it would need some kind of internal support; otherwise the cardboard box would tear and the body would fall through. So you'd need to make a crate within the cardboard box to make it appear as if there were a refrigerator in there, and all that presupposes that there is an explanation for removing the box in the first place. You could try to give the impression they're just removing an empty box, but it would be hard to do if there's a body in there along with a wooden frame." Kory thought some more. "Jan, the piano is off warranty, right?"

Jan said, "It's been over ten years, so yes."

"Could there be a problem with the piano a technician couldn't repair at home?"

"Yes, I suppose," Jan said. "If the soundboard were to crack, but that shouldn't happen to a well-kept ten-year-old piano, especially since we haven't been exposing it to extreme climates."

"This is New York, Jan," Kory said. "It's hot in the summer and snowing in the winter. Would that not constitute climatic extremes?"

Jan shook his head. "No. When I talk about climatic extremes, I mean from humid to dry climates. Moisture affects the wood more than temperature."

Kory said, "I think it gets sufficiently humid in the summer to be a problem."

Jan said, "Maybe for the average piano owner, but we tune my Steinway three times a year. No way would the soundboard crack."

"You know that," Kory said, "but I'll bet the police don't. We just need a believable excuse. You could have been unlucky, right? Ended up with a soundboard of inferior quality? More susceptible to climate changes than the average piano?"

"Yes, Dad, but we're not talking about the *average* piano, this is a Steinway. It's the crown jewel of pianos."

"Again, I don't think the average detective would know that," Kory said. "An observer would see a crate going in, a crate going out, and a week later a crate going in again. We can have a truck painted with the words 'Classical Piano Repair and Restoration.'"

"Grand Repair and Restoration," Jan offered.

"That works," Kory said, glad to help steer Jan's mind clear of the wrapped corpse. "We'll have the piano taken away tomorrow. Saturday is a working day. And during the week that your piano is gone, you'll be gone too. Since the story is you don't have a piano, you'll have to go to Rhodes so that you can practice there. That'll get you away from here. Damon? Can we do this?"

Damon sighed. "If we had months to plan, sure. The body will start to smell in just one day. How are we supposed to get a truck? How do we paint it? How do we get a crate built specifically for a grand? It can all be done, but not overnight. Even if it were possible, it would be risky. You can't paint a rental truck and if you buy a truck—even with cash—that leaves invoices. It's not a good spur-of-the-moment solution."

"There has to be an answer to this," Kory said. "A simple answer; the best answers are the simple answers."

Nobody spoke for a while. Damon said, "We're running out of time and getting nowhere fast."

Kory was deep in concentration. "How about this: we'll take him out the front door as if he's alive."

"It's summertime, you can't cover up the body without drawing attention. You'd have to carry the body out," Damon said. "What are we even talking about here?"

"We could pretend he's drunk," Jan said, "and needs help getting down the steps."

Damon said, "That wouldn't work. His legs would flop around. A drunk would wobble and rock, but he would show signs of life. A witness would see the difference from a mile away."

"He doesn't walk," Kory said. "He leaves in a wheelchair."

Damon said, "We don't have a wheelchair."

"Then we'll have to get one," Kory said. "At a medical supplies store, but I have no idea where to find one and when they would close."

"This is the city that never sleeps, and it's six thirty. We can start by looking at stores around a hospital."

Kory was still thinking. "It's good, I like it, but there are still problems."

"The wheelchair?" Damon asked.

"Yes. It'll have to be seen going in and coming out of the house. We'll seat a live person in it going in, and Mr. Chambers will take his place coming out."

"Once that's done, you two need to leave for Rhodes immediately."

"What about you?" Jan said.

"I can handle myself." Damon smiled, touched by his nephew's concern. "I make a better scapegoat alive than I do dead. Unless he can make me disappear the way we're going to make Mr. Chambers here disappear."

"What about Mom? She must be on her way by now—"

The doorbell rang.

Jan ran to the front door, took a look through the peep-hole, and did an imitation of a frog, his knees fully bent, hopping on his toes.

Kory caught on immediately. "I forgot they were coming," he lied. "It's the bodyguards; they're here to supervise the caterers."

"I've got to go. There's no time to explain this to them. Those morons will shoot first and ask questions later. Do as we planned, but blame all this on me."

"What about Jabber? You can't go out there!"

"If he shoots me out in the open, he won't be able to frame me for anything."

"Okay, but be careful. And call me once you're safely at your hotel. If I don't hear from you in half an hour, the plan changes and I'm calling the police. Go through the back. I'll tell them what really happened once we're all safely in Rhodes."

Kory ran to his son, who was already opening the door for the Frenchmen.

A few moments after the bodyguards entered the town house, he observed Damon walking out of the alley.

Jabber was ready. He was crouched down in his seat, pretending to look for a map in the glove compartment.

He'd already made his decision.

Sure, he could kill Damon from across the street, even with his .38 and all the pedestrians and cars in the way. The satisfaction would be short-lived, however. There was no way to drag Damon's dead carcass across the street and into the car and make it seem as though the SOG had escaped. New Yorkers keep to themselves, but they aren't blind. One of the hundred witnesses would be able to describe Jabber, and the cops would know Damon was dead.

The SOG headed west onto Fifth. He was going back to his hotel, just as he'd told his brother he would.

Perfect.

"Mr. Chambers? Dead? But we must call the police immediately!" *One of the French guys.*

From the audio levels, Jabber knew they were still talking in the foyer. Kory was keeping them away from the body and from the living room phone.

Clever. But the professor still had to convince them not to call the cops without spilling the beans.

"Where were you earlier? I tried calling from Mr. Chambers's office, but there was no answer at either house."

"We were at home, Monsieur; we never received a phone call."

"Then Mr. Chambers dialed a different number." *Kory.*

"Yes, he must have made a mistake." *The other Frog.* "We were at home and then we went to the Waldorf to await Damon's arrival. We were there from five thirty to six, but he never came. As soon as we determined he'd already checked in, we came over to supervise the catering."

"Damon used the meeting to keep us away." *The bodyguard with the deep voice.* "You agreed to this. It is not our fault."

"I never said it was. I ended up coming home with Mr. Chambers. The door was unlocked and Damon was in the house, pointing a gun at Jan."

Bingo. Jabber leaned forward in his seat.

"Damon used loud music to mask Jan's screams. Mr. Chambers acted surprised at first, until Damon realized he was being set up and told us what our attorney had really been up to all these years. See, Mr. Chambers's plan was to have Damon kill Jan so that between my brother and the attorney, they'd still retain full control of the trust. It was supposed to seem like an accident or something; that's why Damon didn't simply shoot Jan."

Bringing Brad into the picture. Smart.

"Damon was about to force Jan into an 'accident' when Mr. Chambers and I intruded upon his nefarious scheme. Mr. Chambers had come by purposely so that he and I could catch Damon right after the fateful act. I arrived at the office early, however, thereby spoiling Mr. Chambers's timing and saving Jan's life. Damon realized he was being double-crossed and shot Mr. Chambers."

The professor could spin some serious BS.

"Why did he let you live?"

Shit. Good question. French asshole.

"He *was* about to kill us. The trust saved our lives. I made an agreement with him: Damon continues to get a percentage of the trust for as long as Jan is alive and has control of the trust. If he were to kill us, Damon would have to go into hiding. The trust would be controlled by Mary or the company and Damon would have nothing."

"So where is your brother now?"

"I don't know. Probably somewhere close. Watching."

"So he agreed to your proposal?"

"There were two conditions. If we call the authorities, he'll know and he'll kill every witness who has seen him alive. That means you two, me, Jan, John, Mary, and Dorothy as well."

"And the other condition?"

"He said we have to get rid of the body."

Jabber laughed. The professor could have talked Nixon out of the Watergate mess.

"I need your help," Kory said.

"What it is you want us to do, Monsieur?" *Jean-Luc.*

"What I've been paying you to do: protect us. And since you weren't here when Jan was almost killed, you can help us now by making sure we're safe from Damon."

"He can do nothing to you if we call the police. The station is just down this block."

"I know where the police station is, thank you. I live here. We can be pretty sure Damon knows where it is as well. The moment police cars come rolling in, he'll be after Dorothy, and right now we have no way of getting in touch with her. We *will* call the police, but not here and not now—he'll be expecting that. We have to catch him by surprise, once we're all safe and in one location."

"You could still call the authorities now; we will protect you."

"No. What happened today proves that he's been a step ahead of us all this time. We can't risk anyone's life on this.

Money is his motivation. He won't harm us as long as we hold our part of the bargain. It's not in his interest."

"Then what are you suggesting, Monsieur?"

"This is what is going to happen: first, you two are going to help us finish cleaning this mess. Then Jan and I are going to Rhodes. You two wait for Dorothy at the recital hall. Don't let her out of the car. Take her straight back to Rhodes—to my mother's estate. Once everyone is there, together, and safely under your protection, then we'll call the police."

"And what are we supposed to do with the body, throw it in a garbage can?"

"Jan and I were working on a plan when you came. Now that you're here, this should be a lot easier." Jabber listened as Kory rehashed his wheelchair idea. "Girard, you look more like Mr. Chambers than anyone else here."

"I don't look at all like him!" *Baritone.* Girard was the baritone.

"You both have the same build."

"He is much older. Okay, yes, I have a belly, and we both are losing most of our hair, but I am taller."

"The height difference won't be noticeable when you're sitting down in the wheelchair. You're going in as a friend from a distant past. A handicapped family friend from Geneva—just in case somebody asks. We need an easy name everyone can remember."

"Alan DuPont?"

"That'll do fine. Hopefully, we'll never have to use it. We're going to need someone to get a wheelchair. It should probably be you, Girard, since you're going to have to go to your house and change into a suit and dress shoes, the attire you wore for Jan's graduation would be quite suitable for someone about to attend a recital. You're probably a size too big for Mr. Chambers, but again, since you'll be seated, nobody will notice. Bring some sports clothing. Athletic shoes and a tracksuit, or shorts and a T-shirt. Make sure the colors are bright and different from your suit. Do you have a hat? Sunglasses?"

"Yes, what kind of a hat?"

"One that you could wear with your suit."

"Then no, I have nothing like that. It has not been in style for a long time, Monsieur."

"You'll have to buy one then. A hat is essential. So, to recap: first you get the wheelchair, then a hat. Go home, change into the suit I mentioned, and put the casual wear and sneakers in a shopping bag. No, better still, a gift bag. You're a visiting friend who's brought a present which you intend to give to Jan after the recital. So you drive back here, park outside the house. Double-park if you must, and when pedestrians aren't looking, get in the backseat and put the hat and the sunglasses on. Jan, Jean-Luc, and I will come, take out the wheelchair from the trunk, open the back door, and put you in the wheelchair and carry you and your gift bag up the steps and into the house. You change into your casual wear and we'll put the suit, shoes, hat, and sunglasses on Mr. Chambers."

"You said he was shot. This happened recently, correct?" *Girard.*

"Right, I see your point. We did cover the wounds, but the towels and plastic bags we wrapped him in should probably be replaced. Okay, Girard, add gauze and medical tape to your shopping list. That should be sufficient to get him into the car without making him look unduly conspicuous and without blood staining through his suit."

"So, what story are you going to tell about Monsieur DuPont?"

"Our blind, severely handicapped friend from Geneva stopped over to say hello and to relieve himself in a convenient location before the recital. If we're unlucky enough to have a nosy neighbor watching, which is unlikely but possible, said neighbor would see a wheelchair with a handicapped man wearing a suit with a matching hat and sunglasses going in the house. After Girard changes and fetches Jean-Luc's car, our hypothetical observer would see the same man, in the same suit, in the same chair being carried out."

"And then? We have a body in the backseat—after, what do we do?" *Girard again.*

"The plan I had for Geneva. Not the kiln, the Newark alternative." *Kory.*

"That is a good idea, but there are two problems." *The other bodyguard, Jean-Luc.* "First, that information is over a decade old. The place might not be there anymore. And then, even if it is, people will be looking for Mr. Chambers."

"I've thought of both of those points. If the place is no longer there, or they conduct business in a manner no longer conducive to our purposes, then don't do the swap—just eighty-six the body. As to your second concern: of course people will be looking for him, but Mr. Chambers is supposed to be leaving on a trip tomorrow for Chile. We'll have to make sure it appears that he's departed as planned. That will buy us until Monday or Tuesday, when his secretary will be looking for him."

"Okay, Monday or Tuesday. And then?"

"And then, we're going to expose him for the criminal he was." *Kory.* "He embezzled funds from my family trust. We'll make it appear that he realized we were on to his scheme and he used this trip to flee the country. We'll have to work out the details later. We are wasting precious time."

"Very well. Show us the body."

Not a peep out of the kid.

Jabber had not heard Kory tell his son to keep his mouth shut. He'd probably signaled Jan before the Frenchmen came in. The professor knew his son had gone soft on Damon. A word out of the kid's mouth, and the bodyguards would have known something was wrong with Kory's story.

Footsteps advanced toward the microphone. Jabber readjusted the squelch on his receiver.

"We will have to wash the floor, every inch. We must burn his clothing, the towels—everything that shows he was here." *Jean-Luc.* "You said Damon shot him with his father's gun, correct? That is a semiautomatic. So there will be shells to collect. The bullet holes will have to be fixed . . ."

"We'll have to worry about that later. We have to be finished with all this before eight." *Kory.*

"Why eight?"

"That's approximately half an hour after sunset, and dark enough so that with the wheelchair, the same suit, hat and sunglasses, it should make it highly improbable for any observer to remark any difference between Girard coming in and Mr. Chambers going out. While Jean-Luc disposes of the body, Girard will drive to the recital to intercept Dorothy, John, and Mary who should be arriving anytime between eight thirty and nine. Jan and I will leave for Rhodes in my car."

"You cannot walk alone to your car in the night. It is in the garage, Monsieur, am I right?" *Girard.*

"Yes."

"Then I will drive you to the garage. I will not leave you until I see that you and Jan are safely on your way."

"Okay, but follow Girard initially and then double back, just in case Damon is waiting."

The phone rang.

"Mr. van Luden's residence."

"Put my brother on the phone, Jean-Luc."

"I don't take orders from murderers—"

"Give me the phone." *The professor.*

"But Monsieur—"

"I told them what you did." *Kory, on the phone line now.*

"Good. I'm at the hotel. Jabber didn't see me or didn't care, so don't call the cops. Continue as planned."

"I'm not going to call the cops. They came to the house . . . I had no choice."

"Good luck, little brother." *Phone connection terminated.*

"He knows I've told you about him. He understands that I had no alternative."

"Do not trust him, Monsieur." *Girard.*

"We don't have to. If we carry out my plan to the letter, we'll be safe and he'll go to prison."

"Where he belongs." *Jean-Luc.*

Jan made a series of phone calls informing his friends that the recital was cancelled. Five minutes later, Jabber spotted Girard leaving the town house.

7:50 p.m.

Girard's car pulled up outside the town house. Though it was too dark for him to actually see, Jabber knew what the Frenchman was supposed to be doing. Less than a minute later, Kory, his kid, and Jean-Luc approached the car. They carried the wheelchair carefully, positioning themselves so that they blocked the view of Girard from every likely angle.

Five minutes later, Girard left the house, wearing Adidas, shorts, and a Hawaiian short-sleeve shirt. He returned in what had to be his partner's Buick Electra, honking his horn once.

The same three men carried out the same wheelchair, this time shielding Brad's dead body from view. They managed to maneuver the corpse into the car and the wheelchair into the trunk without attracting attention.

Jean-Luc drove away first, with Brad as his sole passenger. Girard followed closely behind; the two van Ludens were seated in the back.

Jabber started the ignition. He let two cars pass before he vacated the parking space and started the tail.

Both cars were heading south on Fifth. On Sixty-Fourth, Girard's car took a left, heading east.

Jabber followed him, keeping a careful distance until he saw the car pull in to the garage.

Jabber headed north.

The professor and his son were going to Rhodes and had no reason to hurry.

His plan would work either way but would go more smoothly if he got there first. That way they'd be dead seconds after setting foot in the dark mansion.

Along with the revolver, Jabber had equipped himself with fake FBI creds just in case he ran into any snags offing the kid. The phony ID would come in handy if some highway patrol dipshit were to stop him. He was presently at forty over the limit, and accelerating. If the nimrod didn't feel like extending customary professional courtesy to a fellow law-enforcement officer, there was always the .38.

As expected, there weren't any guards at the place, the video cameras weren't powered, and the gate itself presented no problem. Control of the estate was still technically in company hands. Brad had set up temporary security at the place for the meeting the week before. It was more a tactic to make the van Ludens believe they were safe than a measure to provide real protection from the SOG.

Jabber could have parked the car down the street, but the walk to the main house would have taken too long. He pulled off before arriving at the end of the driveway, plowing over manicured lawn, and hid the car lengthwise behind a wall of trees. The property was huge and it was darker than the inside of a gorilla's ass.

A light was on.

How the fuck did the professor and his kid make it there before him?

No time to check the garage.

No need.

The light burned into her waking eyes.

She must have drifted to sleep on her back. That was most unusual. She always slept on her side. Her back was wet through the nightgown. The fever had broken.

A tall man stood at her bedroom door.

She had a feeling he was a doctor, but she asked anyway. "Who are you?"

He walked over to her. "I'm hurt. You don't remember me?"

Something about his voice severed any comfort she'd derived from the belief that this man might be a well-intentioned physician.

Unzipping his fly, the stranger said, "Maybe you'll remember this."

Dorothy screamed.

Reaching her bedside, he addressed in the steady voice of a hypnotist. "Relax . . . You have no reason to be afraid. It'll be just like old times. Fun shared by friends."

"Oh my God!"

"Give me a minute and you'll be repeating that over and over."

"Don't hurt me."

The stranger smiled. "This is such a wonderful surprise. You weren't supposed to be here. I guess it was destiny."

"Please . . ."

"You beg just like your kid."

"Oh God, you didn't."

His smile revealed a spread of perfect white teeth. "Not yet."

Dorothy threw off the covers and tried to roll away, but he was impossibly fast, holding her arm as he sat down on her legs.

"I wish there was more time. You know, so we could do this right. Don't worry, though, I'll hear them . . . we'll have plenty of time to finish this. Unless you want hubby and the boy to watch—"

Dorothy tried to shake him off, but though he was slender, the focus of his weight was just above her knees. The pain was such that every tiny movement felt as though her legs were on the verge of snapping in two.

He continued to talk, and nothing she did or said could weaken his self-satisfied grin. "If you were drugged, like before, then maybe I wouldn't have to kill you. But your husband broke his end of the bargain, and you were here, so . . ."

"What are you going to—"

Talking over her, he said, "I don't have much of a choice, but because you and I go way back, I'm going to give you a going-away present. I'm going to fill your hot pussy before you die." He laughed as he gripped her panties. "I'll send you from one heaven to the other."

His hand tightened into a fist and he snapped off her last flimsy layer of protection.

"I wish we could talk, but like I was saying, your husband and kid are on their way. Don't worry, though, we're going to come long before they do."

Dorothy went for his eyes, but he caught her wrists, twisting them until she screamed again, this time from physical agony.

He hit her in the diaphragm and suddenly she could neither move nor breathe. Letting go of her arms, he cupped her buttocks with his hands, lifting her off the bed using his torso to force her legs apart. Damon had lifted her exactly the same way when he'd raped her that night in Saint Croix.

Memories of her wedding night—the fragmented nightmare that had feasted on her like vampire bats for nearly twenty years —returned with gruesome clarity.

He kept her raised with one hand as he began unbuckling his belt with the other.

Dorothy's eyes widened.

"I'm not in yet, baby," Jabber said, just before catching the source of her surprise in his peripheral vision.

Jabber snapped to the right as he reached for his gun, shifting his head just enough to avoid the blow. He made a grab for Damon's wrist with his left hand as he tried unholstering his .38 with the other.

The SOG had lost weight, but none of his strength. Damon wrapped his hand around Jabber's arm.

Jabber had his hand on the gun, and as he raised it to fire, Damon yanked his arm, pulling the NSA agent forward while Damon bowed abruptly. Their heads collided. The .38 fell on the covers.

Damon lifted Jabber off the bed by his throat.

Jabber kicked, the tips of his shoes missing their target by inches. The NSA agent tried hooking Damon's wrist, but with the blood supply to his brain dwindling, he was growing weaker by the second. Damon squeezed harder and Jabber's larynx imploded under the crushing force.

Jabber's foot finally made contact, but it was a brushing touch, more of a farewell kiss than a blow.

Damon tossed the unconscious man across the room, where he slammed with his back flat against the wall.

In that same instant, Damon saw the movement. He saw the gun. But nothing could be done without putting himself in the line of fire. Three explosions resounded, almost as one.

Blood smeared across the wall as Jabber slid down the wall into a seated position, his head dangling lifelessly between his knees.

Dorothy pointed the .38 at Damon.

He raised his arms, his left less so than his right, and stepped back slowly. "Easy now."

"Move and you're next."

Damon looked sidelong at Jabber without moving his head. One of the three shots got him in the chest, the other two had damaged the wall. "He's dead."

"My condolences. A friend of yours?"

"I don't kill my friends."

"You didn't kill him, I did."

"Maybe, but he still wasn't my friend."

"Call him what you like, he still worked for you."

Damon shook his head.

"You think I wouldn't recognize the man you sent to threaten me in the clinic?"

Damon didn't speak.

"Answer."

Damon looked up. "Why? You've never listened to me before."

"Because I'm pointing a gun at you."

Damon spoke with closed eyes. "You can believe me, or you can kill me. Either way, Kory and Jan are on their way, and you'll soon know the truth."

Kory answered the doorbell.

John brushed past Girard. "Is Dorothy still here?"

Behind him, Mary said, "Please tell me she's all right."

"See for yourself," Kory said. "Dorothy and Jan are in the drawing room."

Upon seeing her daughter-in-law, Mary took Dorothy's hands into hers. "I'm so sorry, my darling. I called the town house and when nobody answered, I thought I might as well tell them in person that you wouldn't be coming. And then I left the phone off the hook so that you could get your rest."

"Which phone was it?" Kory cut in.

"In the music room," Mary replied. "We were decorating . . ."

Kory ran off before she could finish.

Embarrassed by the urgency with which Kory had scurried away to rectify her error, Mary said, "It was frightfully stupid of me. I had no way of knowing at the time . . . Girard told us about Damon—the horrible things he's done . . . and because of me, we couldn't contact you. Thank goodness you're all right, I'd have never forgiven myself—"

"Don't worry about it," Dorothy said. "I'm okay now. Even my fever has broken."

In the drawing room once again, Kory spoke to his aunt as if he'd never left. "It wasn't your fault. Nobody other than you knew she was here, and you had no reason to be concerned. You naturally assumed she'd be safe."

"Are you implying she *wasn't?*" John asked.

When Dorothy nodded at him, Kory said, "Sit down."

Before they could comply, the phone next to Kory rang. "Hello? Yes, I know. It was off the hook. Dorothy wasn't feeling well, and Aunt Mary . . . yes, she's here. Everyone is here. They're all fine. No. We can't call the police now. Are you still in Newark? Good. It's taken care of? Okay, but don't leave. Girard is going to meet you there. I'll explain later. Can you call us back in twenty minutes? . . . Yes . . . Okay."

"That was Jean-Luc," Kory said. "He's been trying to reach us."

"What was this about you wanting me to rejoin him?" Girard asked. "I thought we were all going to meet here."

"We were." Kory took a breath. "Things have changed." Looking to his wife for support, he said, "What I told you in New York was half fact, half fabrication. Everything I said regarding Mr. Chambers, insofar as it did not pertain to my brother, was completely true, whereas virtually everything I said about Damon was not."

"He killed Mr. Chambers and threatened my daughter," John said. "Are you saying there's more?"

"John, my brother never killed or threatened anyone. He was framed."

"Uncle Damon saved my life, Grandpa."

"Mine too," Dorothy added.

John gave his daughter and his grandson a doubtful glance. To his son-in-law, John said, "Kory?" His frown grew from scorn to outrage. "Is this some kind of joke?"

"Not my brand of humor."

"It was a rhetorical question," John snapped. "Now, you'd better tell me what's going on here."

Dorothy was about to speak, but to everyone's surprise, her father stopped her mid-breath. "I want to hear this from him."

"Then shut up, John, and let the man speak," Mary said.

When Kory reached the point where the bodyguards had arrived at the town house, Girard interrupted him. "But why didn't you tell us? Why did you fabricate such a story about Damon?"

"Because the place was bugged."

"Are you sure?"

"Yes. Damon figured it out and wrote us a message on Jan's sheet music."

"I pretended to be sick to my stomach," Jan said, "so we could go upstairs and talk using a running faucet to mask our voices."

"We had to get back to the living room quickly," Kory said, "so that Jabber would hear us saying we were planning on going to Rhodes alone, and that we would call the police once everyone was here."

"But you weren't alone, of course. Damon was here. You set a trap," Girard said, nodding to himself.

"Actually, we were with him from the moment you dropped us off at the garage where he was waiting for us, until we got here; at which point he left us waiting in the car while he went after Jabber."

"But I still don't understand. Why you didn't tell us?" Girard said. "Why not pass a similar note like the one Damon wrote for you?"

"Jan and I were there. We saw and heard what just took me twelve minutes to summarize. When Damon handed us the note, we didn't need any convincing to know my brother had been framed from the very beginning. When you two came, however, there was no time for me to explain everything on paper. Moreover, we couldn't be sure of how you'd react. Were you to say one thing wrong, Jabber would have heard, and this one-time opportunity to trap him would have been lost."

"Why not just call the police?"

"For the reasons I told you then, and for one important reason which I couldn't divulge at the time: Jabber could have easily escaped, and we would then have lived our lives wondering if he would return, just as we once feared Damon might. One day, he'd come back for his money, and carry out his threats."

"And you're telling us that Mr. Chambers was somehow involved with all of this as well?" John said, his face darkening by the minute.

"He wasn't just involved, he started it all. He used all his resources to devastate our family, all because of his obsession with Martha and this delusion of his that he was once engaged to her."

"He was, I'm afraid," Mary said. "Though the engagement was short-lived. The moment my sister laid eyes on Nicholas, her heart was lost to him."

Kory gave his aunt a look that said he wanted to hear more.

"Your parents felt sorry for him," Mary continued. "That's how he ended up with a job working for Van Luden Enterprises. They tried treating him as one of the family."

"He had some way of showing his gratitude," John said.

Kory spoke to Mary, ignoring his father-in-law. "And he was obsessed with her, right? He followed her?"

"I don't know about that, I wasn't in New York after the war."

"From what we've learned," Kory said, "when he wasn't following her, he was following us."

"Why would he do that?" Mary said, twisting her face in disdain.

"We'll never know. If I were to venture a guess, I'd say that to him, Damon and I were an abomination. Living, walking reminders of the union between the woman he loved and the man who stole her from him."

"Let me get this straight," John said, raising his voice now. "All these years, all these things you've been saying about your brother: 'Damon murdered my dog. Damon kidnapped Dorothy. The marriage was a sham . . . ' All this time you've had us believing a lie?"

"Kory didn't make anyone believe anything," Dorothy pointed out. "We drew our own conclusions. That lunatic attorney and his cousin deceived us all."

"You seem to be taking this well," John shouted. "What about the bodyguards? Was that Mr. Chambers's doing too?"

"No," Dorothy said. "By his own admission, Damon hired Jean-Luc and Girard and kept me in Geneva against my will."

"So why the hell are you *defending* him?"

"Because if he's guilty, then so are you."

"What's that supposed to mean?"

"It means that nobody believed me when I said I wasn't a drunk or a junkie. Damon thought I was in denial; he thought he was helping me by locking me up in his house. The fact is nobody *trusted* me. Not even my own father, so why blame Damon? He was a victim of this as much as anybody. Who listened to him when he claimed he was innocent? Nobody. Least of all me."

"I never thought I'd see the day when my own daughter—"

"If it makes you feel any better," Kory said, "an hour ago she was about to shoot him."

"And I don't see why *you're* shouting," Dorothy said to her father. "I was the one Jabber kidnapped, not you. I was the—"

"Whoa! Wait a second," John said, addressing Kory. "Shoot him? You mean Damon?"

"Yes," Kory said, "this was just before Jan and I came and validated my brother's statements."

"When? Where?"

"Less than half an hour ago," Dorothy said, then elucidated on how the man who had tried to violate and kill her that night had been the same man who had raped her in Saint Croix and then only two days later had blackmailed her in Geneva. "If not for Damon," she concluded, "we'd all be dead."

Before John could think of words to respond, the phone rang again.

Kory turned to Girard. "That would be Jean-Luc. You need to fill him in on what we just said here, then tell him we have another body to dispose of. Have him wait for you there."

Girard spoke to his colleague accelerating as he expounded on the highlights of what he'd learned, reaching a speed of tongue verging on code.

"One moment we're going to our grandson's recital, the next we're thrown into a conspiracy involving two dead bodies and my own daughter."

"That's quite enough, John," Mary said. "Really. You're behaving like a child."

"*I'm* behaving like a child?"

"You know something," Dorothy said, "you need to take an example from your grandson. I think we all do." She looked at her son. "Jan was the only person to have faith in Damon before there was any evidence to exonerate him."

"So where is Damon?" John said, lowering his voice. "Is he here, in this house? Because I'll tell you right now, I can't simply flip a switch and change what I think of him."

"Nobody is expecting you to," Damon said with a laugh, startling everyone except Kory by his sudden appearance. "I mean, if it was so easy and you could change your perspective with a flip of a switch, then you might end up without absolutes. Then where would you be, right?"

John got up. "Don't preach to me. I might be an old man in your eyes, but I can still pack a mean wallop—"

"John Saunders," Mary said, "don't you *dare.*"

He looked reproachfully at his wife and sat back down.

"If it'll make you happy, I'll let you kick my ass later." Turning to his aunt, Damon said, "I heard you talking about a party for Jan? I hope that means you've got some food here. I'm starving."

THE DISPERSED

Saturday, 1:15 a.m.

The exit was there and gone before Girard had time to pull over to the right lane. It took him almost ten minutes to find his way back.

Jean-Luc had been waiting by a pay phone on Elizabeth Avenue, on the north side of I-78, a meeting point thirty blocks from the mortuary. It wasn't safe, but at least there, sitting in a car for hours, the odds of survival were better.

He almost drifted off for the third time when he finally saw Girard's approaching car. He cranked the ignition and pulled out into the street. With the Electra in his rearview mirror, Jean-Luc headed south.

The mortuary was located on Frelinghuysen Avenue, next to Weequalhic Park, just north of Evergreen Cemetery. A dangerous neighborhood for anyone, even armed bodyguards.

A broken lamppost lurked over a vandalized phone booth. The jagged edges of shattered glass protruded from a frame structure supporting a sign that had once read PHONE but was now smothered in graffiti. The metal umbilical cord dangled lifelessly without the phone book it once safeguarded.

"What a joyous place," Girard said in French. "We should move here."

Jean-Luc was in no mood for his partner's asinine humor. "Do you see anyone?"

They looked around once more before Jean-Luc got out his lock pick for the second time that evening. The Garden Tranquility Funeral Home had one simple lock, and this time it took him less than a minute to complete the task. Once inside, he aimed his flashlight at the reception area. On his previous visit, he'd already determined this place had no alarm system. Which made sense. This funeral home, like many in the area, catered mostly to the less affluent rather than to any particular religion, and the only things there to steal were coffins and cadavers.

As his contact had told him years before, this place was little more than a dumping ground for the destitute—ideal for his purposes. Because certain faiths did not allow for a body to be embalmed, after the mourning or viewings were over the bodies destined for cremation were sent directly to the basement. That was what made this one of the few crematoriums that could accommodate their plan.

In the basement now, Jean-Luc and Girard dragged Jabber's corpse and stripped him of his clothes, laying him next to his naked cousin.

"You took a body for him?" Girard said, indicating Mr. Chambers.

"Naturally. It's in the trunk. Now we have to find one that looks roughly like his cousin," Jean-Luc said. "Someone tall, thin. *Putin de mérdes, alors.* I cannot believe I'm having to do this all over again."

After Girard found an appropriate match, he said, "Can we fit them both in your car?"

Jean-Luc gave his partner a curt nod.

Everything was as their contact had said it would be. Nothing had changed in eleven years. The Garden Tranquility Funeral Home still did not place cadavers in bags. Instead, they lay tightly packed, side by side, ready for processing.

All bodies would be cremated early the next morning. At this stage, as was the case with most crematoriums in America, the corpses were not individually identified. The hired hand just counted the cadavers and if the numbers tallied, they were dumped into the furnace. Once the bodies were cremated, the bones were put through a mulching machine, where the ashes fell together into one gray pile. Some of the mélange was then scooped up and offered to the relatives; the rest was disposed of. It was much cheaper for the home to process the bodies en masse, and what the customers didn't know didn't hurt them; and more important, it didn't hurt the business.

By morning, there would be no trace of Mr. Chambers and his cousin. They would forever remain missing, but never missed.

The cover-up for Dorothy's fake suicide had never been intended to actually be carried out. But Kory had insisted it be so perfectly convincing that Damon could have never doubted the veracity of any aspect of the plan.

Had it not been for their current situation, all that painstaking analysis would have been for nothing, since Damon had not probed Jean-Luc on any of the questions his brother had anticipated.

Jean-Luc and Girard drove a hundred miles, going north on I-87 to the Catskills, where they buried the two cadavers they'd taken from the home.

Standing before the mound of soil, observing their handiwork, Girard said, "It is an unfortunate end for these two strangers, no?"

"I believe this is more dignified—if we'd left them to burn, their families would be carrying urns with other people's ashes," Jean-Luc said. "And the count had to be right; there was no other way."

The contact, a man infamous for alleged associations with the mafia, had given them a menu of body-disposal options. Once they'd made their choice—the best, according to Jimmy the Hand, though certainly not the easiest—they were given this address along with complete step-by-step instructions in exchange for $2,500. These instructions included details on the "burn-and-bury" swap—how to take the body "borrowed" from the crematorium eighty miles into the country and bury it six feet deep. Or as Jimmy had phrased it: *Eighty-six the sucker.* Were the replacement corpse ever to be uncovered from its resting place, there'd be no linking it to the body that had been cremated in its place. Back then, the hypothetical plan had been devised for Dorothy's hypothetically dead body.

Eleven years later, Garden Tranquility Funeral Home was still in business, and though they were dealing with two very real and very dead bodies, the instructions still applied.

Which was a great relief. Jean-Luc was uncomfortable with Kory's alternative in case the crematorium was no longer in operation. Simply burying Mr. Chambers and his cousin as they had just buried their replacements was both risky and unsatisfying.

As the family engaged in what would be a long conversation, the evidence bundle Kory had taken from his town house blazed in the main fireplace, making theirs the only smoking chimney that summer in Rhodes.

10:00 a.m.

Getting in had been easier than expected. The uniformed doorman had asked Girard if he could be of any assistance—a deferential way of inquiring who the Frenchman was and what business he had there.

The lobby waiting area had three leather sofas and a matching set of easy chairs. One of the better apartment buildings in Manhattan, no question, and Mr. Chambers owned the entire penthouse floor.

Girard had said he worked for Van Luden Enterprises, which, in a roundabout way, was not entirely untrue. The doorman was about to ring upstairs, but before he could do so, Girard had advised him that Mr. Chambers wasn't at home and produced the two keys he'd removed from the attorney's jacket. If the doorman had wanted to further verify his claims, he could have come upstairs to make sure the keys worked.

He hadn't, of course. To do so would have required him to abandon his post.

Once inside the apartment, Girard put on a pair of thin leather gloves and went to work. Kory had told him that if it couldn't be found, Mr. Chambers's secretary probably had it, in which case Girard was to leave the apartment untouched.

As it turned out, it took him all of two minutes to find the passport. It was in the right-hand drawer of the wooden office desk, nestled in a leather portfolio along with a return ticket on LAN Chile flight 531 to Santiago with one stop in Lima. He pocketed the leather portfolio. Finding the suitcases proved a more challenging task. The damned apartment was huge, and they weren't in Mr. Chambers's bedroom as Girard had expected.

He finally located a storage closet with two hard-cased Samsonites and filled them with all the essentials a wealthy man would take for a one-way trip.

He checked the area, going over everything twice, placing things precisely as instructed.

Once again, Kory had borrowed from his decade-old idea.

Mr. Chambers had planned on destroying the van Luden family, one-by-one, while slowly siphoning away their considerable fortune. Kory had thought it appropriate to chastise him posthumously by making his final criminal act obvious, poorly thought-out, and completely unoriginal.

It would appear as though Mr. Chambers had embezzled ten million dollars and then fled to some remote location in Europe to retire. Instead of leaving for Santiago, the family attorney would drive to Canada, where he would pay in cash for his first-class one-way ticket to Greece.

Still wearing his gloves, Girard got on the phone, and dialed Olympic Reservations.

A sleepless night of talking had capitulated to a quick-rising sun. It was almost noon before they'd started preparations for the matinée. Despite the sleep deprivation, Jan's recital had been a huge success. Damon had hidden himself from public view but had listened to the entire performance in the privacy of the adjoining room.

Eventually, at the dinner table, the last guest gone several hours earlier, fatigue had caught up with them, and for a while nobody spoke.

Damon's head bobbed like a leaf in a gentle breeze while shadows on the corners of his mouth hinted at a smile.

"What is it?" Kory asked.

"I remember dinners like this," Damon said. "You, Mother, and me eating here, at this very table . . ."

"And the quiet," Kory said. "I seem to recall you enforcing the silence most effectively."

"At the time, I believed I was helping Mother."

Kory's eyes narrowed through his glasses. "It seems you've spent the better part of your life trying to please her."

"The better part of my life is now."

Mr. Saunders directed a smirk at his wife. "He weaseled his way out of that one."

"You've been picking on him since last night," Mary said. "Give it a rest."

John carved himself an oversized morsel of sirloin. "He's a tough guy, he can handle it."

"After all this, he shouldn't have to," Mary said.

"You seem to forget." John smiled, pointing his fork at Damon. "I could have taken you up on that offer and knocked your block off last night, but I didn't. I think I deserve some acknowledgment for showing restraint."

Damon raised his glass. "To John Saunders, a man of unrivaled self-control."

"Well, if you're going to be snide about it . . ."

"Then how about a toast to family," Mary suggested.

Six glasses chimed in a crystal chorus.

"Are you sure you want to go through with this?" Dorothy said.

"Positive," Damon said. "I need to do this—for all of us."

"You realize there are no guarantees," Kory said.

John nodded. "You might be wasting a lot of time only to end up empty-handed."

"I realize that," Damon said. "But I don't think it'll be for nothing. Even if I don't turn up any answers, I'll still be helping Kory with his plan."

"But it could be dangerous," Mary warned.

John rolled his eyes. "I thought we had this discussion last night. For Damon, this will be a walk in the park."

"He needs to do this, Grandma," Jan said. "Kinda like the way I need to play the piano."

Damon nodded. "They call it dharma in India. It's like duty, but deeper than that."

"Deeper?" John snickered. "Since when did they open a philosophy branch in the Special Forces?"

"They didn't." Damon laughed. "But if the USO needs a comedian, I'll be sure to recommend you."

They worked on their meal in silence for a while before Damon addressed his aunt. "So, you think you'll be able to handle things on your end?"

"I'm not some helpless damsel," Mary said, her tone affirming her statement. "I have complete faith in my nephew. *Both* of my nephews."

Damon nodded. "Well, after yesterday, nobody in his right mind can question any of my brother's plans."

"I wouldn't have come up with anything if you hadn't discovered the place was bugged," Kory said.

John helped himself to a second serving of baked potatoes. "I never did get how you figured that out. Was that something they taught you in the Army?"

"Not quite." Damon chuckled. "Actually they did teach us to tap into a line, but not how to detect if a place was bugged. Those are things they teach the feds and the spooks too, of course. When Jabber told his cousin that Jan had given me a private recital, I knew the place had to be wired. There was no other way he could have known."

"You can't hear the piano from outside," Jan explained. To his uncle he said, "Dad's right, it couldn't have worked without you."

"Maybe," Damon said, "but how many people do you know who could come up with a multilayered plan in just a matter of minutes? Kory knew all along the bodyguards were coming, and he also knew that he couldn't do any of this without their help, so he came up with a story that had them believing one thing and Jabber another. And for all of it to work, everyone had to be out of harm's way so that I could have a crack at that scumbag one on one."

"Yes, but not everyone ended up being out of harm's way," Kory said, looking at his wife.

"Well, that was entirely my fault," Mary said. "You thought she was going to the recital with us."

"Your fault, my fault," John said. "It's the end result that counts. I'm telling you, Kory played him like he does all the fools who want to imagine they're in his league. He has them believing his overall strategy is brilliant but that he's made a small yet fatal tactical blunder," John said. "You underestimate my son-in-law and it's game over, baby!"

"You mean the way we underestimated Damon?" Mary said.

"What are you talking about?" John said. "I don't think he even plays chess."

"I'm talking about his other qualities," Mary said. "I wasn't referring to his *intellect*."

"What does one thing have to do with the other? I'm discussing strategies and tactics and you are on about emotional gobbledygook."

"It isn't gobbledygook, John," Mary scolded. "There's a lot more to a man than his mind, you know."

John shook his head with phony disgust and finished off the rest of his mashed potatoes.

Kory took his brother aside as the others collected the plates. "You never answered my question."

Damon knew immediately what his brother was talking about. "You're starting to sound like Guru Dev."

"Who?"

"Long story."

"If you don't feel comfortable talking . . ."

"He was my guide."

"I meant about our father," Kory said.

"Oh, I know what you meant," Damon said. "Until yesterday, I didn't really have an answer."

Kory waited.

"Okay," Damon said finally, "but I hope you weren't planning on getting any sleep tonight."

"Tonight is all we have."

"Then what do you say we go for a walk in Rhodes Park?"

"Sounds good to me." Kory smiled. "I know this shortcut . . ."

UNEARTHED

1980

Damon checked the door. The place was closed.

It was six. Too early for dinner in this part of the world, especially in the middle of the summer. He chose a table on the patio of the vacant tavern. From there he could monitor the small road as well as the entrance to the kitchen.

So far so good.

He hadn't come to dine, but he would have welcomed a meal right about then.

From what he'd learned, the locals started trickling in at around nine. That meant the staff should be arriving at least two or three hours earlier.

A bumblebee hovered over the plastic tablecloth, lost interest, and flew away in search of flowers.

His stomach growled for sustenance, but the hunger was good; it kept him alert.

Come what may, this had to work. He was dealing with an unknown, but this time he had the element of surprise. Kory had prepared him for every contingency: worst-case, best-case, and everything in between.

Feasting his senses on the world, Damon was energized, a coiled spring. The Arjuna in him remained as calm as the eye of a hurricane, ever free from the shackles of time.

Barely a faint echo of the young first lieutenant who, in Burlington, Vermont, nineteen years before, had counted every minute as he waited for his bride-to-be at the Mountainview Bar and Grille.

"So, everything is in order? You have the paperwork?"

Stavridis nodded curtly. "This is the third time you ask me."

"Where is she?"

"Please, try to relax, Mr. van Luden, she's coming. Maybe there was a road accident or something making traffic. It has snowed and—"

"I have a bad feeling about this," Damon said. "What if she doesn't come?"

"She will."

"Show me what you have."

Stavridis put out his hand. "Before I forget, give me the keys to your rental car—you will not need it anymore. We have a limousine to take you to the airport."

Damon dug into a tuxedo pocket. "It's a blue Dodge. It's down the block—there's no parking outside."

"Yes," Stavridis said, taking the key, "I know." He eased his way out of the booth and said, "A blue Dodge, you say?"

"It's the only blue car out there, do you want me to come show you?"

"Is not necessary. I will be right back."

When he returned, Damon said, "What took you so long? Did the place suddenly fill up with blue Dodges?"

Stavridis ignored the question, sucked in his belly, and slid back into the booth.

"I don't suppose Dorothy was out there."

"She will be here. Please don't worry." Stavridis produced a wedding certificate and two rings from his briefcase. "This is everything," Stavridis said. As Damon read the wedding certificate, Stavridis added, "It needs signatures, of course. You; Miss Saunders"—he smiled—"soon Mrs. van Luden; me, the witness; and, of course, the Justice of the Peace."

"What about the help I asked for in Geneva? Is that taken care of?"

"Yes, there are two men you can hire. They come with high recommendations."

Damon looked at the rings. Simple gold wedding bands, each with the other's name inscribed on the inside, along with the date, 12/25/61, which would become current in less than two hours. Satisfied, he returned the rings and the certificate to Stavridis. "So I guess this makes you best man?"

"It will be my honor."

"And the travel arrangements?"

Stavridis sighed, no longer bothering to hide his frustration. "The JetStar is fueled and waiting for you at the Burlington Airport. And before you ask me, I tell you: reservations have been confirmed for a honeymoon suite in Saint Croix."

"And we can fly there in the corporate jet nonstop?"

"Of course. The captain said it would take four and a half hours with no headwinds."

Damon consulted his Patek Philippe. The minute hand hadn't moved since the last time he'd looked. "She's supposed to check in with us before she changes into her wedding gown. If she doesn't get here soon, she won't be dressed and ready by midnight."

"She will be here," Stavridis repeated. "I hope she remembers her passport. She told she would bring it, yes?"

Damon nodded. "When she phoned. But it sounded as if she'd been drinking."

"She won't need it for Saint Croix, but she cannot go to Geneva without it."

"I explained that to her."

"Then everything is good."

"Not unless she shows it isn't."

Stavridis smiled. "Women. You will have to get used to this."

Damon did not find consolation in the remark.

"It probably was hard for her to sneak away."

"That's what worries me," Damon said. "She said she'd look for an opportunity in the early evening. Maybe something happened—maybe her father caught her running off with a suitcase."

"It is out of our hand now," Stavridis said. "What can we do? We wait. Unless you want your family to know."

"No." Damon sighed. "I don't mind, but she was adamant it be a secret marriage."

"I'm hungry," Stavridis said. "Have you had dinner?"

Damon shook his head. "I can't eat at a time like this."

Stavridis smiled and snapped his fingers. A waitress came over and took his order: a hamburger with fries. "Tonight is a big night for my friend here," Stavridis said, winking at the waitress. "What do you recommend for him?"

She studied the two men in tuxedos and decided to direct her question to Damon: "Don't tell me you're getting married?"

"That he is," Stavridis said, "that he is."

"Pity. The good ones always marry off young." She took out her pad. "We do a great T-bone."

Stavridis glanced at Damon for a reaction, but he was still searching out the window for Dorothy. "T-bone. No hamburger. T-bone for both of us."

The detective was on his third mouthful when he said, "Eat! You don' like? Trust me, my friend, you'll need your energy tonight. Eat!"

Once Damon swallowed the last morsel on his plate, Stavridis smiled, satisfied his client had been sufficiently nourished. "Now, must have something to drink, yes?"

Damon shook his head, but by the time he could say "I'm fine," Stavridis was already on his way to the bar.

A few minutes later, he placed a large draft beer in front of Damon as he reseated himself in the booth. He lifted his own mug high. "A toast!"

Damon hesitated and looked at his beer.

"To a happy marriage and to good health!"

Damon sighed and nodded, finally raising his mug.

Stavridis reached over and tapped his glass to Damon's. "Come on, be happy! This is your night!"

Stavridis took a long swig of his.

Damon hesitated, allowing himself only a small sip at first.

"One beer never hurt anyone," Stavridis proclaimed. "Drink, you need to relax. This drink could save your life."

Damon waved his hand dismissively. "I don't need to relax, I need a bride."

"She'll be here," Stavridis assured him. "Drink. Time will go by faster. Dorothy will be here, and you will be married before you know it!"

Damon took another miserly sip. Then one more. Tipsy already, the sips gave way to greedy gulps, as if the act of drinking was only making him thirstier.

Stavridis brought two more beers. How many times had he made that trip back and forth? All Damon had to do was count the mugs, but even that simple math had become too cumbersome for him.

Like a voice in a dream, Stavridis announced, "She's here."

"Who? Dorothy? Right. Dorothy? Oh. Oh, good . . . good." Damon made an attempt to get out of the booth. "Whoa."

Stavridis tossed a bill on the table. "Let me help you."

He was leaning on the Greek, trying not to tangle feet.

The waitress came after them. "What about your change?"

Damon couldn't make out Stavridis's reply, even though he was standing only a foot away.

"Do you, Damon van Luden . . ."

Dorothy was standing next to him. Dressed in white, wearing a veil. He wanted to speak, but the ceremony had already begun.

Did he remove the veil and kiss her already?

He was walking up steps. There were only a couple, but they were hard to manage.

White and shiny . . . white leather inside . . . must be the JetStar.

He dozed off, and when he next opened his eyes Dorothy was asleep on the seat next to him. She wasn't wearing the veil anymore. She'd probably had a few . . . God, she was so beautiful. He wanted to tell her, but he drifted off again, revisiting a dark sleep.

The next time, he woke up in a bed. Something soft touching him down there. Dark as ink, he couldn't see a thing.

"Dorothy?"

"Shhh," she said, still working her magic.

He was so hard it hurt.

She was on top of him, moving for him.

The phone on the nightstand was ringing. Where the hell was he? It took Damon seven rings before his hand found the receiver. "Hello." It sounded like a hoarse grunt. Damon gave it a second try.

"Mr. van Luden? This is Stavridis."

"For Christ's sake, what time is it?" Damon's head hurt with every word.

"A quarter to seven. We need to talk. It is urgent. May I come over?"

"Urgent? What's going on?"

"You don't know?" The phone was silent for a few seconds. "It's about Dorothy. . . . I'll explain in person. So . . . can I come?"

Dorothy was nowhere to be seen. "Yes. No. Wait. I need a shower. Give me ten minutes. And see if you can get me some aspirin; I've got the headache from hell." Damon hung up the phone and stripped away the sheets. That's when he saw the red spot. He massaged his temples, feeling slight relief when he released the pressure. He should never have let Stavridis give him that beer.

In the shower, he noticed more blood, this time on his manhood. He knew it was hers, but it was still troubling to see it there. Damon set the water on full cold.

Damon had just put on his robe when the Greek detective knocked on the door. Damon showed him to the patio, bypassing the bedroom with the stained sheets.

From over the treetops, they had a view of the beach and the wind-stirred ocean beyond.

"So you don't know?" Stavridis said. "You were sleeping?"

"Don't know what? What's going on?"

"Your wife was running around naked in the sand, but it's okay now. I took care of everything. You don't have to worry about the complaints."

"Dorothy? Naked?"

"I am afraid so. She was yelling 'I'm free . . . '"

Damon stared at him dumbfounded. "She really said that?" Why was he so surprised? She was free. Free from her father, free to start a new life. Free to be a woman.

"She was drunk," Stavridis said with a frown, as if he'd disapproved of Damon's thoughts. "So were you. A strong man and you cannot handle a few beers?"

"What happened with the complaints?"

"Only one person called," Stavridis said. "I ran out to stop her before she could cause more problems."

"Where is she?"

Stavridis cleared his throat. "Mr. van Luden, you asked me before what I am doing here. Because you were both drunk at the wedding, Van Luden Enterprises said I must chaperone your honeymoon. You are fortunate I came."

"Great. I'll consider myself fortunate. So, where is she?"

"You must understand. I had to do something . . . before the authorities were called. We couldn't let this become a catastrophe. We had to make a decision. It was agreed to shorten your honeymoon."

"Shorten it?"

"She needs help. Medical attention. So we decided to send her to the clinic earlier than planned."

"In Geneva?"

"She is already on her way. I am sorry. I know the plan was to stay here for a week and then she goes to the clinic. You must see we did what's best for her. You can have your honeymoon at the end of the month, when you are finished with your Ranger training and she has removed the poison from her system. You can meet her in Geneva. Go skiing in the Alps. Whatever you desire. But right now, she needs to recover."

The sun had just begun to rise. A couple on the beach below kissed in the sand. Postcard perfect . . . for them.

How the hell had Damon's honeymoon turned into such a mess?

This was not at all what he had expected, but Stavridis was right; they should not have been drunk on their wedding night. Not *that* drunk, at least. And Dorothy needed help, no question there. He wondered if her passion had been alcohol induced. She'd been completely sober on all their dates. She hadn't let him touch her once. Yet she'd been an animal in bed. Maybe her behavior in the past had been a product of good breeding and she'd been holding out for her wedding night. That would have required extraordinary self-restraint, however, especially for an alcoholic.

"All right. I'm not happy with this," Damon said, "but you probably did the right thing. What about when she gets out of the clinic? Have you hired the help we talked about?"

"She won't be released until you return. They told me they will be available for you. Hire them when you need them."

"So what am I supposed to do now?"

"The room is yours for a few more days. When the airplane gets back we will fly you to Eglin. You will continue your training as planned." Stavridis looked Damon in the eyes. "There is something else."

Damon waited.

"Now that you are married and the adventure is over, you need to tell your father-in-law what has happened."

Damon frowned.

"If you don't do the responsible thing—if you do not call him now—Van Luden Enterprises will do this for you. We took the decision to fly her to Geneva. So now the company is more—how you say—tangled? Her father has to be told."

Damon nodded. "I'll call him. This secrecy thing was her idea in the first place—I don't normally operate that way."

A young lady peered through the tavern door. *"Thelete kati kirie? Den ehoume anixi akoma."*

"I don't speak Greek."

She gave Damon a sweet smile. "I'm sorry, we don't serve dinner until nine, but I could make you a salad if you like."

She came back in less than ten minutes with what she called a *choriatiki salata* and a small basket containing a fresh loaf of bread. She asked if Damon would like a beer. He laughed and requested water instead.

"Do you know a Mr. Stavridis? I was told I could find him here."

The girl gave him an enchanting smile. "I am Eleni Stavridi."

Damon was half finished with his salad when he heard the glass door open.

"If you wait, we will have fresh *kokkinisto*." The voice was thick, older, and the accent heavier. The sun had aged his skin like antique leather.

Damon stood. "You're a hard man to find."

The Greek stiffened mid-smile.

Damon pointed at a chair.

Stavridis did not sit. "How did you find me?"

"I was motivated. Also, the fact that you left the States with a barrel of money made you easier to pinpoint. You want to stay invisible, you have to be a bit more subtle with your investments. This tavern is one of three businesses registered under your name."

"Why have you come here? What do you want?"

"Answers."

"What? What answers?"

"Don't play dumb," Damon snapped. "And sit down."

Stavridis did not move.

"I'm not asking," Damon said, pulling out the chair with his free hand. "*Sit.*"

"I don' bother anyone. I have wife. I have daughter—the girl you saw, Eleni."

Damon nodded. "She is very beautiful."

From his expression, it was clear Stavridis had interpreted the statement as a threat.

Damon broke off a piece from the loaf and dipped it in the salad oil on the bottom of the bowl. The crust was crisp, fresh.

"Go!" Stavridis said. "Go now or I call the police."

Eleni showed at the door, hearing her father's raised voice. She couldn't have been more than twenty. She took a step toward him, but he warned her off in Greek and she retreated to the kitchen.

"I'm here because of what Mr. Chambers did to me and my family."

Stavridis was quiet.

"I've come for the truth, and I'll do whatever I have to in order to get it."

"You don' touch my family!" Stavridis shouted. "You leave them *alone*."

"I'm not interested in your family, I just want answers."

"I give you answers but you must promise me you won't hurt them."

"I never said I would."

"Did the lawyer send you here? What did he tell you about me?"

Damon took his time detailing what had happened since he'd last seen Stavridis in Saint Croix, omitting the fact that Mr. Chambers and Jabber were no longer of this world. "You were his henchman. You and his cousin."

"I worked for Mr. Chambers. I don't know about a cousin."

Damon nodded. "That might be true. Before you say another word, let me get something straight: you lie to me, you'll regret it."

"You said you would not hurt my family."

"They're innocent, you're not. If anybody's going to get hurt, it'll be you."

Without asking, Stavridis finished off Damon's glass of water. He refilled the glass from the pitcher and drank some more.

"Now that we understand one another, let's try this once more: did you work with Mr. Chambers's cousin? A man who went by the name of Jabber?"

"In the beginning, I only spoke with the lawyer. Later— much later—there was another. I don' know his name."

"Next question: Were you involved in my mother's death?"

Stavridis's mouth dropped. "What are you saying? No! On my mother's grave, no."

"What about Mr. Chambers? Did *he* do anything to her?"

"I don' know anything about this. I know your mother have heart attack, nothing more."

"Okay," Damon said, softening his tone slightly. "Do you think he could have done it?" Kory had recently done some research and had discovered there was a drug available in the late '50s that could induce a heart attack and it left no traces.

With Mother's preexisting condition, the circumstances of her death had never been put to question.

"Mr. Chambers? The lawyer? Impossible." Stavridis leaned forward. "But I remember at the time he told me he had some *resources* I did not know about."

Damon nodded. Mr. Chambers's resource had been Jabber. During the time Damon was a SOG, Psyops had been experimenting with powerful drugs that could get a man to murder his family and wake up in the morning thinking he'd taken the dog out for a walk. Other drugs caused partial or complete amnesia and were used on kidnapped NVA to make them think they were in Northern Vietnam when in fact they were in a mock village staged for the purposes of getting them to talk. God only knew which of these chemical cocktails Jabber had access to. "So you worked for Mr. Chambers and you had nothing to do with my mother's death, is that what you're saying?"

"Yes. I worked for him," Stavridis said. "When your mother died and you became eighteen, he was afraid you might marry this girl Dorothy."

"And take fifty-percent control of the trust," Damon filled in.

"He did *not* tell me this. He said it was to protect the family money. A man in love can do crazy things . . . In Greece, we have expression: the *muni* pulls boat."

"The what?"

"*Muni,* the woman's thing," Stavridis said, as if Damon should have been familiar with the word. "So he had me watch you like a brother guarding his sister from a suitor. My job was to tell Mr. Chambers if I thought this relationship would lead to marriage. Not such unusual request. I was detective for many years, I have been asked to do stranger things, Mr. van Luden. And he pay very well."

"Not to mention the money you were getting from me."

Stavridis took two more gulps of water. "I told the lawyer what I thought. A young, beautiful girl like that, why not you marry her, right? This worried him. He had me watch closely. I get trust of her father, so to get into her house. It was not hard—he was a lonely man. . . ."

Damon skewered a cucumber.

Stavridis watched as if he was soon to suffer a similar fate. "After several reports, the lawyer was getting very nervous. He took me to his office and told me what he wanted me to do. I'm not proud of this. I have lost my sleep for many years thinking about it. It was a big price to pay to come back home. I went to America to make enough money to bring back to my village and retire. Mr. Chambers took advantage of an immigrant's dream. He fished me with his money. I could not resist. If I helped him, I could return to my country twenty years earlier. It was my dream."

"What exactly did you do for all that money?"

Stavridis took a long time to answer. "I told him everything I told you back then . . . and more. I had the house wired long before I tricked you to have me do so. Dorothy had a friend, Nancy, yes? They talked on the phone all the time. I found out about the party, what they were planning, and what really happened. I told Mr. Chambers. You know what he said?"

Damon waited.

"He told me the seed was planted now; he just needed me to water the tree. But instead of water, he told me to use alcohol. As I said to you back then, I came close to Mr. Saunders. I pretended to be accountant for Van Luden Enterprises. This way, with the meetings I had with him, I could go to his daughter's room, I could go to his alcohol cabinet, no problem. I put empty bottles under her bed and drugs in her dresser. Through Mr. Saunders, I learned about the depression she suffered from her mother's death. I reported this, like I do everything else. After this, it was not hard to give image of her as depressed teenager alcoholic. Especially in a small town like Rhodes. You know? Full of gossiping women, like Greek village. You see, rich or poor, gossip is gossip all over the world."

"What else did he have you do?"

"I reported to him first, then to you . . . but only if he said I could."

"Like when you found out about Kory and Dorothy—you told him about it but not me, right?"

"How did you know?"

"I'm doing the asking here. What did you discover back then that you didn't tell me?"

"In the spring of '61, I heard phone conversations Dorothy had with this friend of hers, Nancy. It was obvious she was seeing you only from pity. She had lost interest in you."

"Because of Kory?"

"I don' think so." Stavridis looked at the thatched canopy without raising his head. "Kory was just a friend at that stage. Don' take personally, she was just a girl—younger than you. At that age they cannot even decide what shoes to wear."

"Stick with the facts, spare me the rest."

"No matter what I told you about her, you would not change your mind. You were young . . . very stubborn. And when you proposed, the lawyer, he was furious."

"But then?"

"Strange, but the next time I spoke with him, he was calm, very sure of himself."

"That must be when he decided to force feed us the marriage so that we'd end up divorced. That way I'd never have control of the trust."

Stavridis creased his brow. "This makes sense to you?"

"Not to me, to Mr. Chambers."

"But why?"

Damon decided to tell him.

"I did not know this thing you say about the trust. Is very complicated."

"Oh yes. And who better to take advantage of a trust than the attorney who'd drafted it in the first place? Since there was no divorce, he'd hoped I'd continue to stay out of his hair so he could steal from the family trust. Then, if the Army didn't get me killed, he was going to find another way to finish me off."

Stavridis raked his fingers on his balding head.

"What happened after I proposed? How did Dorothy react?"

Stavridis shrugged. "Just like I told you."

"You didn't tell me much. All you'd said was that she didn't sound enthusiastic. You were too busy badgering me about her being too young and her drug problems."

"When she spoke with Nancy on the phone, she said she did not know how to tell you she didn't want to marry you. Her friend suggested to her to write a letter."

"You *never* told me that."

"I told the lawyer." Stavridis let out a long sigh. "About this time, something changed. He make me to do strange things, but he would not tell me why I do this. I have to find out for myself. Understand?"

"What strange things?"

"Started when I told the lawyer about this telephone call with Dorothy and Kory—when she told your brother she has a letter she wanted him to give to you."

"Oh, yes, I remember that—you didn't tell me about that until much later, but I'll bet you told Mr. Chambers right away, right?"

"I told the lawyer, yes, and then started the first strange thing: he want me to take photo of this letter. First I had to be sure Kory had not opened it. If so, I had to report this immediately. The boy had given his word to Dorothy, no reason to expect he would not keep it, yes?"

"What if it had been opened?"

"That would have meant he knew Dorothy turned down your proposal. He would have seen the evidence. At the time, you were still at West Point and he probably would not make trip over there to give you the letter. So we didn't have to worry about that."

"But he didn't open the letter," Damon said.

"No. Once Dorothy and her father left for Hawaii, I swapped the envelope and letter with what the lawyer had given to me. It was a work of art—the handwriting . . . it was exactly the same. I checked often to see if the replacement letter was ever opened, but it never was."

"Why would that matter?"

Stavridis's eyes narrowed. "This lawyer was a fox. If Kory had read the forged letter, he would have betrayed his word and this would have forced the boy to secrecy. At the time, I had no signs to make me think those two were involved in more than a platonic sense and Kory did not seem the character to fight you for the girl."

"How wrong you were."

Stavridis said nothing.

"I remember that letter well," Damon said. "She accepted my proposal, but on the condition that I mustn't call or write to her. She said she'd contact me."

"This letter made it seem like her father would object because she was too young—not yet eighteen." Stavridis quoted, "*It is a secret and nobody absolutely nobody must know . . .*'"

"You remember the exact words?" Damon said.

"Yes, because they were taken, one-for-one, from the transcript of her conversation with your brother."

"To what end?"

"In case Kory broke his word and opened the letter *after* I switched it with the forgery. He would have recognized those words and believed she had used the very same line on you. He would have come to the conclusion that she was using both of you and most likely have never mentioned to anyone the letter."

"Until we eloped."

"Yes, but to say what then? That she accepted your proposal? No."

"And if he'd read the original letter?"

"Still, he would not say a word to Dorothy—he had promised he would not read the letter. Once she disappeared that Christmas, of course he could say whatever, but he would not have the letter for proof. But I'm not sure that Mr. Chambers cared about protecting you from criminal charges for the kidnapping."

"And let's not forget rape."

Stavridis sat up. "You didn't!"

"You know damned well I didn't."

"You—" Stavridis turned his head to listen to rising voices from within the tavern.

Eleni was talking with two men. Both youngsters appeared at the glass door, their chests puffed out like pigeons in a mating ritual. One of them was shirtless, his skin cooked to a deep brown.

"Friends or relatives?" Damon asked.

"Children of my wife's cousin."

"They look like good kids," Damon said. "Tell them to get out of here now."

The blood drained from Stavridis's face. *"Figete! Tora!"*

The brothers looked at each other but did not make a move to leave.

Stavridis got up, shouting, both arms flailing. *"Kai pes stin Eleni amesos na paei stin mana tis! Ante! Dromo!"*

They walked away, giving the old man an irreverent shrug. "They're gone?"

"You have my word," Stavridis said. "They will not return."

Damon nodded, and both men sat down. "You were telling me about the letter?"

"Yes . . . Eh . . ."

"Have some water," Damon said. "You look like you need it."

The old man obliged, emptying the glass. "Thank you. Yes . . . this is all with the letter. Oh, I forgot. That summer . . . before the letter—you were given assignment to go to Berlin."

"Right, I remember telling you that," Damon said. "So you went and told Mr. Chambers, and? . . ."

"And this is when he had this idea for center for *apotoxinosi* . . . eh . . . clinic for drug therapy in Switzerland. It would be easy to prove she was drunk at time of her marriage because she would be flown to Geneva and admitted to clinic. They do blood tests there. Standard for every guest."

"Mr. Chambers was sure she'd still be drunk after the long flight from Saint Croix to Geneva?"

Stavridis stared at the tablecloth. "They did not use only alcohol."

"And so Dorothy would have grounds for an annulment," Damon said. "No questions asked. That would void my fifty-percent control before the ink was even dry on paper."

Stavridis shifted forward. "Please, you must understand: they told me nobody would get hurt. It was supposed to make you believe you were married. Then the marriage would be annulled. It was supposed to be simple. They say the worst anyone would suffer would be hangover."

"You weren't suspicious Mr. Chambers wanted to retain control for himself?"

"He told me all this was for the good of the family. You were going to the Army. Like you say, he thought you would die fighting some war and then Dorothy would have inheritance—"

"If I died, she wouldn't have gotten a red penny. He lied to you about the trust. That money would have gone to my aunt."

Stavridis nodded.

"You didn't want to question his motives, did you? You wanted the money and you didn't bother thinking about what the consequences were to me. What did you think she'd do to me after the annulment? I'd be charged with kidnapping and rape; didn't you think of that?"

"What are you talking? You said you did not rape her."

Damon studied him, determined that the old man was not feigning ignorance, and decided to tell him what Jabber had done.

"In the name of God! Why?" Stavridis said.

"I thought you'd know," Damon said. "But let's assume for a second that you didn't. You must have known Dorothy would press charges about the kidnapping, even if you didn't know about the rape."

The old Greek looked ill. "No, you are not right about this. This rape changes everything. Dorothy was supposed to believe she got drunk and you both did something stupid. She would not think you kidnapped her." Stavridis hesitated. "I knew it was wrong. I was drowning in lies but by then, I could not get out of the mess, even if I wanted to."

"Do you realize that he wanted me to go to prison?"

"This makes no sense. Why?"

Damon told him what he'd learned from Jabber about the family attorney.

"*O Theos na me sinhoresi,*" Stavridis said, crossing himself.

"Let's not sidetrack here," Damon said. "You were talking about the letter."

Stavridis cleared his throat, eyeing the empty glass. "After the letter, you kept your promise. You never called or wrote to Dorothy."

"What did you think would have happened to me if I had questioned her about it?"

"You would not have done that," Stavridis muttered.

"He would have had me killed," Damon said, "and you know it."

"Now . . . yes. Then?" Stavridis shook his head. "I had no idea what kind of a man this Mr. Chambers was."

Damon pressed the detective to continue.

"That fall, something unexpected happen. I see signs that maybe Dorothy and your brother were becoming involved. I told the lawyer. He was also very surprised."

"And this messed up his plans because now she was interested in Kory?"

"No so much. They kept it a secret. So secret, I could not get proofs. They were together many times, but I never see them getting close . . . if you understand me."

"And what if she'd made the affair public?"

Stavridis reflected for a moment. "In this case, I think he would not care. It would make annulment of marriage certain, no?"

"And it would also make me appear guilty of kidnapping and rape beyond a shadow of doubt. He could have also waited for Dorothy to annul and then have her killed, framing me for that as well."

The detective did not reply.

"If she'd gone public about her relationship with Kory, though, I'd still have that fake letter in which she accepted my proposal."

"Yes, but you were in training. You had no communications with your home at the time Kory and Dorothy were together. You would never have found out, because your only contact was me."

"That lawyer played me like a trained dog."

"It was not problem because they never told anybody about their relationship and because they kept this affair a secret, so the lawyer thought Kory would say nothing when Dorothy eloped with you . . . and even if he did—"

"Oh, he most certainly did," Damon said. "He pretty much forced Dorothy's father to call the police."

"Yes, well, I wasn't there, I had already left for Greece at that time."

"You're telling me you weren't involved in what happened in Geneva?"

"No. The last job I did for that lawyer was at Saint Croix. After, I packed my suitcases and we took road for Greece."

Damon waited.

"Even as you say, if your brother tried to say the truth about his relationship with Dorothy after she was gone, Mr. Chambers believed nobody would give much gravity to his word."

"He was right about that; they thought the poor guy was lovesick and delusional. We're skipping forward, though. You didn't tell me what happened after you told Mr. Chambers about the letter."

"After I replaced it?"

Damon nodded.

"I called you."

"And?"

"You remember. I told you about the call I monitored between Dorothy and your brother. The call about the letter. I asked you if she had replied to your proposal."

"But you waited until I was in Infantry School to call me, so I'd be out of touch. Just in case I had a wild hair and wanted to talk with people about it, right?"

"Yes. After that, I found out about the trip to Vermont through the phone conversations she was having with Kory. This was confirmed by communications between your aunt and Dorothy's father."

"Right, the Christmas outing I was invited to."

"No. This trip I am talking about happened several weeks before. It was the first snow of the year, if I remember correctly. Only after did they arrange the trip you are talking about."

"So Mr. Chambers hears about plans for a second trip and then?"

"Then they found this girl."

"They?"

"The lawyer told me we would be getting outside help. I asked the man what he was talking exactly. I did not want him involving some amateur. He told me his help was the best and that compared to him *I* was the amateur. I thought: who knows, maybe he had hired a Mafioso."

"What happened with the girl? Who was she? What did they have her do?" Damon asked, once more seeking verification of what he'd heard Jabber say.

"He found a prostitute. Poor thing. She had dreams of becoming a Hollywood actress. They paid her astronomical sums. For a few months, they made her stop selling herself. She had to work only for them. After that, she was told she could do whatever she wanted."

Damon nodded for Stavridis to continue.

"I don't have more. I saw her only twice, I do not even know the girl's name. I didn't deal with her at all."

"Jasmine," Damon said, remembering what Jabber had said to Chambers before all hell broke loose. "Her name was Jasmine. And if you didn't deal with her at all, how do you have all this information on her?"

"I know this only because they believed I had to know."

"Because when Jasmine called me pretending to be a drunken version of Dorothy, I would have told you the moment I'd heard from her. Which I did."

"Right," the detective said, "and if Mr. Chambers had not told me the prostitute was going to call . . ."

"You would have said something to me that would have spoiled their plans, because you knew the real Dorothy would never call me, and certainly not to discuss wedding arrangements."

Damon leaned back, crossing his arms. "So all this business about swapping letters and getting a prostitute to play Dorothy—all that wasn't enough to give you second thoughts?"

Stavridis massaged his forehead. "They gave me information little by little, at last minute. Just enough so I would not get in their way, understand? I tell you, I did not know their entire plan until after."

"I still don't understand how you guys pulled off the fake marriage, and how you got Dorothy to admit herself to the clinic."

"You see, the phone call from this Jasmine girl was critical. She was good actress. She make you believe you were talking with Dorothy. You agreed to elope in Vermont and to go to Caribbean for honeymoon."

"Right, and I called you and you told me all the arrangements were taken care of." Damon took his time digesting what he'd heard. "I'm missing some crucial chunks of history here.

The next time I spoke to you after that phone call was at that Burlington bar and grill. I was waiting for Dorothy. Where was she?"

"She was sedated. Like your brother."

"How?"

"I don' know those things. The lawyer asked me where Dorothy was staying. I told him. This is all."

"So far so good, but Dorothy has always been saying that *I* kidnapped her."

"They make it seem that way. They asked me details, such as what cologne you like. It was Old Spice, if I remember—"

"So Dorothy and Kory must have been accosted from behind. They were probably out cold before they had a chance to identify their attacker."

"From behind, yes . . . they use similar idea during the marriage ceremony."

"I remember the wedding."

"Really?" Stavridis scratched his cheek. "Strange."

"It isn't very clear. They drugged me just like they did her."

The detective looked past Damon. "I'm afraid I drugged you . . . when we were in the bar."

"You insisted on that drink," Damon said. "Now I know why."

"They gave me something to put in your beer. To accelerate the affect of alcohol."

"I didn't need an accelerant. Back then, I couldn't hold my drink."

"This what you think, but not so. You see, Mr. Chambers told me they had tested the drug on you. On Dorothy, too. In your case, you were still at the Academy. Did you ever go out? To the bar with your friends?"

"Rarely; in the beginning they didn't let us out."

"Even this professional he had, this Jabber as you call him—he would not have found you in West Point to test the drug. It must have been when you were on leave. Do you remember being drunk during your vacations?"

"On a few occasions." Damon had cleaned his plate and finished off the last breadcrumb. "Jabber did mention something about body weight. He must have been testing the effects of the drug to calculate the exact doses. Too much and we'd be unconscious; too little and we'd remember things we weren't supposed to."

"They told me they made you drunk so you would believe you had general problem with alcohol. That way, you would not wonder why you got drunk so fast on your wedding night." Stavridis shooed away a street cat. "Before I put drug in your beer, I asked for the keys to your rental car. Do you remember this?"

"Why is that important?"

"Because he used your rental car to kidnap Dorothy."

"So if there were any witnesses who saw the car, it would be linked back to me. When you said *he*, I'm guessing you weren't referring to Mr. Chambers."

"No, not the lawyer, the man he told me about. Tall fellow, like you, with blue eyes."

"That would be Jabber. Did he act as Justice of the Peace, as well?"

Stavridis nodded. "He also pretended to be you when we made this fake ceremony for Dorothy."

"Slow down a bit. I'm drugged and thinking I'm drunk, then what?"

"Then I told you Dorothy has arrived."

"And you dragged me out of the bar and grill . . ."

"Yes, to a place across the street."

"Where the marriage was staged?"

Again, Stavridis nodded.

"Wait," Damon said. "What if I'd refused to drink? This was my wedding night. I distinctly remember not wanting to get drunk."

"I don't know."

"I think you do," Damon said. "If I didn't down that drug, Mr. Chambers would be screwed. I'd be expecting Dorothy to arrive, and when she didn't, I'd seek her out and discover we were both being scammed."

Stavridis said nothing.

"You had to know. You're not dumb."

"I am just guessing . . . but I think—"

"You're *guessing?* Bullshit! You said that Mr. Chambers had to keep you in the loop about everything need-to-know.

This sounds like the weakest link in his plan; he couldn't have afforded not to tell you. He must have made it perfectly clear what would happen if you didn't deliver."

"He told me he would no longer be needing my services."

"Yeah, I'll bet. Your services, mine, Dorothy's. Who else would he have had killed?"

Stavridis sighed. "I suppose anybody who was involved. You are right, he did tell me, but only the last minute. He said if you did not drink, then he would have this man arrange an accident for you and Dorothy in your car. For me, the death would not have been so fast."

"So you got me drugged, you're dragging me out to this place to stage a wedding, what happened then?"

"This Jabber fellow had returned with Dorothy ready in the limousine. At this time, the prostitute was dressed in the white wedding gown for virgin."

"And she wore a veil so I'd never get a good look at her face."

"Like you say, Jabber played Justice of the Peace. I was the witness. He watched you all the time. You were sleeping standing up. You were very heavy, I remember. I had back problems the next day from keeping you on your feet."

"I only remember enough to know it happened."

Stavridis nodded. "That is precisely what they wanted."

"Yeah, well, it worked, and let me guess: if anything had gone wrong, I wouldn't be here to talk about it, right?"

Stavridis gave Damon a nervous glance. "When you had seen enough, Jabber, he tapped you with something—some needle in his hand—and you fell down. I had to drag you out the back door, to the backseat of your car. Dorothy was there, also unconscious. Jabber put on his next costume. A wedding tuxedo, precisely like yours. He left through the front door with the prostitute who was dressed as your bride."

The detective swatted at a fly. "The limousine driver saw them and naturally he thought he was looking at you and Dorothy. They acted drunk. Kissing and making noises in the back as he drove them to the Burlington airport. This was in case there were witnesses, you understand. They painted 'Just Married' on the back window, with these cans you Americans use for dragging on the road. And then the airplane took us to Saint Croix."

"Who was in the jet?"

"First, you and Dorothy, of course, but we changed your clothes to make you look like wedding guests—friends of the bride. You were almost unconscious. Jabber and the prostitute were acting as the drunken newlyweds, but not so much they could not walk. And of course I was there. The cabin was dark all through the flight. The pilots gave us privacy. We had to change Dorothy's clothing again and put on her wedding gown in case you woke up during the flight. Just before the landing, we made her look like wedding guest once more."

"Okay, so these pilots think they've got two drunk couples onboard: the bride and groom and another couple so drunk they can't stand up. And you were what, the chaperone?"

"They were company pilots. The lawyer told me I did not have to worry about them. I don't think they cared if we carried five goats and the devil himself so long as they got paid."

"What if one of us regained consciousness?"

"The cabin was dark. We put you next to each other and Jabber was watching all the time, looking at his watch and waiting with the needle. He gave a few injections. He looked at his watch. Then more injections. I asked him why this was necessary. He said he could not let you go too deep sleep because he needed you awake for later. When we arrived in the island, the seven of us were driven to the hotel in a taxi-van."

"So that's why they chose Saint Croix; it's US soil, so there's no need to worry about customs and immigrations. Wait, you said *seven* passengers?"

"The pilots came with us. We had one honeymoon suite, a room for me, and two rooms for the pilots."

"What about Jasmine and Jabber?"

Stavridis shook his head. "We did not want to show that another suite was rented. Only the pilots knew they were there, and the pilots were told later to forget these details."

"Who registered?"

"It was me. I used the driver's license from everyone. Jabber and the prostitute came to the lobby as bride and groom, pretending to be drunk. The hotel was used to those things. They did not care."

"And what happened then?"

"The prostitute did as she was told. She ran around naked, screaming 'I'm free!'"

"I mean before that," Damon barked.

"I *told* you, we checked in and—"

"No! Earlier, when you had me screwing a prostitute while Jabber was raping Dorothy."

Stavridis's leathery face turned ashen like the painted sadhus Damon had seen in Rishikesh. "I told you, I had nothing to do with that! *You* tell me what happened, I cannot tell you."

"You say there was only *one* honeymoon suite?"

Stavridis nodded. "Yes, the lawyer did not want a record that there was another couple there."

"So Dorothy must have been removed from the bed while Jasmine took her place and Jabber waited to hit me with the drug. Or maybe he had the prostitute do it. Who knows? Once they had me convinced I'd consummated the marriage, Jabber must have moved me somewhere else so that he could rape Dorothy in that very same bed and then drug her back to unconsciousness once he was finished."

Nobody spoke for a while.

"What became of Jasmine?"

Stavridis said nothing.

Damon cocked his head slightly as he glared at the detective.

"They no longer needed her services."

"What about you? After that morning when you told me Dorothy had been shipped off to Geneva because she was running around naked, bothering the natives, what did they need *you* for?"

Stavridis stared at the crumbs on the tablecloth. "They told me Jabber would call the management, to complain about this naked woman. When I hear the yelling stop, they told me to go to the front desk and say I had stopped her from making the noise and I had situation under control. This was a theater, you see. Something for witnesses to remember. The limousine, the airplane trip—all theater, understand?"

"You didn't answer my question."

"I told them I had made special arrangements if my family could not find me."

"What, some letter in a safe-deposit box? They didn't buy that, did they?"

Stavridis gave a feeble shake of his head. "No. They were too clever. I did not know until the last minute about Jasmine. They drowned her in the sea, poor girl. By the time I realized I could be dead like her, it was too late for me to make any arrangements."

"But they let you live?"

"They could not be one hundred percent certain I was lying, no? Also, I told them I was leaving for Greece. I said I would never come back to America."

"And if you did, then what? They'd kill you?"

"Not me," Stavridis said. "My daughter. She was baby then. This Jabber bastard said he'd give my wife a special night, just like for Dorothy. At the time, I thought he was talking about drugging my wife so he can take my daughter. Now, after what you say, I know what he really meant." Stavridis's eyes glazed over. "He told me he would give my baby swimming lessons. The son of a bitch laugh in my face, he said: 'Maybe she will be a better student than the whore.'" Stavridis wiped his mouth. "By telling you this, I put my daughter's life at risk."

Damon realized then why the detective had been so reluctant to talk. "You don't have to worry about him anymore."

Stavridis looked at Damon for a long time.

"He's missing."

"And the lawyer?"

"We no longer needed his services either."

A hint of a smile came to the old man's face. "Sounds like epidemic."

"Yes, and they were the virus."

"And you? What are you going to do?"

"I came here for answers. I got them."

A bird chirped at the afternoon sun, as the leaves rustled on one tree after the other, in answer to a warm summer breeze.

"Your family, Mr. van Luden, do they know?"

"They didn't for years. My brother hated me. Dorothy blamed me for destroying her life, and my son turned out to be my brother's son."

"And now?"

"Now they know some; soon they'll know the rest."

"You are *pallikari.*"

Damon frowned.

"Is not bad word. Means you're okay person."

"Save it—you're off the hook—you don't have to worry about me or anybody else coming near you or your family. Like I said, my brother and I wanted answers. We needed to know exactly how deeply involved you were. Since you didn't have anything to do with killing or raping anyone, I think Kory will agree you weren't a major player."

Stavridis looked away.

"It turns out you weren't the only one. My brother was right: he just recently confirmed there *was* a guy working on the inside, helping Mr. Chambers cook the books. My aunt let him go a few days ago."

"Like the lawyer and his cousin?"

Damon laughed. "No. She just fired the guy, but he'll be lucky to find a job anywhere in the Tri State area doing anything more than flipping burgers. What happened to Mr. Chambers and Jabber was self-defense."

"I see. No problems with the police?"

Damon explained.

"So nobody looked for them?"

Damon told the detective the latest news he'd learned from his brother when he'd phoned him from Athens to advise him on the progress made in locating Stavridis.

Only one person had called asking about the attorney—a Chilean businessman wanting to know why Mr. Chambers had not kept his appointment and if he or someone else from Van Luden Enterprises would like to reschedule the review of their proposal. Mr. Chambers's secretary had phoned the apartment and, unable to locate her boss there, she'd started dialing all the numbers she could find in his Rolodex.

Kory hadn't given her a chance to reach the V's. He'd pre-empted the call, saying he had a few follow-up questions for

Mr. Chambers from their meeting that Friday. When she'd explained that she couldn't locate her boss and that he'd missed a meeting in Santiago, Kory had assured her he'd look into the matter.

As the acting head of Van Luden Enterprises, Mary had ordered an inquiry into the attorney's disappearance using Jean-Luc and Girard as the sole investigators in the case. Jean-Luc had interviewed the doorman who'd said the last he'd seen of Mr. Chambers had been on that Friday. He'd described another man with a French accent who'd claimed to come on behalf of Van Luden Enterprises that very next day. The doorman had asked if he'd done something wrong by letting him into the building. Jean-Luc reassured him, saying that Mr. Chambers had sent the man.

Jean-Luc had kept Mr. Chambers's secretary and the company senior staff apprised of all progress made. He'd told them that none of the furniture in the apartment had been covered, but the A/C had been turned off. It appeared that Mr. Chambers had gone to South America, but he never checked in to his hotel. According to LAN Chile, the ticket could be refunded, but Jean-Luc told the senior staff that neither ticket nor passport had been found.

Ten days into the investigation, Jean-Luc announced he'd discovered that Mr. Chambers had arranged for a ticket to Greece via Canada and that since there were no reservations made from JFK to Toronto, the attorney had most likely walked over the border at Buffalo and taken a taxi from there to Toronto, where he'd caught his flight to Greece. Mary had done a decent job pretending to be shocked.

From her new position as trustee, she had full access to all the financial paperwork related to the trust. Jean-Luc had uncovered the systematic laundering of money over a ten-year period to a Swiss bank account. This was actually Damon's account, and it was made to seem as if Mr. Chambers had intentionally sent money to Switzerland to frame Damon for siphoning money from the fund.

Kory had prepared the grounds for a complete police investigation. Any and all evidence they could gather would lead to the same conclusion Jean-Luc presented to Van Luden

Enterprises at the end of his investigation: Mr. Chambers was guilty of embezzlement and had fled the country to live abroad on the money he'd stolen. The police would ask if the parties involved—the trustees—would like to press charges.

Naturally, the answer would be no. The explanation would be equally simple: Mr. Chambers had served Van Luden Enterprises loyally for forty years. His departure was both distasteful and utterly unwarranted. After so many years with the company, he could have retired with a considerable sum—a golden parachute like few executives before him had ever seen. Instead, he'd chosen to steal, and for that his reputation would suffer, but Van Luden Enterprises would not press charges—it wasn't worth the negative publicity.

As it turned out, the police were never involved.

"Ola edo plironontai," Stavridis said to himself. To Damon he said, "If there is anything I can do for you. Anything at all . . ."

"At the moment, I can't think of anyone I'd like to see framed for drug abuse or force married."

Stavridis gave him a hurt look.

This wasn't the way Damon wanted to leave the old man. He suddenly had an idea. "How're your people-finding skills?"

"It's been a while"—he smiled widely—"but for you, I would find Jimmy Hoffa."

DAMON

Summer 2000
Twenty Years Later

Crimson rose petals glistened on the surface of the Ganges.
Though the day was bright and busy with boats and people
for as far as the eye could see, it appeared to Damon the great
river had swallowed all sound and made still the passage of
time.

He had come occasionally over the years, and while the
Ganges had not spoken to him since those nightly ablutions
three decades earlier, their communion had since grown
deeper roots in the fertile though distant silence.

Vadu had lived almost a full century, just long enough to
witness the birth of a new millennium; now his mortal body was
one with the eternal River of Heaven which flowed from the
Himalayas to the sea in the Bay of Bengal.

Damon had been informed of his friend's death one
month after the Veterans of Foreign Wars convention in Las
Vegas, where he'd met with his team for the first time since the
war. Hiep had tracked him down shortly following the declas-
sification of the SOG through a website created expressly for
effecting such reunions. Senator Tom Dalton, once known as
Snakebite, had insisted on using his political influence to have
RT New York's One-Zero receive commendation for his service to his country. But Damon preferred the arrangement he

already had with the Army: they leave him alone, he returns the favor.

The notice had come too late for Damon to arrive in time and join the many who had been there for the cremation. But this simple immersion ceremony seemed to Damon more befitting. Knowing Vadu, he would have agreed.

In Hindi, gazing down at the river, he said, "Good-bye, old friend."

A reflection of the Ganges danced upon Guru Dev's smiling eyes.

The old master gave him a knowing look.

Palms together, he answered with a gentle bow.

Understanding that the time had come, Madeleine took Damon's hand and they walked away in silence.

EPILOGUE

Run. Don't look back. Run.
But he was already heading for the light . . .

In his parents' bathroom.

His mother was sitting on the floor, with her arms hugging her legs.

She was crying.

Maybe her tummy hurt. Then he saw the blood.

Everywhere.

There was a monster in her bathtub. It had no head.

Yes, it did. The monster was looking the other way. That was hair. That was a nose . . . and . . . and a mouth . . . that was . . . that was . . . Daddy.

Something was wrong with Mommy. She looked happy. *Pretend* happy. Couldn't she see what happened to Daddy?

She whispered, "Don't cry."

Damon wasn't crying.

"Good boy." She smiled, but her eyes were still wet. "You're Mommy's little soldier now."

ACKNOWLEDGMENTS

First and foremost, I would like to thank my copyeditor, Rachelle Mandik, for using her uncanny eye for detail to help iron out the countless wrinkles in my manuscript. She's simply amazing. Thanks also to Pauline Zavitzianos, for helping me discover myself as a writer over the many years that it took me to complete this novel.

Alex Z was an enormous help as a plot sounding board, and has a remarkably keen eye as a proofreader.

Because this novel starts in the middle of the twentieth century, most of my research has come from one-on-one communication with people who have actually lived similar experiences in the time period.

For his law-enforcement-related legal advice, I would like to thank my lifelong friend, NYPD Officer Paul Labbé.

Thanks as well to another great friend, Edward Reiner, for legal advice as a New York state practicing tax attorney in matters pertaining to wills, estates, and trust funds.

For medical advice, I'd like to thank my cousin and friend Dr. Evangelia Razis.

My French, especially my written French, has gotten rusty after decades of disuse, so additional thanks goes to Dean Soldatos and Mike Takahashi for proofreading the short sections written in that language.

I spent more than two years studying the Vietnam era. Much of what I learned could not be included in the book, but it gave me a much deeper perspective on that period in our history. I would like to thank the following men from the US military who were generous enough to spend the time with me to help make this book as historically accurate as possible.

Lt. Col. (Ret.) RG Aguirre has spent many hours with me, working on everything from big-picture issues down to nitty-gritty details such as expressions and military jargon.

From the Special Operations Group, Lynne M. Black Jr.—former MACV/SOG recon team leader, code name Blackjack—as well as USAR Capt. Paul D. Cain have helped me tremendously with specifics related to the SOG, and the entire section on Vietnam, Laos, and Thailand.

I'd like to extend special thanks for their significant contribution on research related primarily to the USMA to Dr. Steve Grove, USMA Historian; and from the Class of '61: Hank Rennagel; Neil S. Grigg, professor at Colorado State University; Maj. Gen. (Ret.) Paul Vallely, US Army; Lt. Col. (Ret.) J. Olejniczak; Jack Dorr; Pete Burgess; Pete Gleichenhaus; John E. Fischer; Mike Brady; Richard Jackson; and Jerry Clements.

www.ingramcontent.com/pod-product-compliance
Lightning Source LLC
Chambersburg PA
CBHW070532030726
47505CB00001B/13